THE
EMERALD
CITY
OF
OZ

NOVELS 6 THROUGH 10
OF THE OZ SERIES

THE EMERALD

CITY OF OZ

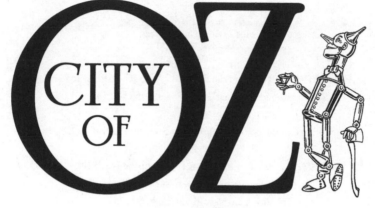

NOVELS 6 THROUGH 10
OF THE OZ SERIES

L. FRANK BAUM

with illustrations
by John R. Neill

FALL RIVER PRESS

New York

FALL RIVER PRESS

New York

An Imprint of Sterling Publishing Co., Inc.
1166 Avenue of the Americas
New York, NY 10036

FALL RIVER PRESS and the distinctive Fall River Press logo are
registered trademarks of Barnes & Noble, Inc.

The Emerald City of Oz was first published in 1910.
The Patchwork Girl of Oz was first published in 1913.
Tik-Tok of Oz was first published in 1914.
The Scarecrow of Oz was first published in 1915.
Rinkitink in Oz was first published in 1915.

ISBN 978-1-4351-5615-9

Manufactured in the United States of America

6 8 10 9 7 5

www.sterlingpublishing.com

CONTENTS

INTRODUCTION

Perhaps I should admit on the title page that this book is "By L. Frank Baum and his correspondents," for I have used many suggestions conveyed to me in letters from children. Once on a time I really imagined myself "an author of fairy tales," but now I am merely an editor or private secretary for a host of youngsters whose ideas I am requested to weave into the thread of my stories.

WHEN L. FRANK BAUM OPENED HIS PREFATORY NOTE TO READERS OF *The Emerald City of Oz* (1910) with the paragraph above, he was not being entirely facetious. His bestselling series of Oz novels, inaugurated with *The Wonderful Wizard of Oz* in 1900, was now a decade old, and it had garnered him a huge audience of fans that made him the envy of other writers for young readers. ("I am almost sure I have as many friends among the children of America as any story writer alive," he wrote in his note "To the Readers" in *Tik-Tok of Oz*.) Those young readers were uninhibited about expressing what they liked and disliked about the Oz adventures, revealing who their favorite characters were, and cajoling the author to keep entertaining them. Baum was very responsive to the whims of his readers, and knew that the best way to please them was to suggest that they played an integral role in the creative process.

Baum clearly enjoyed writing the Oz novels—their imaginative exuberance would not have been possible were he not passionately committed to telling their stories—but there is a sense at the end of *The Emerald City of Oz*, the sixth Oz novel, that he was content to wrap the series up. But no other works that Baum produced were as popular as the Oz novels, and no other projects that he brought to the stage were as successful as the dramatic adaptation of *The Wonderful Wizard of Oz*. When, after a three-year hiatus, he returned to the series with *The Patchwork Girl of Oz* (1913), his motives were as much financial as creative. Extending the Oz series provided him with the earnings he needed to dabble in projects outside of it. In his Prologue to the novel, Baum referred to himself as the Royal Historian of Oz, who was merely transcribing adventures communicated to him via wireless by Dorothy Gale, now a princess in Oz. The meaning to the readers was clear: Oz and its inhabitants were as real as Baum himself. It had many stories to be told, and Baum was the conduit for channeling them to the readers.

This volume collects novels six through ten of the fourteen novels in Baum's Oz series, including *Tik-Tok of Oz* (1914), *The Scarecrow of Oz* (1915), and *Rinkitink in Oz* (1915). For the most part, they follow the same pattern that Baum established in the second Oz novel, *The Marvelous Land of Oz* (1904): the main characters of *The Wonderful Wizard of Oz*—Dorothy, the Scarecrow, the Tin Woodman, and the Cowardly Lion—all reappear, but mostly in roles subordinate to those of characters at the center of the new adventures, including the Patchwork Girl, the clockwork man Tik-Tok, the monarch Rinkitink, the Crooked Magician, Ojo the Unlucky, and the Shaggy Man. In these novels Tik-Tok, who was introduced in *Ozma of Oz* (1907), emerges as a major heroic character in the series, while the scheming King of the Nomes (Baum's variant on traditional fairy tale gnomes), develops into the series' recurring villain. As in other novels, Baum expands the geography of the world of Oz with excursions into the valley of Oogaboo, the Kingdoms of Jinxland and Rinkitink, the Island of Pingaree, and the lands of Regos and Coregos. He also introduces a wild array of magical characters: Hoppers, Horners, Whimsies, Cuttenclips, Tottenhots, Orks, a wooden-legged Grasshopper, and Bilbil the talking goat, to name but a few.

Concluding his prefatory note to *The Emerald City of Oz*, Baum wrote, "My readers know what they want and realize that I try to please them." For the novels collected in this volume, Baum went to creative lengths to ensure that readers pleased with the first five novels in the Oz series would enjoy these just as much.

THE
EMERALD CITY
OF
OZ

CONTENTS

CHAPTER I

HOW THE NOME KING BECAME ANGRY

THE NOME KING WAS IN AN ANGRY MOOD, AND AT SUCH TIMES HE WAS VERY disagreeable. Every one kept away from him, even his Chief Steward Kaliko.

Therefore the King stormed and raved all by himself, walking up and down in his jewel-studded cavern and getting angrier all the time. Then he remembered that it was no fun being angry unless he had some one to frighten and make miserable, and he rushed to his big gong and made it clatter as loud as he could.

In came the Chief Steward, trying not to show the Nome King how frightened he was.

"Send the Chief Counselor here!" shouted the angry monarch.

Kaliko ran out as fast as his spindle legs could carry his fat, round body, and soon the Chief Counselor entered the cavern. The King scowled and said to him:

"I'm in great trouble over the loss of my Magic Belt. Every little while I want to do something magical, and find I can't because the Belt is gone. That makes me angry, and when I'm angry I can't have a good time. Now, what do you advise?"

"Some people," said the Chief Counselor, "enjoy getting angry."

"But not all the time," declared the King. "To be angry once in a while is really good fun, because it makes others so miserable. But to be angry morning, noon and night, as I am, grows monotonous and prevents my gaining any other pleasure in life. Now, what do you advise?"

"Why, if you are angry because you want to do magical things and can't, and if you don't want to get angry at all, my advice is not to want to do magical things."

Hearing this, the King glared at his Counselor with a furious expression and tugged at his own long white whiskers until he pulled them so hard that he yelled with pain.

"You are a fool!" he exclaimed.

"I share that honor with your Majesty," said the Chief Counselor.

The King roared with rage and stamped his foot.

"Ho, there, my guards!" he cried. "Ho" is a royal way of saying, "Come here." So, when the guards had hoed, the King said to them:

"Take this Chief Counselor and throw him away."

Then the guards took the Chief Counselor, and bound him with chains to prevent his struggling, and threw him away. And the King paced up and down his cavern more angry than before.

Finally he rushed to his big gong and made it clatter like a fire-alarm. Kaliko appeared again, trembling and white with fear.

"Fetch my pipe!" yelled the King.

"Your pipe is already here, your Majesty," replied Kaliko.

"Then get my tobacco!" roared the King.

"The tobacco is in your pipe, your Majesty," returned the Steward.

"Then bring a live coal from the furnace!" commanded the King.

"The tobacco is lighted, and your Majesty is already smoking your pipe," answered the Steward.

"Why, so I am!" said the King, who had forgotten this fact; "but you are very rude to remind me of it."

"I am a lowborn, miserable villain," declared the Chief Steward, humbly.

The Nome King could think of nothing to say next, so he puffed away at his pipe and paced up and down the room. Finally he remembered how angry he was, and cried out:

"What do you mean, Kaliko, by being so contented when your monarch is unhappy?"

"What makes you unhappy?" asked the Steward.

"I've lost my Magic Belt. A little girl named Dorothy, who was here with Ozma of Oz, stole my Belt and carried it away with her," said the King, grinding his teeth with rage.

"She captured it in a fair fight," Kaliko ventured to say.

"But I want it! I must have it! Half my power is gone with that Belt!" roared the King.

"You will have to go to the Land of Oz to recover it, and your Majesty can't get to the Land of Oz in any possible way," said the Steward, yawning because he had been on duty ninety-six hours, and was sleepy.

"Why not?" asked the King.

"Because there is a deadly desert all around that fairy country, which no one is able to cross. You know that fact as well as I do, your Majesty. Never mind the lost Belt. You have plenty of power left, for you rule this underground kingdom like a tyrant, and thousands of Nomes obey your commands. I advise you to drink a glass of melted silver, to quiet your nerves, and then go to bed."

The King grabbed a big ruby and threw it at Kaliko's head. The Steward ducked to escape the heavy jewel, which crashed against the door just over his left ear.

"Get out of my sight! Vanish! Go away—and send General Blug here," screamed the Nome King.

Kaliko hastily withdrew, and the Nome King stamped up and down until the General of his armies appeared.

This Nome was known far and wide as a terrible fighter and a cruel, desperate commander. He had fifty thousand Nome soldiers, all well drilled, who feared nothing but their stern master. Yet General Blug was a trifle uneasy when he arrived and saw how angry the Nome King was.

"Ha! So you're here!" cried the King.

"So I am," said the General.

"March your army at once to the Land of Oz, capture and destroy the Emerald City, and bring back to me my Magic Belt!" roared the King.

"You're crazy," calmly remarked the General.

"What's that? What's that? What's that?" And the Nome King danced around on his pointed toes, he was so enraged.

"You don't know what you're talking about," continued the General, seating himself upon a large cut diamond. "I advise you to stand in a corner and count sixty before you speak again. By that time you may be more sensible."

The King looked around for something to throw at General Blug, but as nothing was handy he began to consider that perhaps the man was right and he had been talking foolishly. So he merely threw himself into his glittering throne and tipped his crown over his ear and curled his feet up under him and glared wickedly at Blug.

"In the first place," said the General, "we cannot march across the deadly desert to the Land of Oz; and, if we could, the Ruler of that country, Princess Ozma, has certain fairy powers that would render my army helpless. Had you not lost your Magic Belt we might have some chance of defeating Ozma; but the Belt is gone."

"I want it!" screamed the King. "I must have it."

"Well, then, let us try in a sensible way to get it," replied the General. "The belt was captured by a little girl named Dorothy, who lives in Kansas, in the United States of America."

"But she left it in the Emerald City, with Ozma," declared the King.

"How do you know that?" asked the General.

"One of my spies, who is a Blackbird, flew over the desert to the Land of Oz, and saw the Magic Belt in Ozma's palace," replied the King with a groan.

"Now, that gives me an idea," said General Blug, thoughtfully. "There are two ways to get to the Land of Oz without traveling across the sandy desert."

"What are they?" demanded the King, eagerly.

"One way is *over* the desert, through the air; and the other way is *under* the desert, through the earth."

Hearing this the Nome King uttered a yell of joy and leaped from his throne, to resume his wild walk up and down the cavern.

"That's it, Blug!" he shouted. "That's the idea, General! I'm King of the Under World, and my subjects are all miners. I'll make a secret tunnel under the desert to the Land of Oz—yes! right up to the Emerald City—and you will march your armies there and capture the whole country!"

"Softly, softly, your Majesty. Don't go too fast," warned the General. "My Nomes are good fighters, but they are not strong enough to conquer the Emerald City."

"Are you sure?" asked the King.

"Absolutely certain, your Majesty."

"Then what am I to do?"

"Give up the idea and mind your own business," advised the General. "You have plenty to do trying to rule your underground kingdom."

"But I want that Magic Belt—and I'm going to have it!" roared the Nome King.

"I'd like to see you get it," replied the General, laughing maliciously.

The King was by this time so exasperated that he picked up his scepter, which had a heavy ball, made from a sapphire, at the end of it, and threw it with all his force at General Blug. The sapphire hit the General upon his forehead and knocked him flat upon the ground, where he lay motionless. Then the King rang his gong and told his guards to drag out the General and throw him away; which they did.

This Nome King was named Roquat the Red, and no one loved him. He was a bad man and a powerful monarch, and he had resolved to destroy the Land of Oz and its magnificent Emerald City, to enslave Princess Ozma and little Dorothy and all the Oz people, and recover his Magic Belt. This same Belt had once enabled Roquat the Red to carry out many wicked plans; but that was before Ozma and her people marched to the underground cavern and captured it. The Nome King could not forgive Dorothy or Princess Ozma, and he had determined to be revenged upon them.

But they, for their part, did not know they had so dangerous an enemy. Indeed, Ozma and Dorothy had both almost forgotten that such a person as the Nome King yet lived under the mountains of the Land of Ev—which lay just across the deadly desert to the south of the Land of Oz.

An unsuspected enemy is doubly dangerous.

CHAPTER II

How UNCLE HENRY GOT INTO TROUBLE

DOROTHY GALE LIVED ON A FARM IN KANSAS, WITH HER AUNT EM AND HER UNCLE Henry. It was not a big farm, nor a very good one, because sometimes the rain did not come when the crops needed it, and then everything withered and dried up. Once a cyclone had carried away Uncle Henry's house, so that he was obliged to build another; and as he was a poor man he had to mortgage his farm to get the money to pay for the new house. Then his health became bad and he was too feeble to work. The doctor ordered him to take a sea voyage and he went to Australia and took Dorothy with him. That cost a lot of money, too.

Uncle Henry grew poorer every year, and the crops raised on the farm only bought food for the family. Therefore the mortgage could not be paid. At last the banker who had loaned him the money said that if he did not pay on a certain day, his farm would be taken away from him.

This worried Uncle Henry a good deal, for without the farm he would have no way to earn a living. He was a good man, and worked in the field as hard as he could; and Aunt Em did all the housework, with Dorothy's help. Yet they did not seem to get along.

This little girl, Dorothy, was like dozens of little girls you know. She was loving and usually sweet-tempered, and had a round rosy face and earnest eyes. Life was a serious thing to Dorothy, and a wonderful thing, too, for she had encountered more strange adventures in her short life than many other girls of her age.

Aunt Em once said she thought the fairies must have marked Dorothy at her birth, because she had wandered into strange places and had always been protected by some unseen power. As for Uncle Henry, he thought his little niece merely a dreamer, as her dead mother had been, for he could not quite believe all the curious stories Dorothy told them of the Land of Oz, which she had several times visited. He did not think that she tried to deceive her uncle and aunt, but he imagined that she had dreamed all of those astonishing adventures, and that the dreams had been so real to her that she had come to believe them true.

Whatever the explanation might be, it was certain that Dorothy had been absent from her Kansas home for several long periods, always disappearing unexpectedly, yet always coming back safe and sound, with amazing tales of where she had been and the unusual people she had met. Her uncle and aunt listened to her stories eagerly and in spite of their doubts began to feel that the little girl had gained a lot of experience and wisdom that were unaccountable in this age, when fairies are supposed no longer to exist.

Most of Dorothy's stories were about the Land of Oz, with its beautiful Emerald City and a lovely girl Ruler named Ozma, who was the most faithful friend of the little Kansas girl. When Dorothy told about the riches of this fairy country Uncle Henry would sigh, for he knew that a single one of the great emeralds that were so common there would pay all his debts and leave his farm free. But Dorothy never brought any jewels home with her, so their poverty became greater every year.

When the banker told Uncle Henry that he must pay the money in thirty days or leave the farm, the poor man was in despair, as he knew he could not possibly get the money. So he told his wife, Aunt Em, of his trouble, and she first cried a little and then said that they must be brave and do the best they could, and go away somewhere and try to earn an honest living. But they were getting old and feeble and she feared that they could not take care of Dorothy as well as they had formerly done. Probably the little girl would also be obliged to go to work.

They did not tell their niece the sad news for several days, not wishing to make her unhappy; but one morning the little girl found Aunt Em softly crying while Uncle Henry tried to comfort her. Then Dorothy asked them to tell her what was the matter.

"We must give up the farm, my dear," replied her uncle, sadly, "and wander away into the world to work for our living."

The girl listened quite seriously, for she had not known before how desperately poor they were.

"We don't mind for ourselves," said her aunt, stroking the little girl's head tenderly; "but we love you as if you were our own child, and we are heart-broken to think that you must also endure poverty, and work for a living before you have grown big and strong."

"What could I do to earn money?" asked Dorothy.

"You might do housework for some one, dear, you are so handy; or perhaps you could be a nurse-maid to little children. I'm sure I don't know exactly what you *can* do to earn money, but if your uncle and I are able to support you we will do it willingly, and send you to school. We fear, though, that we shall have much trouble in earning a living for ourselves. No one wants to employ old people who are broken down in health, as we are."

Dorothy smiled.

"Wouldn't it be funny," she said, "for me to do housework in Kansas, when I'm a Princess in the Land of Oz?"

"A Princess!" they both exclaimed, astonished.

"Yes; Ozma made me a Princess some time ago, and she has often begged me to come and live always in the Emerald City," said the child.

Her uncle and aunt looked at each other in amazement. Then the man said:

"Do you suppose you could manage to return to your fairyland, my dear?"

"Oh, yes," replied Dorothy; "I could do that easily."

"How?" asked Aunt Em.

"Ozma sees me every day at four o'clock, in her Magic Picture. She can see me wherever I am, no matter what I am doing. And at that time, if I make a certain secret sign, she will send for me by means of the Magic Belt, which I once captured from the Nome King. Then, in the wink of an eye, I shall be with Ozma in her palace."

The elder people remained silent for some time after Dorothy had spoken. Finally Aunt Em said, with another sigh of regret:

"If that is the case, Dorothy, perhaps you'd better go and live in the Emerald City. It will break our hearts to lose you from our lives, but you will be so much better off with your fairy friends that it seems wisest and best for you to go."

"I'm not so sure about that," remarked Uncle Henry, shaking his gray head doubtfully. "These things all seem real to Dorothy, I know; but I'm afraid our little girl won't find her fairyland just what she has dreamed it to be. It would make me very unhappy to think that she was wandering among strangers who might be unkind to her."

Dorothy laughed merrily at this speech, and then she became very sober again, for she could see how all this trouble was worrying her aunt and uncle, and knew that unless she found a way to help them their future lives would be quite miserable and unhappy. She knew that she *could* help them. She had thought of a way already. Yet she did not tell them at once what it was, because she must ask Ozma's consent before she would be able to carry out her plans.

So she only said:

"If you will promise not to worry a bit about me, I'll go to the Land of Oz this very afternoon. And I'll make a promise, too; that you shall both see me again before the day comes when you must leave this farm."

"The day isn't far away, now," her uncle sadly replied. "I did not tell you of our trouble until I was obliged to, dear Dorothy, so the evil time is near at hand. But if you are quite sure your fairy friends will give you a home, it will be best for you to go to them, as your aunt says."

That was why Dorothy went to her little room in the attic that afternoon, taking with her a small dog named Toto. The dog had curly black hair and big brown eyes and loved Dorothy very dearly.

The child had kissed her uncle and aunt affectionately before she went upstairs, and now she looked around her little room rather wistfully, gazing at the simple trinkets and worn calico and gingham dresses, as if they were old friends. She was tempted at first to make a bundle of them, yet she knew very well that they would be of no use to her in her future life.

She sat down upon a broken-backed chair—the only one the room contained—and holding Toto in her arms waited patiently until the clock struck four.

Then she made the secret signal that had been agreed upon between her and Ozma.

Uncle Henry and Aunt Em waited downstairs. They were uneasy and a good deal excited, for this is a practical humdrum world, and it seemed to them quite impossible that their little niece could vanish from her home and travel instantly to fairyland.

So they watched the stairs, which seemed to be the only way that Dorothy could get out of the farm-house, and they watched them a long time. They heard the clock strike four but there was no sound from above.

Half-past four came, and now they were too impatient to wait any longer. Softly they crept up the stairs to the door of the little girl's room.

"Dorothy! Dorothy!" they called.

There was no answer.

They opened the door and looked in.

The room was empty.

CHAPTER III

How OZMA GRANTED DOROTHY'S REQUEST

I SUPPOSE YOU HAVE READ SO MUCH ABOUT THE MAGNIFICENT EMERALD CITY THAT there is little need for me to describe it here. It is the Capital City of the Land of Oz, which is justly considered the most attractive and delightful fairyland in all the world.

The Emerald City is built all of beautiful marbles in which are set a profusion of emeralds, every one exquisitely cut and of very great size. There are other jewels used in the decorations inside the houses and palaces, such as rubies, diamonds, sapphires, amethysts and turquoises. But in the streets and upon the outside of the buildings only emeralds appear, from which circumstance the place is named the Emerald City of Oz. It has nine thousand, six hundred and fifty-four buildings, in which lived fifty-seven thousand three hundred and eighteen people, up to the time my story opens.

All the surrounding country, extending to the borders of the desert which enclosed it upon every side, was full of pretty and comfortable farm-houses, in which resided those inhabitants of Oz who preferred country to city life.

Altogether there were more than half a million people in the Land of Oz— although some of them, as you will soon learn, were not made of flesh and blood as we are—and every inhabitant of that favored country was happy and prosperous.

No disease of any sort was ever known among the Ozites, and so no one ever died unless he met with an accident that prevented him from living. This happened very seldom, indeed. There were no poor people in the Land of Oz, because there was no such thing as money, and all property of every sort belonged to the Ruler.

The people were her children, and she cared for them. Each person was given freely by his neighbors whatever he required for his use, which is as much as any one may reasonably desire. Some tilled the lands and raised great crops of grain, which was divided equally among the entire population, so that all had enough. There were many tailors and dressmakers and shoemakers and the like, who made things that any who desired them might wear. Likewise there were jewelers who made ornaments for the person, which pleased and beautified the people, and these ornaments also were free to those who asked for them. Each man and woman, no matter what he or she produced for the good of the community, was supplied by the neighbors with food and clothing and a house and furniture and ornaments and games. If by chance the supply ever ran short, more was taken from the great storehouses of the Ruler, which were afterward filled up again when there was more of any article than the people needed.

Every one worked half the time and played half the time, and the people enjoyed the work as much as they did the play, because it is good to be occupied and to have something to do. There were no cruel overseers set to watch them, and no one to rebuke them or to find fault with them. So each one was proud to do all he could for his friends and neighbors, and was glad when they would accept the things he produced.

You will know, by what I have here told you, that the Land of Oz was a remarkable country. I do not suppose such an arrangement would be practical with us, but Dorothy assures me that it works finely with the Oz people.

Oz being a fairy country, the people were, of course, fairy people; but that does not mean that all of them were very unlike the people of our own world. There were all sorts of queer characters among them, but not a single one who was evil, or who possessed a selfish or violent nature. They were peaceful, kind-hearted, loving and merry, and every inhabitant adored the beautiful girl who ruled them, and delighted to obey her every command.

In spite of all I have said in a general way, there were some parts of the Land of Oz not quite so pleasant as the farming country and the Emerald City which was its center. Far away in the South Country there lived in the mountains a band of strange people called Hammer-Heads, because they had no arms and used their flat heads to pound any one who came near them. Their necks were like rubber, so that they could shoot out their heads to quite a distance, and afterward draw them back again to their shoulders. The Hammer-Heads were called the "Wild People," but never harmed any but those who disturbed them in the mountains where they lived.

In some of the dense forests there lived great beasts of every sort; yet these were for the most part harmless and even sociable, and conversed agreeably with those who visited their haunts. The Kalidahs—beasts with bodies like bears and heads like tigers—had once been fierce and bloodthirsty, but even they were now nearly all tamed, although at times one or another of them would get cross and disagreeable.

Not so tame were the Fighting Trees, which had a forest of their own. If any one approached them these curious trees would bend down their branches, twine them around the intruders, and hurl them away.

But these unpleasant things existed only in a few remote parts of the Land of Oz. I suppose every country has some drawbacks, so even this almost perfect fairyland could not be quite perfect. Once there had been wicked witches in the land, too; but now these had all been destroyed; so, as I said, only peace and happiness reigned in Oz.

For some time Ozma had ruled over this fair country, and never was Ruler more popular or beloved. She is said to be the most beautiful girl the world has ever known, and her heart and mind are as lovely as her person.

Dorothy Gale had several times visited the Emerald City and experienced adventures in the Land of Oz, so that she and Ozma had now become firm friends. The girl Ruler had even made Dorothy a Princess of Oz, and had often implored her to come to Ozma's stately palace and live there always; but Dorothy had been loyal to her Aunt Em and Uncle Henry, who had cared for her since she was a baby, and she had refused to leave them because she knew they would be lonely without her.

However, Dorothy now realized that things were going to be different with her uncle and aunt from this time forth, so after giving the matter deep thought she decided to ask Ozma to grant her a very great favor.

A few seconds after she had made the secret signal in her little bedchamber, the Kansas girl was seated in a lovely room in Ozma's palace in the Emerald City of Oz. When the first loving kisses and embraces had been exchanged, the fair Ruler inquired:

"What is the matter, dear? I know something unpleasant has happened to you, for your face was very sober when I saw it in my Magic Picture. And whenever you signal me to transport you to this safe place, where you are always welcome, I know you are in danger or in trouble."

Dorothy sighed.

"This time, Ozma, it isn't I," she replied. "But it's worse, I guess, for Uncle Henry and Aunt Em are in a heap of trouble, and there seems no way for them to get out of it—anyhow, not while they live in Kansas."

"Tell me about it, Dorothy," said Ozma, with ready sympathy.

"Why, you see Uncle Henry is poor; for the farm in Kansas doesn't 'mount to much, as farms go. So one day Uncle Henry borrowed some money, and wrote a letter saying that if he didn't pay the money back they could take his farm for pay. Course he 'spected to pay by making money from the farm; but he just couldn't. An' so they're going to take the farm, and Uncle Henry and Aunt Em won't have any place to live. They're pretty old to do much hard work, Ozma; so I'll have to work for them, unless—"

Ozma had been thoughtful during the story, but now she smiled and pressed her little friend's hand.

"Unless what, dear?" she asked.

Dorothy hesitated, because her request meant so much to them all.

"Well," said she, "I'd like to live here in the Land of Oz, where you've often 'vited me to live. But I can't, you know, unless Uncle Henry and Aunt Em could live here too."

"Of course not," exclaimed the Ruler of Oz, laughing gaily. "So, in order to get you, little friend, we must invite your uncle and aunt to live in Oz, also."

"Oh, will you, Ozma?" cried Dorothy, clasping her chubby little hands eagerly. "Will you bring them here with the Magic Belt, and give them a nice little farm in the Munchkin Country, or the Winkie Country—or some other place?"

"To be sure," answered Ozma, full of joy at the chance to please her little friend. "I have long been thinking of this very thing, Dorothy dear, and often I have had it in my mind to propose it to you. I am sure your uncle and aunt must be good and worthy people, or you would not love them so much; and for *your* friends, Princess, there is always room in the Land of Oz."

Dorothy was delighted, yet not altogether surprised, for she had clung to the hope that Ozma would be kind enough to grant her request. When, indeed, had her powerful and faithful friend refused her anything?

"But you must not call me 'Princess'," she said; "for after this I shall live on the little farm with Uncle Henry and Aunt Em, and princesses ought not to live on farms."

"Princess Dorothy will not," replied Ozma, with her sweet smile. "You are going to live in your own rooms in this palace, and be my constant companion."

"But Uncle Henry——" began Dorothy.

"Oh, he is old, and has worked enough in his lifetime," interrupted the girl Ruler; "so we must find a place for your uncle and aunt where they will be comfortable and happy and need not work more than they care to. When shall we transport them here, Dorothy?"

"I promised to go and see them again before they were turned out of the farmhouse," answered Dorothy; "so—perhaps next Saturday—"

"But why wait so long?" asked Ozma. "And why make the journey back to Kansas again? Let us surprise them, and bring them here without any warning."

"I'm not sure that they believe in the Land of Oz," said Dorothy, "though I've told 'em 'bout it lots of times."

"They'll believe when they see it," declared Ozma; "and if they are told they are to make a magical journey to our fairyland, it may make them nervous. I think the best way will be to use the Magic Belt without warning them, and when they have arrived you can explain to them whatever they do not understand."

"Perhaps that's best," decided Dorothy. "There isn't much use in their staying at the farm until they are put out, 'cause it's much nicer here."

"Then to-morrow morning they shall come here," said Princess Ozma. "I will order Jellia Jamb, who is the palace housekeeper, to have rooms all prepared for them, and after breakfast we will get the Magic Belt and by its aid transport your uncle and aunt to the Emerald City."

"Thank you, Ozma!" cried Dorothy, kissing her friend gratefully.

"And now," Ozma proposed, "let us take a walk in the gardens before we dress for dinner. Come, Dorothy dear!"

CHAPTER IV

How the Nome King Planned Revenge

THE REASON MOST PEOPLE ARE BAD IS BECAUSE THEY DO NOT TRY TO BE GOOD. NOW, the Nome King had never tried to be good, so he was very bad indeed. Having decided to conquer the Land of Oz and to destroy the Emerald City and enslave all its people, King Roquat the Red kept planning ways to do this dreadful thing, and the more he planned the more he believed he would be able to accomplish it.

About the time Dorothy went to Ozma the Nome King called his Chief Steward to him and said:

"Kaliko, I think I shall make you the General of my armies."

"I think you won't," replied Kaliko, positively.

"Why not?" inquired the King, reaching for his scepter with the big sapphire.

"Because I'm your Chief Steward, and know nothing of warfare," said Kaliko, preparing to dodge if anything were thrown at him. "I manage all the affairs of your kingdom better than you could yourself, and you'll never find another Steward as good as I am. But there are a hundred Nomes better fitted to command your army, and your Generals get thrown away so often that I have no desire to be one of them."

"Ah, there is some truth in your remarks, Kaliko," remarked the King, deciding not to throw the scepter. "Summon my army to assemble in the Great Cavern."

Kaliko bowed and retired, and in a few minutes returned to say that the army was assembled. So the King went out upon a balcony that overlooked the Great Cavern, where fifty thousand Nomes, all armed with swords and pikes, stood marshaled in military array.

When they were not required as soldiers all these Nomes were metal workers and miners, and they had hammered so much at the forges and dug so hard with pick and shovel that they had acquired great muscular strength. They were strangely formed creatures, rather round and not very tall. Their toes were curly and their ears broad and flat.

In time of war every Nome left his forge or mine and became part of the great army of King Roquat. The soldiers wore rock-colored uniforms and were excellently drilled.

The King looked upon this tremendous army, which stood silently arrayed before him, and a cruel smile curled the corners of his mouth, for he saw that his legions were very powerful. Then he addressed them from the balcony, saying:

"I have thrown away General Blug, because he did not please me. So I want another General to command this army. Who is next in command?"

"I am," replied Colonel Crinkle, a dapper-looking Nome, as he stepped forward to salute his monarch.

The King looked at him carefully and said:

"I want you to march this army through an underground tunnel, which I am going to bore, to the Emerald City of Oz. When you get there I want you to conquer the Oz people, destroy them and their city, and bring all their gold and silver and precious stones back to my cavern. Also you are to recapture my Magic Belt and return it to me. Will you do this, General Crinkle?"

"No, your Majesty," replied the Nome; "for it can't be done."

"Oh, indeed!" exclaimed the King. Then he turned to his servants and said: "Please take General Crinkle to the torture chamber. There you will kindly slice him into thin slices. Afterward you may feed him to the seven-headed dogs."

"Anything to oblige your Majesty," replied the servants, politely, and led the condemned man away.

When they had gone, the King addressed the army again.

"Listen!" said he. "The General who is to command my armies must promise to carry out my orders. If he fails he will share the fate of poor Crinkle. Now, then, who will volunteer to lead my hosts to the Emerald City?"

For a time no one moved and all were silent. Then an old Nome with white whiskers so long that they were tied around his waist to prevent their tripping him up, stepped out of the ranks and saluted the King.

"I'd like to ask a few questions, your Majesty," he said.

"Go ahead," replied the King.

"These Oz people are quite good, are they not?"

"As good as apple pie," said the King.

"And they are happy, I suppose?" continued the old Nome.

"Happy as the day is long," said the King.

"And contented and prosperous?" inquired the Nome.

"Very much so," said the King.

"Well, your Majesty," remarked he of the white whiskers, "I think I should like to undertake the job, so I'll be your General. I hate good people; I detest happy people; I'm opposed to any one who is contented and prosperous. That is why I am so fond of your Majesty. Make me your General and I'll promise to conquer and destroy the Oz people. If I fail I'm ready to be sliced thin and fed to the seven-headed dogs."

"Very good! Very good, indeed! That's the way to talk!" cried Roquat the Red, who was greatly pleased. "What is your name, General?"

"I'm called Guph, your Majesty."

"Well, Guph, come with me to my private cave and we'll talk it over." Then he turned to the army. "Nomes and soldiers," said he, "you are to obey the commands of General Guph until he becomes dog-feed. Any man who fails to obey his new General will be promptly thrown away. You are now dismissed."

Guph went to the King's private cave and sat down upon an amethyst chair and put his feet on the arm of the King's ruby throne. Then he lighted his pipe and threw the live coal he had taken from his pocket upon the King's left foot and puffed the smoke into the King's eyes and made himself comfortable. For he was a wise old Nome, and he knew that the best way to get along with Roquat the Red was to show that he was not afraid of him.

"I'm ready for the talk, your Majesty," he said.

The King coughed and looked at his new General fiercely.

"Do you not tremble to take such liberties with your monarch?" he asked.

"Oh, no," replied Guph, calmly, and he blew a wreath of smoke that curled around the King's nose and made him sneeze. "You want to conquer the Emerald City, and I'm the only Nome in all your dominions who can conquer it. So you will be very careful not to hurt me until I have carried out your wishes. After that—"

"Well, what then?" inquired the King.

"Then you will be so grateful to me that you won't care to hurt me," replied the General.

"That is a very good argument," said Roquat. "But suppose you fail?"

"Then it's the slicing machine. I agree to that," announced Guph. "But if you do as I tell you there will be no failure. The trouble with you, Roquat, is that you don't think carefully enough. I do. You would go ahead and march through your tunnel into

Oz, and get defeated and driven back. I won't. And the reason I won't is because when I march I'll have all my plans made, and a host of allies to assist my Nomes."

"What do you mean by that?" asked the King.

"I'll explain, King Roquat. You're going to attack a fair country, and a mighty fairy country, too. They haven't much of an army in Oz, but the Princess who rules them has a fairy wand; and the little girl Dorothy has your Magic Belt; and at the North of the Emerald City lives a clever sorceress called Glinda the Good, who commands the spirits of the air. Also I have heard that there is a wonderful Wizard in Ozma's palace, who is so skillful that people used to pay him money in America to see him perform. So you see it will be no easy thing to overcome all this magic."

"We have fifty thousand soldiers!" cried the King, proudly.

"Yes; but they are Nomes," remarked Guph, taking a silk handkerchief from the King's pocket and wiping his own pointed shoes with it. "Nomes are immortals, but they are not strong on magic. When you lost your famous belt the greater part of your own power was gone from you. Against Ozma you and your Nomes would have no show at all."

Roquat's eyes flashed angrily.

"Then away you go to the slicing machine!" he cried.

"Not yet," said the General, filling his pipe from the King's private tobacco pouch.

"What do you propose to do?" asked the monarch.

"I propose to obtain the power we need," answered Guph. "There are a good many evil creatures who have magic powers sufficient to destroy and conquer the

Land of Oz. We will get them on our side, band them all together, and then take Ozma and her people by surprise. It's all very simple and easy when you know how. Alone we should be helpless to injure the Ruler of Oz, but with the aid of the evil powers we can summon we shall easily succeed."

King Roquat was delighted with this idea, for he realized how clever it was.

"Surely, Guph, you are the greatest General I have ever had!" he exclaimed, his eyes sparkling with joy. "You must go at once and make arrangements with the evil powers to assist us, and meantime I'll begin to dig the tunnel."

"I thought you'd agree with me, Roquat," replied the new General. "I'll start this very afternoon to visit the Chief of the Whimsies."

CHAPTER V

How DOROTHY BECAME A PRINCESS

WHEN THE PEOPLE OF THE EMERALD CITY HEARD THAT DOROTHY HAD RETURNED to them every one was eager to see her, for the little girl was a general favorite in the Land of Oz. From time to time some of the folk from the great outside world had found their way into this fairyland, but all except one had been companions of Dorothy and had turned out to be very agreeable people. The exception I speak of was the wonderful Wizard of Oz, a sleight-of-hand performer from Omaha who went up in a balloon and was carried by a current of air to the Emerald City. His queer and puzzling tricks made the people of Oz believe him a great wizard for a time, and he ruled over them until Dorothy arrived on her first visit and showed the Wizard to be a mere humbug. He was a gentle, kindly-hearted little man, and Dorothy grew to like him afterward. When, after an absence, the Wizard returned to the Land of Oz, Ozma received him graciously and gave him a home in a part of the palace.

In addition to the Wizard two other personages from the outside world had been allowed to make their home in the Emerald City. The first was a quaint Shaggy Man, whom Ozma had made the Governor of the Royal Storehouses, and the second a Yellow Hen named Billina, who had a fine house in the gardens back of the palace, where she looked after a large family. Both these had been old comrades of Dorothy, so you see the little girl was quite an important personage in Oz, and the people thought she had brought them good luck, and loved her next best to Ozma. During her several visits this little girl had been the means of destroying two wicked witches who oppressed the people, and she had discovered a live scarecrow who was now one of the most popular personages in all the fairy country. With the Scarecrow's help she had rescued Nick Chopper, a Tin Woodman, who had rusted in a lonely forest, and the tin man was now the Emperor of the Country of the Winkies and much beloved because of his kind heart. No wonder the people thought Dorothy had brought them good luck! Yet, strange as it may seem, she had accomplished all these wonders not because she was a fairy or had any magical powers whatever, but because she was a simple, sweet and true little girl who was honest to herself and to all whom she met. In this world in which we live simplicity and kindness are the only magic wands that work wonders, and in the Land of Oz Dorothy found these same qualities had won for her the love and admiration of the people. Indeed, the little girl had made many warm friends in the fairy country, and the only real grief the Ozites had ever experienced was when Dorothy left them and returned to her Kansas home.

Now she received a joyful welcome, although no one except Ozma knew at first that she had finally come to stay for good and all.

That evening Dorothy had many callers, and among them were such important people as Tik-Tok, a machine man who thought and spoke and moved by clockwork; her old companion the genial Shaggy Man; Jack Pumpkinhead, whose body was brush-wood and whose head was a ripe pumpkin with a face carved upon it; the Cowardly Lion and the Hungry Tiger, two great beasts from the forest, who served Princess Ozma, and Professor H. M. Woggle-Bug, T.E. This woggle-bug was a remarkable creature. He had once been a tiny little bug, crawling around in a school-room, but he was discovered and highly magnified so that he could be seen more plainly, and while in this magnified condition he had escaped. He had always remained big, and he dressed like a dandy and was so full of knowledge and information (which are distinct acquirements) that he had been made a Professor and the head of the Royal College.

Dorothy had a nice visit with these old friends, and also talked a long time with the Wizard, who was little and old and withered and dried up, but as merry and active as a child. Afterward she went to see Billina's fast-growing family of chicks.

Toto, Dorothy's little black dog, also met with a cordial reception. Toto was an especial friend of the Shaggy Man, and he knew every one else. Being the only dog in the Land of Oz, he was highly respected by the people, who believed animals entitled to every consideration if they behaved themselves properly.

Dorothy had four lovely rooms in the palace, which were always reserved for her use and were called "Dorothy's rooms." These consisted of a beautiful sitting room, a dressing room, a dainty bedchamber and a big marble bathroom. And in these rooms were everything that heart could desire, placed there with loving thoughtful-ness by Ozma for her little friend's use. The royal dressmakers had the little girl's measure, so they kept the closets in her dressing room filled with lovely dresses of every description and suitable for every occasion. No wonder Dorothy had refrained from bringing with her her old calico and gingham dresses! Here everything that was dear to a little girl's heart was supplied in profusion, and nothing so rich and beautiful could ever have been found in the biggest department stores in America. Of course Dorothy enjoyed all these luxuries, and the only reason she had heretofore preferred to live in Kansas was because her uncle and aunt loved her and needed her with them.

Now, however, all was to be changed, and Dorothy was really more delighted to know that her dear relatives were to share in her good fortune and enjoy the delights of the Land of Oz, than she was to possess such luxury for herself.

Next morning, at Ozma's request, Dorothy dressed herself in a pretty sky-blue gown of rich silk, trimmed with real pearls. The buckles of her shoes were set with pearls, too, and more of these priceless gems were on a lovely coronet which she wore upon her forehead.

"For," said her friend Ozma, "from this time forth, my dear, you must assume your rightful rank as a Princess of Oz, and being my chosen companion you must dress in a way befitting the dignity of your position."

Dorothy agreed to this, although she knew that neither gowns nor jewels could make her anything else than the simple, unaffected little girl she had always been.

As soon as they had breakfasted—the girls eating together in Ozma's pretty boudoir—the Ruler of Oz said:

"Now, dear friend, we will use the Magic Belt to transport your uncle and aunt from Kansas to the Emerald City. But I think it would be fitting, in receiving such distinguished guests, for us to sit in my Throne Room."

"Oh, they're not very 'stinguished, Ozma," said Dorothy. "They're just plain people, like me."

"Being your friends and relatives, Princess Dorothy, they are certainly distinguished," replied the Ruler, with a smile.

"They—they won't hardly know what to make of all your splendid furniture and things," protested Dorothy, gravely. "It may scare 'em to see your grand Throne Room, an' p'raps we'd better go into the back yard, Ozma, where the cabbages grow an' the chickens are playing. Then it would seem more natural to Uncle Henry and Aunt Em."

"No; they shall first see me in my Throne Room," replied Ozma, decidedly; and when she spoke in that tone Dorothy knew it was not wise to oppose her, for Ozma was accustomed to having her own way.

So together they went to the Throne Room, an immense domed chamber in the center of the palace. Here stood the royal throne, made of solid gold and encrusted with enough precious stones to stock a dozen jewelry stores in our country.

Ozma, who was wearing the Magic Belt, seated herself in the throne, and Dorothy sat at her feet. In the room were assembled many ladies and gentlemen of the court, clothed in rich apparel and wearing fine jewelry. Two immense animals squatted, one on each side of the throne—the Cowardly Lion and the Hungry Tiger. In a balcony high up in the dome an orchestra played sweet music, and beneath the dome two electric fountains sent sprays of colored perfumed water shooting up nearly as high as the arched ceiling.

"Are you ready, Dorothy?" asked the Ruler.

"I am," replied Dorothy; "but I don't know whether Aunt Em and Uncle Henry are ready."

"That won't matter," declared Ozma. "The old life can have very little to interest them, and the sooner they begin the new life here the happier they will be. Here they come, my dear!"

As she spoke, there before the throne appeared Uncle Henry and Aunt Em, who for a moment stood motionless, glaring with white and startled faces at the scene that confronted them. If the ladies and gentlemen present had not been so polite I am sure they would have laughed at the two strangers.

Aunt Em had her calico dress skirt "tucked up," and she wore a faded blue-checked apron. Her hair was rather straggly and she had on a pair of Uncle Henry's old slippers. In one hand she held a dish-towel and in the other a cracked earthenware plate, which she had been engaged in wiping when so suddenly transported to the Land of Oz.

Uncle Henry, when the summons came, had been out in the barn "doin' chores." He wore a ragged and much soiled straw hat, a checked shirt without any collar and blue overalls tucked into the tops of his old cowhide boots.

"By gum!" gasped Uncle Henry, looking around as if bewildered.

"Well, I swan!" gurgled Aunt Em, in a hoarse, frightened voice. Then her eyes fell upon Dorothy, and she said: "D-d-d-don't that look like our little girl—our Dorothy, Henry?"

"Hi, there—look out, Em!" exclaimed the old man, as Aunt Em advanced a step; "take care o' the wild beastses, or you're a goner!"

But now Dorothy sprang forward and embraced and kissed her aunt and uncle affectionately, afterward taking their hands in her own.

"Don't be afraid," she said to them. "You are now in the Land of Oz, where you are to live always, and be comfer'ble an' happy. You'll never have to worry over anything again, 'cause there won't be anything to worry about. And you owe it all to the kindness of my friend Princess Ozma."

Here she led them before the throne and continued:

"Your Highness, this is Uncle Henry. And this is Aunt Em. They want to thank you for bringing them here from Kansas."

Aunt Em tried to "slick" her hair, and she hid the dish-towel and dish under her apron while she bowed to the lovely Ozma. Uncle Henry took off his straw hat and held it awkwardly in his hands.

But the Ruler of Oz rose and came from her throne to greet her newly arrived guests, and she smiled as sweetly upon them as if they had been a King and Queen.

"You are very welcome here, where I have brought you for Princess Dorothy's sake," she said, graciously, "and I hope you will be quite happy in your new home." Then she turned to her courtiers, who were silently and gravely regarding the scene, and added: "I present to my people our Princess Dorothy's beloved Uncle Henry and Aunt Em, who will hereafter be subjects of our kingdom. It will please me to have you show them every kindness and honor in your power, and to join me in making them happy and contented."

Hearing this, all those assembled bowed low and respectfully to the old farmer and his wife, who bobbed their own heads in return.

"And now," said Ozma to them, "Dorothy will show you the rooms prepared for you. I hope you will like them, and shall expect you to join me at luncheon."

So Dorothy led her relatives away, and as soon as they were out of the Throne Room and alone in the corridor Aunt Em squeezed Dorothy's hand and said:

"Child, child! How in the world did we ever get here so quick? And is it all real? And are we to stay here, as she says? And what does it all mean, anyhow?"

Dorothy laughed.

"Why didn't you tell us what you were goin' to do?" inquired Uncle Henry, reproachfully. "If I'd known about it, I'd 'a put on my Sunday clothes."

"I'll 'splain ever'thing as soon as we get to your rooms," promised Dorothy. "You're in great luck, Uncle Henry and Aunt Em; an' so am I! And oh! I'm so happy to have got you here, at last!"

As he walked by the little girl's side Uncle Henry stroked his whiskers thoughtfully.

"'Pears to me, Dorothy, we won't make bang-up fairies," he remarked.

"An' my back hair looks like a fright!" wailed Aunt Em.

"Never mind," returned the little girl, reassuringly. "You won't have anything to do now but to look pretty, Aunt Em; an' Uncle Henry won't have to work till his back aches, that's certain."

"Sure?" they asked, wonderingly, and in the same breath.

"Course I'm sure," said Dorothy. "You're in the Fairyland of Oz, now; an' what's more, you belong to it!"

CHAPTER VI

How Guph Visited the Whimsies

THE NEW GENERAL OF THE NOME KING'S ARMY KNEW PERFECTLY WELL THAT TO fail in his plans meant death for him. Yet he was not at all anxious or worried. He hated every one who was good and longed to make all who were happy unhappy. Therefore he had accepted this dangerous position as General quite willingly, feeling sure in his evil mind that he would be able to do a lot of mischief and finally conquer the Land of Oz.

Yet Guph determined to be careful, and to lay his plans well, so as not to fail. He argued that only careless people fail in what they attempt to do.

The mountains underneath which the Nome King's extensive caverns were located lay grouped just north of the Land of Ev, which lay directly across the deadly desert to the east of the Land of Oz. As the mountains were also on the edge of the desert the Nome King found that he had only to tunnel underneath the desert to reach Ozma's dominions. He did not wish his armies to appear above ground in the Country of the Winkies, which was the part of the Land of Oz nearest to King Roquat's own country, as then the people would give the alarm and enable Ozma to fortify the Emerald City and assemble an army. He wanted to take all the Oz people by surprise; so he decided to run the tunnel clear through to the Emerald City, where he and his hosts could break through the ground without warning and conquer the people before they had time to defend themselves.

Roquat the Red began work at once upon his tunnel, setting a thousand miners at the task and building it high and broad enough for his armies to march through it with ease. The Nomes were used to making tunnels, as all the kingdom in which they lived was underground; so they made rapid progress.

While this work was going on General Guph started out alone to visit the Chief of the Whimsies.

These Whimsies were curious people who lived in a retired country of their own. They had large, strong bodies, but heads so small that they were no bigger than door-knobs. Of course, such tiny heads could not contain any great amount of brains, and the Whimsies were so ashamed of their personal appearance and lack of common-sense that they wore big heads, made of pasteboard, which they fastened over their own little heads. On these pasteboard heads they sewed sheep's wool for hair, and the wool was colored many tints—pink, green and lavender being the favorite colors.

The faces of these false heads were painted in many ridiculous ways, according to the whims of the owners, and these big, burly creatures looked so whimsical and absurd in their queer masks that they were called "Whimsies." They foolishly imag-ined that no one would suspect the little heads that were inside the imitation ones, not knowing that it is folly to try to appear otherwise than as nature has made us.

The Chief of the Whimsies had as little wisdom as the others, and had been cho-sen chief merely because none among them was any wiser or more capable of ruling. The Whimsies were evil spirits and could not be killed. They were hated and feared by every one and were known as terrible fighters because they were so strong and muscular and had not sense enough to know when they were defeated.

General Guph thought the Whimsies would be a great help to the Nomes in the conquest of Oz, for under his leadership they could be induced to fight as long so they could stand up. So he traveled to their country and asked to see the Chief, who lived in a house that had a picture of his grotesque false head painted over the doorway.

The Chief's false head had blue hair, a turned-up nose, and a mouth that stretched half across the face. Big green eyes had been painted upon it, but in the center of the chin were two small holes made in the pasteboard, so that the Chief could see through them with his own tiny eyes; for when the big head was fastened upon his shoulders the eyes in his own natural head were on a level with the false chin.

Said General Guph to the Chief of the Whimsies:

"We Nomes are going to conquer the Land of Oz and capture our King's Magic Belt, which the Oz people stole from him. Then we are going to plunder and destroy the whole country. And we want the Whimsies to help us."

"Will there be any fighting?" asked the Chief.

"Plenty," replied Guph.

That must have pleased the Chief, for he got up and danced around the room three times. Then he seated himself again, adjusted his false head, and said:

"We have no quarrel with Ozma of Oz."

"But you Whimsies love to fight, and here is a splendid chance to do so," urged Guph.

"Wait till I sing a song," said the Chief. Then he lay back in his chair and sang a foolish song that did not seem to the General to mean anything, although he listened carefully. When he had finished, the Chief Whimsie looked at him through the holes in his chin and asked:

"What reward will you give us if we help you?"

The General was prepared for this question, for he had been thinking the matter over on his journey. People often do a good deed without hope of reward, but for an evil deed they always demand payment.

"When we get our Magic Belt," he made reply, "our King, Roquat the Red, will use its power to give every Whimsie a natural head as big and fine as the false head he now wears. Then you will no longer be ashamed because your big strong bodies have such teenty-weenty heads."

"Oh! Will you do that?" asked the Chief, eagerly.

"We surely will," promised the General.

"I'll talk to my people," said the Chief.

So he called a meeting of all the Whimsies and told them of the offer made by the Nomes. The creatures were delighted with the bargain, and at once agreed to fight for the Nome King and help him to conquer Oz.

One Whimsie alone seemed to have a glimmer of sense, for he asked:

"Suppose we fail to capture the Magic Belt? What will happen then, and what good will all our fighting do?"

But they threw him into the river for asking foolish questions, and laughed when the water ruined his pasteboard head before he could swim out again.

So the compact was made and General Guph was delighted with his success in gaining such powerful allies.

But there were other people, too, just as important as the Whimsies, whom the clever old Nome had determined to win to his side.

CHAPTER VII

How Aunt Em Conquered the Lion

"These are your rooms," said Dorothy, opening a door.

Aunt Em drew back at the sight of the splendid furniture and draperies.

"Ain't there any place to wipe my feet?" she asked.

"You will soon change your slippers for new shoes," replied Dorothy. "Don't be afraid, Aunt Em. Here is where you are to live, so walk right in and make yourself at home."

Aunt Em advanced hesitatingly.

"It beats the Topeka Hotel!" she cried, admiringly. "But this place is too grand for us, child. Can't we have some back room in the attic, that's more in our class?"

"No," said Dorothy. "You've got to live here, 'cause Ozma says so. And all the rooms in this palace are just as fine as these, and some are better. It won't do any good to fuss, Aunt Em. You've got to be swell and high-toned in the Land of Oz, whether you want to or not; so you may as well make up your mind to it."

"It's hard luck," replied her aunt, looking around with an awed expression; "but folks can get used to anything, if they try. Eh, Henry?"

"Why, as to that," said Uncle Henry, slowly, "I b'lieve in takin' what's pervided us, an' askin' no questions. I've traveled some, Em, in my time, and you hain't; an' that makes a difference atween us."

Then Dorothy showed them through the rooms. The first was a handsome sitting-room, with windows opening upon the rose gardens. Then came separate bedrooms for Aunt Em and Uncle Henry, with a fine bathroom between them. Aunt Em had a pretty dressing room, besides, and Dorothy opened the closets and showed several exquisite costumes that had been provided for her aunt by the royal dress-makers, who had worked all night to get them ready. Everything that Aunt Em could possibly need was in the drawers and closets, and her dressing-table was covered with engraved gold toilet articles.

Uncle Henry had nine suits of clothes, cut in the popular Munchkin fashion, with knee-breeches, silk stockings and low shoes with jeweled buckles. The hats to match these costumes had pointed tops and wide brims with small gold bells around the edges. His shirts were of fine linen with frilled bosoms, and his vests were richly embroidered with colored silks.

Uncle Henry decided that he would first take a bath and then dress himself in a blue satin suit that had caught his fancy. He accepted his good fortune with calm composure and refused to have a servant to assist him. But Aunt Em was "all of a flutter," as she said, and it took Dorothy and Jellia Jamb, the housekeeper, and two maids a long time to dress her and do up her hair and get her "rigged like a popinjay," as she quaintly expressed it. She wanted to stop and admire everything that caught her eye, and she sighed continually and declared that such finery was too good for an old country woman, and that she never thought she would have to "put on airs" at her time of life.

Finally she was dressed, and when they went into the sitting-room there was Uncle Henry in his blue satin, walking gravely up and down the room. He had trimmed his beard and mustache and looked very dignified and respectable.

"Tell me, Dorothy," he said; "do all the men here wear duds like these?"

"Yes," she replied; "all 'cept the Scarecrow and the Shaggy Man—and of course the Tin Woodman and Tik-Tok, who are made of metal. You'll find all the men at Ozma's court dressed just as you are—only perhaps a little finer."

"Henry, you look like a play-actor," announced Aunt Em, looking at her husband critically.

"An' you, Em, look more highfalutin' than a peacock," he replied.

"I guess you're right," she said, regretfully; "but we're helpless victims of high-toned royalty."

Dorothy was much amused.

"Come with me," she said, "and I'll show you 'round the palace."

She took them through the beautiful rooms and introduced them to all the people they chanced to meet. Also she showed them her own pretty rooms, which were not far from their own.

"So it's all true," said Aunt Em, wide-eyed with amazement, "and what Dorothy told us of this fairy country was plain facts instead of dreams! But where are all the strange creatures you used to know here?"

"Yes; where's the Scarecrow?" inquired Uncle Henry.

"Why, he's just now away on a visit to the Tin Woodman, who is Emp'ror of the Winkie Country," answered the little girl. "You'll see him when he comes back, and you're sure to like him."

"And where's the Wonderful Wizard?" asked Aunt Em.

"You'll see him at Ozma's luncheon, for he lives in this palace," was the reply.

"And Jack Pumpkinhead?"

"Oh, he lives a little way out of town, in his own pumpkin field. We'll go there some time and see him, and we'll call on Professor Woggle-Bug, too. The Shaggy Man will be at the luncheon, I guess, and Tik-Tok. And now I'll take you out to see Billina, who has a house of her own."

So they went into the back yard, and after walking along winding paths some distance through the beautiful gardens they came to an attractive little house where the Yellow Hen sat on the front porch sunning herself.

"Good morning, my dear Mistress," called Billina, fluttering down to meet them. "I was expecting you to call, for I heard you had come back and brought your uncle and aunt with you."

"We're here for good and all, this time, Billina," cried Dorothy, joyfully. "Uncle Henry and Aunt Em belong in Oz now as much as I do!"

"Then they are very lucky people," declared Billina; "for there couldn't be a nicer place to live. But come, my dear; I must show you all my Dorothys. Nine are living and have grown up to be very respectable hens; but one took cold at Ozma's birthday party and died of the pip, and the other two turned out to be horrid roosters, so I had to change their names from Dorothy to Daniel. They all had the letter 'D' engraved upon their gold lockets, you remember, with your picture inside, and 'D' stands for Daniel as well as for Dorothy."

"Did you call both the roosters Daniel?" asked Uncle Henry.

"Yes, indeed. I've nine Dorothys and two Daniels; and the nine Dorothys have eighty-six sons and daughters and over three hundred grandchildren," said Billina, proudly.

"What names do you give 'em all, dear?" inquired the little girl.

"Oh, they are all Dorothys and Daniels, some being Juniors and some Double-Juniors. Dorothy and Daniel are two good names, and I see no object in hunting for others," declared the Yellow Hen. "But just think, Dorothy, what a big chicken family we've grown to be, and our numbers increase nearly every day! Ozma doesn't know what to do with all the eggs we lay, and we are never eaten or harmed in any way, as chickens are in your country. They give us everything to make us contented and happy, and I, my dear, am the acknowledged Queen and Governor of every chicken in Oz, because I'm the eldest and started the whole colony."

"You ought to be very proud, ma'am," said Uncle Henry, who was astonished to hear a hen talk so sensibly.

"Oh, I am," she replied. "I've the loveliest pearl necklace you ever saw. Come in the house and I'll show it to you. And I've nine leg bracelets and a diamond pin for each wing. But I only wear them on state occasions."

They followed the Yellow Hen into the house, which Aunt Em declared was neat as a pin. They could not sit down, because all Billina's chairs were roosting-poles made of silver; so they had to stand while the hen fussily showed them her treasures.

Then they had to go into the back rooms occupied by Billina's nine Dorothys and two Daniels, who were all plump yellow chickens and greeted the visitors very politely. It was easy to see that they were well bred and that Billina had looked after their education.

In the yards were all the children and grandchildren of these eleven elders and they were of all sizes, from well-grown hens to tiny chickens just out of the shell. About fifty fluffy yellow youngsters were at school, being taught good manners and good grammar by a young hen who wore spectacles. They sang in chorus a patriotic song of the Land of Oz, in honor of their visitors, and Aunt Em was much impressed by these talking chickens.

Dorothy wanted to stay and play with the young chickens for a while, but Uncle Henry and Aunt Em had not seen the palace grounds and gardens yet and were eager to get better acquainted with the marvelous and delightful land in which they were to live.

"I'll stay here, and you can go for a walk," said Dorothy. "You'll be perfec'ly safe anywhere, and may do whatever you want to. When you get tired, go back to the palace and find your rooms, and I'll come to you before luncheon is ready."

So Uncle Henry and Aunt Em started out alone to explore the grounds, and Dorothy knew that they couldn't get lost, because all the palace grounds were enclosed by a high wall of green marble set with emeralds.

It was a rare treat to these simple folk, who had lived in the country all their lives and known little enjoyment of any sort, to wear beautiful clothes and live in a palace and be treated with respect and consideration by all around them. They were very happy indeed as they strolled up the shady walks and looked upon the gorgeous flowers and shrubs, feeling that their new home was more beautiful than any tongue could describe.

Suddenly, as they turned a corner and walked through a gap in a high hedge, they came face to face with an enormous Lion, which crouched upon the green lawn and seemed surprised by their appearance.

They stopped short, Uncle Henry trembling with horror and Aunt Em too terrified to scream. Next moment the poor woman clasped her husband around the neck and cried:

"Save me, Henry, save me!"

"Can't even save myself, Em," he returned, in a husky voice, "for the animile looks as if it could eat both of us, an' lick its chops for more! If I only had a gun—"

"Haven't you, Henry? Haven't you?" she asked anxiously.

"Nary gun, Em. So let's die as brave an' graceful as we can. I knew our luck couldn't last!"

"I won't die. I won't be eaten by a lion!" wailed Aunt Em, glaring upon the huge beast. Then a thought struck her, and she whispered: "Henry, I've heard as savage beastses can be conquered by the human eye. I'll eye that lion out o' countenance an' save our lives."

"Try it, Em," he returned, also in a whisper. "Look at him as you do at me when I'm late to dinner."

Aunt Em turned upon the Lion a determined countenance and a wild dilated eye. She glared at the immense beast steadily, and the Lion, who had been quietly blinking at them, began to appear uneasy and disturbed.

"Is anything the matter, ma'am?" he asked, in a mild voice.

At this speech from the terrible beast Aunt Em and Uncle Henry both were startled, and then Uncle Henry remembered that this must be the Lion they had seen in Ozma's Throne Room.

"Hold on, Em!" he exclaimed. "Quit the eagle eye conquest an' take courage. I guess this is the same Cowardly Lion Dorothy has told us about."

"Oh, is it?" she cried, much relieved.

"When he spoke, I got the idea; and when he looked so 'shamed like, I was sure of it," Uncle Henry continued.

Aunt Em regarded the animal with new interest.

"Are you the Cowardly Lion?" she inquired. "Are you Dorothy's friend?"

"Yes'm," answered the Lion, meekly. "Dorothy and I are old chums and are very fond of each other. I'm the King of Beasts, you know, and the Hungry Tiger and I serve Princess Ozma as her body-guards."

"To be sure," said Aunt Em, nodding. "But the King of Beasts shouldn't be cowardly."

"I've heard that said before," remarked the Lion, yawning till he showed his two great rows of sharp white teeth; "but that does not keep me from being frightened whenever I go into battle."

"What do you do, run?" asked Uncle Henry.

"No; that would be foolish, for the enemy would run after me," declared the Lion. "So I tremble with fear and pitch in as hard as I can; and so far I have always won my fight."

"Ah, I begin to understand," said Uncle Henry.

"Were you scared when I looked at you just now?" inquired Aunt Em.

"Terribly scared, madam," answered the Lion, "for at first I thought you were going to have a fit. Then I noticed you were trying to overcome me by the power of your eye, and your glance was so fierce and penetrating that I shook with fear."

This greatly pleased the lady, and she said quite cheerfully:

"Well, I won't hurt you, so don't be scared any more. I just wanted to see what the human eye was good for."

"The human eye is a fearful weapon," remarked the Lion, scratching his nose softly with his paw to hide a smile. "Had I not known you were Dorothy's friends I might have torn you both into shreds in order to escape your terrible gaze."

Aunt Em shuddered at hearing this, and Uncle Henry said hastily:

"I'm glad you knew us. Good morning, Mr. Lion; we'll hope to see you again— by and by—some time in the future."

"Good morning," replied the Lion, squatting down upon the lawn again. "You are likely to see a good deal of me, if you live in the Land of Oz."

CHAPTER VIII

How THE GRAND GALLIPOOT JOINED THE NOMES

AFTER LEAVING THE WHIMSIES, GUPH CONTINUED ON HIS JOURNEY AND PENETRATED far into the Northwest. He wanted to get to the Country of the Growleywogs, and in order to do that he must cross the Ripple Land, which was a hard thing to do. For the Ripple Land was a succession of hills and valleys, all very steep and rocky, and they changed places constantly by rippling. While Guph was climbing a hill it sank down under him and became a valley, and while he was descending into a valley it rose up and carried him to the top of a hill. This was very perplexing to the traveler, and a stranger might have thought he could never cross the Ripple Land at all. But Guph knew that if he kept steadily on he would get to the end at last; so he paid no attention to the changing hills and valleys and plodded along as calmly as if walking upon the level ground.

The result of this wise persistence was that the General finally reached firmer soil and, after penetrating a dense forest, came to the Dominion of the Growleywogs.

No sooner had he crossed the border of this domain when two guards seized him and carried him before the Grand Gallipoot of the Growleywogs, who scowled upon him ferociously and asked him why he dared intrude upon his territory.

"I'm the Lord High General of the Invincible Army of the Nomes, and my name is Guph," was the reply. "All the world trembles when that name is mentioned."

The Growleywogs gave a shout of jeering laughter at this, and one of them caught the Nome in his strong arms and tossed him high into the air. Guph was considerably shaken when he fell upon the hard ground, but he appeared to take no notice of the impertinence and composed himself to speak again to the Grand Gallipoot.

"My master, King Roquat the Red, has sent me here to confer with you. He wishes your assistance to conquer the Land of Oz."

Here the General paused, and the Grand Gallipoot scowled upon him more terribly than ever and said:

"Go on!"

The voice of the Grand Gallipoot was partly a roar and partly a growl. He mumbled his words badly and Guph had to listen carefully in order to understand him.

These Growleywogs were certainly remarkable creatures. They were of gigantic size, yet were all bone and skin and muscle, there being no meat or fat upon their bodies at all. Their powerful muscles lay just underneath their skins, like bunches of tough rope, and the weakest Growleywog was so strong that he could pick up an elephant and toss it seven miles away.

It seems unfortunate that strong people are usually so disagreeable and overbearing that no one cares for them. In fact, to be different from your fellow creatures is always a misfortune. The Growleywogs knew that they were disliked and avoided by every one, so they had become surly and unsociable even among themselves. Guph knew that they hated all people, including the Nomes; but he hoped to win them over, nevertheless, and knew that if he succeeded they would afford him very powerful assistance.

"The Land of Oz is ruled by a namby-pamby girl who is disgustingly kind and good," he continued. "Her people are all happy and contented and have no care or worries whatever."

"Go on!" growled the Grand Gallipoot.

"Once the Nome King enslaved the Royal Family of Ev—another goody-goody lot that we detest," said the General. "But Ozma interfered, although it was none of her business, and marched her army against us. With her was a Kansas girl named Dorothy, and a Yellow Hen, and they marched directly into the Nome King's cavern. There they liberated our slaves from Ev and stole King Roquat's Magic Belt, which they carried away with them. So now our King is making a tunnel under the deadly desert, so we can march through it to the Emerald City. When we get there we mean to conquer and destroy all the land and recapture the Magic Belt."

Again he paused, and again the Grand Gallipoot growled:

"Go on!"

Guph tried to think what to say next, and a happy thought soon occurred to him.

"We want you to help us in this conquest," he announced, "for we need the mighty aid of the Growleywogs in order to make sure that we shall not be defeated. You are the strongest people in all the world, and you hate good and happy creatures as much as we Nomes do. I am sure it will be a real pleasure to you to tear down the

beautiful Emerald City, and in return for your valuable assistance we will allow you to bring back to your country ten thousand people of Oz, to be your slaves."

"Twenty thousand!" growled the Grand Gallipoot.

"All right, we promise you twenty thousand," agreed the General.

The Gallipoot made a signal and at once his attendants picked up General Guph and carried him away to a prison, where the jailor amused himself by sticking pins in the round fat body of the old Nome, to see him jump and hear him yell.

But while this was going on the Grand Gallipoot was talking with his counselors, who were the most important officials of the Growleywogs. When he had stated to them the proposition of the Nome King he said:

"My advice is to offer to help them. Then, when we have conquered the Land of Oz, we will take not only our twenty thousand prisoners but all the gold and jewels we want."

"Let us take the Magic Belt, too," suggested one counselor.

"And rob the Nome King and make him our slave," said another.

"That is a good idea," declared the Grand Gallipoot. "I'd like King Roquat for my own slave. He could black my boots and bring me my porridge every morning while I am in bed."

"There is a famous Scarecrow in Oz. I'll take him for my slave," said a counselor.

"I'll take Tik-Tok, the machine man," said another.

"Give me the Tin Woodman," said a third.

They went on for some time, dividing up the people and the treasure of Oz in advance of the conquest. For they had no doubt at all that they would be able to destroy Ozma's domain. Were they not the strongest people in all the world?

"The deadly desert has kept us out of Oz before," remarked the Grand Gallipoot, "but now that the Nome King is building a tunnel we shall get into the Emerald City very easily. So let us send the little fat General back to his King with our promise to assist him. We will not say that we intend to conquer the Nomes after we have conquered Oz, but we will do so, just the same."

This plan being agreed upon, they all went home to dinner, leaving General Guph still in prison. The Nome had no idea that he had succeeded in his mission, for finding himself in prison he feared the Growleywogs intended to put him to death.

By this time the jailor had tired of sticking pins in the General, and was amusing himself by carefully pulling the Nome's whiskers out by the roots, one at a time. This enjoyment was interrupted by the Grand Gallipoot sending for the prisoner.

"Wait a few hours," begged the jailor. "I haven't pulled out a quarter of his whiskers yet."

"If you keep the Grand Gallipoot waiting, he'll break your back," declared the messenger.

"Perhaps you're right," sighed the jailor. "Take the prisoner away, if you will, but I advise you to kick him at every step he takes. It will be good fun, for he is as soft as a ripe peach."

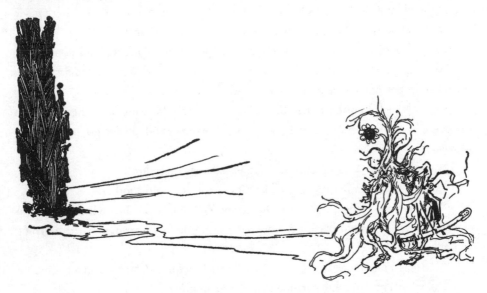

So Guph was led away to the royal castle, where the Grand Gallipoot told him that the Growleywogs had decided to assist the Nomes in conquering the Land of Oz.

"Whenever you are ready," he added, "send me word and I will march with eighteen thousand of my most powerful warriors to your aid."

Guph was so delighted that he forgot all the smarting caused by the pins and the pulling of whiskers. He did not even complain of the treatment he had received, but thanked the Grand Gallipoot and hurried away upon his journey.

He had now secured the assistance of the Whimsies and the Growleywogs; but his success made him long for still more allies. His own life depended upon his conquering Oz, and he said to himself:

"I'll take no chances. I'll be certain of success. Then, when Oz is destroyed, perhaps I shall be a greater man than old Roquat, and I can throw him away and be King of the Nomes myself. Why not? The Whimsies are stronger than the Nomes, and they are my friends. The Growleywogs are stronger than the Whimsies, and they also are my friends. There are some people still stronger than the Growleywogs, and if I can but induce them to aid me I shall have nothing more to fear."

CHAPTER IX

How THE WOGGLE-BUG TAUGHT ATHLETICS

IT DID NOT TAKE DOROTHY LONG TO ESTABLISH HERSELF IN HER NEW HOME, FOR she knew the people and the manners and customs of the Emerald City just as well as she knew the old Kansas farm.

But Uncle Henry and Aunt Em had some trouble in getting used to the finery and pomp and ceremony of Ozma's palace, and felt uneasy because they were obliged to be "dressed up" all the time. Yet every one was very courteous and kind to them and endeavored to make them happy. Ozma, especially, made much of Dorothy's relatives, for her little friend's sake, and she well knew that the awkwardness and strangeness of their new mode of life would all wear off in time.

The old people were chiefly troubled by the fact that there was no work for them to do.

"Ev'ry day is like Sunday, now," declared Aunt Em, solemnly, "and I can't say I like it. If they'd only let me do up the dishes after meals, or even sweep an' dust my own rooms, I'd be a deal happier. Henry don't know what to do with himself either, and once when he stole out an' fed the chickens Billina scolded him for letting 'em eat between meals. I never knew before what a hardship it is to be rich and have everything you want."

These complaints began to worry Dorothy; so she had a long talk with Ozma upon the subject.

"I see I must find them something to do," said the girlish Ruler of Oz, seriously. "I have been watching your uncle and aunt, and I believe they will be more contented if occupied with some light tasks. While I am considering this matter, Dorothy, you might make a trip with them through the Land of Oz, visiting some of the odd corners and introducing your relatives to some of our curious people."

"Oh, that would be fine!" exclaimed Dorothy, eagerly.

"I will give you an escort befitting your rank as a Princess," continued Ozma; "and you may go to some of the places you have not yet visited yourself, as well as some others that you know. I will mark out a plan of the trip for you and have everything in readiness for you to start to-morrow morning. Take your time, dear, and be gone as long as you wish. By the time you return I shall have found some occupation for Uncle Henry and Aunt Em that will keep them from being restless and dissatisfied."

Dorothy thanked her good friend and kissed the lovely Ruler gratefully. Then she ran to tell the joyful news to her uncle and aunt.

Next morning, after breakfast, everything was found ready for their departure.

The escort included Omby Amby, the Captain General of Ozma's army, which consisted merely of twenty-seven officers besides the Captain General. Once Omby Amby had been a private soldier—the only private in the army—but as there was never any fighting to do Ozma saw no need of a private, so she made Omby Amby the highest officer of them all. He was very tall and slim and wore a gay uniform and a fierce mustache. Yet the mustache was the only fierce thing about Omby Amby, whose nature was as gentle as that of a child.

The wonderful Wizard had asked to join the party, and with him came his friend the Shaggy Man, who was shaggy but not ragged, being dressed in fine silks with satin shags and bobtails. The Shaggy Man had shaggy whiskers and hair, but a sweet disposition and a soft, pleasant voice.

There was an open wagon, with three seats for the passengers, and the wagon was drawn by the famous wooden Saw-Horse which had once been brought to life by Ozma by means of a magic powder. The Saw-Horse wore wooden shoes to keep his wooden legs from wearing away, and he was strong and swift. As this curious creature was Ozma's own favorite steed, and very popular with all the people of the Emerald City, Dorothy knew that she had been highly favored by being permitted to use the Saw-Horse on her journey.

In the front seat of the wagon sat Dorothy and the Wizard. Uncle Henry and Aunt Em sat in the next seat and the Shaggy Man and Omby Amby in the third seat. Of course Toto was with the party, curled up at Dorothy's feet, and just as they were about to start Billina came fluttering along the path and begged to be taken with them. Dorothy readily agreed, so the Yellow Hen flew up and perched herself upon the dashboard. She wore her pearl necklace and three bracelets upon each leg, in honor of the occasion.

Dorothy kissed Ozma good-bye, and all the people standing around waved their handkerchiefs, and the band in an upper balcony struck up a military march. Then the Wizard clucked to the Saw-Horse and said: "Gid-dap!" and the wooden animal pranced away and drew behind him the big red wagon and all the passengers, without any effort at all. A servant threw open a gate of the palace enclosure, that they might pass out; and so, with music and shouts following them, the journey was begun.

"It's almost like a circus," said Aunt Em, proudly. "I can't help feelin' high an' mighty in this kind of a turn-out."

Indeed, as they passed down the street, all the people cheered them lustily, and the Shaggy Man and the Wizard and the Captain General all took off their hats and bowed politely in acknowledgment.

When they came to the great wall of the Emerald City the gates were opened by the Guardian who always tended them. Over the gateway hung a dull-colored metal magnet shaped like a horse-shoe, placed against a shield of polished gold.

"That," said the Shaggy Man, impressively, "is the wonderful Love Magnet. I brought it to the Emerald City myself, and all who pass beneath this gateway are both loving and beloved."

"It's a fine thing," declared Aunt Em, admiringly. "If we'd had it in Kansas I guess the man who held a mortgage on the farm wouldn't have turned us out."

"Then I'm glad we didn't have it," returned Uncle Henry. "I like Oz better than Kansas, even; an' this little wood Saw-Horse beats all the critters I ever saw. He don't have to be curried, or fed, or watered, an' he's strong as an ox. Can he talk, Dorothy?"

"Yes, Uncle," replied the child. "But the Saw-Horse never says much. He told me once that he can't talk and think at the same time, so he prefers to think."

"Which is very sensible," declared the Wizard, nodding approvingly. "Which way do we go, Dorothy?"

"Straight ahead into the Quadling Country," she answered. "I've got a letter of interduction to Miss Cuttenclip."

"Oh!" exclaimed the Wizard, much interested. "Are we going there? Then I'm glad I came, for I've always wanted to meet the Cuttenclips."

"Who are they?" inquired Aunt Em.

"Wait till we get there," replied Dorothy, with a laugh; "then you'll see for yourself. I've never seen the Cuttenclips, you know, so I can't 'zactly 'splain 'em to you."

Once free of the Emerald City the Saw-Horse dashed away at tremendous speed. Indeed, he went so fast that Aunt Em had hard work to catch her breath, and Uncle Henry held fast to the seat of the red wagon.

"Gently—gently, my boy!" called the Wizard, and at this the Saw-Horse slackened his speed.

"What's wrong?" asked the animal, slightly turning his wooden head to look at the party with one eye, which was a knot of wood.

"Why, we wish to admire the scenery, that's all," answered the Wizard.

"Some of your passengers," added the Shaggy Man, "have never been out of the Emerald City before, and the country is all new to them."

"If you go too fast you'll spoil all the fun," said Dorothy. "There's no hurry."

"Very well; it is all the same to me," observed the Saw-Horse; and after that he went at a more moderate pace.

Uncle Henry was astonished.

"How can a wooden thing be so intelligent?" he asked.

"Why, I gave him some sawdust brains the last time I fitted his head with new ears," explained the Wizard. "The sawdust was made from hard knots, and now the Saw-Horse is able to think out any knotty problem he meets with."

"I see," said Uncle Henry.

"I don't," remarked Aunt Em; but no one paid any attention to this statement.

Before long they came to a stately building that stood upon a green plain with handsome shade trees grouped here and there.

"What is that?" asked Uncle Henry.

"That," replied the Wizard, "is the Royal Athletic College of Oz, which is directed by Professor H. M. Woggle-Bug, T.E."

"Let's stop and make a call," suggested Dorothy.

So the Saw-Horse drew up in front of the great building and they were met at the door by the learned Woggle-Bug himself. He seemed fully as tall as the Wizard, and was dressed in a red and white checked vest and a blue swallow-tailed coat, and had yellow knee breeches and purple silk stockings upon his slender legs. A tall hat was jauntily set upon his head and he wore spectacles over his big bright eyes.

"Welcome, Dorothy," said the Woggle-Bug; "and welcome to all your friends. We are indeed pleased to receive you at this great Temple of Learning."

"I thought it was an Athletic College," said the Shaggy Man.

"It is, my dear sir," answered the Woggle-Bug, proudly. "Here it is that we teach the youth of our great land scientific College Athletics—in all their purity."

"Don't you teach them anything else?" asked Dorothy. "Don't they get any reading, writing and 'rithmetic?"

"Oh, yes; of course. They get all those, and more," returned the Professor. "But such things occupy little of their time. Please follow me and I will show you how my scholars are usually occupied. This is a class hour and they are all busy."

They followed him to a big field back of the college building, where several hundred young Ozites were at their classes. In one place they played football, in another baseball. Some played tennis, some golf; some were swimming in a big pool. Upon a river which wound through the grounds several crews in racing boats were rowing with great enthusiasm. Other groups of students played basketball and cricket, while in one place a ring was roped in to permit boxing and wrestling by the energetic youths. All the collegians seemed busy and there was much laughter and shouting.

"This college," said Professor Woggle-Bug, complacently, "is a great success. Its educational value is undisputed, and we are turning out many great and valuable citizens every year."

"But when do they study?" asked Dorothy.

"Study?" said the Woggle-Bug, looking perplexed at the question.

"Yes; when do they get their 'rithmetic, and jogerfy, and such things?"

"Oh, they take doses of those every night and morning," was the reply.

"What do you mean by doses?" Dorothy inquired, wonderingly.

"Why, we use the newly invented School Pills, made by your friend the Wizard. These pills we have found to be very effective, and they save a lot of time. Please step this way and I will show you our Laboratory of Learning."

He led them to a room in the building where many large bottles were standing in rows upon shelves.

"These are the Algebra Pills," said the Professor, taking down one of the bottles. "One at night, on retiring, is equal to four hours of study. Here are the Geography Pills—one at night and one in the morning. In this next bottle are the Latin Pills—one three times a day. Then we have the Grammar Pills—one before each meal—and the Spelling Pills, which are taken whenever needed."

"Your scholars must have to take a lot of pills," remarked Dorothy, thoughtfully. "How do they take 'em, in applesauce?"

"No, my dear. They are sugar-coated and are quickly and easily swallowed. I believe the students would rather take the pills than study, and certainly the pills are a more effective method. You see, until these School Pills were invented we wasted a lot of time in study that may now be better employed in practising athletics."

"Seems to me the pills are a good thing," said Omby Amby, who remembered how it used to make his head ache as a boy to study arithmetic.

"They are, sir," declared the Woggle-Bug, earnestly. "They give us an advantage over all other colleges, because at no loss of time our boys become thoroughly conversant with Greek and Latin, Mathematics and Geography, Grammar and Literature. You see they are never obliged to interrupt their games to acquire the lesser branches of learning."

"It's a great invention, I'm sure," said Dorothy, looking admiringly at the Wizard, who blushed modestly at this praise.

"We live in an age of progress," announced Professor Woggle-Bug, pompously. "It is easier to swallow knowledge than to acquire it laboriously from books. Is it not so, my friends?"

"Some folks can swallow anything," said Aunt Em, "but to me this seems too much like taking medicine."

"Young men in college always have to take their medicine, one way or another," observed the Wizard, with a smile; "and, as our Professor says, these School Pills have proved to be a great success. One day while I was making them I happened to drop one of them, and one of Billina's chickens gobbled it up. A few minutes afterward this chick got upon a roost and recited 'The Boy Stood on the Burning Deck' without making a single mistake. Then it recited 'The Charge of the Light Brigade' and afterwards 'Excelsior.' You see, the chicken had eaten an Elocution Pill."

They now bade good-bye to the Professor, and thanking him for his kind reception mounted again into the red wagon and continued their journey.

CHAPTER X

How THE CUTTENCLIPS LIVED

THE TRAVELERS HAD TAKEN NO PROVISIONS WITH THEM BECAUSE THEY KNEW THAT they would be welcomed wherever they might go in the Land of Oz, and that the people would feed and lodge them with genuine hospitality. So about noon they stopped at a farm-house and were given a delicious luncheon of bread and milk, fruits and wheat cakes with maple syrup. After resting a while and strolling through the orchards with their host—a round, jolly farmer—they got into the wagon and again started the Saw-Horse along the pretty, winding road.

There were sign-posts at all the corners, and finally they came to one which read:

☞ TAKE THIS ROAD TO THE CUTTENCLIPS

There was also a hand pointing in the right direction, so they turned the Saw-Horse that way and found it a very good road, but seemingly little traveled.

"I've never been to see the Cuttenclips before," remarked Dorothy.

"Nor I," said the Captain General.

"Nor I," said the Wizard.

"Nor I," said Billina.

"I've hardly been out of the Emerald City since I arrived in this country," added the Shaggy Man.

"Why, none of us has been there, then," exclaimed the little girl. "I wonder what the Cuttenclips are like."

"We shall soon find out," said the Wizard, with a sly laugh. "I've heard they are rather flimsy things."

The farm-houses became fewer as they proceeded, and the path was at times so faint that the Saw-Horse had hard work to keep in the road. The wagon began to jounce, too; so they were obliged to go slowly.

After a somewhat wearisome journey they came in sight of a high wall, painted blue with pink ornaments. This wall was circular, and seemed to enclose a large space. It was so high that only the tops of the trees could be seen above it.

The path led up to a small door in the wall, which was closed and latched. Upon the door was a sign in gold letters reading as follows:

VISITORS are requested to MOVE SLOWLY and CAREFULLY, and to avoid COUGHING or making any BREEZE or DRAUGHT

"That's strange," said the Shaggy Man, reading the sign aloud. "Who *are* the Cuttenclips, anyhow?"

"Why, they're paper dolls," answered Dorothy. "Didn't you know that?"

"Paper dolls! Then let's go somewhere else," said Uncle Henry. "We're all too old to play with dolls, Dorothy."

"But these are different," declared the girl. "They're alive."

"Alive!" gasped Aunt Em, in amazement.

"Yes. Let's go in," said Dorothy.

So they all got out of the wagon, since the door in the wall was not big enough for them to drive the Saw-Horse and wagon through it.

"You stay here, Toto!" commanded Dorothy, shaking her finger at the little dog. "You're so careless that you might make a breeze if I let you inside."

Toto wagged his tail as if disappointed at being left behind; but he made no effort to follow them. The Wizard unlatched the door, which opened outward, and they all looked eagerly inside.

Just before the entrance was drawn up a line of tiny soldiers, with uniforms brightly painted and paper guns upon their shoulders. They were exactly alike, from one end of the line to the other, and all were cut out of paper and joined together in the centers of their bodies.

As the visitors entered the enclosure the Wizard let the door swing back into place, and at once the line of soldiers tumbled over, fell flat upon their backs, and lay fluttering upon the ground.

"Hi, there!" called one of them; "what do you mean by slamming the door and blowing us over?"

"I beg your pardon, I'm sure," said the Wizard, regretfully. "I didn't know you were so delicate."

"We're not delicate!" retorted another soldier, raising his head from the ground. "We are strong and healthy; but we can't stand draughts."

"May I help you up?" asked Dorothy.

"If you please," replied the end soldier. "But do it gently, little girl."

Dorothy carefully stood up the line of soldiers, who first dusted their painted clothes and then saluted the visitors with their paper muskets. From the end it was easy to see that the entire line had been cut out of paper, although from the front the soldiers looked rather solid and imposing.

"I've a letter of introduction from Princess Ozma to Miss Cuttenclip," announced Dorothy.

"Very well," said the end soldier, and blew upon a paper whistle that hung around his neck. At once a paper soldier in a Captain's uniform came out of a paper house near by and approached the group at the entrance. He was not very big, and he walked rather stiffly and uncertainly on his paper legs; but he had a pleasant face, with very red cheeks and very blue eyes, and he bowed so low to the strangers that Dorothy laughed, and the breeze from her mouth nearly blew the Captain over. He wavered and struggled and finally managed to remain upon his feet.

"Take care, Miss!" he said, warningly. "You're breaking the rules, you know, by laughing."

"Oh, I didn't know that," she replied.

"To laugh in this place is nearly as dangerous as to cough," said the Captain. "You'll have to breathe very quietly, I assure you."

"We'll try to," promised the girl. "May we see Miss Cuttenclip, please?"

"You may," promptly returned the Captain. "This is one of her reception days. Be good enough to follow me."

He turned and led the way up a path, and as they followed slowly, because the paper Captain did not move very swiftly, they took the opportunity to gaze around them at this strange paper country.

Beside the path were paper trees, all cut out very neatly and painted a brilliant green color. And back of the trees were rows of cardboard houses, painted in various colors but most of them having green blinds. Some were large and some small, and in the front yards were beds of paper flowers quite natural in appearance. Over some of the porches paper vines were twined, giving them a cozy and shady look.

As the visitors passed along the street a good many paper dolls came to the doors and windows of their houses to look at them curiously. These dolls were nearly all the same height, but were cut into various shapes, some being fat and some lean. The girl dolls wore many beautiful costumes of tissue paper, making them quite fluffy; but their heads and hands were no thicker than the paper of which they were made.

Some of the paper people were on the street, walking along or congregated in groups and talking together; but as soon as they saw the strangers they all fluttered into the houses as fast as they could go, so as to be out of danger.

"Excuse me if I go edgewise," remarked the Captain, as they came to a slight hill. "I can get along faster that way and not flutter so much."

"That's all right," said Dorothy. "We don't mind how you go, I'm sure."

At one side of the street was a paper pump, and a paper boy was pumping paper water into a paper pail. The Yellow Hen happened to brush against this boy with her wing, and he flew into the air and fell into a paper tree, where he stuck until the Wizard gently pulled him out. At the same time the pail went into the air, spilling the paper water, while the paper pump bent nearly double.

"Goodness me!" said the Hen. "If I should flop my wings I believe I'd knock over the whole village!"

"Then don't flop them—please don't!" entreated the Captain. "Miss Cuttenclip would be very much distressed if her village was spoiled."

"Oh, I'll be careful," promised Billina.

"Are not all these paper girls and women named Miss Cuttenclips?" inquired Omby Amby.

"No, indeed," answered the Captain, who was walking better since he began to move edgewise. "There is but one Miss Cuttenclip, who is our Queen, because she made us all. These girls are Cuttenclips, to be sure, but their names are Emily and Polly and Sue and Betty and such things. Only the Queen is called Miss Cuttenclip."

"I must say that this place beats anything I ever heard of," observed Aunt Em. "I used to play with paper dolls myself, an' cut 'em out; but I never thought I'd ever see such things alive."

"I don't see as it's any more curious than hearing hens talk," returned Uncle Henry.

"You're likely to see many queer things in the Land of Oz, sir," said the Wizard. "But a fairy country is extremely interesting when you get used to being surprised."

"Here we are!" called the Captain, stopping before a cottage.

This house was made of wood, and was remarkably pretty in design. In the Emerald City it would have been considered a tiny dwelling, indeed; but in the midst of this paper village it seemed immense. Real flowers were in the garden and real trees grew beside it. Upon the front door was a sign reading:

MISS CUTTENCLIP.

Just as they reached the porch the front door opened and a little girl stood before them. She appeared to be about the same age as Dorothy, and smiling upon her visitors she said, sweetly:

"You are welcome."

All the party seemed relieved to find that here was a real girl, of flesh and blood. She was very dainty and pretty as she stood there welcoming them. Her hair was a golden blonde and her eyes turquoise blue. She had rosy cheeks and lovely white teeth. Over her simple white lawn dress she wore an apron with pink and white checks, and in one hand she held a pair of scissors.

"May we see Miss Cuttenclip, please?" asked Dorothy.

"I am Miss Cuttenclip," was the reply. "Won't you come in?"

She held the door open while they all entered a pretty sitting-room that was littered with all sorts of paper—some stiff, some thin, and some tissue. The sheets and scraps were of all colors. Upon a table were paints and brushes, while several pair of scissors, of different sizes, were lying about.

"Sit down, please," said Miss Cuttenclip, clearing the paper scraps off some of the chairs. "It is so long since I have had any visitors that I am not properly prepared to receive them. But I'm sure you will pardon my untidy room, for this is my workshop."

"Do you make all the paper dolls?" inquired Dorothy.

"Yes; I cut them out with my scissors, and paint the faces and some of the costumes. It is very pleasant work, and I am happy making my paper village grow."

"But how do the paper dolls happen to be alive?" asked Aunt Em.

"The first dolls I made were not alive," said Miss Cuttenclip. "I used to live near the castle of a great Sorceress named Glinda the Good, and she saw my dolls and said they were very pretty. I told her I thought I would like them better if they were alive, and the next day the Sorceress brought me a lot of magic paper. 'This is live paper,' she said, 'and all the dolls you cut out of it will be alive, and able to think and to talk. When you have used it all up, come to me and I will give you more.'

"Of course I was delighted with this present," continued Miss Cuttenclip, "and at once set to work and made several paper dolls, which, as soon as they were cut out, began to walk around and talk to me. But they were so thin that I found that any breeze would blow them over and scatter them dreadfully; so Glinda found this lonely place for me, where few people ever come. She built the wall to keep any wind from blowing away my people, and told me I could build a paper village here and be its Queen. That is why I came here and settled down to work and started the village you now see. It was many years ago that I built the first houses, and I've kept pretty busy and made my village grow finely; and I need not tell you that I am very happy in my work."

"Many years ago!" exclaimed Aunt Em. "Why, how old are you, child?"

"I never keep track of the years," said Miss Cuttenclip, laughing. "You see, I don't grow up at all, but stay just the same as I was when first I came here. Perhaps I'm older even than you are, madam; but I couldn't say for sure."

They looked at the lovely little girl wonderingly, and the Wizard asked:

"What happens to your paper village when it rains?"

"It does not rain here," replied Miss Cuttenclip. "Glinda keeps all the rain storms away; so I never worry about my dolls getting wet. But now, if you will come with me, it will give me pleasure to show you over my paper kingdom. Of course you must go slowly and carefully, and avoid making any breeze."

They left the cottage and followed their guide through the various streets of the village. It was indeed an amazing place, when one considered that it was all made with scissors, and the visitors were not only greatly interested but full of admiration for the skill of little Miss Cuttenclip.

In one place a large group of especially nice paper dolls assembled to greet their Queen, whom it was easy to see they loved early. These dolls marched and danced before the visitors, and then they all waved their paper handkerchiefs and sang in a sweet chorus a song called "The Flag of Our Native Land."

At the conclusion of the song they ran up a handsome paper flag on a tall flagpole, and all of the people of the village gathered around to cheer as loudly as they could—although, of course, their voices were not especially strong.

Miss Cuttenclip was about to make her subjects a speech in reply to this patriotic song, when the Shaggy Man happened to sneeze.

He was a very loud and powerful sneezer at any time, and he had tried so hard to hold in this sneeze that when it suddenly exploded the result was terrible.

The paper dolls were mowed down by dozens, and flew and fluttered in wild confusion in every direction, tumbling this way and that and getting more or less wrinkled and bent.

A wail of terror and grief came from the scattered throng, and Miss Cuttenclip exclaimed:

"Dear me! dear me!" and hurried at once to the rescue of her overturned people.

"Oh, Shaggy Man! How could you?" asked Dorothy, reproachfully.

"I couldn't help it—really I couldn't," protested the Shaggy Man, looking quite ashamed. "And I had no idea it took so little to upset these paper dolls."

"So little!" said Dorothy. "Why, it was 'most as bad as a Kansas cyclone." And then she helped Miss Cuttenclip rescue the paper folk and stand them on their feet again. Two of the cardboard houses had also tumbled over, and the little Queen said she would have to repair them and paste them together before they could be lived in again.

And now, fearing they might do more damage to the flimsy paper people, they decided to go away. But first they thanked Miss Cuttenclip very warmly for her courtesy and kindness to them.

"Any friend of Princess Ozma is always welcome here—unless he sneezes," said the Queen, with a rather severe look at the Shaggy Man, who hung his head. "I like to have visitors admire my wonderful village, and I hope you will call again."

Miss Cuttenclip herself led them to the door in the wall, and as they passed along the street the paper dolls peeped at them half fearfully from the doors and windows. Perhaps they will never forget the Shaggy Man's awful sneeze, and I am sure they were all glad to see the meat people go away.

CHAPTER XI

How THE GENERAL MET THE FIRST AND FOREMOST

ON LEAVING THE GROWLEYWOGS GENERAL GUPH HAD TO RECROSS THE RIPPLE Lands, and he did not find it a pleasant thing to do. Perhaps having his whiskers pulled out one by one and being used as a pin-cushion for the innocent amusement of a good natured jailor had not improved the quality of Guph's temper, for the old Nome raved and raged at the recollection of the wrongs he had suffered, and vowed to take vengeance upon the Growleywogs after he had used them for his purposes and Oz had been conquered. He went on in this furious way until he was half across the Ripple Land. Then he became seasick, and the rest of the way this naughty Nome was almost as miserable as he deserved to be.

But when he reached the plains again and the ground was firm under his feet he began to feel better, and instead of going back home he turned directly west. A squirrel, perched in a tree, saw him take this road and called to him warningly: "Look out!" But he paid no attention. An eagle paused in its flight through the air to look at him wonderingly and say: "Look out!" But on he went.

No one can say that Guph was not brave, for he had determined to visit those dangerous creatures the Phanfasms, who resided upon the very top of the dread Mountain of Phantastico. The Phanfasms were Erbs, and so dreaded by mortals and immortals alike that no one had been near their mountain home for several thousand years. Yet General Guph hoped to induce them to join in his proposed warfare against the good and happy Oz people.

Guph knew very well that the Phanfasms would be almost as dangerous to the Nomes as they would to the Ozites, but he thought himself so clever that he believed he could manage these strange creatures and make them obey him. And there was no doubt at all that if he could enlist the services of the Phanfasms their tremendous power, united to the strength of the Growleywogs and the cunning of the Whimsies would doom the Land of Oz to absolute destruction.

So the old Nome climbed the foothills and trudged along the wild mountain paths until he came to a big gully that encircled the Mountain of Phantastico and marked the boundary line of the dominion of the Phanfasms. This gully was about a third of the way up the mountain, and it was filled to the brim with red-hot molten lava, in which swam fire-serpents and poisonous salamanders. The heat from this mass and its poisonous smell were both so unbearable that even birds hesitated to fly over the gully, but circled around it. All living things kept away from the mountain.

Now Guph had heard, during his long lifetime, many tales of these dreaded Phanfasms; so he had heard of this barrier of melted lava, and also he had been told that there was a narrow bridge that spanned it in one place. So he walked along the edge until he found the bridge. It was a single arch of gray stone, and lying flat upon the bridge was a scarlet alligator, seemingly fast asleep.

When Guph stumbled over the rocks in approaching the bridge the creature opened its eyes, from which tiny flames shot in all directions, and after looking at the intruder very wickedly the scarlet alligator closed its eyelids again and lay still.

Guph saw there was no room for him to pass the alligator on the narrow bridge, so he called out to it:

"Good morning, friend. I don't wish to hurry you, but please tell me if you are coming down, or going up?"

"Neither," snapped the alligator, clicking its cruel jaws together.

The General hesitated.

"Are you likely to stay there long?" he asked.

"A few hundred years or so," said the alligator.

Guph softly rubbed the end of his nose and tried to think what to do.

"Do you know whether the First and Foremost Phanfasm of Phantastico is at home or not?" he presently inquired.

"I expect he is, seeing he is always at home," replied the alligator.

"Ah; who is that coming down the mountain?" asked the Nome, gazing upward.

The alligator turned to look over its shoulder, and at once Guph ran to the bridge and leaped over the sentinel's back before it could turn back again. The scarlet monster made a snap at the Nome's left foot, but missed it by fully an inch.

"Ah ha!" laughed the General, who was now on the mountain path. "I fooled you that time."

"So you did; and perhaps you fooled yourself," retorted the alligator. "Go up the mountain, if you dare, and find out what the First and Foremost will do to you!"

"I will," declared Guph, boldly; and on he went up the path.

At first the scene was wild enough, but gradually it grew more and more awful in appearance. All the rocks had the shapes of frightful beings and even the tree trunks were gnarled and twisted like serpents.

Suddenly there appeared before the Nome a man with the head of an owl. His body was hairy, like that of an ape, and his only clothing was a scarlet scarf twisted around his waist. He bore a huge club in his hand and his round owl eyes blinked fiercely upon the intruder.

"What are you doing here?" he demanded, threatening Guph with his club.

"I've come to see the First and Foremost Phanfasm of Phantastico," replied the General, who did not like the way this creature looked at him, but still was not afraid.

"Ah; you shall see him!" the man said, with a sneering laugh. "The First and Foremost shall decide upon the best way to punish you."

"He will not punish me," returned Guph, calmly, "for I have come here to do him and his people a rare favor. Lead on, fellow, and take me directly to your master."

The owl-man raised his club with a threatening gesture.

"If you try to escape," he said, "beware—"

But here the General interrupted him.

"Spare your threats," said he, "and do not be impertinent, or I will have you severely punished. Lead on, and keep silent!"

This Guph was really a clever rascal, and it seems a pity he was so bad, for in a good cause he might have accomplished much. He realized that he had put himself into a dangerous position by coming to this dreadful mountain, but he also knew that if he showed fear he was lost. So he adopted a bold manner as his best defense. The wisdom of this plan was soon evident, for the Phanfasm with the owl's head turned and led the way up the mountain.

At the very top was a level plain upon which were heaps of rock that at first glance seemed solid. But on looking closer Guph discovered that these rock heaps were dwellings, for each had an opening.

Not a person was to be seen outside the rock huts. All was silent.

The owl-man led the way among the groups of dwellings to one standing in the center. It seemed no better and no worse than any of the others. Outside the entrance to this rock heap the guide gave a low wail that sounded like "Lee-ow-ah!"

Suddenly there bounded from the opening another hairy man. This one wore the head of a bear. In his hand he bore a brass hoop. He glared at the stranger in evident surprise.

"Why have you captured this foolish wanderer and brought him here?" he demanded, addressing the owl-man.

"I did not capture him," was the answer. "He passed the scarlet alligator and came here of his own free will and accord."

The First and Foremost looked at the General.

"Have you tired of life, then?" he asked.

"No, indeed," answered Guph. "I am a Nome, and the Chief General of King Roquat the Red's great army of Nomes. I come of a long-lived race, and I may say that I expect to live a long time yet. Sit down, you Phanfasms—if you can find a seat in this wild haunt—and listen to what I have to say."

With all his knowledge and bravery General Guph did not know that the steady glare from the bear eyes was reading his inmost thoughts as surely as if they had been put into words. He did not know that these despised rock heaps of the Phanfasms were merely deceptions to his own eyes, nor could he guess that he was standing in the midst of one of the most splendid and luxurious cities ever built by magic power. All that he saw was a barren waste of rock heaps, a hairy man with an owl's head and another with a bear's head. The sorcery of the Phanfasms permitted him to see no more.

Suddenly the First and Foremost swung his brass hoop and caught Guph around the neck with it. The next instant, before the General could think what had happened to him, he was dragged inside the rock hut. Here, his eyes still blinded to realities, he perceived only a dim light, by which the hut seemed as rough and rude inside as it was outside. Yet he had a strange feeling that many bright eyes were fastened upon him and that he stood in a vast and extensive hall.

The First and Foremost now laughed grimly and released his prisoner.

"If you have anything to say that is interesting," he remarked, "speak out, before I strangle you."

So Guph spoke out. He tried not to pay any attention to a strange rustling sound that he heard, as of an unseen multitude drawing near to listen to his words. His eyes could see only the fierce bear-man, and to him he addressed his speech. First he told of his plan to conquer the Land of Oz and plunder the country of its riches and enslave its people, who, being fairies, could not be killed. After relating all this, and telling of the tunnel the Nome King was building, he said he had come to ask the First and Foremost to join the Nomes, with his band of terrible warriors, and help them to defeat the Oz people.

The General spoke very earnestly and impressively, but when he had finished the bear-man began to laugh as if much amused, and his laughter seemed to be echoed by a chorus of merriment from an unseen multitude. Then, for the first time, Guph began to feel a trifle worried.

"Who else has promised to help you?" finally asked the First and Foremost.

"The Whimsies," replied the General.

Again the bear-headed Phanfasm laughed.

"Any others?" he inquired.

"Only the Growleywogs," said Guph.

This answer set the First and Foremost laughing anew.

"What share of the spoils am I to have?" was the next question.

"Anything you like, except King Roquat's Magic Belt," replied Guph.

At this the Phanfasm set up a roar of laughter, which had its echo in the unseen chorus, and the bear-man seemed so amused that he actually rolled upon the ground and shouted with merriment.

"Oh, these blind and foolish Nomes!" he said. "How big they seem to themselves and how small they really are!"

Suddenly he arose and seized Guph's neck with one hairy paw, dragging him out of the hut into the open.

Here he gave a curious wailing cry, and, as if in answer, from all the rocky huts on the mountain-top came flocking a horde of Phanfasms, all with hairy bodies, but wearing heads of various animals, birds and reptiles. All were ferocious and repulsive-looking to the deceived eyes of the Nome, and Guph could not repress a shudder of disgust as he looked upon them.

The First and Foremost slowly raised his arms, and in a twinkling his hairy skin fell from him and he appeared before the astonished Nome as a beautiful woman, clothed in a flowing gown of pink gauze. In her dark hair flowers were entwined, and her face was noble and calm.

At the same instant the entire band of Phanfasms was transformed into a pack of howling wolves, running here and there as they snarled and showed their ugly yellow fangs.

The woman now raised her arms, even as the man-bear had done, and in a twinkling the wolves became crawling lizards, while she herself changed into a huge butterfly.

Guph had only time to cry out in fear and take a step backward to avoid the lizards when another transformation occurred, and all returned instantly to the forms they had originally worn.

Then the First and Foremost, who had resumed his hairy body and bear head, turned to the Nome and asked:

"Do you still demand our assistance?"

"More than ever," answered the General, firmly.

"Then tell me: what can you offer the Phanfasms that they have not already?" inquired the First and Foremost.

Guph hesitated. He really did not know what to say. The Nome King's vaunted Magic Belt seemed a poor thing compared to the astonishing magical powers of these people. Gold, jewels and slaves they might secure in any quantity without especial effort. He felt that he was dealing with powers greatly beyond him. There was but one argument that might influence the Phanfasms, who were creatures of evil.

"Permit me to call your attention to the exquisite joy of making the happy unhappy," said he at last. "Consider the pleasure of destroying innocent and harmless people."

"Ah! you have answered me," cried the First and Foremost. "For that reason alone we will aid you. Go home, and tell your bandy-legged King that as soon as his tunnel is finished the Phanfasms will be with him and lead his legions to the conquest of Oz. The deadly desert alone has kept us from destroying Oz long ago, and your underground tunnel is a clever thought. Go home, and prepare for our coming!"

Guph was very glad to be permitted to go with this promise. The owl-man led him back down the mountain path and ordered the scarlet alligator to crawl away and allow the Nome to cross the bridge in safety.

After the visitor had gone a brilliant and gorgeous city appeared upon the mountain top, clearly visible to the eyes of the gaily dressed multitude of Phanfasms that lived there. And the First and Foremost, beautifully arrayed, addressed the others in these words:

"It is time we went into the world and brought sorrow and dismay to its people. Too long have we remained by ourselves upon this mountain top, for while we are thus secluded many nations have grown happy and prosperous, and the chief joy of the race of Phanfasms is to destroy happiness. So I think it is lucky that this messenger from the Nomes arrived among us just now, to remind us that the opportunity has come for us to make trouble. We will use King Roquat's tunnel to conquer the Land of Oz. Then we will destroy the Whimsies, the Growleywogs and the Nomes, and afterward go out to ravage and annoy and grieve the whole world."

The multitude of evil Phanfasms eagerly applauded this plan, which they fully approved.

I am told that the Erbs are the most powerful and merciless of all the evil spirits, and the Phanfasms of Phantastico belong to the race of Erbs.

CHAPTER XII

How THEY MATCHED THE FUDDLES

DOROTHY AND HER FELLOW TRAVELERS RODE AWAY FROM THE CUTTENCLIP VILLAGE and followed the indistinct path as far as the sign-post. Here they took the main road again and proceeded pleasantly through the pretty farming country. When evening came they stopped at a dwelling and were joyfully welcomed and given plenty to eat and good beds for the night.

Early next morning, however, they were up and eager to start, and after a good breakfast they bade their host good-bye and climbed into the red wagon, to which the Saw-Horse had been hitched all night. Being made of wood, this horse never got tired nor cared to lie down. Dorothy was not quite sure whether he ever slept or not, but it was certain that he never did when anybody was around.

The weather is always beautiful in Oz, and this morning the air was cool and refreshing and the sunshine brilliant and delightful.

In about an hour they came to a place where another road branched off. There was a sign-post here which read:

☞ THIS WAY TO FUDDLECUMJIG

"Oh, here is where we turn," said Dorothy, observing the sign.

"What! Are we going to Fuddlecumjig?" asked the Captain General.

"Yes; Ozma thought we would enjoy the Fuddles. They are said to be very interesting," she replied.

"No one would suspect it from their name," said Aunt Em. "Who are they, anyhow? More paper things?"

"I think not," answered Dorothy, laughing; "but I can't say 'zactly, Aunt Em, what they are. We'll find out when we get there."

"Perhaps the Wizard knows," suggested Uncle Henry.

"No; I've never been there before," said the Wizard. "But I've often heard of Fuddlecumjig and the Fuddles, who are said to be the most peculiar people in all the Land of Oz."

"In what way?" asked the Shaggy Man.

"I don't know, I'm sure," said the Wizard.

Just then, as they rode along the pretty green lane toward Fuddlecumjig, they espied a kangaroo sitting by the roadside. The poor animal had its face covered with both its front paws and was crying so bitterly that the tears coursed down its cheeks in two tiny streams and trickled across the road, where they formed a pool in a small hollow.

The Saw-Horse stopped short at this pitiful sight, and Dorothy cried out, with ready sympathy:

"What's the matter, Kangaroo?"

"Boo-hoo! Boo-hoo!" wailed the kangaroo; "I've lost my mi—mi—mi—Oh, boo-hoo! Boo-hoo!"—

"Poor thing," said the Wizard, "she's lost her mister. It's probably her husband, and he's dead."

"No, no, no!" sobbed the kangaroo. "It—it isn't that. I've lost my mi—mi—Oh, boo, boo-hoo!"

"I know," said the Shaggy Man; "she's lost her mirror."

"No; it's my mi—mi—mi—Boo-hoo! My mi—Oh, Boo-hoo!" and the kangaroo cried harder than ever.

"It must be her mince-pie," suggested Aunt Em.

"Or her milk-toast," proposed Uncle Henry.

"I've lost my mi—mi—mittens!" said the kangaroo, getting it out at last.

"Oh!" cried the Yellow Hen, with a cackle of relief. "Why didn't you say so before?"

"Boo-hoo! I—I—couldn't," answered the kangaroo.

"But, see here," said Dorothy, "you don't need mittens in this warm weather."

"Yes, indeed I do," replied the animal, stopping her sobs and removing her paws from her face to look at the little girl reproachfully. "My hands will get all sunburned and tanned without my mittens, and I've worn them so long that I'll probably catch cold without them."

"Nonsense!" said Dorothy. "I never heard before of any kangaroo wearing mittens."

"Didn't you?" asked the animal, as if surprised.

"Never!" repeated the girl. "And you'll probably make yourself sick if you don't stop crying. Where do you live?"

"About two miles beyond Fuddlecumjig," was the answer. "Grandmother Gnit made me the mittens, and she's one of the Fuddles."

"Well, you'd better go home now, and perhaps the old lady will make you another pair," suggested Dorothy. "We're on our way to Fuddlecumjig, and you may hop along beside us."

So they rode on, and the kangaroo hopped beside the red wagon and seemed quickly to have forgotten her loss. By and by the Wizard said to the animal:

"Are the Fuddles nice people?"

"Oh, very nice," answered the kangaroo; "that is, when they're properly put together. But they get dreadfully scattered and mixed up, at times, and then you can't do anything with them."

"What do you mean by their getting scattered?" inquired Dorothy.

"Why, they're made in a good many small pieces," explained the kangaroo; "and whenever any stranger comes near them they have a habit of falling apart and scattering themselves around. That's when they get so dreadfully mixed, and it's a hard puzzle to put them together again."

"Who usually puts them together?" asked Omby Amby.

"Any one who is able to match the pieces. I sometimes put Grandmother Gnit together myself, because I know her so well I can tell every piece that belongs to her.

Then, when she's all matched, she knits for me, and that's how she made my mittens. But it took a good many days hard knitting, and I had to put Grandmother together a good many times, because every time I came near she'd scatter herself."

"I should think she would get used to your coming, and not be afraid," said Dorothy.

"It isn't that," replied the kangaroo. "They're not a bit afraid, when they're put together, and usually they're very jolly and pleasant. It's just a habit they have, to scatter themselves, and if they didn't do it they wouldn't be Fuddles."

The travelers thought upon this quite seriously for a time, while the Saw-Horse continued to carry them rapidly forward. Then Aunt Em remarked:

"I don't see much use our visitin' these Fuddles. If we find them scattered, all we can do is to sweep 'em up, and then go about our business."

"Oh, I b'lieve we'd better go on," replied Dorothy. "I'm getting hungry, and we must try to get some luncheon at Fuddlecumjig. Perhaps the food won't be scattered as badly as the people."

"You'll find plenty to eat there," declared the kangaroo, hopping along in big bounds because the Saw-Horse was going so fast; "and they have a fine cook, too, if you can manage to put him together. There's the town now—just ahead of us!"

They looked ahead and saw a group of very pretty houses standing in a green field a little apart from the main road.

"Some Munchkins came here a few days ago and matched a lot of people together," said the kangaroo. "I think they are together yet, and if you go softly, without making any noise, perhaps they won't scatter."

"Let's try it," suggested the Wizard.

So they stopped the Saw-Horse and got out of the wagon, and, after bidding good-bye to the kangaroo, who hopped away home, they entered the field and very cautiously approached the group of houses.

So silently did they move that soon they saw through the windows of the houses, people moving around, while others were passing to and fro in the yards between the buildings. They seemed much like other people, from a distance, and apparently they did not notice the little party so quietly approaching.

They had almost reached the nearest house when Toto saw a large beetle crossing the path and barked loudly at it. Instantly a wild clatter was heard from the houses and yards. Dorothy thought it sounded like a sudden hailstorm, and the visitors, knowing that caution was no longer necessary, hurried forward to see what had happened.

After the clatter an intense stillness reigned in the town. The strangers entered the first house they came to, which was also the largest, and found the floor strewn with pieces of the people who lived there. They looked much like fragments of wood neatly painted, and were of all sorts of curious and fantastic shapes, no two pieces being in any way alike.

They picked up some of these pieces and looked at them carefully. On one which Dorothy held was an eye, which looked at her pleasantly but with an interested expression, as if it wondered what she was going to do with it. Quite near by she discovered and picked up a nose, and by matching the two pieces together found that they were part of a face.

"If I could find the mouth," she said, "this Fuddle might be able to talk, and tell us what to do next."

"Then let us find it," replied the Wizard, and so all got down on their hands and knees and began examining the scattered pieces.

"I've found it!" cried the Shaggy Man, and ran to Dorothy with a queer-shaped piece that had a mouth on it. But when they tried to fit it to the eye and nose they found the parts wouldn't match together.

"That mouth belongs to some other person," said Dorothy. "You see we need a curve here and a point there, to make it fit the face."

"Well, it must be here some place," declared the Wizard; "so if we search long enough we shall find it."

Dorothy fitted an ear on next, and the ear had a little patch of red hair above it. So while the others were searching for the mouth she hunted for pieces with red hair, and found several of them which, when matched to the other pieces, formed the top of a man's head. She had also found the other eye and the ear by the time Omby Amby in a far corner discovered the mouth. When the face was thus completed all the parts joined together with a nicety that was astonishing.

"Why, it's like a picture puzzle!" exclaimed the little girl. "Let's find the rest of him, and get him all together."

"What's the rest of him like?" asked the Wizard. "Here are some pieces of blue legs and green arms, but I don't know whether they are his or not."

"Look for a white shirt and a white apron," said the head which had been put together, speaking in a rather faint voice. "I'm the cook."

"Oh, thank you," said Dorothy. "It's lucky we started you first, for I'm hungry, and you can be cooking something for us to eat while we match the other folks together."

It was not so very difficult, now that they had a hint as to how the man was dressed, to find the other pieces belonging to him, and as all of them now worked on the cook, trying piece after piece to see if it would fit, they finally had the cook set up complete.

When he was finished he made them a low bow and said:

"I will go at once to the kitchen and prepare your dinner. You will find it something of a job to get all the Fuddles together, so I advise you to begin on the Lord High Chigglewitz, whose first name is Larry. He's a bald-headed fat man and is dressed in a blue coat with brass buttons, a pink vest and drab breeches. A piece of his left knee is missing, having been lost years ago when he scattered himself too carelessly. That makes him limp a little, but he gets along very well with half a knee. As he is the chief personage in this town of Fuddlecumjig, he will be able to welcome you and assist you with the others. So it will be best to work on him while I'm getting your dinner."

"We will," said the Wizard; "and thank you very much, Cook, for the suggestion."

Aunt Em was the first to discover a piece of the Lord High Chigglewitz.

"It seems to me like a fool business, this matching folks together," she remarked; "but as we haven't anything to do till dinner's ready we may as well get rid of some of this rubbish. Here, Henry, get busy and look for Larry's bald head. I've got his pink vest, all right."

They worked with eager interest, and Billina proved a great help to them. The Yellow Hen had sharp eyes and could put her head close to the various pieces that lay scattered around. She would examine the Lord High Chigglewitz and see which piece of him was next needed, and then hunt around until she found it. So before an hour had passed old Larry was standing complete before them.

"I congratulate you, my friends," he said, speaking in a cheerful voice. "You are certainly the cleverest people who ever visited us. I was never matched together so quickly in my life. I'm considered a great puzzle, usually."

"Well," said Dorothy, "there used to be a picture puzzle craze in Kansas, and so I've had some 'sperience matching puzzles. But the pictures were flat, while you are round, and that makes you harder to figure out."

"Thank you, my dear," replied old Larry, greatly pleased. "I feel highly complimented. Were I not a really good puzzle there would be no object in my scattering myself."

"Why do you do it?" asked Aunt Em, severely. "Why don't you behave yourself, and stay put together?"

The Lord High Chigglewitz seemed annoyed by this speech; but he replied, politely:

"Madam, you have perhaps noticed that every person has some peculiarity. Mine is to scatter myself. What your own peculiarity is I will not venture to say; but I shall never find fault with you, whatever you do."

"Now, you've got your diploma, Em," said Uncle Henry, with a laugh, "and I'm glad of it. This is a queer country, and we may as well take people as we find them."

"If we did, we'd leave these folks scattered," she returned, and this retort made everybody laugh good-naturedly.

Just then Omby Amby found a hand with a knitting needle in it, and they decided to put Grandmother Gnit together. She proved an easier puzzle than old Larry, and when she was completed they found her a pleasant old lady who welcomed them cordially. Dorothy told her how the kangaroo had lost her mittens, and Grandmother Gnit promised to set to work at once and make the poor animal another pair.

Then the cook came to call them to dinner, and they found an inviting meal prepared for them. The Lord High Chigglewitz sat at the head of the table and Grandmother Gnit at the foot, and the guests had a merry time and thoroughly enjoyed themselves.

After dinner they went out into the yard and matched several other people together, and this work was so interesting that they might have spent the entire day at Fuddlecumjig had not the Wizard suggested that they resume their journey.

"But I don't like to leave all these poor people scattered," said Dorothy, undecided what to do.

"Oh, don't mind us, my dear," returned old Larry. "Every day or so some of the Gillikins, or Munchkins, or Winkies come here to amuse themselves by matching us together, so there will be no harm in leaving these pieces where they are for a time. But I hope you will visit us again, and if you do you will always be welcome, I assure you."

"Don't you ever match each other?" she inquired.

"Never; for we are no puzzles to ourselves, and so there wouldn't be any fun in it."

They now said good-bye to the queer Fuddles and got into their wagon to continue their journey.

"Those are certainly strange people," remarked Aunt Em, thoughtfully, as they drove away from Fuddlecumjig, "but I really can't see what use they are, at all."

"Why, they amused us all for several hours," replied the Wizard. "That is being of use to us, I'm sure."

"I think they're more fun than playing solitaire or mumbletypeg," declared Uncle Henry, soberly. "For my part, I'm glad we visited the Fuddles."

CHAPTER XIII

How THE GENERAL TALKED TO THE KING

WHEN GENERAL GUPH RETURNED TO THE CAVERN OF THE NOME KING HIS Majesty asked:

"Well, what luck? Will the Whimsies join us?"

"They will," answered the General. "They will fight for us with all their strength and cunning."

"Good!" exclaimed the King. "What reward did you promise them?"

"Your Majesty is to use the Magic Belt to give each Whimsie a large, fine head, in place of the small one he is now obliged to wear."

"I agree to that," said the King. "This is good news, Guph, and it makes me feel more certain of the conquest of Oz."

"But I have other news for you," announced the General.

"Good or bad?"

"Good, your Majesty."

"Then I will hear it," said the King, with interest.

"The Growleywogs will join us."

"No!" cried the astonished King.

"Yes, indeed," said the General. "I have their promise."

"But what reward do they demand?" inquired the King, suspiciously, for he knew how greedy the Growleywogs were.

"They are to take a few of the Oz people for their slaves," replied Guph. He did not think it necessary to tell Roquat that the Growleywogs demanded twenty thousand slaves. It would be time enough for that when Oz was conquered.

"A very reasonable request, I'm sure," remarked the King. "I must congratulate you, Guph, upon the wonderful success of your journey."

"But that is not all," said the General, proudly.

The King seemed astonished.

"Speak out, sir!" he commanded.

"I have seen the First and Foremost Phanfasm of the Mountain of Phantastico, and he will bring his people to assist us."

"What!" cried the King. "The Phanfasms! You don't mean it, Guph!"

"It is true," declared the General, proudly.

The King became thoughtful, and his brows wrinkled.

"I'm afraid, Guph," he said rather anxiously, "that the First and Foremost may prove as dangerous to us as to the Oz people. If he and his terrible band come down from the mountain they may take the notion to conquer the Nomes!"

"Pah! That is a foolish idea," retorted Guph, irritably, but he knew in his heart that the King was right. "The First and Foremost is a particular friend of mine, and will do us no harm. Why, when I was there, he even invited me into his house."

The General neglected to tell the King how he had been jerked into the hut of the First and Foremost by means of the brass hoop. So Roquat the Red looked at his General admiringly and said:

"You are a wonderful Nome, Guph. I'm sorry I did not make you my General before. But what reward did the First and Foremost demand?"

"Nothing at all," answered Guph. "Even the Magic Belt itself could not add to his powers of sorcery. All the Phanfasms wish is to destroy the Oz people, who are good and happy. This pleasure will amply repay them for assisting us."

"When will they come?" asked Roquat, half fearfully.

"When the tunnel is completed," said the General.

"We are nearly half way under the desert now," announced the King; "and that is fast work, because the tunnel has to be drilled through solid rock. But after we have passed the desert it will not take us long to extend the tunnel to the walls of the Emerald City."

"Well, whenever you are ready, we shall be joined by the Whimsies, the Growleywogs and the Phanfasms," said Guph; "so the conquest of Oz is assured without a doubt."

Again the King seemed thoughtful.

"I'm almost sorry we did not undertake the conquest alone," said he. "All of these allies are dangerous people, and they may demand more than you have promised them. It might have been better to have conquered Oz without any out-side assistance."

"We could not do it," said the General, positively.

"Why not, Guph?"

"You know very well. You have had one experience with the Oz people, and they defeated you."

"That was because they rolled eggs at us," replied the King, with a shudder. "My Nomes cannot stand eggs, any more than I can myself. They are poison to all who live underground."

"That is true enough," agreed Guph.

"But we might have taken the Oz people by surprise, and conquered them before they had a chance to get any eggs. Our former defeat was due to the fact that the girl Dorothy had a Yellow Hen with her. I do not know what ever became of that hen, but I believe there are no hens at all in the Land of Oz, and so there could be no eggs there."

"On the contrary," said Guph, "there are now hundreds of chickens in Oz, and they lay heaps of those dangerous eggs. I met a goshawk on my way home, and the bird informed me that he had lately been to Oz to capture and devour some of the young chickens. But they are protected by magic, so the hawk did not get a single one of them."

"That is a very bad report," said the King, nervously. "Very bad, indeed. My Nomes are willing to fight, but they simply can't face hen's eggs—and I don't blame them."

"They won't need to face them," replied Guph. "I'm afraid of eggs myself, and don't propose to take any chances of being poisoned by them. My plan is to send the Whimsies through the tunnel first, and then the Growleywogs and the Phanfasms. By the time we Nomes get there the eggs will all be used up, and we may then pursue and capture the inhabitants at our leisure."

"Perhaps you are right," returned the King, with a dismal sigh. "But I want it distinctly understood that I claim Ozma and Dorothy as my own prisoners. They are rather nice girls, and I do not intend to let any of those dreadful creatures hurt them, or make them their slaves. When I have captured them I will bring them here and transform them into china ornaments to stand on my mantle. They will look very pretty—Dorothy on one end of the mantle and Ozma on the other—and I shall take great care to see they are not broken when the maids dust them."

"Very well, your Majesty. Do what you will with the girls, for all I care. Now that our plans are arranged, and we have the three most powerful bands of evil spirits in the world to assist us, let us make haste to get the tunnel finished as soon as possible."

"It will be ready in three days," promised the King, and hurried away to inspect the work and see that the Nomes kept busy.

CHAPTER XIV

How THE WIZARD PRACTICED SORCERY

"WHERE NEXT?" ASKED THE WIZARD WHEN THEY HAD LEFT THE TOWN OF Fuddlecumjig and the Saw-Horse had started back along the road.

"Why, Ozma laid out this trip," replied Dorothy, "and she 'vised us to see the Rigmaroles next, and then visit the Tin Woodman."

"That sounds good," said the Wizard. "But what road do we take to get to the Rigmaroles?"

"I don't know, 'zactly," returned the little girl; "but it must be somewhere just southwest from here."

"Then why need we go way back to the crossroads?" asked the Shaggy Man. "We might save a lot of time by branching off here."

"There isn't any path," asserted Uncle Henry.

"Then we'd better go back to the sign-posts, and make sure of our way," decided Dorothy.

But after they had gone a short distance farther the Saw-Horse, who had overheard their conversation, stopped and said:

"Here is a path."

Sure enough, a dim path seemed to branch off from the road they were on, and it led across pretty green meadows and past leafy groves, straight toward the southwest.

"That looks like a good path," said Omby Amby. "Why not try it?"

"All right," answered Dorothy. "I'm anxious to see what the Rigmaroles are like, and this path ought to take us there the quickest way."

No one made any objection to the plan, so the Saw-Horse turned into the path, which proved to be nearly as good as the one they had taken to get to the Fuddles.

At first they passed a few retired farm houses, but soon these scattered dwellings were left behind and only the meadows and the trees were before them. But they rode along in cheerful contentment, and Aunt Em got into an argument with Billina about the proper way to raise chickens.

"I do not care to contradict you," said the Yellow Hen, with dignity, "but I have an idea I know more about chickens than human beings do."

"Pshaw!" replied Aunt Em, "I've raised chickens for nearly forty years, Billina, and I know you've got to starve 'em to make 'em lay lots of eggs, and stuff 'em if you want good broilers."

"Broilers!" exclaimed Billina, in horror. "Broil my chickens!"

"Why, that's what they're for, ain't it?" asked Aunt Em, astonished.

"No, Aunt, not in Oz," said Dorothy. "People do not eat chickens here. You see, Billina was the first hen that was ever seen in this country, and I brought her here myself. Everybody liked her an' respected her, so the Oz people wouldn't any more eat her chickens than they would eat Billina."

"Well, I declare," gasped Aunt Em. "How about the eggs?"

"Oh, if we have more eggs than we want to hatch, we allow people to eat them," said Billina. "Indeed, I am very glad the Oz folks like our eggs, for otherwise they would spoil."

"This certainly is a queer country," sighed Aunt Em.

"Excuse me," called the Saw-Horse, "the path has ended and I'd like to know which way to go."

They looked around and, sure enough, there was no path to be seen.

"Well," said Dorothy, "we're going southwest, and it seems just as easy to follow that direction without a path as with one."

"Certainly," answered the Saw-Horse. "It is not hard to draw the wagon over the meadow. I only want to know where to go."

"There's a forest over there across the prairie," said the Wizard, "and it lies in the direction we are going. Make straight for the forest, Saw-Horse, and you're bound to go right."

So the wooden animal trotted on again and the meadow grass was so soft under the wheels that it made easy riding. But Dorothy was a little uneasy at losing the path, because now there was nothing to guide them.

No houses were to be seen at all, so they could not ask their way of any farmer; and although the Land of Oz was always beautiful, wherever one might go, this part of the country was strange to all the party.

"Perhaps we're lost," suggested Aunt Em, after they had proceeded quite a way in silence.

"Never mind," said the Shaggy Man; "I've been lost many a time—and so has Dorothy—and we've always been found again."

"But we may get hungry," remarked Omby Amby. "That is the worst of getting lost in a place where there are no houses near."

"We had a good dinner at the Fuddle town," said Uncle Henry, "and that will keep us from starving to death for a long time."

"No one ever starved to death in Oz," declared Dorothy, positively; "but people may get pretty hungry sometimes."

The Wizard said nothing, and he did not seem especially anxious. The Saw-Horse was trotting along briskly, yet the forest seemed farther away than they had thought when they first saw it. So it was nearly sundown when they finally came to the trees; but now they found themselves in a most beautiful spot, the wide-spreading trees being covered with flowering vines and having soft mosses underneath them.

"This will be a good place to camp," said the Wizard, as the Saw-Horse stopped for further instructions.

"Camp!" they all echoed.

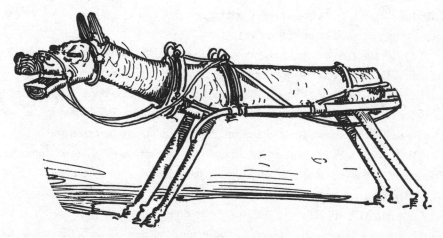

"Certainly," asserted the Wizard. "It will be dark before very long and we cannot travel through this forest at night. So let us make a camp here, and have some supper, and sleep until daylight comes again."

They all looked at the little man in astonishment, and Aunt Em said, with a sniff:

"A pretty camp we'll have, I must say! I suppose you intend us to sleep under the wagon."

"And chew grass for our supper," added the Shaggy Man, laughing.

But Dorothy seemed to have no doubts and was quite cheerful.

"It's lucky we have the wonderful Wizard with us," she said; "because he can do 'most anything he wants to."

"Oh, yes; I forgot we had a Wizard," said Uncle Henry, looking at the little man curiously.

"I didn't," chirped Billina, contentedly.

The Wizard smiled and climbed out of the wagon, and all the others followed him.

"In order to camp," said he, "the first thing we need is tents. Will some one please lend me a handkerchief?"

The Shaggy Man offered him one, and Aunt Em another. He took them both and laid them carefully upon the grass near to the edge of the forest. Then he laid his own handkerchief down, too, and standing a little back from them he waved his left hand toward the handkerchiefs and said:

"Tents of canvas, white as snow,
Let me see how fast you grow!"

Then, lo and behold! the handkerchiefs became tiny tents, and as the travelers looked at them the tents grew bigger and bigger until in a few minutes each one was large enough to contain the entire party.

"This," said the Wizard, pointing to the first tent, "is for the accommodation of the ladies. Dorothy, you and your aunt may step inside and take off your things."

Every one ran to look inside the tent, and they saw two pretty white beds, all ready for Dorothy and Aunt Em, and a silver roost for Billina. Rugs were spread upon the grassy floor and some camp chairs and a table completed the furniture.

"Well, well, well! This beats anything I ever saw or heard of!" exclaimed Aunt Em, and she glanced at the Wizard almost fearfully, as if he might be dangerous because of his great powers.

"Oh, Mr. Wizard! How did you manage to do it?" asked Dorothy.

"It's a trick Glinda the Sorceress taught me, and it is much better magic than I used to practise in Omaha, or when I first came to Oz," he answered. "When the good Glinda found I was to live in the Emerald City always, she promised to help me, because she said the Wizard of Oz ought really to be a clever Wizard, and not a humbug. So we have been much together and I am learning so fast that I expect to be able to accomplish some really wonderful things in time."

"You've done it now!" declared Dorothy. "These tents are just wonderful!"

"But come and see the men's tent," said the Wizard. So they went to the second tent, which had shaggy edges because it has been made from the Shaggy Man's handkerchief, and found that completely furnished also. It contained four neat beds for Uncle Henry, Omby Amby, the Shaggy Man and the Wizard. Also there was a soft rug for Toto to lie upon.

"The third tent," explained the Wizard, "is our dining room and kitchen."

They visited that next, and found a table and dishes in the dining tent, with plenty of those things necessary to use in cooking. The Wizard carried out a big kettle and set it swinging on a crossbar before the tent. While he was doing this Omby Amby and the Shaggy Man brought a supply of twigs from the forest and then they built a fire underneath the kettle.

"Now, Dorothy," said the Wizard, smiling, "I expect you to cook our supper."

"But there is nothing in the kettle," she cried.

"Are you sure?" inquired the Wizard.

"I didn't see anything put in, and I'm almost sure it was empty when you brought it out," she replied.

"Nevertheless," said the little man, winking slyly at Uncle Henry, "you will do well to watch our supper, my dear, and see that it doesn't boil over."

Then the men took some pails and went into the forest to search for a spring of water, and while they were gone Aunt Em said to Dorothy:

"I believe the Wizard is fooling us. I saw the kettle myself, and when he hung it over the fire there wasn't a thing in it but air."

"Don't worry," remarked Billina, confidently, as she nestled in the grass before the fire. "You'll find something in the kettle when it's taken off—and it won't be poor, innocent chickens, either."

"Your hen has very bad manners, Dorothy," said Aunt Em, looking somewhat disdainfully at Billina. "It seems too bad she ever learned how to talk."

There might have been another unpleasant quarrel between Aunt Em and Billina had not the men returned just then with their pails filled with clear, sparkling water. The Wizard told Dorothy that she was a good cook and he believed their supper was ready.

So Uncle Henry lifted the kettle from the fire and poured its contents into a big platter which the Wizard held for him. The platter was fairly heaped with a fine stew, smoking hot, with many kinds of vegetables and dumplings and a rich, delicious gravy.

The Wizard triumphantly placed the platter upon the table in the dining tent and then they all sat down in camp chairs to the feast.

There were several other dishes on the table, all carefully covered, and when the time came to remove these covers they found bread and butter, cakes, cheese, pickles and fruits—including some of the luscious strawberries of Oz.

No one ventured to ask a question as to how these things came there. They contented themselves by eating heartily the good things provided, and Toto and Billina had their full share, you may be sure. After the meal was over, Aunt Em whispered to Dorothy:

"That may have been magic food, my dear, and for that reason perhaps it won't be very nourishing; but I'm willing to say it tasted as good as anything I ever et." Then she added, in a louder tone: "Who's going to do the dishes?"

"No one, madam," answered the Wizard. "The dishes have 'done' themselves."

"La sakes!" ejaculated the good lady, holding up her hands in amazement. For, sure enough, when she looked at the dishes they had a moment before left upon the table, she found them all washed and dried and piled up into neat stacks.

CHAPTER XV

How DOROTHY HAPPENED TO GET LOST

IT WAS A BEAUTIFUL EVENING, SO THEY DREW THEIR CAMP CHAIRS IN A CIRCLE before one of the tents and began to tell stories to amuse themselves and pass away the time before they went to bed.

Pretty soon a zebra was seen coming out of the forest, and he trotted straight up to them and said politely:

"Good evening, people."

The zebra was a sleek little animal and had a slender head, a stubby mane and a paint-brush tail—very like a donkey's. His neatly shaped white body was covered with regular bars of dark brown, and his hoofs were delicate as those of a deer.

"Good evening, friend Zebra," said Omby Amby, in reply to the creature's greeting. "Can we do anything for you?"

"Yes," answered the zebra. "I should like you to settle a dispute that has long been a bother to me, as to whether there is more water or land in the world."

"Who are you disputing with?" asked the Wizard.

"With a soft-shell crab," said the zebra. "He lives in a pool where I go to drink every day, and he is a very impertinent crab, I assure you. I have told him many times that the land is much greater in extent than the water, but he will not be convinced. Even this very evening, when I told him he was an insignificant creature who lived in a small pool, he asserted that the water was greater and more important than the land.

So, seeing your camp, I decided to ask you to settle the dispute for once and all, that I may not be further annoyed by this ignorant crab."

When they had listened to this explanation Dorothy inquired:

"Where is the soft-shell crab?"

"Not far away," replied the zebra. "If you will agree to judge between us I will run and get him."

"Run along, then," said the little girl.

So the animal pranced into the forest and soon came trotting back to them. When he drew near they found a soft-shell crab clinging fast to the stiff hair of the zebra's head, where it held on by one claw.

"Now then, Mr. Crab," said the zebra, "here are the people I told you about; and they know more than you do, who live in a pool, and more than I do, who live in a forest. For they have been travelers all over the world, and know every part of it."

"There's more of the world than Oz," declared the crab, in a stubborn voice.

"That is true," said Dorothy; "but I used to live in Kansas, in the United States, and I've been to California and to Australia—and so has Uncle Henry."

"For my part," added the Shaggy Man, "I've been to Mexico and Boston and many other foreign countries."

"And I," said the Wizard, "have been to Europe and Ireland."

"So you see," continued the zebra, addressing the crab, "here are people of real consequence, who know what they are talking about."

"Then they know there's more water in the world than there is land," asserted the crab, in a shrill, petulant voice.

"They know you are wrong to make such an absurd statement, and they will probably think you are a lobster instead of a crab," retorted the animal.

At this taunt the crab reached out its other claw and seized the zebra's ear, and the creature gave a cry of pain and began prancing up and down, trying to shake off the crab, which clung fast.

"Stop pinching!" cried the zebra. "You promised not to pinch if I would carry you here!"

"And you promised to treat me respectfully," said the crab, letting go the ear.

"Well, haven't I?" demanded the zebra.

"No; you called me a lobster," said the crab.

"Ladies and gentlemen," continued the zebra, "please pardon my poor friend, because he is ignorant and stupid, and does not understand. Also the pinch of his claw is very annoying. So pray tell him that the world contains more land than water, and when he has heard your judgment I will carry him back and dump him into his pool, where I hope he will be more modest in the future."

"But we cannot tell him that," said Dorothy, gravely, "because it would not be true."

"What!" exclaimed the zebra, in astonishment; "do I hear you aright?"

"The soft-shell crab is correct," declared the Wizard. "There is considerably more water than there is land in the world."

"Impossible!" protested the zebra. "Why, I can run for days upon the land, and find but little water."

"Did you ever see an ocean?" asked Dorothy.

"Never," admitted the zebra. "There is no such thing as an ocean in the Land of Oz."

"Well, there are several oceans in the world," said Dorothy, "and people sail in ships upon these oceans for weeks and weeks, and never see a bit of land at all. And the joggerfys will tell you that all the oceans put together are bigger than all the land put together."

At this the crab began laughing in queer chuckles that reminded Dorothy of the way Billina sometimes cackled.

"*Now* will you give up, Mr. Zebra?" it cried, jeeringly; "now will you give up?"

The zebra seemed much humbled.

"Of course I cannot read geographys," he said.

"You could take one of the Wizard's School Pills," suggested Billina, "and that would make you learned and wise without studying."

The crab began laughing again, which so provoked the zebra that he tried to shake the little creature off. This resulted in more ear-pinching, and finally Dorothy told them that if they could not behave they must go back to the forest.

"I'm sorry I asked you to decide this question," said the zebra, crossly. "So long as neither of us could prove we were right we quite enjoyed the dispute; but now I can never drink at that pool again without the soft-shell crab laughing at me. So I must find another drinking place."

"Do! Do, you ignoramus!" shouted the crab, as loudly as his little voice would carry. "Rile some other pool with your clumsy hoofs, and let your betters alone after this!"

Then the zebra trotted back to the forest, bearing the crab with him, and disappeared amid the gloom of the trees. And as it was now getting dark the travelers said good night to one another and went to bed.

Dorothy awoke just as the light was beginning to get strong next morning, and not caring to sleep any later she quietly got out of bed, dressed herself, and left the tent where Aunt Em was yet peacefully slumbering.

Outside she noticed Billina busily pecking around to secure bugs or other food for breakfast, but none of the men in the other tent seemed awake. So the little girl

decided to take a walk in the woods and try to discover some path or road that they
might follow when they again started upon their journey.

She had reached the edge of the forest when the Yellow Hen came fluttering along
and asked where she was going.

"Just to take a walk, Billina; and maybe I'll find some path," said Dorothy.

"Then I'll go along," decided Billina, and scarcely had she spoken when Toto ran
up and joined them.

Toto and the Yellow Hen had become quite friendly by this time, although at first
they did not get along well together. Billina had been rather suspicious of dogs, and
Toto had had an idea that it was every dog's duty to chase a hen on sight. But Dorothy
had talked to them and scolded them for not being agreeable to one another until they
grew better acquainted and became friends.

I won't say they loved each other dearly, but at least they had stopped quarreling
and now managed to get on together very well.

The day was growing lighter every minute and driving the black shadows out
of the forest; so Dorothy found it very pleasant walking under the trees. She went
some distance in one direction, but not finding a path, presently turned in a different
direction. There was no path here, either, although she advanced quite a way into the
forest, winding here and there among the trees and peering through the bushes in an
endeavor to find some beaten track.

"I think we'd better go back," suggested the Yellow Hen, after a time. "The
people will all be up by this time and breakfast will be ready."

"Very well," agreed Dorothy. "Let's see—the camp must be over this way."

She had probably made a mistake about that, for after they had gone far enough to have reached the camp they still found themselves in the thick of the woods. So the little girl stopped short and looked around her, and Toto glanced up into her face with his bright little eyes and wagged his tail as if he knew something was wrong. He couldn't tell much about direction himself, because he had spent his time prowling among the bushes and running here and there; nor had Billina paid much attention to where they were going, being interested in picking bugs from the moss as they passed along. The Yellow Hen now turned one eye up toward the little girl and asked:

"Have you forgotten where the camp is, Dorothy?"

"Yes," she admitted; "have you, Billina?"

"I didn't try to remember," returned Billina. "I'd no idea you would get lost, Dorothy."

"It's the thing we don't expect, Billina, that usually happens," observed the girl, thoughtfully. "But it's no use standing here. Let's go in that direction," pointing a finger at random. "It may be we'll get out of the forest over there."

So on they went again, but this way the trees were closer together, and the vines were so tangled that often they tripped Dorothy up.

Suddenly a voice cried sharply:

"Halt!"

At first Dorothy could see nothing, although she looked around very carefully. But Billina exclaimed:

"Well, I declare!"

"What is it?" asked the little girl: for Toto began barking at something, and following his gaze she discovered what it was.

A row of spoons had surrounded the three, and these spoons stood straight up on their handles and carried swords and muskets. Their faces were outlined in the polished bowls and they looked very stern and severe.

Dorothy laughed at the queer things.

"Who are you?" she asked.

"We're the Spoon Brigade," said one.

"In the service of his Majesty King Kleaver," said another.

"And you are our prisoners," said a third.

Dorothy sat down on an old stump and looked at them, her eyes twinkling with amusement.

"What would happen," she inquired, "if I should set my dog on your Brigade?"

"He would die," replied one of the spoons, sharply. "One shot from our deadly muskets would kill him, big as he is."

"Don't risk it, Dorothy," advised the Yellow Hen. "Remember this is a fairy country, yet none of us three happens to be a fairy."

Dorothy grew sober at this.

"P'raps you're right, Billina," she answered. "But how funny it is, to be captured by a lot of spoons!"

"I do not see anything very funny about it," declared a spoon. "We're the regular military brigade of the kingdom."

"What kingdom?" she asked.

"Utensia," said he.

"I never heard of it before," asserted Dorothy. Then she added, thoughtfully, "I don't believe Ozma ever heard of Utensia, either. Tell me, are you not subjects of Ozma of Oz?"

"We never have heard of her," retorted a spoon. "We are subjects of King Kleaver, and obey only his orders, which are to bring all prisoners to him as soon as they are captured. So step lively, my girl, and march with us, or we may be tempted to cut off a few of your toes with our swords."

This threat made Dorothy laugh again. She did not believe she was in any danger; but here was a new and interesting adventure, so she was willing to be taken to Utensia that she might see what King Kleaver's kingdom was like.

CHAPTER XVI

How DOROTHY VISITED UTENSIA

THERE MUST HAVE BEEN FROM SIX TO EIGHT DOZEN SPOONS IN THE BRIGADE, AND they marched away in the shape of a hollow square, with Dorothy, Billina and Toto in the center of the square. Before they had gone very far Toto knocked over one of the spoons by wagging his tail, and then the Captain of the Spoons told the little dog to be more careful, or he would be punished. So Toto was careful, and the Spoon Brigade moved along with astonishing swiftness, while Dorothy really had to walk fast to keep up with it.

By and by they left the woods and entered a big clearing, in which was the Kingdom of Utensia.

Standing all around the clearing were a good many cookstoves, ranges and grills, of all sizes and shapes, and besides these there were several kitchen cabinets and cupboards and a few kitchen tables. These things were crowded with utensils of all sorts: frying pans, sauce pans, kettles, forks, knives, basting and soup spoons, nutmeg graters, sifters, colanders, meat saws, flat irons, rolling pins and many other things of a like nature.

When the Spoon Brigade appeared with the prisoners a wild shout arose and many of the utensils hopped off their stoves or their benches and ran crowding around Dorothy and the hen and the dog.

"Stand back!" cried the Captain, sternly, and he led his captives through the curious throng until they came before a big range that stood in the center of the

KING KLEAVER

clearing. Beside this range was a butcher's block upon which lay a great cleaver with a keen edge. It rested upon the flat of its back, its legs were crossed and it was smoking a long pipe.

"Wake up, your Majesty," said the Captain. "Here are prisoners."

Hearing this, King Kleaver sat up and looked at Dorothy sharply.

"Gristle and fat!" he cried. "Where did this girl come from?"

"I found her in the forest and brought her here a prisoner," replied the Captain.

"Why did you do that?" inquired the King, puffing his pipe lazily.

"To create some excitement," the Captain answered. "It is so quiet here that we are all getting rusty for want of amusement. For my part, I prefer to see stirring times."

"Naturally," returned the cleaver, with a nod. "I have always said, Captain, without a bit of irony, that you are a sterling officer and a solid citizen, bowled and polished to a degree. But what do you expect me to do with these prisoners?"

"That is for you to decide," declared the Captain. "You are the King."

"To be sure; to be sure," muttered the cleaver, musingly. "As you say, we have had dull times since the steel and grindstone eloped and left us. Command my Counselors and the Royal Courtiers to attend me, as well as the High Priest and the Judge. We'll then decide what can be done."

The Captain saluted and retired and Dorothy sat down on an overturned kettle and asked:

"Have you anything to eat in your kingdom?"

"Here! Get up! Get off from me!" cried a faint voice, at which his Majesty the cleaver said:

"Excuse me, but you're sitting on my friend the Ten-Quart Kettle."

Dorothy at once arose, and the kettle turned right side up and looked at her reproachfully.

"I'm a friend of the King, so no one dares sit on me," said he.

"I'd prefer a chair, anyway," she replied.

"Sit on that hearth," commanded the King.

So Dorothy sat on the hearth-shelf of the big range, and the subjects of Utensia began to gather around in a large and inquisitive throng. Toto lay at Dorothy's feet and Billina flew upon the range, which had no fire in it, and perched there as comfortably as she could.

When all the Counselors and Courtiers had assembled—and these seemed to include most of the inhabitants of the kingdom—the King rapped on the block for order and said:

"Friends and Fellow Utensils! Our worthy Commander of the Spoon Brigade, Captain Dipp, has captured the three prisoners you see before you and brought them here for—for—I don't know what for. So I ask your advice how to act in this matter, and what fate I should mete out to these captives. Judge Sifter, stand on my right. It is your business to sift this affair to the bottom. High Priest Colander, stand on my left and see that no one testifies falsely in this matter."

As these two officials took their places Dorothy asked:

"Why is the colander the High Priest?"

"He's the holiest thing we have in the kingdom," replied King Kleaver.

"Except me," said a sieve. "I'm the whole thing when it comes to holes."

"What we need," remarked the King, rebukingly, "is a wireless sieve. I must speak to Marconi about it. These old fashioned sieves talk too much. Now, it is the duty of the King's Counselors to counsel the King at all times of emergency, so I beg you to speak out and advise me what to do with these prisoners."

"I demand that they be killed several times, until they are dead!" shouted a pepperbox, hopping around very excitedly.

"Compose yourself, Mr. Paprica," advised the King. "Your remarks are piquant and highly-seasoned, but you need a scattering of commonsense. It is only necessary to kill a person once to make him dead; but I do not see that it is necessary to kill this little girl at all."

"I don't, either," said Dorothy.

"Pardon me, but you are not expected to advise me in this matter," replied King Kleaver.

"Why not?" asked Dorothy.

"You might be prejudiced in your own favor, and so mislead us," he said. "Now then, good subjects, who speaks next?"

"I'd like to smooth this thing over, in some way," said a flatiron, earnestly. "We are supposed to be useful to mankind, you know."

"But the girl isn't mankind! She's womankind!" yelled a corkscrew.

"What do you know about it?" inquired the King.

"I'm a lawyer," said the corkscrew, proudly. "I am accustomed to appear at the bar."

"But you're crooked," retorted the King, "and that debars you. You may be a corking good lawyer, Mr. Popp, but I must ask you to withdraw your remarks."

"Very well," said the corkscrew, sadly; "I see I haven't any pull at this court."

"Permit me," continued the flatiron, "to press my suit, your Majesty. I do not wish to gloss over any fault the prisoner may have committed, if such a fault exists; but we owe her some consideration, and that's flat!"

"I'd like to hear from Prince Karver," said the King.

At this a stately carvingknife stepped forward and bowed.

"The Captain was wrong to bring this girl here, and she was wrong to come," he said. "But now that the foolish deed is done let us all prove our mettle and have a slashing good time."

"That's it! that's it!" screamed a fat choppingknife. "We'll make mincemeat of the girl and hash of the chicken and sausage of the dog!"

There was a shout of approval at this and the King had to rap again for order.

"Gentlemen, gentlemen!" he said, "your remarks are somewhat cutting and rather disjointed, as might be expected from such acute intellects. But you give no reasons for your demands."

"See here, Kleaver; you make me tired," exclaimed a saucepan, strutting before the King very impudently. "You're about the worst King that ever reigned in Utensia, and that's saying a good deal. Why don't you run things yourself, instead of asking everybody's advice, like the big, clumsy idiot you are?"

The King sighed.

"I wish there wasn't a saucepan in my kingdom," he said. "You fellows are always stewing, over something, and every once in a while you slop over and make a mess of it. Go hang yourself, sir—by the handle—and don't let me hear from you again."

Dorothy was much shocked by the dreadful language the utensils employed, and she thought that they must have had very little proper training. So she said, addressing the King, who seemed very unfit to rule his turbulent subjects:

"I wish you'd decide my fate right away. I can't stay here all day, trying to find out what you're going to do with me."

"This thing is becoming a regular broil, and it's time I took part in it," observed a big gridiron, coming forward.

"What I'd like to know," said a can-opener, in a shrill voice, "is why the girl came to our forest, anyhow, and why she intruded upon Captain Dipp—who ought to be called Dippy—and who she is, and where she came from, and where she is going, and why and wherefore and therefore and when."

"I'm sorry to see, Sir Jabber," remarked the King to the can-opener, "that you have such a prying disposition. As a matter of fact, all the things you mention are none of our business."

Having said this the King relighted his pipe, which had gone out.

"Tell me, please, what *is* our business?" inquired a potato-masher, winking at Dorothy somewhat impertinently. "I'm fond of little girls, myself, and it seems to me she has as much right to wander in the forest as we have."

"Who accuses the little girl, anyway?" inquired a rolling-pin. "What has she done?"

"I don't know," said the King. "What has she done, Captain Dipp?"

"That's the trouble, your Majesty. She hasn't done anything," replied the Captain.

"What do you want me to do?" asked Dorothy.

This question seemed to puzzle them all. Finally a chafingdish, exclaimed, irritably: "If no one can throw any light on this subject you must excuse me if I go out."

At this a big kitchen fork pricked up its ears and said in a tiny voice:

"Let's hear from Judge Sifter."

"That's proper," returned the King.

So Judge Sifter turned around slowly several times and then said:

"We have nothing against the girl except the stove-hearth upon which she sits. Therefore I order her instantly discharged."

"Discharged!" cried Dorothy. "Why, I never was discharged in my life, and I don't intend to be. If it's all the same to you, I'll resign."

"It's all the same," declared the King. "You are free—you and your companions—and may go wherever you like."

"Thank you," said the little girl. "But haven't you anything to eat in your kingdom? I'm hungry."

"Go into the woods and pick blackberries," advised the King, lying down upon his back again and preparing to go to sleep. "There isn't a morsel to eat in all Utensia, that I know of."

So Dorothy jumped up and said:

"Come on, Toto and Billina. If we can't find the camp we may find some blackberries."

The utensils drew back and allowed them to pass without protest, although Captain Dipp marched the Spoon Brigade in close order after them until they had reached the edge of the clearing.

There the spoons halted; but Dorothy and her companions entered the forest again and began searching diligently for a way back to the camp, that they might rejoin their party.

CHAPTER XVII

How THEY CAME TO BUNBURY

WANDERING THROUGH THE WOODS, WITHOUT KNOWING WHERE YOU ARE GOING or what adventure you are about to meet next, is not as pleasant as one might think. The woods are always beautiful and impressive, and if you are not worried or hungry you may enjoy them immensely; but Dorothy was worried and hungry that morning, so she paid little attention to the beauties of the forest, and hurried along as fast as she could go. She tried to keep in one direction and not circle around, but she was not at all sure that the direction she had chosen would lead her to the camp.

By and by, to her great joy, she came upon a path. It ran to the right and to the left, being lost in the trees in both directions, and just before her, upon a big oak, were fastened two signs, with arms pointing both ways. One sign read:

☛ TAKE THE OTHER ROAD TO BUNBURY

and the second sign read:

☚ TAKE THE OTHER ROAD TO BUNNYBURY

"Well!" exclaimed Billina, eyeing the signs, "this looks as if we were getting back to civilization again."

"I'm not sure about the civil'zation, dear," replied the little girl; "but it looks as if we might get *somewhere*, and that's a big relief, anyhow."

"Which path shall we take?" inquired the Yellow Hen.

Dorothy stared at the signs thoughtfully.

"Bunbury sounds like something to eat," she said. "Let's go there."

"It's all the same to me," replied Billina. She had picked up enough bugs and insects from the moss as she went along to satisfy her own hunger, but the hen knew Dorothy could not eat bugs; nor could Toto.

The path to Bunbury seemed little traveled, but it was distinct enough and ran through the trees in a zigzag course until it finally led them to an open space filled with the queerest houses Dorothy had ever seen. They were all made of crackers, laid out in tiny squares, and were of many pretty and ornamental shapes, having balconies and porches with posts of bread-sticks and roofs shingled with wafer-crackers.

There were walks of bread-crusts leading from house to house and forming streets, and the place seemed to have many inhabitants.

When Dorothy, followed by Billina and Toto, entered the place, they found people walking the streets or assembled in groups talking together, or sitting upon the porches and balconies.

And what funny people they were!

Men, women and children were all made of buns and bread. Some were thin and others fat; some were white, some light brown and some very dark of complexion. A few of the buns, which seemed to form the more important class of the people, were neatly frosted. Some had raisins for eyes and currant buttons on their clothes; others had eyes of cloves and legs of stick cinnamon, and many wore hats and bonnets frosted pink and green.

There was something of a commotion in Bunbury when the strangers suddenly appeared among them. Women caught up their children and hurried into their houses, shutting the cracker doors carefully behind them. Some men ran so hastily that they tumbled over one another, while others, more brave, assembled in a group and faced the intruders defiantly.

Dorothy at once realized that she must act with caution in order not to frighten these shy people, who were evidently unused to the presence of strangers. There was a delightful fragrant odor of fresh bread in the town, and this made the little girl more hungry than ever. She told Toto and Billina to stay back while she slowly advanced toward the group that stood silently awaiting her.

"You must 'scuse me for coming unexpected," she said, softly, "but I really didn't know I was coming here until I arrived. I was lost in the woods, you know, and I'm as hungry as anything."

"Hungry!" they murmured, in a horrified chorus.

"Yes; I haven't had anything to eat since last night's supper," she exclaimed. "Are there any eatables in Bunbury?"

They looked at one another undecidedly, and then one portly bun man, who seemed a person of consequence, stepped forward and said:

"Little girl, to be frank with you, we are all eatables. Everything in Bunbury is eatable to ravenous human creatures like you. But it is to escape being eaten and destroyed that we have secluded ourselves in this out-of-the-way place, and there is neither right nor justice in your coming here to feed upon us."

Dorothy looked at him longingly.

"You're bread, aren't you?" she asked.

"Yes; bread and butter. The butter is inside me, so it won't melt and run. I do the running myself."

At this joke all the others burst into a chorus of laughter, and Dorothy thought they couldn't be much afraid if they could laugh like that.

"Couldn't I eat something besides people?" she asked. "Couldn't I eat just one house, or a side-walk, or something? I wouldn't mind much what it was, you know."

"This is not a public bakery, child," replied the man, sternly. "It's private property."

"I know Mr.—Mr.—"

"My name is C. Bunn, Esquire," said the man. "C stands for Cinnamon, and this place is called after my family, which is the most aristocratic in the town."

"Oh, I don't know about that," objected another of the queer people. "The Grahams and the Browns and Whites are all excellent families, and there is none better of their kind. I'm a Boston Brown, myself."

"I admit you are all desirable citizens," said Mr. Bunn, rather stiffly; "but the fact remains that our town is called Bunbury."

" 'Scuse me," interrupted Dorothy; "but I'm getting hungrier every minute. Now, if you're polite and kind, as I'm sure you ought to be, you'll let me eat *something*. There's so much to eat here that you never will miss it."

Then a big, puffed-up man, of a delicate brown color, stepped forward and said:

"I think it would be a shame to send this child away hungry, especially as she agrees to eat whatever we can spare and not touch our people."

"So do I, Pop," replied a Roll who stood near.

"What, then, do you suggest, Mr. Over?" inquired Mr. Bunn.

"Why, I'll let her eat my back fence, if she wants to. It's made of waffles, and they're very crisp and nice."

"She may also eat my wheelbarrow," added a pleasant looking Muffin. "It's made of nabiscos with a zuzu wheel."

"Very good; very good," remarked Mr. Bunn. "That is certainly very kind of you. Go with Pop Over and Mr. Muffin, little girl, and they will feed you."

"Thank you very much," said Dorothy, gratefully. "May I bring my dog Toto, and the Yellow Hen? They're hungry, too."

"Will you make them behave?" asked the Muffin.

"Of course," promised Dorothy.

"Then come along," said Pop Over.

So Dorothy and Billina and Toto walked up the street and the people seemed no longer to be at all afraid of them. Mr. Muffin's house came first, and as his wheelbarrow stood in the front yard the little girl ate that first. It didn't seem very fresh, but she was so hungry that she was not particular. Toto ate some, too, while Billina picked up the crumbs.

While the strangers were engaged in eating, many of the people came and stood in the street curiously watching them. Dorothy noticed six roguish looking brown children standing all in a row, and she asked:

"Who are you, little ones?"

"We're the Graham Gems," replied one; "and we're all twins."

"I wonder if your mother could spare one or two of you?" asked Billina, who decided that they were fresh baked; but at this dangerous question the six little gems ran away as fast as they could go.

"You musn't say such things, Billina," said Dorothy, reprovingly. "Now let's go into Pop Over's back yard and get the waffles."

"I sort of hate to let that fence go," remarked Mr. Over, nervously, as they walked toward his house. "The neighbors back of us are Soda Biscuits, and I don't care to mix with them."

"But I'm hungry yet," declared the girl. "That wheelbarrow wasn't very big."

"I've got a shortcake piano, but none of my family can play on it," he said, reflectively. "Suppose you eat that."

"All right," said Dorothy; "I don't mind. Anything to be accommodating."

So Mr. Over led her into the house, where she ate the piano, which was of an excellent flavor.

"Is there anything to drink here?" she asked.

"Yes; I've a milk pump and a water pump; which will you have?" he asked.

"I guess I'll try 'em both," said Dorothy.

So Mr. Over called to his wife, who brought into the yard a pail made of some kind of baked dough, and Dorothy pumped the pail full of cool, sweet milk and drank it eagerly.

The wife of Pop Over was several shades darker than her husband.

"Aren't you overdone?" the little girl asked her.

"No indeed," answered the woman. "I'm neither overdone nor done over; I'm just Mrs. Over, and I'm the President of the Bunbury Breakfast Band."

Dorothy thanked them for their hospitality and went away. At the gate Mr. Cinnamon Bunn met her and said he would show her around the town.

"We have some very interesting inhabitants," he remarked, walking stiffly beside her on his stick-cinnamon legs; "and all of us who are in good health are well bred. If you are no longer hungry we will call upon a few of the most important citizens."

Toto and Billina followed behind them, behaving very well, and a little way down the street they came to a handsome residence where Aunt Sally Lunn lived. The old lady was glad to meet the little girl and gave her a slice of white bread and butter which had been used as a door-mat. It was almost fresh and tasted better than anything Dorothy had eaten in the town.

"Where do you get the butter?" she inquired.

"We dig it out of the ground, which, as you may have observed, is all flour and meal," replied Mr. Bunn. "There is a butter mine just at the opposite side of the village. The trees which you see here are all doughleanders and doughderas, and in the season we get quite a crop of dough-nuts off them."

"I should think the flour would blow around and get into your eyes," said Dorothy.

"No," said he; "we are bothered with cracker dust sometimes, but never with flour."

Then he took her to see Johnny Cake, a cheerful old gentleman who lived near by.

"I suppose you've heard of me," said old Johnny, with an air of pride. "I'm a great favorite all over the world."

"Aren't you rather yellow?" asked Dorothy, looking at him critically.

"Maybe, child. But don't think I'm bilious, for I was never in better health in my life," replied the old gentleman. "If anything ailed me, I'd willingly acknowledge the corn."

"Johnny's a trifle stale," said Mr. Bunn, as they went away; "but he's a good mixer and never gets cross-grained. I will now take you to call upon some of my own relatives."

They visited the Sugar Bunns, the Currant Bunns and the Spanish Bunns, the latter having a decidedly foreign appearance. Then they saw the French Rolls, who were very polite to them, and made a brief call upon the Parker H. Rolls, who seemed a bit proud and overbearing.

"But they're not as stuck up as the Frosted Jumbles," declared Mr. Bunn, "who are people I really can't abide. I don't like to be suspicious or talk scandal, but sometimes I think the Jumbles have too much baking powder in them."

Just then a dreadful scream was heard, and Dorothy turned hastily around to find a scene of great excitement a little way down the street. The people were crowding around Toto and throwing at him everything they could find at hand. They pelted the little dog with hard-tack, crackers, and even articles of furniture which were hard baked and heavy enough for missiles.

Toto howled a little as the assortment of bake stuff struck him; but he stood still, with head bowed and tail between his legs, until Dorothy ran up and inquired what the matter was.

"Matter!" cried a rye loafer, indignantly, "why the horrid beast has eaten three of our dear Crumpets, and is now devouring a Salt-rising Biscuit!"

"Oh, Toto! How could you?" exclaimed Dorothy, much distressed.

Toto's mouth was full of his salt-rising victim; so he only whined and wagged his tail. But Billina, who had flown to the top of a cracker house to be in a safe place, called out:

"Don't blame him, Dorothy; the Crumpets dared him to do it."

"Yes, and you pecked out the eyes of a Raisin Bunn—one of our best citizens!" shouted a bread pudding, shaking its fist at the Yellow Hen.

"What's that! What's that?" wailed Mr. Cinnamon Bunn, who had now joined them. "Oh, what a misfortune—what a terrible misfortune!"

"See here," said Dorothy, determined to defend her pets, "I think we've treated you all pretty well, seeing you're eatables, an' reg'lar food for us. I've been kind to you, and eaten your old wheelbarrows and pianos and rubbish, an' not said a word. But Toto and Billina can't be 'spected to go hungry when the town's full of good things they like to eat, 'cause they can't understand your stingy ways as I do."

"You must leave here at once!" said Mr. Bunn, sternly.

"Suppose we won't go?" asked Dorothy, who was now much provoked.

"Then," said he, "we will put you into the great ovens where we are made, and bake you."

Dorothy gazed around and saw threatening looks upon the faces of all. She had not noticed any ovens in the town, but they might be there, nevertheless, for some of the inhabitants seemed very fresh. So she decided to go, and calling to Toto and Billina to follow her she marched up the street with as much dignity as possible, considering that she was followed by the hoots and cries of the buns and biscuits and other bake stuff.

CHAPTER XVIII

How OZMA LOOKED INTO THE MAGIC PICTURE

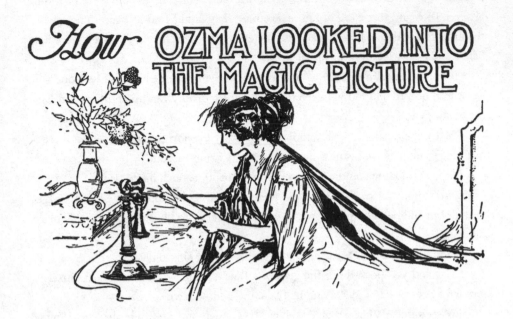

PRINCESS OZMA WAS A VERY BUSY LITTLE RULER, FOR SHE LOOKED CAREFULLY after the comfort and welfare of her people and tried to make them happy. If any quarrels arose she decided them justly; if any one needed counsel or advice she was ready and willing to listen to them.

For a day or two after Dorothy and her companions had started on their trip, Ozma was occupied with the affairs of her kingdom. Then she began to think of some manner of occupation for Uncle Henry and Aunt Em that would be light and easy and yet give the old people something to do.

She soon decided to make Uncle Henry the Keeper of the Jewels, for some one really was needed to count and look after the bins and barrels of emeralds, diamonds, rubies and other precious stones that were in the Royal Storehouses. That would keep Uncle Henry busy enough, but it was harder to find something for Aunt Em to do. The palace was full of servants, so there was no detail of housework that Aunt Em could look after.

While Ozma sat in her pretty room engaged in thought she happened to glance at her Magic Picture.

This was one of the most important treasures in all the Land of Oz. It was a large picture, set in a beautiful gold frame, and it hung in a prominent place upon a wall of Ozma's private room.

Usually this picture seemed merely a country scene, but whenever Ozma looked at it and wished to know what any of her friends or acquaintances were doing, the magic of this wonderful picture was straightway disclosed. For the country scene would gradually fade away and in its place would appear the likeness of the person or persons Ozma might wish to see, surrounded by the actual scenes in which they were then placed. In this way the Princess could view any part of the world she wished, and watch the actions of any one in whom she was interested.

Ozma had often seen Dorothy in her Kansas home by this means, and now, having a little leisure, she expressed a desire to see her little friend again. It was while the travelers were at Fuddlecumjig, and Ozma laughed merrily as she watched in the picture her friends trying to match the pieces of Grandmother Gnit.

"They seem happy and are doubtless having a good time," the girl Ruler said to herself; and then she began to think of the many adventures she herself had encountered with Dorothy.

The images of her friends now faded from the Magic Picture and the old landscape slowly reappeared.

Ozma was thinking of the time when with Dorothy and her army she marched to the Nome King's underground cavern, beyond the Land of Ev, and forced the old monarch to liberate his captives, who belonged to the Royal Family of Ev. That was the time when the Scarecrow nearly frightened the Nome King into fits by throwing one of Billina's eggs at him, and Dorothy had captured King Roquat's Magic Belt and brought it away with her to the Land of Oz.

The pretty Princess smiled at the recollection of this adventure, and then she wondered what had become of the Nome King since then. Merely because she was curious and had nothing better to do, Ozma glanced at the Magic Picture and wished to see in it the King of the Nomes.

Roquat the Red went every day into his tunnel to see how the work was getting along and to hurry his workmen as much as possible. He was there now, and Ozma saw him plainly in the Magic Picture.

She saw the underground tunnel, reaching far underneath the Deadly Desert which separated the Land of Oz from the mountains beneath which the Nome King had his extensive caverns. She saw that the tunnel was being made in the direction of the Emerald City, and knew at once it was being dug so that the army of Nomes could march through it and attack her own beautiful and peaceful country.

"I suppose King Roquat is planning revenge against us," she said, musingly, "and thinks he can surprise us and make us his captives and slaves. How sad it is that any one can have such wicked thoughts! But I must not blame King Roquat too severely, for he is a Nome, and his nature is not so gentle as my own."

Then she dismissed from her mind further thought of the tunnel, for that time, and began to wonder if Aunt Em would not be happy as Royal Mender of the

Stockings of the Ruler of Oz. Ozma wore few holes in her stockings; still, they sometimes needed mending. Aunt Em ought to be able to do that very nicely.

Next day the Princess watched the tunnel again in her Magic Picture, and every day afterward she devoted a few minutes to inspecting the work. It was not especially interesting, but she felt that it was her duty.

Slowly but surely the big arched hole crept through the rocks underneath the deadly desert, and day by day it drew nearer and nearer to the Emerald City.

CHAPTER XIX

How BUNNYBURY WELCOMED THE STRANGERS

DOROTHY LEFT BUNBURY THE SAME WAY SHE HAD ENTERED IT AND WHEN THEY were in the forest again she said to Billina:

"I never thought that things good to eat could be so dis'gree'ble."

"Often I've eaten things that tasted good but were disagreeable afterward," returned the Yellow Hen. "I think, Dorothy, if eatables are going to act badly, it's better before than after you eat them."

"P'raps you're right," said the little girl, with a sigh. "But what shall we do now?"

"Let us follow the path back to the sign-post," suggested Billina. "That will be better than getting lost again."

"Why, we're lost anyhow," declared Dorothy; "but I guess you're right about going back to that sign-post, Billina."

They returned along the path to the place where they had first found it, and at once took "the other road" to Bunnybury. This road was a mere narrow strip, worn hard and smooth but not wide enough for Dorothy's feet to tread. Still it was a guide, and the walking through the forest was not at all difficult.

Before long they reached a high wall of solid white marble, and the path came to an end at this wall.

At first Dorothy thought there was no opening at all in the marble, but on look-ing closely she discovered a small square door about on a level with her head, and underneath this closed door was a bell-push. Near the bell-push a sign was painted in neat letters upon the marble, and the sign read:

No Admittance
Except on Business

This did not discourage Dorothy, however, and she rang the bell.

Pretty soon a bolt was cautiously withdrawn and the marble door swung slowly open. Then she saw it was not really a door, but a window, for several brass bars were placed across it, being set fast in the marble and so close together that the little girl's fingers might barely go between them. Back of the bars appeared the face of a white rabbit—a very sober and sedate face—with an eye-glass held in his left eye and attached to a cord in his button-hole.

"Well! what is it?" asked the rabbit, sharply.

"I'm Dorothy," said the girl, "and I'm lost, and—"

"State your business, please," interrupted the rabbit.

"My business," she replied, "is to find out where I am, and to—"

"No one is allowed in Bunnybury without an order or a letter of introduction from either Ozma of Oz or Glinda the Good," announced the rabbit; "so that settles the matter," and he started to close the window.

"Wait a minute!" cried Dorothy. "I've got a letter from Ozma."

"From the Ruler of Oz?" asked the rabbit, doubtingly.

"Of course. Ozma's my best friend, you know; and I'm a Princess myself," she announced, earnestly.

"Hum—ha! Let me see your letter," returned the rabbit, as if he still doubted her.

So she hunted in her pocket and found the letter Ozma had given her. Then she handed it through the bars to the rabbit, who took it in his paws and opened it. He read it aloud in a pompous voice, as if to let Dorothy and Billina see that he was educated and could read writing. The letter was as follows:

"It will please me to have my subjects greet Princess Dorothy, the bearer of this royal missive, with the same courtesy and consideration they would extend to me."

"Ha—hum! It is signed 'Ozma of Oz,'" continued the rabbit, "and is sealed with the Great Seal of the Emerald City. Well, well, well! How strange! How remarkable!"

"What are you going to do about it?" inquired Dorothy, impatiently.

"We must obey the royal mandate," replied the rabbit. "We are subjects of Ozma of Oz, and we live in her country. Also we are under the protection of the great Sorceress Glinda the Good, who made us promise to respect Ozma's commands."

"Then may I come in?" she asked.

"I'll open the door," said the rabbit. He shut the window and disappeared, but a moment afterward a big door in the wall opened and admitted Dorothy to a small room, which seemed to be a part of the wall and built into it.

Here stood the rabbit she had been talking with, and now that she could see all of him she gazed at the creature in surprise. He was a good sized white rabbit with pink eyes, much like all other white rabbits. But the astonishing thing about him was the manner in which he was dressed. He wore a white satin jacket embroidered with gold, and having diamond buttons. His vest was rose-colored satin, with tourmaline buttons. His trousers were white, to correspond with the jacket, and they were baggy at the knees—like those of a zouave—being tied with knots of rose ribbons. His shoes were of white plush with diamond buckles, and his stockings were rose silk.

The richness and even magnificence of the rabbit's clothing made Dorothy stare at the little creature wonderingly. Toto and Billina had followed her into the room and when he saw them the rabbit ran to a table and sprang upon it nimbly. Then he looked at the three through his monocle and said:

"These companions, Princess, cannot enter Bunnybury with you."

"Why not?" asked Dorothy.

"In the first place they would frighten our people, who dislike dogs above all things on earth; and, secondly, the letter of the Royal Ozma does not mention them."

"But they're my friends," persisted Dorothy, "and go wherever I go."

"Not this time," said the rabbit, decidedly. "You, yourself, Princess, are a welcome visitor, since you come so highly recommended; but unless you consent to leave the dog and the hen in this room I cannot permit you to enter the town."

"Never mind us, Dorothy," said Billina. "Go inside and see what the place is like. You can tell us about it afterward, and Toto and I will rest comfortably here until you return."

This seemed the best thing to do, for Dorothy was curious to see how the rabbit people lived and she was aware of the fact that her friends might frighten the timid little creatures. She had not forgotten how Toto and Billina had misbehaved in Bunbury, and perhaps the rabbit was wise to insist on their staying outside the town.

"Very well," she said, "I'll go in alone. I s'pose you're the King of this town, aren't you?"

"No," answered the rabbit, "I'm merely the Keeper of the Wicket, and a person of little importance, although I try to do my duty. I must now inform you, Princess, that before you enter our town you must consent to reduce."

"Reduce what?" asked Dorothy.

"Your size. You must become the size of the rabbits, although you may retain your own form."

"Wouldn't my clothes be too big for me?" she inquired.

"No; they will reduce when your body does."

"Can *you* make me smaller?" asked the girl.

"Easily," returned the rabbit.

"And will you make me big again, when I'm ready to go away?"

"I will," said he.

"All right, then; I'm willing," she announced.

The rabbit jumped from the table and ran—or rather hopped—to the further wall, where he opened a door so tiny that even Toto could scarcely have crawled through it.

"Follow me," he said.

Now, almost any other little girl would have declared that she could not get through so small a door; but Dorothy had already encountered so many fairy adventures that she believed nothing was impossible in the Land of Oz. So she quietly walked toward the door, and at every step she grew smaller and smaller until, by the time the opening was reached, she could pass through it with ease. Indeed, as she stood beside the rabbit, who sat upon his hind legs and used his paws as hands, her head was just about as high as his own.

Then the Keeper of the Wicket passed through and she followed, after which the door swung shut and locked itself with a sharp click.

Dorothy now found herself in a city so strange and beautiful that she gave a gasp of surprise. The high marble wall extended all around the place and shut out all the rest of the world. And here were marble houses of curious forms, most of them resembling overturned kettles but with delicate slender spires and minarets running far up into the sky. The streets were paved with white marble and in front of each house was a lawn of rich green clover. Everything was as neat as wax, the green and white contrasting prettily together.

But the rabbit people were, after all, the most amazing things Dorothy saw. The streets were full of them, and their costumes were so splendid that the rich dress of the Keeper of the Wicket was commonplace when compared with the others. Silks and satins of delicate hues seemed always used for material, and nearly every costume sparkled with exquisite gems.

But the lady rabbits outshone the gentlemen rabbits in splendor, and the cut of their gowns was really wonderful. They wore bonnets, too, with feathers and jewels in them, and some wheeled baby carriages in which the girl could see wee bunnies. Some were lying asleep while others lay sucking their paws and looking around them with big pink eyes.

As Dorothy was no bigger in size than the grown-up rabbits she had a chance to observe them closely before they noticed her presence. Then they did not seem at all alarmed, although the little girl naturally became the center of attraction and all regarded her with great curiosity.

"Make way!" cried the Keeper of the Wicket, in a pompous voice; "make way for Princess Dorothy, who comes from Ozma of Oz."

Hearing this announcement, the throng of rabbits gave place to them on the walks, and as Dorothy passed along they all bowed their heads respectfully.

Walking thus through several handsome streets they came to a square in the center of the city. In this square were some pretty trees and a statue in bronze of Glinda the Good, while beyond it were the portals of the Royal Palace—an extensive and imposing building of white marble covered with a filigree of frosted gold.

CHAPTER XX

HOW DOROTHY LUNCHED WITH A KING

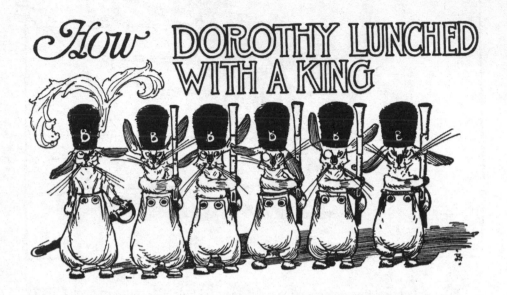

A LINE OF RABBIT SOLDIERS WAS DRAWN UP BEFORE THE PALACE ENTRANCE, AND they wore green and gold uniforms with high shakos upon their heads and held tiny spears in their hands. The Captain had a sword and a white plume in his shako.

"Salute!" called the Keeper of the Wicket. "Salute Princess Dorothy, who comes from Ozma of Oz!"

"Salute!" yelled the Captain, and all the soldiers promptly saluted.

They now entered the great hall of the palace, where they met a gaily dressed attendant, from whom the Keeper of the Wicket inquired if the King were at leisure.

"I think so," was the reply. "I heard his Majesty blubbering and wailing as usual only a few minutes ago. If he doesn't stop acting like a cry-baby I'm going to resign my position here and go to work."

"What's the matter with your King?" asked Dorothy, surprised to hear the rabbit attendant speak so disrespectfully of his monarch.

"Oh, he doesn't want to be King, that's all; and he simply *has* to," was the reply.

"Come!" said the Keeper of the Wicket, sternly; "lead us to his Majesty; and do not air our troubles before strangers, I beg of you."

"Why, if this girl is going to see the King, he'll air his own troubles," returned the attendant.

"That is his royal privilege," declared the Keeper.

So the attendant led them into a room all draped with cloth-of-gold and furnished with satin-covered gold furniture. There was a throne in this room, set on a dais and having a big cushioned seat, and on this seat reclined the Rabbit King. He was lying on his back, with his paws in the air, and whining very like a puppy-dog.

"Your Majesty! your Majesty! Get up. Here's a visitor," called out the attendant.

The King rolled over and looked at Dorothy with one watery pink eye. Then he sat up and wiped his eyes carefully with a silk handkerchief and put on his jeweled crown, which had fallen off.

"Excuse my grief, fair stranger," he said, in a sad voice. "You behold in me the most miserable monarch in all the world. What time is it, Blinkem?"

"One o'clock, your Majesty," replied the attendant to whom the question was addressed.

"Serve luncheon at once!" commanded the King. "Luncheon for two—that's for my visitor and me—and see that the human has some sort of food she's accustomed to."

"Yes, your Majesty," answered the attendant, and went away.

"Tie my shoe, Bristle," said the King to the Keeper of the Wicket. "Ah me! how unhappy I am!"

"What seems to be worrying your Majesty?" asked Dorothy.

"Why, it's this king business, of course," he returned, while the Keeper tied his shoe. "I didn't want to be King of Bunnybury at all, and the rabbits all knew it. So they elected me—to save themselves from such a dreadful fate, I suppose—and here I am, shut up in a palace, when I might be free and happy."

"Seems to me," said Dorothy, "it's a great thing to be a King."

"Were you ever a King?" inquired the monarch.

"No," she answered, laughing.

"Then you know nothing about it," he said. "I haven't inquired who you are, but it doesn't matter. While we're at luncheon, I'll tell you all my troubles. They're a great deal more interesting than anything you can say about yourself."

"Perhaps they are, to you," replied Dorothy.

"Luncheon is served!" cried Blinkem, throwing open the door, and in came a dozen rabbits in livery, all bearing trays which they placed upon the table, where they arranged the dishes in an orderly manner.

"Now clear out—all of you!" exclaimed the King. "Bristle, you may wait outside, in case I want you."

When they had gone and the King was alone with Dorothy he came down from his throne, tossed his crown into a corner and kicked his ermine robe under the table.

"Sit down," he said, "and try to be happy. It's useless for me to try, because I'm always wretched and miserable. But I'm hungry, and I hope you are."

"I am," said Dorothy. "I've only eaten a wheelbarrow and a piano to-day—oh, yes! and a slice of bread and butter that used to be a door-mat."

"That sounds like a square meal," remarked the King, seating himself opposite her; "but perhaps it wasn't a square piano. Eh?"

Dorothy laughed.

"You don't seem so very unhappy now," she said.

"But I am," protested the King, fresh tears gathering in his eyes. "Even my jokes are miserable. I'm wretched, woeful, afflicted, distressed and dismal as an individual can be. Are you not sorry for me?"

"No," answered Dorothy, honestly, "I can't say I am. Seems to me that for a rabbit you're right in clover. This is the prettiest little city I ever saw."

"Oh, the city is good enough," he admitted. "Glinda, the Good Sorceress, made it for us because she was fond of rabbits. I don't mind the city so much, although I wouldn't live here if I had my choice. It is being King that has absolutely ruined my happiness."

"Why wouldn't you live here by choice?" she asked.

"Because it is all unnatural, my dear. Rabbits are out of place in such luxury. When I was young I lived in a burrow in the forest. I was surrounded by enemies and often had to run for my life. It was hard getting enough to eat, at times, and when I found a bunch of clover I had to listen and look for danger while I ate it. Wolves prowled around the hole in which I lived and sometimes I didn't dare stir out for days at a time. Oh, how happy and contented I was then! I was a real rabbit, as nature made me—wild and free!—and I even enjoyed listening to the startled throbbing of my own heart!"

"I've often thought," said Dorothy, who was busily eating, "that it would be fun to be a rabbit."

"It *is* fun—when you're the genuine article," agreed his Majesty. "But look at me now! I live in a marble palace instead of a hole in the ground. I have all I want to eat, without the joy of hunting for it. Every day I must dress in fine clothes and wear that horrible crown till it makes my head ache. Rabbits come to me with all sorts of troubles, when my own troubles are the only ones I care about. When I walk out I can't hop and run; I must strut on my rear legs and wear an ermine robe! And the soldiers salute me and the band plays and the other rabbits laugh and clap their paws and cry out: 'Hail to the King!' Now let me ask you, as a friend and a young lady of good judgment: isn't all this pomp and foolishness enough to make a decent rabbit miserable?"

"Once," said Dorothy, reflectively, "men were wild and unclothed and lived in caves and hunted for food as wild beasts do. But they got civ'lized, in time, and now they'd hate to go back to the old days."

"That is an entirely different case," replied the King. "None of you Humans were civilized in one lifetime. It came to you by degrees. But I have known the forest and

the free life, and that is why I resent being civilized all at once, against my will, and being made a King with a crown and an ermine robe. Pah!"

"If you don't like it, why don't you resign?" she asked.

"Impossible!" wailed the Rabbit, wiping his eyes again with his handkerchief. "There's a beastly law in this town that forbids it. When one is elected a King there's no getting out of it."

"Who made the laws?" inquired Dorothy.

"The same Sorceress who made the town—Glinda the Good. She built the wall, and fixed up the city, and gave us several valuable enchantments, and made the laws. Then she invited all the pink-eyed white rabbits of the forest to come here, after which she left us to our fate."

"What made you 'cept the invitation, and come here?" asked the child.

"I didn't know how dreadful city life was, and I'd no idea I would be elected King," said he, sobbing bitterly. "And—and—now I'm It—with a capital I—and can't escape!"

"I know Glinda," remarked Dorothy, eating for dessert a dish of charlotte russe, "and when I see her again I'll ask her to put another King in your place."

"Will you? Will you, indeed?" asked the King, joyfully.

"I will if you want me to," she replied.

"Hurroo—hurray!" shouted the King; and then he jumped up from the table and danced wildly about the room, waving his napkin like a flag and laughing with glee.

After a time he managed to control his delight and returned to the table.

"When are you likely to see Glinda?" he inquired.

"Oh, p'raps in a few days," said Dorothy.

"And you won't forget to ask her?"

"Of course not."

"Princess," said the Rabbit King, earnestly, "you have relieved me of a great unhappiness, and I am very grateful. Therefore I propose to entertain you, since you are my guest and I am the King, as a slight mark of my appreciation. Come with me to my reception hall."

He then summoned Bristle and said to him: "Assemble all the nobility in the great reception hall, and also tell Blinkem that I want him immediately."

The Keeper of the Wicket bowed and hurried away, and his Majesty turned to Dorothy and continued: "We'll have time for a walk in the gardens before the people get here."

The gardens were back of the palace and were filled with beautiful flowers and fragrant shrubs, with many shade and fruit trees and marble paved walks running in every direction. As they entered this place Blinkem came running to the King, who gave him several orders in a low voice. Then his Majesty rejoined Dorothy and led her through the gardens, which she admired very much.

"What lovely clothes your Majesty wears!" she said, glancing at the rich blue satin costume, embroidered with pearls, in which the King was dressed.

"Yes," he returned, with an air of pride, "this is one of my favorite suits; but I have a good many that are even more elaborate. We have excellent tailors in Bunnybury, and Glinda supplies all the material. By the way, you might ask the Sorceress, when you see her, to permit me to keep my wardrobe."

"But if you go back to the forest you will not need clothes," she said.

"N—o!" he faltered; "that may be so. But I've dressed up so long that I'm used to it, and I don't imagine I'd care to run around naked again. So perhaps the Good Glinda will let me keep the costumes."

"I'll ask her," agreed Dorothy.

Then they left the gardens and went into a fine big reception hall, where rich rugs were spread upon the tiled floors and the furniture was exquisitely carved and studded with jewels. The King's chair was an especially pretty piece of furniture, being in the shape of a silver lily with one leaf bent over to form the seat. The silver was everywhere thickly encrusted with diamonds and the seat was upholstered in white satin.

"Oh, what a splendid chair!" cried Dorothy, clasping her hands admiringly.

"Isn't it?" answered the King, proudly. "It is my favorite seat, and I think it especially becoming to my complexion. While I think of it, I wish you'd ask Glinda to let me keep this lily chair when I go away."

"It wouldn't look very well in a hole in the ground, would it?" she suggested.

"Maybe not; but I'm used to sitting in it and I'd like to take it with me," he answered. "But here come the ladies and gentlemen of the court; so please sit beside me and be presented."

CHAPTER XXI

How THE KING CHANGED HIS MIND

JUST THEN A RABBIT BAND OF NEARLY FIFTY PIECES MARCHED IN, PLAYING UPON golden instruments and dressed in neat uniforms. Following the band came the nobility of Bunnybury, all richly dressed and hopping along on their rear legs. Both the ladies and the gentlemen wore white gloves upon their paws, with their rings on the outside of the gloves, as this seemed to be the fashion here. Some of the lady rabbits carried lorgnettes, while many of the gentlemen rabbits wore monocles in their left eyes.

The courtiers and their ladies paraded past the King, who introduced Princess Dorothy to each couple in a very graceful manner. Then the company seated themselves in chairs and on sofas and looked expectantly at their monarch.

"It is our royal duty, as well as our royal pleasure," he said, "to provide fitting entertainment for our distinguished guest. We will now present the Royal Band of Whiskered Friskers."

As he spoke the musicians, who had arranged themselves in a corner, struck up a dance melody while into the room pranced the Whiskered Friskers. They were eight pretty rabbits dressed only in gauzy purple skirts fastened around their waists with diamond bands. Their whiskers were colored a rich purple, but otherwise they were pure white.

After bowing before the King and Dorothy the Friskers began their pranks, and these were so comical that Dorothy laughed with real enjoyment. They not only danced together, whirling and gyrating around the room, but they leaped over one

another, stood upon their heads and hopped and skipped here and there so nimbly that it was hard work to keep track of them. Finally they all made double somersaults and turned handsprings out of the room.

The nobility enthusiastically applauded, and Dorothy applauded with them.

"They're fine!" she said to the King.

"Yes, the Whiskered Friskers are really very clever," he replied. "I shall hate to part with them when I go away, for they have often amused me when I was very miserable. I wonder if you would ask Glinda—"

"No, it wouldn't do at all," declared Dorothy, positively. "There wouldn't be room in your hole in the ground for so many rabbits, 'spec'ly when you get the lily chair and your clothes there. Don't think of such a thing, your Majesty."

The King sighed. Then he stood up and announced to the company:

"We will now hold a military drill by my picked Body-Guard of Royal Pikemen."

Now the band played a march and a company of rabbit soldiers came in. They wore green and gold uniforms and marched very stiffly but in perfect time. Their spears, or pikes, had slender shafts of polished silver with golden heads, and during the drill they handled these weapons with wonderful dexterity.

"I should think you'd feel pretty safe with such a fine Body-Guard," remarked Dorothy.

"I do," said the King. "They protect me from every harm. I suppose Glinda wouldn't—"

"No," interrupted the girl; "I'm sure she wouldn't. It's the King's own Body-Guard, and when you are no longer King you can't have 'em."

The King did not reply, but he looked rather sorrowful for a time.

When the soldiers had marched out he said to the company:

"The Royal Jugglers will now appear."

Dorothy had seen many jugglers in her lifetime, but never any so interesting as these. There were six of them, dressed in black satin embroidered with queer symbols in silver—a costume which contrasted strongly with their snow-white fur.

First they pushed in a big red ball and three of the rabbit jugglers stood upon its top and made it roll. Then two of them caught up a third and tossed him into the air, all vanishing, until only the two were left. Then one of these tossed the other upward and remained alone of all his fellows. This last juggler now touched the red ball, which fell apart, being hollow, and the five rabbits who had disappeared in the air scrambled out of the hollow ball.

Next they all clung together and rolled swiftly upon the floor. When they came to a stop only one fat rabbit juggler was seen, the others seeming to be inside him. This one leaped lightly into the air and when he came down he exploded and separated into the original six. Then four of them rolled themselves into round balls and the other two tossed them around and played ball with them.

These were but a few of the tricks the rabbit jugglers performed, and they were so skillful that all the nobility and even the King applauded as loudly as did Dorothy.

"I suppose there are no rabbit jugglers in all the world to compare with these," remarked the King. "And since I may not have the Whiskered Friskers or my Body-Guard, you might ask Glinda to let me take away just two or three of these jugglers. Will you?"

"I'll ask her," replied Dorothy, doubtfully.

"Thank you," said the King; "thank you very much. And now you shall listen to the Winsome Waggish Warblers, who have often cheered me in my moments of anguish."

The Winsome Waggish Warblers proved to be a quartette of rabbit singers, two gentlemen and two lady rabbits. The gentlemen Warblers wore full-dress swallow-tailed suits of white satin, with pearls for buttons, while the lady Warblers were gowned in white satin dresses with long trails.

The first song they sang began in this way:

> "When a rabbit gets a habit
>   Of living in a city
> And wearing clothes and furbelows
>   And jewels rare and pretty,

He scorns the Bun who has to run
And burrow in the ground
And pities those whose watchful foes
Are man and gun and hound."

Dorothy looked at the King when she heard this song and noticed that he seemed disturbed and ill at ease.

"I don't like that song," he said to the Warblers. "Give us something jolly and rollicking."

So they sang to a joyous, tinkling melody as follows:

"Bunnies gay
Delight to play
In their fairy town secure;
Ev'ry frisker
Flirts his whisker
At a pink-eyed girl demure.
Ev'ry maid
In silk arrayed
At her partner shyly glances,
Paws are grasped,
Waists are clasped
As they whirl in giddy dances.
Then together
Through the heather
'Neath the moonlight soft they stroll;
Each is very
Blithe and merry,
Gamboling with laughter droll.
Life is fun
To ev'ry one
Guarded by our magic charm
For to dangers
We are strangers,
Safe from any thought of harm."

"You see," said Dorothy to the King, when the song ended, "the rabbits all seem to like Bunnybury except you. And I guess you're the only one that ever has cried or was unhappy and wanted to get back to your muddy hole in the ground."

His Majesty seemed thoughtful, and while the servants passed around glasses of nectar and plates of frosted cakes their King was silent and a bit nervous.

When the refreshments had been enjoyed by all and the servants had retired Dorothy said:

"I must go now, for it's getting late and I'm lost. I've got to find the Wizard and Aunt Em and Uncle Henry and all the rest sometime before night comes, if I poss'bly can."

"Won't you stay with us?" asked the King. "You will be very welcome."

"No, thank you," she replied. "I must get back to my friends. And I want to see Glinda just as soon as I can, you know."

So the King dismissed his court and said he would himself walk with Dorothy to the gate. He did not weep nor groan any more, but his long face was quite solemn and his big ears hung dejectedly on each side of it. He still wore his crown and his ermine and walked with a handsome gold-headed cane.

When they arrived at the room in the wall the little girl found Toto and Billina waiting for her very patiently. They had been liberally fed by some of the attendants and were in no hurry to leave such comfortable quarters.

The Keeper of the Wicket was by this time back in his old place, but he kept a safe distance from Toto. Dorothy bade good-bye to the King as they stood just inside the wall.

"You've been good to me," she said, "and I thank you ever so much. As soon as poss'ble I'll see Glinda and ask her to put another King in your place and send you back into the wild forest. And I'll ask her to let you keep some of your clothes and the lily chair and one or two jugglers to amuse you. I'm sure she will do it, 'cause she's so kind she doesn't like any one to be unhappy."

"Ahem!" said the King, looking rather downcast. "I don't like to trouble you with my misery; so you needn't see Glinda."

"Oh, yes I will," she replied. "It won't be any trouble at all."

"But, my dear," continued the King, in an embarrassed way, "I've been think-ing the subject over carefully, and I find there are a lot of pleasant things here in Bunnybury that I would miss if I went away. So perhaps I'd better stay."

Dorothy laughed. Then she looked grave.

"It won't do for you to be a King and a cry-baby at the same time," she said. "You've been making all the other rabbits unhappy and discontented with your howls about being so miserable. So I guess it's better to have another King."

"Oh, no indeed!" exclaimed the King, earnestly. "If you won't say anything to Glinda I'll promise to be merry and gay all the time, and never cry or wail again."

"Honor bright?" she asked.

"On the royal word of a King I promise it!" he answered.

"All right," said Dorothy. "You'd be a reg'lar lunatic to want to leave Bunnybury for a wild life in the forest, and I'm sure any rabbit outside the city would be glad to take your place."

"Forget it, my dear; forget all my foolishness," pleaded the King, earnestly. "Hereafter I'll try to enjoy myself and do my duty by my subjects."

So then she left him and entered through the little door into the room in the wall, where she grew gradually bigger and bigger until she had resumed her natural size.

The Keeper of the Wicket let them out into the forest and told Dorothy that she had been of great service to Bunnybury because she had brought their dismal King to a realization of the pleasure of ruling so beautiful a city.

"I shall start a petition to have your statue erected beside Glinda's in the public square," said the Keeper. "I hope you will come again, some day, and see it."

"Perhaps I shall," she replied.

Then, followed by Toto and Billina, she walked away from the high marble wall and started back along the narrow path toward the sign-post.

CHAPTER XXII

How THE WIZARD FOUND DOROTHY

When they came to the signpost, there, to their joy, were the tents of the Wizard pitched beside the path and the kettle bubbling merrily over the fire. The Shaggy Man and Omby Amby were gathering firewood while Uncle Henry and Aunt Em sat in their camp chairs talking with the Wizard.

They all ran forward to greet Dorothy, as she approached, and Aunt Em exclaimed: "Goodness gracious, child! Where have you been?"

"You've played hookey the whole day," added the Shaggy Man, reproachfully.

"Well, you see, I've been lost," explained the little girl, "and I've tried awful hard to find the way back to you, but just couldn't do it."

"Did you wander in the forest all day?" asked Uncle Henry.

"You must be a'most starved!" said Aunt Em.

"No," said Dorothy, "I'm not hungry. I had a wheelbarrow and a piano for break-fast, and lunched with a King."

"Ah!" exclaimed the Wizard, nodding with a bright smile. "So you've been hav-ing adventures again."

"She's stark crazy!" cried Aunt Em. "Whoever heard of eating a wheelbarrow?"

"It wasn't very big," said Dorothy; "and it had a zuzu wheel."

"And I ate the crumbs," said Billina, soberly.

"Sit down and tell us about it," begged the Wizard. "We've hunted for you all day, and at last I noticed your footsteps in this path—and the tracks of Billina. We found the path by accident, and seeing it only led to two places I decided you were at either one or the other of those places. So we made camp and waited for you to return. And now, Dorothy, tell us where you have been—to Bunbury or to Bunnybury?"

"Why, I've been to both," she replied; "but first I went to Utensia, which isn't on any path at all."

She then sat down and related the day's adventures, and you may be sure Aunt Em and Uncle Henry were much astonished at the story.

"But after seeing the Cuttenclips and the Fuddles," remarked her uncle, "we ought not to wonder at anything in this strange country."

"Seems like the only common and ordinary folks here are ourselves," rejoined Aunt Em, diffidently.

"Now that we're together again, and one reunited party," observed the Shaggy Man, "what are we to do next?"

"Have some supper and a night's rest," answered the Wizard promptly, "and then proceed upon our journey."

"Where to?" asked the Captain General.

"We haven't visited the Rigmaroles or the Flutterbudgets yet," said Dorothy. "I'd like to see them—wouldn't you?"

"They don't sound very interesting," objected Aunt Em. "But perhaps they are."

"And then," continued the little Wizard, "we will call upon the Tin Woodman and Jack Pumpkinhead and our old friend the Scarecrow, on our way home."

"That will be nice!" cried Dorothy, eagerly.

"Can't say they sound very interesting, either," remarked Aunt Em.

"Why, they're the best friends I have!" asserted the little girl, "and you're sure to like them, Aunt Em, 'cause ever'body likes them."

By this time twilight was approaching, so they ate the fine supper which the Wizard magically produced from the kettle and then went to bed in the cozy tents.

They were all up bright and early next morning, but Dorothy didn't venture to wander from the camp again for fear of more accidents.

"Do you know where there's a road?" she asked the little man.

"No, my dear," replied the Wizard; "but I'll find one."

After breakfast he waved his hand toward the tents and they became handkerchiefs again, which were at once returned to the pockets of their owners. Then they all climbed into the red wagon and the Saw-Horse inquired:

"Which way?"

"Never mind which way," replied the Wizard. "Just go as you please and you're sure to be right. I've enchanted the wheels of the wagon, and they will roll in the right direction, never fear."

As the Saw-Horse started away through the trees Dorothy said:

"If we had one of those new-fashioned airships we could float away over the top of the forest, and look down and find just the places we want."

"Airship? Pah!" retorted the little man, scornfully. "I hate those things, Dorothy, although they are nothing new to either you or me. I was a balloonist for many years, and once my balloon carried me to the Land of Oz, and once to the Vegetable Kingdom. And once Ozma had a Gump that flew all over this kingdom and had sense enough to go where it was told to—which airships won't do. The house which the cyclone brought to Oz all the way from Kansas, with you and Toto in it—was a real airship at the time; so you see we've had plenty of experience flying with the birds."

"Airships are not so bad, after all," declared Dorothy. "Some day they'll fly all over the world, and perhaps bring people even to the Land of Oz."

"I must speak to Ozma about that," said the Wizard, with a slight frown. "It wouldn't do at all, you know, for the Emerald City to become a way-station on an airship line."

"No," said Dorothy, "I don't s'pose it would. But what can we do to prevent it?"

"I'm working out a magic recipe to fuddle men's brains, so they'll never make an airship that will go where they want it to go," the Wizard confided to her. "That won't keep the things from flying, now and then, but it'll keep them from flying to the Land of Oz."

Just then the Saw-Horse drew the wagon out of the forest and a beautiful land-scape lay spread before the travelers' eyes. Moreover, right before them was a good road that wound away through the hills and valleys.

"Now," said the Wizard, with evident delight, "we are on the right track again, and there is nothing more to worry about."

"It's a foolish thing to take chances in a strange country," observed the Shaggy Man. "Had we kept to the roads we never would have been lost. Roads always lead to some place, else they wouldn't be roads."

"This road," added the Wizard, "leads to Rigmarole Town. I'm sure of that because I enchanted the wagon wheels."

Sure enough, after riding along the road for an hour or two they entered a pretty valley where a village was nestled among the hills. The houses were Munchkin shaped, for they were all domes, with windows wider than they were high, and pretty balconies over the front doors.

Aunt Em was greatly relieved to find this town "neither paper nor patchwork," and the only surprising thing about it was that it was so far distant from all other towns.

As the Saw-Horse drew the wagon into the main street the travelers noticed that the place was filled with people, standing in groups and seeming to be engaged in earnest conversation. So occupied with themselves were the inhabitants that they scarcely noticed the strangers at all. So the Wizard stopped a boy and asked:

"Is this Rigmarole Town?"

"Sir," replied the boy, "if you have traveled very much you will have noticed that every town differs from every other town in one way or another and so by observing the methods of the people and the way they live as well as the style of their dwelling places it ought not to be a difficult thing to make up your mind without the trouble of asking questions whether the town bears the appearance of the one you intended to visit or whether perhaps having taken a different road from the one you should have taken you have made an error in your way and arrived at some point where—"

"Land sakes!" cried Aunt Em, impatiently; "what's all this rigmarole about?"

"That's it!" said the Wizard, laughing merrily. "It's a rigmarole because the boy is a Rigmarole and we've come to Rigmarole Town."

"Do they all talk like that?" asked Dorothy, wonderingly.

"He might have said 'yes' or 'no' and settled the question," observed Uncle Henry.

"Not here," said Omby Amby. "I don't believe the Rigmaroles know what 'yes' or 'no' means."

While the boy had been talking several other people had approached the wagon and listened intently to his speech. Then they began talking to one another in long, deliberate speeches, where many words were used but little was said. But when the strangers criticised them so frankly one of the women, who had no one else to talk to, began an address to them, saying:

"It is the easiest thing in the world for a person to say 'yes' or 'no' when a question that is asked for the purpose of gaining information or satisfying the curiosity of the one who has given expression to the inquiry has attracted the attention of an individual who may be competent either from personal experience or the experience of others to answer it with more or less correctness or at least an attempt to satisfy the desire for information on the part of the one who has made the inquiry by—"

"Dear me!" exclaimed Dorothy, interrupting the speech. "I've lost all track of what you are saying."

"Don't let her begin over again, for goodness sake!" cried Aunt Em.

But the woman did not begin again. She did not even stop talking, but went right on as she had begun, the words flowing from her mouth in a stream.

"I'm quite sure that if we waited long enough and listened carefully, some of these people might be able to tell us something, in time," said the Wizard.

"Don't let's wait," returned Dorothy. "I've heard of the Rigmaroles, and wondered what they were like; but now I know, and I'm ready to move on."

"So am I," declared Uncle Henry; "we're wasting time here."

"Why, we're all ready to go," said the Shaggy Man, putting his fingers to his ears to shut out the monotonous babble of those around the wagon.

So the Wizard spoke to the Saw-Horse, who trotted nimbly through the village and soon gained the open country on the other side of it. Dorothy looked back, as they rode away, and noticed that the woman had not yet finished her speech but was talking as glibly as ever, although no one was near to hear her.

"If those people wrote books," Omby Amby remarked with a smile, "it would take a whole library to say the cow jumped over the moon."

"Perhaps some of 'em do write books," asserted the little Wizard. "I've read a few rigmaroles that might have come from this very town."

"Some of the college lecturers and ministers are certainly related to these people," observed the Shaggy Man; "and it seems to me the Land of Oz is a little ahead of the United States in some of its laws. For here, if one can't talk clearly, and straight to the point, they send him to Rigmarole Town; while Uncle Sam lets him roam around wild and free, to torture innocent people."

Dorothy was thoughtful. The Rigmaroles had made a strong impression upon her. She decided that whenever she spoke, after this, she would use only enough words to express what she wanted to say.

THEY WERE SOON AMONG THE PRETTY HILLS AND VALLEYS AGAIN, AND THE SAW-Horse sped up hill and down at a fast and easy pace, the roads being hard and smooth. Mile after mile was speedily covered, and before the ride had grown at all tiresome they sighted another village. The place seemed even larger than Rigmarole Town, but was not so attractive in appearance.

"This must be Flutterbudget Center," declared the Wizard. "You see, it's no trouble at all to find places if you keep to the right road."

"What are the Flutterbudgets like?" inquired Dorothy.

"I do not know, my dear. But Ozma has given them a town all their own, and I've heard that whenever one of the people becomes a Flutterbudget he is sent to this place to live."

"That is true," Omby Amby added; "Flutterbudget Center and Rigmarole Town are called 'the Defensive Settlements of Oz.'"

The village they now approached was not built in a valley, but on top of a hill, and the road they followed wound around the hill like a corkscrew, ascending the hill easily until it came to the town.

"Look out!" screamed a voice. "Look out, or you'll run over my child!"

They gazed around and saw a woman standing upon the sidewalk nervously wringing her hands as she gazed at them appealingly.

"Where is your child?" asked the Saw-Horse.

"In the house," said the woman, bursting into tears; "but if it should happen to be in the road, and you ran over it, those great wheels would crush my darling to jelly. Oh dear! oh dear! Think of my darling child being crushed to jelly by those great wheels!"

"Gid-dap!" said the Wizard, sharply, and the Saw-Horse started on.

They had not gone far before a man ran out of a house shouting wildly: "Help! Help!"

The Saw-Horse stopped short and the Wizard and Uncle Henry and the Shaggy Man and Omby Amby jumped out of the wagon and ran to the poor man's assistance. Dorothy followed them as quickly as she could.

"What's the matter?" asked the Wizard.

"Help! help!" screamed the man; "my wife has cut her finger off and she's bleeding to death!"

Then he turned and rushed back to the house, and all the party went with him. They found a woman in the front dooryard moaning and groaning as if in great pain.

"Be brave, madam!" said the Wizard, consolingly. "You won't die just because you have cut off a finger, you may be sure."

"But I haven't cut off a finger!" she sobbed.

"Then what *has* happened?" asked Dorothy.

"I—I pricked my finger with a needle while I was sewing, and—and the blood came!" she replied. "And now I'll have blood-poisoning, and the doctors will cut off my finger, and that will give me a fever and I shall die!"

"Pshaw!" said Dorothy; "I've pricked my finger many a time, and nothing happened."

"Really?" asked the woman, brightening and wiping her eyes upon her apron.

"Why, it's nothing at all," declared the girl. "You're more scared than hurt."

"Ah, that's because she's a Flutterbudget," said the Wizard, nodding wisely. "I think I know now what these people are like."

"So do I," announced Dorothy.

"Oh, boo-hoo-hoo!" sobbed the woman, giving way to a fresh burst of grief.

"What's wrong now?" asked the Shaggy Man.

"Oh, suppose I had pricked my foot!" she wailed. "Then the doctors would have cut my foot off, and I'd be lamed for life!"

"Surely, ma'am," replied the Wizard, "and if you'd pricked your nose they might cut your head off. But you see you didn't."

"But I might have!" she exclaimed, and began to cry again. So they left her and drove away in their wagon. And her husband came out and began calling "Help!" as he had before; but no one seemed to pay any attention to him.

As the travelers turned into another street they found a man walking excitedly up and down the pavement. He appeared to be in a very nervous condition and the Wizard stopped him to ask:

"Is anything wrong, sir?"

"Everything is wrong," answered the man, dismally. "I can't sleep."

"Why not?" inquired Omby Amby.

"If I go to sleep I'll have to shut my eyes," he explained; "and if I shut my eyes they may grow together, and then I'd be blind for life!"

"Did you ever hear of any one's eyes growing together?" asked Dorothy.

"No," said the man, "I never did. But it would be a dreadful thing, wouldn't it? And the thought of it makes me so nervous I'm afraid to go to sleep."

"There's no help for this case," declared the Wizard; and they went on.

At the next street corner a woman rushed up to them crying:

"Save my baby! Oh, good, kind people, save my baby!"

"Is it in danger?" asked Dorothy, noticing that the child was clasped in her arms and seemed sleeping peacefully.

"Yes, indeed," said the woman, nervously. "If I should go into the house and throw my child out of the window, it would roll way down to the bottom of the hill; and then if there were a lot of tigers and bears down there, they would tear my darling babe to pieces and eat it up!"

"Are there any tigers and bears in this neighborhood?" the Wizard asked.

"I've never heard of any," admitted the woman, "but if there were—"

"Have you any idea of throwing your baby out of the window?" questioned the little man.

"None at all," she said; "but if—"

"All your troubles are due to those 'ifs'," declared the Wizard. "If you were not a Flutterbudget you wouldn't worry."

"There's another 'if'," replied the woman. "Are you a Flutterbudget, too?"

"I will be, if I stay here long," exclaimed the Wizard, nervously.

"Another 'if'!" cried the woman.

But the Wizard did not stop to argue with her. He made the Saw-Horse canter all the way down the hill, and only breathed easily when they were miles away from the village.

After they had ridden in silence for a while Dorothy turned to the little man and asked:

"Do 'ifs' really make Flutterbudgets?"

"I think the 'ifs' help," he answered seriously. "Foolish fears, and worries over nothing, with a mixture of nerves and ifs, will soon make a Flutterbudget of any one."

Then there was another long silence, for all the travelers were thinking over this statement, and nearly all decided it must be true.

The country they were now passing through was everywhere tinted purple, the prevailing color of the Gillikin Country; but as the Saw-Horse ascended a hill they found that upon the other side everything was of a rich yellow hue.

"Aha!" cried the Captain General; "here is the Country of the Winkies. We are just crossing the boundary line."

"Then we may be able to lunch with the Tin Woodman," announced the Wizard, joyfully.

"Must we lunch on tin?" asked Aunt Em.

"Oh, no;" replied Dorothy. "Nick Chopper knows how to feed meat people, and he will give us plenty of good things to eat, never fear. I've been to his castle before."

"Is Nick Chopper the Tin Woodman's name?" asked Uncle Henry.

"Yes; that's one of his names," answered the little girl; "and another of his names is 'Emp'ror of the Winkies.' He's the King of this country, you know, but Ozma rules over all the countries of Oz."

"Does the Tin Woodman keep any Flutterbudgets or Rigmaroles at his castle?" inquired Aunt Em, uneasily.

"No, indeed," said Dorothy, positively. "He lives in a new tin castle, all full of lovely things."

"I should think it would rust," said Uncle Henry.

"He has thousands of Winkies to keep it polished for him," explained the Wizard. "His people love to do anything in their power for their beloved Emperor, so there isn't a particle of rust on all the big castle."

"I suppose they polish their Emperor, too," said Aunt Em.

"Why, some time ago he had himself nickel-plated," the Wizard answered; "so he only needs rubbing up once in a while. He's the brightest man in all the world, is dear Nick Chopper; and the kindest-hearted."

"I helped find him," said Dorothy, reflectively. "Once the Scarecrow and I found the Tin Woodman in the woods, and he was just rusted still, that time, an' no mistake. But we oiled his joints, an' got 'em good and slippery, and after that he went with us to visit the Wizard at the Em'rald City."

"Was that the time the Wizard scared you?" asked Aunt Em.

"He didn't treat us well, at first," acknowledged Dorothy; "for he made us go away and destroy the Wicked Witch. But after we found out he was only a humbug wizard we were not afraid of him."

The Wizard sighed and looked a little ashamed.

"When we try to deceive people we always make mistakes," he said. "But I'm getting to be a real wizard now, and Glinda the Good's magic, that I am trying to practice, can never harm any one."

"You were always a good man," declared Dorothy, "even when you were a bad wizard."

"He's a good wizard now," asserted Aunt Em, looking at the little man admiringly. "The way he made those tents grow out of handkerchiefs was just wonderful! And didn't he enchant the wagon wheels so they'd find the road?"

"All the people of Oz," said the Captain General, "are very proud of their Wizard. He once made some soap-bubbles that astonished the world."

The Wizard blushed at this praise, yet it pleased him. He no longer looked sad, but seemed to have recovered his usual good humor.

The country through which they now rode was thickly dotted with farm-houses, and yellow grain waved in all the fields. Many of the Winkies could be seen working on their farms and the wild and unsettled parts of Oz were by this time left far behind.

These Winkies appeared to be happy, light-hearted folk, and all removed their caps and bowed low when the red wagon with its load of travelers passed by.

It was not long before they saw something glittering in the sunshine far ahead.

"See!" cried Dorothy; "that's the Tin Castle, Aunt Em!"

And the Saw-Horse, knowing his passengers were eager to arrive, broke into a swift trot that soon brought them to their destination.

CHAPTER XXIV

How THE TIN WOODMAN TOLD THE SAD NEWS

THE TIN WOODMAN RECEIVED PRINCESS DOROTHY'S PARTY WITH MUCH GRACE AND cordiality, yet the little girl decided that something must be worrying her old friend, because he was not so merry as usual.

But at first she said nothing about this, for Uncle Henry and Aunt Em were fairly bubbling over with admiration for the beautiful tin castle and its polished tin owner. So her suspicion that something unpleasant had happened was for a time forgotten.

"Where is the Scarecrow?" she asked, when they had all been ushered into the big tin drawing-room of the castle, the Saw-Horse being led around to the tin stable in the rear.

"Why, our old friend has just moved into his new mansion," explained the Tin Woodman. "It has been a long time in building, although my Winkies and many other people from all parts of the country have been busily working upon it. At last, however, it is completed, and the Scarecrow took possession of his new home just two days ago."

"I hadn't heard that he wanted a home of his own," said Dorothy. "Why doesn't he live with Ozma in the Emerald City? He used to, you know; and I thought he was happy there."

"It seems," said the Tin Woodman, "that our dear Scarecrow cannot be contented with city life, however beautiful his surroundings might be. Originally he was a farmer, for he passed his early life in a cornfield, where he was supposed to frighten away the crows."

"I know," said Dorothy, nodding. "I found him, and lifted him down from his pole."

"So now, after a long residence in the Emerald City, his tastes have turned to farm life again," continued the Tin Man. "He feels that he cannot be happy without a farm of his own, so Ozma gave him some land and every one helped him build his mansion, and now he is settled there for good."

"Who designed his house?" asked the Shaggy Man.

"I believe it was Jack Pumpkinhead, who is also a farmer," was the reply.

They were now invited to enter the tin dining room, where luncheon was served.

Aunt Em found, to her satisfaction, that Dorothy's promise was more than fulfilled; for, although the Tin Woodman had no appetite of his own, he respected the appetites of his guests and saw that they were bountifully fed.

They passed the afternoon in wandering through the beautiful gardens and grounds of the palace. The walks were all paved with sheets of tin, brightly polished, and there were tin fountains and tin statues here and there among the trees. The flowers were mostly natural flowers and grew in the regular way; but their host showed them one flower bed which was his especial pride.

"You see, all common flowers fade and die in time," he explained, "and so there are seasons when the pretty blooms are scarce. Therefore I decided to make one tin flower bed all of tin flowers, and my workmen have created them with rare skill. Here you see tin camelias, tin marigolds, tin carnations, tin poppies and tin hollyhocks growing as naturally as if they were real."

Indeed, they were a pretty sight, and glistened under the sunlight like spun silver.

"Isn't this tin hollyhock going to seed?" asked the Wizard, bending over the flowers.

"Why, I believe it is!" exclaimed the Tin Woodman, as if surprised. "I hadn't noticed that before. But I shall plant the tin seeds and raise another bed of tin hollyhocks."

In one corner of the gardens Nick Chopper had established a fish-pond, in which they saw swimming and disporting themselves many pretty tin fishes.

"Would they bite on hooks?" asked Aunt Em, curiously.

The Tin Woodman seemed hurt at this question.

"Madam," said he, "do you suppose I would allow anyone to catch my beautiful fishes, even if they were foolish enough to bite on hooks? No, indeed! Every created thing is safe from harm in my domain, and I would as soon think of killing my little friend Dorothy as killing one of my tin fishes."

"The Emperor is very kind-hearted, ma'am," explained the Wizard. "If a fly happens to light upon his tin body he doesn't rudely brush it off, as some people might do; he asks it politely to find some other resting place."

"What does the fly do then?" inquired Aunt Em.

"Usually it begs his pardon and goes away," said the Wizard, gravely. "Flies like to be treated politely as well as other creatures, and here in Oz they understand what we say to them, and behave very nicely."

"Well," said Aunt Em, "the flies in Kansas, where I came from, don't understand anything but a swat. You have to smash 'em to make 'em behave; and it's the same way with 'skeeters. Do you have 'skeeters in Oz?"

"We have some very large mosquitoes here, which sing as beautifully as song birds," replied the Tin Woodman. "But they never bite or annoy our people, because they are well fed and taken care of. The reason they bite people in your country is because they are hungry—poor things!"

"Yes," agreed Aunt Em; "they're hungry, all right. An' they ain't very particular who they feed on. I'm glad you've got the 'skeeters educated in Oz."

That evening after dinner they were entertained by the Emperor's Tin Cornet Band, which played for them several sweet melodies. Also the Wizard did a few sleight-of-hand tricks to amuse the company; after which they all retired to their cozy tin bedrooms and slept soundly until morning.

After breakfast Dorothy said to the Tin Woodman:

"If you'll tell us which way to go we'll visit the Scarecrow on our way home."

"I will go with you, and show you the way," replied the Emperor; "for I must journey to-day to the Emerald City."

He looked so anxious, as he said this, that the little girl asked:

"There isn't anything wrong with Ozma, is there?"

He shook his tin head.

"Not yet," said he; "but I'm afraid the time has come when I must tell you some very bad news, little friend."

"Oh, what is it?" cried Dorothy.

"Do you remember the Nome King?" asked the Tin Woodman.

"I remember him very well," she replied.

"The Nome King has not a kind heart," said the Emperor, sadly, "and he has been harboring wicked thoughts of revenge, because we once defeated him and liberated his slaves and you took away his Magic Belt. So he has ordered his Nomes to dig a long tunnel underneath the deadly desert, so that he may march his hosts right into the Emerald City. When he gets there he intends to destroy our beautiful country."

Dorothy was much surprised to hear this.

"How did Ozma find out about the tunnel?" she asked.

"She saw it in her Magic Picture."

"Of course," said Dorothy; "I might have known that. And what is she going to do?"

"I cannot tell," was the reply.

"Pooh!" cried the Yellow Hen. "We're not afraid of the Nomes. If we roll a few of our eggs down the tunnel they'll run away back home as fast as they can go."

"Why, that's true enough!" exclaimed Dorothy. "The Scarecrow once conquered all the Nome King's army with some of Billina's eggs."

"But you do not understand all of the dreadful plot," continued the Tin Woodman. "The Nome King is clever, and he knows his Nomes would run from eggs; so he has bargained with many terrible creatures to help him. These evil spirits are not afraid of eggs or anything else, and they are very powerful. So the Nome King will send them through the tunnel first, to conquer and destroy, and then the Nomes will follow after to get their share of the plunder and slaves."

They were all startled to hear this, and every face wore a troubled look.

"Is the tunnel all ready?" asked Dorothy.

"Ozma sent me word yesterday that the tunnel was all completed except for a thin crust of earth at the end. When our enemies break through this crust they will be in the gardens of the royal palace, in the heart of the Emerald City. I offered to arm all my Winkies and march to Ozma's assistance; but she said no."

"I wonder why?" asked Dorothy.

"She answered that all the inhabitants of Oz, gathered together, were not powerful enough to fight and overcome the evil forces of the Nome King. Therefore she refuses to fight at all."

"But they will capture and enslave us, and plunder and ruin all our lovely land!" exclaimed the Wizard, greatly disturbed by this statement.

"I fear they will," said the Tin Woodman, sorrowfully. "And I also fear that those who are not fairies, such as the Wizard, and Dorothy, and her uncle and aunt, as well as Toto and Billina, will be speedily put to death by the conquerors."

"What can be done?" asked Dorothy, shuddering a little at the prospect of this awful fate.

"Nothing can be done!" gloomily replied the Emperor of the Winkies. "But since Ozma refuses my army I will go myself to the Emerald City. The least I may do is to perish beside my beloved Ruler."

CHAPTER XXV

How THE SCARECROW DISPLAYED HIS WISDOM

Probably
The Wisest
Man in All
Oz.

THIS AMAZING NEWS HAD SADDENED EVERY HEART AND ALL WERE NOW ANXIOUS to return to the Emerald City and share Ozma's fate. So they started without loss of time, and as the road led past the Scarecrow's new mansion they determined to make a brief halt there and confer with him.

"The Scarecrow is probably the wisest man in all Oz," remarked the Tin Woodman, when they had started upon their journey. "His brains are plentiful and of excellent quality, and often he has told me things I might never have thought of myself. I must say I rely a good deal upon the Scarecrow's brains in this emergency."

The Tin Woodman rode on the front seat of the wagon, where Dorothy sat between him and the Wizard.

"Has the Scarecrow heard of Ozma's trouble?" asked the Captain General.

"I do not know, sir," was the reply.

"When I was a private," said Omby Amby, "I was an excellent army, as I fully proved in our war against the Nomes. But now there is not a single private left in our army, since Ozma made me the Captain General, so there is no one to fight and defend our lovely Ruler."

"True," said the Wizard. "The present army is composed only of officers, and the business of an officer is to order his men to fight. Since there are no men there can be no fighting."

"Poor Ozma!" whispered Dorothy, with tears in her sweet eyes. "It's dreadful to think of all her lovely fairy country being destroyed. I wonder if we couldn't manage to escape and get back to Kansas by means of the Magic Belt? And we might take Ozma with us and all work hard to get money for her, so she wouldn't be so *very* lonely and unhappy about the loss of her fairyland."

"Do you think there would be any work for *me* in Kansas?" asked the Tin Woodman.

"If you are hollow, they might use you in a canning factory," suggested Uncle Henry. "But I can't see the use of your working for a living. You never eat or sleep or need a new suit of clothes."

"I was not thinking of myself," replied the Emperor, with dignity. "I merely wondered if I could not help to support Dorothy and Ozma."

As they indulged in these sad plans for the future they journeyed in sight of the Scarecrow's new mansion, and even though filled with care and worry over the impending fate of Oz, Dorothy could not help a feeling of wonder at the sight she saw.

The Scarecrow's new house was shaped like an immense ear of corn. The rows of kernels were made of solid gold, and the green upon which the ear stood upright was a mass of sparkling emeralds. Upon the very top of the structure was perched a figure representing the Scarecrow himself, and upon his extended arms, as well as upon his head, were several crows carved out of ebony and having ruby eyes. You may imagine how big this ear of corn was when I tell you that a single gold kernel formed a window, swinging outward upon hinges, while a row of four kernels opened to make the front entrance. Inside there were five stories, each story being a single room.

The gardens around the mansion consisted of cornfields, and Dorothy acknowledged that the place was in all respects a very appropriate home for her good friend the Scarecrow.

"He would have been very happy here, I'm sure," she said, "if only the Nome King had left us alone. But if Oz is destroyed of course this place will be destroyed too."

"Yes," replied the Tin Woodman, "and also my beautiful tin castle, that has been my joy and pride."

"Jack Pumpkinhead's house will go too," remarked the Wizard, "as well as Professor Woggle-Bug's Athletic College, and Ozma's royal palace, and all our other handsome buildings."

"Yes, Oz will indeed become a desert when the Nome King gets through with it," sighed Omby Amby.

The Scarecrow came out to meet them and gave them all a hearty welcome.

"I hear you have decided always to live in the Land of Oz, after this," he said to Dorothy; "and that will delight my heart, for I have greatly disliked our frequent partings. But why are you all so downcast?"

"Have you heard the news?" asked the Tin Woodman.

"No news to make me sad," replied the Scarecrow.

Then Nick Chopper told his friend of the Nome King's tunnel, and how the evil creatures of the North had allied themselves with the underground monarch for the purpose of conquering and destroying Oz. "Well," said the Scarecrow, "it certainly looks bad for Ozma, and all of us. But I believe it is wrong to worry over anything before it happens. It is surely time enough to be sad when our country is despoiled and our people made slaves. So let us not deprive ourselves of the few happy hours remaining to us."

"Ah! that is real wisdom," declared the Shaggy Man, approvingly. "After we become really unhappy we shall regret these few hours that are left to us, unless we enjoy them to the utmost."

"Nevertheless," said the Scarecrow, "I shall go with you to the Emerald City and offer Ozma my services."

"She says we can do nothing to oppose our enemies," announced the Tin Woodman.

"And doubtless she is right, sir," answered the Scarecrow. "Still, she will appreciate our sympathy, and it is the duty of Ozma's friends to stand by her side when the final disaster occurs."

He then led them into his queer mansion and showed them the beautiful rooms in all the five stories. The lower room was a grand reception hall, with a hand-organ in one corner. This instrument the Scarecrow, when alone, could turn to amuse himself, as he was very fond of music. The walls were hung with white silk, upon which flocks of black crows were embroidered in black diamonds. Some of the chairs were made in the shape of big crows and upholstered with cushions of corn-colored silk.

The second story contained a fine banquet room, where the Scarecrow might entertain his guests, and the three stories above that were bed-chambers exquisitely furnished and decorated.

"From these rooms," said the Scarecrow, proudly, "one may obtain fine views of the surrounding cornfields. The corn I grow is always husky, and I call the ears my regiments, because they have so many kernels. Of course I cannot ride my cobs, but I really don't care shucks about that. Taken altogether, my farm will stack up with any in the neighborhood."

The visitors partook of some light refreshment and then hurried away to resume the road to the Emerald City. The Scarecrow found a seat in the wagon between

Omby Amby and the Shaggy Man, and his weight did not add much to the load because he was stuffed with straw.

"You will notice I have one oat-field on my property," he remarked, as they drove away. "Oat-straw is, I have found, the best of all straws to re-stuff myself with when my interior gets musty or out of shape."

"Are you able to re-stuff yourself without help?" asked Aunt Em. "I should think that after the straw was taken out of you there wouldn't be anything left but your clothes."

"You are almost correct, madam," he answered. "My servants do the stuffing, under my direction. For my head, in which are my excellent brains, is a bag tied at the bottom. My face is neatly painted upon one side of the bag, as you may see. My head does not need re-stuffing, as my body does, for all that it requires is to have the face touched up with fresh paint occasionally."

It was not far from the Scarecrow's mansion to the farm of Jack Pumpkinhead, and when they arrived there both Uncle Henry and Aunt Em were much impressed. The farm was one vast pumpkin field, and some of the pumpkins were of enormous size. In one of them, which had been neatly hollowed out, Jack himself lived, and he declared that it was a very comfortable residence. The reason he grew so many pumpkins was in order that he might change his head as often as it became wrinkled or threatened to spoil.

The pumpkin-headed man welcomed his visitors joyfully and offered them several delicious pumpkin pies to eat.

"I don't indulge in pumpkin pies myself, for two reasons," he said. "One reason is that were I to eat pumpkins I would become a cannibal, and the other reason is that I never eat, not being hollow inside."

"Very good reasons," agreed the Scarecrow.

They told Jack Pumpkinhead the dreadful news about the Nome King, and he decided to go with them to the Emerald City and help comfort Ozma.

"I had expected to live here in ease and comfort for many centuries," said Jack, dolefully; "but of course if the Nome King destroys everything in Oz I shall be destroyed too. Really, it seems too bad, doesn't it?"

They were soon on their journey again, and so swiftly did the Saw-Horse draw the wagon over the smooth roads that before twilight fell they had reached the royal palace in the Emerald City, and were at their journey's end.

CHAPTER XXVI

How OZMA REFUSED TO FIGHT FOR HER KINGDOM

OZMA WAS IN HER ROSE GARDEN PICKING A BOUQUET WHEN THE PARTY ARRIVED, and she greeted all her old and new friends as smilingly and sweetly as ever.

Dorothy's eyes were full of tears as she kissed the lovely Ruler of Oz, and she whispered to her:

"Oh, Ozma, Ozma! I'm *so* sorry!"

Ozma seemed surprised.

"Sorry for what, Dorothy?" she asked.

"For all your trouble about the Nome King," was the reply.

Ozma laughed with genuine amusement.

"Why, that has not troubled me a bit, dear Princess," she replied. Then, looking around at the sad faces of her friends, she added: "Have you all been worrying about this tunnel?"

"We have!" they exclaimed in a chorus.

"Well, perhaps it is more serious than I imagined," admitted the fair Ruler; "but I haven't given the matter much thought. After dinner we will all meet together and talk it over."

So they went to their rooms and prepared for dinner, and Dorothy dressed herself in her prettiest gown and put on her coronet, for she thought that this might be the last time she would ever appear as a Princess of Oz.

The Scarecrow, the Tin Woodman and Jack Pumpkinhead all sat at the dinner table, although none of them was made so he could eat. Usually they served to enliven the meal with their merry talk, but to-night all seemed strangely silent and uneasy.

As soon as the dinner was finished Ozma led the company to her own private room in which hung the Magic Picture. When they had seated themselves the Scarecrow was the first to speak.

"Is the Nome King's tunnel finished, Ozma?" he asked.

"It was completed to-day," she replied. "They have built it right under my palace grounds, and it ends in front of the Forbidden Fountain. Nothing but a crust of earth remains to separate our enemies from us, and when they march here they will easily break through this crust and rush upon us."

"Who will assist the Nome King?" inquired the Scarecrow.

"The Whimsies, the Growleywogs and the Phanfasms," she replied. "I watched to-day in my Magic Picture the messengers whom the Nome King sent to all these people to summon them to assemble in his great caverns."

"Let us see what they are doing now," suggested the Tin Woodman.

So Ozma wished to see the Nome King's cavern, and at once the landscape faded from the Magic Picture and was replaced by the scene then being enacted in the jeweled cavern of King Roquat.

A wild and startling scene it was which the Oz people beheld.

Before the Nome King stood the Chief of the Whimsies and the Grand Gallipoot of the Growleywogs, surrounded by their most skillful generals. Very fierce and powerful they looked, so that even the Nome King and General Guph, who stood beside his master, seemed a bit fearful in the presence of their allies.

Now a still more formidable creature entered the cavern. It was the First and Foremost of the Phanfasms and he proudly sat down in King Roquat's own throne and demanded the right to lead his forces through the tunnel in advance of all the others. The First and Foremost now appeared to all eyes in his hairy skin and the bear's head. What his real form was even Roquat did not know.

Through the arches leading into the vast series of caverns that lay beyond the throne room of King Roquat, could be seen ranks upon ranks of the invaders—thousands of Phanfasms, Growleywogs and Whimsies standing in serried lines, while behind them were massed the thousands upon thousands of General Guph's own army of Nomes.

"Listen!" whispered Ozma. "I think we can hear what they are saying."

So they kept still and listened.

"Is all ready?" demanded the First and Foremost, haughtily.

"The tunnel is finally completed," replied General Guph.

"How long will it take us to march to the Emerald City?" asked the Grand Gallipoot of the Growleywogs.

"If we start at midnight," replied the Nome King, "we shall arrive at the Emerald City by daybreak. Then, while all the Oz people are sleeping, we will capture them and make them our slaves. After that we will destroy the city itself and march through the Land of Oz, burning and devastating as we go."

"Good!" cried the First and Foremost. "When we get through with Oz it will be a desert wilderness. Ozma shall be my slave."

"She shall be *my* slave!" shouted the Grand Gallipoot, angrily.

"We'll decide that by and by," said King Roquat, hastily. "Don't let us quarrel now, friends. First let us conquer Oz, and then we will divide the spoils of war in a satisfactory manner."

The First and Foremost smiled wickedly; but he only said:

"I and my Phanfasms go first, for nothing on earth can oppose our power."

They all agreed to that, knowing the Phanfasms to be the mightiest of the combined forces. King Roquat now invited them to attend a banquet he had prepared, where they might occupy themselves in eating and drinking until midnight arrived.

As they had now seen and heard all of the plot against them that they cared to, Ozma allowed her Magic Picture to fade away. Then she turned to her friends and said:

"Our enemies will be here sooner than I expected. What do you advise me to do?"

"It is now too late to assemble our people," said the Tin Woodman, despondently. "If you had allowed me to arm and drill my Winkies we might have put up a good fight and destroyed many of our enemies before we were conquered."

"The Munchkins are good fighters, too," said Omby Amby; "and so are the Gillikins."

"But I do not wish to fight," declared Ozma, firmly. "No one has the right to destroy any living creatures, however evil they may be, or to hurt them or make them unhappy. I will not fight, even to save my kingdom."

"The Nome King is not so particular," remarked the Scarecrow. "He intends to destroy us all and ruin our beautiful country."

"Because the Nome King intends to do evil is no excuse for my doing the same," replied Ozma.

"Self-preservation is the first law of nature," quoted the Shaggy Man.

"True," she said, readily. "I would like to discover a plan to save ourselves without fighting."

That seemed a hopeless task to them, but realizing that Ozma was determined not to fight, they tried to think of some means that might promise escape.

"Couldn't we bribe our enemies, by giving them a lot of emeralds and gold?" asked Jack Pumpkinhead.

"No, because they believe they are able to take everything we have," replied the Ruler.

"I have thought of something," said Dorothy.

"What is it, dear?" asked Ozma.

"Let us use the Magic Belt to wish all of us in Kansas. We will put some emeralds in our pockets, and can sell them in Topeka for enough to pay off the mortgage on Uncle Henry's farm. Then we can all live together and be happy."

"A clever idea!" exclaimed the Scarecrow.

"Kansas is a very good country. I've been there," said the Shaggy Man.

"That seems to me an excellent plan," approved the Tin Woodman.

"No!" said Ozma, decidedly. "Never will I desert my people and leave them to so cruel a fate. I will use the Magic Belt to send the rest of you to Kansas, if you wish, but if my beloved country must be destroyed and my people enslaved I will remain and share their fate."

"Quite right," asserted the Scarecrow, sighing. "I will remain with you."

"And so will I," declared the Tin Woodman and the Shaggy Man and Jack Pumpkinhead, in turn. Tik-Tok, the machine man, also said he intended to stand by Ozma. "For," said he, "I should be of no use at all in Kansas."

"For my part," announced Dorothy, gravely, "if the Ruler of Oz must not desert her people, a Princess of Oz has no right to run away, either. I'm willing to become a slave with the rest of you; so all we can do with the Magic Belt is to use it to send Uncle Henry and Aunt Em back to Kansas."

"I've been a slave all my life," Aunt Em replied, with considerable cheerfulness, "and so has Henry. I guess we won't go back to Kansas, anyway. I'd rather take my chances with the rest of you."

Ozma smiled upon them all gratefully.

"There is no need to despair just yet," she said. "I'll get up early to-morrow morning and be at the Forbidden Fountain when the fierce warriors break through the crust of the earth. I will speak to them pleasantly and perhaps they won't be so very bad, after all."

"Why do they call it the Forbidden Fountain?" asked Dorothy, thoughtfully.

"Don't you know, dear?" returned Ozma, surprised.

"No," said Dorothy. "Of course I've seen the fountain in the palace grounds, ever since I first came to Oz; and I've read the sign which says: 'All Persons are Forbidden to Drink at this Fountain.' But I never knew *why* they were forbidden. The water seems clear and sparkling and it bubbles up in a golden basin all the time."

"That water," declared Ozma, gravely, "is the most dangerous thing in all the Land of Oz. It is the Water of Oblivion."

"What does that mean?" asked Dorothy.

"Whoever drinks at the Forbidden Fountain at once forgets everything he has ever known," Ozma asserted.

"It wouldn't be a bad way to forget our troubles," suggested Uncle Henry.

"That is true; but you would forget everything else, and become as ignorant as a baby," returned Ozma.

"Does it make one crazy?" asked Dorothy.

"No; it only makes one forget," replied the girl Ruler. "It is said that once—long, long ago—a wicked King ruled Oz, and made himself and all his people very miserable and unhappy. So Glinda, the Good Sorceress, placed this fountain here, and the King drank of its water and forgot all his wickedness. His mind became innocent and vacant, and when he learned the things of life again they were all good things. But the people remembered how wicked their King had been, and were still afraid of him. Therefore he made them all drink of the Water of Oblivion and forget everything they had known, so that they became as simple and innocent as their King. After that they all grew wise together, and their wisdom was good, so that peace and happiness reigned in the land. But for fear some one might drink of the water again, and in an instant forget all he had learned, the King put that sign upon the fountain, where it has remained for many centuries up to this very day."

They had all listened intently to Ozma's story, and when she finished speaking there was a long period of silence while all thought upon the curious magical power of the Water of Oblivion.

Finally the Scarecrow's painted face took on a broad smile that stretched the cloth as far as it would go.

"How thankful I am," he said, "that I have such an excellent assortment of brains!"

"I gave you the best brains I ever mixed," declared the Wizard, with an air of pride.

"You did, indeed!" agreed the Scarecrow, "and they work so splendidly that they have found a way to save Oz—to save us all!"

"I'm glad to hear that," said the Wizard. "We never needed saving more than we do just now."

"Do you mean to say you can save us from those awful Phanfasms, and Growleywogs and Whimsies?" asked Dorothy eagerly.

"I'm sure of it, my dear," asserted the Scarecrow, still smiling genially.

"Tell us how!" cried the Tin Woodman.

"Not now," said the Scarecrow. "You may all go to bed, and I advise you to forget your worries just as completely as if you had drunk of the Water of Oblivion in the Forbidden Fountain. I'm going to stay here and tell my plan to Ozma alone, but if you will all be at the Forbidden Fountain  at daybreak, you'll see how easily we will save the kingdom when our enemies break through the crust of earth and come from the tunnel."

So they went away and left the Scarecrow and Ozma alone; but Dorothy could not sleep a wink all night.

"He is only a Scarecrow," she said to herself, "and I'm not sure that his mixed brains are as clever as he thinks they are."

But she knew that if the Scarecrow's plan failed they were all lost; so she tried to have faith in him.

CHAPTER XXVII

How THE FIERCE WARRIORS INVADED OZ

THE NOME KING AND HIS TERRIBLE ALLIES SAT AT THE BANQUET TABLE UNTIL midnight. There was much quarreling between the Growleywogs and Phanfasms, and one of the wee-headed Whimsies got angry at General Guph and choked him until he nearly stopped breathing. Yet no one was seriously hurt, and the Nome King felt much relieved when the clock struck twelve and they all sprang up and seized their weapons.

"Aha!" shouted the First and Foremost. "Now to conquer the Land of Oz!"

He marshaled his Phanfasms in battle array and at his word of command they marched into the tunnel and began the long journey through it to the Emerald City. The First and Foremost intended to take all the treasures in Oz for himself; to kill all who could be killed and enslave the rest; to destroy and lay waste the whole country, and afterward to conquer and enslave the Nomes, the Growleywogs and the Whimsies. And he knew his power was sufficient to enable him to do all these things easily.

Next marched into the tunnel the army of gigantic Growleywogs, with their Grand Gallipoot at their head. They were dreadful beings, indeed, and longed to get to Oz that they might begin to pilfer and destroy. The Grand Gallipoot was a little afraid of the First and Foremost, but had a cunning plan to murder or destroy that powerful being and secure the wealth of Oz for himself. Mighty little of the plunder would the Nome King get, thought the Grand Gallipoot.

The Chief of the Whimsies now marched his false-headed forces into the tunnel. In his wicked little head was a plot to destroy both the First and Foremost and the Grand Gallipoot. He intended to let them conquer Oz, since they insisted on going first; but he would afterward treacherously destroy them, as well as King Roquat, and keep all the slaves and treasure of Ozma's kingdom for himself.

After all his dangerous allies had marched into the tunnel the Nome King and General Guph started to follow them, at the head of fifty thousand Nomes, all fully armed.

"Guph," said the King, "those creatures ahead of us mean mischief. They intend to get everything for themselves and leave us nothing."

"I know," replied the General; "but they are not as clever as they think they are. When you get the Magic Belt you must at once wish the Whimsies and Growley-wogs and Phanfasms all back into their own countries—and the Belt will surely take them there."

"Good!" cried the King. "An excellent plan, Guph. I'll do it. While they are conquering Oz I'll get the Magic Belt, and then only the Nomes will remain to ravage the country."

So you see there was only one thing that all were agreed upon—that Oz should be destroyed.

On, on, on the vast ranks of invaders marched, filling the tunnel from side to side. With a steady tramp, tramp, they advanced, every step taking them nearer to the beautiful Emerald City.

"Nothing can save the Land of Oz!" thought the First and Foremost, scowling until his bear face was as black as the tunnel.

"The Emerald City is as good as destroyed already!" muttered the Grand Gallipoot, shaking his war club fiercely.

"In a few hours Oz will be a desert!" said the Chief of the Whimsies, with an evil laugh.

"My dear Guph," remarked the Nome King to his General, "at last my vengeance upon Ozma of Oz and her people is about to be accomplished."

"You are right!" declared the General. "Ozma is surely lost."

And now the First and Foremost, who was in advance and nearing the Emerald City, began to cough and to sneeze.

"This tunnel is terribly dusty," he growled, angrily. "I'll punish that Nome King for not having it swept clean. My throat and eyes are getting full of dust and I'm as thirsty as a fish!"

The Grand Gallipoot was coughing too, and his throat was parched and dry.

"What a dusty place!" he cried. "I'll be glad when we reach Oz, where we can get a drink."

"Who has any water?" asked the Whimsie Chief, gasping and choking. But none of his followers carried a drop of water, so he hastened on to get through the dusty tunnel to the Land of Oz.

"Where did all this dust come from?" demanded General Guph, trying hard to swallow but finding his throat so dry he couldn't.

"I don't know," answered the Nome King. "I've been in the tunnel every day while it was being built, but I never noticed any dust before."

"Let's hurry!" cried the General. "I'd give half the gold in Oz for a drink of water."

The dust grew thicker and thicker, and the throats and eyes and noses of the invaders were filled with it. But not one halted or turned back. They hurried forward more fierce and vengeful than ever.

CHAPTER XXVIII

How They Drank at the Forbidden Fountain

THE SCARECROW HAD NO NEED TO SLEEP; NEITHER HAD THE TIN WOODMAN OR Tik-Tok or Jack Pumpkinhead. So they all wandered out into the palace grounds and stood beside the sparkling water of the Forbidden Fountain until daybreak. During this time they indulged in occasional conversation.

"Nothing could make me forget what I know," remarked the Scarecrow, gazing into the fountain, "for I cannot drink the Water of Oblivion or water of any kind. And I am glad that this is so, for I consider my wisdom unexcelled."

"You are cer-tain-ly ve-ry wise," agreed Tik-Tok. "For my part, I can on-ly think by ma-chin-er-y, so I do not pre-tend to know as much as you do."

"My tin brains are very bright, but that is all I claim for them," said Nick Chopper, modestly. "Yet I do not aspire to being very wise, for I have noticed that the happiest people are those who do not let their brains oppress them."

"Mine never worry me," Jack Pumpkinhead acknowledged. "There are many seeds of thought in my head, but they do not sprout easily. I am glad that it is so, for if I occupied my days in thinking I should have no time for anything else."

In this cheery mood they passed the hours until the first golden streaks of dawn appeared in the sky. Then Ozma joined them, as fresh and lovely as ever and robed in one of her prettiest gowns.

"Our enemies have not yet arrived," said the Scarecrow, after greeting affectionately the sweet and girlish Ruler.

"They will soon be here," she said, "for I have just glanced at my Magic Picture, and have seen them coughing and choking with the dust in the tunnel."

"Oh, is there dust in the tunnel?" asked the Tin Woodman.

"Yes; Ozma placed it there by means of the Magic Belt," explained the Scarecrow, with one of his broad smiles.

Then Dorothy came to them, Uncle Henry and Aunt Em following close after her. The little girl's eyes were heavy because she had had a sleepless and anxious night. Toto walked by her side, but the little dog's spirits were very much subdued. Billina, who was always up by daybreak, was not long in joining the group by the fountain.

The Wizard and the Shaggy Man next arrived, and soon after appeared Omby Amby, dressed in his best uniform.

"There lies the tunnel," said Ozma, pointing to a part of the ground just before the Forbidden Fountain, "and in a few moments the dreadful invaders will break through the earth and swarm over the land. Let us all stand on the other side of the Fountain and watch to see what happens."

At once they followed her suggestion and moved around the fountain of the Water of Oblivion. There they stood silent and expectant until the earth beyond gave way with a sudden crash and up leaped the powerful form of the First and Foremost, followed by all his grim warriors.

As the leader sprang forward his gleaming eyes caught the play of the fountain and he rushed toward it and drank eagerly of the sparkling water. Many of the other Phanfasms drank, too, in order to clear their dry and dusty throats. Then they stood around and looked at one another with simple, wondering smiles.

The First and Foremost saw Ozma and her companions beyond the fountain, but instead of making an effort to capture her he merely stared at her in pleased admiration—for he had forgotten where he was and why he had come there.

But now the Grand Gallipoot arrived, rushing from the tunnel with a hoarse cry of mingled rage and thirst. He too saw the fountain and hastened to drink of its forbidden waters. The other Growleywogs were not slow to follow suit, and even before they had finished drinking the Chief of the Whimsies and his people came to push them away, while they one and all cast off their false heads that they might slake their thirst at the fountain.

When the Nome King and General Guph arrived they both made a dash to drink, but the General was so mad with thirst that he knocked his King over, and while Roquat lay sprawling upon the ground the General drank heartily of the Water of Oblivion.

This rude act of his General made the Nome King so angry that for a moment he forgot he was thirsty and rose to his feet to glare upon the group of terrible warriors he had brought here to assist him. He saw Ozma and her people, too, and yelled out:

"Why don't you capture them? Why don't you conquer Oz, you idiots? Why do you stand there like a lot of dummies?"

But the great warriors had become like little children. They had forgotten all their enmity against Ozma and against Oz. They had even forgotten who they themselves were, or why they were in this strange and beautiful country. As for the Nome King, they did not recognize him, and wondered who he was.

The sun came up and sent its flood of silver rays to light the faces of the invaders. The frowns and scowls and evil looks were all gone. Even the most monstrous of the creatures there assembled smiled innocently and seemed light-hearted and content merely to be alive.

Not so with Roquat, the Nome King. He had not drunk from the Forbidden Fountain and all his former rage against Ozma and Dorothy now inflamed him as fiercely as ever. The sight of General Guph babbling like a happy child and playing with his hands in the cool waters of the fountain astonished and maddened Red Roquat. Seeing that his terrible allies and his own General refused to act, the Nome King turned to order his great army of Nomes to advance from the tunnel and seize the helpless Oz people.

But the Scarecrow suspected what was in the King's mind and spoke a word to the Tin Woodman. Together they ran at Roquat and grabbing him up tossed him into the great basin of the fountain.

The Nome King's body was round as a ball, and it bobbed up and down in the Water of Oblivion while he spluttered and screamed with fear lest he should drown. And when he cried out his mouth filled with water, which ran down his throat, so that straightway he forgot all he had formerly known just as completely as had all the other invaders.

Ozma and Dorothy could not refrain from laughing to see their dreaded enemies become as harmless as babes. There was no danger now that Oz would be destroyed. The only question remaining to solve was how to get rid of this horde of intruders.

The Shaggy Man kindly pulled the Nome King out of the fountain and set him upon his thin legs. Roquat was dripping wet, but he chattered and laughed and wanted to drink more of the water. No thought of injuring any person was now in his mind.

Before he left the tunnel he had commanded his fifty thousand Nomes to remain there until he ordered them to advance, as he wished to give his allies time to conquer Oz before he appeared with his own army. Ozma did not wish all these Nomes to overrun her land, so she advanced to King Roquat and taking his hand in her own said gently:

"Who are you? What is your name?"

"I don't know," he replied, smiling at her. "Who are you, my dear?"

"My name is Ozma," she said; "and your name is Roquat."

"Oh, is it?" he replied, seeming pleased.

"Yes; you are King of the Nomes," she said.

"Ah; I wonder what the Nomes are!" returned the King, as if puzzled.

"They are underground elves, and that tunnel over there is full of them," she answered. "You have a beautiful cavern at the other end of the tunnel, so you must go to your Nomes and say: 'March home!' Then follow after them and in time you will reach the pretty cavern where you live."

The Nome King was much pleased to learn this, for he had forgotten he had a cavern. So he went to the tunnel and said to his army: "March home!" At once the Nomes turned and marched back through the tunnel, and the King followed after them, laughing with delight to find his orders so readily obeyed.

The Wizard went to General Guph, who was trying to count his fingers, and told him to follow the Nome King, who was his master. Guph meekly obeyed, and so all the Nomes quitted the Land of Oz forever.

But there were still the Phanfasms and Whimsies and Growleywogs standing around in groups, and they were so many that they filled the gardens and trampled upon the flowers and grass because they did not know that the tender plants would be injured by their clumsy feet. But in all other respects they were perfectly harmless and played together like children or gazed with pleasure upon the pretty sights of the royal gardens.

After counseling with the Scarecrow Ozma sent Omby Amby to the palace for the Magic Belt, and when the Captain General returned with it the Ruler of Oz at once clasped the precious Belt around her waist.

"I wish all these strange people—the Whimsies and the Growleywogs and the Phanfasms—safe back in their own homes!" she said.

It all happened in a twinkling, for of course the wish was no sooner spoken than it was granted.

All the hosts of the invaders were gone, and only the trampled grass showed that they had ever been in the Land of Oz.

CHAPTER XXIX

How GLINDA WORKED A MAGIC SPELL

"THAT WAS BETTER THAN FIGHTING," SAID OZMA, WHEN ALL OUR FRIENDS WERE assembled in the palace after the exciting events of the morning; and each and every one agreed with her.

"No one was hurt," said the Wizard, delightedly.

"And no one hurt us," added Aunt Em.

"But, best of all," said Dorothy, "the wicked people have all forgotten their wickedness, and will not wish to hurt any one after this."

"True, Princess," declared the Shaggy Man. "It seems to me that to have reformed all those evil characters is more important than to have saved Oz."

"Nevertheless," remarked the Scarecrow, "I am glad Oz is saved. I can now go back to my new mansion and live happily."

"And I am glad and grateful that my pumpkin farm is saved," said Jack.

"For my part," added the Tin Woodman, "I cannot express my joy that my lovely tin castle is not to be demolished by wicked enemies."

"Still," said Tik-Tok, "o-ther en-e-mies may come to Oz some day."

"Why do you allow your clock-work brains to interrupt our joy?" asked Omby Amby, frowning at the machine man.

"I say what I am wound up to say," answered Tik-Tok.

"And you are right," declared Ozma. "I myself have been thinking of this very idea, and it seems to me there are entirely too many ways for people to get to the Land of Oz. We used to think the deadly desert that surrounds us was enough protection; but that is no longer the case. The Wizard and Dorothy have both come here through the air, and I am told the earth people have invented airships that can fly anywhere they wish them to go."

"Why, sometimes they do, and sometimes they don't," asserted Dorothy.

"But in time the airships may cause us trouble," continued Ozma, "for if the earth folk learn how to manage them we would be overrun with visitors who would ruin our lovely, secluded fairyland."

"That is true enough," agreed the Wizard.

"Also the desert fails to protect us in other ways," Ozma went on, thoughtfully. "Johnny Dooit once made a sand-boat that sailed across it, and the Nome King made a tunnel under it. So I believe something ought to be done to cut us off from the rest of the world entirely, so that no one in the future will ever be able to intrude upon us."

"How will you do that?" asked the Scarecrow.

"I do not know; but in some way I am sure it can be accomplished. To-morrow I will make a journey to the castle of Glinda the Good, and ask her advice."

"May I go with you?" asked Dorothy, eagerly.

"Of course, my dear Princess; and also I invite any of our friends here who would like to undertake the journey."

They all declared they wished to accompany their girl Ruler, for this was indeed an important mission, since the future of the Land of Oz to a great extent depended upon it. So Ozma gave orders to her servants to prepare for the journey on the morrow.

That day she watched her Magic Picture, and when it showed her that all the Nomes had returned through the tunnel to their underground caverns, Ozma used the Magic Belt to close up the tunnel, so that the earth underneath the desert sands became as solid as it was before the Nomes began to dig.

Early the following morning a gay cavalcade set out to visit the famous Sorceress, Glinda the Good. Ozma and Dorothy rode in a chariot drawn by the Cowardly Lion and the Hungry Tiger, while the Saw-Horse drew the red wagon in which rode the rest of the party.

With hearts light and free from care they traveled merrily along through the lovely and fascinating Land of Oz, and in good season reached the stately castle in which resided the Sorceress.

Glinda knew that they were coming.

"I have been reading about you in my Magic Book," she said, as she greeted them in her gracious way.

"What is your Magic Book like?" inquired Aunt Em, curiously.

"It is a record of everything that happens," replied the Sorceress. "As soon as an event takes place, anywhere in the world, it is immediately found printed in my Magic Book. So when I read its pages I am well informed."

"Did it tell how our enemies drank the Water of 'Blivion?" asked Dorothy.

"Yes, my dear; it told all about it. And also it told me you were all coming to my castle, and why."

"Then," said Ozma, "I suppose you know what is in my mind, and that I am seeking a way to prevent any one in the future from discovering the Land of Oz."

"Yes; I know that. And while you were on your journey I have thought of a way to accomplish your desire. For it seems to me unwise to allow too many outside people to come here. Dorothy, with her uncle and aunt, has now returned to Oz to live always, and there is no reason why we should leave any way open for others to travel uninvited to our fairyland. Let us make it impossible for any one ever to communicate with us in any way, after this. Then we may live peacefully and contentedly."

"Your advice is wise," returned Ozma. "I thank you, Glinda, for your promise to assist me."

"But how can you do it?" asked Dorothy. "How can you keep every one from ever finding Oz?"

"By making our country invisible to all eyes but our own," replied the Sorceress, smiling. "I have a magic charm powerful enough to accomplish that wonderful feat, and now that we have been warned of our danger by the Nome King's invasion, I believe we must not hesitate to separate ourselves forever from all the rest of the world."

"I agree with you," said the Ruler of Oz.

"Won't it make any difference to us?" asked Dorothy, doubtfully.

"No, my dear," Glinda answered, assuringly. "We shall still be able to see each other and everything in the Land of Oz. It won't affect us at all; but those who fly through the air over our country will look down and see nothing at all. Those who come to the edge of the desert, or try to cross it, will catch no glimpse of Oz, or know in what direction it lies. No one will try to tunnel to us again because we cannot be seen and therefore cannot be found. In other words, the Land of Oz will entirely disappear from the knowledge of the rest of the world."

"That's all right," said Dorothy, cheerfully. "You may make Oz invis'ble as soon as you please, for all I care."

"It is already invisible," Glinda stated. "I knew Ozma's wishes, and performed the Magic Spell before you arrived."

Ozma seized the hand of the Sorceress and pressed it gratefully.

"Thank you!" she said.

CHAPTER XXX

How THE STORY OF OZ CAME TO AN END

THE WRITER OF THESE OZ STORIES HAS RECEIVED A LITTLE NOTE FROM PRINCESS Dorothy of Oz which, for a time, has made him feel rather discontented. The note was written on a broad white feather from a stork's wing, and it said:

> *"You will never hear anything more about Oz, because we are now cut off forever from all the rest of the world. But Toto and I will always love you and all the other children who love us."*
>
> DOROTHY GALE.

This seemed to me too bad, at first, for Oz is a very interesting fairyland. Still, we have no right to feel grieved, for we have had enough of the history of the Land of Oz to fill six story books, and from its quaint people and their strange adventures we have been able to learn many useful and amusing things.

So good luck to little Dorothy and her companions. May they live long in their invisible country and be very happy!

THE END

THE PATCHWORK GIRL OF OZ

CONTENTS

OJO AND UNC NUNKIE

"WHERE'S THE BUTTER, UNC NUNKIE?" ASKED Ojo.

Unc looked out of the window and stroked his long beard. Then he turned to the Munchkin boy and shook his head.

"Isn't," said he.

"Isn't any butter? That's too bad, Unc. Where's the jam then?" inquired Ojo, standing on a stool so he could look through all the shelves of the cupboard. But Unc Nunkie shook his head again.

"Gone," he said.

"No jam, either? And no cake—no jelly—no apples—nothing but bread?"

"All," said Unc, again stroking his beard as he gazed from the window.

The little boy brought the stool and sat beside his uncle, munching the dry bread slowly and seeming in deep thought.

"Nothing grows in our yard but the bread tree," he mused, "and there are only two more loaves on that tree; and they're not ripe yet. Tell me, Unc; why are we so poor?"

The old Munchkin turned and looked at Ojo. He had kindly eyes, but he hadn't smiled or laughed in so long that the boy had forgotten that Unc Nunkie could look any other way than solemn. And Unc never spoke any more words than he was obliged to, so his little nephew, who lived alone with him, had learned to understand a great deal from one word.

"Why are we so poor, Unc?" repeated the boy.

"Not," said the old Munchkin.

"I think we are," declared Ojo. "What have we got?"

"House," said Unc Nunkie.

"I know; but everyone in the Land of Oz has a place to live. What else, Unc?"

"Bread."

"I'm eating the last loaf that's ripe. There; I've put aside your share, Unc. It's on the table, so you can eat it when you get hungry. But when that is gone, what shall we eat, Unc?"

The old man shifted in his chair but merely shook his head.

"Of course," said Ojo, who was obliged to talk because his uncle would not, "no one starves in the Land of Oz, either. There is plenty for everyone, you know; only, if it isn't just where you happen to be, you must go where it is."

The aged Munchkin wriggled again and stared at his small nephew as if disturbed by his argument.

"By to-morrow morning," the boy went on, "we must go where there is something to eat, or we shall grow very hungry and become very unhappy."

"Where?" asked Unc.

"Where shall we go? I don't know, I'm sure," replied Ojo. "But *you* must know, Unc. You must have traveled, in your time, because you're so old. I don't remember it, because ever since I could remember anything we've lived right here in this lonesome, round house, with a little garden back of it and the thick woods all around. All I've ever seen of the great Land of Oz, Unc dear, is the view of that mountain over at the south, where they say the Hammerheads live—who won't let anybody go by them—and that mountain at the north, where they say nobody lives."

"One," declared Unc, correcting him.

"Oh, yes; one family lives there, I've heard. That's the Crooked Magician, who is named Dr. Pipt, and his wife Margolotte. One year you told me about them; I think it took you a whole year, Unc, to say as much as I've just said about the Crooked Magician and his wife. They live high up on the mountain, and the good Munchkin Country, where the fruits and flowers grow, is just the other side. It's funny you and I should live here all alone, in the middle of the forest, isn't it?"

"Yes," said Unc.

"Then let's go away and visit the Munchkin Country and its jolly, good-natured people. I'd love to get a sight of something besides woods, Unc Nunkie."

"Too little," said Unc.

"Why, I'm not so little as I used to be," answered the boy earnestly. "I think I can walk as far and as fast through the woods as you can, Unc. And now that nothing grows in our back yard that is good to eat, we must go where there is food."

Unc Nunkie made no reply for a time. Then he shut down the window and turned his chair to face the room, for the sun was sinking behind the tree-tops and it was growing cool.

By and by Ojo lighted the fire and the logs blazed freely in the broad fireplace. The two sat in the firelight a long time—the old, white-bearded Munchkin and the little boy. Both were thinking. When it grew quite dark outside, Ojo said:

"Eat your bread, Unc, and then we will go to bed."

But Unc Nunkie did not eat the bread; neither did he go directly to bed. Long after his little nephew was sound asleep in the corner of the room the old man sat by the fire, thinking.

CHAPTER II

THE CROOKED MAGICIAN

JUST AT DAWN NEXT MORNING UNC NUNKIE LAID his hand tenderly on Ojo's head and awakened him.

"Come," he said.

Ojo dressed. He wore blue silk stockings, blue knee-pants with gold buckles, a blue ruffled waist and a jacket of bright blue braided with gold. His shoes were of blue leather and turned up at the toes, which were pointed. His hat had a peaked crown and a flat brim, and around the brim was a row of tiny golden bells that tinkled when he moved. This was the native costume of those who inhabited the Munchkin Country of the Land of Oz, so Unc Nunkie's dress was much like that of his nephew. Instead of shoes, the old man wore boots with turnover tops and his blue coat had wide cuffs of gold braid.

The boy noticed that his uncle had not eaten the bread, and supposed the old man had not been hungry. Ojo was hungry, though; so he divided the piece of bread upon the table and ate his half for breakfast, washing it down with fresh, cool water from the brook. Unc put the other piece of bread in his jacket pocket, after which he again said, as he walked out through the doorway: "Come."

Ojo was well pleased. He was dreadfully tired of living all alone in the woods and wanted to travel and see people. For a long time he had wished to explore the beautiful Land of Oz in which they lived. When they were outside, Unc simply latched the door and started up the path. No one would disturb their little house, even if anyone came so far into the thick forest while they were gone.

At the foot of the mountain that separated the Country of the Munchkins from the Country of the Gillikins, the path divided. One way led to the left and the other to the right—straight up the mountain. Unc Nunkie took this right-hand path and Ojo followed without asking why. He knew it would take them to the house of the Crooked Magician, whom he had never seen but who was their nearest neighbor.

All the morning they trudged up the mountain path and at noon Unc and Ojo sat on a fallen tree-trunk and ate the last of the bread which the old Munchkin had placed in his pocket. Then they started on again and two hours later came in sight of the house of Dr. Pipt.

It was a big house, round, as were all the Munchkin houses, and painted blue, which is the distinctive color of the Munchkin Country of Oz. There was a pretty garden around the house, where blue trees and blue flowers grew in abundance and in one place were beds of blue cabbages, blue carrots and blue lettuce, all of which were delicious to eat. In Dr. Pipt's garden grew bun-trees, cake-trees, cream-puff bushes, blue buttercups which yielded excellent blue butter and a row of chocolate-caramel plants. Paths of blue gravel divided the vegetable and flower beds and a wider path led up to the front door. The place was in a clearing on the mountain, but a little way off was the grim forest, which completely surrounded it.

Unc knocked at the door of the house and a chubby, pleasant-faced woman, dressed all in blue, opened it and greeted the visitors with a smile.

"Ah," said Ojo; "you must be Dame Margolotte, the good wife of Dr. Pipt."

"I am, my dear, and all strangers are welcome to my home."

"May we see the famous Magician, Madam?"

"He is very busy just now," she said, shaking her head doubtfully. "But come in and let me give you something to eat, for you must have traveled far in order to get to our lonely place."

"We have," replied Ojo, as he and Unc entered the house. "We have come from a far lonelier place than this."

"A lonelier place! And in the Munchkin Country?" she exclaimed. "Then it must be somewhere in the Blue Forest."

"It is, good Dame Margolotte."

"Dear me!" she said, looking at the man, "you must be Unc Nunkie, known as the Silent One." Then she looked at the boy. "And you must be Ojo the Unlucky," she added.

"Yes," said Unc.

"I never knew I was called the Unlucky," said Ojo, soberly; "but it is really a good name for me."

"Well," remarked the woman, as she bustled around the room and set the table and brought food from the cupboard, "you were unlucky to live all alone in that dismal forest, which is much worse than the forest around here; but perhaps your luck will change, now you are away from it. If, during your travels, you can manage to lose that 'Un' at the beginning of your name 'Unlucky,' you will then become Ojo the Lucky, which will be a great improvement."

"How can I lose that 'Un,' Dame Margolotte?"

"I do not know how, but you must keep the matter in mind and perhaps the chance will come to you," she replied.

Ojo had never eaten such a fine meal in all his life. There was a savory stew, smoking hot, a dish of blue peas, a bowl of sweet milk of a delicate blue tint and a blue pudding with blue plums in it. When the visitors had eaten heartily of this fare the woman said to them:

"Do you wish to see Dr. Pipt on business or for pleasure?"

Unc shook his head.

"We are traveling," replied Ojo, "and we stopped at your house just to rest and refresh ourselves. I do not think Unc Nunkie cares very much to see the famous Crooked Magician; but for my part I am curious to look at such a great man."

The woman seemed thoughtful.

"I remember that Unc Nunkie and my husband used to be friends, many years ago," she said, "so perhaps they will be glad to meet again. The Magician is very busy, as I said, but if you will promise not to disturb him you may come into his workshop and watch him prepare a wonderful charm."

"Thank you," replied the boy, much pleased. "I would like to do that."

She led the way to a great domed hall at the back of the house, which was the Magician's workshop. There was a row of windows extending nearly around the sides of the circular room, which rendered the place very light, and there was a back door in addition to the one leading to the front part of the house. Before the row of windows a broad seat was built and there were some chairs and benches in the room besides. At one end stood a great fireplace, in which a blue log was blazing with a blue flame, and over the fire hung four kettles in a row, all bubbling and steaming at a great rate. The Magician was stirring all four of these kettles at the same time, two with his hands and two with his feet, to the latter, wooden ladles being strapped, for this man was so very crooked that his legs were as handy as his arms.

Unc Nunkie came forward to greet his old friend, but not being able to shake either his hands or his feet, which were all occupied in stirring, he patted the Magician's bald head and asked: "What?"

"Ah, it's the Silent One," remarked Dr. Pipt, without looking up, "and he wants to know what I'm making. Well, when it is quite finished this compound will be the wonderful Powder of Life, which no one knows how to make but myself. Whenever

it is sprinkled on anything, that thing will at once come to life, no matter what it is. It takes me several years to make this magic Powder, but at this moment I am pleased to say it is nearly done. You see, I am making it for my good wife Margolotte, who wants to use some of it for a purpose of her own. Sit down and make yourself comfortable, Unc Nunkie, and after I've finished my task I will talk to you."

"You must know," said Margolotte, when they were all seated together on the broad window-seat, "that my husband foolishly gave away all the Powder of Life he first made to old Mombi the Witch, who used to live in the Country of the Gillikins, to the north of here. Mombi gave to Dr. Pipt a Powder of Perpetual Youth in exchange for his Powder of Life, but she cheated him wickedly, for the Powder of Youth was no good and could work no magic at all."

"Perhaps the Powder of Life couldn't either," said Ojo.

"Yes; it is perfection," she declared. "The first lot we tested on our Glass Cat, which not only began to live but has lived ever since. She's somewhere around the house now."

"A Glass Cat!" exclaimed Ojo, astonished.

"Yes; she makes a very pleasant companion, but admires herself a little more than is considered modest, and she positively refuses to catch mice," explained Margolotte. "My husband made the cat some pink brains, but they proved to be too high-bred and particular for a cat, so she thinks it is undignified in her to catch mice. Also she has a pretty blood-red heart, but it is made of stone—a ruby, I think—and so is rather hard and unfeeling. I think the next Glass Cat the Magician makes will have neither brains nor heart, for then it will not object to catching mice and may prove of some use to us."

"What did old Mombi the Witch do with the Powder of Life your husband gave her?" asked the boy.

"She brought Jack Pumpkinhead to life, for one thing," was the reply. "I suppose you've heard of Jack Pumpkinhead. He is now living near the Emerald City and is a great favorite with the Princess Ozma, who rules all the Land of Oz."

"No; I've never heard of him," remarked Ojo. "I'm afraid I don't know much about the Land of Oz. You see, I've lived all my life with Unc Nunkie, the Silent One, and there was no one to tell me anything."

"That is one reason you are Ojo the Unlucky," said the woman, in a sympathetic tone. "The more one knows, the luckier he is, for knowledge is the greatest gift in life."

"But tell me, please, what you intend to do with this new lot of the Powder of Life, which Dr. Pipt is making. He said his wife wanted it for some especial purpose."

"So I do," she answered. "I want it to bring my Patchwork Girl to life."

"Oh! A Patchwork Girl? What is that?" Ojo asked, for this seemed even more strange and unusual than a Glass Cat.

"I think I must show you my Patchwork Girl," said Margolotte, laughing at the boy's astonishment, "for she is rather difficult to explain. But first I will tell you that for many years I have longed for a servant to help me with the housework and to cook the meals and wash the dishes. No servant will come here because the place is so lonely and out-of-the-way, so my clever husband, the Crooked Magician, proposed that I make a girl out of some sort of material and he would make her live by sprinkling over her the Powder of Life. This seemed an excellent suggestion and at once Dr. Pipt set to work to make a new batch of his magic powder. He has been at it a long, long while, and so I have had plenty of time to make the girl. Yet that task was not so easy as you may suppose. At first I couldn't think what to make her of, but finally in searching through a chest I came across an old patchwork quilt, which my grandmother once made when she was young."

"What is a patchwork quilt?" asked Ojo.

"A bed-quilt made of patches of different kinds and colors of cloth, all neatly sewed together. The patches are of all shapes and sizes, so a patchwork quilt is a very pretty and gorgeous thing to look at. Sometimes it is called a 'crazy-quilt,' because the patches and colors are so mixed up. We never have used my grandmother's many-colored patchwork quilt, handsome as it is, for we Munchkins do not care for any color other than blue, so it has been packed away in the chest for about a hundred years. When I found it, I said to myself that it would do nicely for my servant girl, for when she was brought to life she would not be proud nor haughty, as the Glass Cat is, for such a dreadful mixture of colors would discourage her from trying to be as dignified as the blue Munchkins are."

"Is blue the only respectable color, then?" inquired Ojo.

"Yes, for a Munchkin. All our country is blue, you know. But in other parts of Oz the people favor different colors. At the Emerald City, where our Princess Ozma lives, green is the popular color. But all Munchkins prefer blue to anything else and when my housework girl is brought to life she will find herself to be of so many unpopular colors that she'll never dare be rebellious or impudent, as servants are sometimes liable to be when they are made the same way their mistresses are."

Unc Nunkie nodded approval.

"Good i-dea," he said; and that was a long speech for Unc Nunkie because it was two words.

"So I cut up the quilt," continued Margolotte, "and made from it a very well-shaped girl, which I stuffed with cotton-wadding. I will show you what a good job I did," and she went to a tall cupboard and threw open the doors.

Then back she came, lugging in her arms the Patchwork Girl, which she set upon the bench and propped up so that the figure would not tumble over.

CHAPTER III

THE PATCHWORK GIRL

OJO EXAMINED THIS CURIOUS CONTRIVANCE WITH WONDER. The Patchwork Girl was taller than he, when she stood upright, and her body was plump and rounded because it had been so neatly stuffed with cotton. Margolotte had first made the girl's form from the patchwork quilt and then she had dressed it with a patchwork skirt and an apron with pockets in it—using the same gay material throughout. Upon the feet she had sewn a pair of red leather shoes with pointed toes. All the fingers and thumbs of the girl's hands had been carefully formed and stuffed and stitched at the edges, with gold plates at the ends to serve as finger-nails.

"She will have to work, when she comes to life," said Margolotte.

The head of the Patchwork Girl was the most curious part of her. While she waited for her husband to finish making his Powder of Life the woman had found ample time to complete the head as her fancy dictated, and she realized that a good servant's head must be properly constructed. The hair was of brown yarn and hung down on her neck in several neat braids. Her eyes were two silver suspender-buttons cut from a pair of the Magician's old trousers, and they were sewed on with black threads, which formed the pupils of the eyes. Margolotte had puzzled over the ears for some time, for these were important if the servant was to hear distinctly, but finally she had made them out of thin plates of gold and attached them in place by means of stitches through tiny holes bored in the metal. Gold is the most common metal in the Land of Oz and is used for many purposes because it is soft and pliable.

The woman had cut a slit for the Patchwork Girl's mouth and sewn two rows of white pearls in it for teeth, using a strip of scarlet plush for a tongue. This mouth Ojo considered very artistic and lifelike, and Margolotte was pleased when the boy praised it. There were almost too many patches on the face of the girl for her to be considered strictly beautiful, for one cheek was yellow and the other red, her chin blue, her forehead purple and the center, where her nose had been formed and padded, a bright yellow.

"You ought to have had her face all pink," suggested the boy.

"I suppose so; but I had no pink cloth," replied the woman. "Still, I cannot see as it matters much, for I wish my Patchwork Girl to be useful rather than ornamental. If I get tired looking at her patched face I can whitewash it."

"Has she any brains?" asked Ojo.

"No; I forgot all about the brains!" exclaimed the woman. "I am glad you reminded me of them, for it is not too late to supply them, by any means. Until she is brought to life I can do anything I please with this girl. But I must be careful not to give her too much brains, and those she has must be such as are fitted to the station she is to occupy in life. In other words, her brains mustn't be very good."

"Wrong," said Unc Nunkie.

"No; I am sure I am right about that," returned the woman.

"He means," explained Ojo, "that unless your servant has good brains she won't know how to obey you properly, nor do the things you ask her to do."

"Well, that may be true," agreed Margolotte; "but, on the contrary, a servant with too much brains is sure to become independent and high-and-mighty and feel above her work. This is a very delicate task, as I said, and I must take care to give the girl just the right quantity of the right sort of brains. I want her to know just enough, but not too much."

With this she went to another cupboard which was filled with shelves. All the shelves were lined with blue glass bottles, neatly labeled by the Magician to show what they contained. One whole shelf was marked: "Brain Furniture," and the bottles on this shelf were labeled as follows: "Obedience," "Cleverness,"

"Judgment," "Courage," "Ingenuity," "Amiability," "Learning," "Truth," "Poesy," "Self Reliance."

"Let me see," said Margolotte; "of those qualities she must have 'Obedience' first of all," and she took down the bottle bearing that label and poured from it upon a dish several grains of the contents. " 'Amiability' is also good and 'Truth.' " She poured into the dish a quantity from each of these bottles. "I think that will do," she continued, "for the other qualities are not needed in a servant."

Unc Nunkie, who with Ojo stood beside her, touched the bottle marked "Cleverness."

"Little," said he.

"A little 'Cleverness'? Well, perhaps you are right, sir," said she, and was about to take down the bottle when the Crooked Magician suddenly called to her excitedly from the fireplace.

"Quick, Margolotte! Come and help me."

She ran to her husband's side at once and helped him lift the four kettles from the fire. Their contents had all boiled away, leaving in the bottom of each kettle a few grains of fine white powder. Very carefully the Magician removed this powder, placing it all together in a golden dish, where he mixed it with a golden spoon. When the mixture was complete there was scarcely a handful, all told.

"That," said Dr. Pipt, in a pleased and triumphant tone, "is the wonderful Powder of Life, which I alone in the world know how to make. It has taken me nearly six years to prepare these precious grains of dust, but the little heap on that dish is worth the price of a kingdom and many a king would give all he has to possess it. When it has become cooled I will place it in a small bottle; but meantime I must watch it carefully, lest a gust of wind blow it away or scatter it."

Unc Nunkie, Margolotte and the Magician all stood looking at the marvelous Powder, but Ojo was more interested just then in the Patchwork Girl's brains. Thinking it both unfair and unkind to deprive her of any good qualities that were handy, the boy took down every bottle on the shelf and poured some of the contents in Margolotte's dish. No one saw him do this, for all were looking at the Powder of Life; but soon the woman remembered what she had been doing, and came back to the cupboard.

"Let's see," she remarked; "I was about to give my girl a little 'Cleverness,' which is the Doctor's substitute for 'Intelligence'—a quality he has not yet learned how to manufacture." Taking down the bottle of "Cleverness" she added some of the powder to the heap on the dish. Ojo became a bit uneasy at this, for he had already put quite a lot of the "Cleverness" powder in the dish; but he dared not interfere and so he comforted himself with the thought that one cannot have too much cleverness.

Margolotte now carried the dish of brains to the bench. Ripping the seam of the patch on the girl's forehead, she placed the powder within the head and then sewed up the seam as neatly and securely as before.

"My girl is all ready for your Powder of Life, my dear," she said to her husband. But the Magician replied:

"This powder must not be used before to-morrow morning; but I think it is now cool enough to be bottled."

He selected a small gold bottle with a pepper-box top, so that the powder might be sprinkled on any object through the small holes. Very carefully he placed the Powder of Life in the gold bottle and then locked it up in a drawer of his cabinet.

"At last," said he, rubbing his hands together gleefully, "I have ample leisure for a good talk with my old friend Unc Nunkie. So let us sit down cosily and enjoy ourselves. After stirring those four kettles for six years I am glad to have a little rest."

"You will have to do most of the talking," said Ojo, "for Unc is called the Silent One and uses few words."

"I know; but that renders your uncle a most agreeable companion and gossip," declared Dr. Pipt. "Most people talk too much, so it is a relief to find one who talks too little."

Ojo looked at the Magician with much awe and curiosity.

"Don't you find it very annoying to be so crooked?" he asked.

"No; I am quite proud of my person," was the reply. "I suppose I am the only Crooked Magician in all the world. Some others are accused of being crooked, but I am the only genuine."

He was really very crooked and Ojo wondered how he managed to do so many things with such a twisted body. When he sat down upon a crooked chair that had been made to fit him, one knee was under his chin and the other near the small of his back; but he was a cheerful man and his face bore a pleasant and agreeable expression.

"I am not allowed to perform magic, except for my own amusement," he told his visitors, as he lighted a pipe with a crooked stem and began to smoke. "Too many people were working magic in the Land of Oz, and so our lovely Princess Ozma put a stop to it. I think she was quite right. There were several wicked Witches who caused a lot of trouble; but now they are all out of business and only the great Sorceress, Glinda the Good, is permitted to practice her arts, which never harm anybody. The Wizard of Oz, who used to be a humbug and knew no magic at all, has been taking lessons of Glinda, and I'm told he is getting to be a pretty good Wizard; but he is merely the assistant of the great Sorceress. I've the right to make a servant girl for my wife, you know, or a Glass Cat to catch our mice—which she refuses to do—but I am forbidden to work magic for others, or to use it as a profession."

"Magic must be a very interesting study," said Ojo.

"It truly is," asserted the Magician. "In my time I've performed some magical feats that were worthy the skill of Glinda the Good. For instance, there's the Powder of Life, and my Liquid of Petrifaction, which is contained in that bottle on the shelf yonder—over the window."

"What does the Liquid of Petrifaction do?" inquired the boy.

"Turns everything it touches to solid marble. It's an invention of my own, and I find it very useful. Once two of those dreadful Kalidahs, with bodies like bears and heads like tigers, came here from the forest to attack us; but I sprinkled some of that Liquid on them and instantly they turned to marble. I now use them as ornamental statuary in my garden. This table looks to you like wood, and once it really was wood; but I sprinkled a few drops of the Liquid of Petrifaction on it and now it is marble. It will never break nor wear out."

"Fine!" said Unc Nunkie, wagging his head and stroking his long gray beard.

"Dear me; what a chatterbox you're getting to be, Unc," remarked the Magician, who was pleased with the compliment. But just then there came a scratching at the back door and a shrill voice cried:

"Let me in! Hurry up, can't you? Let me in!"

Margolotte got up and went to the door.

"Ask like a good cat, then," she said.

"Mee-ee-ow-w-w! There; does that suit your royal highness?" asked the voice, in scornful accents.

"Yes; that's proper cat talk," declared the woman, and opened the door.

At once a cat entered, came to the center of the room and stopped short at the sight of strangers. Ojo and Unc Nunkie both stared at it with wide open eyes, for surely no such curious creature had ever existed before—even in the Land of Oz.

CHAPTER IV

THE GLASS CAT

THE CAT WAS MADE OF GLASS, SO CLEAR AND transparent that you could see through it as easily as through a window. In the top of its head, however, was a mass of delicate pink balls which looked like jewels, and it had a heart made of a blood-red ruby. The eyes were two large emeralds, but aside from these colors all the rest of the animal was clear glass, and it had a spun-glass tail that was really beautiful.

"Well, Doc Pipt, do you mean to introduce us, or not?" demanded the cat, in a tone of annoyance. "Seems to me you are forgetting your manners."

"Excuse me," returned the Magician. "This is Unc Nunkie, the descendant of the former Kings of the Munchkins, before this country became a part of the Land of Oz."

"He needs a hair-cut," observed the cat, washing its face.

"True," replied Unc, with a low chuckle of amusement.

"But he has lived alone in the heart of the forest for many years," the Magician explained; "and, although that is a barbarous country, there are no barbers there."

"Who is the dwarf?" asked the cat.

"That is not a dwarf, but a boy," answered the Magician. "You have never seen a boy before. He is now small because he is young. With more years he will grow big and become as tall as Unc Nunkie."

"Oh. Is that magic?" the glass animal inquired.

"Yes; but it is Nature's magic, which is more wonderful than any art known to man. For instance, my magic made you, and made you live; and it was a poor job because you are useless and a bother to me; but I can't make you grow. You will always be the same size—and the same saucy, inconsiderate Glass Cat, with pink brains and a hard ruby heart."

"No one can regret more than I the fact that you made me," asserted the cat, crouching upon the floor and slowly swaying its spun-glass tail from side to side. "Your world is a very uninteresting place. I've wandered through your gardens and in the forest until I'm tired of it all, and when I come into the house the conversation of your fat wife and of yourself bores me dreadfully."

"That is because I gave you different brains from those we ourselves possess—and much too good for a cat," returned Dr. Pipt.

"Can't you take 'em out, then, and replace 'em with pebbles, so that I won't feel above my station in life?" asked the cat, pleadingly.

"Perhaps so. I'll try it, after I've brought the Patchwork Girl to life," he said.

The cat walked up to the bench on which the Patchwork Girl reclined and looked at her attentively.

"Are you going to make that dreadful thing live?" she asked.

The Magician nodded.

"It is intended to be my wife's servant maid," he said. "When she is alive she will do all our work and mind the house. But you are not to order her around, Bungle, as you do us. You must treat the Patchwork Girl respectfully."

"I won't. I couldn't respect such a bundle of scraps under any circumstances."

"If you don't, there will be more scraps than you will like," cried Margolotte, angrily.

"Why didn't you make her pretty to look at?" asked the cat. "You made me pretty—very pretty, indeed—and I love to watch my pink brains roll around when they're working, and to see my precious red heart beat." She went to a long mirror, as she said this, and stood before it, looking at herself with an air of much pride. "But that poor patched thing will hate herself, when she's once alive," continued the cat. "If I were you I'd use her for a mop, and make another servant that is prettier."

"You have a perverted taste," snapped Margolotte, much annoyed at this frank criticism. "I think the Patchwork Girl is beautiful, considering what she's made of. Even the rainbow hasn't as many colors, and you must admit that the rainbow is a pretty thing."

The Glass Cat yawned and stretched herself upon the floor.

"Have your own way," she said. "I'm sorry for the Patchwork Girl, that's all."

Ojo and Unc Nunkie slept that night in the Magician's house, and the boy was glad to stay because he was anxious to see the Patchwork Girl brought to life. The Glass

Cat was also a wonderful creature to little Ojo, who had never seen or known anything of magic before, although he had lived in the Fairyland of Oz ever since he was born. Back there in the woods nothing unusual ever happened. Unc Nunkie, who might have been King of the Munchkins, had not his people united with all the other countries of Oz in acknowledging Ozma as their sole ruler, had retired into this forgotten forest nook with his baby nephew and they had lived all alone there. Only that the neglected garden had failed to grow food for them, they would always have lived in the solitary Blue Forest; but now they had started out to mingle with other people, and the first place they came to proved so interesting that Ojo could scarcely sleep a wink all night.

Margolotte was an excellent cook and gave them a fine breakfast. While they were all engaged in eating, the good woman said:

"This is the last meal I shall have to cook for some time, for right after breakfast Dr. Pipt has promised to bring my new servant to life. I shall let her wash the breakfast dishes and sweep and dust the house. What a relief it will be!"

"It will, indeed, relieve you of much drudgery," said the Magician. "By the way, Margolotte, I thought I saw you getting some brains from the cupboard, while I was busy with my kettles. What qualities have you given your new servant?"

"Only those that an humble servant requires," she answered. "I do not wish her to feel above her station, as the Glass Cat does. That would make her discontented and unhappy, for of course she must always be a servant."

Ojo was somewhat disturbed as he listened to this, and the boy began to fear he had done wrong in adding all those different qualities of brains to the lot Margolotte had prepared for the servant. But it was too late now for regret, since all the brains were securely sewn up inside the Patchwork Girl's head. He might have confessed what he had done and thus allowed Margolotte and her husband to change the brains; but he was afraid of incurring their anger. He believed that Unc had seen him add to the brains, and Unc had not said a word against it; but then, Unc never did say anything unless it was absolutely necessary.

As soon as breakfast was over they all went into the Magician's big workshop, where the Glass Cat was lying before the mirror and the Patchwork Girl lay limp and lifeless upon the bench.

"Now, then," said Dr. Pipt, in a brisk tone, "we shall perform one of the greatest feats of magic possible to man, even in this marvelous Land of Oz. In no other country could it be done at all. I think we ought to have a little music while the Patchwork Girl comes to life. It is pleasant to reflect that the first sounds her golden ears will hear will be delicious music."

As he spoke he went to a phonograph, which was screwed fast to a small table, and wound up the spring of the instrument and adjusted the big gold horn.

"The music my servant will usually hear," remarked Margolotte, "will be my orders to do her work. But I see no harm in allowing her to listen to this unseen band while she wakens to her first realization of life. My orders will beat the band, afterward."

The phonograph was now playing a stirring march tune and the Magician unlocked his cabinet and took out the gold bottle containing the Powder of Life.

They all bent over the bench on which the Patchwork Girl reclined. Unc Nunkie and Margolotte stood behind, near the windows, Ojo at one side and the Magician in front, where he would have freedom to sprinkle the powder. The Glass Cat came near, too, curious to watch the important scene.

"All ready?" asked Dr. Pipt.

"All is ready," answered his wife.

So the Magician leaned over and shook from the bottle some grains of the wonderful Powder, and they fell directly on the Patchwork Girl's head and arms.

CHAPTER V

A TERRIBLE ACCIDENT

"IT WILL TAKE A FEW MINUTES FOR THIS POWDER to do its work," remarked the Magician, sprinkling the body up and down with much care.

But suddenly the Patchwork Girl threw up one arm, which knocked the bottle of powder from the crooked man's hand and sent it flying across the room. Unc Nunkie and Margolotte were so startled that they both leaped backward and bumped together, and Unc's head joggled the shelf above them and upset the bottle containing the Liquid of Petrifaction.

The Magician uttered such a wild cry that Ojo jumped away and the Patchwork Girl sprang after him and clasped her stuffed arms around him in terror. The Glass Cat snarled and hid under the table, and so it was that when the powerful Liquid of Petrifaction was spilled it fell only upon the wife of the Magician and the uncle of Ojo. With these two the charm worked promptly. They stood motionless and stiff as marble statues, in exactly the positions they were in when the Liquid struck them.

Ojo pushed the Patchwork Girl away and ran to Unc Nunkie, filled with a terrible fear for the only friend and protector he had ever known. When he grasped Unc's hand it was cold and hard. Even the long gray beard was solid marble. The Crooked Magician was dancing around the room in a frenzy of despair, calling upon his wife to forgive him, to speak to him, to come to life again!

The Patchwork Girl, quickly recovering from her fright, now came nearer and looked from one to another of the people with deep interest. Then she looked at herself and laughed. Noticing the mirror, she stood before it and examined her extraordinary features with amazement—her button eyes, pearl bead teeth and puffy nose. Then, addressing her reflection in the glass, she exclaimed:

> "Whee, but there's a gaudy dame!
> Makes a paint-box blush with shame.
> Razzle-dazzle, fizzle-fazzle!
> Howdy-do, Miss What's-your-name?"

She bowed, and the reflection bowed. Then she laughed again, long and merrily, and the Glass Cat crept out from under the table and said:

"I don't blame you for laughing at yourself. Aren't you horrid?"

"Horrid?" she replied. "Why, I'm thoroughly delightful. I'm an Original, if you please, and therefore incomparable. Of all the comic, absurd, rare and amusing creatures the world contains, I must be the supreme freak. Who but poor Margolotte could have managed to invent such an unreasonable being as I? But I'm glad—I'm awfully glad!—that I'm just what I am, and nothing else."

"Be quiet, will you?" cried the frantic Magician; "be quiet and let me think! If I don't think I shall go mad."

"Think ahead," said the Patchwork Girl, seating herself in a chair. "Think all you want to. I don't mind."

"Gee! but I'm tired playing that tune," called the phonograph, speaking through its horn in a brazen, scratchy voice. "If you don't mind, Pipt, old boy, I'll cut it out and take a rest."

The Magician looked gloomily at the music-machine.

"What dreadful luck!" he wailed, despondently. "The Powder of Life must have fallen on the phonograph."

He went up to it and found that the gold bottle that contained the precious powder had dropped upon the stand and scattered its life-giving grains over the machine. The phonograph was very much alive, and began dancing a jig with the legs of the table to which it was attached, and this dance so annoyed Dr. Pipt that he kicked the thing into a corner and pushed a bench against it, to hold it quiet.

"You were bad enough before," said the Magician, resentfully; "but a live phonograph is enough to drive every sane person in the Land of Oz stark crazy."

"No insults, please," answered the phonograph in a surly tone. "You did it, my boy; don't blame me."

"You've bungled everything, Dr. Pipt," added the Glass Cat, contemptuously.

"Except me," said the Patchwork Girl, jumping up to whirl merrily around the room.

"I think," said Ojo, almost ready to cry through grief over Unc Nunkie's sad fate, "it must all be my fault, in some way. I'm called Ojo the Unlucky, you know."

"That's nonsense, kiddie," retorted the Patchwork Girl cheerfully. "No one can be unlucky who has the intelligence to direct his own actions. The unlucky ones are those who beg for a chance to think, like poor Dr. Pipt here. What's the row about, anyway, Mr. Magic-maker?"

"The Liquid of Petrifaction has accidentally fallen upon my dear wife and Unc Nunkie and turned them into marble," he sadly replied.

"Well, why don't you sprinkle some of that powder on them and bring them to life again?" asked the Patchwork Girl.

The Magician gave a jump.

"Why, I hadn't thought of that!" he joyfully cried, and grabbed up the golden bottle, with which he ran to Margolotte.

Said the Patchwork Girl:

> "Higgledy, piggledy, dee—
> What fools magicians be!
> His head's so thick
> He can't think quick,
> So he takes advice from me."

Standing upon the bench, for he was so crooked he could not reach the top of his wife's head in any other way, Dr. Pipt began shaking the bottle. But not a grain of powder came out. He pulled off the cover, glanced within, and then threw the bottle from him with a wail of despair.

"Gone—gone! Every bit gone," he cried. "Wasted on that miserable phonograph when it might have saved my dear wife!"

Then the Magician bowed his head on his crooked arms and began to cry.

Ojo was sorry for him. He went up to the sorrowful man and said softly:

"You can make more Powder of Life, Dr. Pipt."

"Yes; but it will take me six years—six long, weary years of stirring four kettles with both feet and both hands," was the agonized reply. "Six years! while poor Margolotte stands watching me as a marble image."

"Can't anything else be done?" asked the Patchwork Girl.

The Magician shook his head. Then he seemed to remember something and looked up.

"There is one other compound that would destroy the magic spell of the Liquid of Petrifaction and restore my wife and Unc Nunkie to life," said he. "It may be hard to find the things I need to make this magic compound, but if they were found I could do in an instant what will otherwise take six long, weary years of stirring kettles with both hands and both feet."

"All right; let's find the things, then," suggested the Patchwork Girl. "That seems a lot more sensible than those stirring times with the kettles."

"That's the idea, Scraps," said the Glass Cat, approvingly. "I'm glad to find you have decent brains. Mine are exceptionally good. You can see 'em work; they're pink."

"Scraps?" repeated the girl. "Did you call me 'Scraps'? Is that my name?"

"I—I believe my poor wife had intended to name you 'Angeline,' " said the Magician.

"But I like 'Scraps' best," she replied with a laugh. "It fits me better, for my patchwork is all scraps, and nothing else. Thank you for naming me, Miss Cat. Have you any name of your own?"

"I have a foolish name that Margolotte once gave me, but which is quite undignified for one of my importance," answered the cat. "She called me 'Bungle.' "

"Yes," sighed the Magician; "you were a sad bungle, taken all in all. I was wrong to make you as I did, for a more useless, conceited and brittle thing never before existed."

"I'm not so brittle as you think," retorted the cat. "I've been alive a good many years, for Dr. Pipt experimented on me with the first magic Powder of Life he ever made, and so far I've never broken or cracked or chipped any part of me."

"You seem to have a chip on your shoulder," laughed the Patchwork Girl, and the cat went to the mirror to see.

"Tell me," pleaded Ojo, speaking to the Crooked Magician, "what must we find to make the compound that will save Unc Nunkie?"

"First," was the reply, "I must have a six-leaved clover. That can only be found in the green country around the Emerald City, and six-leaved clovers are very scarce, even there."

"I'll find it for you," promised Ojo.

"The next thing," continued the Magician, "is the left wing of a yellow butterfly. That color can only be found in the yellow country of the Winkies, West of the Emerald City."

"I'll find it," declared Ojo. "Is that all?"

"Oh, no; I'll get my Book of Recipes and see what comes next."

Saying this, the Magician unlocked a drawer of his cabinet and drew out a small book covered with blue leather. Looking through the pages he found the recipe he wanted and said: "I must have a gill of water from a dark well."

"What kind of a well is that, sir?" asked the boy.

"One where the light of day never penetrates. The water must be put in a gold bottle and brought to me without any light ever reaching it."

"I'll get the water from the dark well," said Ojo.

"Then I must have three hairs from the tip of a Woozy's tail, and a drop of oil from a live man's body."

Ojo looked grave at this.

"What is a Woozy, please?" he inquired.

"Some sort of an animal. I've never seen one, so I can't describe it," replied the Magician.

"If I can find a Woozy, I'll get the hairs from its tail," said Ojo. "But is there ever any oil in a man's body?"

The Magician looked in the book again, to make sure.

"That's what the recipe calls for," he replied, "and of course we must get everything that is called for, or the charm won't work. The book doesn't say 'blood'; it says 'oil,' and there must be oil somewhere in a live man's body or the book wouldn't ask for it."

"All right," returned Ojo, trying not to feel discouraged; "I'll try to find it."

The Magician looked at the little Munchkin boy in a doubtful way and said:

"All this will mean a long journey for you; perhaps several long journeys; for you must search through several of the different countries of Oz in order to get the things I need."

"I know it, sir; but I must do my best to save Unc Nunkie."

"And also my poor wife Margolotte. If you save one you will save the other, for both stand there together and the same compound will restore them both to life. Do the best you can, Ojo, and while you are gone I shall begin the six years' job of making a new batch of the Powder of Life. Then, if you should unluckily fail to secure any one of the things needed, I will have lost no time. But if you succeed you must return here as quickly as you can, and that will save me much tiresome stirring of four kettles with both feet and both hands."

"I will start on my journey at once, sir," said the boy.

"And I will go with you," declared the Patchwork Girl.

"No, no!" exclaimed the Magician. "You have no right to leave this house. You are only a servant and have not been discharged."

Scraps, who had been dancing up and down the room, stopped and looked at him. "What is a servant?" she asked.

"One who serves. A—a sort of slave," he explained.

"Very well," said the Patchwork Girl, "I'm going to serve you and your wife by helping Ojo find the things you need. You need a lot, you know, such as are not easily found."

"It is true," sighed Dr. Pipt. "I am well aware that Ojo has undertaken a serious task."

Scraps laughed, and resuming her dance she said:

> "Here's a job for a boy of brains:
> A drop of oil from a live man's veins;
> A six-leaved clover; three nice hairs
> From a Woozy's tail, the book declares
> Are needed for the magic spell,
> And water from a pitch-dark well.
> The yellow wing of a butterfly
> To find must Ojo also try,
> And if he gets them without harm,
> Doc Pipt will make the magic charm;
> But if he doesn't get 'em, Unc
> Will always stand a marble chunk."

The Magician looked at her thoughtfully.

"Poor Margolotte must have given you some of the quality of poesy, by mistake," he said. "And, if that is true, I didn't make a very good article when I prepared it, or else you got an overdose or an underdose. However, I believe I shall let you go with Ojo, for my poor wife will not need your services until she is restored to life. Also I think you may be able to help the boy, for your head seems to contain some thoughts I did not expect to find in it. But be very careful of yourself, for you're a souvenir of my dear Margolotte. Try not to get ripped, or your stuffing may fall out. One of your eyes seems loose, and you may have to sew it on tighter. If you talk too much you'll wear out your scarlet plush tongue, which ought to have been hemmed on the edges. And remember you belong to me and must return here as soon as your mission is accomplished."

"I'm going with Scraps and Ojo," announced the Glass Cat.

"You can't," said the Magician.

"Why not?"

"You'd get broken in no time, and you couldn't be a bit of use to the boy and the Patchwork Girl."

"I beg to differ with you," returned the cat, in a haughty tone. "Three heads are better than two, and my pink brains are beautiful. You can see 'em work."

"Well, go along," said the Magician, irritably. "You're only an annoyance, anyhow, and I'm glad to get rid of you."

"Thank you for nothing, then," answered the cat, stiffly.

Dr. Pipt took a small basket from a cupboard and packed several things in it. Then he handed it to Ojo.

"Here is some food and a bundle of charms," he said. "It is all I can give you, but I am sure you will find friends on your journey who will assist you in your search. Take care of the Patchwork Girl and bring her safely back, for she ought to prove useful to my wife. As for the Glass Cat—properly named Bungle—if she bothers you I now give you my permission to break her in two, for she is not respectful and does not obey me. I made a mistake in giving her the pink brains, you see."

Then Ojo went to Unc Nunkie and kissed the old man's marble face very tenderly.

"I'm going to try to save you, Unc," he said, just as if the marble image could hear him; and then he shook the crooked hand of the Crooked Magician, who was already busy hanging the four kettles in the fireplace, and picking up his basket left the house.

The Patchwork Girl followed him, and after them came the Glass Cat.

CHAPTER VI

THE JOURNEY

OJO HAD NEVER TRAVELED
before and so he only knew that the path down
the mountainside led into the open Munchkin
Country, where large numbers of people dwelt.
Scraps was quite new and not supposed to know
anything of the Land of Oz, while the Glass
Cat admitted she had never wandered very far
away from the Magician's house. There was
only one path before them, at the beginning,
so they could not miss their way, and for a time
they walked through the thick forest in silent
thought, each one impressed with the importance of the adventure they had undertaken.

Suddenly the Patchwork Girl laughed.
It was funny to see her laugh, because her
cheeks wrinkled up, her nose tipped, her silver
button eyes twinkled and her mouth curled at the
corners in a comical way.

"Has something pleased you?" asked Ojo,
who was feeling solemn and joyless through
thinking upon his uncle's sad fate.

"Yes," she answered. "Your world pleases
me, for it's a queer world, and life in it is queerer
still. Here am I, made from an old bedquilt and
intended to be a slave to Margolotte, rendered free as air by
an accident that none of you could foresee. I am enjoying life and seeing the world,
while the woman who made me is standing helpless as a block of wood. If that isn't
funny enough to laugh at, I don't know what is."

"You're not seeing much of the world yet, my poor, innocent Scraps," remarked
the cat. "The world doesn't consist wholly of the trees that are on all sides of us."

"But they're part of it; and aren't they pretty trees?" returned Scraps, bobbing her head until her brown yarn curls fluttered in the breeze. "Growing between them I can see lovely ferns and wild-flowers, and soft green mosses. If the rest of your world is half as beautiful I shall be glad I'm alive."

"I don't know what the rest of the world is like, I'm sure," said the cat; "but I mean to find out."

"I have never been out of the forest," Ojo added; "but to me the trees are gloomy and sad and the wild-flowers seem lonesome. It must be nicer where there are no trees and there is room for lots of people to live together."

"I wonder if any of the people we shall meet will be as splendid as I am," said the Patchwork Girl. "All I have seen, so far, have pale, colorless skins and clothes as blue as the country they live in, while I am of many gorgeous colors—face and body and clothes. That is why I am bright and contented, Ojo, while you are blue and sad."

"I think I made a mistake in giving you so many sorts of brains," observed the boy. "Perhaps, as the Magician said, you have an overdose, and they may not agree with you."

"What had you to do with my brains?" asked Scraps.

"A lot," replied Ojo. "Old Margolotte meant to give you only a few—just enough to keep you going—but when she wasn't looking I added a good many more, of the best kinds I could find in the Magician's cupboard."

"Thanks," said the girl, dancing along the path ahead of Ojo and then dancing back to his side. "If a few brains are good, many brains must be better."

"But they ought to be evenly balanced," said the boy, "and I had no time to be careful. From the way you're acting, I guess the dose was badly mixed."

"Scraps hasn't enough brains to hurt her, so don't worry," remarked the cat, which was trotting along in a very dainty and graceful manner. "The only brains worth considering are mine, which are pink. You can see 'em work."

After walking a long time they came to a little brook that trickled across the path, and here Ojo sat down to rest and eat something from his basket. He found that the Magician had given him part of a loaf of bread and a slice of cheese. He broke off some of the bread and was surprised to find the loaf just as large as it was before. It was the same way with the cheese: however much he broke off from the slice, it remained exactly the same size.

"Ah," said he, nodding wisely; "that's magic. Dr. Pipt has enchanted the bread and the cheese, so it will last me all through my journey, however much I eat."

"Why do you put those things into your mouth?" asked Scraps, gazing at him in astonishment. "Do you need more stuffing? Then why don't you use cotton, such as I am stuffed with?"

"I don't need that kind," said Ojo.

"But a mouth is to talk with, isn't it?"

"It is also to eat with," replied the boy. "If I didn't put food into my mouth, and eat it, I would get hungry and starve."

"Ah, I didn't know that," she said. "Give me some."

Ojo handed her a bit of the bread and she put it in her mouth.

"What next?" she asked, scarcely able to speak.

"Chew it and swallow it," said the boy.

Scraps tried that. Her pearl teeth were unable to chew the bread and beyond her mouth there was no opening. Being unable to swallow she threw away the bread and laughed.

"I must get hungry and starve, for I can't eat," she said.

"Neither can I," announced the cat; "but I'm not fool enough to try. Can't you understand that you and I are superior people and not made like these poor humans?"

"Why should I understand that, or anything else?" asked the girl. "Don't bother my head by asking conundrums, I beg of you. Just let me discover myself in my own way."

With this she began amusing herself by leaping across the brook and back again.

"Be careful, or you'll fall in the water," warned Ojo.

"Never mind."

"You'd better. If you get wet you'll be soggy and can't walk. Your colors might run, too," he said.

"Don't my colors run whenever I run?" she asked.

"Not in the way I mean. If they get wet, the reds and greens and yellows and purples of your patches might run into each other and become just a blur—no color at all, you know."

"Then," said the Patchwork Girl, "I'll be careful, for if I spoiled my splendid colors I would cease to be beautiful."

"Pah!" sneered the Glass Cat, "such colors are not beautiful; they're ugly, and in bad taste. Please notice that my body has no color at all. I'm transparent, except for my exquisite red heart and my lovely pink brains—you can see 'em work."

"Shoo—shoo—shoo!" cried Scraps, dancing around and laughing. "And your horrid green eyes, Miss Bungle! You can't see your eyes, but we can, and I notice you're very proud of what little color you have. Shoo, Miss Bungle, shoo—shoo—shoo! If you were all colors and many colors, as I am, you'd be too stuck up for anything." She leaped over the cat and back again, and the startled Bungle crept close to a tree to escape her. This made Scraps laugh more heartily than ever, and she said:

"Whoop-te-doodle-doo!

The cat has lost her shoe.

Her tootsie's bare, but she don't care,

So what's the odds to you?"

"Dear me, Ojo," said the cat; "don't you think the creature is a little bit crazy?"

"It may be," he answered, with a puzzled look.

"If she continues her insults I'll scratch off her suspender-button eyes," declared the cat.

"Don't quarrel, please," pleaded the boy, rising to resume the journey. "Let us be good comrades and as happy and cheerful as possible, for we are likely to meet with plenty of trouble on our way."

It was nearly sundown when they came to the edge of the forest and saw spread out before them a delightful landscape. There were broad blue fields stretching for miles over the valley, which was dotted everywhere with pretty, blue domed houses, none of which, however, was very near to the place where they stood. Just at the point where the path left the forest stood a tiny house covered with leaves from the trees, and before this stood a Munchkin man with an axe in his hand. He seemed very much surprised when Ojo and Scraps and the Glass Cat came out of the woods, but as the Patchwork Girl approached nearer he sat down upon a bench and laughed so hard that he could not speak for a long time.

This man was a woodchopper and lived all alone in the little house. He had bushy blue whiskers and merry blue eyes and his blue clothes were quite old and worn.

"Mercy me!" exclaimed the woodchopper, when at last he could stop laughing. "Who would think such a funny harlequin lived in the Land of Oz? Where did you come from, Crazy-quilt?"

"Do you mean me?" asked the Patchwork Girl.

"Of course," he replied.

"You misjudge my ancestry. I'm not a crazy-quilt; I'm patchwork," she said.

"There's no difference," he replied, beginning to laugh again. "When my old grandmother sews such things together she calls it a crazy-quilt; but I never thought such a jumble could come to life."

"It was the Magic Powder that did it," explained Ojo.

"Oh, then you have come from the Crooked Magician on the mountain. I might have known it, for—Well, I declare! here's a glass cat. But the Magician will get in trouble for this; it's against the law for anyone to work magic except Glinda the Good and the royal Wizard of Oz. If you people—or things—or glass spectacles—or crazy-quilts—or whatever you are, go near the Emerald City, you'll be arrested."

"We're going there, anyhow," declared Scraps, sitting upon the bench and swinging her stuffed legs.

> "If any of us takes a rest,
>   We'll be arrested sure,
>   And get no restitution
> 'Cause the rest we must endure."

"I see," said the woodchopper, nodding; "you're as crazy as the crazy-quilt you're made of."

"She really *is* crazy," remarked the Glass Cat. "But that isn't to be wondered at when you remember how many different things she's made of. For my part, I'm made of pure glass—except my jewel heart and my pretty pink brains. Did you notice my brains, stranger? You can see 'em work."

"So I can," replied the woodchopper; "but I can't see that they accomplish much. A glass cat is a useless sort of thing, but a Patchwork Girl is really useful. She makes me laugh, and laughter is the best thing in life. There was once a woodchopper, a friend of mine, who was made all of tin, and I used to laugh every time I saw him."

"A tin woodchopper?" said Ojo. "That is strange."

"My friend wasn't always tin," said the man, "but he was careless with his axe, and used to chop himself very badly. Whenever he lost an arm or a leg he had it replaced with tin; so after a while he was all tin."

"And could he chop wood then?" asked the boy.

"He could if he didn't rust his tin joints. But one day he met Dorothy in the forest and went with her to the Emerald City, where he made his fortune. He is now one of the favorites of Princess Ozma, and she has made him the Emperor of the Winkies— the Country where all is yellow."

"Who is Dorothy?" inquired the Patchwork Girl.

"A little maid who used to live in Kansas, but is now a Princess of Oz. She's Ozma's best friend, they say, and lives with her in the royal palace."

"Is Dorothy made of tin?" inquired Ojo.

"Is she patchwork, like me?" inquired Scraps.

"No," said the man; "Dorothy is flesh, just as I am. I know of only one tin person, and that is Nick Chopper, the Tin Woodman; and there will never be but one Patchwork Girl, for any magician that sees you will refuse to make another one like you."

"I suppose we shall see the Tin Woodman, for we are going to the Country of the Winkies," said the boy.

"What for?" asked the woodchopper.

"To get the left wing of a yellow butterfly."

"It is a long journey," declared the man, "and you will go through lonely parts of Oz and cross rivers and traverse dark forests before you get there."

"Suits me all right," said Scraps. "I'll get a chance to see the country."

"You're crazy, girl. Better crawl into a rag-bag and hide there; or give yourself to some little girl to play with. Those who travel are likely to meet trouble; that's why I stay at home."

The woodchopper then invited them all to stay the night at his little hut, but they were anxious to get on and so left him and continued along the path, which was broader, now, and more distinct.

They expected to reach some other house before it grew dark, but the twilight was brief and Ojo soon began to fear they had made a mistake in leaving the woodchopper.

"I can scarcely see the path," he said at last. "Can you see it, Scraps?"

"No," replied the Patchwork Girl, who was holding fast to the boy's arm so he could guide her.

"I can see," declared the Glass Cat. "My eyes are better than yours, and my pink brains—"

"Never mind your pink brains, please," said Ojo hastily; "just run ahead and show us the way. Wait a minute and I'll tie a string to you; for then you can lead us."

He got a string from his pocket and tied it around the cat's neck, and after that the creature guided them along the path. They had proceeded in this way for about an hour when a twinkling blue light appeared ahead of them.

"Good! there's a house at last," cried Ojo. "When we reach it the good people will surely welcome us and give us a night's lodging." But however far they walked the light seemed to get no nearer, so by and by the cat stopped short, saying:

"I think the light is traveling, too, and we shall never be able to catch up with it. But here is a house by the roadside, so why go farther?"

"Where is the house, Bungle?"

"Just here beside us, Scraps."

Ojo was now able to see a small house near the pathway. It was dark and silent, but the boy was tired and wanted to rest, so he went up to the door and knocked.

"Who is there?" cried a voice from within.

"I am Ojo the Unlucky, and with me are Miss Scraps Patchwork and the Glass Cat," he replied.

"What do you want?" asked the Voice.

"A place to sleep," said Ojo.

"Come in, then; but don't make any noise, and you must go directly to bed," returned the Voice.

Ojo unlatched the door and entered. It was very dark inside and he could see nothing at all. But the cat exclaimed: "Why, there's no one here!"

"There must be," said the boy. "Some one spoke to me."

"I can see everything in the room," replied the cat, "and no one is present but ourselves. But here are three beds, all made up, so we may as well go to sleep."

"What is sleep?" inquired the Patchwork Girl.

"It's what you do when you go to bed," said Ojo.

"But why do you go to bed?" persisted the Patchwork Girl.

"Here, here! You are making altogether too much noise," cried the Voice they had heard before. "Keep quiet, strangers, and go to bed."

The cat, which could see in the dark, looked sharply around for the owner of the Voice, but could discover no one, although the Voice had seemed close beside them. She arched her back a little and seemed afraid. Then she whispered to Ojo: "Come!" and led him to a bed.

With his hands the boy felt of the bed and found it was big and soft, with feather pillows and plenty of blankets. So he took off his shoes and hat and crept into the bed. Then the cat led Scraps to another bed and the Patchwork Girl was puzzled to know what to do with it.

"Lie down and keep quiet," whispered the cat, warningly.

"Can't I sing?" asked Scraps.

"No."

"Can't I whistle?" asked Scraps.

"No."

"Can't I dance till morning, if I want to?" asked Scraps.

"You must keep quiet," said the cat, in a soft voice.

"I don't want to," replied the Patchwork Girl, speaking as loudly as usual. "What right have you to order me around? If I want to talk, or yell, or whistle—"

Before she could say anything more an unseen hand seized her firmly and threw her out of the door, which closed behind her with a sharp slam. She found herself bumping and rolling in the road and when she got up and tried to open the door of the house again she found it locked.

"What has happened to Scraps?" asked Ojo.

"Never mind. Let's go to sleep, or something will happen to us," answered the Glass Cat.

So Ojo snuggled down in his bed and fell asleep, and he was so tired that he never wakened until broad daylight.

CHAPTER VII

THE TROUBLESOME PHONOGRAPH

WHEN THE BOY OPENED HIS EYES NEXT morning he looked carefully around the room. These small Munchkin houses seldom had more than one room in them. That in which Ojo now found himself had three beds, set all in a row on one side of it. The Glass Cat lay asleep on one bed, Ojo was in the second, and the third was neatly made up and smoothed for the day. On the other side of the room was a round table on which breakfast was already placed, smoking hot. Only one chair was drawn up to the table, where a place was set for one person. No one seemed to be in the room except the boy and Bungle.

Ojo got up and put on his shoes. Finding a toilet stand at the head of his bed he washed his face and hands and brushed his hair. Then he went to the table and said:

"I wonder if this is my breakfast?"

"Eat it!" commanded a voice at his side, so near that Ojo jumped. But no person could he see.

He was hungry, and the breakfast looked good; so he sat down and ate all he wanted. Then, rising, he took his hat and wakened the Glass Cat.

"Come on, Bungle," said he; "we must go."

He cast another glance about the room and, speaking to the air, he said: "Whoever lives here has been kind to me, and I'm much obliged."

There was no answer, so he took his basket and went out the door, the cat following him. In the middle of the path sat the Patchwork Girl, playing with pebbles she had picked up.

"Oh, there you are!" she exclaimed cheerfully. "I thought you were never coming out. It has been daylight a long time."

"What did you do all night?" asked the boy.

"Sat here and watched the stars and the moon," she replied. "They're interesting. I never saw them before, you know."

"Of course not," said Ojo.

"You were crazy to act so badly and get thrown outdoors," remarked Bungle, as they renewed their journey.

"That's all right," said Scraps. "If I hadn't been thrown out I wouldn't have seen the stars, nor the big gray wolf."

"What wolf?" inquired Ojo.

"The one that came to the door of the house three times during the night."

"I don't see why that should be," said the boy, thoughtfully; "there was plenty to eat in that house, for I had a fine breakfast, and I slept in a nice bed."

"Don't you feel tired?" asked the Patchwork Girl, noticing that the boy yawned.

"Why, yes; I'm as tired as I was last night; and yet I slept very well."

"And aren't you hungry?"

"It's strange," replied Ojo. "I had a good breakfast, and yet I think I'll now eat some of my crackers and cheese."

Scraps danced up and down the path. Then she sang:

> "Kizzle-kazzle-kore;
> The wolf is at the door,
> There's nothing to eat but a bone without meat,
> And a bill from the grocery store."

"What does that mean?" asked Ojo.

"Don't ask me," replied Scraps. "I say what comes into my head, but of course I know nothing of a grocery store or bones without meat or—very much else."

"No," said the cat; "she's stark, staring, raving crazy, and her brains can't be pink, for they don't work properly."

"Bother the brains!" cried Scraps. "Who cares for 'em, anyhow? Have you noticed how beautiful my patches are in this sunlight?"

Just then they heard a sound as of footsteps pattering along the path behind them and all three turned to see what was coming. To their astonishment they beheld a small

round table running as fast as its four spindle legs could carry it, and to the top was screwed fast a phonograph with a big gold horn.

"Hold on!" shouted the phonograph. "Wait for me!"

"Goodness me; it's that music thing which the Crooked Magician scattered the Powder of Life over," said Ojo.

"So it is," returned Bungle, in a grumpy tone of voice; and then, as the phonograph overtook them, the Glass Cat added sternly: "What are you doing here, anyhow?"

"I've run away," said the music thing. "After you left, old Dr. Pipt and I had a dreadful quarrel and he threatened to smash me to pieces if I didn't keep quiet. Of course I wouldn't do that, because a talking-machine is supposed to talk and make a noise—and sometimes music. So I slipped out of the house while the Magician was stirring his four kettles and I've been running after you all night. Now that I've found such pleasant company, I can talk and play tunes all I want to."

Ojo was greatly annoyed by this unwelcome addition to their party. At first he did not know what to say to the newcomer, but a little thought decided him not to make friends.

"We are traveling on important business," he declared, "and you'll excuse me if I say we can't be bothered."

"How very impolite!" exclaimed the phonograph.

"I'm sorry; but it's true," said the boy. "You'll have to go somewhere else."

"This is very unkind treatment, I must say," whined the phonograph, in an injured tone. "Everyone seems to hate me, and yet I was intended to amuse people."

"It isn't you we hate, especially," observed the Glass Cat; "it's your dreadful music. When I lived in the same room with you I was much annoyed by your squeaky horn. It growls and grumbles and clicks and scratches so it spoils the music, and your machinery rumbles so that the racket drowns every tune you attempt."

"That isn't my fault; it's the fault of my records. I must admit that I haven't a clear record," answered the machine.

"Just the same, you'll have to go away," said Ojo.

"Wait a minute," cried Scraps. "This music thing interests me. I remember to have heard music when I first came to life, and I would like to hear it again. What is your name, my poor abused phonograph?"

"Victor Columbia Edison," it answered.

"Well, I shall call you 'Vic' for short," said the Patchwork Girl. "Go ahead and play something."

"It'll drive you crazy," warned the cat.

"I'm crazy now, according to your statement. Loosen up and reel out the music, Vic."

"The only record I have with me," explained the phonograph, "is one the Magician attached just before we had our quarrel. It's a highly classical composition."

"A what?" inquired Scraps.

"It is classical music, and is considered the best and most puzzling ever manufactured. You're supposed to like it, whether you do or not, and if you don't, the proper thing is to look as if you did. Understand?"

"Not in the least," said Scraps.

"Then, listen!"

At once the machine began to play and in a few minutes Ojo put his hands to his ears to shut out the sounds and the cat snarled and Scraps began to laugh.

"Cut it out, Vic," she said. "That's enough."

But the phonograph continued playing the dreary tune, so Ojo seized the crank, jerked it free and threw it into the road. However, the moment the crank struck the ground it bounded back to the machine again and began winding it up. And still the music played.

"Let's run!" cried Scraps, and they all started and ran down the path as fast as they could go. But the phonograph was right behind them and could run and play at the same time. It called out, reproachfully:

"What's the matter? Don't you love classical music?"

"No, Vic," said Scraps, halting. "We will passical the classical and preserve what joy we have left. I haven't any nerves, thank goodness, but your music makes my cotton shrink."

"Then turn over my record. There's a rag-time tune on the other side," said the machine.

"What's rag-time?"

"The opposite of classical."

"All right," said Scraps, and turned over the record.

The phonograph now began to play a jerky jumble of sounds which proved so bewildering that after a moment Scraps stuffed her patchwork apron into the gold horn and cried: "Stop—stop! That's the other extreme. It's extremely bad!"

Muffled as it was, the phonograph played on.

"If you don't shut off that music I'll smash your record," threatened Ojo.

The music stopped, at that, and the machine turned its horn from one to another and said with great indignation: "What's the matter now? Is it possible you can't appreciate rag-time?"

"Scraps ought to, being rags herself," said the cat; "but I simply can't stand it; it makes my whiskers curl."

"It is, indeed, dreadful!" exclaimed Ojo, with a shudder.

"It's enough to drive a crazy lady mad," murmured the Patchwork Girl. "I'll tell you what, Vic," she added as she smoothed out her apron and put it on again, "for some reason or other you've missed your guess. You're not a concert; you're a nuisance."

"Music hath charms to soothe the savage breast," asserted the phonograph sadly.

"Then we're not savages. I advise you to go home and beg the Magician's pardon."

"Never! He'd smash me."

"That's what we shall do, if you stay here," Ojo declared.

"Run along, Vic, and bother some one else," advised Scraps. "Find some one who is real wicked, and stay with him till he repents. In that way you can do some good in the world."

The music thing turned silently away and trotted down a side path, toward a distant Munchkin village.

"Is that the way *we* go?" asked Bungle anxiously.

"No," said Ojo; "I think we shall keep straight ahead, for this path is the widest and best. When we come to some house we will inquire the way to the Emerald City."

CHAPTER VIII

THE FOOLISH OWL AND THE WISE DONKEY

ON THEY WENT, AND HALF AN HOUR'S steady walking brought them to a house somewhat better than the two they had already passed. It stood close to the roadside and over the door was a sign that read: "Miss Foolish Owl and Mr. Wise Donkey: Public Advisers."

When Ojo read this sign aloud Scraps said laughingly: "Well, here is a place to get all the advice we want, maybe more than we need. Let's go in."

The boy knocked at the door.

"Come in!" called a deep bass voice.

So they opened the door and entered the house, where a little light-brown donkey, dressed in a blue apron and a blue cap, was engaged in dusting the furniture with a blue cloth. On a shelf over the window sat a great blue owl with a blue sunbonnet on her head, blinking her big round eyes at the visitors.

"Good morning," said the donkey, in his deep voice, which seemed bigger than he was. "Did you come to us for advice?"

"Why, we came, anyhow," replied Scraps, "and now we are here we may as well have some advice. It's free, isn't it?"

"Certainly," said the donkey. "Advice doesn't cost anything—unless you follow it. Permit me to say, by the way, that you are the queerest lot of travelers that ever came to my shop. Judging you merely by appearances, I think you'd better talk to the Foolish Owl yonder."

They turned to look at the bird, which fluttered its wings and stared back at them with its big eyes.

"Hoot-ti-toot-ti-toot!" cried the owl.

> "Fiddle-cum-foo,
> Howdy-do?
> Riddle-cum, tiddle-cum,
> Too-ra-la-loo!"

"That beats your poetry, Scraps," said Ojo.

"It's just nonsense!" declared the Glass Cat.

"But it's good advice for the foolish," said the donkey, admiringly. "Listen to my partner, and you can't go wrong."

Said the owl in a grumbling voice:

> "Patchwork Girl has come to life;
> No one's sweetheart, no one's wife;
> Lacking sense and loving fun,
> She'll be snubbed by everyone."

"Quite a compliment! Quite a compliment, I declare," exclaimed the donkey, turning to look at Scraps. "You are certainly a wonder, my dear, and I fancy you'd make a splendid pincushion. If you belonged to me, I'd wear smoked glasses when I looked at you."

"Why?" asked the Patchwork Girl.

"Because you are so gay and gaudy."

"It is my beauty that dazzles you," she asserted. "You Munchkin people all strut around in your stupid blue color, while I—"

"You are wrong in calling me a Munchkin," interrupted the donkey, "for I was born in the Land of Mo and came to visit the Land of Oz on the day it was shut off from all the rest of the world. So here I am obliged to stay, and I confess it is a very pleasant country to live in."

"Hoot-ti-toot!" cried the owl;

> "Ojo's searching for a charm,
> 'Cause Unc Nunkie's come to harm.
> Charms are scarce; they're hard to get;
> Ojo's got a job, you bet!"

"Is the owl so very foolish?" asked the boy.

"Extremely so," replied the donkey. "Notice what vulgar expressions she uses. But I admire the owl for the reason that she *is* positively foolish. Owls are supposed to be so very wise, generally, that a foolish one is unusual, and you perhaps know that anything or anyone unusual is sure to be interesting to the wise."

The owl flapped its wings again, muttering these words:

> "It's hard to be a glassy cat—
> No cat can be more hard than that;
> She's so transparent, every act
> Is clear to us, and that's a fact."

"Have you noticed my pink brains?" inquired Bungle, proudly. "You can see 'em work."

"Not in the daytime," said the donkey. "She can't see very well by day, poor thing. But her advice is excellent. I advise you all to follow it."

"The owl hasn't given us any advice, as yet," the boy declared.

"No? Then what do you call all those sweet poems?"

"Just foolishness," replied Ojo. "Scraps does the same thing."

"Foolishness! Of course! To be sure! The Foolish Owl must be foolish or she wouldn't be the Foolish Owl. You are very complimentary to my partner, indeed," asserted the donkey, rubbing his front hoofs together as if highly pleased.

"The sign says that *you* are wise," remarked Scraps to the donkey. "I wish you would prove it."

"With great pleasure," returned the beast. "Put me to the test, my dear Patches, and I'll prove my wisdom in the wink of an eye."

"What is the best way to get to the Emerald City?" asked Ojo.

"Walk," said the donkey.

"I know; but what road shall I take?" was the boy's next question.

"The road of yellow bricks, of course. It leads directly to the Emerald City."

"And how shall we find the road of yellow bricks?"

"By keeping along the path you have been following. You'll come to the yellow bricks pretty soon, and you'll know them when you see them because they're the only yellow things in the blue country."

"Thank you," said the boy. "At last you have told me something."

"Is that the extent of your wisdom?" asked Scraps.

"No," replied the donkey; "I know many other things, but they wouldn't interest you. So I'll give you a last word of advice: move on, for the sooner you do that the sooner you'll get to the Emerald City of Oz."

"Hoot-ti-toot-ti-toot-ti-too!" screeched the owl;

> "Off you go! fast or slow,
> Where you're going you don't know.
> Patches, Bungle, Munchkin lad,
> Facing fortunes good and bad,
> Meeting dangers grave and sad,
> Sometimes worried, sometimes glad—
> Where you're going you don't know,
> Nor do I, but off you go!"

"Sounds like a hint, to me," said the Patchwork Girl.

"Then let's take it and go," replied Ojo.

They said good-bye to the Wise Donkey and the Foolish Owl and at once resumed their journey.

CHAPTER IX

THEY MEET THE WOOZY

"THERE SEEM TO BE VERY FEW HOUSES around here, after all," remarked Ojo, after they had walked for a time in silence.

"Never mind," said Scraps; "we are not looking for houses, but rather the road of yellow bricks. Won't it be funny to run across something yellow in this dismal blue country?"

"There are worse colors than yellow in this country," asserted the Glass Cat, in a spiteful tone.

"Oh; do you mean the pink pebbles you call your brains, and your red heart and green eyes?" asked the Patchwork Girl.

"No; I mean you, if you must know it," growled the cat.

"You're jealous!" laughed Scraps. "You'd give your whiskers for a lovely variegated complexion like mine."

"I wouldn't!" retorted the cat. "I've the clearest complexion in the world, and I don't employ a beauty-doctor, either."

"I see you don't," said Scraps.

"Please don't quarrel," begged Ojo. "This is an important journey, and quarreling makes me discouraged. To be brave, one must be cheerful, so I hope you will be as good-tempered as possible."

They had traveled some distance when suddenly they faced a high fence which barred any further progress straight ahead. It ran directly across the road and enclosed a small forest of tall trees, set close together. When the group of adventurers peered through the bars of the fence they thought this forest looked more gloomy and forbidding than any they had ever seen before.

They soon discovered that the path they had been following now made a bend and passed around the enclosure, but what made Ojo stop and look thoughtful was a sign painted on the fence which read:

"BEWARE OF THE WOOZY!"

"That means," he said, "that there's a Woozy inside that fence, and the Woozy must be a dangerous animal or they wouldn't tell people to beware of it."

"Let's keep out, then," replied Scraps. "That path is outside the fence, and Mr. Woozy may have all his little forest to himself, for all we care."

"But one of our errands is to find a Woozy," Ojo explained. "The Magician wants me to get three hairs from the end of a Woozy's tail."

"Let's go on and find some other Woozy," suggested the cat. "This one is ugly and dangerous, or they wouldn't cage him up. Maybe we shall find another that is tame and gentle."

"Perhaps there isn't any other, at all," answered Ojo. "The sign doesn't say: 'Beware *a* Woozy'; it says: 'Beware *the* Woozy,' which may mean there's only one in all the Land of Oz."

"Then," said Scraps, "suppose we go in and find him? Very likely if we ask him politely to let us pull three hairs out of the tip of his tail he won't hurt us."

"It would hurt *him*, I'm sure, and that would make him cross," said the cat.

"You needn't worry, Bungle," remarked the Patchwork Girl; "for if there is danger you can climb a tree. Ojo and I are not afraid; are we, Ojo?"

"I am, a little," the boy admitted; "but this danger must be faced, if we intend to save poor Unc Nunkie. How shall we get over the fence?"

"Climb," answered Scraps, and at once she began climbing up the rows of bars. Ojo followed and found it more easy than he had expected. When they got to the top of the fence they began to get down on the other side and soon were in the forest. The Glass Cat, being small, crept between the lower bars and joined them.

Here there was no path of any sort, so they entered the woods, the boy leading the way, and wandered through the trees until they were nearly in the center of the forest. They now came upon a clear space in which stood a rocky cave.

So far they had met no living creature, but when Ojo saw the cave he knew it must be the den of the Woozy.

It is hard to face any savage beast without a sinking of the heart, but still more terrifying is it to face an unknown beast, which you have never seen even a picture of.

So there is little wonder that the pulses of the Munchkin boy beat fast as he and his companions stood facing the cave. The opening was perfectly square, and about big enough to admit a goat.

"I guess the Woozy is asleep," said Scraps. "Shall I throw in a stone, to waken him?"

"No; please don't," answered Ojo, his voice trembling a little. "I'm in no hurry."

But he had not long to wait, for the Woozy heard the sound of voices and came trotting out of his cave. As this is the only Woozy that has ever lived, either in the Land of Oz or out of it, I must describe it to you.

The creature was all squares and flat surfaces and edges. Its head was an exact square, like one of the building-blocks a child plays with; therefore it had no ears, but heard sounds through two openings in the upper corners. Its nose, being in the center of a square surface, was flat, while the mouth was formed by the opening of the lower edge of the block. The body of the Woozy was much larger than its head, but was likewise block-shaped—being twice as long as it was wide and high. The tail was square and stubby and perfectly straight, and the four legs were made in the same way, each being four-sided. The animal was covered with a thick, smooth skin and had no hair at all except at the extreme end of its tail, where there grew exactly three stiff, stubby hairs. The beast was dark blue in color and his face was not fierce nor ferocious in expression, but rather good-humored and droll.

Seeing the strangers, the Woozy folded his hind legs as if they had been hinged and sat down to look his visitors over.

"Well, well," he exclaimed; "what a queer lot you are! At first I thought some of those miserable Munchkin farm-ers had come to annoy me, but I am relieved to find you in their stead. It is plain to me that you are a remarkable group—as remarkable in your way as I am in mine—and so you are welcome to my domain. Nice place, isn't it? But lonesome— dreadfully lonesome."

"Why did they shut you up here?" asked Scraps, who was regarding the queer, square creature with much curiosity.

"Because I eat up all the honey-bees which the Munchkin farmers who live around here keep to make them honey."

"Are you fond of eating honey-bees?" inquired the boy.

"Very. They are really delicious. But the farmers did not like to lose their bees and so they tried to destroy me. Of course they couldn't do that."

"Why not?"

"My skin is so thick and tough that nothing can get through it to hurt me. So, finding they could not destroy me, they drove me into this forest and built a fence around me. Unkind, wasn't it?"

"But what do you eat now?" asked Ojo.

"Nothing at all. I've tried the leaves from the trees and the mosses and creeping vines, but they don't seem to suit my taste. So, there being no honey-bees here, I've eaten nothing for years.

"You must be awfully hungry," said the boy. "I've got some bread and cheese in my basket. Would you like that kind of food?"

"Give me a nibble and I will try it; then I can tell you better whether it is grateful to my appetite," returned the Woozy.

So the boy opened his basket and broke a piece off the loaf of bread. He tossed it toward the Woozy, who cleverly caught it in his mouth and ate it in a twinkling.

"That's rather good," declared the animal. "Any more?"

"Try some cheese," said Ojo, and threw down a piece.

The Woozy ate that, too, and smacked its long, thin lips.

"That's mighty good!" it exclaimed. "Any more?"

"Plenty," replied Ojo. So he sat down on a stump and fed the Woozy bread and cheese for a long time; for, no matter how much the boy broke off, the loaf and the slice remained just as big.

"That'll do," said the Woozy, at last; "I'm quite full. I hope the strange food won't give me indigestion."

"I hope not," said Ojo. "It's what I eat."

"Well, I must say I'm much obliged, and I'm glad you came," announced the beast. "Is there anything I can do in return for your kindness?"

"Yes," said Ojo earnestly, "you have it in your power to do me a great favor, if you will."

"What is it?" asked the Woozy. "Name the favor and I will grant it."

"I—I want three hairs from the tip of your tail," said Ojo, with some hesitation.

"Three hairs! Why, that's all I have—on my tail or anywhere else," exclaimed the beast.

"I know; but I want them very much."

"They are my sole ornaments, my prettiest feature," said the Woozy, uneasily. "If I give up those three hairs I—I'm just a blockhead."

"Yet I must have them," insisted the boy, firmly, and he then told the Woozy all about the accident to Unc Nunkie and Margolotte, and how the three hairs were to be a part of the magic charm that would restore them to life. The beast listened with attention and when Ojo had finished the recital it said, with a sigh:

"I always keep my word, for I pride myself on being square. So you may have the three hairs, and welcome. I think, under such circumstances, it would be selfish in me to refuse you."

"Thank you! Thank you very much," cried the boy, joyfully. "May I pull out the hairs now?"

"Any time you like," answered the Woozy.

So Ojo went up to the queer creature and taking hold of one of the hairs began to pull. He pulled harder. He pulled with all his might; but the hair remained fast.

"What's the trouble?" asked the Woozy, which Ojo had dragged here and there all around the clearing in his endeavor to pull out the hair.

"It won't come," said the boy, panting.

"I was afraid of that," declared the beast. "You'll have to pull harder."

"I'll help you," exclaimed Scraps, coming to the boy's side. "You pull the hair, and I'll pull you, and together we ought to get it out easily."

"Wait a jiffy," called the Woozy, and then it went to a tree and hugged it with its front paws, so that its body couldn't be dragged around by the pull. "All ready, now. Go ahead!"

Ojo grasped the hair with both hands and pulled with all his strength, while Scraps seized the boy around his waist and added her strength to his. But the hair wouldn't budge. Instead, it slipped out of Ojo's hands and he and Scraps both rolled upon the ground in a heap and never stopped until they bumped against the rocky cave.

"Give it up," advised the Glass Cat, as the boy arose and assisted the Patchwork Girl to her feet. "A dozen strong men couldn't pull out those hairs. I believe they're clinched on the under side of the Woozy's thick skin."

"Then what shall I do?" asked the boy, despairingly. "If on our return I fail to take these three hairs to the Crooked Magician, the other things I have come to seek will be of no use at all, and we cannot restore Unc Nunkie and Margolotte to life."

"They're goners, I guess," said the Patchwork Girl.

"Never mind," added the cat. "I can't see that old Unc and Margolotte are worth all this trouble, anyhow."

But Ojo did not feel that way. He was so disheartened that he sat down upon a stump and began to cry.

The Woozy looked at the boy thoughtfully.

"Why don't you take me with you?" asked the beast. "Then, when at last you get to the Magician's house, he can surely find some way to pull out those three hairs."

Ojo was overjoyed at this suggestion.

"That's it!" he cried, wiping away the tears and springing to his feet with a smile. "If I take the three hairs to the Magician, it won't matter if they are still in your body."

"It can't matter in the least," agreed the Woozy.

"Come on, then," said the boy, picking up his basket; "let us start at once. I have several other things to find, you know."

But the Glass Cat gave a little laugh and inquired in her scornful way:

"How do you intend to get the beast out of this forest?"

That puzzled them all for a time.

"Let us go to the fence, and then we may find a way," suggested Scraps. So they walked through the forest to the fence, reaching it at a point exactly opposite that where they had entered the enclosure.

"How did you get in?" asked the Woozy.

"We climbed over," answered Ojo.

"I can't do that," said the beast. "I'm a very swift runner, for I can overtake a honey-bee as it flies; and I can jump very high, which is the reason they made such a tall fence to keep me in. But I can't climb at all, and I'm too big to squeeze between the bars of the fence."

Ojo tried to think what to do.

"Can you dig?" he asked.

"No," answered the Woozy, "for I have no claws. My feet are quite flat on the bottom of them. Nor can I gnaw away the boards, as I have no teeth."

"You're not such a terrible creature, after all," remarked Scraps.

"You haven't heard me growl, or you wouldn't say that," declared the Woozy. "When I growl, the sound echoes like thunder all through the valleys and woodlands, and children tremble with fear, and women cover their heads with their aprons, and big men run and hide. I suppose there is nothing in the world so terrible to listen to as the growl of a Woozy."

"Please don't growl, then," begged Ojo, earnestly.

"There is no danger of my growling, for I am not angry. Only when angry do I utter my fearful, ear-splitting, soul-shuddering growl. Also, when I am angry, my eyes flash fire, whether I growl or not."

"Real fire?" asked Ojo.

"Of course, real fire. Do you suppose they'd flash imitation fire?" inquired the Woozy, in an injured tone.

"In that case, I've solved the riddle," cried Scraps, dancing with glee. "Those fence-boards are made of wood, and if the Woozy stands close to the fence and lets his eyes flash fire, they might set fire to the fence and burn it up. Then he could walk away with us easily, being free."

"Ah, I have never thought of that plan, or I would have been free long ago," said the Woozy. "But I cannot flash fire from my eyes unless I am very angry."

"Can't you get angry 'bout something, please?" asked Ojo.

"I'll try. You just say 'Krizzle-Kroo' to me."

"Will that make you angry?" inquired the boy.

"Terribly angry."

"What does it mean?" asked Scraps.

"I don't know; that's what makes me so angry," replied the Woozy.

He then stood close to the fence, with his head near one of the boards, and Scraps called out "Krizzle-Kroo!" Then Ojo said "Krizzle-Kroo!" and the Glass Cat said "Krizzle-Kroo!" The Woozy began to tremble with anger and small sparks darted from his eyes. Seeing this, they all cried "Krizzle-Kroo!" together, and that made the beast's eyes flash fire so fiercely that the fence-board caught the sparks and began to smoke. Then it burst into flame, and the Woozy stepped back and said triumphantly:

"Aha! That did the business, all right. It was a happy thought for you to yell all together, for that made me as angry as I have ever been. Fine sparks, weren't they?"

"Reg'lar fireworks," replied Scraps, admiringly.

In a few moments the board had burned to a distance of several feet, leaving an opening big enough for them all to pass through. Ojo broke some branches from a tree and with them whipped the fire until it was extinguished.

"We don't want to burn the whole fence down," said he, "for the flames would attract the attention of the Munchkin farmers, who would then come and capture the Woozy again. I guess they'll be rather surprised when they find he's escaped."

"So they will," declared the Woozy, chuckling gleefully. "When they find I'm gone the farmers will be badly scared, for they'll expect me to eat up their honey-bees, as I did before."

"That reminds me," said the boy, "that you must promise not to eat honey-bees while you are in our company."

"None at all?"

"Not a bee. You would get us all into trouble, and we can't afford to have any more trouble than is necessary. I'll feed you all the bread and cheese you want, and that must satisfy you."

"All right; I'll promise," said the Woozy, cheerfully. "And when I promise anything you can depend on it, 'cause I'm square."

"I don't see what difference that makes," observed the Patchwork Girl, as they found the path and continued their journey. "The shape doesn't make a thing honest, does it?"

"Of course it does," returned the Woozy, very decidedly. "No one could trust that Crooked Magician, for instance, just because he *is* crooked; but a square Woozy couldn't do anything crooked if he wanted to."

"I am neither square nor crooked," said Scraps, looking down at her plump body.

"No; you're round, so you're liable to do anything," asserted the Woozy. "Do not blame me, Miss Gorgeous, if I regard you with suspicion. Many a satin ribbon has a cotton back."

Scraps didn't understand this, but she had an uneasy misgiving that she had a cotton back herself. It would settle down, at times, and make her squat and dumpy, and then she had to roll herself in the road until her body stretched out again.

CHAPTER X

SHAGGY MAN TO THE RESCUE

THEY HAD NOT GONE VERY FAR BEFORE
Bungle, who had run on ahead, came
bounding back to say that the road of
yellow bricks was just before them. At
once they hurried forward to see what this
famous road looked like.

It was a broad road, but not straight,
for it wandered over hill and dale and
picked out the easiest places to go. All its
length and breadth was paved with smooth
bricks of a bright yellow color, so it was
smooth and level except in a few places
where the bricks had crumbled or been
removed, leaving holes that might cause
the unwary to stumble.

"I wonder," said Ojo, looking up and
down the road, "which way to go."

"Where are you bound for?" asked
the Woozy.

"The Emerald City," he replied.

"Then go west," said the Woozy. "I
know this road pretty well, for I've chased
many a honey-bee over it."

"Have you ever been to the Emerald City?" asked Scraps.

"No. I am very shy by nature, as you may have noticed, so I haven't mingled
much in society."

"Are you afraid of men?" inquired the Patchwork Girl.

"Me? With my heart-rending growl—my horrible, shudderful growl? I should
say not. I am not afraid of anything," declared the Woozy.

"I wish I could say the same," sighed Ojo. "I don't think we need be afraid when we get to the Emerald City, for Unc Nunkie has told me that Ozma, our girl Ruler, is very lovely and kind, and tries to help everyone who is in trouble. But they say there are many dangers lurking on the road to the great Fairy City, and so we must be very careful."

"I hope nothing will break me," said the Glass Cat, in a nervous voice. "I'm a little brittle, you know, and can't stand many hard knocks."

"If anything should fade the colors of my lovely patches it would break my heart," said the Patchwork Girl.

"I'm not sure you have a heart," Ojo reminded her.

"Then it would break my cotton," persisted Scraps. "Do you think they are all fast colors, Ojo?" she asked anxiously.

"They seem fast enough when you run," he replied; and then, looking ahead of them, he exclaimed: "Oh, what lovely trees!"

They were certainly pretty to look upon and the travelers hurried forward to observe them more closely.

"Why, they are not trees at all," said Scraps; "they are just monstrous plants."

That is what they really were: masses of great broad leaves which rose from the ground far into the air, until they towered twice as high as the top of the Patchwork Girl's head, who was a little taller than Ojo. The plants formed rows on both sides of the road and from each plant rose a dozen or more of the big broad leaves, which swayed continually from side to side, although no wind was blowing. But the most curious thing about the swaying leaves was their color. They seemed to have a general groundwork of blue, but here and there other colors glinted at times through the blue—gorgeous yellows, turning to pink, purple, orange and scarlet, mingled with more sober browns and grays—each appearing as a blotch or stripe anywhere on a leaf and then disappearing, to be replaced by some other color of a different shape.

The changeful coloring of the great leaves was very beautiful, but it was bewildering, as well, and the novelty of the scene drew our travelers close to the line of plants, where they stood watching them with rapt interest.

Suddenly a leaf bent lower than usual and touched the Patchwork Girl. Swiftly it enveloped her in its embrace, covering her completely in its thick folds, and then it swayed back upon its stem.

"Why, she's gone!" gasped Ojo, in amazement, and listening carefully he thought he could hear the muffled screams of Scraps coming from the center of the folded leaf. But, before he could think what he ought to do to save her, another leaf bent down and captured the Glass Cat, rolling around the little creature until she was completely hidden, and then straightening up again upon its stem.

"Look out," cried the Woozy. "Run! Run fast, or you are lost."

Ojo turned and saw the Woozy running swiftly up the road. But the last leaf of the row of plants seized the beast even as he ran and instantly he disappeared from sight.

The boy had no chance to escape. Half a dozen of the great leaves were bending toward him from different directions and as he stood hesitating one of them clutched him in its embrace. In a flash he was in the dark. Then he felt himself gently lifted until he was swaying in the air, with the folds of the leaf hugging him on all sides.

At first he struggled hard to escape, crying out in anger: "Let me go! Let me go!" But neither struggles nor protests had any effect whatever. The leaf held him firmly and he was a prisoner.

Then Ojo quieted himself and tried to think. Despair fell upon him when he remembered that all his little party had been captured, even as he was, and there was none to save them.

"I might have expected it," he sobbed, miserably. "I'm Ojo the Unlucky, and something dreadful was sure to happen to me."

He pushed against the leaf that held him and found it to be soft, but thick and firm. It was like a great bandage all around him and he found it difficult to move his body or limbs in order to change their position.

The minutes passed and became hours. Ojo wondered how long one could live in such a condition and if the leaf would gradually sap his strength and even his life, in order to feed itself. The little Munchkin boy had never heard of any person dying in the Land of Oz, but he knew one could suffer a great deal of pain. His greatest fear at this time was that he would always remain imprisoned in the beautiful leaf and never see the light of day again.

No sound came to him through the leaf; all around was intense silence. Ojo wondered if Scraps had stopped screaming, or if the folds of the leaf prevented his hearing her. By and by he thought he heard a whistle, as of some one whistling a tune. Yes; it really must be some one whistling, he decided, for he could follow the strains of a pretty Munchkin melody that Unc Nunkie used to sing to him. The sounds were low and sweet and, although they reached Ojo's ears very faintly, they were clear and harmonious.

Could the leaf whistle, Ojo wondered? Nearer and nearer came the sounds and then they seemed to be just the other side of the leaf that was hugging him.

Suddenly the whole leaf toppled and fell, carrying the boy with it, and while he sprawled at full length the folds slowly relaxed and set him free. He scrambled quickly to his feet and found that a strange man was standing before him—a man so curious in appearance that the boy stared with round eyes.

He was a big man, with shaggy whiskers, shaggy eyebrows, shaggy hair—but kindly blue eyes that were gentle as those of a cow. On his head was a green velvet hat with a jeweled band, which was all shaggy around the brim. Rich but shaggy laces were at his throat; a coat with shaggy edges was decorated with diamond buttons; the velvet breeches had jeweled buckles at the knees and shags all around the bottoms. On his breast hung a medallion bearing a picture of Princess Dorothy of Oz, and in his hand, as he stood looking at Ojo, was a sharp knife shaped like a dagger.

"Oh!" exclaimed Ojo, greatly astonished at the sight of this stranger; and then he added: "Who has saved me, sir?"

"Can't you see?" replied the other, with a smile; "I'm the Shaggy Man."

"Yes; I can see that," said the boy, nodding. "Was it you who rescued me from the leaf?"

"None other, you may be sure. But take care, or I shall have to rescue you again."

Ojo gave a jump, for he saw several broad leaves leaning toward him; but the Shaggy Man began to whistle again, and at the sound the leaves all straightened up on their stems and kept still.

The man now took Ojo's arm and led him up the road, past the last of the great plants, and not till he was safely beyond their reach did he cease his whistling.

"You see, the music charms 'em," said he. "Singing or whistling—it doesn't matter which—makes 'em behave, and nothing else will. I always whistle as I go by 'em and so they always let me alone. To-day as I went by, whistling, I saw a leaf curled and knew there must be something inside it. I cut down the leaf with my knife and—out you popped. Lucky I passed by, wasn't it?"

"You were very kind," said Ojo, "and I thank you. Will you please rescue my companions, also?"

"What companions?" asked the Shaggy Man.

"The leaves grabbed them all," said the boy. "There's a Patchwork Girl and—"

"A what?"

"A girl made of patchwork, you know. She's alive and her name is Scraps. And there's a Glass Cat—"

"Glass?" asked the Shaggy Man.

"All glass."

"And alive?"

"Yes," said Ojo; "she has pink brains. And there's a Woozy—"

"What's a Woozy?" inquired the Shaggy Man.

"Why, I—I—can't describe it," answered the boy, greatly perplexed. "But it's a queer animal with three hairs on the tip of its tail that won't come out and—"

"What won't come out?" asked the Shaggy Man; "the tail?"

"The hairs won't come out. But you'll see the Woozy, if you'll please rescue it, and then you'll know just what it is."

"Of course," said the Shaggy Man, nodding his shaggy head. And then he walked back among the plants, still whistling, and found the three leaves which were curled around Ojo's traveling companions. The first leaf he cut down released Scraps, and on seeing her the Shaggy Man threw back his shaggy head, opened wide his mouth and laughed so shaggily and yet so merrily that Scraps liked him at once. Then he took off his hat and made her a low bow, saying:

"My dear, you're a wonder. I must introduce you to my friend the Scarecrow."

When he cut down the second leaf he rescued the Glass Cat, and Bungle was so frightened that she scampered away like a streak and soon had joined Ojo, when she sat beside him panting and trembling. The last plant of all the row had captured the Woozy, and a big bunch in the center of the curled leaf showed plainly where he was. With his sharp knife the Shaggy Man sliced off the stem of the leaf and as it fell and unfolded out trotted the Woozy and escaped beyond the reach of any more of the dangerous plants.

CHAPTER XI

A GOOD FRIEND

SOON THE ENTIRE PARTY WAS GATHERED on the road of yellow bricks, quite beyond the reach of the beautiful but treacherous plants. The Shaggy Man, staring first at one and then at the other, seemed greatly pleased and interested.

"I've seen queer things since I came to the Land of Oz," said he, "but never anything queerer than this band of adventurers. Let us sit down a while, and have a talk and get acquainted."

"Haven't you always lived in the Land of Oz?" asked the Munchkin boy.

"No; I used to live in the big, outside world. But I came here once with Dorothy, and Ozma let me stay."

"How do you like Oz?" asked Scraps. "Isn't the country and the climate grand?"

"It's the finest country in all the world, even if it is a fairyland, and I'm happy every minute I live in it," said the Shaggy Man. "But tell me something about yourselves."

So Ojo related the story of his visit to the house of the Crooked Magician, and how he met there the Glass Cat, and how the Patchwork Girl was brought to life and of the terrible accident to Unc Nunkie and Margolotte. Then he told how he had set out to find the five different things which the Magician needed to make a charm that would restore the marble figures to life, one requirement being three hairs from a Woozy's tail.

"We found the Woozy," explained the boy, "and he agreed to give us the three hairs; but we couldn't pull them out. So we had to bring the Woozy along with us."

"I see," returned the Shaggy Man, who had listened with interest to the story. "But perhaps I, who am big and strong, can pull those three hairs from the Woozy's tail."

"Try it, if you like," said the Woozy.

So the Shaggy Man tried it, but pull as hard as he could he failed to get the hairs out of the Woozy's tail. So he sat down again and wiped his shaggy face with a shaggy silk handkerchief and said:

"It doesn't matter. If you can keep the Woozy until you get the rest of the things you need, you can take the beast and his three hairs to the Crooked Magician and let him find a way to extract 'em. What are the other things you are to find?"

"One," said Ojo, "is a six-leaved clover."

"You ought to find that in the fields around the Emerald City," said the Shaggy Man. "There is a law against picking six-leaved clovers, but I think I can get Ozma to let you have one."

"Thank you," replied Ojo. "The next thing is the left wing of a yellow butterfly."

"For that you must go to the Winkie Country," the Shaggy Man declared. "I've never noticed any butterflies there, but that is the yellow country of Oz and it's ruled by a good friend of mine, the Tin Woodman."

"Oh, I've heard of him!" exclaimed Ojo. "He must be a wonderful man."

"So he is, and his heart is wonderfully kind. I'm sure the Tin Woodman will do all in his power to help you to save your Unc Nunkie and poor Margolotte."

"The next thing I must find," said the Munchkin boy, "is a gill of water from a dark well."

"Indeed! Well, that is more difficult," said the Shaggy Man, scratching his left ear in a puzzled way. "I've never heard of a dark well; have you?"

"No," said Ojo.

"Do you know where one may be found?" inquired the Shaggy Man.

"I can't imagine," said Ojo.

"Then we must ask the Scarecrow."

"The Scarecrow! But surely, sir, a scarecrow can't know anything."

"Most scarecrows don't, I admit," answered the Shaggy Man. "But this Scarecrow of whom I speak is very intelligent. He claims to possess the best brains in all Oz."

"Better than mine?" asked Scraps.

"Better than mine?" echoed the Glass Cat. "Mine are pink, and you can see 'em work."

"Well, you can't see the Scarecrow's brains work, but they do a lot of clever thinking," asserted the Shaggy Man. "If anyone knows where a dark well is, it's my friend the Scarecrow."

"Where does he live?" inquired Ojo.

"He has a splendid castle in the Winkie Country, near to the palace of his friend the Tin Woodman, and he is often to be found in the Emerald City, where he visits Dorothy at the royal palace."

"Then we will ask him about the dark well," said Ojo.

"But what else does this Crooked Magician want?" asked the Shaggy Man.

"A drop of oil from a live man's body."

"Oh; but there isn't such a thing."

"That is what I thought," replied Ojo; "but the Crooked Magician said it wouldn't be called for by the recipe if it couldn't be found, and therefore I must search until I find it."

"I wish you good luck," said the Shaggy Man, shaking his head doubtfully; "but I imagine you'll have a hard job getting a drop of oil from a live man's body. There's blood in a body, but no oil."

"There's cotton in mine," said Scraps, dancing a little jig.

"I don't doubt it," returned the Shaggy Man admiringly. "You're a regular comforter and as sweet as patchwork can be. All you lack is dignity."

"I hate dignity," cried Scraps, kicking a pebble high in the air and then trying to catch it as it fell. "Half the fools and all the wise folks are dignified, and I'm neither the one nor the other."

"She's just crazy," explained the Glass Cat.

The Shaggy Man laughed.

"She's delightful, in her way," he said. "I'm sure Dorothy will be pleased with her, and the Scarecrow will dote on her. Did you say you were traveling toward the Emerald City?"

"Yes," replied Ojo. "I thought that the best place to go, at first, because the six-leaved clover may be found there."

"I'll go with you," said the Shaggy Man, "and show you the way."

"Thank you," exclaimed Ojo. "I hope it won't put you out any."

"No," said the other, "I wasn't going anywhere in particular. I've been a rover all my life, and although Ozma has given me a suite of beautiful rooms in her palace I still get the wandering fever once in a while and start out to roam the country over. I've been away from the Emerald City several weeks, this time, and now that I've met you and your friends I'm sure it will interest me to accompany you to the great city of Oz and introduce you to my friends."

"That will be very nice," said the boy, gratefully.

"I hope your friends are not dignified," observed Scraps.

"Some are, and some are not," he answered; "but I never criticise my friends. If they are really true friends, they may be anything they like, for all of me."

"There's some sense in that," said Scraps, nodding her queer head in approval. "Come on, and let's get to the Emerald City as soon as possible." With this she ran up the path, skipping and dancing, and then turned to await them.

"It is quite a distance from here to the Emerald City," remarked the Shaggy Man, "so we shall not get there to-day, nor to-morrow. Therefore let us take the jaunt in an easy manner. I'm an old traveler and have found that I never gain anything by being in a hurry. 'Take it easy' is my motto. If you can't take it easy, take it as easy as you can."

After walking some distance over the road of yellow bricks Ojo said he was hungry and would stop to eat some bread and cheese. He offered a portion of the food to the Shaggy Man, who thanked him but refused it.

"When I start out on my travels," said he, "I carry along enough square meals to last me several weeks. Think I'll indulge in one now, as long as we're stopping anyway."

Saying this, he took a bottle from his pocket and shook from it a tablet about the size of one of Ojo's finger-nails.

"That," announced the Shaggy Man, "is a square meal, in condensed form. Invention of the great Professor Woggle-Bug, of the Royal College of Athletics. It contains soup, fish, roast meat, salad, apple-dumplings, ice cream and chocolate-drops, all boiled down to this small size, so it can be conveniently carried and swallowed when you are hungry and need a square meal."

"I'm square," said the Woozy. "Give me one, please."

So the Shaggy Man gave the Woozy a tablet from his bottle and the beast ate it in a twinkling.

"You have now had a six course dinner," declared the Shaggy Man.

"Pshaw!" said the Woozy, ungratefully, "I want to taste something. There's no fun in that sort of eating."

"One should only eat to sustain life," replied the Shaggy Man, "and that tablet is equal to a peck of other food."

"I don't care for it. I want something I can chew and taste," grumbled the Woozy.

"You are quite wrong, my poor beast," said the Shaggy Man in a tone of pity. "Think how tired your jaws would get chewing a square meal like this, if it were not condensed to the size of a small tablet—which you can swallow in a jiffy."

"Chewing isn't tiresome; it's fun," maintained the Woozy. "I always chew the honey-bees when I catch them. Give me some bread and cheese, Ojo."

"No, no! You've already eaten a big dinner!" protested the Shaggy Man.

"May be," answered the Woozy; "but I guess I'll fool myself by munching some bread and cheese. I may not be hungry, having eaten all those things you gave me, but I consider this eating business a matter of taste, and I like to realize what's going into me."

Ojo gave the beast what he wanted, but the Shaggy Man shook his shaggy head reproachfully and said there was no animal so obstinate or hard to convince as a Woozy.

At this moment a patter of footsteps was heard, and looking up they saw the live phonograph standing before them. It seemed to have passed through many adventures since Ojo and his comrades last saw the machine, for the varnish of its wooden case was all marred and dented and scratched in a way that gave it an aged and disreputable appearance.

"Dear me!" exclaimed Ojo, staring hard. "What has happened to you?"

"Nothing much," replied the phonograph in a sad and depressed voice. "I've had enough things thrown at me, since I left you, to stock a department store and furnish half a dozen bargain-counters."

"Are you so broken up that you can't play?" asked Scraps.

"No; I still am able to grind out delicious music. Just now I've a record on tap that is really superb," said the phonograph, growing more cheerful.

"That is too bad," remarked Ojo. "We've no objection to you as a machine, you know; but as a music-maker we hate you."

"Then why was I ever invented?" demanded the machine, in a tone of indignant protest.

They looked at one another inquiringly, but no one could answer such a puzzling question. Finally the Shaggy Man said:

"I'd like to hear the phonograph play."

Ojo sighed. "We've been very happy since we met you, sir," he said.

"I know. But a little misery, at times, makes one appreciate happiness more. Tell me, Phony, what is this record like, which you say you have on tap?"

"It's a popular song, sir. In all civilized lands the common people have gone wild over it."

"Makes civilized folks wild folks, eh? Then it's dangerous."

"Wild with joy, I mean," explained the phonograph. "Listen. This song will prove a rare treat to you, I know. It made the author rich—for an author. It is called 'My Lulu.'"

Then the phonograph began to play. A strain of odd, jerky sounds was followed by these words, sung by a man through his nose with great vigor of expression:

> "Ah wants mah Lulu, mah coal-black Lulu;
> Ah wants mah loo-loo, loo-loo, loo-loo, Lu!
> Ah loves mah Lulu, mah coal-black Lulu,
> There ain't nobody else loves loo-loo, Lu!"

"Here—shut that off!" cried the Shaggy Man, springing to his feet. "What do you mean by such impertinence?"

"It's the latest popular song," declared the phonograph, speaking in a sulky tone of voice.

"A popular song?"

"Yes. One that the feeble-minded can remember the words of and those ignorant of music can whistle or sing. That makes a popular song popular, and the time is coming when it will take the place of all other songs."

"That time won't come to us, just yet," said the Shaggy Man, sternly: "I'm something of a singer myself, and I don't intend to be throttled by any Lulus like your coal-black one. I shall take you all apart, Mr. Phony, and scatter your pieces far and wide over the country, as a matter of kindness to the people you might meet if allowed to run around loose. Having performed this painful duty I shall—"

But before he could say more the phonograph turned and dashed up the road as fast as its four table-legs could carry it, and soon it had entirely disappeared from their view.

The Shaggy Man sat down again and seemed well pleased. "Some one else will save me the trouble of scattering that phonograph," said he; "for it is not possible that such a music-maker can last long in the Land of Oz. When you are rested, friends, let us go on our way."

During the afternoon the travelers found themselves in a lonely and uninhabited part of the country. Even the fields were no longer cultivated and the country began to resemble a wilderness. The road of yellow bricks seemed to have been neglected and became uneven and more difficult to walk upon. Scrubby underbrush grew on either side of the way, while huge rocks were scattered around in abundance.

But this did not deter Ojo and his friends from trudging on, and they beguiled the journey with jokes and cheerful conversation. Toward evening they reached a crystal spring which gushed from a tall rock by the roadside and near this spring stood a deserted cabin. Said the Shaggy Man, halting here:

"We may as well pass the night here, where there is shelter for our heads and good water to drink. Road beyond here is pretty bad; worst we shall have to travel; so let's wait until morning before we tackle it."

They agreed to this and Ojo found some brushwood in the cabin and made a fire on the hearth. The fire delighted Scraps, who danced before it until Ojo warned her she might set fire to herself and burn up. After that the Patchwork Girl kept at a respectful distance from the darting flames, but the Woozy lay down before the fire like a big dog and seemed to enjoy its warmth.

For supper the Shaggy Man ate one of his tablets, but Ojo stuck to his bread and cheese as the most satisfying food. He also gave a portion to the Woozy.

When darkness came on and they sat in a circle on the cabin floor, facing the fire-light—there being no furniture of any sort in the place—Ojo said to the Shaggy Man:

"Won't you tell us a story?"

"I'm not good at stories," was the reply; "but I sing like a bird."

"Raven, or crow?" asked the Glass Cat.

"Like a song bird. I'll prove it. I'll sing a song I composed myself. Don't tell anyone I'm a poet; they might want me to write a book. Don't tell 'em I can sing, or they'd want me to make records for that awful phonograph. Haven't time to be a public benefactor, so I'll just sing you this little song for your own amusement."

They were glad enough to be entertained, and listened with interest while the Shaggy Man chanted the following verses to a tune that was not unpleasant:

"I'll sing a song of Ozland, where wondrous creatures dwell
And fruits and flowers and shady bowers abound in every dell,
Where magic is a science and where no one shows surprise
If some amazing thing takes place before his very eyes.

Our Ruler's a bewitching girl whom fairies love to please;
She's always kept her magic sceptre to enforce decrees
To make her people happy, for her heart is kind and true
And to aid the needy and distressed is what she longs to do.

And then there's Princess Dorothy, as sweet as any rose,
A lass from Kansas, where they don't grow fairies, I suppose;
And there's the brainy Scarecrow, with a body stuffed with straw,
Who utters words of wisdom rare that fill us all with awe.

I'll not forget Nick Chopper, the Woodman made of Tin,
Whose tender heart thinks killing time is quite a dreadful sin,
Nor old Professor Woggle-Bug, who's highly magnified
And looks so big to everyone that he is filled with pride.

Jack Pumpkinhead's a dear old chum who might be called a chump,
But won renown by riding round upon a magic Gump;
The Saw-Horse is a splendid steed and though he's made of wood
He does as many thrilling stunts as any meat horse could.

And now I'll introduce a beast that ev'ryone adores—
The Cowardly Lion shakes with fear 'most ev'ry time he roars,
And yet he does the bravest things that any lion might,
Because he knows that cowardice is not considered right.

There's Tik-Tok—he's a clockwork man and quite a funny sight—
He talks and walks mechanically, when he's wound up tight;
And we've a Hungry Tiger who would babies love to eat
But never does because we feed him other kinds of meat.

It's hard to name all of the freaks this noble Land's acquired;
'Twould make my song so very long that you would soon be tired;
But give attention while I mention one wise Yellow Hen
And Nine fine Tiny Piglets living in a golden pen.

Just search the whole world over—sail the seas from coast to coast—
No other nation in creation queerer folks can boast;
And now our rare museum will include a cat of glass,
A Woozy, and—last but not least—a crazy Patchwork Lass."

Ojo was so pleased with this song that he applauded the singer by clapping his hands, and Scraps followed suit by clapping her padded fingers together, although they made no noise. The cat pounded on the floor with her glass paws—gently, so as not to break them—and the Woozy, which had been asleep, woke up to ask what the row was about.

"I seldom sing in public, for fear they might want me to start an opera company," remarked the Shaggy Man, who was pleased to know his effort was appreciated. "Voice, just now, is a little out of training; rusty, perhaps."

"Tell me," said the Patchwork Girl earnestly, "do all those queer people you mention really live in the Land of Oz?"

"Every one of 'em. I even forgot one thing: Dorothy's Pink Kitten."

"For goodness sake!" exclaimed Bungle, sitting up and looking interested. "A Pink Kitten? How absurd! Is it glass?"

"No; just ordinary kitten."

"Then it can't amount to much. I have pink brains, and you can see 'em work."

"Dorothy's kitten is all pink—brains and all—except blue eyes. Name's Eureka. Great favorite at the royal palace," said the Shaggy Man, yawning.

The Glass Cat seemed annoyed.

"Do you think a pink kitten—common meat—is as pretty as I am?" she asked.

"Can't say. Tastes differ, you know," replied the Shaggy Man, yawning again. "But here's a pointer that may be of service to you: make friends with Eureka and you'll be solid at the palace."

"I'm solid now; solid glass."

"You don't understand," rejoined the Shaggy Man, sleepily. "Anyhow, make friends with the Pink Kitten and you'll be all right. If the Pink Kitten despises you, look out for breakers."

"Would anyone at the royal palace break a Glass Cat?"

"Might. You never can tell. Advise you to purr soft and look humble—if you can. And now I'm going to bed."

Bungle considered the Shaggy Man's advice so carefully that her pink brains were busy long after the others of the party were fast asleep.

CHAPTER XII

THE GIANT PORCUPINE

NEXT MORNING THEY STARTED OUT bright and early to follow the road of yellow bricks toward the Emerald City. The little Munchkin boy was beginning to feel tired from the long walk, and he had a great many things to think of and consider besides the events of the journey. At the wonderful Emerald City, which he would presently reach, were so many strange and curious people that he was half afraid of meeting them and wondered if they would prove friendly and kind. Above all else, he could not drive from his mind the important errand on which he had come, and he was determined to devote every energy to finding the things that were necessary to prepare the magic recipe. He believed that until dear Unc Nunkie was restored to life he could feel no joy in anything, and often he wished that Unc could be with him, to see all the astonishing things Ojo was seeing. But alas Unc Nunkie was now a marble statue in the house of the Crooked Magician and Ojo must not falter in his efforts to save him.

The country through which they were passing was still rocky and deserted, with here and there a bush or a tree to break the dreary landscape. Ojo noticed one tree, especially, because it had such long, silky leaves and was so beautiful in shape. As he approached it he studied the tree earnestly, wondering if any fruit grew on it or if it bore pretty flowers.

Suddenly he became aware that he had been looking at that tree a long time—at least for five minutes—and it had remained in the same position, although the boy had continued to walk steadily on. So he stopped short, and when he stopped, the tree and all the landscape, as well as his companions, moved on before him and left him far behind.

Ojo uttered such a cry of astonishment that it aroused the Shaggy Man, who also halted. The others then stopped, too, and walked back to the boy.

"What's wrong?" asked the Shaggy Man.

"Why, we're not moving forward a bit, no matter how fast we walk," declared Ojo. "Now that we have stopped, we are moving backward! Can't you see? Just notice that rock."

Scraps looked down at her feet and said: "The yellow bricks are not moving."

"But the whole road is," answered Ojo.

"True; quite true," agreed the Shaggy Man. "I know all about the tricks of this road, but I have been thinking of something else and didn't realize where we were."

"It will carry us back to where we started from," predicted Ojo, beginning to be nervous.

"No," replied the Shaggy Man; "it won't do that, for I know a trick to beat this tricky road. I've traveled this way before, you know. Turn around, all of you, and walk backward."

"What good will that do?" asked the cat.

"You'll find out, if you obey me," said the Shaggy Man.

So they all turned their backs to the direction in which they wished to go and began walking backward. In an instant Ojo noticed they were gaining ground and as they proceeded in this curious way they soon passed the tree which had first attracted his attention to their difficulty.

"How long must we keep this up, Shags?" asked Scraps, who was constantly tripping and tumbling down, only to get up again with a laugh at her mishap.

"Just a little way farther," replied the Shaggy Man.

A few minutes later he called to them to turn about quickly and step forward, and as they obeyed the order they found themselves treading solid ground.

"That task is well over," observed the Shaggy Man. "It's a little tiresome to walk backward, but that is the only way to pass this part of the road, which has a trick of sliding back and carrying with it anyone who is walking upon it."

With new courage and energy they now trudged forward and after a time came to a place where the road cut through a low hill, leaving high banks on either side of it. They were traveling along this cut, talking together, when the Shaggy Man seized Scraps with one arm and Ojo with another and shouted: "Stop!"

"What's wrong now?" asked the Patchwork Girl.

"See there!" answered the Shaggy Man, pointing with his finger.

Directly in the center of the road lay a motionless object that bristled all over with sharp quills, which resembled arrows. The body was as big as a ten-bushel-basket, but the projecting quills made it appear to be four times bigger.

"Well, what of it?" asked Scraps.

"That is Chiss, who causes a lot of trouble along this road," was the reply.

"Chiss! What is Chiss?

"I think it is merely an overgrown porcupine, but here in Oz they consider Chiss an evil spirit. He's different from a reg'lar porcupine, because he can throw his quills in any direction, which an American porcupine cannot do. That's what makes old Chiss so dangerous. If we get too near, he'll fire those quills at us and hurt us badly."

"Then we will be foolish to get too near," said Scraps.

"I'm not afraid," declared the Woozy. "The Chiss is cowardly, I'm sure, and if it ever heard my awful, terrible, frightful growl, it would be scared stiff."

"Oh; can you growl?" asked the Shaggy Man.

"That is the only ferocious thing about me," asserted the Woozy with evident pride. "My growl makes an earthquake blush and the thunder ashamed of itself. If I growled at that creature you call Chiss, it would immediately think the world had cracked in two and bumped against the sun and moon, and that would cause the monster to run as far and as fast as its legs could carry it."

"In that case," said the Shaggy Man, "you are now able to do us all a great favor. Please growl."

"But you forget," returned the Woozy; "my tremendous growl would also frighten you, and if you happen to have heart disease you might expire."

"True; but we must take that risk," decided the Shaggy Man, bravely. "Being warned of what is to occur we must try to bear the terrific noise of your growl; but Chiss won't expect it, and it will scare him away."

The Woozy hesitated.

"I'm fond of you all, and I hate to shock you," it said.

"Never mind," said Ojo.

"You may be made deaf."

"If so, we will forgive you."

"Very well, then," said the Woozy in a determined voice, and advanced a few steps toward the giant porcupine. Pausing to look back, it asked: "All ready?"

"All ready!" they answered.

"Then cover up your ears and brace yourselves firmly. Now, then—look out!"

The Woozy turned toward Chiss, opened wide its mouth and said:

"Quee-ee-ee-eek."

"Go ahead and growl," said Scraps.

"Why, I—I *did* growl!" retorted the Woozy, who seemed much astonished.

"What, that little squeak?" she cried.

"It is the most awful growl that ever was heard, on land or sea, in caverns or in the sky," protested the Woozy. "I wonder you stood the shock so well. Didn't you feel the ground tremble? I suppose Chiss is now quite dead with fright."

The Shaggy Man laughed merrily.

"Poor Wooz!" said he; "your growl wouldn't scare a fly."

The Woozy seemed to be humiliated and surprised. It hung its head a moment, as if in shame or sorrow, but then it said with renewed confidence: "Anyhow, my eyes can flash fire; and good fire, too; good enough to set fire to a fence!"

"That is true," declared Scraps; "I saw it done myself. But your ferocious growl isn't as loud as the tick of a beetle—or one of Ojo's snores when he's fast asleep."

"Perhaps," said the Woozy, humbly, "I have been mistaken about my growl. It has always sounded very fearful to me, but that may have been because it was so close to my ears."

"Never mind," Ojo said soothingly; "it is a great talent to be able to flash fire from your eyes. No one else can do that."

As they stood hesitating what to do Chiss stirred and suddenly a shower of quills came flying toward them, almost filling the air, they were so many. Scraps realized in an instant that they had gone too near to Chiss for safety, so she sprang in front of Ojo and shielded him from the darts, which stuck their points into her own body until she resembled one of those targets they shoot arrows at in archery games. The Shaggy Man dropped flat on his face to avoid the shower, but one quill struck him in the leg and went far in. As for the Glass Cat, the quills rattled off her body without making even a scratch, and the skin of the Woozy was so thick and tough that he was not hurt at all.

When the attack was over they all ran to the Shaggy Man, who was moaning and groaning, and Scraps promptly pulled the quill out of his leg. Then up he jumped and ran over to Chiss, putting his foot on the monster's neck and holding it a prisoner. The body of the great porcupine was now as smooth as leather, except for the holes where the quills had been, for it had shot every single quill in that one wicked shower.

"Let me go!" it shouted angrily. "How dare you put your foot on Chiss?"

"I'm going to do worse than that, old boy," replied the Shaggy Man. "You have annoyed travelers on this road long enough, and now I shall put an end to you."

"You can't!" returned Chiss. "Nothing can kill me, as you know perfectly well."

"Perhaps that is true," said the Shaggy Man in a tone of disappointment. "Seems to me I've been told before that you can't be killed. But if I let you go, what will you do?"

"Pick up my quills again," said Chiss in a sulky voice.

"And then shoot them at more travelers? No; that won't do. You must promise me to stop throwing quills at people."

"I won't promise anything of the sort," declared Chiss.

"Why not?"

"Because it is my nature to throw quills, and every animal must do what Nature intends it to do. It isn't fair for you to blame me. If it were wrong for me to throw quills, then I wouldn't be made with quills to throw. The proper thing for you to do is to keep out of my way."

"Why, there's some sense in that argument," admitted the Shaggy Man, thoughtfully; "but people who are strangers, and don't know you are here, won't be able to keep out of your way."

"Tell you what," said Scraps, who was trying to pull the quills out of her own body, "let's gather up all the quills and take them away with us; then old Chiss won't have any left to throw at people."

"Ah, that's a clever idea. You and Ojo must gather up the quills while I hold Chiss a prisoner; for, if I let him go, he will get some of his quills and be able to throw them again."

So Scraps and Ojo picked up all the quills and tied them in a bundle so they might easily be carried. After this the Shaggy Man released Chiss and let him go, knowing that he was harmless to injure anyone.

"It's the meanest trick I ever heard of," muttered the porcupine gloomily. "How would you like it, Shaggy Man, if I took all your shags away from you?"

"If I threw my shags and hurt people, you would be welcome to capture them," was the reply.

Then they walked on and left Chiss standing in the road sullen and disconsolate. The Shaggy Man limped as he walked, for his wound still hurt him, and Scraps was much annoyed because the quills had left a number of small holes in her patches.

When they came to a flat stone by the roadside the Shaggy Man sat down to rest, and then Ojo opened his basket and took out the bundle of charms the Crooked Magician had given him.

"I am Ojo the Unlucky," he said, "or we would never have met that dreadful porcupine. But I will see if I can find anything among these charms which will cure your leg."

Soon he discovered that one of the charms was labeled: "For flesh wounds," and this the boy separated from the others. It was only a bit of dried root, taken from some unknown shrub, but the boy rubbed it upon the wound made by the quill and in a few moments the place was healed entirely and the Shaggy Man's leg was as good as ever.

"Rub it on the holes in my patches," suggested Scraps, and Ojo tried it, but without any effect.

"The charm you need is a needle and thread," said the Shaggy Man. "But do not worry, my dear; those holes do not look badly, at all."

"They'll let in the air, and I don't want people to think I'm airy, or that I've been stuck up," said the Patchwork Girl.

"You were certainly stuck up until we pulled out those quills," observed Ojo, with a laugh.

So now they went on again and coming presently to a pond of muddy water they tied a heavy stone to the bundle of quills and sunk it to the bottom of the pond, to avoid carrying it farther.

CHAPTER XIII

SCRAPS AND THE SCARECROW

FROM HERE ON THE COUNTRY IMPROVED and the desert places began to give way to fertile spots; still no houses were yet to be seen near the road. There were some hills, with valleys between them, and on reaching the top of one of these hills the travelers found before them a high wall, running to the right and the left as far as their eyes could reach. Immediately in front of them, where the wall crossed the roadway, stood a gate having stout iron bars that extended from top to bottom. They found, on coming nearer, that this gate was locked with a great padlock, rusty through lack of use.

"Well," said Scraps, "I guess we'll stop here."

"It's a good guess," replied Ojo. "Our way is barred by this great wall and gate. It looks as if no one had passed through in many years."

"Looks are deceiving," declared the Shaggy Man, laughing at their disappointed faces, "and this barrier is the most deceiving thing in all Oz."

"It prevents our going any farther, anyhow," said Scraps. "There is no one to mind the gate and let people through, and we've no key to the padlock."

"True," replied Ojo, going a little nearer to peep through the bars of the gate. "What shall we do, Shaggy Man? If we had wings we might fly over the wall, but we cannot climb it and unless we get to the Emerald City I won't be able to find the things to restore Unc Nunkie to life."

"All very true," answered the Shaggy Man, quietly; "but I know this gate, having passed through it many times."

"How?" they all eagerly inquired.

"I'll show you how," said he. He stood Ojo in the middle of the road and placed Scraps just behind him, with her padded hands on his shoulders. After the Patchwork Girl came the Woozy, who held a part of her skirt in his mouth. Then, last of all, was the Glass Cat, holding fast to the Woozy's tail with her glass jaws.

"Now," said the Shaggy Man, "you must all shut your eyes tight, and keep them shut until I tell you to open them."

"I can't," objected Scraps. "My eyes are buttons, and they won't shut."

So the Shaggy Man tied his red handkerchief over the Patchwork Girl's eyes and examined all the others to make sure they had their eyes fast shut and could see nothing.

"What's the game, anyhow—blind-man's-buff?" asked Scraps.

"Keep quiet!" commanded the Shaggy Man, sternly. "All ready? Then follow me."

He took Ojo's hand and led him forward over the road of yellow bricks, toward the gate. Holding fast to one another they all followed in a row, expecting every

minute to bump against the iron bars. The Shaggy Man also had his eyes closed, but marched straight ahead, nevertheless, and after he had taken one hundred steps, by actual count, he stopped and said:

"Now you may open your eyes."

They did so, and to their astonishment found the wall and the gateway far behind them, while in front the former Blue Country of the Munchkins had given way to green fields, with pretty farm-houses scattered among them.

"That wall," explained the Shaggy Man, "is what is called an optical illusion. It is quite real while you have your eyes open, but if you are not looking at it the barrier doesn't exist at all. It's the same way with many other evils in life; they seem to exist, and yet it's all seeming and not true. You will notice that the wall—or what we thought was a wall—separates the Munchkin Country from the green country that surrounds the Emerald City, which lies exactly in the center of Oz. There are two roads of yellow bricks through the Munchkin Country, but the one we followed is the best of the two. Dorothy once traveled the other way, and met with more dangers than we did. But all our troubles are over for the present, as another day's journey will bring us to the great Emerald City."

They were delighted to know this, and proceeded with new courage. In a couple of hours they stopped at a farm-house, where the people were very hospitable and invited them to dinner. The farm folk regarded Scraps with much curiosity but no great astonishment, for they were accustomed to seeing extraordinary people in the Land of Oz.

The woman of this house got her needle and thread and sewed up the holes made by the porcupine quills in the Patchwork Girl's body, after which Scraps was assured she looked as beautiful as ever.

"You ought to have a hat to wear," remarked the woman, "for that would keep the sun from fading the colors of your face. I have some patches and scraps put away,

and if you will wait two or three days I'll make you a lovely hat that will match the rest of you."

"Never mind the hat," said Scraps, shaking her yarn braids; "it's a kind offer, but we can't stop. I can't see that my colors have faded a particle, as yet; can you?"

"Not much," replied the woman. "You are still very gorgeous, in spite of your long journey."

The children of the house wanted to keep the Glass Cat to play with, so Bungle was offered a good home if she would remain; but the cat was too much interested in Ojo's adventures and refused to stop.

"Children are rough playmates," she remarked to the Shaggy Man, "and although this home is more pleasant than that of the Crooked Magician I fear I would soon be smashed to pieces by the boys and girls."

After they had rested themselves they renewed their journey, finding the road now smooth and pleasant to walk upon and the country growing more beautiful the nearer they drew to the Emerald City.

By and by Ojo began to walk on the green grass, looking carefully around him.

"What are you trying to find?" asked Scraps.

"A six-leaved clover," said he.

"Don't do that!" exclaimed the Shaggy Man, earnestly. "It's against the law to pick a six-leaved clover. You must wait until you get Ozma's consent."

"She wouldn't know it," declared the boy.

"Ozma knows many things," said the Shaggy Man. "In her room is a Magic Picture that shows any scene in the Land of Oz where strangers or travelers happen to be. She may be watching the picture of us even now, and noticing everything that we do."

"Does she always watch the Magic Picture?" asked Ojo.

"Not always, for she has many other things to do; but, as I said, she may be watching us this very minute."

"I don't care," said Ojo, in an obstinate tone of voice; "Ozma's only a girl."

The Shaggy Man looked at him in surprise.

"You ought to care for Ozma," said he, "if you expect to save your uncle. For, if you displease our powerful Ruler, your journey will surely prove a failure; whereas, if you make a friend of Ozma, she will gladly assist you. As for her being a girl, that is another reason why you should obey her laws, if you are courteous and polite. Everyone in Oz loves Ozma and hates her enemies, for she is as just as she is powerful."

Ojo sulked a while, but finally returned to the road and kept away from the green clover. The boy was moody and bad tempered for an hour or two afterward, because he could really see no harm in picking a six-leaved clover, if he found one, and in spite of what the Shaggy Man had said he considered Ozma's Law to be unjust.

They presently came to a beautiful grove of tall and stately trees, through which the road wound in sharp curves—first one way and then another. As they were walking through this grove they heard some one in the distance singing, and the sounds grew nearer and nearer until they could distinguish the words, although the bend in the road still hid the singer. The song was something like this:

> "Here's to the hale old bale of straw
>   That's cut from the waving grain,
>   The sweetest sight man ever saw
>   In forest, dell or plain.
>   It fills me with a crunkling joy
>   A straw-stack to behold,
>   For then I pad this lucky boy
>   With strands of yellow gold."

"Ah!" exclaimed the Shaggy Man; "here comes my friend the Scarecrow."

"What, a live Scarecrow?" asked Ojo.

"Yes; the one I told you of. He's a splendid fellow, and very intelligent. You'll like him, I'm sure."

Just then the famous Scarecrow of Oz came around the bend in the road, riding astride a wooden Saw-Horse which was so small that its rider's legs nearly touched the ground.

The Scarecrow wore the blue dress of the Munchkins, in which country he was made, and on his head was set a peaked hat with a flat brim trimmed with tinkling bells. A rope was tied around his waist to hold him in shape, for he was stuffed with straw in every part of him except the top of his head, where at one time the Wizard of Oz had placed sawdust, mixed with needles and pins, to sharpen his wits. The head itself was merely a bag of cloth, fastened to the body at the neck, and on the front of this bag was painted the face—ears, eyes, nose and mouth.

The Scarecrow's face was very interesting, for it bore a comical and yet winning expression, although one eye was a bit larger than the other and the ears were not mates. The Munchkin farmer who had made the Scarecrow had neglected to sew him together with close stitches and therefore some of the straw with which he was stuffed was inclined to stick out between the seams. His hands consisted of padded white gloves, with the fingers long and rather limp, and on his feet he wore Munchkin boots of blue leather with broad turns at the tops of them.

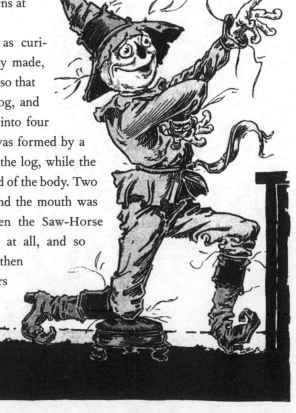

The Saw-Horse was almost as curious as its rider. It had been rudely made, in the beginning, to saw logs upon, so that its body was a short length of a log, and its legs were stout branches fitted into four holes made in the body. The tail was formed by a small branch that had been left on the log, while the head was a gnarled bump on one end of the body. Two knots of wood formed the eyes, and the mouth was a gash chopped in the log. When the Saw-Horse first came to life it had no ears at all, and so could not hear; but the boy who then owned him had whittled two ears out of bark and stuck them in the head, after which the Saw-Horse heard very distinctly.

This queer wooden horse was a great favorite with Princess Ozma, who had caused the bottoms of its legs to be shod with plates of gold, so the wood would not wear away. Its saddle was made of cloth-of-gold richly encrusted with precious gems. It had never worn a bridle.

As the Scarecrow came in sight of the party of travelers, he reined in his wooden steed and dismounted, greeting the Shaggy Man with a smiling nod. Then he turned to stare at the Patchwork Girl in wonder, while she in turn stared at him.

"Shags," he whispered, drawing the Shaggy Man aside, "pat me into shape, there's a good fellow!"

While his friend punched and patted the Scarecrow's body, to smooth out the humps, Scraps turned to Ojo and whispered: "Roll me out, please; I've sagged down dreadfully from walking so much and men like to see a stately figure."

She then fell upon the ground and the boy rolled her back and forth like a rolling-pin, until the cotton had filled all the spaces in her patchwork covering and the body had lengthened to its fullest extent. Scraps and the Scarecrow both finished their hasty toilets at the same time, and again they faced each other.

"Allow me, Miss Patchwork," said the Shaggy Man, "to present my friend, the Right Royal Scarecrow of Oz. Scarecrow, this is Miss Scraps Patches; Scraps, this is the Scarecrow. Scarecrow—Scraps; Scraps—Scarecrow."

They both bowed with much dignity.

"Forgive me for staring so rudely," said the Scarecrow, "but you are the most beautiful sight my eyes have ever beheld."

"That is a high compliment from one who is himself so beautiful," murmured Scraps, casting down her suspender-button eyes by lowering her head. "But, tell me, good sir, are you not a trifle lumpy?"

"Yes, of course; that's my straw, you know. It bunches up, sometimes, in spite of all my efforts to keep it even. Doesn't your straw ever bunch?"

"Oh, I'm stuffed with cotton," said Scraps. "It never bunches, but it's inclined to pack down and make me sag."

"But cotton is a high-grade stuffing. I may say it is even more stylish, not to say aristocratic, than straw," said the Scarecrow politely. "Still, it is but proper that one so entrancingly lovely should have the best stuffing there is going. I—er—I'm *so* glad I've met you, Miss Scraps! Introduce us again, Shaggy."

"Once is enough," replied the Shaggy Man, laughing at his friend's enthusiasm.

"Then tell me where you found her, and—Dear me, what a queer cat! What are *you* made of—gelatine?"

"Pure glass," answered the cat, proud to have attracted the Scarecrow's attention. "I am much more beautiful than the Patchwork Girl. I'm transparent, and Scraps isn't; I've pink brains—you can see 'em work; and I've a ruby heart, finely polished, while Scraps hasn't any heart at all."

"No more have I," said the Scarecrow, shaking hands with Scraps, as if to congratulate her on the fact. "I've a friend, the Tin Woodman, who has a heart, but I find I get along pretty well without one. And so—Well, well! here's a little Munchkin boy, too. Shake hands, my little man. How are you?"

Ojo placed his hand in the flabby stuffed glove that served the Scarecrow for a hand, and the Scarecrow pressed it so cordially that the straw in his glove crackled.

Meantime, the Woozy had approached the Saw-Horse and begun to sniff at it. The Saw-Horse resented this familiarity and with a sudden kick pounded the Woozy squarely on its head with one gold-shod foot.

"Take that, you monster!" it cried angrily.

The Woozy never even winked.

"To be sure," he said; "I'll take anything I have to. But don't make me angry, you wooden beast, or my eyes will flash fire and burn you up."

The Saw-Horse rolled its knot eyes wickedly and kicked again, but the Woozy trotted away and said to the Scarecrow:

"What a sweet disposition that creature has! I advise you to chop it up for kindling-wood and use me to ride upon. My back is flat and you can't fall off."

"I think the trouble is that you haven't been properly introduced," said the Scarecrow, regarding the Woozy with much wonder, for he had never seen such a queer animal before.

"The Saw-Horse is the favorite steed of Princess Ozma, the Ruler of the Land of Oz, and he lives in a stable decorated with pearls and emeralds, at the rear of the royal palace. He is swift as the wind, untiring, and is kind to his friends. All the people of Oz respect the Saw-Horse highly, and when I visit Ozma she sometimes allows me to ride him—as I am doing to-day. Now you know what an important personage the Saw-Horse is, and if some one—perhaps yourself—will tell me your name, your rank and station, and your history, it will give me pleasure to relate them to the Saw-Horse. This will lead to mutual respect and friendship."

The Woozy was somewhat abashed by this speech and did not know how to reply. But Ojo said:

"This square beast is called the Woozy, and he isn't of much importance except that he has three hairs growing on the tip of his tail."

The Scarecrow looked and saw that this was true.

"But," said he, in a puzzled way, "what makes those three hairs important? The Shaggy Man has thousands of hairs, but no one has ever accused him of being important."

So Ojo related the sad story of Unc Nunkie's transformation into a marble statue, and told how he had set out to find the things the Crooked Magician wanted, in order to make a charm that would restore his uncle to life. One of the requirements was three hairs from a Woozy's tail, but not being able to pull out the hairs they had been obliged to take the Woozy with them.

The Scarecrow looked grave as he listened and he shook his head several times, as if in disapproval.

"We must see Ozma about this matter," he said. "That Crooked Magician is breaking the law by practicing magic without a license, and I'm not sure Ozma will allow him to restore your uncle to life."

"Already I have warned the boy of that," declared the Shaggy Man.

At this Ojo began to cry. "I want my Unc Nunkie!" he exclaimed. "I know how he can be restored to life, and I'm going to do it— Ozma or no Ozma! What right has this girl Ruler to keep my Unc Nunkie a statue forever?"

"Don't worry about that just now," advised

the Scarecrow. "Go on to the Emerald City, and when you reach it have the Shaggy Man take you to see Dorothy. Tell her your story and I'm sure she will help you. Dorothy is Ozma's best friend, and if you can win her to your side your uncle is pretty safe to live again." Then he turned to the Woozy and said: "I'm afraid you are not important enough to be introduced to the Saw-Horse, after all."

"I'm a better beast than he is," retorted the Woozy, indignantly. "My eyes can flash fire, and his can't."

"Is this true?" inquired the Scarecrow, turning to the Munchkin boy.

"Yes," said Ojo, and told how the Woozy had set fire to the fence.

"Have you any other accomplishments?" asked the Scarecrow.

"I have a most terrible growl—that is, *sometimes*," said the Woozy, as Scraps laughed merrily and the Shaggy Man smiled. But the Patchwork Girl's laugh made the Scarecrow forget all about the Woozy. He said to her:

"What an admirable young lady you are, and what jolly good company! We must be better acquainted, for never before have I met a girl with such exquisite coloring or such natural, artless manners."

"No wonder they call you the Wise Scarecrow," replied Scraps.

"When you arrive at the Emerald City I will see you again," continued the Scarecrow. "Just now I am going to call upon an old friend—an ordinary young lady named Jinjur—who has promised to repaint my left ear for me. You may have noticed that the paint on my left ear has peeled off and faded, which affects my hearing on that side. Jinjur always fixes me up when I get weather-worn."

"When do you expect to return to the Emerald City?" asked the Shaggy Man.

"I'll be there this evening, for I'm anxious to have a long talk with Miss Scraps. How is it, Saw-Horse; are you equal to a swift run?"

"Anything that suits you suits me," returned the wooden horse.

So the Scarecrow mounted to the jeweled saddle and waved his hat, when the Saw-Horse darted away so swiftly that they were out of sight in an instant.

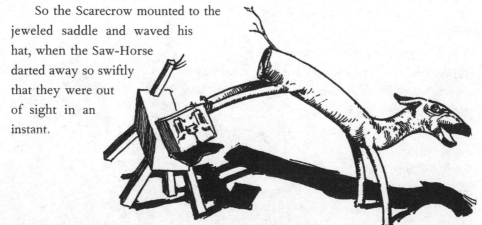

CHAPTER XIV

OJO BREAKS THE LAW

"WHAT A QUEER MAN," REMARKED THE MUNCHKIN BOY, WHEN THE party had resumed its journey.

"And so nice and polite," added Scraps, bobbing her head. "I think he is the handsomest man I've seen since I came to life."

"Handsome is as handsome does," quoted the Shaggy Man; "but we must admit that no living scarecrow is handsomer. The chief merit of my friend is that he is a great thinker, and in Oz it is considered good policy to follow his advice."

"I didn't notice any brains in his head," observed the Glass Cat.

"You can't see 'em work, but they're there, all right," declared the Shaggy Man. "I hadn't much confidence in his brains myself, when first I came to Oz, for a humbug Wizard gave them to him; but I was soon convinced that the Scarecrow is really wise; and, unless his brains make him so, such wisdom is unaccountable."

"Is the Wizard of Oz a humbug?" asked Ojo.

"Not now. He was once, but he has reformed and now assists Glinda the Good, who is the Royal Sorceress of Oz and the only one licensed to practice magic or sorcery. Glinda has taught our old Wizard a good many clever things, so he is no longer a humbug."

They walked a little while in silence and then Ojo said:

"If Ozma forbids the Crooked Magician to restore Unc Nunkie to life, what shall I do?"

The Shaggy Man shook his head.

"In that case you can't do anything," he said. "But don't be discouraged yet. We will go to Princess Dorothy and tell her your troubles, and then we will let her talk to

Ozma. Dorothy has the kindest little heart in the world, and she has been through so many troubles herself that she is sure to sympathize with you."

"Is Dorothy the little girl who came here from Kansas?" asked the boy.

"Yes. In Kansas she was Dorothy Gale. I used to know her there, and she brought me to the Land of Oz. But now Ozma has made her a Princess, and Dorothy's Aunt Em and Uncle Henry are here, too." Here the Shaggy Man uttered a long sigh, and then he continued: "It's a queer country, this Land of Oz; but I like it, nevertheless."

"What is queer about it?" asked Scraps.

"You, for instance," said he.

"Did you see no girls as beautiful as I am in your own country?" she inquired.

"None with the same gorgeous, variegated beauty," he confessed. "In America a girl stuffed with cotton wouldn't be alive, nor would anyone think of making a girl out of a patchwork quilt."

"What a queer country America must be!" she exclaimed in great surprise. "The Scarecrow, whom you say is wise, told me I am the most beautiful creature he has ever seen."

"I know; and perhaps you are—from a scarecrow point of view," replied the Shaggy Man; but why he smiled as he said it Scraps could not imagine.

As they drew nearer to the Emerald City the travelers were filled with admiration for the splendid scenery they beheld. Handsome houses stood on both sides of the road and each had a green lawn before it as well as a pretty flower garden.

"In another hour," said the Shaggy Man, "we shall come in sight of the walls of the Royal City."

He was walking ahead, with Scraps, and behind them came the Woozy and the Glass Cat. Ojo had lagged behind, for in spite of the warnings he had received the boy's eyes were fastened on the clover that bordered the road of yellow bricks and he was eager to discover if such a thing as a six-leaved clover really existed.

Suddenly he stopped short and bent over to examine the ground more closely. Yes; here at last was a clover with six spreading leaves. He counted them carefully, to make sure. In an instant his heart leaped with joy, for this was one of the important things he had come for—one of the things that would restore dear Unc Nunkie to life.

He glanced ahead and saw that none of his companions was looking back. Neither were any other people about, for it was midway between two houses. The temptation was too strong to be resisted.

"I might search for weeks and weeks, and never find another six-leaved clover," he told himself, and quickly plucking the stem from the plant he placed the prized clover in his basket, covering it with the other things he carried there. Then, trying to look as if nothing had happened, he hurried forward and overtook his comrades.

The Emerald City, which is the most splendid as well as the most beautiful city in any fairyland, is surrounded by a high, thick wall of green marble, polished smooth

and set with glistening emeralds. There are four gates, one facing the Munchkin Country, one facing the Country of the Winkies, one facing the Country of the Quadlings and one facing the Country of the Gillikins. The Emerald City lies directly in the center of these four important countries of Oz. The gates had bars of pure gold, and on either side of each gateway were built high towers, from which floated gay banners. Other towers were set at distances along the walls, which were broad enough for four people to walk abreast upon.

This enclosure, all green and gold and glittering with precious gems, was indeed a wonderful sight to greet our travelers, who first observed it from the top of a little hill; but beyond the wall was the vast city it surrounded, and hundreds of jeweled spires, domes and minarets, flaunting flags and banners, reared their crests far above the towers of the gateways. In the center of the city our friends could see the tops of many magnificent trees, some nearly as tall as the spires of the buildings, and the Shaggy Man told them that these trees were in the royal gardens of Princess Ozma.

They stood a long time on the hilltop, feasting their eyes on the splendor of the Emerald City.

"Whee!" exclaimed Scraps, clasping her padded hands in ecstacy, "that'll do for me to live in, all right. No more of the Munchkin Country for these patches—and no more of the Crooked Magician!"

"Why, you belong to Dr. Pipt," replied Ojo, looking at her in amazement. "You were made for a servant, Scraps, so you are personal property and not your own mistress."

"Bother Dr. Pipt! If he wants me, let him come here and get me. I'll not go back to his den of my own accord; that's certain. Only one place in the Land of Oz is fit to live in, and that's the Emerald City. It's lovely! It's almost as beautiful as I am, Ojo."

"In this country," remarked the Shaggy Man, "people live wherever our Ruler tells them to. It wouldn't do to have everyone live in the Emerald City, you know, for some must plow the land and raise grains and fruits and vegetables, while others chop wood in the forests, or fish in the rivers, or herd the sheep and the cattle."

"Poor things!" said Scraps.

"I'm not sure they are not happier than the city people," replied the Shaggy Man. "There's a freedom and independence in country life that not even the Emerald City can give one. I know that lots of the city people would like to get back to the land. The Scarecrow lives in the country, and so do the Tin Woodman and Jack Pumpkinhead; yet all three would be welcome to live in Ozma's palace if they cared to. Too much splendor becomes tiresome, you know. But, if we're to reach the Emerald City before sundown, we must hurry, for it is yet a long way off."

The entrancing sight of the city had put new energy into them all and they hurried forward with lighter steps than before. There was much to interest them along the roadway, for the houses were now set more closely together and they met a good many people who were coming or going from one place or another. All these seemed happy-faced, pleasant people, who nodded graciously to the strangers as they passed, and exchanged words of greeting.

At last they reached the great gateway, just as the sun was setting and adding its red glow to the glitter of the emeralds on the green walls and spires. Somewhere inside the city a band could be heard playing sweet music; a soft, subdued hum, as of many voices, reached their ears; from the neighboring yards came the low mooing of cows waiting to be milked.

They were almost at the gate when the golden bars slid back and a tall soldier stepped out and faced them. Ojo thought he had never seen so tall a man before. The soldier wore a handsome green and gold uniform, with a tall hat in which was a waving plume, and he had a belt thickly encrusted with jewels. But the most peculiar thing about him was his long green beard, which fell far below his waist and perhaps made him seem taller than he really was.

"Halt!" said the Soldier with the Green Whiskers, not in a stern voice but rather in a friendly tone.

They halted before he spoke and stood looking at him.

"Good evening, Colonel," said the Shaggy Man. "What's the news since I left? Anything important?"

"Billina has hatched out thirteen new chickens," replied the Soldier with the Green Whiskers, "and they're the cutest little fluffy yellow balls you ever saw. The Yellow Hen is mighty proud of those children, I can tell you."

"She has a right to be," agreed the Shaggy Man. "Let me see; that's about seven thousand chicks she has hatched out; isn't it, General?"

"That, at least," was the reply. "You will have to visit Billina and congratulate her."

"It will give me pleasure to do that," said the Shaggy Man. "But you will observe that I have brought some strangers home with me. I am going to take them to see Dorothy."

"One moment, please," said the soldier, barring their way as they started to enter the gate. "I am on duty, and I have orders to execute. Is anyone in your party named Ojo the Unlucky?"

"Why, that's me!" cried Ojo, astonished at hearing his name on the lips of a stranger.

The Soldier with the Green Whiskers nodded. "I thought so," said he, "and I am sorry to announce that it is my painful duty to arrest you."

"Arrest me!" exclaimed the boy. "What for?"

"I haven't looked to see," answered the soldier. Then he drew a paper from his breast pocket and glanced at it. "Oh, yes; you are to be arrested for willfully breaking one of the Laws of Oz."

"Breaking a law!" said Scraps. "Nonsense, Soldier; you're joking."

"Not this time," returned the soldier, with a sigh. "My dear child—what are you, a rummage sale or a guess-me-quick?—in me you behold the Body-Guard of our gracious Ruler, Princess Ozma, as well as the Royal Army of Oz and the Police Force of the Emerald City."

"And only one man!" exclaimed the Patchwork Girl.

"Only one, and plenty enough. In my official positions I've had nothing to do for a good many years—so long that I began to fear I was absolutely useless—until to-day. An hour ago I was called to the presence of her Highness, Ozma of Oz, and told to arrest a boy named Ojo the Unlucky, who was journeying from the Munchkin Country to the Emerald City and would arrive in a short time. This command so astonished me that I nearly fainted, for it is the first time anyone has merited arrest since I can remember. You are rightly named Ojo the Unlucky, my poor boy, since you have broken a Law of Oz.

"But you are wrong," said Scraps. "Ozma is wrong—you are all wrong—for Ojo has broken no law."

"Then he will soon be free again," replied the Soldier with the Green Whiskers. "Anyone accused of crime is given a fair trial by our Ruler and has every chance to prove his innocence. But just now Ozma's orders must be obeyed."

With this he took from his pocket a pair of handcuffs made of gold and set with rubies and diamonds, and these he snapped over Ojo's wrists.

CHAPTER XV

OZMA'S PRISONER

THE BOY WAS SO BEWILDERED BY THIS CALAMITY THAT HE MADE NO resistance at all. He knew very well he was guilty, but it surprised him that Ozma also knew it. He wondered how she had found out so soon that he had picked the six-leaved clover. He handed his basket to Scraps and said:

"Keep that, until I get out of prison. If I never get out, take it to the Crooked Magician, to whom it belongs."

The Shaggy Man had been gazing earnestly in the boy's face, uncertain whether to defend him or not; but something he read in Ojo's expression made him draw back and refuse to interfere to save him. The Shaggy Man was greatly surprised and grieved, but he knew that Ozma never made mistakes and so Ojo must really have broken the Law of Oz.

The Soldier with the Green Whiskers now led them all through the gate and into a little room built in the wall. Here sat a jolly little man, richly dressed in green and having around his neck a heavy gold chain to which a number of great golden keys were attached. This was the Guardian of the Gate and at the moment they entered his room he was playing a tune upon a mouth-organ.

"Listen!" he said, holding up his hand for silence. "I've just composed a tune called 'The Speckled Alligator.' It's in patch-time, which is much superior to rag-time, and I've composed it in honor of the Patchwork Girl, who has just arrived."

"How did you know I had arrived?" asked Scraps, much interested.

"It's my business to know who's coming, for I'm the Guardian of the Gate. Keep quiet while I play you 'The Speckled Alligator.'"

It wasn't a very bad tune, nor a very good one, but all listened respectfully while he shut his eyes and swayed his head from side to side and blew the notes from the little instrument. When it was all over the Soldier with the Green Whiskers said:

"Guardian, I have here a prisoner."

"Good gracious! A prisoner?" cried the little man, jumping up from his chair. "Which one? Not the Shaggy Man?"

"No; this boy."

"Ah; I hope his fault is as small as himself," said the Guardian of the Gate. "But what can he have done, and what made him do it?"

"Can't say," replied the soldier. "All I know is that he has broken the law."

"But no one ever does that!"

"Then he must be innocent, and soon will be released. I hope you are right, Guardian. Just now I am ordered to take him to prison. Get me a prisoner's robe from your Official Wardrobe."

The Guardian unlocked a closet and took from it a white robe, which the soldier threw over Ojo. It covered him from head to foot, but had two holes just in front of his eyes, so he could see where to go. In this attire the boy presented a very quaint appearance.

As the Guardian unlocked a gate leading from his room into the streets of the Emerald City, the Shaggy Man said to Scraps:

"I think I shall take you directly to Dorothy, as the Scarecrow advised, and the Glass Cat and the Woozy may come with us. Ojo must go to prison with the Soldier with the Green Whiskers, but he will be well treated and you need not worry about him."

"What will they do with him?" asked Scraps.

"That I cannot tell. Since I came to the Land of Oz no one has ever been arrested or imprisoned—until Ojo broke the law."

"Seems to me that girl Ruler of yours is making a big fuss over nothing," remarked Scraps, tossing her yarn hair out of her eyes with a jerk of her patched head. "I don't know what Ojo has done, but it couldn't be anything very bad, for you and I were with him all the time."

The Shaggy Man made no reply to this speech and presently the Patchwork Girl forgot all about Ojo in her admiration of the wonderful city she had entered.

They soon separated from the Munchkin boy, who was led by the Soldier with the Green Whiskers down a side street toward the prison. Ojo felt very miserable and greatly ashamed of himself, but he was beginning to grow angry because he was treated in such a disgraceful manner. Instead of entering the splendid Emerald City as a respectable traveler who was entitled to a welcome and to hospitality, he was being brought in as a criminal, handcuffed and in a robe that told all he met of his deep disgrace.

Ojo was by nature gentle and affectionate and if he had disobeyed the Law of Oz it was to restore his dear Unc Nunkie to life. His fault was more thoughtless than wicked, but that did not alter the fact that he had committed a fault. At first he had felt sorrow and remorse, but the more he thought about the unjust treatment he had received—unjust merely because he considered it so—the more he resented his arrest, blaming Ozma for making foolish laws and then punishing folks who broke them. Only a six-leaved clover! A tiny green plant growing neglected and trampled under foot. What harm could there be in picking it? Ojo began to think Ozma must be a very bad and oppressive Ruler for such a lovely fairyland as Oz. The Shaggy Man said the people loved her; but how could they?

The little Munchkin boy was so busy thinking these things—which many guilty prisoners have thought before him—that he scarcely noticed all the splendor of the city streets through which they passed. Whenever they met any of the happy, smiling people, the boy turned his head away in shame, although none knew who was beneath the robe.

By and by they reached a house built just beside the great city wall, but in a quiet, retired place. It was a pretty house, neatly painted and with many windows. Before it was a garden filled with blooming flowers. The Soldier with the Green Whiskers led Ojo up the gravel path to the front door, on which he knocked.

A woman opened the door and, seeing Ojo in his white robe, exclaimed:

"Goodness me! A prisoner at last. But what a small one, Soldier."

"The size doesn't matter, Tollydiggle, my dear. The fact remains that he is a prisoner," said the soldier. "And, this being the prison, and you the jailor, it is my duty to place the prisoner in your charge."

"True. Come in, then, and I'll give you a receipt for him."

They entered the house and passed through a hall to a large circular room, where the woman pulled the robe off from Ojo and looked at him with kindly interest. The boy, on his part, was gazing around him in amazement, for never had he dreamed of such a magnificent apartment as this in which he stood. The roof of the dome was of colored glass, worked into beautiful designs. The walls were paneled with plates of gold decorated with gems of great size and many colors, and upon the tiled floor were soft rugs delightful to walk upon. The furniture was framed in gold and upholstered in satin brocade and it consisted of easy chairs, divans and stools in great variety. Also there were several tables with mirror tops and cabinets filled with rare and curious things. In one place a case filled with books stood against the wall, and elsewhere Ojo saw a cupboard containing all sorts of games.

"May I stay here a little while before I go to prison?" asked the boy, pleadingly.

"Why, this is your prison," replied Tollydiggle, "and in me behold your jailor. Take off those handcuffs, Soldier, for it is impossible for anyone to escape from this house."

"I know that very well," replied the soldier and at once unlocked the handcuffs and released the prisoner.

The woman touched a button on the wall and lighted a big chandelier that hung suspended from the ceiling, for it was growing dark outside. Then she seated herself at a desk and asked:

"What name?"

"Ojo the Unlucky," answered the Soldier with the Green Whiskers.

"Unlucky? Ah, that accounts for it," said she. "What crime?"

"Breaking a Law of Oz."

"All right. There's your receipt, Soldier; and now I'm responsible for the prisoner. I'm glad of it, for this is the first time I've ever had anything to do, in my official capacity," remarked the jailor, in a pleased tone.

"It's the same with me, Tollydiggle," laughed the soldier. "But my task is finished and I must go and report to Ozma that I've done my duty like a faithful police force, a loyal army and an honest body-guard—as I hope I am."

Saying this, he nodded farewell to Tollydiggle and Ojo and went away.

"Now, then," said the woman briskly, "I must get you some supper, for you are doubtless hungry. What would you prefer: planked whitefish, omelet with jelly or mutton-chops with gravy?"

Ojo thought about it. Then he said: "I'll take the chops, if you please."

"Very well; amuse yourself while I'm gone; I won't be long," and then she went out by a door and left the prisoner alone.

Ojo was much astonished, for not only was this unlike any prison he had ever heard of, but he was being treated more as a guest than a criminal. There were many windows and they had no locks. There were three doors to the room and none were bolted. He cautiously opened one of the doors and found it led into a hallway. But he had no intention of trying to escape. If his jailor was willing to trust him in this way he would not betray her trust, and moreover a hot supper was being prepared for him and his prison was very pleasant and comfortable. So he took a book from the case and sat down in a big chair to look at the pictures.

This amused him until the woman came in with a large tray and spread a cloth on one of the tables. Then she arranged his supper, which proved the most varied and delicious meal Ojo had ever eaten in his life.

Tollydiggle sat near him while he ate, sewing on some fancy work she held in her lap. When he had finished she cleared the table and then read to him a story from one of the books.

"Is this really a prison?" he asked, when she had finished reading.

"Indeed it is," she replied. "It is the only prison in the Land of Oz."

"And am I a prisoner?"

"Bless the child! Of course."

"Then why is the prison so fine, and why are you so kind to me?" he earnestly asked.

Tollydiggle seemed surprised by the question, but she presently answered:

"We consider a prisoner unfortunate. He is unfortunate in two ways—because he has done something wrong and because he is deprived of his liberty. Therefore we should treat him kindly, because of his misfortune, for otherwise he would become hard and bitter and would not be sorry he had done wrong. Ozma thinks that one who has committed a fault did so because he was not strong and brave; therefore she puts him in prison to make him strong and brave. When that is accomplished he is no longer a prisoner, but a good and loyal citizen and everyone is glad that he is now strong enough to resist doing wrong. You see, it is kindness that makes one strong and brave; and so we are kind to our prisoners."

Ojo thought this over very carefully. "I had an idea," said he, "that prisoners were always treated harshly, to punish them."

"That would be dreadful!" cried Tollydiggle. "Isn't one punished enough in knowing he has done wrong? Don't you wish, Ojo, with all your heart, that you had not been disobedient and broken a Law of Oz?"

"I—I hate to be different from other people," he admitted.

"Yes; one likes to be respected as highly as his neighbors are," said the woman. "When you are tried and found guilty, you will be obliged to make amends, in some way. I don't know just what Ozma will do to you, because this is the first time one of us has broken a law; but you may be sure she will be just and merciful. Here in the Emerald City people are too happy and contented ever to do wrong; but perhaps you came from some faraway corner of our land, and having no love for Ozma carelessly broke one of her laws."

"Yes," said Ojo, "I've lived all my life in the heart of a lonely forest, where I saw no one but dear Unc Nunkie."

"I thought so," said Tollydiggle. "But now we have talked enough, so let us play a game until bedtime."

CHAPTER XVI

PRINCESS DOROTHY

DOROTHY GALE WAS SITTING IN ONE OF HER ROOMS IN the royal palace, while curled up at her feet was a little black dog with a shaggy coat and very bright eyes. She wore a plain white frock, without any jewels or other ornaments except an emerald-green hair-ribbon, for Dorothy was a simple little girl and had not been in the least spoiled by the magnificence surrounding her. Once the child had lived on the Kansas prairies, but she seemed marked for adventure, for she had made several trips to the Land of Oz before she came to live there for good. Her very best friend was the beautiful Ozma of Oz, who loved Dorothy so well that she kept her in her own palace, so as to be near her. The girl's Uncle Henry and Aunt Em—the only relatives she had in the world—had also been brought here by Ozma and given a pleasant home. Dorothy knew almost everybody in Oz, and it was she who had discovered the Scarecrow, the Tin Woodman and the Cowardly Lion, as well as Tik-Tok the Clockwork Man. Her life was very pleasant now, and although she had been made a Princess of Oz by her friend Ozma she did not care much to be a Princess and remained as sweet as when she had been plain Dorothy Gale of Kansas.

Dorothy was reading in a book this evening when Jellia Jamb, the favorite servant-maid of the palace, came to say that the Shaggy Man wanted to see her.

"All right," said Dorothy; "tell him to come right up."

"But he has some queer creatures with him—some of the queerest I've ever laid eyes on," reported Jellia.

"Never mind; let 'em all come up," replied Dorothy.

But when the door opened to admit not only the Shaggy Man, but Scraps, the Woozy and the Glass Cat, Dorothy jumped up and looked at her strange visitors in amazement. The Patchwork Girl was the most curious of all and Dorothy was uncertain at first whether Scraps was really alive or only a dream or a nightmare. Toto, her dog, slowly uncurled himself and going to the Patchwork Girl sniffed at her inquiringly; but soon he lay down again, as if to say he had no interest in such an irregular creation.

"You're a new one to me," Dorothy said reflectively, addressing the Patchwork Girl. "I can't imagine where you've come from."

"Who, me?" asked Scraps, looking around the pretty room instead of at the girl. "Oh, I came from a bed-quilt, I guess. That's what they say, anyhow. Some call it a crazy-quilt and some a patchwork quilt. But my name is Scraps—and now you know all about me."

"Not quite all," returned Dorothy with a smile. "I wish you'd tell me how you came to be alive."

"That's an easy job," said Scraps, sitting upon a big upholstered chair and making the springs bounce her up and down. "Margolotte wanted a slave, so she made me out of an old bed-quilt she didn't use. Cotton stuffing, suspender-button eyes, red velvet tongue, pearl beads for teeth. The Crooked Magician made a Powder of Life, sprinkled me with it and— here I am. Perhaps you've noticed my different colors. A very refined 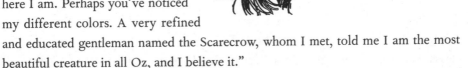 and educated gentleman named the Scarecrow, whom I met, told me I am the most beautiful creature in all Oz, and I believe it."

"Oh! Have you met our Scarecrow, then?" asked Dorothy, a little puzzled to understand the brief history related.

"Yes; isn't he jolly?"

"The Scarecrow has many good qualities," replied Dorothy. "But I'm sorry to hear all this 'bout the Crooked Magician. Ozma'll be mad as hops when she hears he's been doing magic again. She told him not to."

"He only practices magic for the benefit of his own family," explained Bungle, who was keeping at a respectful distance from the little black dog.

"Dear me," said Dorothy; "I hadn't noticed you before. Are you glass, or what?"

"I'm glass, and transparent, too, which is more than can be said of some folks," answered the cat. "Also I have some lovely pink brains; you can see 'em work."

"Oh; is that so? Come over here and let me see."

The Glass Cat hesitated, eyeing the dog.

"Send that beast away and I will," she said.

"Beast! Why, that's my dog Toto, an' he's the kindest dog in all the world. Toto knows a good many things, too; 'most as much as I do, I guess."

"Why doesn't he say anything?" asked Bungle.

"He can't talk, not being a fairy dog," explained Dorothy. "He's just a common United States dog; but that's a good deal; and I understand him, and he understands me, just as well as if he could talk."

Toto, at this, got up and rubbed his head softly against Dorothy's hand, which she held out to him, and he looked up into her face as if he had understood every word she had said.

"This cat, Toto," she said to him, "is made of glass, so you mustn't bother it, or chase it, any more than you do my Pink Kitten. It's prob'ly brittle and might break if it bumped against anything."

"Woof!" said Toto, and that meant he understood.

The Glass Cat was so proud of her pink brains that she ventured to come close to Dorothy, in order that the girl might "see 'em work." This was really interesting, but when Dorothy patted the cat she found the glass cold and hard and unresponsive, so she decided at once that Bungle would never do for a pet.

"What do you know about the Crooked Magician who lives on the mountain?" asked Dorothy.

"He made me," replied the cat; "so I know all about him. The Patchwork Girl is new—three or four days old—but I've lived with Dr. Pipt for years; and, though I don't much care for him, I will say that he has always refused to work magic for any of the people who come to his house. He thinks there's no harm in doing magic things for his own family, and he made me out of glass because the meat cats drink too much milk. He also made Scraps come to life so she could do the housework for his wife Margolotte."

"Then why did you both leave him?" asked Dorothy.

"I think you'd better let me explain that," interrupted the Shaggy Man, and then he told Dorothy all of Ojo's story, and how Unc Nunkie and Margolotte had accidentally been turned to marble by the Liquid of Petrifaction. Then he related how the boy had started out in search of the things needed to make the magic charm, which would restore the unfortunates to life, and how he had found the Woozy and taken him along because he could not pull the three hairs out of its tail. Dorothy listened to all this with much interest, and thought that so far Ojo had acted very well. But when the Shaggy Man told her of the Munchkin boy's arrest by the Soldier with the Green Whiskers, because he was accused of wilfully breaking a Law of Oz, the little girl was greatly shocked.

"What do you s'pose he's done?" she asked.

"I fear he has picked a six-leaved clover," answered the Shaggy Man, sadly. "I did not see him do it, and I warned him that to do so was against the law; but perhaps that is what he did, nevertheless."

"I'm sorry 'bout that," said Dorothy gravely, "for now there will be no one to help his poor uncle and Margolotte—'cept this Patchwork Girl, the Woozy and the Glass Cat."

"Don't mention it," said Scraps. "That's no affair of mine. Margolotte and Unc Nunkie are perfect strangers to me, for the moment I came to life they came to marble."

"I see," remarked Dorothy with a sigh of regret; "the woman forgot to give you a heart."

"I'm glad she did," retorted the Patchwork Girl. "A heart must be a great annoyance to one. It makes a person feel sad or sorry or devoted or sympathetic—all of which sensations interfere with one's happiness."

"I have a heart," murmured the Glass Cat. "It's made of a ruby; but I don't imagine I shall let it bother me about helping Unc Nunkie and Margolotte."

"That's a pretty hard heart of yours," said Dorothy. "And the Woozy, of course—"

"Why, as for me," observed the Woozy, who was reclining on the floor with his legs doubled under him, so that he looked much like a square box, "I have never seen those unfortunate people you are speaking of, and yet I am sorry for them, having at times been unfortunate myself. When I was shut up in that forest I longed for some one to help me, and by and by Ojo came and did help me. So I'm willing to help his uncle. I'm only a stupid beast, Dorothy, but I can't help that, and if you'll tell me what to do to help Ojo and his uncle, I'll gladly do it."

Dorothy walked over and patted the Woozy on his square head.

"You're not pretty," she said, "but I like you. What are you able to do; anything 'special?"

"I can make my eyes flash fire—real fire—when I'm angry. When anyone says: 'Krizzle-Kroo' to me I get angry, and then my eyes flash fire."

"I don't see as fireworks could help Ojo's uncle," remarked Dorothy. "Can you do anything else?"

"I—I thought I had a very terrifying growl," said the Woozy, with hesitation; "but perhaps I was mistaken."

"Yes," said the Shaggy Man, "you were certainly wrong about that." Then he turned to Dorothy and added: "What will become of the Munchkin boy?"

"I don't know," she said, shaking her head thoughtfully. "Ozma will see him 'bout it, of course, and then she'll punish him. But how, I don't know, 'cause no one ever has been punished in Oz since I knew anything about the place. Too bad, Shaggy Man, isn't it?"

While they were talking Scraps had been roaming around the room and looking at all the pretty things it contained. She had carried Ojo's basket in her hand, until now, when she decided to see what was inside it. She found the bread and cheese, which she had no use for, and the bundle of charms, which were curious but quite a mystery to her. Then, turning these over, she came upon the six-leaved clover which the boy had plucked.

Scraps was quick-witted, and although she had no heart she recognized the fact that Ojo was her first friend. She knew at once that because the boy had taken the clover he had been imprisoned, and she understood that Ojo had given her the basket so they would not find the clover in his possession and have proof of his crime. So, turning her head to see that no one noticed her, she took the clover from the basket and dropped it into a golden vase that stood on Dorothy's table. Then she came forward and said to Dorothy:

"I wouldn't care to help Ojo's uncle, but I will help Ojo. He did not break the law—no one can prove he did—and that green-whiskered soldier had no right to arrest him."

"Ozma ordered the boy's arrest," said Dorothy, "and of course she knew what she was doing. But if you can prove Ojo is innocent they will set him free at once."

"They'll have to prove him guilty, won't they?" asked Scraps.

"I s'pose so."

"Well, they can't do that," declared the Patchwork Girl.

As it was nearly time for Dorothy to dine with Ozma, which she did every evening, she rang for a servant and ordered the Woozy taken to a nice room and given plenty of such food as he liked best.

"That's honey-bees," said the Woozy.

"You can't eat honey-bees, but you'll be given something just as nice," Dorothy told him. Then she had the Glass Cat taken to another room for the night and the Patchwork Girl she kept in one of her own rooms, for she was much interested in the strange creature and wanted to talk with her again and try to understand her better.

CHAPTER XVII

OZMA AND HER FRIENDS

THE SHAGGY MAN HAD A ROOM OF HIS OWN in the royal palace, so there he went to change his shaggy suit of clothes for another just as shaggy but not so dusty from travel. He selected a costume of pea-green and pink satin and velvet, with embroidered shags on all the edges and iridescent pearls for ornaments. Then he bathed in an alabaster pool and brushed his shaggy hair and whiskers the wrong way to make them still more shaggy. This accomplished, and arrayed in his splendid shaggy garments, he went to Ozma's banquet hall and found the Scarecrow, the Wizard and Dorothy already assembled there. The Scarecrow had made a quick trip and returned to the Emerald City with his left ear freshly painted.

A moment later, while they all stood in waiting, a servant threw open a door, the orchestra struck up a tune and Ozma of Oz entered.

Much has been told and written concerning the beauty of person and character of this sweet girl Ruler of the Land of Oz—the richest, the happiest and most delightful fairyland of which we have any knowledge. Yet with all her queenly qualities Ozma was a real girl and enjoyed the things in life that other real girls enjoy. When she sat on her splendid emerald throne in the great Throne Room of her palace and made laws and settled disputes and tried to keep all her subjects happy and contented, she was as dignified and demure as any Queen might be; but when she had thrown aside her jeweled robe of state and her sceptre, and had retired to her private apartments, the girl—joyous, light-hearted and free— replaced the sedate Ruler.

In the banquet hall to-night were gathered only old and trusted friends, so here Ozma was herself—a mere girl. She greeted Dorothy with a kiss, the Shaggy Man with a smile, the little old Wizard with a friendly handshake and then she pressed the Scarecrow's stuffed arm and cried merrily:

"What a lovely left ear! Why, it's a hundred times better than the old one."

"I'm glad you like it," replied the Scarecrow, well pleased. "Jinjur did a neat job, didn't she? And my hearing is now perfect. Isn't it wonderful what a little paint will do, if it's properly applied?"

"It really *is* wonderful," she agreed, as they all took their seats; "but the Saw-Horse must have made his legs twinkle to have carried you so far in one day. I didn't expect you back before to-morrow, at the earliest."

"Well," said the Scarecrow, "I met a charming girl on the road and wanted to see more of her, so I hurried back."

Ozma laughed.

"I know," she returned; "it's the Patchwork Girl. She is certainly bewildering, if not strictly beautiful."

"Have you seen her, then?" the straw man eagerly asked.

"Only in my Magic Picture, which shows me all scenes of interest in the Land of Oz."

"I fear the picture didn't do her justice," said the Scarecrow.

"It seemed to me that nothing could be more gorgeous," declared Ozma. "Whoever made that patchwork quilt, from which Scraps was formed, must have selected the gayest and brightest bits of cloth that ever were woven."

"I am glad you like her," said the Scarecrow in a satisfied tone. Although the straw man did not eat, not being made so he could, he often dined with Ozma and her companions, merely for the pleasure of talking with them. He sat at the table and had a napkin and plate, but the servants knew better than to offer him food. After a little while he asked: "Where is the Patchwork Girl now?"

"In my room," replied Dorothy. "I've taken a fancy to her; she's so queer and—and—uncommon."

"She's half crazy, I think," added the Shaggy Man.

"But she is so beautiful!" exclaimed the Scarecrow, as if that fact disarmed all criticism. They all laughed at his enthusiasm, but the Scarecrow was quite serious. Seeing that he was interested in Scraps they forbore to say anything against her. The little band of friends Ozma had gathered around her was so quaintly assorted that much care must be exercised to avoid hurting their feelings or making any one of them unhappy. It was this considerate kindness that held them close friends and enabled them to enjoy one another's society.

Another thing they avoided was conversing on unpleasant subjects, and for that reason Ojo and his troubles were not mentioned during the dinner. The Shaggy Man, however, related his adventures with the monstrous plants which had seized and enfolded the travelers, and told how he had robbed Chiss, the giant porcupine, of the quills which it was accustomed to throw at people. Both Dorothy and Ozma were pleased with this exploit and thought it served Chiss right.

Then they talked of the Woozy, which was the most remarkable animal any of them had ever before seen—except, perhaps, the live Saw-Horse. Ozma had never known that her dominions contained such a thing as a Woozy, there being but one in existence and this being confined in his forest for many years. Dorothy said she believed the Woozy was a good beast, honest and faithful; but she added that she did not care much for the Glass Cat.

"Still," said the Shaggy Man, "the Glass Cat is very pretty and if she were not so conceited over her pink brains no one would object to her as a companion."

The Wizard had been eating silently until now, when he looked up and remarked:

"That Powder of Life which is made by the Crooked Magician is really a wonderful thing. But Dr. Pipt does not know its true value and he uses it in the most foolish ways."

"I must see about that," said Ozma, gravely. Then she smiled again and continued in a lighter tone: "It was Dr. Pipt's famous Powder of Life that enabled me to become the Ruler of Oz."

"I've never heard that story," said the Shaggy Man, looking at Ozma questioningly.

"Well, when I was a baby girl I was stolen by an old Witch named Mombi and transformed into a boy," began the girl Ruler. "I did not know who I was and when I grew big enough to work, the Witch made me wait upon her and carry wood for the fire and hoe in the garden. One day she came back from a journey bringing some of the Powder of Life, which Dr. Pipt had given her. I had made a pumpkin-headed man and set it up in her path to frighten her, for I was fond of fun and hated the Witch. But she knew what the figure was and to test her Powder of Life she sprinkled some of it on the man I had made. It came to life and is now our dear friend Jack Pumpkinhead. That night I ran away with Jack to escape punishment, and I took old Mombi's Powder of Life with me. During our journey we came upon a wooden Saw-Horse standing by the road and I used the magic powder to bring it to life. The Saw-Horse has been with me ever since. When I got to the Emerald City the good Sorceress, Glinda, knew who I was and restored me to my proper person, when I became the rightful Ruler of this land. So you see had not old Mombi brought home the Powder of Life I might never have run away from her and become Ozma of Oz, nor would we have had Jack Pumpkinhead and the Saw-Horse to comfort and amuse us."

That story interested the Shaggy Man very much, as well as the others, who had often heard it before. The dinner being now concluded, they all went to Ozma's drawing-room, where they passed a pleasant evening before it came time to retire.

CHAPTER XVIII

OJO IS FORGIVEN

THE NEXT MORNING THE SOLDIER WITH the Green Whiskers went to the prison and took Ojo away to the royal palace, where he was summoned to appear before the girl Ruler for judgment. Again the soldier put upon the boy the jeweled handcuffs and white prisoner's robe with the peaked top and holes for the eyes. Ojo was so ashamed, both of his disgrace and the fault he had committed, that he was glad to be covered up in this way, so that people could not see him or know who he was. He followed the Soldier with the Green Whiskers very willingly, anxious that his fate might be decided as soon as possible.

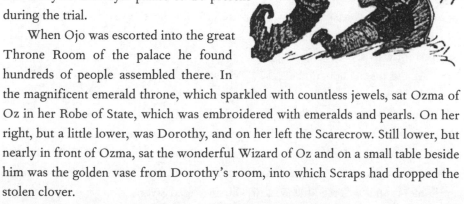

The inhabitants of the Emerald City were polite people and never jeered at the unfortunate; but it was so long since they had seen a prisoner that they cast many curious looks toward the boy and many of them hurried away to the royal palace to be present during the trial.

When Ojo was escorted into the great Throne Room of the palace he found hundreds of people assembled there. In the magnificent emerald throne, which sparkled with countless jewels, sat Ozma of Oz in her Robe of State, which was embroidered with emeralds and pearls. On her right, but a little lower, was Dorothy, and on her left the Scarecrow. Still lower, but nearly in front of Ozma, sat the wonderful Wizard of Oz and on a small table beside him was the golden vase from Dorothy's room, into which Scraps had dropped the stolen clover.

At Ozma's feet crouched two enormous beasts, each the largest and most power-ful of its kind. Although these beasts were quite free, no one present was alarmed by them; for the Cowardly Lion and the Hungry Tiger were well known and respected in the Emerald City and they always guarded the Ruler when she held high court in the Throne Room. There was still another beast present, but this one Dorothy held in her arms, for it was her constant companion, the little dog Toto. Toto knew the Cowardly Lion and the Hungry Tiger and often played and romped with them, for they were good friends.

Seated on ivory chairs before Ozma, with a clear space between them and the throne, were many of the nobility of the Emerald City, lords and ladies in beautiful costumes, and officials of the kingdom in the royal uniforms of Oz. Behind these courtiers were others of less importance, filling the great hall to the very doors.

At the same moment that the Soldier with the Green Whiskers arrived with Ojo, the Shaggy Man entered from a side door, escorting the Patchwork Girl, the Woozy and the Glass Cat. All these came to the vacant space before the throne and stood fac-ing the Ruler.

"Hullo, Ojo," said Scraps; "how are you?"

"All right," he replied; but the scene awed the boy and his voice trembled a little with fear. Nothing could awe the Patchwork Girl, and although the Woozy was somewhat uneasy in these splendid surroundings the Glass Cat was delighted with the sumptuousness of the court and the impressiveness of the occasion—pretty big words but quite expressive.

At a sign from Ozma the soldier removed Ojo's white robe and the boy stood face to face with the girl who was to decide his punishment. He saw at a glance how lovely and sweet she was, and his heart gave a bound of joy, for he hoped she would be merciful.

Ozma sat looking at the prisoner a long time. Then she said gently:

"One of the Laws of Oz forbids anyone to pick a six-leaved clover. You are accused of having broken this law, even after you had been warned not to do so."

Ojo hung his head and while he hesitated how to reply the Patchwork Girl stepped forward and spoke for him.

"All this fuss is about nothing at all," she said, facing Ozma unabashed. "You can't prove he picked the six-leaved clover, so you've no right to accuse him of it. Search him, if you like, but you won't find the clover; look in his basket and you'll find it's not there. He hasn't got it, so I demand that you set this poor Munchkin boy free."

The people of Oz listened to this defiance in amazement and wondered at the queer Patchwork Girl who dared talk so boldly to their Ruler. But Ozma sat silent and motionless and it was the little Wizard who answered Scraps.

"So the clover hasn't been picked, eh?" he said. "I think it has. I think the boy hid it in his basket, and then gave the basket to you. I also think you dropped the clover into this vase, which stood in Princess Dorothy's room, hoping to get rid of it so it would not prove the boy guilty. You're a stranger here, Miss Patches, and so you don't know that nothing can be hidden from our powerful Ruler's Magic Picture—nor from the watchful eyes of the humble Wizard of Oz. Look, all of you!" With these words he waved his hands toward the vase on the table, which Scraps now noticed for the first time.

From the mouth of the vase a plant sprouted, slowly growing before their eyes until it became a beautiful bush, and on the topmost branch appeared the six-leaved clover which Ojo had unfortunately picked.

The Patchwork Girl looked at the clover and said: "Oh, so you've found it. Very well; prove he picked it, if you can."

Ozma turned to Ojo.

"Did you pick the six-leaved clover?" she asked.

"Yes," he replied. "I knew it was against the law, but I wanted to save Unc Nunkie and I was afraid if I asked your consent to pick it you would refuse me."

"What caused you to think that?" asked the Ruler.

"Why, it seemed to me a foolish law, unjust and unreasonable. Even now I can see no harm in picking a six-leaved clover. And I—I had not seen the Emerald City, then, nor you, and I thought a girl who would make such a silly law would not be likely to help anyone in trouble."

Ozma regarded him musingly, her chin resting upon her hand; but she was not angry. On the contrary she smiled a little at her thoughts and then grew sober again.

"I suppose a good many laws seem foolish to those people who do not understand them," she said; "but no law is ever made without some purpose, and that purpose is usually to protect all the people and guard their welfare. As you are a stranger, I will explain this law which to you seems so foolish. Years ago there were many Witches and Magicians in the Land of Oz, and one of the things they often used in making their magic charms and transformations was a six-leaved clover. These Witches and Magicians caused so much trouble among my people, often using their powers for evil rather than good, that I decided to forbid anyone to practice magic or sorcery except Glinda the Good and her assistant, the Wizard of Oz, both of whom I can trust to use their arts only to benefit my people and to make them happier. Since I issued that law the Land of Oz has been far more peaceful and quiet; but I learned that some of the Witches and Magicians were still practicing magic on the sly and using the six-leaved clovers to make their potions and charms. Therefore I made another law forbidding anyone from plucking a six-leaved clover or from gathering other plants and herbs which the Witches boil in their kettles to work magic with. That has almost put an end

to wicked sorcery in our land, so you see the law was not a foolish one, but wise and just; and, in any event, it is wrong to disobey a law."

Ojo knew she was right and felt greatly mortified to realize he had acted and spoken so ridiculously. But he raised his head and looked Ozma in the face, saying:

"I am sorry I have acted wrongly and broken your law. I did it to save Unc Nunkie, and thought I would not be found out. But I am guilty of this act and whatever punishment you think I deserve I will suffer willingly."

"I demand that you set this poor Munchkin Boy free"

Ozma smiled more brightly, then, and nodded graciously.

"You are forgiven," she said. "For, although you have committed a serious fault, you are now penitent and I think you have been punished enough. Soldier, release Ojo the Lucky and—"

"I beg your pardon; I'm Ojo the *Un*lucky," said the boy.

"At this moment you are lucky," said she. "Release him, Soldier, and let him go free."

The people were glad to hear Ozma's decree and murmured their approval. As the royal audience was now over, they began to leave the Throne Room and soon there were none remaining except Ojo and his friends and Ozma and her favorites.

The girl Ruler now asked Ojo to sit down and tell her all his story, which he did, beginning at the time he had left his home in the forest and ending with his arrival at the Emerald City and his arrest. Ozma listened attentively and was thoughtful for some moments after the boy had finished speaking. Then she said:

"The Crooked Magician was wrong to make the Glass Cat and the Patchwork Girl, for it was against the law. And if he had not unlawfully kept the bottle of Liquid of Petrifaction standing on his shelf, the accident to his wife Margolotte and to Unc Nunkie could not have occurred. I can understand, however, that Ojo, who loves his uncle, will be unhappy unless he can save him. Also I feel it is wrong to leave those two victims standing as marble statues, when they ought to be alive. So I propose we allow Dr. Pipt to make the magic charm which will save them, and that we assist Ojo to find the things he is seeking. What do you think, Wizard?"

"That is perhaps the best thing to do," replied the Wizard. "But after the Crooked Magician has restored those poor people to life you must take away his magic powers."

"I will," promised Ozma.

"Now tell me, please, what magic things must you find?" continued the Wizard, addressing Ojo.

"The three hairs from the Woozy's tail I have," said the boy. "That is, I have the Woozy, and the hairs are in his tail. The six-leaved clover I—I—"

"You may take it and keep it," said Ozma. "That will not be breaking the law, for it is already picked, and the crime of picking it is forgiven."

"Thank you!" cried Ojo gratefully. Then he continued: "The next thing I must find is a gill of water from a dark well."

The Wizard shook his head. "That," said he, "will be a hard task, but if you travel far enough you may discover it."

"I am willing to travel for years, if it will save Unc Nunkie," declared Ojo, earnestly.

"Then you'd better begin your journey at once," advised the Wizard.

Dorothy had been listening with interest to this conversation. Now she turned to Ozma and asked: "May I go with Ojo, to help him?"

"Would you like to?" returned Ozma.

"Yes. I know Oz pretty well, but Ojo doesn't know it at all. I'm sorry for his uncle and poor Margolotte and I'd like to help save them. May I go?"

"If you wish to," replied Ozma.

"If Dorothy goes, then I must go to take care of her," said the Scarecrow, decidedly. "A dark well can only be discovered in some out-of-the-way place, and there may be dangers there."

"You have my permission to accompany Dorothy," said Ozma. "And while you are gone I will take care of the Patchwork Girl."

"I'll take care of myself," announced Scraps, "for I'm going with the Scarecrow and Dorothy. I promised Ojo to help him find the things he wants and I'll stick to my promise."

"Very well," replied Ozma. "But I see no need for Ojo to take the Glass Cat and the Woozy."

"I prefer to remain here," said the cat. "I've nearly been nicked half a dozen times, already, and if they're going into dangers it's best for me to keep away from them."

"Let Jellia Jamb keep her till Ojo returns," suggested Dorothy. "We won't need to take the Woozy, either, but he ought to be saved because of the three hairs in his tail."

"Better take me along," said the Woozy. "My eyes can flash fire, you know, and I can growl—a little."

"I'm sure you'll be safer here," Ozma decided, and the Woozy made no further objection to the plan.

After consulting together they decided that Ojo and his party should leave the very next day to search for the gill of water from a dark well, so they now separated to make preparations for the journey.

Ozma gave the Munchkin boy a room in the palace for that night and the afternoon he passed with Dorothy—getting acquainted, as she said—and receiving advice from the Shaggy Man as to where they must go. The Shaggy Man had wandered in many parts of Oz, and so had Dorothy, for that matter, yet neither of them knew where a dark well was to be found.

"If such a thing is anywhere in the settled parts of Oz," said Dorothy, "we'd prob'ly have heard of it long ago. If it's in the wild parts of the country, no one there would need a dark well. P'raps there isn't such a thing."

"Oh, there must be!" returned Ojo, positively; "or else the recipe of Dr. Pipt wouldn't call for it."

"That's true," agreed Dorothy; "and, if it's anywhere in the Land of Oz, we're bound to find it."

"Well, we're bound to *search* for it, anyhow," said the Scarecrow. "As for finding it, we must trust to luck."

"Don't do that," begged Ojo, earnestly. "I'm called Ojo the Unlucky, you know."

CHAPTER XIX

TROUBLE WITH THE TOTTENHOTS

A DAY'S JOURNEY FROM THE EMERALD CITY brought the little band of adventurers to the home of Jack Pumpkinhead, which was a house formed from the shell of an immense pumpkin. Jack had made it himself and was very proud of it. There was a door, and several windows, and through the top was stuck a stovepipe that led from a small stove inside. The door was reached by a flight of three steps and there was a good floor on which was arranged some furniture that was quite comfortable.

It is certain that Jack Pumpkinhead might have had a much finer house to live in had he wanted it, for Ozma loved the stupid fellow, who had been her earliest companion; but Jack preferred his pumpkin house, as it matched himself very well, and in this he was not so stupid, after all.

The body of this remarkable person was made of wood, branches of trees of various sizes having been used for the purpose. This wooden framework was covered by a red shirt—with white spots in it—blue trousers, a yellow vest, a jacket of green-and-gold and stout leather shoes. The neck was a sharpened stick on which the pumpkin head was set, and the eyes, ears, nose and mouth were carved on the skin of the pumpkin, very like a child's jack-o'-lantern.

The house of this interesting creation stood in the center of a vast pumpkin-field, where the vines grew in profusion and bore pumpkins of extraordinary size as well as those which were smaller. Some of the pumpkins now ripening on the vines were almost as large as Jack's house, and he told Dorothy he intended to add another pumpkin to his mansion.

The travelers were cordially welcomed to this quaint domicile and invited to pass the night there, which they had planned to do. The Patchwork Girl was greatly interested in Jack and examined him admiringly.

"You are quite handsome," she said; "but not as really beautiful as the Scarecrow."

Jack turned, at this, to examine the Scarecrow critically, and his old friend slyly winked one painted eye at him.

"There is no accounting for tastes," remarked the Pumpkinhead, with a sigh. "An old crow once told me I was very fascinating, but of course the bird might have been mistaken. Yet I have noticed that the crows usually avoid the Scarecrow, who is a very honest fellow, in his way, but stuffed. I am not stuffed, you will observe; my body is good solid hickory."

"I adore stuffing," said the Patchwork Girl.

"Well, as for that, my head is stuffed with pumpkin-seeds," declared Jack. "I use them for brains, and when they are fresh I am intellectual. Just now, I regret to say, my seeds are rattling a bit, so I must soon get another head."

"Oh; do you change your head?" asked Ojo.

"To be sure. Pumpkins are not permanent, more's the pity, and in time they spoil. That is why I grow such a great field of pumpkins—that I may select a new head whenever necessary."

"Who carves the faces on them?" inquired the boy.

"I do that myself. I lift off my old head, place it on a table before me, and use the face for a pattern to go by. Sometimes the faces I carve are better than others—more expressive and cheerful, you know—but I think they average very well."

Before she had started on the journey Dorothy had packed a knapsack with the things she might need, and this knapsack the Scarecrow carried strapped to his back. The little girl wore a plain gingham dress and a checked sunbonnet, as she knew they were best fitted for travel. Ojo also had brought along his basket, to which Ozma had added a bottle of "Square Meal Tablets" and some fruit. But Jack Pumpkinhead grew a lot of things in his garden besides pumpkins, so he cooked for them a fine vegetable soup and gave Dorothy, Ojo and Toto, the only ones who found it necessary to eat, a pumpkin pie and some green cheese. For beds they must use the sweet dried grasses which Jack had strewn along one side of the room, but that satisfied Dorothy and Ojo very well. Toto, of course, slept beside his little mistress.

The Scarecrow, Scraps and the Pumpkinhead were tireless and had no need to sleep, so they sat up and talked together all night; but they stayed outside the house, under the bright stars, and talked in low tones so as not to disturb the sleepers. During the conversation the Scarecrow explained their quest for a dark well, and asked Jack's advice where to find it.

The Pumpkinhead considered the matter gravely.

"That is going to be a difficult task," said he, "and if I were you I'd take any ordinary well and enclose it, so as to make it dark."

"I fear that wouldn't do," replied the Scarecrow. "The well must be naturally dark, and the water must never have seen the light of day, for otherwise the magic charm might not work at all."

"How much of the water do you need?" asked Jack.

"A gill."

"How much is a gill?"

"Why—a gill is a gill, of course," answered the Scarecrow, who did not wish to display his ignorance.

"I know!" cried Scraps. "Jack and Jill went up the hill to fetch—"

"No, no; that's wrong," interrupted the Scarecrow. "There are two kinds of gills, I think; one is a girl, and the other is—"

"A gillyflower," said Jack.

"No; a measure."

"How big a measure?"

"Well, I'll ask Dorothy."

So next morning they asked Dorothy, and she said:

"I don't just know how much a gill is, but I've brought along a gold flask that holds a pint. That's more than a gill, I'm sure, and the Crooked Magician may measure it to suit himself. But the thing that's bothering us most, Jack, is to find the well."

Jack gazed around the landscape, for he was standing in the doorway of his house.

"This is a flat country, so you won't find any dark wells here," said he. "You must go into the mountains, where rocks and caverns are."

"And where is that?" asked Ojo.

"In the Quadling Country, which lies south of here," replied the Scarecrow. "I've known all along that we must go to the mountains."

"So have I," said Dorothy.

"But—goodness me!—the Quadling Country is full of dangers," declared Jack. "I've never been there myself, but—"

"I have," said the Scarecrow. "I've faced the dreadful Hammerheads, which have no arms and butt you like a goat; and I've faced the Fighting Trees, which bend down their branches to pound and whip you, and had many other adventures there."

"It's a wild country," remarked Dorothy, soberly, "and if we go there we're sure to have troubles of our own. But I guess we'll have to go, if we want that gill of water from the dark well."

So they said good-bye to the Pumpkinhead and resumed their travels, heading now directly toward the South Country, where mountains and rocks and caverns and forests of great trees abounded. This part of the Land of Oz, while it belonged to Ozma and owed her allegiance, was so wild and secluded that many queer peoples hid in its jungles and lived in their own way, without even a knowledge that they had a Ruler in the Emerald City. If they were left alone, these creatures never troubled the inhabitants of the rest of Oz, but those who invaded their domains encountered many dangers from them.

It was a two days' journey from Jack Pumkinhead's house to the edge of the Quadling Country, for neither Dorothy nor Ojo could walk very fast and they often stopped by the wayside to rest. The first night they slept on the broad fields, among the buttercups and daisies, and the Scarecrow covered the children with a gauze blanket taken from his knapsack, so they would not be chilled by the night air. Toward evening of the second day they reached a sandy plain where walking was difficult; but some distance before them they saw a group of palm trees, with many curious black dots under them; so they trudged bravely on to reach that place by dark and spend the night under the shelter of the trees.

The black dots grew larger as they advanced and although the light was dim Dorothy thought they looked like big kettles turned upside down. Just beyond this place a jumble of huge, jagged rocks lay scattered, rising to the mountains behind them.

Our travelers preferred to attempt to climb these rocks by daylight, and they realized that for a time this would be their last night on the plains.

Twilight had fallen by the time they came to the trees, beneath which were the
black, circular objects they had marked from a distance. Dozens of them were scattered around and Dorothy bent near to one, which was about as tall as she was, to
examine it more closely. As she did so the top flew open and out popped a dusky
creature, rising its length into the air and then plumping down upon the ground just
beside the little girl. Another and another popped out of the circular, pot-like dwelling, while from all the other black objects came popping more creatures—very like
jumping-jacks when their boxes are unhooked—until fully a hundred stood gathered
around our little group of travelers.

By this time Dorothy had discovered they were people, tiny and curiously
formed, but still people. Their skins were dusky and their hair stood straight up,
like wires, and was brilliant scarlet in color. Their bodies were bare except for skins
fastened around their waists and they wore bracelets on their ankles and wrists, and
necklaces, and great pendant earrings.

Toto crouched beside his mistress and wailed as if he did not like these strange
creatures a bit. Scraps began to mutter something about "hoppity, poppity, jumpity,
dump!" but no one paid any attention to her. Ojo kept close to the Scarecrow and
the Scarecrow kept close to Dorothy; but the little girl turned to the queer creatures
and asked:

"Who are you?"

They answered this question all together, in a sort of chanting chorus, the words being as follows:

"We're the jolly Tottenhots;
We do not like the day,
But in the night 'tis our delight
To gambol, skip and play.

"We hate the sun and from it run,
The moon is cool and clear,
So on this spot each Tottenhot
Waits for it to appear.

"We're ev'ry one chock full of fun,
And full of mischief, too;
But if you're gay and with us play
We'll do no harm to you."

"Glad to meet you, Tottenhots," said the Scarecrow solemnly. "But you mustn't expect us to play with you all night, for we've traveled all day and some of us are tired."

"And we never gamble," added the Patchwork Girl. "It's against the law."

These remarks were greeted with shouts of laughter by the impish creatures and one seized the Scarecrow's arm and was astonished to find the straw man whirl around so easily. So the Tottenhot raised the Scarecrow high in the air and tossed him over the heads of the crowd. Some one caught him and tossed him back, and so with shouts of glee they continued throwing the Scarecrow here and there, as if he had been a basket-ball.

Presently another imp seized Scraps and began to throw her about, in the same way. They found her a little heavier than the Scarecrow but still light enough to be tossed like a sofa-cushion, and they were enjoying the sport immensely when Dorothy, angry and indignant at the treatment her friends were receiving, rushed among the Tottenhots and began slapping and pushing them until she had rescued the Scarecrow and the Patchwork Girl and held them close on either side of her. Perhaps she would not have accomplished this victory so easily had not Toto helped her, barking and snapping at the bare legs of the imps until they were glad to flee from his attack. As for Ojo, some of the creatures had attempted to toss him, also, but finding his body too heavy they threw him to the ground and a row of the imps sat on him and held him from assisting Dorothy in her battle.

The little brown folks were much surprised at being attacked by the girl and the dog, and one or two who had been slapped hardest began to cry. Then suddenly they gave a shout, all together, and disappeared in a flash into their various houses, the tops of which closed with a series of pops that sounded like a bunch of firecrackers being exploded.

The adventurers now found themselves alone, and Dorothy asked anxiously:

"Is anybody hurt?"

"Not me," answered the Scarecrow. "They have given my straw a good shaking up and taken all the lumps out of it. I am now in splendid condition and am really obliged to the Tottenhots for their kind treatment."

"I feel much the same way," said Scraps. "My cotton stuffing had sagged a good deal with the day's walking and they've loosened it up until I feel as plump as a sausage. But the play was a little rough and I'd had quite enough of it when you interfered."

"Six of them sat on me," said Ojo, "but as they are so little they didn't hurt me much."

Just then the roof of the house in front of them opened and a Tottenhot stuck his head out, very cautiously, and looked at the strangers.

"Can't you take a joke?" he asked, reproachfully; "haven't you any fun in you at all?"

"If I had such a quality," replied the Scarecrow, "your people would have knocked it out of me. But I don't bear grudges. I forgive you."

"So do I," added Scraps. "That is, if you behave yourselves after this."

"It was just a little rough-house, that's all," said the Tottenhot. "But the question is not if *we* will behave, but if *you* will behave? We can't be shut up here all night, because this is our time to play; nor do we care to come out and be chewed up by a savage beast or slapped by an angry girl. That slapping hurts like sixty; some of my folks are crying about it. So here's the proposition: you let us alone and we'll let you alone."

"You began it," declared Dorothy.

"Well, you ended it, so we won't argue the matter. May we come out again? Or are you still cruel and slappy?"

"Tell you what we'll do," said Dorothy. "We're all tired and want to sleep until morning. If you'll let us get into your house, and stay there until daylight, you can play outside all you want to."

"That's a bargain!" cried the Tottenhot eagerly, and he gave a queer whistle that brought his people popping out of their houses on all sides. When the house before them was vacant, Dorothy and Ojo leaned over the hole and looked in, but could see nothing because it was so dark. But if the Tottenhots slept there all day the children thought they could sleep there at night, so Ojo lowered himself down and found it was not very deep.

"There's a soft cushion all over," said he. "Come on in."

Dorothy handed Toto to the boy and then climbed in herself. After her came Scraps and the Scarecrow, who did not wish to sleep but preferred to keep out of the way of the mischievous Tottenhots.

There seemed no furniture in the round den, but soft cushions were strewn about the floor and these they found made very comfortable beds. They did not close the

hole in the roof but left it open to admit air. It also admitted the shouts and ceaseless laughter of the impish Tottenhots as they played outside, but Dorothy and Ojo, being weary from their journey, were soon fast asleep.

Toto kept an eye open, however, and uttered low, threatening growls whenever the racket made by the creatures outside became too boisterous; and the Scarecrow and the Patchwork Girl sat leaning against the wall and talked in whispers all night long. No one disturbed the travelers until daylight, when in popped the Tottenhot who owned the place and invited them to vacate his premises.

CHAPTER XX

THE CAPTIVE YOOP

As they were preparing to leave, Dorothy asked: "Can you tell us where there is a dark well?"

"Never heard of such a thing," said the Tottenhot. "We live our lives in the dark, mostly, and sleep in the daytime; but we've never seen a dark well, or anything like one."

"Does anyone live on those mountains beyond here?" asked the Scarecrow.

"Lots of people. But you'd better not visit them. We never go there," was the reply.

"What are the people like?" Dorothy inquired.

"Can't say. We've been told to keep away from the mountain paths, and so we obey. This sandy desert is good enough for us, and we're not disturbed here," declared the Tottenhot.

So they left the man snuggling down to sleep in his dusky dwelling, and went out into the sunshine, taking the path that led toward the rocky places. They soon found it hard climbing, for the rocks were uneven and full of sharp points and edges, and now there was no path at all. Clambering here and there among the boulders they kept steadily on, gradually rising higher and higher until finally they came to a great rift in a part of the mountain, where the rock seemed to have split in two and left high walls on either side.

"S'pose we go this way," suggested Dorothy; "it's much easier walking than to climb over the hills."

"How about that sign?" asked Ojo.

"What sign?" she inquired.

The Munchkin boy pointed to some words painted on the wall of rock beside them, which Dorothy had not noticed. The words read:

"LOOK OUT FOR YOOP."

The girl eyed this sign a moment and then turned to the Scarecrow, asking:

"Who is Yoop; or what is Yoop?"

The straw man shook his head. Then she looked at Toto and the dog said "Woof!"

"Only way to find out is to go on," said Scraps.

This being quite true, they went on. As they proceeded, the walls of rock on either side grew higher and higher. Presently they came upon another sign which read:

"BEWARE THE CAPTIVE YOOP."

"Why, as for that," remarked Dorothy, "if Yoop is a captive there's no need to beware of him. Whatever Yoop happens to be, I'd much rather have him a captive than running around loose."

"So had I," agreed the Scarecrow, with a nod of his painted head.

"Still," said Scraps, reflectively:

> "Yoop-te-hoop-te-loop-te-goop!
> Who put noodles in the soup?
> We may beware but we don't care,
> And dare go where we scare the Yoop.

"Dear me! Aren't you feeling a little queer, just now?" Dorothy asked the Patchwork Girl.

"Not queer, but crazy," said Ojo. "When she says those things I'm sure her brains get mixed somehow and work the wrong way.

"I don't see why we are told to beware the Yoop unless he is dangerous," observed the Scarecrow in a puzzled tone.

"Never mind; we'll find out all about him when we get to where he is," replied the little girl.

The narrow canyon turned and twisted this way and that, and the rift was so small that they were able to touch both walls at the same time by stretching out their arms. Toto had run on ahead, frisking playfully, when suddenly he uttered a sharp bark of fear and came running back to them with his tail between his legs, as dogs do when they are frightened.

"Ah," said the Scarecrow, who was leading the way, "we must be near Yoop."

Just then, as he rounded a sharp turn, the straw man stopped so suddenly that all the others bumped against him.

"What is it?" asked Dorothy, standing on tip-toes to look over his shoulder. But then she saw what it was and cried "Oh!" in a tone of astonishment.

In one of the rock walls—that at their left—was hollowed a great cavern, in front of which was a row of thick iron bars, the tops and bottoms being firmly fixed in the solid rock. Over this cavern was a big sign, which Dorothy read with much curiosity, speaking the words aloud that all might know what they said:

"MISTER YOOP—HIS CAVE
The Largest Untamed Giant in Captivity.
Height, 21 Feet.—(And yet he has but 2 feet.)
Weight, 1640 Pounds.—(But he waits all the time.)
Age, 400 Years 'and Up' (as they say in the Department Store advertisements.)
Temper, Fierce and Ferocious.—(Except when asleep.)
Appetite, Ravenous.—(Prefers Meat People and Orange Marmalade.)

Strangers Approaching this cave do so at Their Own Peril!
P.S.—Don't feed the Giant yourself."

"Very well," said Ojo, with a sigh; "let's go back."

"It's a long way back," declared Dorothy.

"So it is," remarked the Scarecrow, "and it means a tedious climb over those sharp rocks if we can't use this passage. I think it will be best to run by the Giant's cave as fast as we can go. Mister Yoop seems to be asleep just now."

But the Giant wasn't asleep. He suddenly appeared at the front of his cavern, seized the iron bars in his great hairy hands and shook them until they rattled in their sockets. Yoop was so tall that our friends had to tip their heads way back to look into his face, and they noticed he was dressed all in pink velvet, with silver buttons and braid. The Giant's boots were of pink leather and had tassels on them and his hat was decorated with an enormous pink ostrich feather, carefully curled.

"Yo-ho!" he said in a deep bass voice; "I smell dinner."

"I think you are mistaken," replied the Scarecrow. "There is no orange marmalade around here."

"Ah, but I eat other things," asserted Mister Yoop. "That is, I eat them when I can get them. But this is a lonely place, and no good meat has passed by my cave for many years; so I'm hungry."

"Haven't you eaten anything in many years?" asked Dorothy.

"Nothing except six ants and a monkey. I thought the monkey would taste like meat people, but the flavor was different. I hope you will taste better, for you seem plump and tender."

"Oh, I'm not going to be eaten," said Dorothy.

"Why not?"

"I shall keep out of your way," she answered.

"How heartless!" wailed the Giant, shaking the bars again. "Consider how many years it is since I've eaten a single plump little girl! They tell me meat is going up, but if I can manage to catch you I'm sure it will soon be going down. And I'll catch you if I can."

With this the Giant pushed his big arms, which looked like tree-trunks (except that tree-trunks don't wear pink velvet) between the iron bars, and the arms were so long that they touched the opposite wall of the rock passage. Then he extended them as far as he could reach toward our travelers and found he could almost touch the Scarecrow—but not quite.

"Come a little nearer, please," begged the Giant.

"I'm a Scarecrow."

"A Scarecrow? Ugh! I don't care a straw for a scarecrow. Who is that bright-colored delicacy behind you?"

"Me?" asked Scraps. "I'm a Patchwork Girl, and I'm stuffed with cotton."

"Dear me," sighed the Giant in a disappointed tone; "that reduces my dinner from four to two—and the dog. I'll save the dog for dessert."

Toto growled, keeping a good distance away.

"Back up," said the Scarecrow to those behind him. "Let us go back a little way and talk this over."

So they turned and went around the bend in the passage, where they were out of sight of the cave and Mister Yoop could not hear them.

"My idea," began the Scarecrow, when they had halted, "is to make a dash past the cave, going on a run."

"He'd grab us," said Dorothy.

"Well, he can't grab but one at a time, and I'll go first. As soon as he grabs me the rest of you can slip past him, out of his reach, and he will soon let me go because I am not fit to eat."

They decided to try this plan and Dorothy took Toto in her arms, so as to protect him. She followed just after the Scarecrow. Then came Ojo, with Scraps the last of the four. Their hearts beat a little faster than usual as they again approached the Giant's cave, this time moving swiftly forward.

It turned out about the way the Scarecrow had planned. Mister Yoop was quite astonished to see them come flying toward him, and thrusting his arms between the bars he seized the Scarecrow in a firm grip. In the next instant he realized, from the way the straw crunched between his fingers, that he had captured the non-eatable man, but during that instant of delay Dorothy and Ojo had slipped by the Giant and were out of reach. Uttering a howl of rage the monster threw the Scarecrow after them with one hand and grabbed Scraps with the other.

The poor Scarecrow went whirling through the air and so cleverly was he aimed that he struck Ojo's back and sent the boy tumbling head over heels, and he tripped Dorothy and sent her, also, sprawling upon the ground. Toto flew out of the little girl's arms and landed some distance ahead, and all were so dazed that it was a moment before they could scramble to their feet again. When they did so they turned to look toward the Giant's cave, and at that moment the ferocious Mister Yoop threw the Patchwork Girl at them.

Down went all three again, in a heap, with Scraps on top. The Giant roared so terribly that for a time they were afraid he had broken loose; but he hadn't. So they sat in the road and looked at one another in a rather bewildered way, and then began to feel glad.

"We did it!" exclaimed the Scarecrow, with satisfaction. "And now we are free to go on our way."

"Mister Yoop is very impolite," declared Scraps. "He jarred me terribly. It's lucky my stitches are so fine and strong, for otherwise such harsh treatment might rip me up the back."

"Allow me to apologize for the Giant," said the Scarecrow, raising the Patchwork Girl to her feet and dusting her skirt with his stuffed hands. "Mister Yoop is a perfect stranger to me, but I fear, from the rude manner in which he has acted, that he is no gentleman."

Dorothy and Ojo laughed at this statement and Toto barked as if he understood the joke, after which they all felt better and resumed the journey in high spirits.

"Of course," said the little girl, when they had walked a way along the passage, "it was lucky for us the Giant was caged; for, if he had happened to be loose, he—he—"

"Perhaps, in that case, he wouldn't be hungry any more," said Ojo gravely.

CHAPTER XXI

HIP HOPPER ᵀᴴᴱ CHAMPION

THEY MUST HAVE HAD GOOD COURAGE TO CLIMB ALL THOSE rocks, for after getting out of the canyon they encountered more rock hills to be surmounted. Toto could jump from one rock to another quite easily, but the others had to creep and climb with care, so that after a whole day of such work Dorothy and Ojo found themselves very tired.

As they gazed upward at the great mass of tumbled rocks that covered the steep incline, Dorothy gave a little groan and said:

"That's going to be a ter'ble hard climb, Scarecrow. I wish we could find the dark well without so much trouble."

"Suppose," said Ojo, "you wait here and let me do the climbing, for it's on my account we're searching for the dark well. Then, if I don't find anything, I'll come back and join you."

"No," replied the little girl, shaking her head positively, "we'll all go together, for that way we can help each other. If you went alone, something might happen to you, Ojo."

So they began the climb and found it indeed difficult, for a way. But presently, in creeping over the big crags, they found a path at their feet which wound in and out among the masses of rock and was quite smooth and easy to walk upon. As the path gradually ascended the mountain, although in a roundabout way, they decided to follow it.

"This must be the road to the Country of the Hoppers," said the Scarecrow.

"Who are the Hoppers?" asked Dorothy.

"Some people Jack Pumpkinhead told me about," he replied.

"I didn't hear him," replied the girl.

"No; you were asleep," explained the Scarecrow. "But he told Scraps and me that the Hoppers and the Horners live on this mountain."

"He said *in* the mountain," declared Scraps; "but of course he meant *on* it."

"Didn't he say what the Hoppers and Horners were like?" inquired Dorothy.

"No; he only said they were two separate nations, and that the Horners were the most important."

"Well, if we go to their country we'll find out all about 'em," said the girl. "But I've never heard Ozma mention those people, so they can't be *very* important."

"Is this mountain in the Land of Oz?" asked Scraps.

"Course it is," answered Dorothy. "It's in the South Country of the Quadlings. When one comes to the edge of Oz, in any direction, there is nothing more to be seen at all. Once you could see sandy desert all around Oz; but now it's diff'rent, and no other people can see us, any more than we can see them."

"If the mountain is under Ozma's rule, why doesn't she know about the Hoppers and the Horners?" Ojo asked.

"Why, it's a fairyland," explained Dorothy, "and lots of queer people live in places so tucked away that those in the Emerald City never even hear of 'em. In the middle of the country it's diff'rent, but when you get around the edges you're sure to run into strange little corners that surprise you. I know, for I've traveled in Oz a good deal, and so has the Scarecrow."

"Yes," admitted the straw man, "I've been considerable of a traveler, in my time, and I like to explore strange places. I find I learn much more by traveling than by staying at home."

During this conversation they had been walking up the steep pathway and now found themselves well up on the mountain. They could see nothing around them, for the rocks beside their path were higher than their heads. Nor could they see far in front of them, because the path was so crooked. But suddenly they stopped, because the path ended and there was no place to go. Ahead was a big rock lying against the side of the mountain, and this blocked the way completely.

"There wouldn't be a path, though, if it didn't go somewhere," said the Scarecrow, wrinkling his forehead in deep thought.

"This is somewhere, isn't it?" asked the Patchwork Girl, laughing at the bewildered looks of the others.

"The path is locked, the way is blocked,
    Yet here we've innocently flocked;
    And now we're here it's rather queer
    There's no front door that can be knocked."

"Please don't, Scraps," said Ojo. "You make me nervous."

"Well," said Dorothy, "I'm glad of a little rest, for that's a drea'ful steep path."

As she spoke she leaned against the edge of the big rock that stood in their way. To her surprise it slowly swung backward and showed behind it a dark hole that looked like the mouth of a tunnel.

"Why, here's where the path goes to!" she exclaimed.

"So it is," answered the Scarecrow. "But the question is, do we want to go where the path does?"

"It's underground; right inside the mountain," said Ojo, peering into the dark hole. "Perhaps there's a well there; and, if there is, it's sure to be a dark one."

"Why, that's true enough!" cried Dorothy with eagerness. "Let's go in, Scarecrow; 'cause, if others have gone, we're pretty safe to go, too."

Toto looked in and barked, but he did not venture to enter until the Scarecrow had bravely gone first. Scraps followed closely after the straw man and then Ojo and Dorothy timidly stepped inside the tunnel. As soon as all of them had passed the big rock, it slowly turned and filled up the opening again; but now they were no longer in the dark, for a soft, rosy light enabled them to see around them quite distinctly.

It was only a passage, wide enough for two of them to walk abreast—with Toto in between them—and it had a high, arched roof. They could not see where the light which flooded the place so pleasantly came from, for there were no lamps anywhere visible. The passage ran straight for a little way and then made a bend to the right and another sharp turn to the left, after which it went straight again. But there were no side passages, so they could not lose their way.

After proceeding some distance, Toto, who had gone on ahead, began to bark loudly. They ran around a bend to see what was the matter and found a man sitting on the floor of the passage and leaning his back against the wall. He had probably been asleep before Toto's barks aroused him, for he was now rubbing his eyes and staring at the little dog with all his might.

There was something about this man that Toto objected to, and when he slowly rose to his foot they saw what it was. He had but one leg, set just below the middle of his round, fat body; but it was a stout leg and had a broad, flat foot at the bottom of it, on which the man seemed to stand very well. He had never had but this one leg, which looked something like a pedestal, and when Toto ran up and made a grab at the man's ankle he hopped first one way and then another in a very active manner, looking so frightened that Scraps laughed aloud.

Toto was usually a well behaved dog, but this time he was angry and snapped at the man's leg again and again. This filled the poor fellow with fear, and in hopping out of Toto's reach he suddenly lost his balance and tumbled heel over head upon the

floor. When he sat up he kicked Toto on the nose and made the dog howl angrily, but Dorothy now ran forward and caught Toto's collar, holding him back.

"Do you surrender?" she asked the man.

"Who? Me?" asked the Hopper.

"Yes; you," said the little girl.

"Am I captured?" he inquired.

"Of course. My dog has captured you," she said.

"Well," replied the man, "if I'm captured I must surrender, for it's the proper thing to do. I like to do everything proper, for it saves one a lot of trouble."

"It does, indeed," said Dorothy. "Please tell us who you are."

"I'm Hip Hopper—Hip Hopper, the Champion."

"Champion what?" she asked in surprise.

"Champion wrestler. I'm a very strong man, and that ferocious animal which you are so kindly holding is the first living thing that has ever conquered me."

"And you are a Hopper?" she continued.

"Yes. My people live in a great city not far from here. Would you like to visit it?"

"I'm not sure," she said with hesitation. "Have you any dark wells in your city?"

"I think not. We have wells, you know, but they're all well lighted, and a well lighted well cannot well be a dark well. But there may be such a thing as a very dark well in the Horner Country, which is a black spot on the face of the earth."

"Where is the Horner Country?" Ojo inquired.

"The other side of the mountain. There's a fence between the Hopper Country and the Horner Country, and a gate in the fence; but you can't pass through just now, because we are at war with the Horners."

"That's too bad," said the Scarecrow. "What seems to be the trouble?"

"Why, one of them made a very insulting remark about my people. He said we were lacking in understanding, because we had only one leg to a person. I can't see that legs have anything to do with understanding things. The Horners each have two legs, just as you have. That's one leg too many, it seems to me."

"No," declared Dorothy, "it's just the right number."

"You don't need them," argued the Hopper, obstinately. "You've only one head, and one body, and one nose and mouth. Two legs are quite unnecessary, and they spoil one's shape."

"But how can you walk, with only one leg?" asked Ojo.

"Walk! Who wants to walk?" exclaimed the man. "Walking is a terribly awkward way to travel. I hop, and so do all my people. It's so much more graceful and agreeable than walking."

"I don't agree with you," said the Scarecrow. "But tell me, is there any way to get to the Horner Country without going through the city of the Hoppers?"

"Yes; there is another path from the rocky lowlands, outside the mountain, that leads straight to the entrance of the Horner Country. But it's a long way around, so you'd better come with me. Perhaps they will allow you to go through the gate; but we expect to conquer them this afternoon, if we get time, and then you may go and come as you please."

They thought it best to take the Hopper's advice, and asked him to lead the way. This he did in a series of hops, and he moved so swiftly in this strange manner that those with two legs had to run to keep up with him.

CHAPTER XXII

THE JOKING HORNERS

IT WAS NOT LONG BEFORE THEY LEFT THE passage and came to a great cave, so high that it must have reached nearly to the top of the mountain within which it lay. It was a magnificent cave, illumined by the soft, invisible light, so that everything in it could be plainly seen. The walls were of polished marble, white with veins of delicate colors running through it, and the roof was arched and carved in designs both fantastic and beautiful.

Built beneath this vast dome was a pretty village—not very large, for there seemed not more than fifty houses altogether—and the dwellings were of marble and artistically designed. No grass nor flowers nor trees grew in this cave, so the yards surrounding the houses were smooth and bare and had low walls around them to mark their boundaries.

In the streets and the yards of the houses were many people, all having one leg growing below their bodies and all hopping here and there whenever they moved. Even the children stood firmly upon their single legs and never lost their balance.

"All hail, Champion!" cried a man in the first group of Hoppers they met; "whom have you captured?"

"No one," replied the Champion in a gloomy voice; "these strangers have captured me."

"Then," said another, "we will rescue you, and capture them, for we are greater in number."

"No," answered the Champion, "I can't allow it. I've surrendered, and it isn't polite to capture those you've surrendered to."

"Never mind that," said Dorothy. "We will give you your liberty and set you free."

"Really?" asked the Champion in joyous tones.

"Yes," said the little girl; "your people may need you to help conquer the Horners."

At this all the Hoppers looked downcast and sad. Several more had joined the group by this time and quite a crowd of curious men, women and children surrounded the strangers.

"This war with our neighbors is a terrible thing," remarked one of the women. "Some one is almost sure to get hurt."

"Why do you say that, madam?" inquired the Scarecrow.

"Because the horns of our enemies are sharp, and in battle they will try to stick those horns into our warriors," she replied.

"How many horns do the Horners have?" asked Dorothy.

"Each has one horn in the center of his forehead," was the answer.

"Oh, then they're unicorns," declared the Scarecrow.

"No; they're Horners. We never go to war with them if we can help it, on account of their dangerous horns; but this insult was so great and so unprovoked that our brave men decided to fight, in order to be revenged," said the woman.

"What weapons do you fight with?" the Scarecrow asked.

"We have no weapons," explained the Champion. "Whenever we fight the Horners, our plan is to push them back, for our arms are longer than theirs."

"Then you are better armed," said Scraps.

"Yes; but they have those terrible horns, and unless we are careful they prick us with the points," returned the Champion with a shudder. "That makes a war with them dangerous, and a dangerous war cannot be a pleasant one."

"I see very clearly," remarked the Scarecrow, "that you are going to have trouble in conquering those Horners—unless we help you."

"Oh!" cried the Hoppers in a chorus; "can you help us? Please do! We will be greatly obliged! It would please us very much!" and by these exclamations the Scarecrow knew that his speech had met with favor.

"How far is it to the Horner Country?" he asked.

"Why, it's just the other side of the fence," they answered, and the Champion added:

"Come with me, please, and I'll show you the Horners."

So they followed the Champion and several others through the streets and just beyond the village came to a very high picket fence, built all of marble, which seemed to divide the great cave into two equal parts.

But the part inhabited by the Horners was in no way as grand in appearance as that of the Hoppers. Instead of being marble, the walls and roof were of dull gray rock and the square houses were plainly made of the same material. But in extent the city was much larger than that of the Hoppers and the streets were thronged with numerous people who busied themselves in various ways.

Looking through the open pickets of the fence our friends watched the Horners, who did not know they were being watched by strangers, and found them very unusual in appearance. They were little folks in size and had bodies round as balls and short legs and arms. Their heads were round, too, and they had long, pointed ears and a horn set in the center of the forehead. The horns did not seem very terrible, for they were not more than six inches long; but they were ivory white and sharp pointed, and no wonder the Hoppers feared them.

The skins of the Horners were light brown, but they wore snow-white robes and were bare-footed. Dorothy thought the most striking thing about them was their hair, which grew in three distinct colors on each and every head—red, yellow and green. The red was at the bottom and sometimes hung over their eyes; then came a broad circle of yellow and the green was at the top and formed a brush-shaped top-knot.

None of the Horners was yet aware of the presence of strangers, who watched the little brown people for a time and then went to the big gate in the center of the dividing fence. It was locked on both sides and over the latch was a sign reading:

"WAR IS DECLARED"

"Can't we go through?" asked Dorothy.

"Not now," answered the Champion.

"I think," said the Scarecrow, "that if I could talk with those Horners they would apologize to you, and then there would be no need to fight."

"Can't you talk from this side?" asked the Champion.

"Not so well," replied the Scarecrow. "Do you suppose you could throw me over that fence? It is high, but I am very light."

"We can try it," said the Hopper. "I am perhaps the strongest man in my country, so I'll undertake to do the throwing. But I won't promise you will land on your feet."

"No matter about that," returned the Scarecrow. "Just toss me over and I'll be satisfied."

So the Champion picked up the Scarecrow and balanced him a moment, to see how much he weighed, and then with all his strength tossed him high into the air.

Perhaps if the Scarecrow had been a trifle heavier he would have been easier to throw and would have gone a greater distance; but, as it was, instead of going over the fence he landed just on top of it, and one of the sharp pickets caught him in the middle of his back and held him fast prisoner. Had he been face downward the Scarecrow might have managed to free himself, but lying on his back on the picket his hands waved in the air of the Horner Country while his feet kicked the air of the Hopper Country; so there he was.

"Are you hurt?" called the Patchwork Girl anxiously.

"Course not," said Dorothy. "But if he wiggles that way he may tear his clothes. How can we get him down, Mr. Champion?"

The Champion shook his head.

"I don't know," he confessed. "If he could scare Horners as well as he does crows, it might be a good idea to leave him there."

"This is terrible," said Ojo, almost ready to cry. "I s'pose it's because I am Ojo the Unlucky that everyone who tries to help me gets into trouble."

"You are lucky to have anyone to help you," declared Dorothy. "But don't worry. We'll rescue the Scarecrow, somehow."

"I know how," announced Scraps. "Here, Mr. Champion; just throw me up to the Scarecrow. I'm nearly as light as he is, and when I'm on top the fence I'll pull our friend off the picket and toss him down to you."

"All right," said the Champion, and he picked up the Patchwork Girl and threw her in the same manner he had the Scarecrow. He must have used more strength this time, however, for Scraps sailed far over the top of the fence and, without being able to grab the Scarecrow at all, tumbled to the ground in the Horner Country, where her

stuffed body knocked over two men and a woman and made a crowd that had collected there run like rabbits to get away from her.

Seeing the next moment that she was harmless, the people slowly returned and
gathered around the Patchwork Girl, regarding her with astonishment. One of them
wore a jeweled star in his hair, just above his horn, and this seemed a person of importance. He spoke for the rest of his people, who treated him with great respect.

"Who are you, Unknown Being?" he asked.

"Scraps," she said, rising to her feet and patting her cotton wadding smooth where
it had bunched up.

"And where did you come from?" he continued.

"Over the fence. Don't be silly. There's no other place I *could* have come from,"
she replied.

He looked at her thoughtfully.

"You are not a Hopper," said he, "for you have two legs. They're not very well
shaped, but they are two in number. And that strange creature on top the fence—
why doesn't he stop kicking?—must be your brother, or father, or son, for he also
has two legs."

"You must have been to visit the Wise Donkey," said Scraps, laughing so merrily
that the crowd smiled with her, in sympathy. "But that reminds me, Captain—
or King—"

"I am Chief of the Horners, and my name is Jak."

"Of course; Little Jack Horner; I might have known it. But the reason I volplaned
over the fence was so I could have a talk with you about the Hoppers."

"What about the Hoppers?" asked the Chief, frowning.

"You've insulted them, and you'd better beg their pardon," said Scraps. "If you
don't, they'll probably hop over here and conquer you."

"We're not afraid—as long as the gate is locked," declared the Chief. "And we
didn't insult them at all. One of us made a joke that the stupid Hoppers couldn't see."

The Chief smiled as he said this and the smile made his face look quite jolly.

"What was the joke?" asked Scraps.

"A Horner said they have less understanding than we, because they've only one
leg. Ha, ha! You see the point, don't you? If you stand on your legs, and your legs are
under you, then—ha, ha, ha!—then your legs are your under-standing. Hee, hee, hee!
Ho, ho! My, but that's a fine joke. And the stupid Hoppers couldn't see it! They couldn't
see that with only one leg they must have less under-standing than we who have two
legs. Ha, ha, ha! Hee, hee! Ho, ho!" The Chief wiped the tears of laughter from his eyes
with the bottom hem of his white robe, and all the other Horners wiped their eyes on
their robes, for they had laughed just as heartily as their Chief at the absurd joke.

"Then," said Scraps, "their understanding of the understanding you meant led to the misunderstanding."

"Exactly; and so there's no need for us to apologize," returned the Chief.

"No need for an apology, perhaps, but much need for an explanation," said Scraps decidedly. "You don't want war, do you?"

"Not if we can help it," admitted Jak Horner. "The question is, who's going to explain the joke to the Horners? You know it spoils any joke to be obliged to explain it, and this is the best joke I ever heard."

"Who made the joke?" asked Scraps.

"Diksey Horner. He is working in the mines, just now, but he'll be home before long. Suppose we wait and talk with him about it? Maybe he'll be willing to explain his joke to the Hoppers."

"All right," said Scraps. "I'll wait, if Diksey isn't too long."

"No, he's short; he's shorter than I am. Ha, ha, ha! Say! that's a better joke than Diksey's. He won't be too long, because he's short. Hee, hee, ho!"

The other Horners who were standing by roared with laughter and seemed to like their Chief's joke as much as he did. Scraps thought it was odd that they could be so easily amused, but decided there could be little harm in people who laughed so merrily.

CHAPTER XXIII

PEACE IS DECLARED

"COME WITH ME TO MY DWELLING AND I'LL INTRODUCE you to my daughters," said the Chief. "We're bringing them up according to a book of rules that was written by one of our leading old bachelors, and everyone says they're a remarkable lot of girls."

So Scraps accompanied him along the street to a house that seemed on the outside exceptionally grimy and dingy. The streets of this city were not paved nor had any attempt been made to beautify the houses or their surroundings, and having noticed this condition Scraps was astonished when the Chief ushered her into his home.

Here was nothing grimy or faded, indeed. On the contrary, the room was of dazzling brilliance and beauty, for it was lined throughout with an exquisite metal that resembled translucent frosted silver. The surface of this metal was highly ornamented in raised designs representing men, animals, flowers and trees, and from the metal itself was radiated the soft light which flooded the room. All the furniture was made of the same glorious metal, and Scraps asked what it was.

"That's radium," answered the Chief. "We Horners spend all our time digging radium from the mines under this mountain, and we use it to decorate our homes and make them pretty and cosy. It is a medicine, too, and no one can ever be sick who lives near radium."

"Have you plenty of it?" asked the Patchwork Girl.

"More than we can use. All the houses in this city are decorated with it, just the same as mine is."

"Why don't you use it on your streets, then, and the outside of your houses, to make them as pretty as they are within?" she inquired.

"Outside? Who cares for the outside of anything?" asked the Chief. "We Horners don't live on the outside of our homes; we live inside. Many people are like those stupid Hoppers, who love to make an outside show. I suppose you strangers thought their city more beautiful than ours, because you judged from appearances and they have handsome marble houses and marble streets; but if you entered one of their stiff dwellings you would find it bare and uncomfortable, as all their show is on the outside. They have an idea that what is not seen by others is not important, but with us the rooms we live in are our chief delight and care, and we pay no attention to outside show."

"Seems to me," said Scraps, musingly, "it would be better to make it all pretty—inside and out."

"Seems? Why, you're all seams, my girl!" said the Chief; and then he laughed heartily at his latest joke and a chorus of small voices echoed the chorus with "tee-hee-hee! ha, ha!"

Scraps turned around and found a row of girls seated in radium chairs ranged along one wall of the room. There were nineteen of them, by actual count, and they were of all sizes from a tiny child to one almost a grown woman. All were neatly dressed in spotless white robes and had brown skins, horns on their foreheads and three-colored hair.

"These," said the Chief, "are my sweet daughters. My dears, I introduce to you Miss Scraps Patchwork, a lady who is traveling in foreign parts to increase her store of wisdom."

The nineteen Horner girls all arose and made a polite courtesy, after which they resumed their seats and rearranged their robes properly.

"Why do they sit so still, and all in a row?" asked Scraps.

"Because it is ladylike and proper," replied the Chief.

"But some are just children, poor things! Don't they ever run around and play and laugh, and have a good time?"

"No, indeed," said the Chief. "That would be improper in young ladies, as well as in those who will sometime become young ladies. My daughters are being brought up according to the rules and regulations laid down by a leading bachelor who has given the subject much study and is himself a man of taste and culture. Politeness is his great hobby, and he claims that if a child is allowed to do an impolite thing one cannot expect the grown person to do anything better."

"Is it impolite to romp and shout and be jolly?" asked Scraps.

"Well, sometimes it is, and sometimes it isn't," replied the Horner, after considering the question. "By curbing such inclinations in my daughters we keep on the safe side. Once in a while I make a good joke, as you have heard, and then I permit my daughters to laugh decorously; but they are never allowed to make a joke themselves."

"That old bachelor who made the rules ought to be skinned alive!" declared Scraps, and would have said more on the subject had not the door opened to admit a little Horner man whom the Chief introduced as Diksey.

"What's up, Chief?" asked Diksey, winking nineteen times at the nineteen girls, who demurely cast down their eyes because their father was looking.

The Chief told the man that his joke had not been understood by the dull Hoppers, who had become so angry that they had declared war. So the only way to avoid a terrible battle was to explain the joke so they could understand it.

"All right," replied Diksey, who seemed a good-natured man; "I'll go at once to the fence and explain. I don't want any war with the Hoppers, for wars between nations always cause hard feelings."

So the Chief and Diksey and Scraps left the house and went back to the marble picket fence. The Scarecrow was still stuck on the top of his picket but had now ceased to struggle. On the other side of the fence were Dorothy and Ojo, looking between the pickets; and there, also, were the Champion and many other Hoppers.

Diksey went close to the fence and said:

"My good Hoppers, I wish to explain that what I said about you was a joke. You have but one leg each, and we have two legs each. Our legs are under us, whether one or two, and we stand on them. So, when I said you had less understanding than we, I did not mean that you had less understanding, you understand, but that you had less standundering, so to speak. Do you understand that?"

The Hoppers thought it over carefully. Then one said:

"That is clear enough; but where does the joke come in?"

Dorothy laughed, for she couldn't help it, although all the others were solemn enough.

"I'll tell you where the joke comes in," she said, and took the Hoppers away to a distance, where the Horners could not hear them. "You know," she then explained, "those neighbors of yours are not very bright, poor things, and what they think is a joke isn't a joke at all—it's true, don't you see?"

"True that we have less understanding?" asked the Champion.

"Yes; it's true because you don't understand such a poor joke; if you did, you'd be no wiser than they are."

"Ah, yes; of course," they answered, looking very wise.

"So I'll tell you what to do," continued Dorothy. "Laugh at their poor joke and tell 'em it's pretty good for a Horner. Then they won't dare say you have less under-standing, because you understand as much as they do."

The Hoppers looked at one another questioningly and blinked their eyes and tried to think what it all meant; but they couldn't figure it out.

"What do you think, Champion?" asked one of them.

"I think it is dangerous to think of this thing any more than we can help," he replied. "Let us do as this girl says and laugh with the Horners, so as to make them believe we see the joke. Then there will be peace again and no need to fight."

They readily agreed to this and returned to the fence laughing as loud and as hard as they could, although they didn't feel like laughing a bit. The Horners were much surprised.

"That's a fine joke—for a Horner—and we are much pleased with it," said the Champion, speaking between the pickets. "But please don't do it again."

"I won't," promised Diksey. "If I think of another such joke I'll try to forget it."

"Good!" cried the Chief Horner. "The war is over and peace is declared."

There was much joyful shouting on both sides of the fence and the gate was unlocked and thrown wide open, so that Scraps was able to rejoin her friends.

"What about the Scarecrow?" she asked Dorothy.

"We must get him down, somehow or other," was the reply.

"Perhaps the Horners can find a way," suggested Ojo. So they all went through the gate and Dorothy asked the Chief Horner how they could get the Scarecrow off the fence. The Chief didn't know how, but Diksey said:

"A ladder's the thing."

"Have you one?" asked Dorothy.

"To be sure. We use ladders in our mines," said he. Then he ran away to get the ladder, and while he was gone the Horners gathered around and welcomed the strangers to their country, for through them a great war had been avoided.

In a little while Diksey came back with a tall ladder which he placed against the fence. Ojo at once climbed to the top of the ladder and Dorothy went about halfway up and Scraps stood at the foot of it. Toto ran around it and barked. Then Ojo pulled the Scarecrow away from the picket and passed him down to Dorothy, who in turn lowered him to the Patchwork Girl.

As soon as he was on his feet and standing on solid ground the Scarecrow said:

"Much obliged. I feel much better. I'm not stuck on that picket any more."

The Horners began to laugh, thinking this was a joke, but the Scarecrow shook himself and patted his straw a little and said to Dorothy: "Is there much of a hole in my back?"

The little girl examined him carefully.

"There's quite a hole," she said. "But I've got a needle and thread in the knapsack and I'll sew you up again."

"Do so," he begged earnestly, and again the Hoppers laughed, to the Scarecrow's great annoyance.

While Dorothy was sewing up the hole in the straw man's back Scraps examined the other parts of him.

"One of his legs is ripped, too!" she exclaimed.

"Oho!" cried little Diksey; "that's bad. Give him the needle and thread and let him mend his ways."

"Ha, ha, ha!" laughed the Chief, and the other Horners at once roared with laughter.

"What's funny?" inquired the Scarecrow sternly.

"Don't you see?" asked Diksey, who had laughed even harder than the others. "That's a joke. It's by odds the best joke I ever made. You walk with your legs, and so that's the way you walk, and your legs are the ways. See? So, when you mend your legs, you mend your ways. Ho, ho, ho! hee, hee! I'd no idea I could make such a fine joke!"

"Just wonderful!" echoed the Chief. "How do you manage to do it, Diksey?"

"I don't know," said Diksey modestly. "Perhaps it's the radium, but I rather think it's my splendid intellect."

"If you don't quit it," the Scarecrow told him, "there'll be a worse war than the one you've escaped from."

Ojo had been deep in thought, and now he asked the Chief: "Is there a dark well in any part of your country?"

"A dark well? None that ever I heard of," was the answer.

"Oh, yes," said Diksey, who overheard the boy's question. "There's a very dark well down in my radium mine."

"Is there any water in it?" Ojo eagerly asked.

"Can't say; I've never looked to see. But we can find out."

So, as soon as the Scarecrow was mended, they decided to go with Diksey to the mine. When Dorothy had patted the straw man into shape again he declared he felt as good as new and equal to further adventures.

"Still," said he, "I prefer not to do picket duty again. High life doesn't seem to agree with my constitution." And then they hurried away to escape the laughter of the Horners, who thought this was another joke.

CHAPTER XXIV

OJO FINDS THE DARK WELL

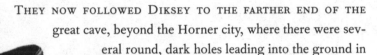

THEY NOW FOLLOWED DIKSEY TO THE FARTHER END OF THE great cave, beyond the Horner city, where there were several round, dark holes leading into the ground in a slanting direction. Diksey went to one of these holes and said:

"Here is the mine in which lies the dark well you are seeking. Follow me and step carefully and I'll lead you to the place."

He went in first and after him came Ojo, and then Dorothy, with the Scarecrow behind her. The Patchwork Girl entered last of all, for Toto kept close beside his little mistress.

A few steps beyond the mouth of the opening it was pitch dark. "You won't lose your way, though," said the Horner, "for there's only one way to go. The mine's mine and I know every step of the way. How's that for a joke, eh? The mine's mine." Then he chuckled gleefully as they followed him silently down the steep slant. The hole was just big enough to permit them to walk upright, although the Scarecrow, being much the taller of the party, often had to bend his head to keep from hitting the top.

The floor of the tunnel was difficult to walk upon because it had been worn smooth as glass, and pretty soon Scraps, who was some distance behind the others, slipped and fell head foremost. At once she began to slide downward, so swiftly that

when she came to the Scarecrow she knocked him off his feet and sent him tumbling against Dorothy, who tripped up Ojo. The boy fell against the Horner, so that all went tumbling down the slide in a regular mix-up, unable to see where they were going because of the darkness.

Fortunately, when they reached the bottom the Scarecrow and Scraps were in front, and the others bumped against them, so that no one was hurt. They found themselves in a vast cave which was dimly lighted by the tiny grains of radium that lay scattered among the loose rocks.

"Now," said Diksey, when they had all regained their feet, "I will show you where the dark well is. This is a big place, but if we hold fast to each other we won't get lost."

They took hold of hands and the Horner led them into a dark corner, where he halted.

"Be careful," said he warningly. "The well is at your feet."

"All right," replied Ojo, and kneeling down he felt in the well with his hand and found that it contained a quantity of water. "Where's the gold flask, Dorothy?" he asked, and the little girl handed him the flask, which she had brought with her.

Ojo knelt again and by feeling carefully in the dark managed to fill the flask with the unseen water that was in the well. Then he screwed the top of the flask firmly in place and put the precious water in his pocket.

"All right!" he said again, in a glad voice; "now we can go back."

They returned to the mouth of the tunnel and began to creep cautiously up the incline. This time they made Scraps stay behind, for fear she would slip again; but they all managed to get up in safety and the Munchkin boy was very happy when he stood in the Horner city and realized that the water from the dark well, which he and his friends had traveled so far to secure, was safe in his jacket pocket.

CHAPTER XXV

THEY BRIBE THE LAZY QUADLING

"Now," said Dorothy, as they stood on the mountain path, having left behind them the cave in which dwelt the Hoppers and the Horners, "I think we must find a road into the Country of the Winkies, for there is where Ojo wants to go next."

"Is there such a road?" asked the Scarecrow.

"I don't know," she replied. "I s'pose we can go back the way we came, to Jack Pumpkinhead's house, and then turn into the Winkie Country; but that seems like running 'round a haystack, doesn't it?"

"Yes," said the Scarecrow. "What is the next thing Ojo must get?"

"A yellow butterfly," answered the boy.

"That means the Winkie Country, all right, for it's the yellow country of Oz," remarked Dorothy. "I think, Scarecrow, we ought to take him to the Tin Woodman, for he's the Emp'ror of the Winkies and will help us to find what Ojo wants."

"Of course," replied the Scarecrow, brightening at the suggestion. "The Tin Woodman will do anything we ask him, for he's one of my dearest friends. I believe we can take a crosscut into his country and so get to his castle a day sooner than if we travel back the way we came."

"I think so, too," said the girl; "and that means we must keep to the left."

They were obliged to go down the mountain before they found any path that led in the direction they wanted to go, but among the tumbled rocks at the foot of the mountain was a faint trail which they decided to follow. Two or three hours' walk along this trail brought them to a clear, level country, where there were a few farms and some scattered houses. But they knew they were still in the Country of the Quadlings, because everything had a bright red color. Not that the trees and grasses were red, but the fences and houses were painted that color and all the wild-flowers that bloomed by the wayside had red blossoms. This part of the Quadling Country seemed peaceful and prosperous, if rather lonely, and the road was now more distinct and easier to follow.

But just as they were congratulating themselves upon the progress they had made they came upon a broad river which swept along between high banks, and here the road ended and there was no bridge of any sort to allow them to cross.

"This is queer," mused Dorothy, looking at the water reflectively. "Why should there be any road, if the river stops everyone walking along it?"

"Wow!" said Toto, gazing earnestly into her face.

"That's the best answer you'll get," declared the Scarecrow, with his comical smile, "for no one knows any more than Toto about this road."

Said Scraps:

> "Ev'ry time I see a river,
> I have chills that make me shiver,
> For I never can forget
> All the water's very wet.
> If my patches get a soak
> It will be a sorry joke;
> So to swim I'll never try
> Till I find the water dry."

"Try to control yourself, Scraps," said Ojo; "you're getting crazy again. No one intends to swim that river."

"No," decided Dorothy, "we couldn't swim it if we tried. It's too big a river, and the water moves awful fast."

"There ought to be a ferryman with a boat," said the Scarecrow; "but I don't see any."

"Couldn't we make a raft?" suggested Ojo.

"There's nothing to make one of," answered Dorothy.

"Wow!" said Toto again, and Dorothy saw he was looking along the bank of the river.

"Why, he sees a house over there!" cried the little girl. "I wonder we didn't notice it ourselves. Let's go and ask the people how to get 'cross the river."

A quarter of a mile along the bank stood a small, round house, painted bright red, and as it was on their side of the river they hurried toward it. A chubby little man, dressed all in red, came out to greet them, and with him were two children, also in red costumes. The man's eyes were big and staring as he examined the Scarecrow and the Patchwork Girl, and the children shyly hid behind him and peeked timidly at Toto.

"Do you live here, my good man?" asked the Scarecrow.

"I think I do, Most Mighty Magician," replied the Quadling, bowing low; "but whether I'm awake or dreaming I can't be positive, so I'm not sure where I live. If you'll kindly pinch me I'll find out all about it."

"You're awake," said Dorothy, "and this is no magician, but just the Scarecrow."

"But he's alive," protested the man, "and he oughtn't to be, you know. And that other dreadful person—the girl who is all patches—seems to be alive, too."

"Very much so," declared Scraps, making a face at him. "But that isn't your affair, you know."

"I've a right to be surprised, haven't I?" asked the man meekly.

"I'm not sure; but anyhow you've no right to say I'm dreadful. The Scarecrow, who is a gentleman of great wisdom, thinks I'm beautiful," retorted Scraps.

"Never mind all that," said Dorothy. "Tell us, good Quadling, how we can get across the river."

"I don't know," replied the Quadling.

"Don't you ever cross it?" asked the girl.

"Never."

"Don't travelers cross it?"

"Not to my knowledge," said he.

They were much surprised to hear this, and the man added: "It's a pretty big river, and the current is strong. I know a man who lives on the opposite bank, for I've seen him there a good many years; but we've never spoken because neither of us has ever crossed over."

"That's queer," said the Scarecrow. "Don't you own a boat?"

The man shook his head.

"Nor a raft?"

"Where does this river go to?" asked Dorothy.

"That way," answered the man, pointing with one hand, "it goes into the Country of the Winkies, which is ruled by the Tin Emperor, who must be a mighty magician because he's all made of tin, and yet he's alive. And that way," pointing with the other hand, "the river runs between two mountains where dangerous people dwell."

The Scarecrow looked at the water before them.

"The current flows toward the Winkie Country," said he; "and so, if we had a boat, or a raft, the river would float us there more quickly and more easily than we could walk."

"That is true," agreed Dorothy; and then they all looked thoughtful and wondered what could be done.

"Why can't the man make us a raft?" asked Ojo.

"Will you?" inquired Dorothy, turning to the Quadling.

The chubby man shook his head.

"I'm too lazy," he said. "My wife says I'm the laziest man in all Oz, and she is a truthful woman. I hate work of any kind, and making a raft is hard work."

"I'll give you my em'rald ring," promised the girl.

"No; I don't care for emeralds. If it were a ruby, which is the color I like best, I might work a little while."

"I've got some Square Meal Tablets," said the Scarecrow. "Each one is the same as a dish of soup, a fried fish, a mutton pot-pie, lobster salad, charlotte russe and lemon jelly—all made into one little tablet that you can swallow without trouble."

"Without trouble!" exclaimed the Quadling, much interested; "then those tablets would be fine for a lazy man. It's such hard work to chew when you eat."

"I'll give you six of those tablets if you'll help us make a raft," promised the Scarecrow. "They're a combination of food which people who eat are very fond of. I never eat, you know, being straw; but some of my friends eat regularly. What do you say to my offer, Quadling?"

"I'll do it," decided the man. "I'll help, and you can do most of the work. But my wife has gone fishing for red eels to-day, so some of you will have to mind the children."

Scraps promised to do that, and the children were not so shy when the Patchwork Girl sat down to play with them. They grew to like Toto, too, and the little dog allowed them to pat him on his head, which gave the little ones much joy.

There were a number of fallen trees near the house and the Quadling got his axe and chopped them into logs of equal length. He took his wife's clothesline to bind these logs together, so that they would form a raft, and Ojo found some strips of wood and nailed them along the tops of the logs, to render them more firm. The Scarecrow and Dorothy helped roll the logs together and carry the strips of wood, but it took so long to make the raft that evening came just as it was finished, and with evening the Quadling's wife returned from her fishing.

The woman proved to be cross and bad-tempered, perhaps because she had only caught one red eel during all the day. When she found that her husband had used her clothesline, and the logs she had wanted for firewood, and the boards she had intended to mend the shed with, and a lot of gold nails, she became very angry. Scraps wanted to shake the woman, to make her behave, but Dorothy talked to her in a gentle tone and told the Quadling's wife she was a Princess of Oz and a friend of Ozma and that when she got back to the Emerald City she would send them a lot of things to repay them for the raft, including a new clothesline. This promise pleased the woman and she soon became more pleasant, saying they could stay the night at her house and begin their voyage on the river next morning.

This they did, spending a pleasant evening with the Quadling family and being entertained with such hospitality as the poor people were able to offer them. The man groaned a good deal and said he had overworked himself by chopping the logs, but the Scarecrow gave him two more tablets than he had promised, which seemed to comfort the lazy fellow.

CHAPTER XXVI

THE TRICK RIVER

NEXT MORNING THEY PUSHED THE RAFT into the water and all got aboard. The Quadling man had to hold the log craft fast while they took their places, and the flow of the river was so powerful that it nearly tore the raft from his hands. As soon as they were all seated upon the logs he let go and away it floated and the adventurers had begun their voyage toward the Winkie Country.

The little house of the Quadlings was out of sight almost before they had cried their good-byes, and the Scarecrow said in a pleased voice: "It won't take us long to get to the Winkie Country, at this rate."

They had floated several miles down the stream and were enjoying the ride when suddenly the raft slowed up, stopped short, and then began to float back the way it had come.

"Why, what's wrong?" asked Dorothy, in astonishment; but they were all just as bewildered as she was and at first no one could answer the question. Soon, however, they realized the truth: that the current of the river had reversed and the water was now flowing in the opposite direction— toward the mountains.

They began to recognize the scenes they had passed, and by and by they came in sight of the little house of the Quadlings again. The man was standing on the river bank and he called to them:

"How do you do? Glad to see you again. I forgot to tell you that the river changes its direction every little while. Sometimes it flows one way, and sometimes the other."

They had no time to answer him, for the raft was swept past the house and a long distance on the other side of it.

"We're going just the way we don't want to go," said Dorothy, "and I guess the best thing we can do is to get to land before we're carried any farther."

But they could not get to land. They had no oars, nor even a pole to guide the raft with. The logs which bore them floated in the middle of the stream and were held fast in that position by the strong current.

So they sat still and waited and, even while they were wondering what could be done, the raft slowed down, stopped, and began drifting the other way—in the direction it had first followed. After a time they repassed the Quadling house and the man was still standing on the bank. He cried out to them:

"Good day! Glad to see you again. I expect I shall see you a good many times, as you go by, unless you happen to swim ashore."

By that time they had left him behind and were headed once more straight toward the Winkie Country.

"This is pretty hard luck," said Ojo in a discouraged voice. "The Trick River keeps changing, it seems, and here we must float back and forward forever, unless we manage in some way to get ashore."

"Can you swim?" asked Dorothy.

"No; I'm Ojo the Unlucky."

"Neither can I. Toto can swim a little, but that won't help us to get to shore."

"I don't know whether I could swim, or not," remarked Scraps; "but if I tried it I'd surely ruin my lovely patches."

"My straw would get soggy in the water and I would sink," said the Scarecrow.

So there seemed no way out of their dilemma and being helpless they simply sat still. Ojo, who was on the front of the raft, looked over into the water and thought he saw some large fishes swimming about. He found a loose end of the clothesline which fastened the logs together, and taking a gold nail from his pocket he bent it nearly double, to form a hook, and tied it to the end of the line. Having baited the hook with some bread which he broke from his loaf, he dropped the line into the water and almost instantly it was seized by a great fish.

They knew it was a great fish, because it pulled so hard on the line that it dragged the raft forward even faster than the current of the river had carried it. The fish was frightened, and it was a strong swimmer. As the other end of the clothesline was bound around the logs he could not get it away, and as he had greedily swallowed the gold hook at the first bite he could not get rid of that, either.

When they reached the place where the current had before changed, the fish was still swimming ahead in its wild attempt to escape. The raft slowed down, yet it did not stop, because the fish would not let it. It continued to move in the same direction it had been going. As the current reversed and rushed backward on its course it failed to drag the raft with it. Slowly, inch by inch, they floated on, and the fish tugged and tugged and kept them going.

"I hope he won't give up," said Ojo anxiously. "If the fish can hold out until the current changes again, we'll be all right."

The fish did not give up, but held the raft bravely on its course, till at last the water in the river shifted again and floated them the way they wanted to go. But now the captive fish found its strength failing. Seeking a refuge, it began to drag the raft toward the shore. As they did not wish to land in this place the boy cut the rope with his pocket-knife and set the fish free, just in time to prevent the raft from grounding.

The next time the river backed up the Scarecrow managed to seize the branch of a tree that overhung the water and they all assisted him to hold fast and prevent the raft from being carried backward. While they waited here, Ojo spied a long broken branch lying upon the bank, so he leaped ashore and got it. When he had stripped off the side shoots he believed he could use the branch as a pole, to guide the raft in case of emergency.

They clung to the tree until they found the water flowing the right way, when they let go and permitted the raft to resume its voyage. In spite of these pauses they were really making good progress toward the Winkie Country and having found a way to conquer the adverse current their spirits rose considerably. They could see little of the country through which they were passing, because of the high banks, and they met with no boats or other craft upon the surface of the river.

Once more the trick river reversed its current, but this time the Scarecrow was on guard and used the pole to push the raft toward a big rock which lay in the water. He believed the rock would prevent their floating backward with the current, and so it did. They clung to this anchorage until the water resumed its proper direction, when they allowed the raft to drift on.

Floating around a bend they saw ahead a high bank of water, extending across the entire river, and toward this they were being irresistibly carried. There being no way to arrest the progress of the raft they clung fast to the logs and let the river sweep them on. Swiftly the raft climbed the bank of water and slid down on the other side, plunging its edge deep into the water and drenching them all with spray.

As again the raft righted and drifted on, Dorothy and Ojo laughed at the ducking they had received; but Scraps was much dismayed and the Scarecrow took out his handkerchief and wiped the water off the Patchwork Girl's patches as well as he was able to. The sun soon dried her and the colors of her patches proved good, for they did not run together nor did they fade.

After passing the wall of water the current did not change or flow backward any more but continued to sweep them steadily forward. The banks of the river grew lower, too, permitting them to see more of the country, and presently they discovered yellow buttercups and dandelions growing amongst the grass, from which evidence they knew they had reached the Winkie Country.

"Don't you think we ought to land?" Dorothy asked the Scarecrow.

"Pretty soon," he replied. "The Tin Woodman's castle is in the southern part of the Winkie Country, and so it can't be a great way from here."

Fearing they might drift too far, Dorothy and Ojo now stood up and raised the Scarecrow in their arms, as high as they could, thus allowing him a good view of the country. For a time he saw nothing he recognized, but finally he cried:

"There it is! There it is!"

"What?" asked Dorothy.

"The Tin Woodman's tin castle. I can see its turrets glittering in the sun. It's quite a way off, but we'd better land as quickly as we can."

They let him down and began to urge the raft toward the shore by means of the pole. It obeyed very well, for the current was more sluggish now, and soon they had reached the bank and landed safely.

The Winkie Country was really beautiful, and across the fields they could see afar the silvery sheen of the tin castle. With light hearts they hurried toward it, being fully rested by their long ride on the river.

By and by they began to cross an immense field of splendid yellow lilies, the delicate fragrance of which was very delightful.

"How beautiful they are!" cried Dorothy, stopping to admire the perfection of these exquisite flowers.

"Yes," said the Scarecrow, reflectively, "but we must be careful not to crush or injure any of these lilies."

"Why not?" asked Ojo.

"The Tin Woodman is very kind-hearted," was the reply, "and he hates to see any living thing hurt in any way."

"Are flowers alive?" asked Scraps.

"Yes, of course. And these flowers belong to the Tin Woodman. So, in order not to offend him, we must not tread on a single blossom."

"Once," said Dorothy, "the Tin Woodman stepped on a beetle and killed the little creature. That made him very unhappy and he cried until his tears rusted his joints, so he couldn't move 'em."

"What did he do then?" asked Ojo.

"Put oil on them, until the joints worked smooth again."

"Oh!" exclaimed the boy, as if a great discovery had flashed across his mind. But he did not tell anybody what the discovery was and kept the idea to himself.

It was a long walk, but a pleasant one, and they did not mind it a bit. Late in the afternoon they drew near to the wonderful tin castle of the Emperor of the Winkies, and Ojo and Scraps, who had never seen it before, were filled with amazement.

Tin abounded in the Winkie Country and the Winkies were said to be the most skillful tinsmiths in all the world. So the Tin Woodman had employed them in building his magnificent castle, which was all of tin, from the ground to the tallest turret, and so brightly polished that it glittered in the sun's rays more gorgeously than silver. Around the grounds of the castle ran a tin wall, with tin gates; but the gates stood wide open because the Emperor had no enemies to disturb him.

When they entered the spacious grounds our travelers found more to admire. Tin fountains sent sprays of clear water far into the air and there were many beds of tin flowers, all as perfectly formed as any natural flowers might be. There were tin trees, too, and here and there shady bowers of tin, with tin benches and chairs to sit upon. Also, on the sides of the pathway leading up to the front door of the castle, were rows of tin statuary, very cleverly executed. Among these Ojo recognized statues of Dorothy, Toto, the Scarecrow, the Wizard, the Shaggy Man, Jack Pumpkinhead and Ozma, all standing upon neat pedestals of tin.

Toto was well acquainted with the residence of the Tin Woodman and, being assured a joyful welcome, he ran ahead and barked so loudly at the front door that the Tin Woodman heard him and came out in person to see if it were really his old friend Toto. Next moment the tin man had clasped the Scarecrow in a warm embrace and then turned to hug Dorothy. But now his eye was arrested by the strange sight of the Patchwork Girl, and he gazed upon her in mingled wonder and admiration.

CHAPTER XXVII

THE TIN WOODMAN OBJECTS

THE TIN WOODMAN WAS ONE OF THE most important personages in all Oz. Though Emperor of the Winkies, he owed allegiance to Ozma, who ruled all the land, and the girl and the tin man were warm personal friends. He was something of a dandy and kept his tin body brilliantly polished and his tin joints well oiled. Also he was very courteous in manner and so kind and gentle that everyone loved him. The Emperor greeted Ojo and Scraps with cordial hospitality and ushered the entire party into his handsome tin parlor, where all the furniture and pictures were made of tin. The walls were paneled with tin and from the tin ceiling hung tin chandeliers.

The Tin Woodman wanted to know, first of all, where Dorothy had found the Patchwork Girl, so between them the visitors told the story of how Scraps was made, as well as the accident to Margolotte and Unc Nunkie and how Ojo had set out upon a journey to procure the things needed for the Crooked Magician's magic charm. Then Dorothy told of their adventures in the Quadling Country and how at last they succeeded in getting the water from a dark well. While the little girl was relating these adventures the Tin Woodman sat in an easy chair listening with intense interest, while the others sat grouped around him. Ojo, however, had kept his eyes fixed upon the body of the tin Emperor, and now he noticed that under the joint of his left knee a tiny drop of oil was forming. He watched this drop of oil with a fast-beating heart, and feeling in his pocket brought out a tiny vial of crystal, which he held secreted in his hand.

Presently the Tin Woodman changed his position, and at once Ojo, to the astonishment of all, dropped to the floor and held his crystal vial under the Emperor's knee joint. Just then the drop of oil fell, and the boy caught it in his bottle and immediately corked it tight. Then, with a red face and embarrassed manner, he rose to confront the others.

"What in the world were you doing?" asked the Tin Woodman.

"I caught a drop of oil that fell from your knee-joint," confessed Ojo.

"A drop of oil!" exclaimed the Tin Woodman. "Dear me, how careless my valet must have been in oiling me this morning. I'm afraid I shall have to scold the fellow, for I can't be dropping oil wherever I go."

"Never mind," said Dorothy. "Ojo seems glad to have the oil, for some reason."

"Yes," declared the Munchkin boy, "I am glad. For one of the things the Crooked Magician sent me to get was a drop of oil from a live man's body. I had no idea, at first, that there was such a thing; but it's now safe in the little crystal vial."

"You are very welcome to it, indeed," said the Tin Woodman. "Have you now secured all the things you were in search of?"

"Not quite all," answered Ojo. "There were five things I had to get, and I have found four of them. I have the three hairs in the tip of a Woozy's tail, a six-leaved clover, a gill of water from a dark well and a drop of oil from a live man's body. The last thing is the easiest of all to get, and I'm sure that my dear Unc Nunkie—and good Margolotte, as well—will soon be restored to life."

The Munchkin boy said this with much pride and pleasure.

"Good!" exclaimed the Tin Woodman; "I congratulate you. But what is the fifth and last thing you need, in order to complete the magic charm?"

"The left wing of a yellow butterfly," said Ojo. "In this yellow country, and with your kind assistance, that ought to be very easy to find."

The Tin Woodman stared at him in amazement.

"Surely you are joking!" he said.

"No," replied Ojo, much surprised; "I am in earnest."

"But do you think for a moment that I would permit you, or anyone else, to pull the left wing from a yellow butterfly?" demanded the Tin Woodman sternly.

"Why not, sir?"

"Why not? You ask me why not? It would be cruel—one of the most cruel and heartless deeds I ever heard of," asserted the Tin Woodman. "The butterflies are among the prettiest of all created things, and they are very sensitive to pain. To tear a wing from one would cause it exquisite torture and it would soon die in great agony. I would not permit such a wicked deed under any circumstances!"

Ojo was astounded at hearing this. Dorothy, too, looked grave and disconcerted, but she knew in her heart that the Tin Woodman was right. The Scarecrow nodded his head in approval of his friend's speech, so it was evident that he agreed with the Emperor's decision. Scraps looked from one to another in perplexity.

"Who cares for a butterfly?" she asked.

"Don't you?" inquired the Tin Woodman.

"Not the snap of a finger, for I have no heart," said the Patchwork Girl. "But I want to help Ojo, who is my friend, to rescue the uncle whom he loves, and I'd kill a dozen useless butterflies to enable him to do that."

The Tin Woodman sighed regretfully.

"You have kind instincts," he said, "and with a heart you would indeed be a fine creature. I cannot blame you for your heartless remark, as you cannot understand the feelings of those who possess hearts. I, for instance, have a very neat and responsive heart which the wonderful Wizard of Oz once gave me, and so I shall never—never— *never* permit a poor yellow butterfly to be tortured by anyone."

"The yellow country of the Winkies," said Ojo sadly, "is the only place in Oz where a yellow butterfly can be found."

"I'm glad of that," said the Tin Woodman. "As I rule the Winkie Country, I can protect my butterflies."

"Unless I get the wing—just one left wing—" said Ojo miserably, "I can't save Unc Nunkie."

"Then he must remain a marble statue forever," declared the Tin Emperor, firmly.

Ojo wiped his eyes, for he could not hold back the tears.

"I'll tell you what to do," said Scraps. "We'll take a whole yellow butterfly, alive and well, to the Crooked Magician, and let him pull the left wing off."

"No you won't," said the Tin Woodman. "You can't have one of my dear little butterflies to treat in that way."

"Then what in the world shall we do?" asked Dorothy.

They all became silent and thoughtful. No one spoke for a long time. Then the Tin Woodman suddenly roused himself and said:

"We must all go back to the Emerald City and ask Ozma's advice. She's a wise little girl, our Ruler, and she may find a way to help Ojo save his Unc Nunkie."

So the following morning the party started on the journey to the Emerald City, which they reached in due time without any important adventure. It was a sad journey for Ojo, for without the wing of the yellow butterfly he saw no way to save Unc Nunkie—unless he waited six years for the Crooked Magician to make a new lot of the Powder of Life. The boy was utterly discouraged, and as he walked along he groaned aloud.

"Is anything hurting you?" inquired the Tin Woodman in a kindly tone, for the Emperor was with the party.

"I'm Ojo the Unlucky," replied the boy. "I might have known I would fail in anything I tried to do."

"Why are you Ojo the Unlucky?" asked the tin man.

"Because I was born on a Friday."

"Friday is not unlucky," declared the Emperor. "It's just one of seven days. Do you suppose all the world becomes unlucky one-seventh of the time?"

"It was the thirteenth day of the month," said Ojo.

"Thirteen! Ah, that is indeed a lucky number," replied the Tin Woodman. "All my good luck seems to happen on the thirteenth. I suppose most people never notice the good luck that comes to them with the number 13, and yet if the least bit of bad luck falls on that day, they blame it to the number, and not to the proper cause."

"Thirteen's my lucky number, too," remarked the Scarecrow.

"And mine," said Scraps. "I've just thirteen patches on my head."

"But," continued Ojo, "I'm left-handed."

"Many of our greatest men are that way," asserted the Emperor. "To be left-handed is usually to be two-handed; the right-handed people are usually one-handed."

"And I've a wart under my right arm," said Ojo.

"How lucky!" cried the Tin Woodman. "If it were on the end of your nose it might be unlucky, but under your arm it is luckily out of the way."

"For all those reasons," said the Munchkin boy, "I have been called Ojo the Unlucky."

"Then we must turn over a new leaf and call you henceforth Ojo the Lucky," declared the tin man. "Every reason you have given is absurd. But I have noticed that those who continually dread ill luck and fear it will overtake them, have no time to take advantage of any good fortune that comes their way. Make up your mind to be Ojo the Lucky."

"How can I?" asked the boy, "when all my attempts to save my dear uncle have failed?"

"Never give up, Ojo," advised Dorothy. "No one ever knows what's going to happen next."

Ojo did not reply, but he was so dejected that even their arrival at the Emerald City failed to interest him.

The people joyfully cheered the appearance of the Tin Woodman, the Scarecrow and Dorothy, who were all three general favorites, and on entering the royal palace word came to them from Ozma that she would at once grant them an audience.

Dorothy told the girl Ruler how successful they had been in their quest until they came to the item of the yellow butterfly, which the Tin Woodman positively refused to sacrifice to the magic potion.

"He is quite right," said Ozma, who did not seem a bit surprised. "Had Ojo told me that one of the things he sought was the wing of a yellow butterfly I would have informed him, before he started out, that he could never secure it. Then you would have been saved the troubles and annoyances of your long journey."

"I didn't mind the journey at all," said Dorothy; "it was fun."

"As it has turned out," remarked Ojo, "I can never get the things the Crooked Magician sent me for; and so, unless I wait the six years for him to make the Powder of Life, Unc Nunkie cannot be saved."

Ozma smiled.

"Dr. Pipt will make no more Powder of Life, I promise you," said she. "I have sent for him and had him brought to this palace, where he now is, and his four kettles have been destroyed and his book of recipes burned up. I have also had brought here the marble statues of your uncle and of Margolotte, which are standing in the next room."

They were all greatly astonished at this announcement.

"Oh, let me see Unc Nunkie! Let me see him at once, please!" cried Ojo eagerly.

"Wait a moment," replied Ozma, "for I have something more to say. Nothing that happens in the Land of Oz escapes the notice of our wise Sorceress, Glinda the Good. She knew all about the magic-making of Dr. Pipt, and how he had brought the Glass Cat and the Patchwork Girl to life, and the accident to Unc Nunkie and Margolotte, and of Ojo's quest and his journey with Dorothy. Glinda also knew that Ojo would fail to find all the things he sought, so she sent for our Wizard and instructed him what to do. Something is going to happen in this palace, presently, and that 'something' will, I am sure, please you all. And now," continued the girl Ruler, rising from her chair, "you may follow me into the next room."

CHAPTER XXVIII

THE WONDERFUL WIZARD OF OZ

WHEN OJO ENTERED THE ROOM HE RAN QUICKLY to the statue of Unc Nunkie and kissed the marble face affectionately.

"I did my best, Unc," he said, with a sob, "but it was no use!"

Then he drew back and looked around the room, and the sight of the assembled company quite amazed him.

Aside from the marble statues of Unc Nunkie and Margolotte, the Glass Cat was there, curled up on a rug; and the Woozy was there, sitting on its square hind legs and looking on the scene with solemn interest; and there was the Shaggy Man, in a suit of shaggy pea-green satin, and at a table sat the little Wizard, looking quite important and as if he knew much more than he cared to tell.

Last of all, Dr. Pipt was there, and the Crooked Magician sat humped up in a chair, seeming very dejected but keeping his eyes fixed on the lifeless form of his wife Margolotte, whom he fondly loved but whom he now feared was lost to him forever.

Ozma took a chair which Jellia Jamb wheeled forward for the Ruler, and back of her stood the Scarecrow, the Tin Woodman and Dorothy, as well as the Cowardly Lion and the Hungry Tiger. The Wizard now arose and made a low bow to Ozma and another less deferent bow to the assembled company.

"Ladies and gentlemen and beasts," he said, "I beg to announce that our Gracious Ruler has permitted me to obey the commands of the great Sorceress, Glinda the

Good, whose humble Assistant I am proud to be. We have discovered that the Crooked Magician has been indulging in his magical arts contrary to law, and therefore, by Royal Edict, I hereby deprive him of all power to work magic in the future. He is no longer a crooked magician, but a simple Munchkin; he is no longer even crooked, but a man like other men."

As he pronounced these words the Wizard waved his hand toward Dr. Pipt and instantly every crooked limb straightened out and became perfect. The former magician, with a cry of joy, sprang to his feet, looked at himself in wonder, and then fell back in his chair and watched the Wizard with fascinated interest.

"The Glass Cat, which Dr. Pipt lawlessly made," continued the Wizard, "is a pretty cat, but its pink brains made it so conceited that it was a disagreeable companion to everyone. So the other day I took away the pink brains and replaced them with transparent ones, and now the Glass Cat is so modest and well behaved that Ozma has decided to keep her in the palace as a pet."

"I thank you," said the cat, in a soft voice.

"The Woozy has proved himself a good Woozy and a faithful friend," the Wizard went on, "so we will send him to the Royal Menagerie, where he will have good care and plenty to eat all his life."

"Much obliged," said the Woozy. "That beats being fenced up in a lonely forest and starved."

"As for the Patchwork Girl," resumed the Wizard, "she is so remarkable in appearance, and so clever and good tempered, that our Gracious Ruler intends to preserve her carefully, as one of the curiosities of the curious Land of Oz. Scraps may live in the palace, or wherever she pleases, and be nobody's servant but her own."

"That's all right," said Scraps.

"We have all been interested in Ojo," the little Wizard continued, "because his love for his unfortunate uncle has led him bravely to face all sorts of dangers, in order that he might rescue him. The Munchkin boy has a loyal and generous heart and has done his best to restore Unc Nunkie to life. He has failed, but there are others more powerful than the Crooked Magician, and there are more ways than Dr. Pipt knew of to destroy the charm of the Liquid of Petrifaction. Glinda the Good has told me of one way, and you shall now learn how great is the knowledge and power of our peerless Sorceress."

As he said this the Wizard advanced to the statue of Margolotte and made a magic pass, at the same time muttering a magic word that none could hear distinctly. At once the woman moved, turned her head wonderingly this way and that, to note all who stood before her, and seeing Dr. Pipt, ran forward and threw herself into her husband's outstretched arms.

Then the Wizard made the magic pass and spoke the magic word before the statue of Unc Nunkie. The old Munchkin immediately came to life and with a low bow to the Wizard said: "Thanks."

But now Ojo rushed up and threw his arms joyfully about his uncle, and the old man hugged his little nephew tenderly and stroked his hair and wiped away the boy's tears with a handkerchief, for Ojo was crying from pure happiness.

Ozma came forward to congratulate them.

"I have given to you, my dear Ojo and Unc Nunkie, a nice house just outside the walls of the Emerald City," she said, "and there you shall make your future home and be under my protection."

"Didn't I say you were Ojo the Lucky?" asked the Tin Woodman, as everyone crowded around to shake Ojo's hand.

"Yes; and it is true!" replied Ojo, gratefully.

Tik-Tok of Oz

CONTENTS

CHAPTER I

ANN'S ARMY

"I WON'T!" CRIED ANN; "I WON'T SWEEP THE FLOOR. IT IS BENEATH MY DIGNITY."

"Some one must sweep it," replied Ann's younger sister, Salye; "else we shall soon be wading in dust. And you are the eldest, and the head of the family."

"I'm Queen of Oogaboo," said Ann, proudly. "But," she added with a sigh, "my kingdom is the smallest and the poorest in all the Land of Oz."

This was quite true. Away up in the mountains, in a far corner of the beautiful Fairyland of Oz, lies a small valley which is named Oogaboo, and in this valley lived a few people who were usually happy and contented and never cared to wander over the mountain pass into the more settled parts of the land. They knew that all of Oz, including their own territory, was ruled by a beautiful Princess named Ozma, who lived in the splendid Emerald City; yet the simple folk of Oogaboo never visited Ozma. They had a royal family of their own—not especially to rule over them, but just as a matter of pride. Ozma permitted the various parts of her country to have their Kings and Queens and Emperors and the like, but all were ruled over by the lovely girl Queen of the Emerald City.

The King of Oogaboo used to be a man named Jol Jemkiph Soforth, who for many years did all the drudgery of deciding disputes and telling his people when to plant cabbages and pickle onions. But the King's wife had a sharp tongue and small respect for the King, her husband; therefore one night King Jol crept over the pass into the Land of Oz and disappeared from Oogaboo for good and all. The Queen waited a few years for him to return and then started in search of him, leaving her eldest daughter, Ann Soforth, to act as Queen.

Now, Ann had not forgotten when her birthday came, for that meant a party and feasting and dancing, but she had quite forgotten how many years the birthdays marked. In a land where people live always, this is not considered a cause for regret, so we may justly say that Queen Ann of Oogaboo was old enough to make jelly—and let it go at that.

But she didn't make jelly, or do any more of the housework than she could help. She was an ambitious woman and constantly resented the fact that her kingdom was so tiny and her people so stupid and unenterprising. Often she wondered what had become of her father and mother, out beyond the pass, in the wonderful Land of Oz, and the fact that they did not return to Oogaboo led Ann to suspect that they had found a better place to live. So, when Salye refused to sweep the floor of the living room in the palace, and Ann would not sweep it, either, she said to her sister:

"I'm going away. This absurd Kingdom of Oogaboo tires me."

"Go, if you want to," answered Salye; "but you are very foolish to leave this place."

"Why?" asked Ann.

"Because in the Land of Oz, which is Ozma's country, you will be a nobody, while here you are a Queen."

"Oh, yes! Queen over eighteen men, twenty-seven women and forty-four children!" returned Ann bitterly.

"Well, there are certainly more people than that in the great Land of Oz," laughed Salye. "Why don't you raise an army and conquer them, and be Queen of all Oz?" she asked, trying to taunt Ann and so to anger her. Then she made a face at her sister and went into the back yard to swing in the hammock.

Her jeering words, however, had given Queen Ann an idea. She reflected that Oz was reported to be a peaceful country and Ozma a mere girl who ruled with gentleness to all and was obeyed because her people loved her. Even in Oogaboo the story was told that Ozma's sole army consisted of twenty-seven fine officers, who wore beautiful uniforms but carried no weapons, because there was no one to fight. Once there had been a Private Soldier, besides the officers, but Ozma had made him a Captain General and taken away his gun for fear it might accidentally hurt some one.

The more Ann thought about the matter the more she was convinced it would be easy to conquer the Land of Oz and set herself up as Ruler in Ozma's place, if she but had an army to do it with. Afterward she could go out into the world and conquer other lands, and then perhaps she could find a way to the moon, and conquer that. She had a warlike spirit that preferred trouble to idleness.

It all depended on an army, Ann decided. She carefully counted in her mind all the men of her kingdom. Yes; there were exactly eighteen of them, all told. That would not make a very big army, but by surprising Ozma's unarmed officers her men might easily subdue them. "Gentle people are always afraid of those that bluster," Ann told herself. "I don't wish to shed any blood, for that would shock my nerves and I might faint; but if we threaten and flash our weapons I am sure the people of Oz will fall upon their knees before me and surrender."

This argument, which she repeated to herself more than once, finally determined the Queen of Oogaboo to undertake the audacious venture.

"Whatever happens," she reflected, "can make me no more unhappy than my staying shut up in this miserable valley and sweeping floors and quarreling with Sister Salye; so I will venture all, and win what I may."

That very day she started out to organize her army.

The first man she came to was Jo Apple, so called because he had an apple orchard.

"Jo," said Ann, "I am going to conquer the world, and I want you to join my army."

"Don't ask me to do such a fool thing, for I must politely refuse Your Majesty," said Jo Apple.

"I have no intention of asking you. I shall command you, as Queen of Oogaboo, to join," said Ann.

"In that case, I suppose I must obey," the man remarked, in a sad voice. "But I pray you to consider that I am a very important citizen, and for that reason am entitled to an office of high rank."

"You shall be a General," promised Ann.

"With gold epaulets and a sword?" he asked.

"Of course," said the Queen.

Then she went to the next man, whose name was Jo Bunn, as he owned an orchard where graham-buns and wheat-buns, in great variety, both hot and cold, grew on the trees.

"Jo," said Ann, "I am going to conquer the world, and I command you to join my army."

"Impossible!" he exclaimed. "The bun crop has to be picked."

"Let your wife and children do the picking," said Ann.

"But I'm a man of great importance, Your Majesty," he protested.

"For that reason you shall be one of my Generals, and wear a cocked hat with gold braid, and curl your mustaches and clank a long sword," she promised.

So he consented, although sorely against his will, and the Queen walked on to the next cottage. Here lived Jo Cone, so called because the trees in his orchard bore crops of excellent ice-cream cones.

"Jo," said Ann, "I am going to conquer the world, and you must join my army."

"Excuse me, please," said Jo Cone. "I am a bad fighter. My good wife conquered me years ago, for she can fight better than I. Take her, Your Majesty, instead of me, and I'll bless you for the favor."

"This must be an army of men—fierce, ferocious warriors," declared Ann, looking sternly upon the mild little man.

"And you will leave my wife here in Oogaboo?" he asked.

"Yes; and make you a General."

"I'll go," said Jo Cone, and Ann went on to the cottage of Jo Clock, who had an orchard of clock-trees. This man at first insisted that he would not join the army, but Queen Ann's promise to make him a General finally won his consent.

"How many Generals are there in your army?" he asked.

"Four, so far," replied Ann.

"And how big will the army be?" was his next question.

"I intend to make every one of the eighteen men in Oogaboo join it," she said.

"Then four Generals are enough," announced Jo Clock. "I advise you to make the rest of them Colonels."

Ann tried to follow his advice. The next four men she visited—who were Jo Plum, Jo Egg, Jo Banjo and Jo Cheese, named after the trees in their orchards—she made Colonels of her army; but the fifth one, Jo Nails, said Colonels and Generals were getting to be altogether too common in the Army of Oogaboo and he preferred to be a Major. So Jo Nails, Jo Cake, Jo Ham and Jo Stockings were all four made Majors, while the next four—Jo Sandwich, Jo Padlocks, Jo Sundae and Jo Buttons—were appointed Captains of the army.

But now Queen Ann was in a quandary. There remained but two other men in all Oogaboo, and if she made these two Lieutenants, while there were four Captains, four Majors, four Colonels and four Generals, there was likely to be jealousy in her army, and perhaps mutiny and desertions.

One of these men, however, was Jo Candy, and he would not go at all. No promises could tempt him, nor could threats move him. He said he must remain at home to harvest his crop of jackson-balls, lemon-drops, bonbons and chocolate-creams. Also he had large fields of crackerjack and buttered pop corn to be mowed and threshed, and he was determined not to disappoint the children of Oogaboo by going away to conquer the world and so let the candy crop spoil.

Finding Jo Candy so obstinate, Queen Ann let him have his own way and continued her journey to the house of the eighteenth and last man in Oogaboo, who was a young fellow named Jo Files. This Files had twelve trees which bore steel files of various sorts; but also he had nine book-trees, on which grew a choice selection of

story-books. In case you have never seen books growing upon trees, I will explain that those in Jo Files' orchard were enclosed in broad green husks which, when fully ripe, turned to a deep red color. Then the books were picked and husked and were ready to read. If they were picked too soon, the stories were found to be confused and uninteresting and the spelling bad. However, if allowed to ripen perfectly, the stories were fine reading and the spelling and grammar excellent.

Files freely gave his books to all who wanted them, but the people of Oogaboo cared little for books and so he had to read most of them himself, before they spoiled. For, as you probably know, as soon as the books were read the words disappeared and the leaves withered and faded—which is the worst fault of all books which grow upon trees.

When Queen Ann spoke to this young man Files, who was both intelligent and ambitious, he said he thought it would be great fun to conquer the world. But he called her attention to the fact that he was far superior to the other men of her army. Therefore, he would not be one of her Generals or Colonels or Majors or Captains, but claimed the honor of being sole Private.

Ann did not like this idea at all.

"I hate to have a Private soldier in my army," she said; "they're so common. I am told that Princess Ozma once had a Private Soldier, but she made him her Captain General, which is good evidence that the Private was unnecessary."

"Ozma's army doesn't fight," returned Files; "but your army must fight like fury in order to conquer the world. I have read in my books that it is always the Private soldiers who do the fighting, for no officer is ever brave enough to face the foe. Also, it stands to reason that your officers must have some one to command and to issue their orders to; therefore I'll be the one. I long to slash and slay the enemy and become a hero. Then, when we return to Oogaboo, I'll take all the marbles away from the children and melt them up and make a marble statue of myself for all to look upon and admire."

Ann was much pleased with Private Files. He seemed indeed to be such a warrior as she needed in her enterprise, and her hopes of success took a sudden bound when Files told her he knew where a gun-tree grew and would go there at once and pick the ripest and biggest musket the tree bore.

CHAPTER II

OUT OF OOGABOO

THREE DAYS LATER THE GRAND ARMY OF OOGABOO ASSEMBLED IN THE SQUARE IN front of the royal palace. The sixteen officers were attired in gorgeous uniforms and carried sharp, glittering swords. The Private had picked his gun and, although it was not a very big weapon, Files tried to look fierce and succeeded so well that all his commanding officers were secretly afraid of him.

The women were there, protesting that Queen Ann Soforth had no right to take their husbands and fathers from them; but Ann commanded them to keep silent, and that was the hardest order to obey they had ever received.

The Queen appeared before her army dressed in an imposing uniform of green, covered with gold braid. She wore a green soldier-cap with a purple plume in it and looked so royal and dignified that everyone in Oogaboo except the army was glad she was going. The army was sorry she was not going alone.

"Form ranks!" she cried in her shrill voice.

Salye leaned out of the palace window and laughed.

"I believe your army can run better than it can fight," she observed.

"Of course," replied General Bunn, proudly. "We're not looking for trouble, you know, but for plunder. The more plunder and the less fighting we get, the better we shall like our work."

"For my part," said Files, "I prefer war and carnage to anything. The only way to become a hero is to conquer, and the story-books all say that the easiest way to conquer is to fight."

"That's the idea, my brave man!" agreed Ann. "To fight is to conquer and to conquer is to secure plunder and to secure plunder is to become a hero. With such noble determination to back me, the world is mine! Good-bye, Salye. When we return we shall be rich and famous. Come, Generals; let us march."

At this the Generals straightened up and threw out their chests. Then they swung their glittering swords in rapid circles and cried to the Colonels:

"For—ward March!"

Then the Colonels shouted to the Majors: "For—ward March!" and the Majors yelled to the Captains: "For—ward March!" and the Captains screamed to the Private:

"For—ward March!"

So Files shouldered his gun and began to march, and all the officers followed after him. Queen Ann came last of all, rejoicing in her noble army and wondering why she had not decided long ago to conquer the world.

In this order the procession marched out of Oogaboo and took the narrow mountain pass which led into the lovely Fairyland of Oz.

CHAPTER III

MAGIC MYSTIFIES THE MARCHERS

PRINCESS OZMA WAS ALL UNAWARE THAT THE ARMY OF OOGABOO, LED BY THEIR ambitious Queen, was determined to conquer her kingdom. The beautiful girl Ruler of Oz was busy with the welfare of her subjects and had no time to think of Ann Soforth and her disloyal plans. But there was one who constantly guarded the peace and happiness of the Land of Oz and this was the Official Sorceress of the Kingdom, Glinda the Good.

In her magnificent castle, which stands far north of the Emerald City where Ozma holds her court, Glinda owns a wonderful magic Record Book, in which is printed every event that takes place anywhere, just as soon as it happens.

The smallest things and the biggest things are all recorded in this book. If a child stamps its foot in anger, Glinda reads about it; if a city burns down, Glinda finds the fact noted in her book.

The Sorceress always reads her Record Book every day, and so it was she knew that Ann Soforth, Queen of Oogaboo, had foolishly assembled an army of sixteen officers and one Private Soldier, with which she intended to invade and conquer the Land of Oz.

There was no danger but that Ozma, supported by the magic arts of Glinda the Good and the powerful Wizard of Oz—both her firm friends—could easily defeat a far more imposing army than Ann's; but it would be a shame to have the peace of Oz interrupted by any sort of quarreling or fighting. So Glinda did not even mention the matter to Ozma, or to anyone else. She merely went into a great chamber of her castle, known as the Magic Room, where she performed a magical ceremony which caused the mountain pass that led from Oogaboo to make several turns and twists. The result was that when Ann and her army came to the end of the pass they were not in the Land of Oz at all, but in an adjoining territory that was quite distinct from Ozma's domain and separated from Oz by an invisible barrier.

As the Oogaboo people emerged into this country, the pass they had traversed disappeared behind them and it was not likely they would ever find their way back into the valley of Oogaboo. They were greatly puzzled, indeed, by their surroundings and did not know which way to go. None of them had ever visited Oz, so it took them some time to discover they were not in Oz at all, but in an unknown country.

"Never mind," said Ann, trying to conceal her disappointment; "we have started out to conquer the world, and here is part of it. In time, as we pursue our victorious journey, we will doubtless come to Oz; but, until we get there, we may as well conquer whatever land we find ourselves in."

"Have we conquered this place, Your Majesty?" anxiously inquired Major Cake.

"Most certainly," said Ann. "We have met no people, as yet, but when we do, we will inform them that they are our slaves."

"And afterward we will plunder them of all their possessions," added General Apple.

"They may not possess anything," objected Private Files; "but I hope they will fight us, just the same. A peaceful conquest wouldn't be any fun at all."

"Don't worry," said the Queen. "*We* can fight, whether our foes do or not; and perhaps we would find it more comfortable to have the enemy surrender promptly."

It was a barren country and not very pleasant to travel in. Moreover, there was little for them to eat, and as the officers became hungry they became fretful. Many would have deserted had they been able to find their way home, but as the Oogaboo people were now hopelessly lost in a strange country they considered it more safe to keep together than to separate.

Queen Ann's temper, never very agreeable, became sharp and irritable as she and her army tramped over the rocky roads without encountering either people or plunder. She scolded her officers until they became surly, and a few of them were disloyal enough to ask her to hold her tongue. Others began to reproach her for leading them into difficulties and in the space of three unhappy days every man was mourning for his orchard in the pretty valley of Oogaboo.

Files, however, proved a different sort. The more difficulties he encountered the more cheerful he became, and the sighs of the officers were answered by the merry whistle of the Private. His pleasant disposition did much to encourage Queen Ann and before long she consulted the Private Soldier more often than she did his superiors.

It was on the third day of their pilgrimage that they encountered their first adventure. Toward evening the sky was suddenly darkened and Major Nails exclaimed:

"A fog is coming toward us."

"I do not think it is a fog," replied Files, looking with interest at the approaching cloud. "It seems to me more like the breath of a Rak."

"What is a Rak?" asked Ann, looking about fearfully.

"A terrible beast with a horrible appetite," answered the soldier, growing a little paler than usual. "I have never seen a Rak, to be sure, but I have read of them in the story-books that grew in my orchard, and if this is indeed one of those fearful monsters, we are not likely to conquer the world."

Hearing this, the officers became quite worried and gathered closer about their soldier.

"What is the thing like?" asked one.

"The only picture of a Rak that I ever saw in a book was rather blurred," said Files, "because the book was not quite ripe when it was picked. But the creature can fly in the air and run like a deer and swim like a fish. Inside its body is a glowing furnace of fire, and the Rak breathes in air and breathes out smoke, which darkens the sky for miles around, wherever it goes. It is bigger than a hundred men and feeds on any living thing."

The officers now began to groan and to tremble, but Files tried to cheer them, saying:

"It may not be a Rak, after all, that we see approaching us, and you must not forget that we people of Oogaboo, which is part of the Fairyland of Oz, cannot be killed."

"Nevertheless," said Captain Buttons, "if the Rak catches us, and chews us up into small pieces, and swallows us—what will happen then?"

"Then each small piece will still be alive," declared Files.

"I cannot see how that would help us," wailed Colonel Banjo. "A hamburger steak is a hamburger steak, whether it is alive or not!"

"I tell you, this may not be a Rak," persisted Files. "We will know, when the cloud gets nearer, whether it is the breath of a Rak or not. If it has no smell at all, it is probably a fog; but if it has an odor of salt and pepper, it is a Rak and we must prepare for a desperate fight."

They all eyed the dark cloud fearfully. Before long it reached the frightened group and began to envelop them. Every nose sniffed the cloud—and every one detected in it the odor of salt and pepper.

"The Rak!" shouted Private Files, and with a howl of despair the sixteen officers fell to the ground, writhing and moaning in anguish. Queen Ann sat down upon a rock and faced the cloud more bravely, although her heart was beating fast. As for Files, he calmly loaded his gun and stood ready to fight the foe, as a soldier should.

They were now in absolute darkness, for the cloud which covered the sky and the setting sun was black as ink. Then through the gloom appeared two round, glowing balls of red, and Files at once decided these must be the monster's eyes.

He raised his gun, took aim and fired.

There were several bullets in the gun, all gathered from an excellent bullet-tree in Oogaboo, and they were big and hard. They flew toward the monster and struck it, and with a wild, weird cry the Rak came fluttering down and its huge body fell plump upon the forms of the sixteen officers, who thereupon screamed louder than before.

"Badness me!" moaned the Rak. "See what you've done with that dangerous gun of yours!"

"I can't see," replied Files, "for the cloud formed by your breath darkens my sight!"

"Don't tell me it was an accident," continued the Rak, reproachfully, as it still flapped its wings in a helpless manner. "Don't claim you didn't know the gun was loaded, I beg of you!"

"I don't intend to," replied Files. "Did the bullets hurt you very badly?"

"One has broken my jaw, so that I can't open my mouth. You will notice that my voice sounds rather harsh and husky, because I have to talk with my teeth set close together. Another bullet broke my left wing, so that I can't fly; and still another broke my right leg, so that I can't walk. It was the most careless shot I ever heard of!"

"Can't you manage to lift your body off from my commanding officers?" inquired Files. "From their cries I'm afraid your great weight is crushing them."

"I hope it is," growled the Rak. "I want to crush them, if possible, for I have a bad disposition. If only I could open my mouth, I'd eat all of you, although my appetite is poorly this warm weather."

With this the Rak began to roll its immense body sidewise, so as to crush the officers more easily; but in doing this it rolled completely off from them and the entire sixteen scrambled to their feet and made off as fast as they could run.

Private Files could not see them go but he knew from the sound of their voices that they had escaped, so he ceased to worry about them.

"Pardon me if I now bid you good-bye," he said to the Rak. "The parting is caused by our desire to continue our journey. If you die, do not blame me, for I was obliged to shoot you as a matter of self-protection."

"I shall not die," answered the monster, "for I bear a charmed life. But I beg you not to leave me!"

"Why not?" asked Files.

"Because my broken jaw will heal in about an hour, and then I shall be able to eat you. My wing will heal in a day and my leg will heal in a week, when I shall be as well as ever. Having shot me, and so caused me all this annoyance, it is only fair and just that you remain here and allow me to eat you as soon as I can open my jaws."

"I beg to differ with you," returned the soldier firmly. "I have made an engagement with Queen Ann of Oogaboo to help her conquer the world, and I cannot break my word for the sake of being eaten by a Rak."

"Oh; that's different," said the monster. "If you've an engagement, don't let me detain you."

So Files felt around in the dark and grasped the hand of the trembling Queen, whom he led away from the flapping, sighing Rak. They stumbled over the stones for a way but presently began to see dimly the path ahead of them, as they got farther and farther away from the dreadful spot where the wounded monster lay.

By and by they reached a little hill and could see the last rays of the sun flooding a pretty valley beyond, for now they had passed beyond the cloudy breath of the Rak. Here were huddled the sixteen officers, still frightened and panting from their run. They had halted only because it was impossible for them to run any farther.

Queen Ann gave them a severe scolding for their cowardice, at the same time praising Files for his courage.

"We are wiser than he, however," muttered General Clock, "for by running away we are now able to assist Your Majesty in conquering the world; whereas, had Files been eaten by the Rak, he would have deserted your army."

After a brief rest they descended into the valley, and as soon as they were out of sight of the Rak the spirits of the entire party rose quickly. Just at dusk they came to a brook, on the banks of which Queen Ann commanded them to make camp for the night.

Each officer carried in his pocket a tiny white tent. This, when placed upon the ground, quickly grew in size until it was large enough to permit the owner to enter it and sleep within its canvas walls. Files was obliged to carry a knapsack, in which was not only his own tent but an elaborate pavilion for Queen Ann, besides a bed and chair and a magic table. This table, when set upon the ground in Ann's pavilion, became of large size, and in a drawer of the table was contained the Queen's supply of extra clothing, her manicure and toilet articles and other necessary things. The royal bed was the only one in the camp, the officers and Private sleeping in hammocks attached to their tent poles.

There was also in the knapsack a flag bearing the royal emblem of Oogaboo, and this flag Files flew upon its staff every night, to show that the country they were in had been conquered by the Queen of Oogaboo. So far, no one but themselves had seen the flag, but Ann was pleased to see it flutter in the breeze and considered herself already a famous conqueror.

CHAPTER IV

BETSY BRAVES THE BILLOWS

THE WAVES DASHED AND THE LIGHTNING FLASHED AND THE THUNDER ROLLED AND the ship struck a rock. Betsy Bobbin was running across the deck and the shock sent her flying through the air until she fell with a splash into the dark blue water. The same shock caught Hank, a thin little, sad-faced mule, and tumbled him also into the sea, far from the ship's side.

When Betsy came up, gasping for breath because the wet plunge had surprised her, she reached out in the dark and grabbed a bunch of hair. At first she thought it was the end of a rope, but presently she heard a dismal "Hee-haw!" and knew she was holding fast to the end of Hank's tail.

Suddenly the sea was lighted up by a vivid glare. The ship, now in the far distance, caught fire, blew up and sank beneath the waves.

Betsy shuddered at the sight, but just then her eye caught a mass of wreckage floating near her and she let go the mule's tail and seized the rude raft, pulling herself up so that she rode upon it in safety. Hank also saw the raft and swam to it, but he was so clumsy he never would have been able to climb upon it had not Betsy helped him to get aboard.

They had to crowd close together, for their support was only a hatch-cover torn from the ship's deck; but it floated them fairly well and both the girl and the mule knew it would keep them from drowning.

The storm was not over, by any means, when the ship went down. Blinding bolts of lightning shot from cloud to cloud and the clamor of deep thunderclaps echoed far over the sea. The waves tossed the little raft here and there as a child tosses a rubber ball and Betsy had a solemn feeling that for hundreds of watery miles in every direction there was no living thing besides herself and the small donkey.

Perhaps Hank had the same thought, for he gently rubbed his nose against the frightened girl and said "Hee-haw!" in his softest voice, as if to comfort her.

"You'll protect me, Hank dear, won't you?" she cried helplessly, and the mule said "Hee-haw!" again, in tones that meant a promise.

On board the ship, during the days that preceded the wreck, when the sea was calm, Betsy and Hank had become good friends; so, while the girl might have preferred a more powerful protector in this dreadful emergency, she felt that the mule would do all in a mule's power to guard her safety.

All night they floated, and when the storm had worn itself out and passed away with a few distant growls, and the waves had grown smaller and easier to ride, Betsy stretched herself out on the wet raft and fell asleep.

Hank did not sleep a wink. Perhaps he felt it his duty to guard Betsy. Anyhow, he crouched on the raft beside the tired sleeping girl and watched patiently until the first light of dawn swept over the sea.

The light wakened Betsy Bobbin. She sat up, rubbed her eyes and stared across the water.

"Oh, Hank; there's land ahead!" she exclaimed.

"Hee-haw!" answered Hank in his plaintive voice.

The raft was floating swiftly toward a very beautiful country and as they drew near Betsy could see banks of lovely flowers showing brightly between leafy trees. But no people were to be seen at all.

CHAPTER V

THE ROSES REPULSE THE REFUGEES

GENTLY THE RAFT GRATED ON THE SANDY BEACH. THEN BETSY EASILY WADED ashore, the mule following closely behind her. The sun was now shining and the air was warm and laden with the fragrance of roses.

"I'd like some breakfast, Hank," remarked the girl, feeling more cheerful now that she was on dry land; "but we can't eat the flowers, although they do smell mighty good."

"Hee-haw!" replied Hank and trotted up a little pathway to the top of the bank.

Betsy followed and from the eminence looked around her. A little way off stood a splendid big greenhouse, its thousands of crystal panes glittering in the sunlight.

"There ought to be people somewhere 'round," observed Betsy thoughtfully; "gardeners, or somebody. Let's go and see, Hank. I'm getting hungrier ev'ry minute."

So they walked toward the great greenhouse and came to its entrance without meeting with anyone at all. A door stood ajar, so Hank went in first, thinking if there was any danger he could back out and warn his companion. But Betsy was close at his heels and the moment she entered was lost in amazement at the wonderful sight she saw.

The greenhouse was filled with magnificent rosebushes, all growing in big pots. On the central stem of each bush bloomed a splendid Rose, gorgeously colored and deliciously fragrant, and in the center of each Rose was the face of a lovely girl.

As Betsy and Hank entered, the heads of the Roses were drooping and their eyelids were closed in slumber; but the mule was so amazed that he uttered a loud "Hee-haw!" and at the sound of his harsh voice the rose leaves fluttered, the Roses raised their heads and a hundred startled eyes were instantly fixed upon the intruders.

"I—I beg your pardon!" stammered Betsy, blushing and confused.

"O-o-o-h!" cried the Roses, in a sort of sighing chorus; and one of them added: "What a horrid noise!"

"Why, that was only Hank," said Betsy, and as if to prove the truth of her words the mule uttered another loud "Hee-haw!"

At this all the Roses turned on their stems as far as they were able and trembled as if some one were shaking their bushes. A dainty Moss Rose gasped: "Dear me! How dreadfully dreadful!"

"It isn't dreadful at all," said Betsy, somewhat indignant. "When you get used to Hank's voice it will put you to sleep."

The Roses now looked at the mule less fearfully and one of them asked:

"Is that savage beast named Hank?"

"Yes; Hank's my comrade, faithful and true," answered the girl, twining her arms around the little mule's neck and hugging him tight. "Aren't you, Hank?"

Hank could only say in reply: "Hee-haw!" and at his bray the Roses shivered again.

"Please go away!" begged one. "Can't you see you're frightening us out of a week's growth?"

"Go away!" echoed Betsy. "Why, we've no place to go. We've just been wrecked."

"Wrecked?" asked the Roses in a surprised chorus.

"Yes; we were on a big ship and the storm came and wrecked it," explained the girl. "But Hank and I caught hold of a raft and floated ashore to this place, and—we're tired and hungry. What country *is* this, please?"

"This is the Rose Kingdom," replied the Moss Rose, haughtily, "and it is devoted to the culture of the rarest and fairest Roses grown."

"I believe it," said Betsy, admiring the pretty blossoms.

"But only Roses are allowed here," continued a delicate Tea Rose, bending her brows in a frown; "therefore you must go away before the Royal Gardener finds you and casts you back into the sea."

"Oh! Is there a Royal Gardener, then?" inquired Betsy.

"To be sure."

"And is he a Rose, also?"

"Of course not; he's a man—a wonderful man," was the reply.

"Well, I'm not afraid of a man," declared the girl, much relieved, and even as she spoke the Royal Gardener popped into the greenhouse—a spading fork in one hand and a watering pot in the other.

He was a funny little man, dressed in a rose-colored costume, with ribbons at his knees and elbows, and a bunch of ribbons in his hair. His eyes were small and twinkling, his nose sharp and his face puckered and deeply lined.

"O-ho!" he exclaimed, astonished to find strangers in his greenhouse, and when Hank gave a loud bray the Gardener threw the watering pot over the mule's head and danced around with his fork, in such agitation that presently he fell over the handle of the implement and sprawled at full length upon the ground.

Betsy laughed and pulled the watering pot off from Hank's head. The little mule was angry at the treatment he had received and backed toward the Gardener threateningly.

"Look out for his heels!" called Betsy warningly and the Gardener scrambled to his feet and hastily hid behind the Roses.

"You are breaking the law!" he shouted, sticking out his head to glare at the girl and the mule.

"What law?" asked Betsy.

"The Law of the Rose Kingdom. No strangers are allowed in these domains."

"Not when they're shipwrecked?" she inquired.

"The law doesn't except shipwrecks," replied the Royal Gardener, and he was about to say more when suddenly there was a crash of glass and a man came tumbling through the roof of the greenhouse and fell plump to the ground.

CHAPTER VI

SHAGGY SEEKS HIS STRAY BROTHER

THIS SUDDEN ARRIVAL WAS A QUEER LOOKING MAN, DRESSED ALL IN GARMENTS SO shaggy that Betsy at first thought he must be some animal. But the stranger ended his fall in a sitting position and then the girl saw it was really a man. He held an apple in his hand, which he had evidently been eating when he fell, and so little was he jarred or flustered by the accident that he continued to munch this apple as he calmly looked around him.

"Good gracious!" exclaimed Betsy, approaching him. "Who *are* you, and where did you come from?"

"Me? Oh, I'm Shaggy Man," said he, taking another bite of the apple. "Just dropped in for a short call. Excuse my seeming haste."

"Why, I s'pose you couldn't help the haste," said Betsy.

"No. I climbed an apple tree, outside; branch gave way and—here I am."

As he spoke the Shaggy Man finished his apple, gave the core to Hank—who ate it greedily—and then stood up to bow politely to Betsy and the Roses.

The Royal Gardener had been frightened nearly into fits by the crash of glass and the fall of the shaggy stranger into the bower of Roses, but now he peeped out from behind a bush and cried in his squeaky voice:

"You're breaking the law! You're breaking the law!"

Shaggy stared at him solemnly.

"Is the glass the law in this country?" he asked.

"Breaking the glass is breaking the law," squeaked the Gardener, angrily. "Also, to intrude in any part of the Rose Kingdom is breaking the law."

"How do you know?" asked Shaggy.

"Why, it's printed in a book," said the Gardener, coming forward and taking a small book from his pocket. "Page thirteen. Here it is: 'If any stranger enters the Rose Kingdom he shall at once be condemned by the Ruler and put to death.' So you see, strangers," he continued triumphantly, "it's death for you all and your time has come!"

But just here Hank interposed. He had been stealthily backing toward the Royal Gardener, whom he disliked, and now the mule's heels shot out and struck the little man in the middle. He doubled up like the letter "U" and flew out of the door so swiftly—never touching the ground—that he was gone before Betsy had time to wink.

But the mule's attack frightened the girl.

"Come," she whispered, approaching the Shaggy Man and taking his hand; "let's go somewhere else. They'll surely kill us if we stay here!"

"Don't worry, my dear," replied Shaggy, patting the child's head. "I'm not afraid of anything, so long as I have the Love Magnet."

"The Love Magnet! Why, what is that?" asked Betsy.

"It's a charming little enchantment that wins the heart of everyone who looks upon it," was the reply. "The Love Magnet used to hang over the gateway to the Emerald City, in the Land of Oz; but when I started on this journey our beloved Ruler, Ozma of Oz, allowed me to take it with me."

"Oh!" cried Betsy, staring hard at him; "are you really from the wonderful Land of Oz?"

"Yes. Ever been there, my dear?"

"No; but I've heard about it. And do you know Princess Ozma?"

"Very well indeed."

"And—and Princess Dorothy?"

"Dorothy's an old chum of mine," declared Shaggy.

"Dear me!" exclaimed Betsy. "And why did you ever leave such a beautiful land as Oz?"

"On an errand," said Shaggy, looking sad and solemn. "I'm trying to find my dear little brother."

"Oh! Is he lost?" questioned Betsy, feeling very sorry for the poor man.

"Been lost these ten years," replied Shaggy, taking out a handkerchief and wiping a tear from his eye. "I didn't know it until lately, when I saw it recorded in the magic Record Book of the Sorceress Glinda, in the Land of Oz. So now I'm trying to find him."

"Where was he lost?" asked the girl sympathetically.

"Back in Colorado, where I used to live before I went to Oz. Brother was a miner, and dug gold out of a mine. One day he went into his mine and never came out. They searched for him, but he was not there. Disappeared entirely," Shaggy ended miserably.

"For goodness sake! What do you s'pose became of him?" she asked.

"There is only one explanation," replied Shaggy, taking another apple from his pocket and eating it to relieve his misery. "The Nome King probably got him."

"The Nome King! Who is he?"

"Why, he's sometimes called the Metal Monarch, and his name is Ruggedo. Lives in some underground cavern. Claims to own all the metals hidden in the earth. Don't ask me why."

"Why?"

"'Cause I don't know. But this Ruggedo gets wild with anger if anyone digs gold out of the earth, and my private opinion is that he captured brother and carried him off to his underground kingdom. No—don't ask me why. I see you're dying to ask me why. But I don't know."

"But—dear me!—in that case you will never find your lost brother!" exclaimed the girl.

"Maybe not; but it's my duty to try," answered Shaggy. "I've wandered so far without finding him, but that only proves he is not where I've been looking. What I seek now is the hidden passage to the underground cavern of the terrible Metal Monarch."

"Well," said Betsy doubtfully, "it strikes me that if you ever manage to get there the Metal Monarch will make you, too, his prisoner."

"Nonsense!" answered Shaggy, carelessly. "You mustn't forget the Love Magnet."

"What about it?" she asked.

"When the fierce Metal Monarch sees the Love Magnet, he will love me dearly and do anything I ask."

"It must be wonderful," said Betsy, with awe.

"It is," the man assured her. "Shall I show it to you?"

"Oh, do!" she cried; so Shaggy searched in his shaggy pocket and drew out a small silver magnet, shaped like a horseshoe.

The moment Betsy saw it she began to like the Shaggy Man better than before. Hank also saw the Magnet and crept up to Shaggy to rub his head lovingly against the man's knee.

But they were interrupted by the Royal Gardener, who stuck his head into the greenhouse and shouted angrily:

"You are all condemned to death! Your only chance to escape is to leave here instantly."

This startled little Betsy, but the Shaggy Man merely waved the Magnet toward the Gardener, who, seeing it, rushed forward and threw himself at Shaggy's feet, murmuring in honeyed words:

"Oh, you lovely, lovely man! How fond I am of you! Every shag and bobtail that decorates you is dear to me—all I have is yours! But for goodness' sake get out of here before you die the death."

"I'm not going to die," declared Shaggy Man.

"You must. It's the law," exclaimed the Gardener, beginning to weep real tears. "It breaks my heart to tell you this bad news, but the law says that all strangers must be condemned by the Ruler to die the death."

"No Ruler has condemned us yet," said Betsy.

"Of course not," added Shaggy. "We haven't even seen the Ruler of the Rose Kingdom."

"Well, to tell the truth," said the Gardener, in a perplexed tone of voice, "we haven't any real Ruler, just now. You see, all our Rulers grow on bushes in the Royal Gardens, and the last one we had got mildewed and withered before his time. So we had to plant him, and at this time there is no one growing on the Royal Bushes who is ripe enough to pick."

"How do you know?" asked Betsy.

"Why, I'm the Royal Gardener. Plenty of royalties are growing, I admit; but just now they are all green. Until one ripens, I am supposed to rule the Rose Kingdom myself, and see that its Laws are obeyed. Therefore, much as I love you, Shaggy, I must put you to death."

"Wait a minute," pleaded Betsy. "I'd like to see those Royal Gardens before I die."

"So would I," added Shaggy Man. "Take us there, Gardener."

"Oh, I can't do that," objected the Gardener. But Shaggy again showed him the Love Magnet and after one glance at it the Gardener could no longer resist.

He led Shaggy, Betsy and Hank to the end of the great greenhouse and carefully unlocked a small door. Passing through this they came into the splendid Royal Garden of the Rose Kingdom.

It was all surrounded by a tall hedge and within the enclosure grew several enormous rosebushes having thick green leaves of the texture of velvet. Upon these bushes grew the members of the Royal Family of the Rose Kingdom—men, women and children in all stages of maturity. They all seemed to have a light green hue, as if unripe or not fully developed, their flesh and clothing being alike green. They stood

perfectly lifeless upon their branches, which swayed softly in the breeze, and their wide-open eyes stared straight ahead, unseeing and unintelligent.

While examining these curious growing people, Betsy passed behind a big central bush and at once uttered an exclamation of surprise and pleasure. For there, blooming in perfect color and shape, stood a Royal Princess, whose beauty was amazing.

"Why, she's ripe!" cried Betsy, pushing aside some of the broad leaves to observe her more clearly.

"Well, perhaps so," admitted the Gardener, who had come to the girl's side; "but she's a girl, and so we can't use her for a Ruler."

"No, indeed!" came a chorus of soft voices, and looking around Betsy discovered that all the Roses had followed them from the greenhouse and were now grouped before the entrance.

"You see," explained the Gardener, "the subjects of Rose Kingdom don't want a girl Ruler. They want a King."

"A King! We want a King!" repeated the chorus of Roses.

"Isn't she Royal?" inquired Shaggy, admiring the lovely Princess.

"Of course, for she grows on a Royal Bush. This Princess is named Ozga, as she is a distant cousin of Ozma of Oz; and, were she but a man, we would joyfully hail her as our Ruler."

The Gardener then turned away to talk with his Roses and Betsy whispered to her companion: "Let's pick her, Shaggy."

"All right," said he. "If she's royal, she has the right to rule this Kingdom, and if we pick her she will surely protect us and prevent our being hurt, or driven away."

So Betsy and Shaggy each took an arm of the beautiful Rose Princess and a little twist of her feet set her free of the branch upon which she grew. Very gracefully she stepped down from the bush to the ground, where she bowed low to Betsy and Shaggy and said in a delightfully sweet voice: "I thank you."

But at the sound of these words the Gardener and the Roses turned and discovered that the Princess had been picked, and was now alive. Over every face flashed an expression of resentment and anger, and one of the Roses cried aloud:

"Audacious mortals! What have you done?"

"Picked a Princess for you, that's all," replied Betsy, cheerfully.

"But we won't have her! We want a King!" exclaimed a Jacque Rose, and another added with a voice of scorn: "No girl shall rule over us!"

The newly-picked Princess looked from one to another of her rebellious subjects in astonishment. A grieved look came over her exquisite features.

"Have I no welcome here, pretty subjects?" she asked gently. "Have I not come from my Royal Bush to be your Ruler?"

"You were picked by mortals, without our consent," replied the Moss Rose, coldly; "so we refuse to allow you to rule us."

"Turn her out, Gardener, with the others!" cried the Tea Rose.

"Just a second, please!" called Shaggy, taking the Love Magnet from his pocket. "I guess this will win their love, Princess. Here—take it in your hand and let the Roses see it."

Princess Ozga took the Magnet and held it poised before the eyes of her subjects; but the Roses regarded it with calm disdain.

"Why, what's the matter?" demanded Shaggy in surprise. "The Magnet never failed to work before!"

"I know," said Betsy, nodding her head wisely. "These Roses have no hearts."

"That's it," agreed the Gardener. "They're pretty, and sweet, and alive; but still they are Roses. Their stems have thorns, but no hearts."

The Princess sighed and handed the Magnet to the Shaggy Man.

"What shall I do?" she asked sorrowfully.

"Turn her out, Gardener, with the others!" commanded the Roses. "We will have no Ruler until a man-rose—a King—is ripe enough to pick."

"Very well," said the Gardener meekly. "You must excuse me, my dear Shaggy, for opposing your wishes, but you and the others, including Ozga, must get out of Rose Kingdom immediately, if not before."

"Don't you love me, Gardy?" asked Shaggy, carelessly displaying the Magnet.

"I do. I dote on thee!" answered the Gardener earnestly; "but no true man will neglect his duty for the sake of love. My duty is to drive you out, so—out you go!"

With this he seized a garden fork and began jabbing it at the strangers, in order to force them to leave. Hank the mule was not afraid of the fork and when he got his heels near to the Gardener the man fell back to avoid a kick.

But now the Roses crowded around the outcasts and

it was soon discovered that beneath their draperies of green leaves were many sharp thorns which were more dangerous than Hank's heels. Neither Betsy nor Ozga nor Shaggy nor the mule cared to brave those thorns and when they pressed away from them they found themselves slowly driven through the garden door into the greenhouse. From there they were forced out at the entrance and so through the territory of the flower-strewn Rose Kingdom, which was not of very great extent.

The Rose Princess was sobbing bitterly; Betsy was indignant and angry; Hank uttered defiant "Hee-haws" and the Shaggy Man whistled softly to himself.

The boundary of the Rose Kingdom was a deep gulf, but there was a drawbridge in one place and this the Royal Gardener let down until the outcasts had passed over it. Then he drew it up again and returned with his Roses to the greenhouse, leaving the four queerly assorted comrades to wander into the bleak and unknown country that lay beyond.

"I don't mind, much," remarked Shaggy, as he led the way over the stony, barren ground. "I've got to search for my long-lost little brother, anyhow, so it won't matter where I go."

"Hank and I will help you find your brother," said Betsy in her most cheerful voice. "I'm so far away from home now that I don't s'pose I'll ever find my way back; and, to tell the truth, it's more fun traveling around and having adventures than sticking at home. Don't you think so, Hank?"

"Hee-haw!" said Hank, and the Shaggy Man thanked them both.

"For my part," said Princess Ozga of Roseland, with a gentle sigh, "I must remain forever exiled from my kingdom. So I, too, will be glad to help the Shaggy Man find his lost brother."

"That's very kind of you, ma'am," said Shaggy. "But unless I can find the underground cavern of Ruggedo,* the Metal Monarch, I shall never find poor brother."

"Doesn't anyone know where it is?" inquired Betsy.

"*Some* one must know, of course," was Shaggy's reply. "But we are not the ones. The only way to succeed is for us to keep going until we find a person who can direct us to Ruggedo's cavern."

"We may find it ourselves, without any help," suggested Betsy. "Who knows?"

"No one knows that, except the person who's writing this story," said Shaggy. "But we won't find anything—not even supper—unless we travel on. Here's a path. Let's take it and see where it leads to."

---

* This King was formerly named "Roquat," but after he drank of the "Waters of Oblivion" he forgot his own name and had to take another.

CHAPTER VII

POLYCHROME'S PITIFUL PLIGHT

The Rain King got too much water in his basin and spilled some over the brim. That made it rain in a certain part of the country—a real hard shower, for a time—and sent the Rainbow scampering to the place to show the gorgeous colors of his glorious bow as soon as the mist of rain had passed and the sky was clear.

The coming of the Rainbow is always a joyous event to earth folk, yet few have ever seen it close by. Usually the Rainbow is so far distant that you can observe its splendid hues but dimly, and that is why we seldom catch sight of the dancing Daughters of the Rainbow.

In the barren country where the rain had just fallen there appeared to be no human beings at all; but the Rainbow appeared, just the same, and dancing gayly upon its arch were the Rainbow's Daughters, led by the fairylike Polychrome, who is so dainty and beautiful that no girl has ever quite equaled her in loveliness.

Polychrome was in a merry mood and danced down the arch of the bow to the ground, daring her sisters to follow her. Laughing and gleeful, they also touched the ground with their twinkling feet; but all the Daughters of the Rainbow knew that this was a dangerous pastime, so they quickly climbed upon their bow again.

All but Polychrome. Though the sweetest and merriest of them all, she was likewise the most reckless. Moreover, it was an unusual sensation to pat the cold, damp earth with her rosy toes. Before she realized it the bow had lifted and disappeared in the billowy blue sky, and here was Polychrome standing helpless upon a rock, her gauzy draperies floating about her like brilliant cobwebs and not a soul—fairy or mortal—to help her regain her lost bow!

"Dear me!" she exclaimed, a frown passing across her pretty face, "I'm caught again. This is the second time my carelessness has left me on earth while my sisters returned to our Sky Palaces. The first time I enjoyed some pleasant adventures, but this is a lonely, forsaken country and I shall be very unhappy until my Rainbow comes again and I can climb aboard. Let me think what is best to be done."

She crouched low upon the flat rock, drew her draperies about her and bowed her head.

It was in this position that Betsy Bobbin spied Polychrome as she came along the stony path, followed by Hank, the Princess and Shaggy. At once the girl ran up to the radiant Daughter of the Rainbow and exclaimed:

"Oh, what a lovely, lovely creature!"

Polychrome raised her golden head. There were tears in her blue eyes.

"I'm the most miserable girl in the whole world!" she sobbed.

The others gathered around her.

"Tell us your troubles, pretty one," urged the Princess.

"I—I've lost my bow!" wailed Polychrome.

"Take me, my dear," said Shaggy Man in a sympathetic tone, thinking she meant "beau" instead of "bow."

"I don't want you!" cried Polychrome, stamping her foot imperiously; "I want my *Rainbow*."

"Oh; that's different," said Shaggy. "But try to forget it. When I was young I used to cry for the Rainbow myself, but I couldn't have it. Looks as if *you* couldn't have it, either; so please don't cry."

Polychrome looked at him reproachfully.

"I don't like you," she said.

"No?" replied Shaggy, drawing the Love Magnet from his pocket; "not a little bit?—just a wee speck of a like?"

"Yes, yes!" said Polychrome, clasping her hands in ecstasy as she gazed at the enchanted talisman; "I love you, Shaggy Man!"

"Of course you do," said he calmly; "but I don't take any credit for it. It's the Love Magnet's powerful charm. But you seem quite alone and friendless, little Rainbow. Don't you want to join our party until you find your father and sisters again?"

"Where are you going?" she asked.

"We don't just know that," said Betsy, taking her hand; "but we're trying to find Shaggy's long-lost brother, who has been captured by the terrible Metal Monarch. Won't you come with us, and help us?"

Polychrome looked from one to another of the queer party of travelers and a bewitching smile suddenly lighted her face.

"A donkey, a mortal maid, a Rose Princess and a Shaggy Man!" she exclaimed. "Surely you need help, if you intend to face Ruggedo."

"Do you know him, then?" inquired Betsy.

"No, indeed. Ruggedo's caverns are beneath the earth's surface, where no Rainbow can ever penetrate. But I've heard of the Metal Monarch. He is also called the Nome King, you know, and he has made trouble for a good many people—mortals and fairies—in his time," said Polychrome.

"Do you fear him, then?" asked the Princess, anxiously.

"No one can harm a Daughter of the Rainbow," said Polychrome proudly. "I'm a sky fairy."

"Then," said Betsy, quickly, "you will be able to tell us the way to Ruggedo's cavern."

"No," returned Polychrome, shaking her head, "that is one thing I cannot do. But I will gladly go with you and help you search for the place."

This promise delighted all the wanderers and after the Shaggy Man had found the path again they began moving along it in a more happy mood. The Rainbow's Daughter danced lightly over the rocky trail, no longer sad, but with her beautiful features wreathed in smiles. Shaggy came next, walking steadily and now and then supporting the Rose Princess, who followed him. Betsy and Hank brought up the rear, and if she tired with walking the girl got upon Hank's back and let the stout little donkey carry her for a while.

At nightfall they came to some trees that grew beside a tiny brook and here they made camp and rested until morning. Then away they tramped, finding berries and fruits here and there which satisfied the hunger of Betsy, Shaggy and Hank, so that they were well content with their lot.

It surprised Betsy to see the Rose Princess partake of their food, for she considered her a fairy; but when she mentioned this to Polychrome, the Rainbow's Daughter explained that when Ozga was driven out of her Rose Kingdom she ceased to be a fairy and would never again be more than a mere mortal. Polychrome, however, was a fairy wherever she happened to be, and if she sipped a few dewdrops by moonlight for refreshment no one ever saw her do it.

As they continued their wandering journey, direction meant very little to them, for they were hopelessly lost in this strange country. Shaggy said it would be best to go toward the mountains, as the natural entrance to Ruggedo's underground cavern was likely to be hidden in some rocky, deserted place; but mountains seemed all around them except in the one direction that they had come from, which led to the Rose Kingdom and the sea. Therefore it mattered little which way they traveled.

By and by they espied a faint trail that looked like a path and after following this for some time they reached a crossroads. Here were many paths, leading in various directions, and there was a sign-post so old that there were now no words upon the sign. At one side was an old well, with a chain windlass for drawing water, yet there was no house or other building anywhere in sight.

While the party halted, puzzled which way to proceed, the mule approached the well and tried to look into it.

"He's thirsty," said Betsy.

"It's a dry well," remarked Shaggy. "Probably there has been no water in it for many years. But, come; let us decide which way to travel."

No one seemed able to decide that. They sat down in a group and tried to consider which road might be the best to take. Hank, however, could not keep away from the well and finally he reared up on his hind legs, got his head over the edge and uttered a loud "Hee-haw!" Betsy watched her animal friend curiously.

"I wonder if he sees anything down there?" she said.

At this, Shaggy rose and went over to the well to investigate, and Betsy went with him. The Princess and Polychrome, who had become fast friends, linked arms and sauntered down one of the roads, to find an easy path.

"Really," said Shaggy, "there does seem to be something at the bottom of this old well."

"Can't we pull it up, and see what it is?" asked the girl.

There was no bucket at the end of the windlass chain, but there was a big hook that at one time was used to hold a bucket. Shaggy let down this hook, dragged it around on the bottom and then pulled it up. An old hoopskirt came with it, and Betsy laughed and threw it away. The thing frightened Hank, who had never seen a hoopskirt before, and he kept a good distance away from it.

Several other objects the Shaggy Man captured with the hook and drew up, but none of these was important.

"This well seems to have been the dump for all the old rubbish in the country," he said, letting down the hook once more. "I guess I've captured everything now. No—the hook has caught again. Help me, Betsy! Whatever this thing is, it's heavy."

She ran up and helped him turn the windlass and after much effort a confused mass of copper came in sight.

"Good gracious!" exclaimed Shaggy. "Here is a surprise, indeed!"

"What is it?" inquired Betsy, clinging to the windlass and panting for breath.

For answer the Shaggy Man grasped the bundle of copper and dumped it upon the ground, free of the well. Then he turned it over with his foot, spread it out, and to Betsy's astonishment the thing proved to be a copper man.

"Just as I thought," said Shaggy, looking hard at the object. "But unless there are two copper men in the world this is the most astonishing thing I ever came across."

At this moment the Rainbow's Daughter and the Rose Princess approached them, and Polychrome said:

"What have you found, Shaggy One?"

"Either an old friend, or a stranger," he replied.

"Oh, here's a sign on his back!" cried Betsy, who had knelt down to examine the man. "Dear me; how funny! Listen to this."

Then she read the following words, engraved upon the copper plates of the man's body:

SMITH & TINKER'S
Patent Double-Action, Extra-Responsive,
Thought-Creating, Perfect-Talking
MECHANICAL MAN
Fitted with our Special Clockwork Attachment.
Thinks, Speaks, Acts, and Does Everything but Live.

"Isn't he wonderful!" exclaimed the Princess.

"Yes; but here's more," said Betsy, reading from another engraved plate:

DIRECTIONS FOR USING:
For THINKING:—Wind the Clockwork Man under
his left arm, (marked No. 1).
For SPEAKING:—Wind the Clockwork Man under
his right arm, (marked No. 2).
For WALKING and ACTION:—Wind Clockwork Man
in the middle of his back, (marked No. 3).
N. B.—This Mechanism is guaranteed to work perfectly for a thousand years.

"If he's guaranteed for a thousand years," said Polychrome, "he ought to work yet."

"Of course," replied Shaggy. "Let's wind him up."

In order to do this they were obliged to set the copper man upon his feet, in an upright position, and this was no easy task. He was inclined to topple over, and had to be propped again and again. The girls assisted Shaggy, and at last Tik-Tok seemed to be balanced and stood alone upon his broad feet.

"Yes," said Shaggy, looking at the copper man carefully, "this must be, indeed, my old friend Tik-Tok, whom I left ticking merrily in the Land of Oz. But how he came to this lonely place, and got into that old well, is surely a mystery."

"If we wind him, perhaps he will tell us," suggested Betsy. "Here's the key, hanging to a hook on his back. What part of him shall I wind up first?"

"His thoughts, of course," said Polychrome, "for it requires thought to speak or move intelligently."

So Betsy wound him under his left arm, and at once little flashes of light began to show in the top of his head, which was proof that he had begun to think.

"Now, then," said Shaggy, "wind up his phonograph."

"What's that?" she asked.

"Why, his talking-machine. His thoughts may be interesting, but they don't tell us anything."

So Betsy wound the copper man under his right arm, and then from the interior of his copper body came in jerky tones the words: "Ma-ny thanks!"

"Hurrah!" cried Shaggy, joyfully, and he slapped Tik-Tok upon the back in such a hearty manner that the copper man lost his balance and tumbled to the ground in a heap. But the clockwork that enabled him to speak had been wound up and he kept saying: "Pick-me-up! Pick-me-up! Pick-me-up!" until they had again raised him and balanced him upon his feet, when he added politely: "Ma-ny thanks!"

"He won't be self-supporting until we wind up his action," remarked Shaggy; so Betsy wound it, as tight as she could—for the key turned rather hard—and then Tik-Tok lifted his feet, marched around in a circle and ended by stopping before the group and making them all a low bow.

"How in the world did you happen to be in that well, when I left you safe in Oz?" inquired Shaggy.

"It is a long sto-ry," replied Tik-Tok, "but I'll tell it in a few words. Af-ter you had gone in search of your broth-er, Oz-ma saw you wan-der-ing in strange lands when-ev-er she looked in her mag-ic pic-ture, and she also saw your broth-er in the Nome King's cavern; so she sent me to tell you where to find your broth-er and told me to help you if I could. The Sor-cer-ess, Glin-da the Good, trans-port-ed me to this place in the wink of an eye; but here I met the Nome King him-self—old Rug-ge-do, who is called in these parts the Met-al Mon-arch. Rug-ge-do knew what I had come for, and he was so an-gry that he threw me down the well. Af-ter my works ran down I was help-less un-til you came a-long and pulled me out a-gain. Ma-ny thanks."

"This is, indeed, good news," said Shaggy. "I suspected that my brother was the prisoner of Ruggedo; but now I know it. Tell us, Tik-Tok, how shall we get to the Nome King's underground cavern?"

"The best way is to walk," said Tik-Tok. "We might crawl, or jump, or roll o-ver and o-ver un-til we get there; but the best way is to walk."

"I know; but which road shall we take?"

"My ma-chin-er-y is-n't made to tell that," replied Tik-Tok.

"There is more than one entrance to the underground cavern," said Polychrome; "but old Ruggedo has cleverly concealed every opening, so that earth dwellers cannot intrude in his domain. If we find our way underground at all, it will be by chance."

"Then," said Betsy, "let us select any road, haphazard, and see where it leads us."

"That seems sensible," declared the Princess. "It may require a lot of time for us to find Ruggedo, but we have more time than anything else."

"If you keep me wound up," said Tik-Tok, "I will last a thou-sand years."

"Then the only question to decide is which way to go," added Shaggy, looking first at one road and then at another.

But while they stood hesitating, a peculiar sound reached their ears—a sound like the tramping of many feet.

"What's coming?" cried Betsy; and then she ran to the left-hand road and glanced along the path. "Why, it's an army!" she exclaimed. "What shall we do, hide or run?"

"Stand still," commanded Shaggy. "I'm not afraid of an army. If they prove to be friendly, they can help us; if they are enemies, I'll show them the Love Magnet."

CHAPTER VIII

TIK-TOK TACKLES A TOUGH TASK

WHILE SHAGGY AND HIS COMPANIONS STOOD HUDDLED IN A GROUP AT ONE SIDE, the Army of Oogaboo was approaching along the pathway, the tramp of their feet being now and then accompanied by a dismal groan as one of the officers stepped on a sharp stone or knocked his funnybone against his neighbor's sword-handle.

Then out from among the trees marched Private Files, bearing the banner of Oogaboo, which fluttered from a long pole. This pole he stuck in the ground just in front of the well and then he cried in a loud voice:

"I hereby conquer this territory in the name of Queen Ann Soforth of Oogaboo, and all the inhabitants of the land I proclaim her slaves!"

Some of the officers now stuck their heads out of the bushes and asked:

"Is the coast clear, Private Files?"

"There is no coast here," was the reply, "but all's well."

"I hope there's water in it," said General Cone, mustering courage to advance to the well; but just then he caught a glimpse of Tik-Tok and Shaggy and at once fell upon his knees, trembling and frightened, and cried out:

"Mercy, kind enemies! Mercy! Spare us, and we will be your slaves forever!"

The other officers, who had now advanced into the clearing, likewise fell upon their knees and begged for mercy.

Files turned around and, seeing the strangers for the first time, examined them with much curiosity. Then, discovering that three of the party were girls, he lifted his cap and made a polite bow.

"What's all this?" demanded a harsh voice, as Queen Ann reached the place and beheld her kneeling army.

"Permit us to introduce ourselves," replied Shaggy, stepping forward. "This is Tik-Tok, the Clockwork Man—who works better than some meat people. And here is Princess Ozga of Roseland, just now unfortunately exiled from her Kingdom of Roses. I next present Polychrome, a sky fairy, who lost her bow by an accident and can't find her way home. The small girl here is Betsy Bobbin, from some unknown earthly paradise called Oklahoma, and with her you see Mr. Hank, a mule with a long tail and a short temper."

"Puh!" said Ann, scornfully; "a pretty lot of vagabonds you are, indeed; all lost or strayed, I suppose, and not worth a Queen's plundering. I'm sorry I've conquered you."

"But you haven't conquered us yet," called Betsy indignantly.

"No," agreed Files, "that is a fact. But if my officers will kindly command me to conquer you, I will do so at once, after which we can stop arguing and converse more at our ease."

The officers had by this time risen from their knees and brushed the dust from their trousers. To them the enemy did not look very fierce, so the Generals and Colonels and Majors and Captains gained courage to face them and began strutting in their most haughty manner.

"You must understand," said Ann, "that I am the Queen of Oogaboo, and this is my invincible army. We are busy conquering the world, and since you seem to be a part of the world, and are obstructing our journey, it is necessary for us to conquer you—unworthy though you may be of such high honor."

"That's all right," replied Shaggy. "Conquer us as often as you like. We don't mind."

"But we won't be anybody's slaves," added Betsy, positively.

"We'll see about that," retorted the Queen, angrily. "Advance, Private Files, and bind the enemy hand and foot!"

But Private Files looked at pretty Betsy and fascinating Polychrome and the beautiful Rose Princess and shook his head.

"It would be impolite, and I won't do it," he asserted.

"You must!" cried Ann. "It is your duty to obey orders."

"I haven't received any orders from my officers," objected the Private.

But the Generals now shouted: "Forward, and bind the prisoners!" and the Colonels and Majors and Captains repeated the command, yelling it as loud as they could.

All this noise annoyed Hank, who had been eyeing the Army of Oogaboo with strong disfavor. The mule now dashed forward and began backing upon the officers and kicking fierce and dangerous heels at them. The attack was so sudden that the officers scattered like dust in a whirlwind, dropping their swords as they ran and trying to seek refuge behind the trees and bushes.

Betsy laughed joyously at the comical rout of the "noble army," and Polychrome danced with glee. But Ann was furious at this ignoble defeat of her gallant forces by one small mule.

"Private Files, I command you to do your duty!" she cried again, and then she herself ducked to escape the mule's heels—for Hank made no distinction in favor of a lady who was an open enemy. Betsy grabbed her champion by the forelock, however,

and so held him fast, and when the officers saw that the mule was restrained from further attacks they crept fearfully back and picked up their discarded swords.

"Private Files, seize and bind these prisoners!" screamed the Queen.

"No," said Files, throwing down his gun and removing the knapsack which was strapped to his back, "I resign my position as the Army of Oogaboo. I enlisted to fight the enemy and become a hero, but if you want some one to bind harmless girls you will have to hire another Private."

Then he walked over to the others and shook hands with Shaggy and Tik-Tok.

"Treason!" shrieked Ann, and all the officers echoed her cry.

"Nonsense," said Files. "I've the right to resign if I want to."

"Indeed you haven't!" retorted the Queen. "If you resign it will break up my army, and then I cannot conquer the world." She now turned to the officers and said: "I must ask you to do me a favor. I know it is undignified in officers to fight, but unless you immediately capture Private Files and force him to obey my orders there will be no plunder for any of us. Also it is likely you will all suffer the pangs of hunger, and when we meet a powerful foe you are liable to be captured and made slaves."

The prospect of this awful fate so frightened the officers that they drew their swords and rushed upon Files, who stood beside Shaggy, in a truly ferocious manner. The next instant, however, they halted and again fell upon their knees; for there, before them, was the glistening Love Magnet, held in the hand of the smiling Shaggy Man, and the sight of this magic talisman at once won the heart of every Oogabooite. Even Ann saw the Love Magnet, and forgetting all enmity and anger threw herself upon Shaggy and embraced him lovingly.

Quite disconcerted by this unexpected effect of the Magnet, Shaggy disengaged himself from the Queen's encircling arms and quickly hid the talisman in his pocket. The adventurers from Oogaboo were now his firm friends, and there was no more talk about conquering and binding any of his party.

"If you insist on conquering anyone," said Shaggy, "you may march with me to the underground Kingdom of Ruggedo. To conquer the world, as you have set out to do, you must conquer everyone under its surface as well as those upon its surface, and no one in all the world needs conquering so much as Ruggedo."

"Who is he?" asked Ann.

"The Metal Monarch, King of the Nomes."

"Is he rich?" inquired Major Stockings in an anxious voice.

"Of course," answered Shaggy. "He owns all the metal that lies underground— gold, silver, copper, brass and tin. He has an idea he also owns all the metals above ground, for he says all metal was once a part of his kingdom. So, by conquering the Metal Monarch, you will win all the riches in the world."

"Ah!" exclaimed General Apple, heaving a deep sigh, "that would be plunder worth our while. Let's conquer him, Your Majesty."

The Queen looked reproachfully at Files, who was sitting next to the lovely Princess and whispering in her ear.

"Alas," said Ann, "I have no longer an army. I have plenty of brave officers, indeed, but no Private Soldier for them to command. Therefore I cannot conquer Ruggedo and win all his wealth."

"Why don't you make one of your officers the Private?" asked Shaggy; but at once every officer began to protest and the Queen of Oogaboo shook her head as she replied:

"That is impossible. A Private Soldier must be a terrible fighter, and my officers are unable to fight. They are exceptionally brave in commanding others to fight, but could not themselves meet the enemy and conquer."

"Very true, Your Majesty," said Colonel Plum, eagerly. "There are many kinds of bravery and one cannot be expected to possess them all. I myself am brave as a lion in all ways until it comes to fighting, but then my nature revolts. Fighting is unkind and liable to be injurious to others; so, being a gentleman, I never fight."

"Nor I!" shouted each of the other officers.

"You see," said Ann, "how helpless I am. Had not Private Files proved himself a traitor and a deserter, I would gladly have conquered this Ruggedo; but an army without a Private Soldier is like a bee without a stinger."

"I am not a traitor, Your Majesty," protested Files. "I resigned in a proper manner, not liking the job. But there are plenty of people to take my place. Why not make Shaggy Man the Private Soldier?"

"He might be killed," said Ann, looking tenderly at Shaggy, "for he is mortal, and able to die. If anything happened to him, it would break my heart."

"It would hurt me worse than that," declared Shaggy. "You must admit, Your Majesty, that I am commander of this expedition, for it is my brother we are seeking, rather than plunder. But I and my companions would like the assistance of your army, and if you help us to conquer Ruggedo and to rescue my brother from captivity we will allow you to keep all the gold and jewels and other plunder you may find."

This prospect was so tempting that the officers began whispering together and presently Colonel Cheese said: "Your Majesty, by combining our brains we have just evolved a most brilliant idea. We will make the Clockwork Man the Private Soldier!"

"Who? Me?" asked Tik-Tok. "Not for a sin-gle sec-ond! I cannot fight, and you must not for-get that it was Rug-ge-do who threw me in the well."

"At that time you had no gun," said Polychrome. "But if you join the army of Oogaboo you will carry the gun that Mr. Files used."

"A sol-dier must be a-ble to run as well as to fight," protested Tik-Tok, "and if my works run down, as they of-ten do, I could nei-ther run nor fight."

"I'll keep you wound up, Tik-Tok," promised Betsy.

"Why, it isn't a bad idea," said Shaggy. "Tik-Tok will make an ideal soldier, for nothing can injure him except a sledge hammer. And, since a Private Soldier seems to be necessary to this Army, Tik-Tok is the only one of our party fitted to undertake the job."

"What must I do?" asked Tik-Tok.

"Obey orders," replied Ann. "When the officers command you to do anything, you must do it; that is all."

"And that's enough, too," said Files.

"Do I get a salary?" inquired Tik-Tok.

"You get your share of the plunder," answered the Queen.

"Yes," remarked Files, "one-half of the plunder goes to Queen Ann, the other half is divided among the officers, and the Private gets the rest."

"That will be sat-is-fac-tor-y," said Tik-Tok, picking up the gun and examining it wonderingly, for he had never before seen such a weapon.

Then Ann strapped the knapsack to Tik-Tok's copper back and said: "Now we are ready to march to Ruggedo's kingdom and conquer it. Officers, give the command to march."

"Fall—in!" yelled the Generals, drawing their swords.

"Fall—in!" cried the Colonels, drawing their swords.

"Fall—in!" shouted the Majors, drawing their swords.

"Fall—in!" bawled the Captains, drawing their swords.

Tik-Tok looked at them and then around him in surprise.

"Fall in what? The well?" he asked.

"No," said Queen Ann, "you must fall in marching order."

"Cannot I march with-out fall-ing in-to it?" asked the Clockwork Man.

"Shoulder your gun and stand ready to march," advised Files; so Tik-Tok held the gun straight and stood still.

"What next?" he asked.

The Queen turned to Shaggy.

"Which road leads to the Metal Monarch's cavern?"

"We don't know, Your Majesty," was the reply.

"But this is absurd!" said Ann with a frown. "If we can't get to Ruggedo, it is certain that we can't conquer him."

"You are right," admitted Shaggy; "but I did not say we could not get to him. We have only to discover the way, and that was the matter we were considering when you and your magnificent army arrived here."

"Well, then, get busy and discover it," snapped the Queen.

That was no easy task. They all stood looking from one road to another in perplexity. The paths radiated from the little clearing like the rays of the midday sun, and each path seemed like all the others.

Files and the Rose Princess, who had by this time become good friends, advanced a little way along one of the roads and found that it was bordered by pretty wild flowers.

"Why don't you ask the flowers to tell you the way?" he said to his companion.

"The flowers?" returned the Princess, surprised at the question.

"Of course," said Files. "The field-flowers must be second-cousins to a Rose Princess, and I believe if you ask them they will tell you."

She looked more closely at the flowers. There were hundreds of white daisies, golden buttercups, bluebells and daffodils growing by the roadside, and each flowerhead was firmly set upon its slender but stout stem. There were even a few wild roses scattered here and there and perhaps it was the sight of these that gave the Princess courage to ask the important question.

She dropped to her knees, facing the flowers, and extended both her arms pleadingly toward them.

"Tell me, pretty cousins," she said in her sweet, gentle voice, "which way will lead us to the Kingdom of Ruggedo, the Nome King?"

At once all the stems bent gracefully to the right and the flower heads nodded once—twice—thrice in that direction.

"That's it!" cried Files joyfully. "Now we know the way."

Ozga rose to her feet and looked wonderingly at the field-flowers, which had now resumed their upright position.

"Was it the wind, do you think?" she asked in a low whisper.

"No, indeed," replied Files. "There is not a breath of wind stirring. But these lovely blossoms are indeed your cousins and answered your question at once, as I knew they would."

CHAPTER IX

RUGGEDO'S RAGE IS RASH AND RECKLESS

THE WAY TAKEN BY THE ADVENTURERS LED UP HILL AND DOWN DALE AND WOUND here and there in a fashion that seemed aimless. But always it drew nearer to a range of low mountains and Files said more than once that he was certain the entrance to Ruggedo's cavern would be found among these rugged hills.

In this he was quite correct. Far underneath the nearest mountain was a gorgeous chamber hollowed from the solid rock, the walls and roof of which glittered with thousands of magnificent jewels. Here, on a throne of virgin gold, sat the famous Nome King, dressed in splendid robes and wearing a superb crown cut from a single blood-red ruby.

Ruggedo, the Monarch of all the Metals and Precious Stones of the Underground World, was a round little man with a flowing white beard, a red face, bright eyes and a scowl that covered all his forehead. One would think, to look at him, that he ought to be jolly; one might think, considering his enormous wealth, that he ought to be happy; but this was not the case. The Metal Monarch was surly and cross because mortals had dug so much treasure out of the earth and kept it above ground, where all the power of Ruggedo and his Nomes was unable to recover it. He hated not only the mortals but also the fairies who live upon the earth or above it, and instead of being content with the riches he still possessed he was unhappy because he did not own all the gold and jewels in the world.

Ruggedo had been nodding, half asleep, in his chair when suddenly he sat upright, uttered a roar of rage and began pounding upon a huge gong that stood beside him.

The sound filled the vast cavern and penetrated to many caverns beyond, where countless thousands of Nomes were working at their unending tasks, hammering out gold and silver and other metals, or melting ores in great furnaces, or polishing glittering gems. The Nomes trembled at the sound of the King's gong and whispered fearfully to one another that something unpleasant was sure to happen; but none dared pause in his task.

The heavy curtains of cloth-of-gold were pushed aside and Kaliko, the King's High Chamberlain, entered the royal presence.

"What's up, Your Majesty?" he asked, with a wide yawn, for he had just wakened.

"Up?" roared Ruggedo, stamping his foot viciously. "Those foolish mortals are up, that's what! And they want to come down."

"Down here?" inquired Kaliko.

"Yes!"

"How do you know?" continued the Chamberlain, yawning again.

"I feel it in my bones," said Ruggedo. "I can always feel it when those hateful earth-crawlers draw near to my kingdom. I am positive, Kaliko, that mortals are this very minute on their way here to annoy me—and I hate mortals more than I do catnip tea!"

"Well, what's to be done?" demanded the Nome.

"Look through your spyglass, and see where the invaders are," commanded the King.

So Kaliko went to a tube in the wall of rock and put his eye to it. The tube ran from the cavern up to the side of the mountain and turned several curves and corners, but as it was a magic spyglass Kaliko was able to see through it just as easily as if it had been straight.

"Ho—hum," said he. "I see 'em, Your Majesty."

"What do they look like?" inquired the Monarch.

"That's a hard question to answer, for a queerer assortment of creatures I never yet beheld," replied the Nome. "However, such a collection of curiosities may prove dangerous. There's a copper man, worked by machinery—"

"Bah! that's only Tik-Tok," said Ruggedo. "I'm not afraid of him. Why, only the other day I met the fellow and threw him down a well."

"Then some one must have pulled him out again," said Kaliko. "And there's a little girl—"

"Dorothy?" asked Ruggedo, jumping up in fear.

"No; some other girl. In fact, there are several girls, of various sizes; but Dorothy is not with them, nor is Ozma."

"That's good!" exclaimed the King, sighing in relief.

Kaliko still had his eye to the spyglass.

"I see," said he, "an army of men from Oogaboo. They are all officers and carry swords. And there is a Shaggy Man—who seems very harmless—and a little donkey with big ears."

"Pooh!" cried Ruggedo, snapping his fingers in scorn. "I've no fear of such a mob as that. A dozen of my Nomes can destroy them all in a jiffy."

"I'm not so sure of that," said Kaliko. "The people of Oogaboo are hard to destroy, and I believe the Rose Princess is a fairy. As for Polychrome, you know very well that the Rainbow's Daughter cannot be injured by a Nome."

"Polychrome! Is she among them?" asked the King.

"Yes; I have just recognized her."

"Then these people are coming here on no peaceful errand," declared Ruggedo, scowling fiercely. "In fact, no one ever comes here on a peaceful errand. I hate every-body, and everybody hates me!"

"Very true," said Kaliko.

"I must in some way prevent these people from reaching my dominions. Where are they now?"

"Just now they are crossing the Rubber Country, Your Majesty."

"Good! Are your magnetic rubber wires in working order?"

"I think so," replied Kaliko. "Is it your Royal Will that we have some fun with these invaders?"

"It is," answered Ruggedo. "I want to teach them a lesson they will never forget."

Now, Shaggy had no idea that he was in a Rubber Country, nor had any of his companions. They noticed that everything around them was of a dull gray color and that the path upon which they walked was soft and springy, yet they had no suspicion that the rocks and trees were rubber and even the path they trod was made of rubber.

Presently they came to a brook where sparkling water dashed through a deep channel and rushed away between high rocks far down the mountain-side. Across the brook were stepping-stones, so placed that travelers might easily leap from one to another and in that manner cross the water to the farther bank.

Tik-Tok was marching ahead, followed by his officers and Queen Ann. After them came Betsy Bobbin and Hank, Polychrome and Shaggy, and last of all the Rose Princess with Files. The Clockwork Man saw the stream and the stepping-stones and, without making a pause, placed his foot upon the first stone.

The result was astonishing. First he sank down in the soft rubber, which then rebounded and sent Tik-Tok soaring high in the air, where he turned a succession of flip-flops and alighted upon a rubber rock far in the rear of the party.

General Apple did not see Tik-Tok bound, so quickly had he disappeared; therefore he also stepped upon the stone (which you will guess was connected with Kaliko's magnetic rubber wire) and instantly shot upward like an arrow. General Cone came next and met with a like fate, but the others now noticed that something was wrong and with one accord they halted the column and looked back along the path.

There was Tik-Tok, still bounding from one rubber rock to another, each time rising a less distance from the ground. And there was General Apple, bounding away in another direction, his three-cornered hat jammed over his eyes and his long sword thumping him upon the arms and head as it swung this way and that. And there, also, appeared General Cone, who had struck a rubber rock headforemost and was so crumpled up that his round body looked more like a bouncing-ball than the form of a man.

Betsy laughed merrily at the strange sight and Polychrome echoed her laughter. But Ozga was grave and wondering, while Queen Ann became angry at seeing the chief officers of the Army of Oogaboo bounding around in so undignified a manner. She shouted to them to stop, but they were unable to obey, even though they would have been glad to do so. Finally, however, they all ceased bounding and managed to get upon their feet and rejoin the army.

"Why did you do that?" demanded Ann, who seemed greatly provoked.

"Don't ask them why," said Shaggy earnestly. "I knew you would ask them why, but you ought not to do it. The reason is plain. Those stones are rubber; therefore they are not stones. Those rocks around us are rubber, and therefore they are not rocks. Even this path is not a path; it's rubber. Unless we are very careful, your Majesty, we are all likely to get the bounce, just as your poor officers and Tik-Tok did."

"Then let's be careful," remarked Files, who was full of wisdom; but Polychrome wanted to test the quality of the rubber, so she began dancing. Every step sent her higher and higher into the air, so that she resembled a big butterfly fluttering lightly. Presently she made a great bound and bounded way across the stream, landing lightly and steadily on the other side.

"There is no rubber over here," she called to them. "Suppose you all try to bound over the stream, without touching the stepping-stones."

Ann and her officers were reluctant to undertake such a risky adventure, but Betsy at once grasped the value of the suggestion and began jumping up and down until she found herself bounding almost as high as Polychrome had done. Then she suddenly leaned forward and the next bound took her easily across the brook, where she alighted by the side of the Rainbow's Daughter.

"Come on, Hank!" called the girl, and the donkey tried to obey. He managed to bound pretty high but when he tried to bound across the stream he misjudged the distance and fell with a splash into the middle of the water.

"Hee-haw!" he wailed, struggling toward the far bank. Betsy rushed forward to help him out, but when the mule stood safely beside her she was amazed to find he was not wet at all.

"It's dry water," said Polychrome, dipping her hand into the stream and showing how the water fell from it and left it perfectly dry.

"In that case," returned Betsy, "they can all walk through the water."

She called to Ozga and Shaggy to wade across, assuring them the water was shallow and would not wet them. At once they followed her advice, avoiding the rubber stepping-stones, and made the crossing with ease. This encouraged the entire party to wade through the dry water, and in a few minutes all had assembled on the bank and renewed their journey along the path that led to the Nome King's dominions.

When Kaliko again looked through his magic spyglass he exclaimed:

"Bad luck, Your Majesty! All the invaders have passed the Rubber Country and now are fast approaching the entrance to your caverns."

Ruggedo raved and stormed at the news and his anger was so great that several times, as he strode up and down his jeweled cavern, he paused to kick Kaliko upon his shins, which were so sensitive that the poor Nome howled with pain. Finally the King said:

"There's no help for it; we must drop these audacious invaders down the Hollow Tube."

Kaliko gave a jump, at this, and looked at his master wonderingly.

"If you do that, Your Majesty," he said, "you will make Tititi-Hoochoo very angry."

"Never mind that," retorted Ruggedo. "Tititi-Hoochoo lives on the other side of the world, so what do I care for his anger?"

Kaliko shuddered and uttered a little groan.

"Remember his terrible powers," he pleaded, "and remember that he warned you, the last time you slid people through the Hollow Tube, that if you did it again he would take vengeance upon you."

The Metal Monarch walked up and down in silence, thinking deeply.

"Of two dangers," said he, "it is wise to choose the least. What do you suppose these invaders want?"

"Let the Long-Eared Hearer listen to them," suggested Kaliko.

"Call him here at once!" commanded Ruggedo eagerly.

So in a few minutes there entered the cavern a Nome with enormous ears, who bowed low before the King.

"Strangers are approaching," said Ruggedo, "and I wish to know their errand. Listen carefully to their talk and tell me why they are coming here, and what for."

The Nome bowed again and spread out his great ears, swaying them gently up and down and back and forth. For half an hour he stood silent, in an attitude of listening, while both the King and Kaliko grew impatient at the delay. At last the Long-Eared Hearer spoke:

"Shaggy Man is coming here to rescue his brother from captivity," said he.

"Ha, the Ugly One!" exclaimed Ruggedo. "Well, Shaggy Man may have his ugly brother, for all I care. He's too lazy to work and is always getting in my way. Where is the Ugly One now, Kaliko?"

"The last time Your Majesty stumbled over the prisoner you commanded me to send him to the Metal Forest, which I did. I suppose he is still there."

"Very good. The invaders will have a hard time finding the Metal Forest," said the King, with a grin of malicious delight, "for half the time I can't find it myself. Yet I created the forest and made every tree, out of gold and silver, so as to keep the precious metals in a safe place and out of the reach of mortals. But tell me, Hearer, do the strangers want anything else?"

"Yes, indeed they do!" returned the Nome. "The Army of Oogaboo is determined to capture all the rich metals and rare jewels in your kingdom, and the officers and their Queen have arranged to divide the spoils and carry them away."

When he heard this Ruggedo uttered a bellow of rage and began dancing up and down, rolling his eyes, clicking his teeth together and swinging his arms furiously. Then, in an ecstasy of anger he seized the long ears of the Hearer and pulled and twisted them cruelly; but Kaliko grabbed up the King's sceptre and rapped him over the knuckles with it, so that Ruggedo let go the ears and began to chase his Royal Chamberlain around the throne.

The Hearer took advantage of this opportunity to slip away from the cavern and escape, and after the King had tired himself out chasing Kaliko he threw himself into his throne and panted for breath, while he glared wickedly at his defiant subject.

"You'd better save your strength to fight the enemy," suggested Kaliko. "There will be a terrible battle when the Army of Oogaboo gets here."

"The army won't get here," said the King, still coughing and panting. "I'll drop 'em down the Hollow Tube—every man Jack and every girl Jill of 'em!"

"And defy Tititi-Hoochoo?" asked Kaliko.

"Yes. Go at once to my Chief Magician and order him to turn the path toward the Hollow Tube, and to make the top of the Tube invisible, so they'll all fall into it."

Kaliko went away shaking his head, for he thought Ruggedo was making a great mistake. He found the Magician and had the path twisted so that it led directly to the opening of the Hollow Tube, and this opening he made invisible.

Having obeyed the orders of his master, the Royal Chamberlain went to his private room and began to write letters of recommendation of himself, stating that he was an honest man, a good servant and a small eater.

"Pretty soon," he said to himself, "I shall have to look for another job, for it is certain that Ruggedo has ruined himself by this reckless defiance of the mighty Tititi-Hoochoo. And in seeking a job nothing is so effective as a letter of recommendation."

CHAPTER X

A TERRIBLE TUMBLE THROUGH A TUBE

I SUPPOSE THAT POLYCHROME, AND PERHAPS QUEEN ANN AND HER ARMY, MIGHT have been able to dispel the enchantment of Ruggedo's Chief Magician had they known that danger lay in their pathway; for the Rainbow's Daughter was a fairy and as Oogaboo is a part of the Land of Oz its inhabitants cannot easily be deceived by such common magic as the Nome King could command. But no one suspected any especial danger until after they had entered Ruggedo's cavern, and so they were journeying along in quite a contented manner when Tik-Tok, who marched ahead, suddenly disappeared.

The officers thought he must have turned a corner, so they kept on their way and all of them likewise disappeared—one after another. Queen Ann was rather surprised at this, and in hastening forward to learn the reason she also vanished from sight.

Betsy Bobbin had tired her feet by walking, so she was now riding upon the back of the stout little mule, facing backward and talking to Shaggy and Polychrome, who were just behind. Suddenly Hank pitched forward and began falling and Betsy would have tumbled over his head had she not grabbed the mule's shaggy neck with both arms and held on for dear life.

All around was darkness, and they were not falling directly downward but seemed to be sliding along a steep incline. Hank's hoofs were resting upon some smooth substance over which he slid with the swiftness of the wind. Once Betsy's heels flew up and struck a similar substance overhead. They were, indeed, descending the "Hollow Tube" that led to the other side of the world.

"Stop, Hank—stop!" cried the girl; but Hank only uttered a plaintive "Hee-haw!" for it was impossible for him to obey.

After several minutes had passed and no harm had befallen them, Betsy gained courage. She could see nothing at all, nor could she hear anything except the rush of air past her ears as they plunged downward along the Tube. Whether she and Hank were alone, or the others were with them, she could not tell. But had some one been able to take a flash-light photograph of the Tube at that time a most curious picture would have resulted. There was Tik-Tok, flat upon his back and sliding headfore-most down the incline. And there were the Officers of the Army of Oogaboo, all tangled up in a confused crowd, flapping their arms and trying to shield their faces from the clanking swords, which swung back and forth during the swift journey and pommeled everyone within their reach. Now followed Queen Ann, who had struck the Tube in a sitting position and went flying along with a dash and abandon that thoroughly bewildered the poor lady, who had no idea what had happened to her. Then, a little distance away, but unseen by the others in the inky darkness, slid Betsy and Hank, while behind them were Shaggy and Polychrome and finally Files and the Princess.

When first they tumbled into the Tube all were too dazed to think clearly, but the trip was a long one, because the cavity led straight through the earth to a place just opposite the Nome King's dominions, and long before the adventurers got to the end they had begun to recover their wits.

"This is awful, Hank!" cried Betsy in a loud voice, and Queen Ann heard her and called out: "Are you safe, Betsy?"

"Mercy, no!" answered the little girl. "How could anyone be safe when she's going about sixty miles a minute?" Then, after a pause, she added: "But where do you s'pose we're going to, Your Maj'sty?"

"Don't ask her that, please don't!" said Shaggy, who was not too far away to overhear them. "And please don't ask me why, either."

"Why?" said Betsy.

"No one can tell where we are going until we get there," replied Shaggy, and then he yelled "Ouch!" for Polychrome had overtaken him and was now sitting on his head.

The Rainbow's Daughter laughed merrily, and so infectious was this joyous laugh that Betsy echoed it and Hank said "Hee-haw!" in a mild and sympathetic tone of voice.

"I'd like to know where and when we'll arrive, just the same," exclaimed the little girl.

"Be patient and you'll find out, my dear," said Polychrome. "But isn't this an odd experience? Here am I, whose home is in the skies, making a journey through the center of the earth—where I never expected to be!"

"How do you know we're in the center of the earth?" asked Betsy, her voice trembling a little through nervousness.

"Why, we can't be anywhere else," replied Polychrome. "I have often heard of this passage, which was once built by a Magician who was a great traveler. He thought it would save him the bother of going around the earth's surface, but he tumbled through the Tube so fast that he shot out at the other end and hit a star in the sky, which at once exploded."

"The star exploded?" asked Betsy wonderingly.

"Yes; the Magician hit it so hard."

"And what became of the Magician?" inquired the girl.

"No one knows that," answered Polychrome. "But I don't think it matters much."

"It matters a good deal, if we also hit the stars when we come out," said Queen Ann, with a moan.

"Don't worry," advised Polychrome. "I believe the Magician was going the other way, and probably he went much faster than we are going."

"It's fast enough to suit me," remarked Shaggy, gently removing Polychrome's heel from his left eye. "Couldn't you manage to fall all by yourself, my dear?"

"I'll try," laughed the Rainbow's Daughter.

All this time they were swiftly falling through the Tube, and it was not so easy for them to talk as you may imagine when you read their words. But although they were so helpless and altogether in the dark as to their fate, the fact that they were able to converse at all cheered them, considerably.

Files and Ozga were also conversing as they clung tightly to one another, and the young fellow bravely strove to reassure the Princess, although he was terribly frightened, both on her account and on his own.

An hour, under such trying circumstances, is a very long time, and for more than an hour they continued their fearful journey. Then, just as they began to fear the Tube would never end, Tik-Tok popped out into broad daylight and, after making a graceful circle in the air, fell with a splash into a great marble fountain.

Out came the officers, in quick succession, tumbling heels over head and striking the ground in many undignified attitudes.

"For the love of sassafras!" exclaimed a Peculiar Person who was hoeing pink violets in a garden. "What can all this mean?"

For answer, Queen Ann sailed up from the Tube, took a ride through the air as high as the treetops, and alighted squarely on top of the Peculiar Person's head, smashing a jeweled crown over his eyes and tumbling him to the ground.

The mule was heavier and had Betsy clinging to his back, so he did not go so high up. Fortunately for his little rider he struck the ground upon his four feet. Betsy was jarred a trifle but not hurt and when she looked around her she saw the Queen and the Peculiar Person struggling together upon the ground, where the man was trying to choke Ann and she had both hands in his bushy hair and was pulling with all her might. Some of the officers, when they got upon their feet, hastened to separate the combatants and sought to restrain the Peculiar Person so that he could not attack their Queen again.

By this time, Shaggy, Polychrome, Ozga and Files had all arrived and were curiously examining the strange country in which they found themselves and which they knew to be exactly on the opposite side of the world from the place where they had fallen into the Tube. It was a lovely place, indeed, and seemed to be the garden of some great Prince, for through the vistas of trees and shrubbery could be seen the towers of an immense castle. But as yet the only inhabitant to greet them was the Peculiar Person just mentioned, who had shaken off the grasp of the officers without effort and was now trying to pull the battered crown from off his eyes.

Shaggy, who was always polite, helped him to do this and when the man was free and could see again he looked at his visitors with evident amazement.

"Well, well, well!" he exclaimed. "Where did you come from and how did you get here?"

Betsy tried to answer him, for Queen Ann was surly and silent.

"I can't say, exac'ly where we came from, 'cause I don't know the name of the place," said the girl, "but the way we got here was through the Hollow Tube."

"Don't call it a 'hollow' Tube, please," exclaimed the Peculiar Person in an irritated tone of voice. "If it's a tube, it's sure to be hollow."

"Why?" asked Betsy.

"Because all tubes are made that way. But this Tube is private property and everyone is forbidden to fall into it."

"We didn't do it on purpose," explained Betsy, and Polychrome added:

"I am quite sure that Ruggedo, the Nome King, pushed us down that Tube."

"Ha! Ruggedo! Did you say Ruggedo?" cried the man, becoming much excited.

"That is what she said," replied Shaggy, "and I believe she is right. We were on our way to conquer the Nome King when suddenly we fell into the Tube."

"Then you are enemies of Ruggedo?" inquired the peculiar Person.

"Not exac'ly enemies," said Betsy, a little puzzled by the question, "'cause we don't know him at all; but we started out to conquer him, which isn't as friendly as it might be."

"True," agreed the man. He looked thoughtfully from one to another of them for a while and then he turned his head over his shoulder and said: "Never mind the fire and pincers, my good brothers. It will be best to take these strangers to the Private Citizen."

"Very well, Tubekins," responded a voice, deep and powerful, that seemed to come out of the air, for the speaker was invisible.

All our friends gave a jump, at this. Even Polychrome was so startled that her gauze draperies fluttered like a banner in a breeze. Shaggy shook his head and sighed; Queen Ann looked very unhappy; the officers clung to each other, trembling violently.

But soon they gained courage to look more closely at the Peculiar Person. As he was a type of all the inhabitants of this extraordinary land whom they afterward met, I will try to tell you what he looked like.

His face was beautiful, but lacked expression. His eyes were large and blue in color and his teeth finely formed and white as snow. His hair was black and bushy and seemed inclined to curl at the ends. So far no one could find any fault with his appearance. He wore a robe of scarlet, which did not cover his arms and extended no lower than his bare knees. On the bosom of the robe was embroidered a terrible dragon's head, as horrible to look at as the man was beautiful. His arms and legs were left bare and the skin of one arm was bright yellow and the skin of the other arm a vivid green. He had one blue leg and one pink one, while both his feet—which showed through the open sandals he wore—were jet black.

Betsy could not decide whether these gorgeous colors were dyes or the natural tints of the skin, but while she was thinking it over the man who had been called "Tubekins" said:

"Follow me to the Residence—all of you!"

But just then a Voice exclaimed: "Here's another of them, Tubekins, lying in the water of the fountain."

"Gracious!" cried Betsy; "it must be Tik-Tok, and he'll drown."

"Water is a bad thing for his clockworks, anyhow," agreed Shaggy, as with one accord they all started for the fountain. But before they could reach it, invisible hands raised Tik-Tok from the marble basin and set him upon his feet beside it, water dripping from every joint of his copper body.

"Ma—ny tha—tha—tha—thanks!" he said; and then his copper jaws clicked together and he could say no more. He next made an attempt to walk but after several awkward trials found he could not move his joints.

Peals of jeering laughter from persons unseen greeted Tik-Tok's failure, and the new arrivals in this strange land found it very uncomfortable to realize that there were many creatures around them who were invisible, yet could be heard plainly.

"Shall I wind him up?" asked Betsy, feeling very sorry for Tik-Tok.

"I think his machinery is wound; but he needs oiling," replied Shaggy.

At once an oil-can appeared before him, held on a level with his eyes by some unseen hand. Shaggy took the can and tried to oil Tik-Tok's joints. As if to assist him, a strong current of warm air was directed against the copper man, which quickly dried

him. Soon he was able to say "Ma-ny thanks!" quite smoothly and his joints worked fairly well.

"Come!" commanded Tubekins, and turning his back upon them he walked up the path toward the castle.

"Shall we go?" asked Queen Ann, uncertainly; but just then she received a shove that almost pitched her forward on her head; so she decided to go. The officers who hesitated received several energetic kicks, but could not see who delivered them; therefore they also decided—very wisely—to go. The others followed willingly enough, for unless they ventured upon another terrible journey through the Tube they must make the best of the unknown country they were in, and the best seemed to be to obey orders.

CHAPTER XI

THE FAMOUS FELLOWSHIP OF FAIRIES

AFTER A SHORT WALK THROUGH VERY BEAUTIFUL GARDENS THEY CAME TO THE castle and followed Tubekins through the entrance and into a great domed chamber, where he commanded them to be seated.

From the crown which he wore, Betsy had thought this man must be the King of the country they were in, yet after he had seated all the strangers upon benches that were ranged in a semicircle before a high throne, Tubekins bowed humbly before the vacant throne and in a flash became invisible and disappeared.

The hall was an immense place, but there seemed to be no one in it beside themselves. Presently, however, they heard a low cough near them, and here and there was the faint rustling of a robe and a slight patter as of footsteps. Then suddenly there rang out the clear tone of a bell and at the sound all was changed.

Gazing around the hall in bewilderment they saw that it was filled with hundreds of men and women, all with beautiful faces and staring blue eyes and all wearing scarlet robes and jeweled crowns upon their heads. In fact, these people seemed exact duplicates of Tubekins and it was difficult to find any mark by which to tell them apart.

"My! what a lot of Kings and Queens!" whispered Betsy to Polychrome, who sat beside her and appeared much interested in the scene but not a bit worried.

"It is certainly a strange sight," was Polychrome's reply; "but I cannot see how there can be more than one King, or Queen, in any one country, for were these all rulers, no one could tell who was Master."

One of the Kings who stood near and overheard this remark turned to her and said: "One who is Master of himself is always a King, if only to himself. In this favored land all Kings and Queens are equal, and it is our privilege to bow before one supreme Ruler—the Private Citizen."

"Who's he?" inquired Betsy.

As if to answer her, the clear tones of the bell again rang out and instantly there appeared seated in the throne the man who was lord and master of all these royal ones. This fact was evident when with one accord they fell upon their knees and touched their foreheads to the floor.

The Private Citizen was not unlike the others, except that his eyes were black instead of blue and in the centers of the black irises glowed red sparks that seemed like coals of fire. But his features were very beautiful and dignified and his manner composed and stately. Instead of the prevalent scarlet robe, he wore one of white, and the same dragon's head that decorated the others was embroidered upon its bosom.

"What charge lies against these people, Tubekins?" he asked in quiet, even tones.

"They came through the forbidden Tube, O Mighty Citizen," was the reply.

"You see, it was this way," said Betsy. "We were marching to the Nome King, to conquer him and set Shaggy's brother free, when on a sudden—"

"Who are you?" demanded the Private Citizen sternly.

"Me? Oh, I'm Betsy Bobbin, and—"

"Who is the leader of this party?" asked the Citizen.

"Sir, I am Queen Ann of Oogaboo, and—"

"Then keep quiet," said the Citizen. "Who is the leader?"

No one answered for a moment. Then General Bunn stood up.

"Sit down!" commanded the Citizen. "I can see that sixteen of you are merely officers, and of no account."

"But we have an army," said General Clock, blusteringly, for he didn't like to be told he was of no account.

"Where is your army?" asked the Citizen.

"It's me," said Tik-Tok, his voice sounding a little rusty. "I'm the on-ly Pri-vate Sol-dier in the par-ty."

Hearing this, the Citizen rose and bowed respectfully to the Clockwork Man.

"Pardon me for not realizing your importance before," said he. "Will you oblige me by taking a seat beside me on my throne?"

Betsy

Tik-Tok rose and walked over to the throne, all the Kings and Queens making way for him. Then with clanking steps he mounted the platform and sat on the broad seat beside the Citizen.

Ann was greatly provoked at this mark of favor shown to the humble Clockwork Man, but Shaggy seemed much pleased that his old friend's importance had been recognized by the ruler of this remarkable country. The Citizen now began to question Tik-Tok, who told in his mechanical voice about Shaggy's quest of his lost brother, and how Ozma of Oz had sent the Clockwork Man to assist him, and how they had fallen in with Queen Ann and her people from Oogaboo. Also he told how Betsy and Hank and Polychrome and the Rose Princess had happened to join their party.

"And you intended to conquer Ruggedo, the Metal Monarch and King of the Nomes?" asked the Citizen.

"Yes. That seemed the on-ly thing for us to do," was Tik-Tok's reply. "But he was too cle-ver for us. When we got close to his cav-ern he made our path lead to the Tube, and made the op-en-ing in-vis-i-ble, so that we all fell in-to it be-fore we knew it was there. It was an eas-y way to get rid of us and now Rug-ge-do is safe and we are far a-way in a strange land."

The Citizen was silent a moment and seemed to be thinking. Then he said:

"Most noble Private Soldier, I must inform you that by the laws of our country anyone who comes through the Forbidden Tube must be tortured for nine days and ten nights and then thrown back into the Tube. But it is wise to disregard laws when they conflict with justice, and it seems that you and your followers did not disobey our laws willingly, being forced into the Tube by Ruggedo. Therefore the Nome King is alone to blame, and he alone must be punished."

"That suits me," said Tik-Tok. "But Rug-ge-do is on the o-ther side of the world where he is a-way out of your reach."

The Citizen drew himself up proudly.

"Do you imagine anything in the world or upon it can be out of the reach of the Great Jinjin?" he asked.

"Oh! Are you, then, the Great Jinjin?" inquired Tik-Tok.

"I am."

"Then your name is Ti-ti-ti-Hoo-choo?"

"It is."

Queen Ann gave a scream and began to tremble. Shaggy was so disturbed that he took out a handkerchief and wiped the perspiration from his brow. Polychrome looked sober and uneasy for the first time, while Files put his arms around the Rose Princess as if to protect her. As for the officers, the name of the great Jinjin set them moaning and weeping at a great rate and every one fell upon his knees before the throne, begging for mercy. Betsy was worried at seeing her companions so disturbed, but did not know what it was all about. Only Tik-Tok was unmoved at the discovery.

"Then," said he, "if you are Ti-ti-ti-Hoo-choo, and think Rug-ge-do is to blame, I am sure that some-thing queer will hap-pen to the King of the Nomes."

"I wonder what 'twill be," said Betsy.

The Private Citizen—otherwise known as Tititi-Hoochoo, the Great Jinjin— looked at the little girl steadily.

"I will presently decide what is to happen to Ruggedo," said he in a hard, stern voice. Then, turning to the throng of Kings and Queens, he continued: "Tik-Tok has spoken truly, for his machinery will not allow him to lie, nor will it allow his thoughts to think falsely. Therefore these people are not our enemies and must be treated with consideration and justice. Take them to your palaces and entertain them as guests until to-morrow, when I command that they be brought again to my Residence. By then I shall have formed my plans."

No sooner had Tititi-Hoochoo spoken than he disappeared from sight. Immediately after, most of the Kings and Queens likewise disappeared. But several of them remained visible and approached the strangers with great respect. One of the lovely Queens said to Betsy:

"I trust you will honor me by being my guest. I am Erma, Queen of Light."

"May Hank come with me?" asked the girl.

"The King of Animals will care for your mule," was the reply. "But do not fear for him, for he will be treated royally. All of your party will be reunited on the morrow."

"I—I'd like to have *some* one with me," said Betsy, pleadingly.

Queen Erma looked around and smiled upon Polychrome.

"Will the Rainbow's Daughter be an agreeable companion?" she asked.

"Oh, yes!" exclaimed the girl.

So Polychrome and Betsy became guests of the Queen of Light, while other beautiful Kings and Queens took charge of the others of the party.

The two girls followed Erma out of the hall and through the gardens of the Residence to a village of pretty dwellings. None of these was so large or imposing as the castle of the Private Citizen, but all were handsome enough to be called palaces—as, in fact, they really were.

CHAPTER XII

THE LOVELY LADY OF LIGHT

THE PALACE OF THE QUEEN OF LIGHT STOOD ON A LITTLE EMINENCE AND WAS A MASS of crystal windows, surmounted by a vast crystal dome. When they entered the portals Erma was greeted by six lovely maidens, evidently of high degree, who at once aroused Betsy's admiration. Each bore a wand in her hand, tipped with an emblem of light, and their costumes were also emblematic of the lights they represented. Erma introduced them to her guests and each made a graceful and courteous acknowledgment.

First was Sunlight, radiantly beautiful and very fair; the second was Moonlight, a soft, dreamy damsel with nut-brown hair; next came Starlight, equally lovely but inclined to be retiring and shy. These three were dressed in shimmering robes of silvery white. The fourth was Daylight, a brilliant damsel with laughing eyes and frank manners, who wore a variety of colors. Then came Firelight, clothed in a fleecy flame-colored robe that wavered around her shapely form in a very attractive manner. The sixth maiden, Electra, was the most beautiful of all, and Betsy thought from the first that both Sunlight and Daylight regarded Electra with envy and were a little jealous of her.

But all were cordial in their greetings to the strangers and seemed to regard the Queen of Light with much affection, for they fluttered around her in a flashing, radiant group as she led the way to her regal drawing-room.

This apartment was richly and cosily furnished, the upholstery being of many tints, and both Betsy and Polychrome enjoyed resting themselves upon the downy divans after their strenuous adventures of the day.

The Queen sat down to chat with her guests, who noticed that Daylight was the only maiden now seated beside Erma. The others had retired to another part of the room, where they sat modestly with entwined arms and did not intrude themselves at all.

The Queen told the strangers all about this beautiful land, which is one of the chief residences of fairies who minister to the needs of mankind. So many important fairies lived there that, to avoid rivalry, they had elected as their Ruler the only important personage in the country who had no duties to mankind to perform and was, in effect, a Private Citizen. This Ruler, or Jinjin, as was his title, bore the name of Tititi-Hoochoo, and the most singular thing about him was that he had no heart. But instead of this he possessed a high degree of Reason and Justice and while he showed no mercy in his judgments he never punished unjustly or without reason. To wrong-doers Tititi-Hoochoo was as terrible as he was heartless, but those who were innocent of evil had nothing to fear from him.

All the Kings and Queens of this fairyland paid reverence to Jinjin, for as they expected to be obeyed by others they were willing to obey the one in authority over them.

The inhabitants of the Land of Oz had heard many tales of this fearfully just Jinjin, whose punishments were always equal to the faults committed. Polychrome also knew of him, although this was the first time she had ever seen him face to face. But to Betsy the story was all new, and she was greatly interested in Tititi-Hoochoo, whom she no longer feared.

Time sped swiftly during their talk and suddenly Betsy noticed that Moonlight was sitting beside the Queen of Light, instead of Daylight.

"But tell me, please," she pleaded, "why do you all wear a dragon's head embroidered on your gowns?"

Erma's pleasant face became grave as she answered:

"The Dragon, as you must know, was the first living creature ever made; therefore the Dragon is the oldest and wisest of living things. By good fortune the Original Dragon, who still lives, is a resident of this land and supplies us with wisdom whenever we are in need of it. He is old as the world and remembers everything that has happened since the world was created."

"Did he ever have any children?" inquired the girl.

"Yes, many of them. Some wandered into other lands, where men, not understanding them, made war upon them; but many still reside in this country. None, however, is as wise as the Original Dragon, for whom we have great respect. As he was the first resident here, we wear the emblem of the dragon's head to show that we are the favored people who alone have the right to inhabit this fairyland, which in beauty almost equals the Fairyland of Oz, and in power quite surpasses it."

"I understand about the dragon, now," said Polychrome, nodding her lovely head. Betsy did not quite understand, but she was at present interested in observing the changing lights. As Daylight had given way to Moonlight, so now Starlight sat at the right hand of Erma the Queen, and with her coming a spirit of peace and content seemed to fill the room. Polychrome, being herself a fairy, had many questions to ask about the various Kings and Queens who lived in this far-away, secluded place, and before Erma had finished answering them a rosy glow filled the room and Firelight took her place beside the Queen.

Betsy liked Firelight, but to gaze upon her warm and glowing features made the little girl sleepy, and presently she began to nod. Thereupon Erma rose and took Betsy's hand gently in her own.

"Come," said she; "the feast time has arrived and the feast is spread."

"That's nice," exclaimed the small mortal. "Now that I think of it, I'm awful hungry. But p'raps I can't eat your fairy food."

The Queen smiled and led her to a doorway. As she pushed aside a heavy drapery a flood of silvery light greeted them, and Betsy saw before her a splendid banquet hall, with a table spread with snowy linen and crystal and silver. At one side was a broad, throne-like seat for Erma and beside her now sat the brilliant maid Electra. Polychrome was placed on the Queen's right hand and Betsy upon her left. The other five messengers of light now waited upon them, and each person was supplied with just the food she liked best. Polychrome found her dish of dewdrops, all fresh and sparkling, while Betsy was so lavishly served that she decided she had never in her life eaten a dinner half so good.

"I s'pose," she said to the Queen, "that Miss Electra is the youngest of all these girls."

"Why do you suppose that?" inquired Erma, with a smile.

"'Cause electric'ty is the newest light we know of. Didn't Mr. Edison discover it?"

"Perhaps he was the first mortal to discover it," replied the Queen. "But electricity was a part of the world from its creation, and therefore my Electra is as old as Daylight or Moonlight, and equally beneficent to mortals and fairies alike."

Betsy was thoughtful for a time. Then she remarked, as she looked at the six messengers of light:

"We couldn't very well do without any of 'em; could we?"

Erma laughed softly. "*I* couldn't, I'm sure," she replied, "and I think mortals would miss any one of my maidens, as well. Daylight cannot take the place of Sunlight, which gives us strength and energy. Moonlight is of value when Daylight, worn out with her long watch, retires to rest. If the moon in its course is hidden behind the earth's rim, and my sweet Moonlight cannot cheer us, Starlight takes her place, for the skies always lend her power. Without Firelight we should miss much of our warmth and comfort, as well as much cheer when the walls of houses encompass us. But always, when other lights forsake us, our glorious Electra is ready to flood us with bright rays. As Queen of Light, I love all my maidens, for I know them to be faithful and true."

"I love 'em too!" declared Betsy. "But sometimes, when I'm *real* sleepy, I can get along without any light at all."

"Are you sleepy now?" inquired Erma, for the feast had ended.

"A little," admitted the girl.

So Electra showed her to a pretty chamber where there was a soft, white bed, and waited patiently until Betsy had undressed and put on a shimmery silken nightrobe that lay beside her pillow. Then the light-maid bade her good night and opened the door.

When she closed it after her Betsy was in darkness. In six winks the little girl was fast asleep.

CHAPTER XIII

THE JINJIN'S JUST JUDGMENT

ALL THE ADVENTURERS WERE REUNITED NEXT MORNING WHEN THEY WERE BROUGHT from various palaces to the Residence of Tititi-Hoochoo and ushered into the great Hall of State.

As before, no one was visible except our friends and their escorts until the first bell sounded. Then in a flash the room was seen to be filled with the beautiful Kings and Queens of the land. The second bell marked the appearance in the throne of the mighty Jinjin, whose handsome countenance was as composed and expressionless as ever.

All bowed low to the Ruler. Their voices softly murmured: "We greet the Private Citizen, mightiest of Rulers, whose word is law and whose law is just."

Tititi-Hoochoo bowed in acknowledgment. Then, looking around the brilliant assemblage, and at the little group of adventurers before him, he said:

"An unusual thing has happened. Inhabitants of other lands than ours, who are different from ourselves in many ways, have been thrust upon us through the Forbidden Tube, which one of our people foolishly made years ago and was properly punished for his folly. But these strangers had no desire to come here and were wickedly thrust into the Tube by a cruel King on the other side of the world, named

Ruggedo. This King is an immortal, but he is not good. His magic powers hurt mankind more than they benefit them. Because he had unjustly kept the Shaggy Man's brother a prisoner, this little band of honest people, consisting of both mortals and immortals, determined to conquer Ruggedo and to punish him. Fearing they might succeed in this, the Nome King misled them so that they fell into the Tube.

"Now, this same Ruggedo has been warned by me, many times, that if ever he used this Forbidden Tube in any way he would be severely punished. I find, by referring to the Fairy Records, that this King's servant, a Nome named Kaliko, begged his master not to do such a wrong act as to drop these people into the Tube and send them tumbling into our country. But Ruggedo defied me and my orders.

"Therefore these strangers are innocent of any wrong. It is only Ruggedo who deserves punishment, and I will punish him." He paused a moment and then continued in the same cold, merciless voice:

"These strangers must return through the Tube to their own side of the world; but I will make their fall more easy and pleasant than it was before. Also I shall send with them an Instrument of Vengeance, who in my name will drive Ruggedo from his underground caverns, take away his magic powers and make him a homeless wanderer on the face of the earth—a place he detests."

There was a little murmur of horror from the Kings and Queens at the severity of this punishment, but no one uttered a protest, for all realized that the sentence was just.

"In selecting my Instrument of Vengeance," went on Tititi-Hoochoo, "I have realized that this will be an unpleasant mission. Therefore no one of us who is blameless should be forced to undertake it. In this wonderful land it is seldom one is guilty of wrong, even in the slightest degree, and on examining the Records I found no King or Queen had erred. Nor had any among their followers or servants done any wrong. But finally I came to the Dragon Family, which we highly respect, and then it was that I discovered the error of Quox.

"Quox, as you well know, is a young dragon who has not yet acquired the wisdom of his race. Because of this lack, he has been disrespectful toward his most ancient ancestor, the Original Dragon, telling him once to mind his own business and again saying that the Ancient One had grown foolish with age. We are aware that dragons are not the same as fairies and cannot be altogether guided by our laws, yet such disrespect as Quox has shown should not be unnoticed by us. Therefore I have selected Quox as my royal Instrument of Vengeance and he shall go through the Tube with these people and inflict upon Ruggedo the punishment I have decreed."

All had listened quietly to this speech and now the Kings and Queens bowed gravely to signify their approval of the Jinjin's judgment.

Tititi-Hoochoo turned to Tubekins.

"I command you," said he, "to escort these strangers to the Tube and see that they all enter it."

The King of the Tube, who had first discovered our friends and brought them to the Private Citizen, stepped forward and bowed. As he did so, the Jinjin and all the Kings and Queens suddenly disappeared and only Tubekins remained visible.

"All right," said Betsy, with a sigh; "I don't mind going back so *very* much, 'cause the Jinjin promised to make it easy for us."

Indeed, Queen Ann and her officers were the only ones who looked solemn and seemed to fear the return journey. One thing that bothered Ann was her failure to conquer this land of Tititi-Hoochoo. As they followed their guide through the gardens to the mouth of the Tube she said to Shaggy:

"How can I conquer the world, if I go away and leave this rich country unconquered?"

"You can't," he replied. "Don't ask me why, please, for if you don't know I can't inform you."

"Why not?" said Ann; but Shaggy paid no atten tion to the question.

This end of the Tube had a silver rim and around it was a gold railing to which was attached a sign that read:

> "IF YOU ARE OUT, STAY THERE.
> IF YOU ARE IN, DON'T COME OUT."

On a little silver plate just inside the Tube was engraved the words:

> *"Burrowed and built by*
> *Hiergargo the Magician,*
> *In the Year of the World*
> *1 9 6 2 5 4 7 8*
> *For his own exclusive uses."*

"He was some builder, I must say," remarked Betsy, when she had read the inscription; "but if he had known about that star I guess he'd have spent his time playing solitaire."

"Well, what are we waiting for?" inquired Shaggy, who was impatient to start.

"Quox," replied Tubekins. "But I think I hear him coming."

"Is the young dragon invisible?" asked Ann, who had never seen a live dragon and was a little fearful of meeting one.

"No, indeed," replied the King of the Tube. "You'll see him in a minute; but before you part company I'm sure you'll wish he *was* invisible."

"Is he dangerous, then?" questioned Files.

"Not at all. But Quox tires me dreadfully," said Tubekins, "and I prefer his room to his company."

At that instant a scraping sound was heard, drawing nearer and nearer until from between two big bushes appeared a huge dragon, who approached the party, nodded his head and said: "Good morning."

Had Quox been at all bashful I am sure he would have felt uncomfortable at the astonished stare of every eye in the group—except Tubekins, of course, who was not astonished because he had seen Quox so often.

Betsy had thought a "young" dragon must be a small dragon, yet here was one so enormous that the girl decided he must be full grown, if not overgrown. His body was a lovely sky-blue in color and it was thickly set with glittering silver scales, each one as big as a serving-tray. Around his neck was a pink ribbon with a bow just under his left ear, and below the ribbon appeared a chain of pearls to which was attached a golden locket about as large around as the end of a bass drum. This locket was set with many large and beautiful jewels.

The head and face of Quox were not especially ugly, when you consider that he was a dragon; but his eyes were so large that it took him a long time to wink and his teeth seemed very sharp and terrible when they showed, which they did whenever the beast smiled. Also his nostrils were quite large and wide, and those who stood near him were liable to smell brimstone—especially when he breathed out fire, as it is the nature of dragons to do. To the end of his long tail was attached a big electric light.

Perhaps the most singular thing about the dragon's appearance at this time was the fact that he had a row of seats attached to his back, one seat for each member of the party. These seats were double, with curved backs, so that two could sit in them, and there were twelve of these double seats, all strapped firmly around the dragon's thick body and placed one behind the other, in a row that extended from his shoulders nearly to his tail.

"Aha!" exclaimed Tubekins; "I see that Tititi-Hoochoo has transformed Quox into a carryall."

"I'm glad of that," said Betsy. "I hope, Mr. Dragon, you won't mind our riding on your back."

"Not a bit," replied Quox. "I'm in disgrace just now, you know, and the only way to redeem my good name is to obey the orders of the Jinjin. If he makes me a beast of burden, it is only a part of my punishment, and I must bear it like a dragon. I don't blame you people at all, and I hope you'll enjoy the ride. Hop on, please. All aboard for the other side of the world!"

Silently they took their places. Hank sat in the front seat with Betsy, so that he could rest his front hoofs upon the dragon's head. Behind them were Shaggy and Polychrome, then Files and the Princess, and Queen Ann and Tik-Tok. The officers rode in the rear seats. When all had mounted to their places the dragon looked very like one of those sightseeing wagons so common in big cities—only he had legs instead of wheels.

"All ready?" asked Quox, and when they said they were he crawled to the mouth of the Tube and put his head in.

"Good-bye, and good luck to you!" called Tubekins; but no one thought to reply, because just then the dragon slid his great body into the Tube and the journey to the other side of the world had begun.

At first they went so fast that they could scarcely catch their breaths, but presently Quox slowed up and said with a sort of cackling laugh:

"My scales! but that is some tumble. I think I shall take it easy and fall slower, or I'm likely to get dizzy. Is it very far to the other side of the world?"

"Haven't you ever been through this Tube before?" inquired Shaggy.

"Never. Nor has anyone else in our country; at least, not since I was born."

"How long ago was that?" asked Betsy.

"That I was born? Oh, not very long ago. I'm only a mere child. If I had not been sent on this journey, I would have celebrated my three thousand and fifty-sixth birthday next Thursday. Mother was going to make me a birthday cake with three thousand and fifty-six candles on it; but now, of course, there will be no celebration, for I fear I shall not get home in time for it."

"Three thousand and fifty-six years!" cried Betsy. "Why, I had no idea anything could live that long!"

"My respected Ancestor, whom I would call a stupid old humbug if I had not reformed, is so old that I am a mere baby compared with him," said Quox. "He dates from the beginning of the world, and insists on telling us stories of things that happened fifty thousand years ago, which are of no interest at all to youngsters like me. In fact, Grandpa isn't up to date. He lives altogether in the past, so I can't see any good reason for his being alive to-day. . . . Are you people able to see your way, or shall I turn on more light?"

"Oh, we can see very nicely, thank you; only there's nothing to see but ourselves," answered Betsy.

This was true. The dragon's big eyes were like headlights on an automobile and illuminated the Tube far ahead of them. Also he curled his tail upward so that the electric light on the end of it enabled them to see one another quite clearly. But the Tube itself was only dark metal, smooth as glass but exactly the same from one of its ends to the other. Therefore there was no scenery of interest to beguile the journey.

They were now falling so gently that the trip was proving entirely comfortable, as the Jinjin had promised it would be; but this meant a longer journey and the only way they could make time pass was to engage in conversation. The dragon seemed a willing and persistent talker and he was of so much interest to them that they encouraged him to chatter. His voice was a little gruff but not unpleasant when one became used to it.

"My only fear," said he presently, "is that this constant sliding over the surface of the Tube will dull my claws. You see, this hole isn't straight down, but on a steep slant, and so instead of tumbling freely through the air I must skate along the Tube. Fortunately, there is a file in my tool-kit, and if my claws get dull they can be sharpened again."

"Why do you want sharp claws?" asked Betsy.

"They are my natural weapons, and you must not forget that I have been sent to conquer Ruggedo."

"Oh, you needn't mind about that," remarked Queen Ann, in her most haughty manner; "for when we get to Ruggedo I and my invincible army can conquer him without your assistance."

"Very good," returned the dragon, cheerfully. "That will save me a lot of bother—if you succeed. But I think I shall file my claws, just the same."

He gave a long sigh, as he said this, and a sheet of flame, several feet in length, shot from his mouth. Betsy shuddered and Hank said "Hee-haw!" while some of the officers screamed in terror. But the dragon did not notice that he had done anything unusual.

"Is there fire inside of you?" asked Shaggy.

"Of course," answered Quox. "What sort of a dragon would I be if my fire went out?"

"What keeps it going?" Betsy inquired.

"I've no idea. I only know it's there," said Quox. "The fire keeps me alive and enables me to move; also to think and speak."

"Ah! You are ver-y much like my-self," said Tik-Tok. "The on-ly dif-fer-ence is that I move by clock-work, while you move by fire."

"I don't see a particle of likeness between us, I must confess," retorted Quox, gruffly. "You are not a live thing; you're a dummy."

"But I can do things, you must ad-mit," said Tik-Tok.

"Yes, when you are wound up," sneered the dragon. "But if you run down, you are helpless."

"What would happen to you, Quox, if you ran out of gasoline?" inquired Shaggy, who did not like this attack upon his friend.

"I don't use gasoline."

"Well, suppose you ran out of fire."

"What's the use of supposing that?" asked Quox. "My great-great-great-grand-father has lived since the world began, and he has never once run out of fire to keep him going. But I will confide to you that as he gets older he shows more smoke and less fire. As for Tik-Tok, he's well enough in his way, but he's merely copper. And the Metal Monarch knows copper through and through. I wouldn't be surprised if Ruggedo melted Tik-Tok in one of his furnaces and made copper pennies of him."

"In that case, I would still keep going," remarked Tik-Tok, calmly.

"Pennies do," said Betsy regretfully.

"This is all nonsense," said the Queen, with irritation. "Tik-Tok is my great army—all but the officers—and I believe he will be able to conquer Ruggedo with ease. What do you think, Polychrome?"

"You might let him try," answered the Rainbow's Daughter, with her sweet ring-ing laugh, that sounded like the tinkling of tiny bells. "And if Tik-Tok fails, you have still the big fire-breathing dragon to fall back on."

"Ah!" said the dragon, another sheet of flame gushing from his mouth and nos-trils; "it's a wise little girl, this Polychrome. Anyone would know she is a fairy."

CHAPTER XIV

THE LONG-EARED HEARER LEARNS BY LISTENING

DURING THIS TIME RUGGEDO, THE METAL MONARCH AND KING OF THE NOMES, WAS trying to amuse himself in his splendid jeweled cavern. It was hard work for Ruggedo to find amusement to-day, for all the Nomes were behaving well and there was no one to scold or to punish. The King had thrown his sceptre at Kaliko six times, without hitting him once. Not that Kaliko had done anything wrong. On the contrary, he had obeyed the King in every way but one: he would not stand still, when commanded to do so, and let the heavy sceptre strike him.

We can hardly blame Kaliko for this, and even the cruel Ruggedo forgave him; for he knew very well that if he mashed his Royal Chamberlain he could never find another so intelligent and obedient. Kaliko could make the Nomes work when their King could not, for the Nomes hated Ruggedo and there were so many thousands of the quaint little underground people that they could easily have rebelled and defied the King had they dared to do so. Sometimes, when Ruggedo abused them worse than usual, they grew sullen and threw down their hammers and picks. Then, however hard the King scolded or whipped them, they would not work until Kaliko came and begged them to. For Kaliko was one of themselves and was as much abused by the King as any Nome in the vast series of caverns.

But to-day all the little people were working industriously at their tasks and Ruggedo, having nothing to do, was greatly bored. He sent for the Long-Eared Hearer and asked him to listen carefully and report what was going on in the big world.

"It seems," said the Hearer, after listening for a while, "that the women in America have clubs."

"Are there spikes in them?" asked Ruggedo, yawning.

"I cannot hear any spikes, Your Majesty," was the reply.

"Then their clubs are not as good as my sceptre. What else do you hear?'

"There's a war.

"Bah! there's always a war. What else?"

For a time the Hearer was silent, bending forward and spreading out his big ears to catch the slightest sound. Then suddenly he said:

"Here is an interesting thing, Your Majesty. These people are arguing as to who shall conquer the Metal Monarch, seize his treasure and drive him from his dominions."

"What people?" demanded Ruggedo, sitting up straight in his throne.

"The ones you threw down the Hollow Tube."

"Where are they now?"

"In the same Tube, and coming back this way," said the Hearer.

Ruggedo got out of his throne and began to pace up and down the cavern.

"I wonder what can be done to stop them," he mused.

"Well," said the Hearer, "if you could turn the Tube upside down, they would be falling the other way, Your Majesty."

Ruggedo glared at him wickedly, for it was impossible to turn the Tube upside down and he believed the Hearer was slyly poking fun at him. Presently he asked:

"How far away are those people now?"

"About nine thousand three hundred and six miles, seventeen furlongs, eight feet and four inches—as nearly as I can judge from the sound of their voices," replied the Hearer.

"Aha! Then it will be some time before they arrive," said Ruggedo, "and when they get here I shall be ready to receive them."

He rushed to his gong and pounded upon it so fiercely that Kaliko came bounding into the cavern with one shoe off and one shoe on, for he was just dressing himself after a swim in the hot bubbling lake of the Underground Kingdom.

"Kaliko, those invaders whom we threw down the Tube are coming back again!" he exclaimed.

"I thought they would," said the Royal Chamberlain, pulling on the other shoe. "Tititi-Hoochoo would not allow them to remain in his kingdom, of course, and so I've been expecting them back for some time. That was a very foolish action of yours, Rug."

"What, to throw them down the Tube?"

"Yes. Tititi-Hoochoo has forbidden us to throw even rubbish into the Tube."

"Pooh! what do I care for the Jinjin?" asked Ruggedo scornfully. "He never leaves his own kingdom, which is on the other side of the world."

"True; but he might send some one through the Tube to punish you," suggested Kaliko.

"I'd like to see him do it! Who could conquer my thousands of Nomes?"

"Why, they've been conquered before, if I remember aright," answered Kaliko with a grin. "Once I saw you running from a little girl named Dorothy, and her friends, as if you were really afraid."

"Well, I *was* afraid, that time," admitted the Nome King, with a deep sigh, "for Dorothy had a Yellow Hen that laid eggs!"

The King shuddered as he said "eggs," and Kaliko also shuddered, and so did the Long-Eared Hearer; for eggs are the only things that the Nomes greatly dread. The reason for this is that eggs belong on the earth's surface, where birds and fowl of all sorts live, and there is something about a hen's egg, especially, that fills a Nome with horror. If by chance the inside of an egg touches one of these underground people, he withers up and blows away and that is the end of him—unless he manages quickly to speak a magical word which only a few of the Nomes know. Therefore Ruggedo and his followers had very good cause to shudder at the mere mention of eggs.

"But Dorothy," said the King, "is not with this band of invaders; nor is the Yellow Hen. As for Tititi-Hoochoo, he has no means of knowing that we are afraid of eggs."

"You mustn't be too sure of that," Kaliko warned him. "Tititi-Hoochoo knows a great many things, being a fairy, and his powers are far superior to any we can boast."

Ruggedo shrugged impatiently and turned to the Hearer.

"Listen," said he, "and tell me if you hear any eggs coming through the Tube."

The Long-Eared one listened and then shook his head. But Kaliko laughed at the King.

"No one can hear an egg, Your Majesty," said he. "The only way to discover the truth is to look through the Magic Spyglass."

"That's it!" cried the King. "Why didn't I think of it before? Look at once, Kaliko!"

So Kaliko went to the Spyglass and by uttering a mumbled charm he caused the other end of it to twist around, so that it pointed down the opening of the Tube. Then

he put his eye to the glass and was able to gaze along all the turns and windings of the Magic Spyglass and then deep into the Tube, to where our friends were at that time falling.

"Dear me!" he exclaimed. "Here comes a dragon."

"A big one?" asked Ruggedo.

"A monster. He has an electric light on the end of his tail, so I can see him very plainly. And the other people are all riding upon his back."

"How about the eggs?" inquired the King.

Kaliko looked again.

"I can see no eggs at all," said he; "but I imagine that the dragon is as dangerous as eggs. Probably Tititi-Hoochoo has sent him here to punish you for dropping those strangers into the Forbidden Tube. I warned you not to do it, Your Majesty."

This news made the Nome King anxious. For a few minutes he paced up and down, stroking his long beard and thinking with all his might. After this he turned to Kaliko and said:

"All the harm a dragon can do is to scratch with his claws and bite with his teeth."

"That is not all, but it's quite enough," returned Kaliko earnestly. "On the other hand, no one can hurt a dragon, because he's the toughest creature alive. One flop of his huge tail could smash a hundred Nomes to pancakes, and with teeth and claws he could tear even you or me into small bits, so that it would be almost impossible to put us together again. Once, a few hundred years ago, while wandering through some deserted caverns, I came upon a small piece of a Nome lying on the rocky floor. I asked the piece of Nome what had happened to it. Fortunately the mouth was a part of this piece—the mouth and the left eye—so it was able to tell me that a fierce dragon was the cause. It had attacked the poor Nome and scattered him in every direction, and as there was no friend near to collect his pieces and put him together, they had been separated for a great many years. So you see, Your Majesty, it is not in good taste to sneer at a dragon."

The King had listened attentively to Kaliko. Said he:

"It will only be necessary to chain this dragon which Tititi-Hoochoo has sent here, in order to prevent his reaching us with his claws and teeth."

"He also breathes flames," Kaliko reminded him.

"My Nomes are not afraid of fire, nor am I," said Ruggedo.

"Well, how about the Army of Oogaboo?"

"Sixteen cowardly officers and Tik-Tok! Why, I could defeat them single-handed; but I won't try to. I'll summon my army of Nomes to drive the invaders out of my territory, and if we catch any of them I intend to stick needles into them until they hop with pain."

"I hope you won't hurt any of the girls," said Kaliko.

"I'll hurt 'em all!" roared the angry Metal Monarch. "And that braying Mule I'll make into hoof-soup, and feed it to my Nomes, that it may add to their strength."

"Why not be good to the strangers and release your prisoner, the Shaggy Man's brother?" suggested Kaliko.

"Never!"

"It may save you a lot of annoyance. And you don't want the Ugly One."

"I don't want him; that's true. But I won't allow anybody to order me around. I'm King of the Nomes and I'm the Metal Monarch, and I shall do as I please and what I please and when I please!"

With this speech Ruggedo threw his sceptre at Kaliko's head, aiming it so well that the Royal Chamberlain had to fall flat upon the floor in order to escape it. But the Hearer did not see the sceptre coming and it swept past his head so closely that it broke off the tip of one of his long ears. He gave a dreadful yell that quite startled Ruggedo, and the King was sorry for the accident because those long ears of the Hearer were really valuable to him.

So the Nome King forgot to be angry with Kaliko and ordered his Chamberlain to summon General Guph and the army of Nomes and have them properly armed. They were then to march to the mouth of the Tube, where they could seize the travelers as soon as they appeared.

CHAPTER XV

THE DRAGON DEFIES DANGER

ALTHOUGH THE JOURNEY THROUGH THE TUBE WAS LONGER, THIS TIME, THAN BEFORE, it was so much more comfortable that none of our friends minded it at all. They talked together most of the time and as they found the dragon good-natured and fond of the sound of his own voice they soon became well acquainted with him and accepted him as a companion.

"You see," said Shaggy, in his frank way, "Quox is on our side, and therefore the dragon is a good fellow. If he happened to be an enemy, instead of a friend, I am sure I should dislike him very much, for his breath smells of brimstone, he is very conceited and he is so strong and fierce that he would prove a dangerous foe."

"Yes, indeed," returned Quox, who had listened to this speech with pleasure; "I suppose I am about as terrible as any living thing. I am glad you find me conceited, for that proves I know my good qualities. As for my breath smelling of brimstone, I really can't help it, and I once met a man whose breath smelled of onions, which I consider far worse."

"I don't," said Betsy; "I love onions."

"And I love brimstone," declared the dragon, "so don't let us quarrel over one another's peculiarities."

Saying this, he breathed a long breath and shot a flame fifty feet from his mouth. The brimstone made Betsy cough, but she remembered about the onions and said nothing.

They had no idea how far they had gone through the center of the earth, nor when to expect the trip to end. At one time the little girl remarked:

"I wonder when we'll reach the bottom of this hole. And isn't it funny, Shaggy Man, that what is the bottom to us now, was the top when we fell the other way?"

"What puzzles me," said Files, "is that we are able to fall both ways."

"That," announced Tik-Tok, "is be-cause the world is round."

"Exactly," responded Shaggy. "The machinery in your head is in fine working order, Tik-Tok. You know, Betsy, that there is such a thing as the Attraction of Gravitation, which draws everything toward the center of the earth. That is why we fall out of bed, and why everything clings to the surface of the earth."

"Then why doesn't everything go on down to the center of the earth?" inquired the little girl.

"I was afraid you were going to ask me that," replied Shaggy in a sad tone. "The reason, my dear, is that the earth is so solid that other solid things can't get through it. But when there's a hole, as there is in this case, we drop right down to the center of the world."

"Why don't we stop there?" asked Betsy.

"Because we go so fast that we acquire speed enough to carry us right up to the other end."

"I don't understand that, and it makes my head ache to try to figure it out," she said after some thought. "One thing draws us to the center and another thing pushes us away from it. But——"

"Don't ask me why, please," interrupted the Shaggy Man. "If you can't understand it, let it go at that."

"Do *you* understand it?" she inquired.

"All the magic isn't in fairyland," he said gravely. "There's lots of magic in all Nature, and you may see it as well in the United States, where you and I once lived, as you can here."

"I never did," she replied.

"Because you were so used to it all that you didn't realize it was magic. Is anything more wonderful than to see a flower grow and blossom, or to get light out of the electricity in the air? The cows that manufacture milk for us must have machinery fully as remarkable as that in Tik-Tok's copper body, and perhaps you've noticed that——"

And then, before Shaggy could finish his speech, the strong light of day suddenly broke upon them, grew brighter, and completely enveloped them. The dragon's claws

no longer scraped against the metal Tube, for he shot into the open air a hundred feet
or more and sailed so far away from the slanting hole that when he landed it was on
the peak of a mountain and just over the entrance to the many underground caverns
of the Nome King.

Some of the officers tumbled off their seats when Quox struck the ground, but
most of the dragon's passengers only felt a slight jar. All were glad to be on solid earth
again and they at once dismounted and began to look about them. Queerly enough,
as soon as they had left the dragon, the seats that were strapped to the monster's back
disappeared, and this probably happened because there was no further use for them

and because Quox looked far more dignified in just his silver scales. Of course he still wore the forty yards of ribbon around his neck, as well as the great locket, but these only made him look "dressed up," as Betsy remarked.

Now the army of Nomes had gathered thickly around the mouth of the Tube, in order to be ready to capture the band of invaders as soon as they popped out. There were, indeed, hundreds of Nomes assembled, and they were led by Guph, their most famous General. But they did not expect the dragon to fly so high, and he shot out of the Tube so suddenly that it took them by surprise. When the Nomes had rubbed the astonishment out of their eyes and regained their wits, they discovered the dragon quietly seated on the mountainside far above their heads, while the other strangers were standing in a group and calmly looking down upon them.

General Guph was very angry at the escape, which was no one's fault but his own.

"Come down here and be captured!" he shouted, waving his sword at them.

"Come up here and capture us—if you dare!" replied Queen Ann, who was winding up the clockwork of her Private Soldier, so he could fight more briskly.

Guph's first answer was a roar of rage at the defiance; then he turned and issued a command to his Nomes. These were all armed with sharp spears and with one accord they raised these spears and threw them straight at their foes, so that they rushed through the air in a perfect cloud of flying weapons.

Some damage might have been done had not the dragon quickly crawled before the others, his body being so big that it shielded every one of them, including Hank. The spears rattled against the silver scales of Quox and then fell harmlessly to the ground. They were magic spears, of course, and all straightway bounded back into the hands of those who had thrown them, but even Guph could see that it was useless to repeat the attack.

It was now Queen Ann's turn to attack, so the Generals yelled "For—ward march!" and the Colonels and Majors and Captains repeated the command and the valiant Army of Oogaboo, which seemed to be composed mainly of Tik-Tok, marched forward in single column toward the Nomes, while Betsy and Polychrome cheered and Hank gave a loud "Hee-haw!" and Shaggy shouted "Hooray!" and Queen Ann screamed: "At 'em, Tik-Tok—at 'em!"

The Nomes did not await the Clockwork Man's attack but in a twinkling disappeared into the underground caverns. They made a great mistake in being so hasty, for Tik-Tok had not taken a dozen steps before he stubbed his copper toe on a rock and fell flat to the ground, where he cried: "Pick me up! Pick me up! Pick me up!" until Shaggy and Files ran forward and raised him to his feet again.

The dragon chuckled softly to himself as he scratched his left ear with his hind claw, but no one was paying much attention to Quox just then.

It was evident to Ann and her officers that there could be no fighting unless the enemy was present, and in order to find the enemy they must boldly enter the underground Kingdom of the Nomes. So bold a step demanded a council of war.

"Don't you think I'd better drop in on Ruggedo and obey the orders of the Jinjin?" asked Quox.

"By no means!" returned Queen Ann. "We have already put the army of Nomes to flight and all that yet remains is to force our way into those caverns, and conquer the Nome King and all his people."

"That seems to me something of a job," said the dragon, closing his eyes sleepily. "But go ahead, if you like, and I'll wait here for you. Don't be in any hurry on my account. To one who lives thousands of years the delay of a few days means nothing at all, and I shall probably sleep until the time comes for me to act."

Ann was provoked at this speech.

"You may as well go back to Tititi-Hoochoo now," she said, "for the Nome King is as good as conquered already."

But Quox shook his head. "No," said he; "I'll wait."

CHAPTER XVI

THE NAUGHTY NOME

Shaggy Man had said nothing during the conversation between Queen Ann and Quox, for the simple reason that he did not consider the matter worth an argument. Safe within his pocket reposed the Love Magnet, which had never failed to win every heart. The Nomes, he knew, were not like the heartless Roses and therefore could be won to his side as soon as he exhibited the magic talisman.

Shaggy's chief anxiety had been to reach Ruggedo's kingdom and now that the entrance lay before him he was confident he would be able to rescue his lost brother. Let Ann and the dragon quarrel as to who should conquer the Nomes, if they liked; Shaggy would let them try, and if they failed he had the means of conquest in his own pocket.

But Ann was positive she could not fail, for she thought her army could do anything. So she called the officers together and told them how to act, and she also instructed Tik-Tok what to do and what to say.

"Please do not shoot your gun except as a last resort," she added, "for I do not wish to be cruel or to shed any blood—unless it is absolutely necessary."

"All right," replied Tik-Tok; "but I do not think Rug-ge-do would bleed if I filled him full of holes and put him in a ci-der press."

Then the officers fell in line, the four Generals abreast and then the four Colonels and the four Majors and the four Captains. They drew their glittering swords and commanded Tik-Tok to march, which he did. Twice he fell down, being tripped by the rough rocks, but when he struck the smooth path he got along better. Into the gloomy mouth of the cavern entrance he stepped without hesitation, and after him proudly pranced the officers and Queen Ann. The others held back a little, waiting to see what would happen.

Of course the Nome King knew they were coming and was prepared to receive them. Just within the rocky passage that led to the jeweled throne-room was a deep pit, which was usually covered. Ruggedo had ordered the cover removed and it now stood open, scarcely visible in the gloom.

The pit was so large around that it nearly filled the passage and there was barely room for one to walk around it by pressing close to the rock walls. This Tik-Tok did, for his copper eyes saw the pit clearly and he avoided it; but the officers marched straight into the hole and tumbled in a heap on the bottom. An instant later Queen Ann also walked into the pit, for she had her chin in the air and was careless where she placed her feet. Then one of the Nomes pulled a lever which replaced the cover on the pit and made the officers of Oogaboo and their Queen fast prisoners.

As for Tik-Tok, he kept straight on to the cavern where Ruggedo sat in his throne and there he faced the Nome King and said:

"I here-by con-quer you in the name of Queen Ann So-forth of Oo-ga-boo, whose Ar-my I am, and I de-clare that you are her pris-on-er!"

Ruggedo laughed at him.

"Where is this famous Queen?" he asked.

"She'll be here in a min-ute," said Tik-Tok. "Per-haps she stopped to tie her shoe-string."

"Now, see here, Tik-Tok," began the Nome King, in a stern voice, "I've had enough of this nonsense. Your Queen and her officers are all prisoners, having fallen into my power, so perhaps you'll tell me what you mean to do."

"My or-ders were to con-quer you," replied Tik-Tok, "and my ma-chin-er-y has done the best it knows how to car-ry out those or-ders."

Ruggedo pounded on his gong and Kaliko appeared, followed closely by General Guph.

"Take this copper man into the shops and set him to work hammering gold," commanded the King. "Being run by machinery he ought to be a steady worker. He ought never to have been made, but since he exists I shall hereafter put him to good use."

"If you try to cap-ture me," said Tik-Tok, "I shall fight."

"Don't do that!" exclaimed General Guph, earnestly, "for it will be useless to resist and you might hurt some one."

But Tik-Tok raised his gun and took aim and not knowing what damage the gun might do the Nomes were afraid to face it.

While he was thus defying the Nome King and his high officials, Betsy Bobbin rode calmly into the royal cavern, seated upon the back of Hank the mule. The little girl had grown tired of waiting for "something to happen" and so had come to see if Ruggedo had been conquered.

"Nails and nuggets!" roared the King; "how dare you bring that beast here and enter my presence unannounced?"

"There wasn't anybody to announce me," replied Betsy. "I guess your folks were all busy. Are you conquered yet?"

"No!" shouted the King, almost beside himself with rage.

"Then please give me something to eat, for I'm awful hungry," said the girl. "You see, this conquering business is a good deal like waiting for a circus parade; it takes a long time to get around and don't amount to much anyhow."

The Nomes were so much astonished at this speech that for a time they could only glare at her silently, not finding words to reply. The King finally recovered the use of his tongue and said:

"Earth-crawler! this insolence to my majesty shall be your death-warrant. You are an ordinary mortal, and to stop a mortal from living is so easy a thing to do that I will not keep you waiting half so long as you did for my conquest."

"I'd rather you wouldn't stop me from living," remarked Betsy, getting off Hank's back and standing beside him. "And it would be a pretty cheap King who killed a visitor while she was hungry. If you'll give me something to eat, I'll talk this killing business over with you afterward; only, I warn you now that I don't approve of it, and never will."

Her coolness and lack of fear impressed the Nome King, although he bore an intense hatred toward all mortals.

"What do you wish to eat?" he asked gruffly.

"Oh, a ham-sandwich would do, or perhaps a couple of hard-boiled eggs—"

"Eggs!" shrieked the three Nomes who were present, shuddering till their teeth chattered.

"What's the matter?" asked Betsy wonderingly. "Are eggs as high here as they are at home?"

"Guph," said the King in an agitated voice, turning to his General, "let us destroy this rash mortal at once! Seize her and take her to the Slimy Cave and lock her in."

Guph glanced at Tik-Tok, whose gun was still pointed, but just then Kaliko stole softly behind the copper man and kicked his knee-joints so that they suddenly bent forward and tumbled Tik-Tok to the floor, his gun falling from his grasp.

Then Guph, seeing Tik-Tok helpless, made a grab at Betsy. At the same time Hank's heels shot out and caught the General just where his belt was buckled. He rose into the air swift as a cannon-ball, struck the Nome King fairly and flattened his Majesty against the wall of rock on the opposite side of the cavern. Together they fell to the floor in a dazed and crumpled condition, seeing which Kaliko whispered to Betsy:

"Come with me—quick!—and I will save you."

She looked into Kaliko's face inquiringly and thought he seemed honest and good-natured, so she decided to follow him. He led her and the mule through several passages and into a small cavern very nicely and comfortably furnished.

"This is my own room," said he, "but you are quite welcome to use it. Wait here a minute and I'll get you something to eat."

When Kaliko returned he brought a tray containing some broiled mushrooms, a loaf of mineral bread and some petroleum-butter. The butter Betsy could not eat, but the bread was good and the mushrooms delicious.

"Here's the door key," said Kaliko, "and you'd better lock yourself in."

"Won't you let Polychrome and the Rose Princess come here, too?" she asked.

"I'll see. Where are they?"

"I don't know. I left them outside," said Betsy.

"Well, if you hear three raps on the door, open it," said Kaliko; "but don't let anyone in unless they give the three raps."

"All right," promised Betsy, and when Kaliko left the cosy cavern she closed and locked the door.

In the meantime Ann and her officers, finding themselves prisoners in the pit, had shouted and screamed until they were tired out, but no one had come to their assistance. It was very dark and damp in the pit and they could not climb out because the walls were higher than their heads and the cover was on. The Queen was first angry and then annoyed and then discouraged; but the officers were only afraid. Every one of the poor fellows heartily wished he was back in Oogaboo caring for his orchard, and some were so unhappy that they began to reproach Ann for causing them all this trouble and danger.

Finally the Queen sat down on the bottom of the pit and leaned her back against the wall. By good luck her sharp elbow touched a secret spring in the wall and a big flat rock swung inward. Ann fell over backward, but the next instant she jumped up and cried to the others:

"A passage! A passage! Follow me, my brave men, and we may yet escape."

Then she began to crawl through the passage, which was as dark and dank as the pit, and the officers followed her in single file. They crawled, and they crawled, and they kept on crawling, for the passage was not big enough to allow them to stand upright. It turned this way and twisted that, sometimes like a corkscrew and sometimes zigzag, but seldom ran for long in a straight line.

"It will never end—never!" moaned the officers, who were rubbing all the skin off their knees on the rough rocks.

"It *must* end," retorted Ann courageously, "or it never would have been made. We don't know where it will lead us to, but any place is better than that loathsome pit."

So she crawled on, and the officers crawled on, and while they were crawling through this awful underground passage Polychrome and Shaggy and Files and the Rose Princess, who were standing outside the entrance to Ruggedo's domains, were wondering what had become of them.

CHAPTER XVII

A TRAGIC
TRANSFORMATION

"Don't let us worry," said Shaggy to his companions, "for it may take the Queen some time to conquer the Metal Monarch, as Tik-Tok has to do everything in his slow, mechanical way."

"Do you suppose they are likely to fail?" asked the Rose Princess.

"I do, indeed," replied Shaggy. "This Nome King is really a powerful fellow and has a legion of Nomes to assist him, whereas our bold Queen commands a Clockwork Man and a band of faint-hearted officers."

"She ought to have let Quox do the conquering," said Polychrome, dancing lightly upon a point of rock and fluttering her beautiful draperies. "But perhaps the dragon was wise to let her go first, for when she fails to conquer Ruggedo she may become more modest in her ambitions."

"Where is the dragon now?" inquired Ozga.

"Up there on the rocks," replied Files. "Look, my dear; you may see him from here. He said he would take a little nap while we were mixing up with Ruggedo, and he added that after we had gotten into trouble he would wake up and conquer the Nome King in a jiffy, as his master the Jinjin has ordered him to do."

"Quox means well," said Shaggy, "but I do not think we shall need his services; for just as soon as I am satisfied that Queen Ann and her army have failed to conquer

Ruggedo, I shall enter the caverns and show the King my Love Magnet. That he cannot resist; therefore the conquest will be made with ease."

This speech of Shaggy Man's was overheard by the Long-Eared Hearer, who was at that moment standing by Ruggedo's side. For when the King and Guph had recovered from Hank's kick and had picked themselves up, their first act was to turn Tik-Tok on his back and put a heavy diamond on top of him, so that he could not get up again. Then they carefully put his gun in a corner of the cavern and the King sent Guph to fetch the Long-Eared Hearer.

The Hearer was still angry at Ruggedo for breaking his ear, but he acknowledged the Nome King to be his master and was ready to obey his commands. Therefore he repeated Shaggy's speech to the King, who at once realized that his kingdom was in grave danger. For Ruggedo knew of the Love Magnet and its powers and was horrified at the thought that Shaggy might show him the magic talisman and turn all the hatred in his heart into love. Ruggedo was proud of his hatred and abhorred love of any sort.

"Really," said he, "I'd rather he conquered and lose my wealth and my kingdom than gaze at that awful Love Magnet. What can I do to prevent the Shaggy Man from taking it out of his pocket?"

Kaliko returned to the cavern in time to overhear this question, and being a loyal Nome and eager to serve his King, he answered by saying:

"If we can manage to bind the Shaggy Man's arms, tight to his body, he could not get the Love Magnet out of his pocket."

"True!" cried the King in delight at this easy solution of the problem. "Get at once a dozen Nomes, with ropes, and place them in the passage where they can seize and bind Shaggy as soon as he enters."

This Kaliko did, and meanwhile the watchers outside the entrance were growing more and more uneasy about their friends.

"I don't worry so much about the Oogaboo people," said Polychrome, who had grown sober with waiting, and perhaps a little nervous, "for they could not be killed, even though Ruggedo might cause them much suffering and perhaps destroy them utterly. But we should not have allowed Betsy and Hank to go alone into the caverns. The little girl is mortal and possesses no magic powers whatever, so if Ruggedo captures her she will be wholly at his mercy."

"That is indeed true," replied Shaggy. "I wouldn't like to have anything happen to dear little Betsy, so I believe I'll go in right away and put an end to all this worry."

"We may as well go with you," asserted Files, "for by means of the Love Magnet you can soon bring the Nome King to reason."

So it was decided to wait no longer. Shaggy walked through the entrance first, and after him came the others. They had no thought of danger to themselves, and Shaggy, who was going along with his hands thrust into his pockets, was much surprised when a rope shot out from the darkness and twined around his body, pinning down his arms so securely that he could not even withdraw his hands from the pockets. Then appeared several grinning Nomes, who speedily tied knots in the ropes and then led the prisoner along the passage to the cavern. No attention was paid to the others, but Files and the Princess followed on after Shaggy, determined not to desert their friend and hoping that an opportunity might arise to rescue him.

As for Polychrome, as soon as she saw that trouble had overtaken Shaggy she turned and ran lightly back through the passage and out of the entrance. Then she easily leaped from rock to rock until she paused beside the great dragon, who lay fast asleep.

"Wake up, Quox!" she cried. "It is time for you to act."

But Quox did not wake up. He lay as one in a trance, absolutely motionless, with his enormous eyes tight closed. The eyelids had big silver scales on them, like all the rest of his body.

Polychrome might have thought Quox was dead had she not known that dragons do not die easily or had she not observed his huge body swelling as he breathed. She picked up a piece of rock and pounded against his eyelids with it, saying:

"Wake up, Quox—wake up!" But he would not waken.

"Dear me, how unfortunate!" sighed the lovely Rainbow's Daughter. "I wonder what is the best and surest way to waken a dragon. All our friends may be captured and destroyed while this great beast lies asleep."

She walked around Quox two or three times, trying to discover some tender place on his body where a thump or a punch might be felt; but he lay extended along the rocks with his chin flat upon the ground and his legs drawn underneath his body, and all that one could see was his thick sky-blue skin—thicker than that of a rhinoceros—and his silver scales.

Then, despairing at last of wakening the beast, and worried over the fate of her friends, Polychrome again ran down to the entrance and hurried along the passage into the Nome King's cavern.

Here she found Ruggedo lolling in his throne and smoking a long pipe. Beside him stood General Guph and Kaliko, and ranged before the King were the Rose Princess, Files and the Shaggy Man. Tik-Tok still lay upon the floor, weighted down by the big diamond.

Ruggedo was now in a more contented frame of mind. One by one he had met the invaders and easily captured them. The dreaded Love Magnet was indeed in Shaggy's pocket, only a few feet away from the King, but Shaggy was powerless to show it and unless Ruggedo's eyes beheld the talisman it could not affect him. As for Betsy Bobbin and her mule, he believed Kaliko had placed them in the Slimy Cave, while Ann and her officers he thought safely imprisoned in the pit. Ruggedo had no fear of Files or Ozga, but to be on the safe side he had ordered golden handcuffs placed upon their wrists. These did not cause them any great annoyance but prevented them from making an attack, had they been inclined to do so.

The Nome King, thinking himself wholly master of the situation, was laughing and jeering at his prisoners when Polychrome, exquisitely beautiful and dancing like a ray of light, entered the cavern.

"Oho!" cried the King; "a Rainbow under ground, eh?" and then he stared hard at Polychrome, and still harder, and then he sat up and pulled the wrinkles out of his robe and arranged his whiskers. "On my word," said he, "you are a very captivating creature; moreover, I perceive you are a fairy."

"I am Polychrome, the Rainbow's Daughter," she said proudly.

"Well," replied Ruggedo, "I like you. The others I hate. I hate everybody—but you! Wouldn't you like to live always in this beautiful cavern, Polychrome? See! the jewels that stud the walls have every tint and color of your Rainbow—and they are not so elusive. I'll have fresh dewdrops gathered for your feasting every day and you shall be Queen of all my Nomes and pull Kaliko's nose whenever you like."

"No, thank you," laughed Polychrome. "My home is in the sky, and I'm only on a visit to this solid, sordid earth. But tell me, Ruggedo, why my friends have been wound with cords and bound with chains?"

"They threatened me," answered Ruggedo. "The fools did not know how powerful I am."

"Then, since they are now helpless, why not release them and send them back to the earth's surface?"

"Because I hate 'em and mean to make 'em suffer for their invasion. But I'll make a bargain with you, sweet Polly. Remain here and live with me and I'll set all these people free. You shall be my daughter or my wife or my aunt or grandmother—whichever you like—only stay here to brighten my gloomy kingdom and make me happy!"

Polychrome looked at him wonderingly. Then she turned to Shaggy and asked: "Are you sure he hasn't seen the Love Magnet?"

"I'm positive," answered Shaggy. "But you seem to be something of a Love Magnet yourself, Polychrome."

She laughed again and said to Ruggedo: "Not even to rescue my friends would I live in your kingdom. Nor could I endure for long the society of such a wicked monster as you."

"You forget," retorted the King, scowling darkly, "that you also are in my power."

"Not so, Ruggedo. The Rainbow's Daughter is beyond the reach of your spite or malice."

"Seize her!" suddenly shouted the King, and General Guph sprang forward to obey. Polychrome stood quite still, yet when Guph attempted to clutch her his hands met in air, and now the Rainbow's Daughter was in another part of the room, as smiling and composed as before.

Several times Guph endeavored to capture her and Ruggedo even came down from his throne to assist his General; but never could they lay hands upon the lovely

sky fairy, who flitted here and there with the swiftness of light and constantly defied them with her merry laughter as she evaded their efforts.

So after a time they abandoned the chase and Ruggedo returned to his throne and wiped the perspiration from his face with a finely-woven handkerchief of cloth-of-gold.

"Well," said Polychrome, "what do you intend to do now?"

"I'm going to have some fun, to repay me for all my bother," replied the Nome King. Then he said to Kaliko: "Summon the executioners."

Kaliko at once withdrew and presently returned with a score of Nomes, all of whom were nearly as evil looking as their hated master. They bore great golden pincers, and prods of silver, and clamps and chains and various wicked-looking instruments, all made of precious metals and set with diamonds and rubies.

"Now, Pang," said Ruggedo, addressing the leader of the executioners, "fetch the Army of Oogaboo and their Queen from the pit and torture them here in my presence—as well as in the presence of their friends. It will be great sport."

"I hear Your Majesty, and I obey Your Majesty," answered Pang, and went with his Nomes into the passage. In a few minutes he returned and bowed to Ruggedo.

"They're all gone," said he.

"Gone!" exclaimed the Nome King. "Gone where?"

"They left no address, Your Majesty; but they are not in the pit."

"Picks and puddles!" roared the King; "who took the cover off?"

"No one," said Pang. "The cover was there, but the prisoners were not under it."

"In that case," snarled the King, trying to control his disappointment, "go to the Slimy Cave and fetch hither the girl and the donkey. And while we are torturing them Kaliko must take a hundred Nomes and search for the escaped prisoners—the Queen of Oogaboo and her officers. If he does not find them, I will torture Kaliko."

Kaliko went away looking sad and disturbed, for he knew the King was cruel and unjust enough to carry out this threat. Pang and the executioners also went away, in another direction, but when they came back Betsy Bobbin was not with them, nor was Hank.

"There is no one in the Slimy Cave, Your Majesty," reported Pang.

"Jumping jellycakes!" screamed the King. "Another escape? Are you sure you found the right cave?"

"There is but one Slimy Cave, and there is no one in it," returned Pang positively.

Ruggedo was beginning to be alarmed as well as angry. However, these disappointments but made him the more vindictive and he cast an evil look at the other prisoners and said:

"Never mind the girl and the donkey. Here are four, at least, who cannot escape my vengeance. Let me see; I believe I'll change my mind about Tik-Tok. Have the gold crucible heated to a white, seething heat, and then we'll dump the copper man into it and melt him up."

"But, Your Majesty," protested Kaliko, who had returned to the room after sending a hundred Nomes to search for the Oogaboo people, "you must remember that Tik-Tok is a very curious and interesting machine. It would be a shame to deprive the world of such a clever contrivance."

"Say another word, and you'll go into the furnace with him!" roared the King. "I'm getting tired of you, Kaliko, and the first thing you know I'll turn you into a potato and make Saratoga-chips of you! The next to consider," he added more mildly, "is the Shaggy Man. As he owns the Love Magnet, I think I'll transform him into a dove, and then we can practice shooting at him with Tik-Tok's gun. Now, this is a very interesting ceremony and I beg you all to watch me closely and see that I've nothing up my sleeve."

He came out of his throne to stand before the Shaggy Man, and then he waved his hands, palms downward, in seven semicircles over his victim's head, saying in a low but clear tone of voice the magic wugwa:

"Adi, edi, idi, odi, udi, oo-i-oo!
Idu, ido, idi, ide, ida, woo!"

The effect of this well-known sorcery was instantaneous. Instead of the Shaggy Man, a pretty dove lay fluttering upon the floor, its wings confined by tiny cords wound around them. Ruggedo gave an order to Pang, who cut the cords with a pair of scissors. Being freed, the dove quickly flew upward and alighted on the shoulder of the Rose Princess, who stroked it tenderly.

"Very good! Very good!" cried Ruggedo, rubbing his hands gleefully together. "One enemy is out of my way, and now for the others."

(Perhaps my readers should be warned not to attempt the above transformation; for, although the exact magical formula has been described, it is unlawful in all civilized countries for anyone to transform a person into a dove by muttering the words Ruggedo used. There were no laws to prevent the Nome King from performing this transformation, but if it should be attempted in any other country, and the magic worked, the magician would be severely punished.)

When Polychrome saw Shaggy Man transformed into a dove and realized that Ruggedo was about do something as dreadful to the Princess and Files, and that Tik-Tok would soon be melted in a crucible, she turned and ran from the cavern, through the passage and back to the place where Quox lay asleep.

CHAPTER XVIII
A CLEVER CONQUEST

THE GREAT DRAGON STILL HAD HIS EYES CLOSED AND WAS EVEN SNORING IN A manner that resembled distant thunder; but Polychrome was now desperate, because any further delay meant the destruction of her friends. She seized the pearl necklace, to which was attached the great locket, and jerked it with all her strength.

The result was encouraging. Quox stopped snoring and his eyelids flickered. So Polychrome jerked again—and again—till slowly the great lids raised and the dragon looked at her steadily. Said he, in a sleepy tone:

"What's the matter, little Rainbow?"

"Come quick!" exclaimed Polychrome. "Ruggedo has captured all our friends and is about to destroy them."

"Well, well," said Quox, "I suspected that would happen. Step a little out of my path, my dear, and I'll make a rush for the Nome King's cavern."

She fell back a few steps and Quox raised himself on his stout legs, whisked his long tail and in an instant had slid down the rocks and made a dive through the entrance.

Along the passage he swept, nearly filling it with his immense body, and now he poked his head into the jeweled cavern of Ruggedo.

But the King had long since made arrangements to capture the dragon, whenever he might appear. No sooner did Quox stick his head into the room than a thick chain fell from above and encircled his neck. Then the ends of the chain were drawn tight—for in an adjoining cavern a thousand Nomes were pulling on them—and so the dragon could advance no further toward the King. He could not use his teeth or his claws and as his body was still in the passage he had not even room to strike his foes with his terrible tail.

Ruggedo was delighted with the success of his stratagem. He had just transformed the Rose Princess into a fiddle and was about to transform Files into a fiddle bow, when the dragon appeared to interrupt him. So he called out:

"Welcome, my dear Quox, to my royal entertainment. Since you are here, you shall witness some very neat magic, and after I have finished with Files and Tik-Tok I mean to transform you into a tiny lizard—one of the chameleon sort—and you shall live in my cavern and amuse me."

"Pardon me for contradicting Your Majesty," returned Quox in a quiet voice, "but I don't believe you'll perform any more magic."

"Eh? Why not?" asked the King in surprise.

"There's a reason," said Quox. "Do you see this ribbon around my neck?"

"Yes; and I'm astonished that a dignified dragon should wear such a silly thing."

"Do you see it plainly?" persisted the dragon, with a little chuckle of amusement.

"I do," declared Ruggedo.

"Then you no longer possess any magical powers, and are as helpless as a clam," asserted Quox. "My great master, Tititi-Hoochoo, the Jinjin, enchanted this ribbon in such a way that whenever Your Majesty looked upon it all knowledge of magic would desert you instantly, nor will any magical formula you can remember ever perform your bidding."

"Pooh! I don't believe a word of it!" cried Ruggedo, half frightened, nevertheless. Then he turned toward Files and tried to transform him into a fiddle bow. But he could not remember the right words or the right pass of the hands and after several trials he finally gave up the attempt.

By this time the Nome King was so alarmed that he was secretly shaking in his shoes.

"I told you not to anger Tititi-Hoochoo," grumbled Kaliko, "and now you see the result of your disobedience."

Ruggedo promptly threw his sceptre at his Royal Chamberlain, who dodged it with his usual cleverness, and then he said with an attempt to swagger:

"Never mind; I don't need magic to enable me to destroy these invaders; fire and the sword will do the business and I am still King of the Nomes and lord and master of my Underground Kingdom!"

"Again I beg to differ with Your Majesty," said Quox. "The Great Jinjin commands you to depart instantly from this kingdom and seek the earth's surface, where you will wander for all time to come, without a home or country, without a friend or follower, and without any more riches than you can carry with you in your pockets. The Great Jinjin is so generous that he will allow you to fill your pockets with jewels or gold, but you must take nothing more."

Ruggedo now stared at the dragon in amazement.

"Does Tititi-Hoochoo condemn me to such a fate?" he asked in a hoarse voice.

"He does," said Quox.

"And just for throwing a few strangers down the Forbidden Tube?"

"Just for that," repeated Quox in a stern, gruff voice.

"Well, I won't do it. And your crazy old Jinjin can't make me do it, either!" declared Ruggedo. "I intend to remain here, King of the Nomes, until the end of the world, and I defy your Tititi-Hoochoo and all his fairies—as well as his clumsy messenger, whom I have been obliged to chain up!"

The dragon smiled again, but it was not the sort of smile that made Ruggedo feel very happy. Instead, there was something so cold and merciless in the dragon's expression that the condemned Nome King trembled and was sick at heart.

There was little comfort for Ruggedo in the fact that the dragon was now chained, although he had boasted of it. He glared at the immense head of Quox as if fascinated and there was fear in the old King's eyes as he watched his enemy's movements.

For the dragon was now moving; not abruptly, but as if he had something to do and was about to do it. Very deliberately he raised one claw, touched the catch of the great jeweled locket that was suspended around his neck, and at once it opened wide.

Nothing much happened at first; half a dozen hen's eggs rolled out upon the floor and then the locket closed with a sharp click. But the effect upon the Nomes of this simple thing was astounding. General Guph, Kaliko, Pang and his band of executioners were all standing close to the door that led to the vast series of underground caverns which constituted the dominions of the Nomes, and as soon as they saw the eggs they raised a chorus of frantic screams and rushed through the door, slamming it in Ruggedo's face and placing a heavy bronze bar across it.

Ruggedo, dancing with terror and uttering loud cries, now leaped upon the seat of his throne to escape the eggs, which had rolled steadily toward him. Perhaps these eggs, sent by the wise and crafty Tititi-Hoochoo, were in some way enchanted, for they all rolled directly after Ruggedo and when they reached the throne where he had taken refuge they began rolling up the legs to the seat.

This was too much for the King to bear. His horror of eggs was real and absolute and he made a leap from the throne to the center of the room and then ran to a far corner.

The eggs followed, rolling slowly but steadily in his direction. Ruggedo threw his sceptre at them, and then his ruby crown, and then he drew off his heavy golden sandals and hurled these at the advancing eggs. But the eggs dodged every missile and continued to draw nearer. The King stood trembling, his eyes staring in terror, until they were but half a yard distant; then with an agile leap he jumped clear over them and made a rush for the passage that led to the outer entrance.

Of course the dragon was in his way, being chained in the passage with his head in the cavern, but when he saw the King making toward him he crouched as low as he could and dropped his chin to the floor, leaving a small space between his body and the roof of the passage.

Ruggedo did not hesitate an instant. Impelled by fear, he leaped to the dragon's nose and then scrambled to his back, where he succeeded in squeezing himself through the opening. After the head was passed there was more room and he slid along the dragon's scales to his tail and then ran as fast as his legs would carry him to the entrance. Not pausing here, so great was his fright, the King dashed on down the mountain path, but before he had gone very far he stumbled and fell.

When he picked himself up he observed that no one was following him, and while he recovered his breath he happened to think of the decree of the Jinjin—that he should be driven from his kingdom and made a wanderer on the face of the earth. Well, here he was, driven from his cavern in truth; driven by those dreadful eggs; but he would go back and defy them; he would not submit to losing his precious kingdom and his tyrannical powers, all because Tititi-Hoochoo had said he must.

So, although still afraid, Ruggedo nerved himself to creep back along the path to the entrance, and when he arrived there he saw the six eggs lying in a row just before the arched opening.

At first he paused a safe distance away to consider the case, for the eggs were now motionless. While he was wondering what could be done, he remembered there was a magical charm which would destroy eggs and render them harmless to Nomes. There were nine passes to be made and six verses of incantation to be recited; but Ruggedo knew them all. Now that he had ample time to be exact, he carefully went through the entire ceremony.

But nothing happened. The eggs did not disappear, as he had expected; so he repeated the charm a second time. When that also failed, he remembered, with a moan of despair, that his magic power had been taken away from him and in the future he could do no more than any common mortal.

And there were the eggs, forever barring him from the kingdom which he had ruled so long with absolute sway! He threw rocks at them, but could not hit a single egg. He raved and scolded and tore his hair and beard, and danced in helpless passion, but that did nothing to avert the just judgment of the Jinjin, which Ruggedo's own evil deeds had brought upon him.

From this time on he was an outcast—a wanderer upon the face of the earth—and he had even forgotten to fill his pockets with gold and jewels before he fled from his former kingdom!

CHAPTER XIX

KING KALIKO

After the King had made good his escape Files said to the dragon, in a sad voice:

"Alas! why did you not come before? Because you were sleeping instead of conquering, the lovely Rose Princess has become a fiddle without a bow, while poor Shaggy sits there a cooing dove!"

"Don't worry," replied Quox. "Tititi-Hoochoo knows his business, and I had my orders from the Great Jinjin himself. Bring the fiddle here and touch it lightly to my pink ribbon."

Files obeyed and at the moment of contact with the ribbon the Nome King's charm was broken and the Rose Princess herself stood before them as sweet and smiling as ever.

The dove, perched on the back of the throne, had seen and heard all this, so without being told what to do it flew straight to the dragon and alighted on the ribbon. Next instant Shaggy was himself again and Quox said to him grumblingly:

"Please get off my left toe, Shaggy Man, and be more particular where you step."

"I beg your pardon!" replied Shaggy, very glad to resume his natural form. Then he ran to lift the heavy diamond off Tik-Tok's chest and to assist the Clockwork Man to his feet.

"Ma-ny thanks!" said Tik-Tok. "Where is the wick-ed King who want-ed to melt me in a cru-ci-ble?"

"He has gone, and gone for good," answered Polychrome, who had managed to squeeze into the room beside the dragon and had witnessed the occurrences with much interest. "But I wonder where Betsy Bobbin and Hank can be, and if any harm has befallen them."

"We must search the cavern until we find them," declared Shaggy; but when he went to the door leading to the other caverns he found it shut and barred.

"I've a pretty strong push in my forehead," said Quox, "and I believe I can break down that door, even though it's made of solid gold."

"But you are a prisoner, and the chains that hold you are fastened in some other room, so that we cannot release you," Files said anxiously.

"Oh, never mind that," returned the dragon. "I have remained a prisoner only because I wished to be one," and with this he stepped forward and burst the stout chains as easily as if they had been threads.

But when he tried to push in the heavy metal door, even his mighty strength failed, and after several attempts he gave it up and squatted himself in a corner to think of a better way.

"I'll o-pen the door," asserted Tik-Tok, and going to the King's big gong he pounded upon it until the noise was almost deafening.

Kaliko, in the next cavern, was wondering what had happened to Ruggedo and if he had escaped the eggs and outwitted the dragon. But when he heard the sound of the gong, which had so often called him into the King's presence, he decided that Ruggedo had been victorious; so he took away the bar, threw open the door and entered the royal cavern.

Great was his astonishment to find the King gone and the enchantments removed from the Princess and Shaggy. But the eggs were also gone and so Kaliko advanced to the dragon, whom he knew to be Tititi-Hoochoo's messenger, and bowed humbly before the beast.

"What is your will?" he inquired.

"Where is Betsy?" demanded the dragon.

"Safe in my own private room," said Kaliko.

"Go and get her!" commanded Quox.

So Kaliko went to Betsy's room and gave three raps upon the door. The little girl had been asleep, but she heard the raps and opened the door.

"You may come out now," said Kaliko. "The King has fled in disgrace and your friends are asking for you."

So Betsy and Hank returned with the Royal Chamberlain to the throne cav-ern, where she was received with great joy by her friends. They told her what had

happened to Ruggedo and she told them how kind Kaliko had been to her. Quox did not have much to say until the conversation was ended, but then he turned to Kaliko and asked:

"Do you suppose you could rule your Nomes better than Ruggedo has done?"

"Me?" stammered the Chamberlain, greatly surprised by the question. "Well, I couldn't be a worse King, I'm sure."

"Would the Nomes obey you?" inquired the dragon.

"Of course," said Kaliko. "They like me better than ever they did Ruggedo."

"Then hereafter you shall be the Metal Monarch, King of the Nomes, and Tititi-Hoochoo expects you to rule your kingdom wisely and well," said Quox.

"Hooray!" cried Betsy; "I'm glad of that. King Kaliko, I salute Your Majesty and wish you joy in your gloomy old kingdom!"

"We all wish him joy," said Polychrome; and then the others made haste to congratulate the new King.

"Will you release my dear brother?" asked Shaggy.

"The Ugly One? Very willingly," replied Kaliko. "I begged Ruggedo long ago to send him away, but he would not do so. I also offered to help your brother to escape, but he would not go."

"He's so conscientious!" said Shaggy, highly pleased. "All of our family have noble natures. But is my dear brother well?" he added anxiously.

"He eats and sleeps very steadily," replied the new King.

"I hope he doesn't work too hard," said Shaggy.

"He doesn't work at all. In fact, there is nothing he can do in these dominions as well as our Nomes, whose numbers are so great that it worries us to keep them all busy. So your brother has only to amuse himself."

"Why, it's more like visiting, than being a prisoner," asserted Betsy.

"Not exactly," returned Kaliko. "A prisoner cannot go where or when he pleases, and is not his own master."

"Where is my brother now?" inquired Shaggy.

"In the Metal Forest."

"Where is that?"

"The Metal Forest is in the Great Domed Cavern, the largest in all our dominions," replied Kaliko. "It is almost like being out of doors, it is so big, and Ruggedo made the wonderful forest to amuse himself, as well as to tire out his hard-working Nomes. All the trees are gold and silver and the ground is strewn with precious stones, so it is a sort of treasury."

"Let us go there at once and rescue my dear brother," pleaded Shaggy earnestly.

Kaliko hesitated.

"I don't believe I can find the way," said he. "Ruggedo made three secret passages to the Metal Forest, but he changes the location of these passages every week, so that no one can get to the Metal Forest without his permission. However, if we look sharp, we may be able to discover one of these secret ways."

"That reminds me to ask what has become of Queen Ann and the Officers of Oogaboo," said Files.

"I'm sure I can't say," replied Kaliko.

"Do you suppose Ruggedo destroyed them?"

"Oh, no; I'm quite sure he didn't. They fell into the big pit in the passage, and we put the cover on to keep them there; but when the executioners went to look for them they had all disappeared from the pit and we could find no trace of them."

"That's funny," remarked Betsy thoughtfully. "I don't believe Ann knew any magic, or she'd have worked it before. But to disappear like that *seems* like magic; now, doesn't it?"

They agreed that it did, but no one could explain the mystery.

"However," said Shaggy, "they are gone, that is certain, so we cannot help them or be helped by them. And the important thing just now is to rescue my dear brother from captivity."

"Why do they call him the Ugly One?" asked Betsy.

"I do not know," confessed Shaggy. "I cannot remember his looks very well, it is so long since I have seen him; but all of our family are noted for their handsome faces."

Betsy laughed and Shaggy seemed rather hurt; but Polychrome relieved his embarrassment by saying softly: "One can be ugly in looks, but lovely in disposition."

"Our first task," said Shaggy, a little comforted by this remark, "is to find one of those secret passages to the Metal Forest."

"True," agreed Kaliko. "So I think I will assemble the chief Nomes of my kingdom in this throne room and tell them that I am their new King. Then I can ask them to assist us in searching for the secret passages.

"That's a good idea," said the dragon, who seemed to be getting sleepy again.

Kaliko went to the big gong and pounded on it just as Ruggedo used to do; but no one answered the summons.

"Of course not," said he, jumping up from the throne, where he had seated himself. "That is my call, and I am still the Royal Chamberlain, and will be until I appoint another in my place."

So he ran out of the room and found Guph and told him to answer the summons of the King's gong. Having returned to the royal cavern, Kaliko first pounded the gong and then sat in the throne, wearing Ruggedo's discarded ruby crown and holding in his hand the sceptre which Ruggedo had so often thrown at his head.

When Guph entered he was amazed.

"Better get out of that throne before old Ruggedo comes back," he said warningly.

"He isn't coming back, and I am now the King of the Nomes, in his stead," announced Kaliko.

"All of which is quite true," asserted the dragon, and all of those who stood around the throne bowed respectfully to the new King.

Seeing this, Guph also bowed, for he was glad to be rid of such a hard master as Ruggedo. Then Kaliko, in quite a kingly way, informed Guph that he was appointed the Royal Chamberlain, and promised not to throw the sceptre at his head unless he deserved it.

All this being pleasantly arranged, the new Chamberlain went away to tell the news to all the Nomes of the Underground Kingdom, every one of whom would be delighted with the change in Kings.

CHAPTER XX

QUOX QUIETLY QUITS

WHEN THE CHIEF NOMES ASSEMBLED BEFORE THEIR NEW KING THEY JOYFULLY saluted him and promised to obey his commands. But, when Kaliko questioned them, none knew the way to the Metal Forest, although all had assisted in its making. So the King instructed them to search carefully for one of the passages and to bring him the news as soon as they had found it.

Meantime Quox had managed to back out of the rocky corridor and so regain the open air and his old station on the mountain-side, and there he lay upon the rocks, sound asleep, until the next day. The others of the party were all given as good rooms as the caverns of the Nomes afforded, for King Kaliko felt that he was indebted to them for his promotion and was anxious to be as hospitable as he could.

Much wonderment had been caused by the absolute disappearance of the sixteen officers of Oogaboo and their Queen. Not a Nome had seen them, nor were they discovered during the search for the passages leading to the Metal Forest. Perhaps no one was unhappy over their loss, but all were curious to know what had become of them.

On the next day, when our friends went to visit the dragon, Quox said to them: "I must now bid you good-bye, for my mission here is finished and I must depart for the other side of the world, where I belong."

"Will you go through the Tube again?" asked Betsy.

"To be sure. But it will be a lonely trip this time, with no one to talk to, and I cannot invite any of you to go with me. Therefore, as soon as I slide into the hole I shall go to sleep, and when I pop out at the other end I will wake up at home."

They thanked the dragon for befriending them and wished him a pleasant journey. Also they sent their thanks to the great Jinjin, whose just condemnation of Ruggedo had served their interests so well. Then Quox yawned and stretched himself and ambled over to the Tube, into which he slid headforemost and disappeared.

They really felt as if they had lost a friend, for the dragon had been both kind and sociable during their brief acquaintance with him; but they knew it was his duty to return to his own country. So they went back to the caverns to renew the search for the hidden passages that led to the forest, but for three days all efforts to find them proved in vain.

It was Polychrome's custom to go every day to the mountain and watch for her father, the Rainbow, for she was growing tired with wandering upon the earth and longed to rejoin her sisters in their sky palaces. And on the third day, while she sat motionless upon a point of rock, whom should she see slyly creeping up the mountain but Ruggedo!

The former King looked very forlorn. His clothes were soiled and torn and he had no sandals upon his feet or hat upon his head. Having left his crown and sceptre behind when he fled, the old Nome no longer seemed kingly, but more like a beggerman.

Several times had Ruggedo crept up to the mouth of the caverns, only to find the six eggs still on guard. He knew quite well that he must accept his fate and become a homeless wanderer, but his chief regret now was that he had neglected to fill his pockets with gold and jewels. He was aware that a wanderer with wealth at his command would fare much better than one who was a pauper, so he still loitered around the caverns wherein he knew so much treasure was stored, hoping for a chance to fill his pockets.

That was how he came to recollect the Metal Forest.

"Aha!" said he to himself, "I alone know the way to that Forest, and once there I can fill my pockets with the finest jewels in all the world."

He glanced at his pockets and was grieved to find them so small. Perhaps they might be enlarged, so that they would hold more. He knew of a poor woman who lived in a cottage at the foot of the mountain, so he went to her and begged her to sew pockets all over his robe, paying her with the gift of a diamond ring which he had worn upon his finger. The woman was delighted to possess so valuable a ring and she sewed as many pockets on Ruggedo's robe as she possibly could.

Then he returned up the mountain and, after gazing cautiously around to make sure he was not observed, he touched a spring in a rock and it swung slowly backward, disclosing a broad passageway. This he entered, swinging the rock in place behind him.

However, Ruggedo had failed to look as carefully as he might have done, for Polychrome was seated only a little distance off and her clear eyes marked exactly the manner in which Ruggedo had released the hidden spring. So she rose and hurried into the cavern, where she told Kaliko and her friends of her discovery.

"I've no doubt that that is a way to the Metal Forest," exclaimed Shaggy. "Come, let us follow Ruggedo at once and rescue my poor brother!"

They agreed to this and King Kaliko called together a band of Nomes to assist them by carrying torches to light their way.

"The Metal Forest has a brilliant light of its own," said he, "but the passage across the valley is likely to be dark."

Polychrome easily found the rock and touched the spring, so in less than an hour after Ruggedo had entered they were all in the passage and following swiftly after the former King.

"He means to rob the forest, I'm sure," said Kaliko; "but he will find he is no longer of any account in this kingdom and I will have my Nomes throw him out."

"Then please throw him as hard as you can," said Betsy, "for he deserves it. I don't mind an honest, out-an'-out enemy, who fights square; but changing girls into fiddles and ordering 'em put into Slimy Caves is mean and tricky, and Ruggedo doesn't deserve any sympathy. But you'll have to let him take as much treasure as he can get in his pockets, Kaliko."

"Yes, the Jinjin said so; but we won't miss it much. There is more treasure in the Metal Forest than a million Nomes could carry in their pockets."

It was not difficult to walk through this passage, especially when the torches lighted the way, so they made good progress. But it proved to be a long distance and Betsy had tired herself with walking and was seated upon the back of the mule when the passage made a sharp turn and a wonderful and glorious light burst upon them. The next moment they were all standing upon the edge of the marvelous Metal Forest.

It lay under another mountain and occupied a great domed cavern, the roof of which was higher than a church steeple. In this space the industrious Nomes had built, during many years of labor, the most beautiful forest in the world. The trees—trunks, branches and leaves—were all of solid gold, while the bushes and underbrush were formed of filigree silver, virgin pure. The trees towered as high as natural live oaks do and were of exquisite workmanship.

On the ground were thickly strewn precious gems of every hue and size, while here and there among the trees were paths pebbled with cut diamonds of the clearest water. Taken all together, more treasure was gathered in this Metal Forest than is contained in all the rest of the world—if we except the Land of Oz, where perhaps its value is equaled in the famous Emerald City.

Our friends were so amazed at the sight that for a while they stood gazing in silent wonder. Then Shaggy exclaimed:

"My brother! My dear lost brother! Is he indeed a prisoner in this place?"

"Yes," replied Kaliko. "The Ugly One has been here for two or three years, to my positive knowledge."

"But what could he find to eat?" inquired Betsy. "It's an awfully swell place to live in, but one can't breakfast on rubies and di'monds, or even gold."

"One doesn't need to, my dear," Kaliko assured her. "The Metal Forest does not fill all of this great cavern, by any means. Beyond these gold and silver trees are other trees of the real sort, which bear foods very nice to eat. Let us walk in that direction, for I am quite sure we will find Shaggy's brother in that part of the cavern, rather than in this."

So they began to tramp over the diamond-pebbled paths, and at every step they were more and more bewildered by the wondrous beauty of the golden trees with their glittering foliage.

Suddenly they heard a scream. Jewels scattered in every direction as some one hidden among the bushes scampered away before them. Then a loud voice cried: "Halt!" and there was the sound of a struggle.

CHAPTER XXI

A BASHFUL BROTHER

WITH FAST BEATING HEARTS THEY ALL RUSHED FORWARD AND, BEYOND A GROUP OF stately metal trees, came full upon a most astonishing scene.

There was Ruggedo in the hands of the officers of Oogaboo, a dozen of whom were clinging to the old Nome and holding him fast in spite of his efforts to escape. There also was Queen Ann, looking grimly upon the scene of strife; but when she observed her former companions approaching she turned away in a shamefaced manner.

For Ann and her officers were indeed a sight to behold. Her Majesty's clothing, once so rich and gorgeous, was now worn and torn into shreds by her long crawl through the tunnel, which, by the way, had led her directly into the Metal Forest. It was, indeed, one of the three secret passages, and by far the most difficult of the three. Ann had not only torn her pretty skirt and jacket, but her crown had become bent and battered and even her shoes were so cut and slashed that they were ready to fall from her feet.

The officers had fared somewhat worse than their leader, for holes were worn in the knees of their trousers, while sharp points of rock in the roof and sides of the tunnel had made rags of every inch of their once brilliant uniforms. A more tattered and woeful army never came out of a battle, than these harmless victims of the rocky passage. But it had seemed their only means of escape from the cruel Nome King; so they had crawled on, regardless of their sufferings.

When they reached the Metal Forest their eyes beheld more plunder than they had ever dreamed of; yet they were prisoners in this huge dome and could not escape with the riches heaped about them. Perhaps a more unhappy and homesick lot of "conquerors" never existed than this band from Oogaboo.

After several days of wandering in their marvelous prison they were frightened by the discovery that Ruggedo had come among them. Rendered desperate by their sad condition, the officers exhibited courage for the first time since they left home and, ignorant of the fact that Ruggedo was no longer King of the Nomes, they threw themselves upon him and had just succeeded in capturing him when their fellow adventurers reached the spot.

"Goodness gracious!" cried Betsy. "What has happened to you all?"

Ann came forward to greet them, sorrowful and indignant.

"We were obliged to escape from the pit through a small tunnel, which was lined with sharp and jagged rocks," said she, "and not only was our clothing torn to rags but our flesh is so bruised and sore that we are stiff and lame in every joint. To add to our troubles we find we are still prisoners; but now that we have succeeded in capturing the wicked Metal Monarch we shall force him to grant us our liberty."

"Ruggedo is no longer Metal Monarch, or King of the Nomes," Files informed her. "He has been deposed and cast out of his kingdom by Quox; but here is the new King, whose name is Kaliko, and I am pleased to assure Your Majesty that he is our friend."

"Glad to meet Your Majesty, I'm sure," said Kaliko, bowing as courteously as if the Queen still wore splendid raiment.

The officers, having heard this explanation, now set Ruggedo free; but, as he had no place to go, he stood by and faced his former servant, who was now King in his place, in a humble and pleading manner.

"What are you doing here?" asked Kaliko sternly.

"Why, I was promised as much treasure as I could carry in my pockets," replied Ruggedo; "so I came here to get it, not wishing to disturb Your Majesty."

"You were commanded to leave the country of the Nomes forever!" declared Kaliko.

"I know; and I'll go as soon as I have filled my pockets," said Ruggedo, meekly.

"Then fill them, and be gone," returned the new King.

Ruggedo obeyed. Stooping down, he began gathering up jewels by the handful and stuffing them into his many pockets. They were heavy things, these diamonds and rubies and emeralds and amethysts and the like, so before long Ruggedo was staggering with the weight he bore, while the pockets were not yet filled. When he could no longer stoop over without falling, Betsy and Polychrome and the Rose Princess came to his assistance, picking up the finest gems and tucking them into his pockets.

At last these were all filled and Ruggedo presented a comical sight, for surely no man ever before had so many pockets, or any at all filled with such a choice collection of precious stones. He neglected to thank the young ladies for their kindness, but gave them a surly nod of farewell and staggered down the path by the way he had come. They let him depart in silence, for with all he had taken, the masses of jewels upon the ground seemed scarcely to have been disturbed, so numerous were they. Also they hoped they had seen the last of the degraded King.

"I'm awful glad he's gone," said Betsy, sighing deeply. "If he doesn't get reckless and spend his wealth foolishly, he's got enough to start a bank when he gets to Oklahoma."

"But my brother—my dear brother! Where is he?" inquired Shaggy anxiously. "Have you seen him, Queen Ann?"

"What does your brother look like?" asked the Queen.

Shaggy hesitated to reply, but Betsy said: "He's called the Ugly One. Perhaps you'll know him by that."

"The only person we have seen in this cavern," said Ann, "has run away from us whenever we approached him. He hides over yonder, among the trees that are not gold, and we have never been able to catch sight of his face. So I cannot tell whether he is ugly or not."

"That must be my dear brother!" exclaimed Shaggy.

"Yes, it must be," assented Kaliko. "No one else inhabits this splendid dome, so there can be no mistake."

"But why does he hide among those green trees, instead of enjoying all these glittery golden ones?" asked Betsy.

"Because he finds food among the natural trees," replied Kaliko, "and I remember that he has built a little house there, to sleep in. As for these glittery golden trees, I will admit they are very pretty at first sight. One cannot fail to admire them, as well as the rich jewels scattered beneath them; but if one has to look at them always, they become pretty tame."

"I believe that is true," declared Shaggy. "My dear brother is very wise to prefer real trees to the imitation ones. But come; let us go there and find him."

Shaggy started for the green grove at once, and the others followed him, being curious to witness the final rescue of his long-sought, long-lost brother.

Not far from the edge of the grove they came upon a small hut, cleverly made of twigs and golden branches woven together. As they approached the place they caught a glimpse of a form that darted into the hut and slammed the door tight shut after him.

Shaggy Man ran to the door and cried aloud:

"Brother! Brother!"

"Who calls," demanded a sad, hollow voice from within.

"It is Shaggy—your own loving brother—who has been searching for you a long time and has now come to rescue you."

"Too late!" replied the gloomy voice. "No one can rescue me now."

"Oh, but you are mistaken about that," said Shaggy. "There is a new King of the Nomes, named Kaliko, in Ruggedo's place, and he has promised you shall go free."

"Free! I dare not go free!" said the Ugly One, in a voice of despair.

"Why not, Brother?" asked Shaggy, anxiously.

"Do you know what they have done to me?" came the answer through the closed door.

"No. Tell me, Brother, what have they done?"

"When Ruggedo first captured me I was very handsome. Don't you remember, Shaggy?"

"Not very well, Brother; you were so young when I left home. But I remember that mother thought you were beautiful."

"She was right! I am sure she was right," wailed the prisoner. "But Ruggedo wanted to injure me—to make me ugly in the eyes of all the world—so he performed a wicked enchantment. I went to bed beautiful—or you might say handsome—to be very modest I will merely claim that I was good-looking—and I wakened the next morning the homeliest man in all the world! I am so repulsive that when I look in a mirror I frighten myself."

"Poor Brother!" said Shaggy softly, and all the others were silent from sympathy.

"I was so ashamed of my looks," continued the voice of Shaggy's brother, "that I tried to hide; but the cruel King Ruggedo forced me to appear before all the legion of Nomes, to whom he said: 'Behold the Ugly One!' But when the Nomes saw my face they all fell to laughing and jeering, which prevented them from working at their tasks. Seeing this, Ruggedo became angry and pushed me into a tunnel, closing the rock entrance so that I could not get out. I followed the length of the tunnel until I reached this huge dome, where the marvelous Metal Forest stands, and here I have remained ever since."

"Poor Brother!" repeated Shaggy. "But I beg you now to come forth and face us, who are your friends. None here will laugh or jeer, however unhandsome you may be."

"No, indeed," they all added pleadingly.

But the Ugly One refused the invitation.

"I cannot," said he; "indeed, I cannot face strangers, ugly as I am."

Shaggy Man turned to the group surrounding him.

"What shall I do?" he asked in sorrowful tones. "I cannot leave my dear brother here, and he refuses to come out of that house and face us."

"I'll tell you," replied Betsy. "Let him put on a mask."

"The very idea I was seeking!" exclaimed Shaggy joyfully; and then he called out: "Brother, put a mask over your face, and then none of us can see what your features are like."

"I have no mask," answered the Ugly One.

"Look here," said Betsy; "he can use my handkerchief."

Shaggy looked at the little square of cloth and shook his head.

"It isn't big enough," he objected; "I'm sure it isn't big enough to hide a man's face. But he can use mine."

Saying this he took from his pocket his own handkerchief and went to the door of the hut.

"Here, my Brother," he called, "take this handkerchief and make a mask of it. I will also pass you my knife, so that you may cut holes for the eyes, and then you must tie it over your face."

The door slowly opened, just far enough for the Ugly One to thrust out his hand and take the handkerchief and the knife. Then it closed again.

"Don't forget a hole for your nose," cried Betsy. "You must breathe, you know."

For a time there was silence. Queen Ann and her army sat down upon the ground to rest. Betsy sat on Hank's back. Polychrome danced lightly up and down the jeweled paths while Files and the Princess wandered through the groves arm in arm. Tik-Tok, who never tired, stood motionless.

By and by a noise sounded from within the hut.

"Are you ready?" asked Shaggy.

"Yes, Brother," came the reply, and the door was thrown open to allow the Ugly One to step forth.

Betsy might have laughed aloud had she not remembered how sensitive to ridicule Shaggy's brother was, for the handkerchief with which he had masked his features was a red one covered with big white polka dots. In this two holes had been cut—in front of the eyes—while two smaller ones before the nostrils allowed the man to breathe freely. The cloth was then tightly drawn over the Ugly One's face and knotted at the back of his neck.

He was dressed in clothes that had once been good, but now were sadly worn and frayed. His silk stockings had holes in them, and his shoes were stub-toed and needed blackening. "But what can you expect," whispered Betsy, "when the poor man has been a prisoner for so many years?"

Shaggy had darted forward, and embraced his newly found brother with both his arms. The brother also embraced Shaggy, who then led him forward and introduced him to all the assembled company.

"This is the new Nome King," he said when he came to Kaliko. "He is our friend, and has granted you your freedom."

"That is a kindly deed," replied Ugly in a sad voice, "but I dread to go back to the world in this direful condition. Unless I remain forever masked, my dreadful face would curdle all the milk and stop all the clocks."

"Can't the enchantment be broken in some way?" inquired Betsy.

Shaggy looked anxiously at Kaliko, who shook his head.

"I am sure *I* can't break the enchantment," he said. "Ruggedo was fond of magic, and learned a good many enchantments that we Nomes know nothing of."

"Perhaps Ruggedo himself might break his own enchantment," suggested Ann; "but unfortunately we have allowed the old King to escape."

"Never mind, my dear Brother," said Shaggy consolingly; "I am very happy to have found you again, although I may never see your face. So let us make the most of this joyful reunion."

The Ugly One was affected to tears by this tender speech, and the tears began to wet the red handkerchief; so Shaggy gently wiped them away with his coat sleeve.

CHAPTER XXII

KINDLY KISSES

"Won't you be dreadful sorry to leave this lovely place?" Betsy asked the Ugly One.

"No, indeed," said he. "Jewels and gold are cold and heartless things, and I am sure I would presently have died of loneliness had I not found the natural forest at the edge of the artificial one. Anyhow, without these real trees I should soon have starved to death."

Betsy looked around at the quaint trees.

"I don't just understand that," she admitted. "What could you find to eat here?"

"The best food in the world," Ugly answered. "Do you see that grove at your left?" he added, pointing it out; "well, such trees as those do not grow in your country, or in any other place but this cavern. I have named them 'Hotel Trees,' because they bear a certain kind of table d'hote fruit called 'Three-Course Nuts.' "

"That's funny!" said Betsy. "What are the 'Three-Course Nuts' like?"

"Something like cocoanuts, to look at," explained the Ugly One. "All you have to do is to pick one of them and then sit down and eat your dinner. You first unscrew the top part and find a cupfull of good soup. After you've eaten that, you unscrew the middle part and find a hollow filled with meat and potatoes, vegetables and a fine salad. Eat that, and unscrew the next section, and you come to the dessert in the bottom of the nut. That is pie and cake, cheese and crackers, and nuts and raisins. The

Three-Course Nuts are not all exactly alike in flavor or in contents, but they are all good and in each one may be found a complete three-course dinner."

"But how about breakfasts?" inquired Betsy.

"Why, there are Breakfast Trees for that, which grow over there at the right. They bear nuts, like the others, only the nuts contain coffee or chocolate, instead of soup; oatmeal instead of meat-and-potatoes, and fruits instead of dessert. Sad as has been my life in this wonderful prison, I must admit that no one could live more luxuriously in the best hotel in the world than I have lived here; but I will be glad to get into the open air again and see the good old sun and the silvery moon and the soft green grass and the flowers that are kissed by the morning dew. Ah, how much more lovely are those blessed things than the glitter of gems or the cold gleam of gold!"

"Of course," said Betsy. "I once knew a little boy who wanted to catch the measles, because all the little boys in his neighborhood but him had 'em, and he was really unhappy 'cause he couldn't catch 'em, try as he would. So I'm pretty certain that the things we want, and can't have, are not good for us. Isn't that true, Shaggy?"

"Not always, my dear," he gravely replied. "If we didn't want anything, we would never get anything, good or bad. I think our longings are natural, and if we act as nature prompts us we can't go far wrong."

"For my part," said Queen Ann, "I think the world would be a dreary place without the gold and jewels."

"All things are good in their way," said Shaggy; "but we may have too much of any good thing. And I have noticed that the value of anything depends upon how scarce it is, and how difficult it is to obtain."

"Pardon me for interrupting you," said King Kaliko, coming to their side, "but now that we have rescued Shaggy's brother I would like to return to my royal cavern. Being the King of the Nomes, it is my duty to look after my restless subjects and see that they behave themselves."

So they all turned and began walking through the Metal Forest to the other side of the great domed cave, where they had first entered it. Shaggy and his brother walked side by side and both seemed rejoiced that they were together after their long separation. Betsy didn't dare look at the polka-dot handkerchief, for fear she would laugh aloud; so she walked behind the two brothers and led Hank by holding fast to his left ear.

When at last they reached the place where the passage led to the outer world, Queen Ann said, in a hesitating way that was unusual with her:

"I have not conquered this Nome Country, nor do I expect to do so; but I would like to gather a few of these pretty jewels before I leave this place."

"Help yourself, ma'am," said King Kaliko, and at once the officers of the army took advantage of his royal permission and began filling their pockets, while Ann tied a lot of diamonds in a big handkerchief.

This accomplished, they all entered the passage, the Nomes going first to light the way with their torches. They had not proceeded far when Betsy exclaimed:

"Why, there are jewels here, too!"

All eyes were turned upon the ground and they found a regular trail of jewels strewn along the rock floor.

"This is queer!" said Kaliko, much surprised. "I must send some of my Nomes to gather up these gems and replace them in the Metal Forest, where they belong. I wonder how they came to be here?"

All the way along the passage they found this trail of jewels, but when they neared the end the mystery was explained. For there, squatted upon the floor with his back to the rock wall, sat old Ruggedo, puffing and blowing as if he was all tired out. Then they realized it was he who had scattered the jewels, from his many pockets, which one by one had burst with the weight of their contents as he had stumbled along the passage.

"But I don't mind," said Ruggedo, with a deep sigh. "I now realize that I could not have carried such a weighty load very far, even had I managed to escape from this passage with it. The woman who sewed the pockets on my robe used poor thread, for which I shall thank her."

"Have you any jewels left?" inquired Betsy.

He glanced into some of the remaining pockets.

"A few," said he, "but they will be sufficient to supply my wants, and I no longer have any desire to be rich. If some of you will kindly help me to rise, I'll get out of here and leave you, for I know you all despise me and prefer my room to my company."

Shaggy and Kaliko raised the old King to his feet, when he was confronted by Shaggy's brother, whom he now noticed for the first time. The queer and unexpected appearance of the Ugly One so startled Ruggedo that he gave a wild cry and began to tremble, as if he had seen a ghost.

"Wh—wh—who is this?" he faltered.

"I am that helpless prisoner whom your cruel magic transformed from a handsome man into an ugly one!" answered Shaggy's brother, in a voice of stern reproach.

"Really, Ruggedo," said Betsy, "you ought to be ashamed of that mean trick."

"I am, my dear," admitted Ruggedo, who was now as meek and humble as formerly he had been cruel and vindictive.

"Then," returned the girl, "you'd better do some more magic and give the poor man his own face again."

"I wish I could," answered the old King; "but you must remember that Tititi-Hoochoo has deprived me of all my magic powers. However, I never took the trouble to learn just how to break the charm I cast over Shaggy's brother, for I intended he should always remain ugly."

"Every charm," remarked pretty Polychrome, "has its antidote; and, if you knew this charm of ugliness, Ruggedo, you must have known how to dispel it."

He shook his head.

"If I did, I—I've forgotten," he stammered regretfully.

"Try to think!" pleaded Shaggy, anxiously. "*Please* try to think!"

Ruggedo ruffled his hair with both hands, sighed, slapped his chest, rubbed his ear, and stared stupidly around the group.

"I've a faint recollection that there *was* one thing that would break the charm," said he; "but misfortune has so addled my brain that I can't remember what it was."

"See here, Ruggedo," said Betsy, sharply, "we've treated you pretty well, so far, but we won't stand for any nonsense, and if you know what's good for yourself you'll think of that charm!"

"Why?" he demanded, turning to look wonderingly at the little girl.

"Because it means so much to Shaggy's brother. He's dreadfully ashamed of himself, the way he is now, and you're to blame for it. Fact is, Ruggedo, you've done so much wickedness in your life that it won't hurt you to do a kind act now."

Ruggedo blinked at her, and sighed again, and then tried very hard to think.

"I seem to remember, dimly," said he, "that a certain kind of a kiss will break the charm of ugliness."

"What kind of a kiss?"

"What kind? Why, it was— it was— it was either the kiss of a Mortal Maid; or— or— the kiss of a Mortal Maid who had once been a fairy; or— or the kiss of one who is still a fairy. I can't remember which. But of course no maid, mortal or fairy, would ever consent to kiss a person so ugly—so dreadfully, fearfully, terribly ugly—as Shaggy's brother."

"I'm not so sure of that," said Betsy, with admirable courage; "I'm a Mortal Maid, and if it is *my* kiss that will break this awful charm, I—I'll do it!"

"Oh, you really couldn't," protested Ugly. "I would be obliged to remove my mask, and when you saw my face, nothing could induce you to kiss me, generous as you are."

"Well, as for that," said the little girl, "I needn't see your face at all. Here's my plan: You stay in this dark passage, and we'll send away the Nomes with their torches. Then you'll take off the handkerchief, and I—I'll kiss you."

"This is awfully kind of you, Betsy!" said Shaggy, gratefully.

"Well, it surely won't kill me," she replied; "and, if it makes you and your brother happy, I'm willing to take some chances."

So Kaliko ordered the torch-bearers to leave the passage, which they did by going through the rock opening. Queen Ann and her army also went out; but the others were so interested in Betsy's experiment that they remained grouped at the mouth of the passageway. When the big rock swung into place, closing tight the opening, they were left in total darkness.

"Now, then," called Betsy in a cheerful voice, "have you got that handkerchief off your face, Ugly?"

"Yes," he replied.

"Well, where are you, then?" she asked, reaching out her arms.

"Here," said he.

"You'll have to stoop down, you know."

He found her hands and clasping them in his own stooped until his face was near to that of the little girl. The others heard a clear, smacking kiss, and then Betsy exclaimed:

"There! I've done it, and it didn't hurt a bit!"

"Tell me, dear brother; is the charm broken?" asked Shaggy.

"I do not know," was the reply. "It may be, or it may not be. I cannot tell."

"Has anyone a match?" inquired Betsy.

"I have several," said Shaggy.

"Then let Ruggedo strike one of them and look at your brother's face, while we all turn our backs. Ruggedo made your brother ugly, so I guess he can stand the horror of looking at him, if the charm isn't broken."

Agreeing to this, Ruggedo took the match and lighted it. He gave one look and then blew out the match.

"Ugly as ever!" he said with a shudder. "So it wasn't the kiss of a Mortal Maid, after all."

"Let me try," proposed the Rose Princess, in her sweet voice. "I am a Mortal Maid who was once a fairy. Perhaps my kiss will break the charm."

Files did not wholly approve of this, but he was too generous to interfere. So the Rose Princess felt her way through the darkness to Shaggy's brother and kissed him.

Ruggedo struck another match, while they all turned away.

"No," announced the former King; "that didn't break the charm, either. It must be the kiss of a fairy that is required—or else my memory has failed me altogether."

"Polly," said Betsy, pleadingly, "won't *you* try?"

"Of course I will!" answered Polychrome, with a merry laugh. "I've never kissed a mortal man in all the thousands of years I have existed, but I'll do it to please our faithful Shaggy Man, whose unselfish affection for his ugly brother deserves to be rewarded."

Even as Polychrome was speaking she tripped lightly to the side of the Ugly One and quickly touched his cheek with her lips.

"Oh, thank you—thank you!" he fervently cried. "I've changed, this time, I know. I can feel it! I'm different. Shaggy—dear Shaggy—I am myself again!"

Files, who was near the opening, touched the spring that released the big rock and it suddenly swung backward and let in a flood of daylight.

Everyone stood motionless, staring hard at Shaggy's brother, who, no longer masked by the polka-dot handkerchief, met their gaze with a glad smile.

"Well," said Shaggy Man, breaking the silence at last and drawing a long, deep breath of satisfaction, "you are no longer the Ugly One, my dear brother; but, to be entirely frank with you, the face that belongs to you is no more handsome than it ought to be."

"I think he's rather good looking," remarked Betsy, gazing at the man critically.

"In comparison with what he was," said King Kaliko, "he is really beautiful. You, who never beheld his ugliness, may not understand that; but it was my misfortune to look at the Ugly One many times, and I say again that, in comparison with what he was, the man is now beautiful."

"All right," returned Betsy, briskly, "we'll take your word for it, Kaliko. And now let us get out of this tunnel and into the world again."

CHAPTER XXIII

RUGGEDO REFORMS

IT DID NOT TAKE THEM LONG TO REGAIN THE ROYAL CAVERN OF THE NOME KING, where Kaliko ordered served to them the nicest refreshments the place afforded.

Ruggedo had come trailing along after the rest of the party and while no one paid any attention to the old King they did not offer any objection to his presence or command him to leave them. He looked fearfully to see if the eggs were still guarding the entrance, but they had now disappeared; so he crept into the cavern after the others and humbly squatted down in a corner of the room.

There Betsy discovered him. All of the little girl's companions were now so happy at the success of Shaggy's quest for his brother, and the laughter and merriment seemed so general, that Betsy's heart softened toward the friendless old man who had once been their bitter enemy, and she carried to him some of the food and drink.

Ruggedo's eyes filled with tears at this unexpected kindness. He took the child's hand in his own and pressed it gratefully.

"Look here, Kaliko," said Betsy, addressing the new King, "what's the use of being hard on Ruggedo? All his magic power is gone, so he can't do any more harm, and I'm sure he's sorry he acted so badly to everybody."

"Are you?" asked Kaliko, looking down at his former master.

"I am," said Ruggedo. "The girl speaks truly. I'm sorry and I'm harmless. I don't want to wander through the wide world, on top of the ground, for I'm a Nome. No Nome can ever be happy any place but underground."

"That being the case," said Kaliko, "I will let you stay here as long as you behave yourself; but, if you try to act badly again, I shall drive you out, as Tititi-Hoochoo has commanded, and you'll have to wander."

"Never fear. I'll behave," promised Ruggedo. "It is hard work being a King, and harder still to be a good King. But now that I am a common Nome I am sure I can lead a blameless life."

They were all pleased to hear this and to know that Ruggedo had really reformed.

"I hope he'll keep his word," whispered Betsy to Shaggy; "but if he gets bad again we will be far away from the Nome Kingdom and Kaliko will have to 'tend to the old Nome himself."

Polychrome had been a little restless during the last hour or two. The lovely Daughter of the Rainbow knew that she had now done all in her power to assist her earth friends, and so she began to long for her sky home.

"I think," she said, after listening intently, "that it is beginning to rain. The Rain King is my uncle, you know, and perhaps he has read my thoughts and is going to help me. Anyway, I must take a look at the sky and make sure."

So she jumped up and ran through the passage to the outer entrance, and they all followed after her and grouped themselves on a ledge of the mountain-side. Sure enough, dark clouds had filled the sky and a slow, drizzling rain had set in.

"It can't last for long," said Shaggy, looking upward, "and when it stops we shall lose the sweet little fairy we have learned to love. Alas," he continued, after a moment, "the clouds are already breaking in the west, and—see!—isn't that the Rainbow coming?"

Betsy didn't look at the sky; she looked at Polychrome, whose happy, smiling face surely foretold the coming of her father to take her to the Cloud Palaces. A moment later a gleam of sunshine flooded the mountain and a gorgeous Rainbow appeared.

With a cry of gladness Polychrome sprang upon a point of rock and held out her arms. Straightway the Rainbow descended until its end was at her very feet, when with a graceful leap she sprang upon it and was at once clasped in the arms of her radiant sisters, the Daughters of the Rainbow. But Polychrome released herself to lean over the edge of the glowing arch and nod, and smile and throw a dozen kisses to her late comrades.

"Good-bye!" she called, and they all shouted "Good-bye!" in return and waved their hands to their pretty friend.

Slowly the magnificent bow lifted and melted into the sky, until the eyes of the earnest watchers saw only fleecy clouds flitting across the blue.

"I'm dreadful sorry to see Polychrome go," said Betsy, who felt like crying; "but I s'pose she'll be a good deal happier with her sisters in the sky palaces."

"To be sure," returned Shaggy, nodding gravely. "It's her home, you know, and those poor wanderers who, like ourselves, have no home, can realize what that means to her."

"Once," said Betsy, "I, too, had a home. Now, I've only—only—dear old Hank!"

She twined her arms around her shaggy friend who was not human, and he said: "Hee-haw!" in a tone that showed he understood her mood. And the shaggy friend who was human stroked the child's head tenderly and said: "You're wrong about that, Betsy dear. I will never desert you."

"Nor I!" exclaimed Shaggy's brother, in earnest tones.

The little girl looked up at them gratefully, and her eyes smiled through their tears.

"All right," she said. "It's raining again, so let's go back into the cavern."

Rather soberly, for all loved Polychrome and would miss her, they reëntered the dominions of the Nome King.

CHAPTER XXIV

DOROTHY IS DELIGHTED

"WELL," SAID QUEEN ANN, WHEN ALL WERE AGAIN SEATED IN KALIKO'S ROYAL cavern, "I wonder what we shall do next. If I could find my way back to Oogaboo I'd take my army home at once, for I'm sick and tired of these dreadful hardships."

"Don't you want to conquer the world?" asked Betsy.

"No; I've changed my mind about that," admitted the Queen. "The world is too big for one person to conquer and I was happier with my own people in Oogaboo. I wish—Oh, how earnestly I wish—that I was back there this minute!"

"So do I!" yelled every officer in a fervent tone.

Now, it is time for the reader to know that in the far-away Land of Oz the lovely Ruler, Ozma, had been following the adventures of her Shaggy Man, and Tik-Tok, and all the others they had met. Day by day Ozma, with the wonderful Wizard of Oz seated beside her, had gazed upon a Magic Picture in a radium frame, which occupied one side of the Ruler's cosy boudoir in the palace of the Emerald City. The singular thing about this Magic Picture was that it showed whatever scene Ozma wished to see, with the figures all in motion, just as it was taking place. So Ozma and the Wizard had watched every action of the adventurers from the time Shaggy had met shipwrecked

Betsy and Hank in the Rose Kingdom, at which time the Rose Princess, a distant cousin of Ozma, had been exiled by her heartless subjects.

When Ann and her people so earnestly wished to return to Oogaboo, Ozma was sorry for them and remembered that Oogaboo was a corner of the Land of Oz. She turned to her attendant and asked:

"Cannot your magic take these unhappy people to their old home, Wizard?"

"It can, Your Highness," replied the little Wizard.

"I think the poor Queen has suffered enough in her misguided effort to conquer the world," said Ozma, smiling at the absurdity of the undertaking, "so no doubt she will hereafter be contented in her own little kingdom. Please send her there, Wizard, and with her the officers and Files."

"How about the Rose Princess?" asked the Wizard.

"Send her to Oogaboo with Files," answered Ozma. "They have become such good friends that I am sure it would make them unhappy to separate them."

"Very well," said the Wizard, and without any fuss or mystery whatever he performed a magical rite that was simple and effective. Therefore those seated in the Nome King's cavern were both startled and amazed when all the people of Oogaboo suddenly disappeared from the room, and with them the Rose Princess. At first they could not understand it at all; but presently Shaggy suspected the truth, and believing that Ozma was now taking an interest in the party he drew from his pocket a tiny instrument which he placed against his ear.

Ozma, observing this action in her Magic Picture, at once caught up a similar instrument from a table beside her and held it to her own ear. The two instruments recorded the same delicate vibrations of sound and formed a wireless telephone, an invention of the Wizard. Those separated by any distance were thus enabled to converse together with perfect ease and without any wire connection.

"Do you hear me, Shaggy Man?" asked Ozma.

"Yes, Your Highness," he replied.

"I have sent the people of Oogaboo back to their own little valley," announced the Ruler of Oz; "so do not worry over their disappearance."

"That was very kind of you," said Shaggy. "But Your Highness must permit me to report that my own mission here is now ended. I have found my lost brother, and he is now beside me, freed from the enchantment of ugliness which Ruggedo cast upon him. Tik-Tok has served me and my comrades faithfully, as you requested him to do, and I hope you will now transport the Clockwork Man back to your Fairyland of Oz."

"I will do that," replied Ozma. "But how about yourself, Shaggy?"

"I have been very happy in Oz," he said, "but my duty to others forces me to exile myself from that delightful land. I must take care of my new-found brother, for one thing, and I have a new comrade in a dear little girl named Betsy Bobbin, who has no home to go to, and no other friends but me and a small donkey named Hank. I have promised Betsy never to desert her as long as she needs a friend, and so I must give up the delights of the Land of Oz forever."

He said this with a sigh of regret, and Ozma made no reply but laid the tiny instrument on her table, thus cutting off all further communication with the Shaggy Man. But the lovely Ruler of Oz still watched her Magic Picture, with a thoughtful expression upon her face, and the little Wizard of Oz watched Ozma and smiled softly to himself.

In the cavern of the Nome King Shaggy replaced the wireless telephone in his pocket and turning to Betsy said in as cheerful a voice as he could muster:

"Well, little comrade, what shall we do next?"

"I don't know, I'm sure," she answered with a puzzled face. "I'm kind of sorry our adventures are over, for I enjoyed them, and now that Queen Ann and her people are gone, and Polychrome is gone, and—dear me!—where's Tik-Tok, Shaggy?"

"He also has disappeared," said Shaggy, looking around the cavern and nodding wisely. "By this time he is in Ozma's palace in the Land of Oz, which is his home."

"Isn't it your home, too?" asked Betsy.

"It used to be, my dear; but now my home is wherever you and my brother are. We are wanderers, you know, but if we stick together I am sure we shall have a good time."

"Then," said the girl, "let us get out of this stuffy, underground cavern and go in search of new adventures. I'm sure it has stopped raining."

"I'm ready," said Shaggy, and then they bade good-bye to King Kaliko, and thanked him for his assistance, and went out to the mouth of the passage.

The sky was now clear and a brilliant blue in color; the sun shone brightly and even this rugged, rocky country seemed delightful after their confinement underground. There were but four of them now—Betsy and Hank, and Shaggy and his brother—and the little party made their way down the mountain and followed a faint path that led toward the southwest.

During this time Ozma had been holding a conference with the Wizard, and later with Tik-Tok, whom the magic of the Wizard had quickly transported to Ozma's palace. Tik-Tok had only words of praise for Betsy Bobbin, "who," he said, "is al-most as nice as Dor-o-thy her-self."

"Let us send for Dorothy," said Ozma, and summoning her favorite maid, who was named Jellia Jamb, she asked her to request Princess Dorothy to attend her at once. So a few moments later Dorothy entered Ozma's room and greeted her and the Wizard and Tik-Tok with the same gentle smile and simple manner that had won for the little girl the love of everyone she met.

"Did you want to see me, Ozma?" she asked.

"Yes, dear. I am puzzled how to act, and I want your advice."

"I don't b'lieve it's worth much," replied Dorothy, "but I'll do the best I can. What is it all about, Ozma?"

"You all know," said the girl Ruler, addressing her three friends, "what a serious thing it is to admit any mortals into this Fairyland of Oz. It is true I have invited several mortals to make their home here, and all of them have proved true and loyal subjects. Indeed, no one of you three was a native of Oz. Dorothy and the Wizard came here from the United States, and Tik-Tok came from the Land of Ev. But of course he is not a mortal. Shaggy is another American, and he is the cause of all my worry, for our dear Shaggy will not return here and desert the new friends he has found in his recent adventures, because he believes they need his services."

"Shaggy Man was always kind-hearted," remarked Dorothy. "But who are these new friends he has found?"

"One is his brother, who for many years has been a prisoner of the Nome King, our old enemy Ruggedo. This brother seems a kindly, honest fellow, but he has done nothing to entitle him to a home in the Land of Oz."

"Who else?" asked Dorothy.

"I have told you about Betsy Bobbin, the little girl who was shipwrecked—in much the same way you once were—and has since been following the Shaggy Man in his search for his lost brother. You remember her, do you not?"

"Oh, yes!" exclaimed Dorothy. "I've often watched her and Hank in the Magic Picture, you know. She's a dear little girl, and old Hank is a darling! Where are they now?"

"Look and see," replied Ozma with a smile at her friend's enthusiasm.

Dorothy turned to the picture, which showed Betsy and Hank, with Shaggy and his brother, trudging along the rocky paths of a barren country.

"Seems to me," she said, musingly, "that they're a good way from any place to sleep, or any nice things to eat."

"You are right," said Tik-Tok. "I have been in that coun-try, and it is a wil-der-ness."

"It is the country of the Nomes," explained the Wizard, "who are so mischievous that no one cares to live near them. I'm afraid Shaggy and his friends will endure many hardships before they get out of that rocky place, unless—"

He turned to Ozma and smiled.

"Unless I ask you to transport them all here?" she asked.

"Yes, your Highness."

"Could your magic do that?" inquired Dorothy.

"I think so," said the Wizard.

"Well," said Dorothy, "as far as Betsy and Hank are concerned, I'd like to have them here in Oz. It would be such fun to have a girl playmate of my own age, you see. And Hank is such a dear little mule!"

Ozma laughed at the wistful expression in the girl's eyes, and then she drew Dorothy to her and kissed her.

"Am I not your friend and playmate?" she asked.

Dorothy flushed.

"You know how dearly I love you, Ozma!" she cried. "But you're so busy ruling all this Land of Oz that we can't always be together."

"I know, dear. My first duty is to my subjects, and I think it would be a delight to us all to have Betsy with us. There's a pretty suite of rooms just opposite your own where she can live, and I'll build a golden stall for Hank in the stable where the Saw-Horse lives. Then we'll introduce the mule to the Cowardly Lion and the Hungry Tiger, and I'm sure they will soon become firm friends. But I cannot very well admit Betsy and Hank into Oz unless I also admit Shaggy's brother."

"And, unless you admit Shaggy's brother, you will keep out poor Shaggy, whom we are all very fond of," said the Wizard.

"Well, why not ad-mit him?" demanded Tik-Tok.

"The Land of Oz is not a refuge for all mortals in distress," explained Ozma. "I do not wish to be unkind to Shaggy Man, but his brother has no claim on me."

"The Land of Oz isn't crowded," suggested Dorothy.

"Then you advise me to admit Shaggy's brother?" inquired Ozma.

"Well, we can't afford to lose our Shaggy Man, can we?"

"No, indeed!" returned Ozma. "What do you say, Wizard?"

"I'm getting my magic ready to transport them all."

"And you, Tik-Tok?"

"Shag-gy's broth-er is a good fel-low, and we can't spare Shag-gy."

"So, then, the question is settled," decided Ozma. "Perform your magic, Wizard!"

He did so, placing a silver plate upon a small standard and pouring upon the plate a small quantity of pink powder which was contained in a crystal vial. Then he muttered a rather difficult incantation which the sorceress Glinda the Good had taught him, and it all ended in a puff of perfumed smoke from the silver plate. This smoke was so pungent that it made both Ozma and Dorothy rub their eyes for a moment.

"You must pardon these disagreeable fumes," said the Wizard. "I assure you the smoke is a very necessary part of my wizardry."

"Look!" cried Dorothy, pointing to the Magic Picture; "they're gone! All of them are gone."

Indeed, the picture now showed the same rocky landscape as before, but the three people and the mule had disappeared from it.

"They are gone," said the Wizard, polishing the silver plate and wrapping it in a fine cloth, "because they are here."

At that moment Jellia Jamb entered the room.

"Your Highness," she said to Ozma, "the Shaggy Man and another man are in the waiting room and ask to pay their respects to you. Shaggy is crying like a baby, but he says they are tears of joy."

"Send them here at once, Jellia!" commanded Ozma.

"Also," continued the maid, "a girl and a small-sized mule have mysteriously arrived, but they don't seem to know where they are or how they came here. Shall I send them here, too?"

"Oh, no!" exclaimed Dorothy, eagerly jumping up from her chair; "I'll go to meet Betsy myself, for she'll feel awful strange in this big palace."

And she ran down the stairs two at a time to greet her new friend, Betsy Bobbin.

CHAPTER XXV

THE LAND OF LOVE

"WELL, IS 'HEE-HAW' ALL YOU ARE ABLE TO SAY?" INQUIRED THE SAW-HORSE, as he examined Hank with his knot eyes and slowly wagged the branch that served him for a tail.

They were in a beautiful stable in the rear of Ozma's palace, where the wooden Saw-Horse—very much alive—lived in a gold-paneled stall, and where there were rooms for the Cowardly Lion and the Hungry Tiger, which were filled with soft cushions for them to lie upon and golden troughs for them to eat from.

Beside the stall of the Saw-Horse had been placed another for Hank, the mule. This was not quite so beautiful as the other, for the Saw-Horse was Ozma's favorite steed; but Hank had a supply of cushions for a bed (which the Saw-Horse did not need because he never slept) and all this luxury was so strange to the little mule that he could only stand still and regard his surroundings and his queer companions with wonder and amazement.

The Cowardly Lion, looking very dignified, was stretched out upon the marble floor of the stable, eyeing Hank with a calm and critical gaze, while near by crouched the huge Hungry Tiger, who seemed equally interested in the new animal that had just arrived. The Saw-Horse, standing stiffly before Hank, repeated his question:

"Is 'hee-haw' all you are able to say?"

Hank moved his ears in an embarrassed manner.

"I have never said anything else, until now," he replied; and then he began to tremble with fright to hear himself talk.

"I can well understand that," remarked the Lion, wagging his great head with a swaying motion. "Strange things happen in this Land of Oz, as they do everywhere else. I believe you came here from the cold, civilized, outside world, did you not?"

"I did," replied Hank. "One minute I was outside of Oz—and the next minute I was inside! That was enough to give me a nervous shock, as you may guess; but to find myself able to talk, as Betsy does, is a marvel that staggers me."

"That is because you are in the Land of Oz," said the Saw-Horse. "All animals talk, in this favored country, and you must admit it is more sociable than to bray your dreadful 'hee-haw,' which nobody can understand."

"Mules understand it very well," declared Hank.

"Oh, indeed! Then there must be other mules in your outside world," said the Tiger, yawning sleepily.

"There are a great many in America," said Hank. "Are you the only Tiger in Oz?"

"No," acknowledged the Tiger, "I have many relatives living in the Jungle Country; but I am the only Tiger living in the Emerald City."

"There are other Lions, too," said the Saw-Horse; "but I am the only horse, of any description, in this favored Land."

"That is why this Land is favored," said the Tiger. "You must understand, friend Hank, that the Saw-Horse puts on airs because he is shod with plates of gold, and because our beloved Ruler, Ozma of Oz, likes to ride upon his back."

"Betsy rides upon *my* back," declared Hank proudly.

"Who is Betsy?"

"The dearest, sweetest girl in all the world!"

The Saw-Horse gave an angry snort and stamped his golden feet. The Tiger crouched and growled. Slowly the great Lion rose to his feet, his mane bristling.

"Friend Hank," said he, "either you are mistaken in judgment or you are willfully trying to deceive us. The dearest, sweetest girl in the world is our Dorothy, and I will fight anyone—animal or human—who dares to deny it!"

"So will I!" snarled the Tiger, showing two rows of enormous white teeth.

"You are all wrong!" asserted the Saw-Horse in a voice of scorn. "No girl living can compare with my mistress, Ozma of Oz!"

Hank slowly turned around until his heels were toward the others. Then he said stubbornly:

"I am not mistaken in my statement, nor will I admit there can be a sweeter girl alive than Betsy Bobbin. If you want to fight, come on—I'm ready for you!"

While they hesitated, eyeing Hank's heels doubtfully, a merry peal of laughter startled the animals and turning their heads they beheld three lovely girls standing just within the richly carved entrance to the stable. In the center was Ozma, her arms encircling the waists of Dorothy and Betsy, who stood on either side of her. Ozma was nearly half a head taller than the two other girls, who were almost of one size. Unobserved, they had listened to the talk of the animals, which was a very strange experience indeed to little Betsy Bobbin.

"You foolish beasts!" exclaimed the Ruler of Oz, in a gentle but chiding tone of voice. "Why should you fight to defend us, who are all three loving friends and in no sense rivals? Answer me!" she continued, as they bowed their heads sheepishly.

"I have the right to express my opinion, your Highness," pleaded the Lion.

"And so have the others," replied Ozma. "I am glad you and the Hungry Tiger love Dorothy best, for she was your first friend and companion. Also I am pleased that my Saw-Horse loves me best, for together we have endured both joy and sorrow. Hank has proved his faith and loyalty by defending his own little mistress; and so you are all right in one way, but wrong in another. Our Land of Oz is a Land of Love, and here friendship outranks every other quality. Unless you can all be friends, you cannot retain our love."

They accepted this rebuke very meekly.

"All right," said the Saw-Horse, quite cheerfully; "shake hoofs, friend Mule."

Hank touched his hoof to that of the wooden horse.

"Let us be friends and rub noses," said the Tiger. So Hank modestly rubbed noses with the big beast.

The Lion merely nodded and said, as he crouched before the mule:

"Any friend of a friend of our beloved Ruler is a friend of the Cowardly Lion. That seems to cover your case. If ever you need help or advice, friend Hank, call on me."

"Why, this is as it should be," said Ozma, highly pleased to see them so fully reconciled. Then she turned to her companions: "Come, my dears, let us resume our walk."

As they turned away Betsy said wonderingly:

"Do all the animals in Oz talk as we do?"

"Almost all," answered Dorothy. "There's a Yellow Hen here, and she can talk, and so can her chickens; and there's a Pink Kitten upstairs in my room who talks very nicely; but I've a little fuzzy black dog, named Toto, who has been with me in Oz a long time, and he's never said a single word but 'bow-wow!'"

"Do you know why?" asked Ozma.

"Why, he's a Kansas dog; so I s'pose he's different from these fairy animals," replied Dorothy.

"Hank isn't a fairy animal, any more than Toto," said Ozma, "yet as soon as he came under the spell of our fairyland he found he could talk. It was the same way with Billina, the Yellow Hen whom you brought here at one time. The same spell has affected Toto, I assure you; but he's a wise little dog and while he knows everything that is said to him he prefers not to talk."

"Goodness me!" exclaimed Dorothy. "I never s'pected Toto was fooling me all this time." Then she drew a small silver whistle from her pocket and blew a shrill note upon it. A moment later there was a sound of scurrying footsteps, and a shaggy black dog came running up the path.

Dorothy knelt down before him and shaking her finger just above his nose she said:

"Toto, haven't I always been good to you?"

Toto looked up at her with his bright black eyes and wagged his tail.

"Bow-wow!" he said, and Betsy knew at once that meant yes, as well as Dorothy and Ozma knew it, for there was no mistaking the tone of Toto's voice.

"That's a dog answer," said Dorothy. "How would you like it, Toto, if I said nothing to you but 'bow-wow'?"

Toto's tail was wagging furiously now, but otherwise he was silent.

"Really, Dorothy," said Betsy, "he can talk with his bark and his tail just as well as we can. Don't you understand such dog language?"

"Of course I do," replied Dorothy. "But Toto's got to be more sociable. See here, sir!" she continued, addressing the dog, "I've just learned, for the first time, that you can say words—if you want to. Don't you want to, Toto?"

"Woof!" said Toto, and that meant "no."

"Not just one word, Toto, to prove you're as good as any other animal in Oz?"

"Woof!"

"Just one word, Toto—and then you may run away."

He looked at her steadily a moment.

"All right. Here I go!" he said, and darted away as swift as an arrow.

Dorothy clapped her hands in delight, while Betsy and Ozma both laughed heartily at her pleasure and the success of her experiment. Arm in arm they sauntered away through the beautiful gardens of the palace, where magnificent flowers bloomed in abundance and fountains shot their silvery sprays far into the air. And by and by, as they turned a corner, they came upon Shaggy Man and his brother, who were seated together upon a golden bench.

The two arose to bow respectfully as the Ruler of Oz approached them.

"How are you enjoying our Land of Oz?" Ozma asked the stranger.

"I am very happy here, Your Highness," replied Shaggy's brother. "Also I am very grateful to you for permitting me to live in this delightful place."

"You must thank Shaggy for that," said Ozma. "Being his brother, I have made you welcome here."

"When you know Brother better," said Shaggy earnestly, "you will be glad he has become one of your loyal subjects. I am just getting acquainted with him myself, and I find much in his character to admire."

Leaving the brothers, Ozma and the girls continued their walk. Presently Betsy exclaimed:

"Shaggy's brother can't ever be as happy in Oz as *I* am. Do you know, Dorothy, I didn't believe any girl could ever have such a good time—*anywhere*—as I'm having now?"

"I know," answered Dorothy. "I've felt that way myself, lots of times."

"I wish," continued Betsy, dreamily, "that every little girl in the world could live in the Land of Oz; and every little boy, too!"

Ozma laughed at this.

"It is quite fortunate for us, Betsy, that your wish cannot be granted," said she, "for all that army of girls and boys would crowd us so that we would have to move away."

"Yes," agreed Betsy, after a little thought, "I guess that's true."

THE END

THE
SCARECROW
OF OZ

CONTENTS

CHAPTER I

THE GREAT WHIRLPOOL

"Seems to me," said Cap'n Bill, as he sat beside Trot under the big acacia tree, looking out over the blue ocean, "seems to me, Trot, as how the more we know, the more we find we don't know."

"I can't quite make that out, Cap'n Bill," answered the little girl in a serious voice, after a moment's thought, during which her eyes followed those of the old sailor-man across the glassy surface of the sea. "Seems to me that all we learn is jus' so much gained."

"I know; it looks that way at first sight," said the sailor, nodding his head; "but those as knows the least have a habit of thinkin' they know all there is to know, while them as knows the most admits what a turr'ble big world this is. It's the knowing ones that realize one lifetime ain't long enough to git more'n a few dips o' the oars of knowledge."

Trot didn't answer. She was a very little girl, with big, solemn eyes and an earnest, simple manner. Cap'n Bill had been her faithful companion for years and had taught her almost everything she knew.

He was a wonderful man, this Cap'n Bill. Not so very old, although his hair was grizzled—what there was of it. Most of his head was bald as an egg and as shiny as oilcloth, and this made his big ears stick out in a funny way. His eyes had a gentle look and were pale blue in color, and his round face was rugged and bronzed. Cap'n Bill's left leg was missing, from the knee down, and that was why the sailor no longer sailed the seas. The wooden leg he wore was good enough to stump around with on land, or even to take Trot out for a row or a sail on the ocean, but when it came to "runnin' up aloft" or performing active duties on shipboard, the old sailor was not equal to the task. The loss of his leg had ruined his career and the old sailor found comfort in devoting himself to the education and companionship of the little girl.

The accident to Cap'n Bill's leg had happened at about the time Trot was born, and "ever since then" he had lived with Trot's mother as "a star boarder," having enough money saved up to pay for his weekly "keep." He loved the baby and often held her on his lap; her first ride was on Cap'n Bill's shoulders, for she had no baby-carriage; and when she began to toddle around, the child and the sailor became close comrades and enjoyed many strange adventures together. It is said the fairies had been present at Trot's birth and had marked her forehead with their invisible mystic signs, so that she was able to see and do many wonderful things.

The acacia tree was on top of a high bluff, but a path ran down the bank in a zigzag way to the water's edge, where Cap'n Bill's boat was moored to a rock by means of a stout cable. It had been a hot, sultry afternoon, with scarcely a breath of air stirring, so Cap'n Bill and Trot had been quietly sitting beneath the shade of the tree, waiting for the sun to get low enough for them to take a row.

They had decided to visit one of the great caves which the waves had washed out of the rocky coast during many years of steady effort. The caves were a source of continual delight to both the girl and the sailor, who loved to explore their awesome depths.

"I b'lieve, Cap'n," remarked Trot, at last, "that it's time for us to start."

The old man cast a shrewd glance at the sky, the sea and the motionless boat. Then he shook his head.

"Mebbe it's time, Trot," he answered, "but I don't jes' like the looks o' things this afternoon."

"What's wrong?" she asked wonderingly.

"Can't say as to that. Things is too quiet to suit me, that's all. No breeze, not a ripple a-top the water, nary a gull a-flyin' anywhere, an' the end o' the hottest day o' the year. I ain't no weather-prophet, Trot, but any sailor would know the signs is ominous."

"There's nothing wrong that I can see," said Trot. "If there was a cloud in the sky even as big as my thumb, we might worry about it; but—look, Cap'n!—the sky is as clear as can be."

He looked again and nodded.

"P'r'aps we can make the cave, all right," he agreed, not wishing to disappoint her. "It's only a little way out, an' we'll be on the watch; so come along, Trot."

Together they descended the winding path to the beach. It was no trouble for the girl to keep her footing on the steep way, but Cap'n Bill, because of his wooden leg, had to hold on to rocks and roots now and then to save himself from tumbling. On a level path he was as spry as anyone, but to climb up hill or down required some care.

They reached the boat safely and while Trot was untying the rope Cap'n Bill reached into a crevice of the rock and drew out several tallow candles and a box of wax matches, which he thrust into the capacious pockets of his "sou'wester." This sou'wester was a short coat of oilskin which the old sailor wore on all occasions—when he wore a coat at all—and the pockets always contained a variety of objects, useful and ornamental, which made even Trot wonder where they all came from and why Cap'n Bill should treasure them. The jackknives—a big one and a little one—the bits of cord, the fishhooks, the nails: these were handy to have on certain occasions. But bits of shell, and tin boxes with unknown contents, buttons, pincers, bottles of curious stones and the like, seemed quite unnecessary to carry around. That was Cap'n Bill's business, however, and now that he added the candles and the matches to his collection Trot made no comment, for she knew these last were to light their way through the caves.

The sailor always rowed the boat, for he handled the oars with strength and skill. Trot sat in the stern and steered. The place where they embarked was a little bight or circular bay, and the boat cut across a much larger bay toward a distant headland where the caves were located, right at the water's edge. They were nearly a mile from shore and about halfway across the bay when Trot suddenly sat up straight and exclaimed: "What's that, Cap'n?"

He stopped rowing and turned half around to look.

"That, Trot," he slowly replied, "looks to me mighty like a whirlpool."

"What makes it, Cap'n?"

"A whirl in the air makes the whirl in the water. I was afraid as we'd meet with trouble, Trot. Things didn't look right. The air was too still."

"It's coming closer," said the girl.

The old man grabbed the oars and began rowing with all his strength.

" 'Tain't comin' closer to us, Trot," he gasped; "it's we that are comin' closer to the whirlpool. The thing is drawin' us to it like a magnet!"

Trot's sun-bronzed face was a little paler as she grasped the tiller firmly and tried to steer the boat away; but she said not a word to indicate fear.

The swirl of the water as they came nearer made a roaring sound that was fearful to listen to. So fierce and powerful was the whirlpool that it drew the surface of the sea into the form of a great basin, slanting downward toward the center, where a big hole had been made in the ocean—a hole with walls of water that were kept in place by the rapid whirling of the air.

The boat in which Trot and Cap'n Bill were riding was just on the outer edge of this saucer-like slant, and the old sailor knew very well that unless he could quickly force the little craft away from the rushing current they would soon be drawn into the great black hole that yawned in the middle. So he exerted all his might and pulled as he had never pulled before. He pulled so hard that the left oar snapped in two and sent Cap'n Bill sprawling upon the bottom of the boat.

He scrambled up quickly enough and glanced over the side. Then he looked at Trot, who sat quite still, with a serious, far-away look in her sweet eyes. The boat was now speeding swiftly of its own accord, following the line of the circular basin round and round and gradually drawing nearer to the great hole in the center. Any further effort to escape the whirlpool was useless, and realizing this fact Cap'n Bill turned toward Trot and put an arm around her, as if to shield her from the awful fate before them. He did not try to speak, because the roar of the waters would have drowned the sound of his voice.

These two faithful comrades had faced dangers before, but nothing to equal that which now faced them. Yet Cap'n Bill, noting the look in Trot's eyes and remembering how often she had been protected by unseen powers, did not quite give way to despair.

The great hole in the dark water—now growing nearer and nearer—looked very terrifying; but they were both brave enough to face it and await the result of the adventure.

CHAPTER II

THE CAVERN UNDER THE SEA

THE CIRCLES WERE SO MUCH SMALLER AT THE BOTTOM OF THE BASIN, AND THE BOAT moved so much more swiftly, that Trot was beginning to get dizzy with the motion, when suddenly the boat made a leap and dived headlong into the murky depths of the hole. Whirling like tops, but still clinging together, the sailor and the girl were separated from their boat and plunged down—down—down—into the farthermost recesses of the great ocean.

At first their fall was swift as an arrow, but presently they seemed to be going more moderately and Trot was almost sure that unseen arms were about her, supporting her and protecting her. She could see nothing, because the water filled her eyes and blurred her vision, but she clung fast to Cap'n Bill's sou'wester, while other arms clung fast to her, and so they gradually sank down and down until a full stop was made, when they began to ascend again.

But it seemed to Trot that they were not rising straight to the surface from where they had come. The water was no longer whirling them and they seemed to be drawn in a slanting direction through still, cool ocean depths. And then—in much quicker time than I have told it—up they popped to the surface and were cast at full length upon a sandy beach, where they lay choking and gasping for breath and wondering what had happened to them.

Trot was the first to recover. Disengaging herself from Cap'n Bill's wet embrace and sitting up, she rubbed the water from her eyes and then looked around her. A soft, bluish-green glow lighted the place, which seemed to be a sort of cavern, for above and on either side of her were rugged rocks. They had been cast upon a beach of clear sand, which slanted upward from the pool of water at their feet—a pool which doubtless led into the big ocean that fed it. Above the reach of the waves of the pool were more rocks, and still more and more, into the dim windings and recesses of which the glowing light from the water did not penetrate.

The place looked grim and lonely, but Trot was thankful that she was still alive and had suffered no severe injury during her trying adventure under water. At her side Cap'n Bill was sputtering and coughing, trying to get rid of the water he had swallowed. Both of them were soaked through, yet the cavern was warm and comfortable and a wetting did not dismay the little girl in the least.

She crawled up the slant of sand and gathered in her hand a bunch of dried seaweed, with which she mopped the face of Cap'n Bill and cleared the water from his eyes and ears. Presently the old man sat up and stared at her intently. Then he nodded his bald head three times and said in a gurgling voice:

"Mighty good, Trot; mighty good! We didn't reach Davy Jones's locker that time, did we? Though why we didn't, an' why we're here, is more'n I kin make out."

"Take it easy, Cap'n," she replied. "We're safe enough, I guess, at least for the time being."

He squeezed the water out of the bottoms of his loose trousers and felt of his wooden leg and arms and head, and finding he had brought all of his person with him he gathered courage to examine closely their surroundings.

"Where d'ye think we are, Trot?" he presently asked.

"Can't say, Cap'n. P'r'aps in one of our caves."

He shook his head. "No," said he, "I don't think that, at all. The distance we came up didn't seem half as far as the distance we went down; an' you'll notice there ain't any outside entrance to this cavern whatever. It's a reg'lar dome over this pool o' water, and unless there's some passage at the back, up yonder, we're fast pris'ners."

Trot looked thoughtfully over her shoulder.

"When we're rested," she said, "we will crawl up there and see if there's a way to get out."

Cap'n Bill reached in the pocket of his oilskin coat and took out his pipe. It was still dry, for he kept it in an oilskin pouch with his tobacco. His matches were in a tight tin box, so in a few moments the old sailor was smoking contentedly. Trot knew it helped him to think when he was in any difficulty. Also, the pipe did much to restore the old sailor's composure, after his long ducking and his terrible fright—a fright that was more on Trot's account than his own.

The sand was dry where they sat, and soaked up the water that dripped from their clothing. When Trot had squeezed the wet out of her hair she began to feel much like her old self again. By and by they got upon their feet and crept up the incline to the scattered boulders above. Some of these were of huge size, but by passing between some and around others, they were able to reach the extreme rear of the cavern.

"Yes," said Trot, with interest, "here's a round hole."

"And it's black as night inside it," remarked Cap'n Bill.

"Just the same," answered the girl, "we ought to explore it, and see where it goes, 'cause it's the only poss'ble way we can get out of this place."

Cap'n Bill eyed the hole doubtfully

"It may be a way out o' here, Trot," he said, "but  it may be a way into a far worse place than this. I'm not sure but our best plan is to stay right here."

Trot wasn't sure, either, when she thought of it in that light. After a while she made her way back to the sands again, and Cap'n Bill followed her. As they sat down, the child looked thoughtfully at the sailor's bulging pockets.

"How much food have we got, Cap'n?" she asked.

"Half a dozen ship's biscuits an' a hunk o' cheese," he replied. "Want some now, Trot?"

She shook her head, saying:

"That ought to keep us alive 'bout three days if we're careful of it."

"Longer'n that, Trot," said Cap'n Bill, but his voice was a little troubled and unsteady.

"But if we stay here we're bound to starve in time," continued the girl, "while if we go into the dark hole—"

"Some things are more hard to face than starvation," said the sailor-man, gravely. "We don't know what's inside that dark hole, Trot, nor where it might lead us to."

"There's a way to find that out," she persisted.

Instead of replying, Cap'n Bill began searching in his pockets. He soon drew out a little package of fish-hooks and a long line. Trot watched him join them together. Then he crept a little way up the slope and turned over a big rock. Two or three small crabs began scurrying away over the sands and the old sailor caught them and put one on his hook and the others in his pocket. Coming back to the pool he swung the hook over his shoulder and circled it around his head and cast it nearly into the center of the water, where he allowed it to sink gradually, paying out the line as far as it would go. When the end was reached, he began drawing it in again, until the crab bait was floating on the surface.

Trot watched him cast the line a second time, and a third. She decided that either there were no fishes in the pool or they would not bite the crab bait. But Cap'n Bill was an old fisherman and not easily discouraged. When the crab got away he put another on the hook. When the crabs were all gone he climbed up the rocks and found some more.

Meantime Trot tired of watching him and lay down upon the sands, where she fell fast asleep. During the next two hours her clothing dried completely, as did that of the old sailor. They were both so used to salt water that there was no danger of taking cold.

Finally the little girl was wakened by a splash beside her and a grunt of satisfaction from Cap'n Bill. She opened her eyes to find that the Cap'n had landed a silver-scaled fish weighing about two pounds. This cheered her considerably and she hurried to scrape together a heap of seaweed, while Cap'n Bill cut up the fish with his jackknife and got it ready for cooking.

They had cooked fish with seaweed before. Cap'n Bill wrapped his fish in some of the weed and dipped it in the water to dampen it. Then he lighted a match and set fire to Trot's heap, which speedily burned down to a glowing bed of ashes. Then they laid the wrapped fish on the ashes, covered it with more seaweed, and allowed this to catch fire and burn to embers. After feeding the fire with seaweed for some time, the sailor finally decided that their supper was ready, so he scattered the ashes and drew out the bits of fish, still encased in their smoking wrappings. When these wrappings were removed, the fish was found thoroughly cooked and both Trot and Cap'n Bill ate of it freely. It had a slight flavor of seaweed and would have been better with a sprinkling of salt.

The soft glow which until now had lighted the cavern, began to grow dim, but there was a great quantity of seaweed in the place, so after they had eaten their fish they kept the fire alive for a time by giving it a handful of fuel now and then.

From an inner pocket the sailor drew a small flask of battered metal and unscrewing the cap handed it to Trot. She took but one swallow of the water, although she wanted more, and she noticed that Cap'n Bill merely wet his lips with it.

"S'pose," said she, staring at the glowing seaweed fire and speaking slowly, "that we can catch all the fish we need; how 'bout the drinking-water, Cap'n?"

He moved uneasily but did not reply. Both of them were thinking about the dark hole, but while Trot had little fear of it the old man could not overcome his dislike to enter the place. He knew that Trot was right, though. To remain in the cavern, where they now were, could only result in slow but sure death.

It was nighttime up on the earth's surface, so the little girl became drowsy and soon fell asleep. After a time the old sailor slumbered on the sands beside her. It was very still and nothing disturbed them for hours. When at last they awoke the cavern was light again.

They had divided one of the biscuits and were munching it for breakfast when they were startled by a sudden splash in the pool. Looking toward it they saw emerging from the water the most curious creature either of them had ever beheld. It wasn't a fish, Trot decided, nor was it a beast. It had wings, though, and queer wings they were: shaped like an inverted chopping-bowl and covered with tough skin instead of feathers. It had four legs—much like the legs of a stork, only double the number—and its head was shaped a good deal like that of a poll parrot, with a beak that curved downward in front and upward at the edges, and was half bill and half mouth. But to call it a bird was out of the question, because it had no feathers whatever except a crest of wavy plumes of a scarlet color on the very top of its head. The strange creature must have weighed as much as Cap'n Bill, and as it floundered and struggled to get out of the water to the sandy beach it was so big and unusual that both Trot and her companion stared at it in wonder—in wonder that was not unmixed with fear.

CHAPTER III

THE ORK

THE EYES THAT REGARDED THEM, AS THE CREATURE STOOD DRIPPING BEFORE THEM, were bright and mild in expression, and the queer addition to their party made no attempt to attack them and seemed quite as surprised by the meeting as they were.

"I wonder," whispered Trot, "what it is."

"Who, me?" exclaimed the creature in a shrill, high-pitched voice. "Why, I'm an Ork."

"Oh!" said the girl. "But what is an Ork?"

"I am," he repeated, a little proudly, as he shook the water from his funny wings; "and if ever an Ork was glad to be out of the water and on dry land again, you can be mighty sure that I'm that especial, individual Ork!"

"Have you been in the water long?" inquired Cap'n Bill, thinking it only polite to show an interest in the strange creature.

"Why, this last ducking was about ten minutes, I believe, and that's about nine minutes and sixty seconds too long for comfort," was the reply. "But last night I was in an awful pickle, I assure you. The whirlpool caught me, and—"

"Oh, were you in the whirlpool, too?" asked Trot eagerly.

He gave her a glance that was somewhat reproachful.

"I believe I was mentioning the fact, young lady, when your desire to talk interrupted me," said the Ork. "I am not usually careless in my actions, but that whirlpool was so busy yesterday that I thought I'd see what mischief it was up to. So I flew a little too near it and the suction of the air drew me down into the depths of the ocean. Water and I are natural enemies, and it would have conquered me this time had not a bevy of pretty mermaids come to my assistance and dragged me away from the whirling water and far up into a cavern, where they deserted me."

"Why, that's about the same thing that happened to us," cried Trot. "Was your cavern like this one?"

"I haven't examined this one yet," answered the Ork; "but if they happen to be alike I shudder at our fate, for the other one was a prison, with no outlet except by means of the water. I stayed there all night, however, and this morning I plunged into the pool, as far down as I could go, and then swam as hard and as far as I could. The rocks scraped my back, now and then, and I barely escaped the clutches of an ugly sea-monster; but by and by I came to the surface to catch my breath, and found myself here. That's the whole story, and as I see you have something to eat I entreat you to give me a share of it. The truth is, I'm half starved."

With these words the Ork squatted down beside them. Very reluctantly Cap'n Bill drew another biscuit from his pocket and held it out. The Ork promptly seized it in one of its front claws and began to nibble the biscuit in much the same manner a parrot might have done.

"We haven't much grub," said the sailor-man, "but we're willin' to share it with a comrade in distress."

"That's right," returned the Ork, cocking its head sidewise in a cheerful manner, and then for a few minutes there was silence while they all ate of the biscuits. After a while Trot said:

"I've never seen or heard of an Ork before. Are there many of you?"

"We are rather few and exclusive, I believe," was the reply. "In the country where I was born we are the absolute rulers of all living things, from ants to elephants."

"What country is that?" asked Cap'n Bill.

"Orkland."

"Where does it lie?"

"I don't know, exactly. You see, I have a restless nature, for some reason, while all the rest of my race are quiet and contented Orks and seldom stray far from home. From childhood days I loved to fly long distances away, although father often warned me that I would get into trouble by so doing.

" 'It's a big world, Flipper, my son,' he would say, 'and I've heard that in parts of it live queer two-legged creatures called Men, who war upon all other living things and would have little respect for even an Ork.'

"This naturally aroused my curiosity and after I had completed my education and left school I decided to fly out into the world and try to get a glimpse of the creatures called Men. So I left home without saying good-bye, an act I shall always regret. Adventures were many, I found. I sighted men several times, but have never before been so close to them as now. Also I had to fight my way through the air, for I met gigantic birds, with fluffy feathers all over them, which attacked me fiercely. Besides, it kept me busy escaping from floating airships. In my rambling I had lost all track of distance or direction, so that when I wanted to go home I had no idea where my country was located. I've now been trying to find it for several months and it was during one of my flights over the ocean that I met the whirlpool and became its victim."

Trot and Cap'n Bill listened to this recital with much interest, and from the friendly tone and harmless appearance of the Ork they judged he was not likely to prove so disagreeable a companion as at first they had feared he might be.

The Ork sat upon its haunches much as a cat does, but used the finger-like claws of its front legs almost as cleverly as if they were hands. Perhaps the most curious thing about the creature was its tail, or what ought to have been its tail. This queer arrangement of skin, bones and muscle was shaped like the propellers used on boats and airships, having fan-like surfaces and being pivoted to its body. Cap'n Bill knew something of mechanics, and observing the propeller-like tail of the Ork he said:

"I s'pose you're a pretty swift flyer?"

"Yes, indeed; the Orks are admitted to be Kings of the Air."

"Your wings don't seem to amount to much," remarked Trot.

"Well, they are not very big," admitted the Ork, waving the four hollow skins gently to and fro, "but they serve to support my body in the air while I speed along by means of my tail. Still, taken altogether, I'm very handsomely formed, don't you think?"

Trot did not like to reply, but Cap'n Bill nodded gravely. "For an Ork," said he, "you're a wonder. I've never seen one afore, but I can imagine you're as good as any."

That seemed to please the creature and it began walking around the cavern, making its way easily up the slope. While it was gone, Trot and Cap'n Bill each took another sip from the water-flask, to wash down their breakfast.

"Why, here's a hole—an exit—an outlet!" exclaimed the Ork from above.

"We know," said Trot. "We found it last night."

"Well, then, let's be off," continued the Ork, after sticking its head into the black hole and sniffing once or twice. "The air seems fresh and sweet, and it can't lead us to any worse place than this."

The girl and the sailor-man got up and climbed to the side of the Ork.

"We'd about decided to explore this hole before you came," explained Cap'n Bill; "but it's a dangerous place to navigate in the dark, so wait till I light a candle."

"What is a candle?" inquired the Ork.

"You'll see in a minute," said Trot.

The old sailor drew one of the candles from his right-side pocket and the tin matchbox from his left-side pocket. When he lighted the match the Ork gave a startled jump and eyed the flame suspiciously; but Cap'n Bill proceeded to light the candle and the action interested the Ork very much.

"Light," it said, somewhat nervously, "is valuable in a hole of this sort. The candle is not dangerous, I hope?"

"Sometimes it burns your fingers," answered Trot, "but that's about the worst it can do—'cept to blow out when you don't want it to."

Cap'n Bill shielded the flame with his hand and crept into the hole. It wasn't any too big for a grown man, but after he had crawled a few feet it grew larger. Trot came close behind him and then the Ork followed.

"Seems like a reg'lar tunnel," muttered the sailor-man, who was creeping along awkwardly because of his wooden leg. The rocks, too, hurt his knees.

For nearly half an hour the three moved slowly along the tunnel, which made many twists and turns and sometimes slanted downward and sometimes upward. Finally Cap'n Bill stopped short, with an exclamation of disappointment, and held the flickering candle far ahead to light the scene.

"What's wrong?" demanded Trot, who could see nothing because the sailor's form completely filled the hole.

"Why, we've come to the end of our travels, I guess," he replied.

"Is the hole blocked?" inquired the Ork.

"No; it's wuss nor that," replied Cap'n Bill sadly. "I'm on the edge of a precipice. Wait a minute an' I'll move along and let you see for yourselves. Be careful, Trot, not to fall."

Then he crept forward a little and moved to one side, holding the candle so that the girl could see to follow him. The Ork came next and now all three knelt on a narrow ledge of rock which dropped straight away and left a huge black space which the tiny flame of the candle could not illuminate.

"H-m!" said the Ork, peering over the edge; "this doesn't look very promising, I'll admit. But let me take your candle, and I'll fly down and see what's below us."

"Aren't you afraid?" asked Trot.

"Certainly I'm afraid," responded the Ork. "But if we intend to escape we can't stay on this shelf forever. So, as I notice you poor creatures cannot fly, it is my duty to explore the place for you."

Cap'n Bill handed the Ork the candle, which had now burned to about half its length. The Ork took it in one claw rather cautiously and then tipped its body forward and slipped over the edge. They heard a queer buzzing sound, as the tail revolved, and a brisk flapping of the peculiar wings, but they were more interested just then in following with their eyes the tiny speck of light which marked the location of the candle. This light first made a great circle, then dropped slowly downward and suddenly was extinguished, leaving everything before them black as ink.

"Hi, there! How did that happen?" cried the Ork.

"It blew out, I guess," shouted Cap'n Bill. "Fetch it here."

"I can't see where you are," said the Ork.

So Cap'n Bill got out another candle and lighted it, and its flame enabled the Ork to fly back to them. It alighted on the edge and held out the bit of candle.

"What made it stop burning?" asked the creature.

"The wind," said Trot. "You must be more careful, this time."

"What's the place like?" inquired Cap'n Bill.

"I don't know, yet; but there must be a bottom to it, so I'll try to find it."

With this the Ork started out again and this time sank downward more slowly. Down, down, down it went, till the candle was a mere spark, and then it headed away to the left and Trot and Cap'n Bill lost all sight of it.

In a few minutes, however, they saw the spark of light again, and as the sailor still held the second lighted candle the Ork made straight toward them. It was only a few yards distant when suddenly it dropped the candle with a cry of pain and next moment alighted, fluttering wildly, upon the rocky ledge.

"What's the matter?" asked Trot.

"It bit me!" wailed the Ork. "I don't like your candles. The thing began to disappear slowly as soon as I took it in my claw, and it grew smaller and smaller until just now it turned and bit me—a most unfriendly thing to do. Oh—oh! Ouch, what a bite!"

"That's the nature of candles, I'm sorry to say," explained Cap'n Bill, with a grin. "You have to handle 'em mighty keerful. But tell us, what did you find down there?"

"I found a way to continue our journey," said the Ork, nursing tenderly the claw which had been burned. "Just below us is a great lake of black water, which looked so cold and wicked that it made me shudder; but away at the left there's a big tunnel, which we can easily walk through. I don't know where it leads to, of course, but we must follow it and find out."

"Why, we can't get to it," protested the little girl. "We can't fly, as you do, you must remember."

"No, that's true," replied the Ork musingly. "Your bodies are built very poorly, it seems to me, since all you can do is crawl upon the earth's surface. But you may ride upon my back, and in that way I can promise you a safe journey to the tunnel."

"Are you strong enough to carry us?" asked Cap'n Bill, doubtfully.

"Yes, indeed; I'm strong enough to carry a dozen of you, if you could find a place to sit," was the reply; "but there's only room between my wings for one at a time, so I'll have to make two trips."

"All right; I'll go first," decided Cap'n Bill.

He lit another candle for Trot to hold while they were gone and to light the Ork on his return to her, and then the old sailor got upon the Ork's back, where he sat with his wooden leg sticking straight out sidewise.

"If you start to fall, clasp your arms around my neck," advised the creature.

"If I start to fall, it's good night an' pleasant dreams," said Cap'n Bill.

"All ready?" asked the Ork.

"Start the buzz-tail," said Cap'n Bill, with a tremble in his voice. But the Ork flew away so gently that the old man never even tottered in his seat.

Trot watched the light of Cap'n Bill's candle till it disappeared in the far distance. She didn't like to be left alone on this dangerous ledge, with a lake of black water hundreds of feet below her; but she was a brave little girl and waited patiently for the return of the Ork. It came even sooner than she had expected and the creature said to her:

"Your friend is safe in the tunnel. Now, then, get aboard and I'll carry you to him in a jiffy."

I'm sure not many little girls would have cared to take that awful ride through the huge black cavern on the back of a skinny Ork. Trot didn't care for it, herself, but it just had to be done and so she did it as courageously as possible. Her heart beat fast and she was so nervous she could scarcely hold the candle in her fingers as the Ork sped swiftly through the darkness.

It seemed like a long ride to her, yet in reality the Ork covered the distance in a wonderfully brief period of time and soon Trot stood safely beside Cap'n Bill on the level floor of a big arched tunnel. The sailor-man was very glad to greet his little comrade again and both were grateful to the Ork for his assistance.

"I dunno where this tunnel leads to," remarked Cap'n Bill, "but it surely looks more promisin' than that other hole we crept through."

"When the Ork is rested," said Trot, "we'll travel on and see what happens."

"Rested!" cried the Ork, as scornfully as his shrill voice would allow. "That bit of flying didn't tire me at all. I'm used to flying days at a time, without ever once stopping."

"Then let's move on," proposed Cap'n Bill. He still held in his hand one lighted candle, so Trot blew out the other flame and placed her candle in the sailor's big pocket. She knew it was not wise to burn two candles at once.

The tunnel was straight and smooth and very easy to walk through, so they made good progress. Trot thought that the tunnel began about two miles from the cavern where they had been cast by the whirlpool, but now it was impossible to guess the miles traveled, for they walked steadily for hours and hours without any change in their surroundings.

Finally Cap'n Bill stopped to rest.

"There's somethin' queer about this 'ere tunnel, I'm certain," he declared, wagging his head dolefully. "Here's three candles gone a'ready, an' only three more left us, yet the tunnel's the same as it was when we started. An' how long it's goin' to keep up, no one knows."

"Couldn't we walk without a light?" asked Trot. "The way seems safe enough."

"It does right now," was the reply, "but we can't tell when we are likely to come to another gulf, or somethin' jes' as dangerous. In that case we'd be killed afore we knew it."

"Suppose I go ahead?" suggested the Ork. "I don't fear a fall, you know, and if anything happens I'll call out and warn you."

"That's a good idea," declared Trot, and Cap'n Bill thought so, too. So the Ork started off ahead, quite in the dark, and hand in hand the two followed him.

When they had walked in this way for a good long time the Ork halted and demanded food. Cap'n Bill had not mentioned food because there was so little left— only three biscuits and a lump of cheese about as big as his two fingers—but he gave the Ork half of a biscuit, sighing as he did so. The creature didn't care for the cheese, so the sailor divided it between himself and Trot. They lighted a candle and sat down in the tunnel while they ate.

"My feet hurt me," grumbled the Ork. "I'm not used to walking and this rocky passage is so uneven and lumpy that it hurts me to walk upon it."

"Can't you fly along?" asked Trot.

"No; the roof is too low," said the Ork.

After the meal they resumed their journey, which Trot began to fear would never end. When Cap'n Bill noticed how tired the little girl was, he paused and lighted a match and looked at his big silver watch.

"Why, it's night!" he exclaimed. "We've tramped all day, an' still we're in this awful passage, which mebbe goes straight through the middle of the world, an' mebbe is a circle—in which case we can keep walkin' till doomsday. Not knowin' what's before us so well as we know what's behind us, I propose we make a stop, now, an' try to sleep till mornin'."

"That will suit me," asserted the Ork, with a groan. "My feet are hurting me dreadfully and for the last few miles I've been limping with pain."

"My foot hurts, too," said the sailor, looking for a smooth place on the rocky floor to sit down.

"*Your* foot!" cried the Ork. "Why, you've only one to hurt you, while I have four. So I suffer four times as much as you possibly can. Here; hold the candle while I look at the bottoms of my claws. I declare," he said, examining them by the flickering light, "there are bunches of pain all over them!"

"P'r'aps," said Trot, who was very glad to sit down beside her companions, "you've got corns."

"Corns? Nonsense! Orks never have corns," protested the creature, rubbing its sore feet tenderly.

"Then mebbe they're—they're— What do you call 'em, Cap'n Bill? Something 'bout the Pilgrim's Progress, you know."

"Bunions," said Cap'n Bill.

"Oh, yes; mebbe you've got bunions."

"It is possible," moaned the Ork. "But whatever they are, another day of such walking on them would drive me crazy."

"I'm sure they'll feel better by mornin'," said Cap'n Bill, encouragingly. "Go to sleep an' try to forget your sore feet."

The Ork cast a reproachful look at the sailor-man, who didn't see it. Then the creature asked plaintively: "Do we eat now, or do we starve?"

"There's only half a biscuit left for you," answered Cap'n Bill. "No one knows how long we'll have to stay in this dark tunnel, where there's nothing whatever to eat; so I advise you to save that morsel o' food till later."

"Give it me now!" demanded the Ork. "If I'm going to starve, I'll do it all at once—not by degrees."

Cap'n Bill produced the biscuit and the creature ate it in a trice. Trot was rather hungry and whispered to Cap'n Bill that she'd take part of her share; but the old man secretly broke his own half-biscuit in two, saving Trot's share for a time of greater need.

He was beginning to be worried over the little girl's plight and long after she was asleep and the Ork was snoring in a rather disagreeable manner, Cap'n Bill sat with his back to a rock and smoked his pipe and tried to think of some way to escape from this seemingly endless tunnel. But after a time he also slept, for hobbling on a wooden leg all day was tiresome, and there in the dark slumbered the three adventurers for many hours, until the Ork roused itself and kicked the old sailor with one foot.

"It must be another day," said he.

CHAPTER IV

DAYLIGHT AT LAST

CAP'N BILL RUBBED HIS EYES, LIT A MATCH AND CONSULTED HIS WATCH.

"Nine o'clock. Yes, I guess it's another day, sure enough. Shall we go on?" he asked.

"Of course," replied the Ork. "Unless this tunnel is different from everything else in the world, and has no end, we'll find a way out of it sooner or later."

The sailor gently wakened Trot. She felt much rested by her long sleep and sprang to her feet eagerly.

"Let's start, Cap'n," was all she said.

They resumed the journey and had only taken a few steps when the Ork cried "Wow!" and made a great fluttering of its wings and whirling of its tail. The others, who were following a short distance behind, stopped abruptly.

"What's the matter?" asked Cap'n Bill.

"Give us a light," was the reply. "I think we've come to the end of the tunnel." Then, while Cap'n Bill lighted a candle, the creature added: "If that is true, we needn't have wakened so soon, for we were almost at the end of this place when we went to sleep."

The sailor-man and Trot came forward with a light. A wall of rock really faced the tunnel, but now they saw that the opening made a sharp turn to the left. So they followed on, by a narrower passage, and then made another sharp turn—this time to the right.

"Blow out the light, Cap'n," said the Ork, in a pleased voice. "We've struck daylight."

Daylight at last! A shaft of mellow light fell almost at their feet as Trot and the sailor turned the corner of the passage, but it came from above, and raising their eyes they found they were at the bottom of a deep, rocky well, with the top far, far above their heads. And here the passage ended.

For a while they gazed in silence, at least two of them being filled with dismay at the sight. But the Ork merely whistled softly and said cheerfully:

"That was the toughest journey I ever had the misfortune to undertake, and I'm glad it's over. Yet, unless I can manage to fly to the top of this pit, we are entombed here forever."

"Do you think there is room enough for you to fly in?" asked the little girl anxiously; and Cap'n Bill added:

"It's a straight-up shaft, so I don't see how you'll ever manage it."

"Were I an ordinary bird—one of those horrid feathered things—I wouldn't even make the attempt to fly out," said the Ork. "But my mechanical propeller tail can accomplish wonders, and whenever you're ready I'll show you a trick that is worth while."

"Oh!" exclaimed Trot; "do you intend to take us up, too?"

"Why not?"

"I thought," said Cap'n Bill, "as you'd go first, an' then send somebody to help us by lettin' down a rope."

"Ropes are dangerous," replied the Ork, "and I might not be able to find one to reach all this distance. Besides, it stands to reason that if I can get out myself I can also carry you two with me."

"Well, I'm not afraid," said Trot, who longed to be on the earth's surface again.

"S'pose we fall?" suggested Cap'n Bill, doubtfully.

"Why, in that case we would all fall together," returned the Ork. "Get aboard, little girl; sit across my shoulders and put both your arms around my neck."

Trot obeyed and when she was seated on the Ork, Cap'n Bill inquired:

"How 'bout me, Mr. Ork?"

"Why, I think you'd best grab hold of my rear legs and let me carry you up in that manner," was the reply.

Cap'n Bill looked way up at the top of the well, and then he looked at the Ork's slender, skinny legs and heaved a deep sigh.

"It's goin' to be some dangle, I guess; but if you don't waste too much time on the way up, I may be able to hang on," said he.

"All ready, then!" cried the Ork, and at once his whirling tail began to revolve. Trot felt herself rising into the air; when the creature's legs left the ground Cap'n Bill grasped two of them firmly and held on for dear life. The Ork's body was tipped straight upward, and Trot had to embrace the neck very tightly to keep from sliding off. Even in this position the Ork had trouble in escaping the rough sides of the well. Several times it exclaimed "Wow!" as it bumped its back, or a wing hit against some jagged projection; but the tail kept whirling with remarkable swiftness and the daylight grew brighter and brighter. It was, indeed, a long journey from the bottom to the top, yet almost before Trot realized they had come so far, they popped out of the hole into the clear air and sunshine and a moment later the Ork alighted gently upon the ground.

The release was so sudden that even with the creature's care for its passengers Cap'n Bill struck the earth with a shock that sent him rolling heel over head; but by the time Trot had slid down from her seat the old sailor-man was sitting up and looking around him with much satisfaction.

"It's sort o' pretty here," said he.

"Earth is a beautiful place!" cried Trot.

"I wonder where on earth we are?" pondered the Ork, turning first one bright eye and then the other to this side and that. Trees there were, in plenty, and shrubs and flowers and green turf. But there were no houses; there were no paths; there was no sign of civilization whatever.

"Just before I settled down on the ground I thought I caught a view of the ocean," said the Ork. "Let's see if I was right." Then he flew to a little hill, near by, and Trot and Cap'n Bill followed him more slowly. When they stood on the top of the hill they could see the blue waves of the ocean in front of them, to the right of them, and at the left of them. Behind the hill was a forest that shut out the view.

"I hope it ain't an island, Trot," said Cap'n Bill gravely.

"If it is, I s'pose we're prisoners," she replied.

"Ezzackly so, Trot."

"But, even so, it's better than those terr'ble underground tunnels and caverns," declared the girl.

"You are right, little one," agreed the Ork. "Anything above ground is better than the best that lies underground. So let's not quarrel with our fate but be thankful we've escaped."

"We are, indeed!" she replied. "But I wonder if we can find something to eat in this place?"

"Let's explore an' find out," proposed Cap'n Bill. "Those trees over at the left look like cherry-trees."

On the way to them the explorers had to walk through a tangle of vines and Cap'n Bill, who went first, stumbled and pitched forward on his face.

"Why, it's a melon!" cried Trot delightedly, as she saw what had caused the sailor to fall.

Cap'n Bill rose to his foot, for he was not at all hurt, and examined the melon. Then he took his big jackknife from his pocket and cut the melon open. It was quite ripe and looked delicious; but the old man tasted it before he permitted Trot to eat any. Deciding it was good he gave her a big slice and then offered the Ork some. The creature looked at the fruit somewhat disdainfully, at first, but once he had tasted its flavor he ate of it as heartily as did the others. Among the vines they discovered many other melons, and Trot said gratefully: "Well, there's no danger of our starving, even if this *is* an island."

"Melons," remarked Cap'n Bill, "are both food an' water. We couldn't have struck anything better."

Farther on they came to the cherry-trees, where they obtained some of the fruit, and at the edge of the little forest were wild plums. The forest itself consisted entirely of nut trees—walnuts, filberts, almonds and chestnuts—so there would be plenty of wholesome food for them while they remained there.

Cap'n Bill and Trot decided to walk through the forest, to discover what was on the other side of it, but the Ork's feet were still so sore and "lumpy" from walking on the rocks that the creature said he preferred to fly over the tree-tops and meet them on the other side. The forest was not large, so by walking briskly for fifteen minutes they reached its farthest edge and saw before them the shore of the ocean.

"It's an island, all right," said Trot, with a sigh.

"Yes, and a pretty island, too," said Cap'n Bill, trying to conceal his disappointment on Trot's account. "I guess, partner, if the wuss comes to the wuss, I could build a raft—or even a boat—from those trees, so's we could sail away in it."

The little girl brightened at this suggestion.

"I don't see the Ork anywhere," she remarked, looking around. Then her eyes lighted upon something and she exclaimed: "Oh, Cap'n Bill! Isn't that a house, over there to the left?"

Cap'n Bill, looking closely, saw a shed-like structure built at one edge of the forest.

"Seems like it, Trot. Not that I'd call it much of a house, but it's a buildin', all right. Let's go over an' see if it's occypied."

CHAPTER V

THE LITTLE OLD MAN OF THE ISLAND

A FEW STEPS BROUGHT THEM TO THE SHED, WHICH WAS MERELY A ROOF OF BOUGHS built over a square space, with some branches of trees fastened to the sides to keep off the wind. The front was quite open and faced the sea, and as our friends came nearer they observed a little man, with a long pointed beard, sitting motionless on a stool and staring thoughtfully out over the water.

"Get out of the way, please," he called in a fretful voice. "Can't you see you are obstructing my view?"

"Good morning," said Cap'n Bill, politely.

"It isn't a good morning!" snapped the little man. "I've seen plenty of mornings better than this. Do you call it a good morning when I'm pestered with such a crowd as you?"

Trot was astonished to hear such words from a stranger whom they had greeted quite properly, and Cap'n Bill grew red at the little man's rudeness. But the sailor said, in a quiet tone of voice:

"Are you the only one as lives on this 'ere island?"

"Your grammar's bad," was the reply. "But this is my own exclusive island, and I'll thank you to get off it as soon as possible."

"We'd like to do that," said Trot, and then she and Cap'n Bill turned away and walked down to the shore, to see if any other land was in sight.

The little man rose and followed them, although both were now too provoked to pay any attention to him.

"Nothin' in sight, partner," reported Cap'n Bill, shading his eyes with his hand; "so we'll have to stay here for a time, anyhow. It isn't a bad place, Trot, by any means."

"That's all you know about it!" broke in the little man. "The trees are altogether too green and the rocks are harder than they ought to be. I find the sand very grainy and the water dreadfully wet. Every breeze makes a draught and the sun shines in the daytime, when there's no need of it, and disappears just as soon as it begins to get dark. If you remain here you'll find the island very unsatisfactory."

Trot turned to look at him, and her sweet face was grave and curious.

"I wonder who you are," she said.

"My name is Pessim," said he, with an air of pride. "I'm called the Observer."

"Oh. What do you observe?" asked the little girl.

"Everything I see," was the reply, in a more surly tone. Then Pessim drew back with a startled exclamation and looked at some footprints in the sand. "Why, good gracious me!" he cried in distress.

"What's the matter now?" asked Cap'n Bill.

"Someone has pushed the earth in! Don't you see it?

"It isn't pushed in far enough to hurt anything," said Trot, examining the footprints.

"Everything hurts that isn't right," insisted the man. "If the earth were pushed in a mile, it would be a great calamity, wouldn't it?"

"I s'pose so," admitted the little girl.

"Well, here it is pushed in a full inch! That's a twelfth of a foot, or a little more than a millionth part of a mile. Therefore it is one-millionth part of a calamity—Oh, dear! How dreadful!" said Pessim in a wailing voice.

"Try to forget it, sir," advised Cap'n Bill, soothingly. "It's beginning to rain. Let's get under your shed and keep dry."

"Raining! Is it really raining?" asked Pessim, beginning to weep.

"It is," answered Cap'n Bill, as the drops began to descend, "and I don't see any way to stop it—although I'm some observer myself."

"No; we can't stop it, I fear," said the man. "Are you very busy just now?"

"I won't be after I get to the shed," replied the sailor-man.

"Then do me a favor, please," begged Pessim, walking briskly along behind them, for they were hastening to the shed.

"Depends on what it is," said Cap'n Bill.

"I wish you would take my umbrella down to the shore and hold it over the poor fishes till it stops raining. I'm afraid they'll get wet," said Pessim.

Trot laughed, but Cap'n Bill thought the little man was poking fun at him and so he scowled upon Pessim in a way that showed he was angry.

They reached the shed before getting very wet, although the rain was now coming down in big drops. The roof of the shed protected them and while they stood watching the rainstorm something buzzed in and circled around Pessim's head. At once the Observer began beating it away with his hands, crying out:

"A bumblebee! A bumblebee! The queerest bumblebee I ever saw!"

Cap'n Bill and Trot both looked at it and the little girl said in surprise:

"Dear me! It's a wee little Ork!"

"That's what it is, sure enough," exclaimed Cap'n Bill.

Really, it wasn't much bigger than a big bumblebee, and when it came toward Trot she allowed it to alight on her shoulder.

"It's me, all right," said a very small voice in her ear; "but I'm in an awful pickle, just the same!"

"What, are you *our* Ork, then?" demanded the girl, much amazed.

"No, I'm my own Ork. But I'm the only Ork you know," replied the tiny creature.

"What's happened to you?" asked the sailor, putting his head close to Trot's shoulder in order to hear the reply better. Pessim also put his head close, and the Ork said:

"You will remember that when I left you I started to fly over the trees, and just as I got to this side of the forest I saw a bush that was loaded down with the most luscious fruit you can imagine. The fruit was about the size of a gooseberry and of a lovely lavender color. So I swooped down and picked off one in my bill and ate it. At once I began to grow small. I could feel myself shrinking, shrinking away, and it frightened me terribly, so that I alighted on the ground to think over what was happening. In a few seconds I had shrunk to the size you now see me; but there I remained, getting no smaller, indeed, but no larger. It is certainly a dreadful affliction! After I had recovered somewhat from the shock I began to search for you. It is not so easy to find one's way when a creature is so small, but fortunately I spied you here in this shed and came to you at once."

Cap'n Bill and Trot were much astonished at this story and felt grieved for the poor Ork, but the little man Pessim seemed to think it a good joke. He began laughing when he heard the story and laughed until he choked, after which he lay down on the ground and rolled and laughed again, while the tears of merriment coursed down his wrinkled cheeks.

"Oh, dear! Oh, dear!" he finally gasped, sitting up and wiping his eyes. "This is too rich! It's almost too joyful to be true."

"I don't see anything funny about it," remarked Trot indignantly.

"You would if you'd had my experience," said Pessim, getting upon his feet and gradually resuming his solemn and dissatisfied expression of countenance. "The same thing happened to me."

"Oh, did it? And how did you happen to come to this island?" asked the girl.

"I didn't come; the neighbors brought me," replied the little man, with a frown at the recollection. "They said I was quarrelsome and fault-finding and blamed me because I told them all the things that went wrong, or never were right, and because I told them how things ought to be. So they brought me here and left me all alone, saying that if I quarreled with myself, no one else would be made unhappy. Absurd, wasn't it?"

"Seems to me," said Cap'n Bill, "those neighbors did the proper thing."

"Well," resumed Pessim, "when I found myself King of this island I was obliged to live upon fruits, and I found many fruits growing here that I had never seen before. I tasted several and found them good and wholesome. But one day I ate a lavender berry—as the Ork did—and immediately I grew so small that I was scarcely two inches high. It was a very unpleasant condition and like the Ork I became frightened.

I could not walk very well nor very far, for every lump of earth in my way seemed a mountain, every blade of grass a tree and every grain of sand a rocky boulder. For several days I stumbled around in an agony of fear. Once a tree toad nearly gobbled me up, and if I ran out from the shelter of the bushes the gulls and cormorants swooped down upon me. Finally I decided to eat another berry and become nothing at all, since life, to one as small as I was, had become a dreary nightmare.

"At last I found a small tree that I thought bore the same fruit as that I had eaten. The berry was dark purple instead of light lavender, but otherwise it was quite similar. Being unable to climb the tree, I was obliged to wait underneath it until a sharp breeze arose and shook the limbs so that a berry fell. Instantly I seized it and taking a last view of the world—as I then thought—I ate the berry in a twinkling. Then, to my surprise, I began to grow big again, until I became of my former stature, and so I have since remained. Needless to say, I have never eaten again of the lavender fruit, nor do any of the beasts or birds that live upon this island eat it."

They had all three listened eagerly to this amazing tale, and when it was finished the Ork exclaimed:

"Do you think, then, that the deep purple berry is the antidote for the lavender one?"

"I'm sure of it," answered Pessim.

"Then lead me to the tree at once!" begged the Ork, "for this tiny form I now have terrifies me greatly."

Pessim examined the Ork closely.

"You are ugly enough as you are," said he. "Were you any larger you might be dangerous."

"Oh, no," Trot assured him; "the Ork has been our good friend. Please take us to the tree."

Then Pessim consented, although rather reluctantly. He led them to the right, which was the east side of the island, and in a few minutes brought them near to the edge of the grove which faced the shore of the ocean. Here stood a small tree bearing berries of a deep purple color. The fruit looked very enticing and Cap'n Bill reached up and selected one that seemed especially plump and ripe.

The Ork had remained perched upon Trot's shoulder but now it flew down to the ground. It was so difficult for Cap'n Bill to kneel down, with his wooden leg, that the little girl took the berry from him and held it close to the Ork's head.

"It's too big to go into my mouth," said the little creature, looking at the fruit sidewise.

"You'll have to make sev'ral mouthfuls of it, I guess," said Trot; and that is what the Ork did. He pecked at the soft, ripe fruit with his bill and ate it up very quickly, because it was good.

Even before he had finished the berry they could see the Ork begin to grow. In a few minutes he had regained his natural size and was strutting before them, quite delighted with his transformation.

"Well, well! What do you think of me now?" he asked proudly.

"You are very skinny and remarkably ugly," declared Pessim.

"You are a poor judge of Orks," was the reply. "Anyone can see that I'm much handsomer than those dreadful things called birds, which are all fluff and feathers."

"Their feathers make soft beds," asserted Pessim.

"And my skin would make excellent drumheads," retorted the Ork. "Nevertheless, a plucked bird or a skinned Ork would be of no value to himself, so we needn't brag of our usefulness after we are dead. But for the sake of argument, friend Pessim, I'd like to know what good *you* would be, were you not alive?"

"Never mind that," said Cap'n Bill. "He isn't much good as he is."

"I am King of this island, allow me to say, and you're intruding on my property," declared the little man, scowling upon them. "If you don't like me—and I'm sure you don't, for no one else does—why don't you go away and leave me to myself?"

"Well, the Ork can fly, but we can't," explained Trot, in answer. "We don't want to stay here a bit, but I don't see how we can get away."

"You can go back into the hole you came from."

Cap'n Bill shook his head; Trot shuddered at the thought; the Ork laughed aloud.

"You may be King here," the creature said to Pessim, "but we intend to run this island to suit ourselves, for we are three and you are one, and the balance of power lies with us."

The little man made no reply to this, although as they walked back to the shed his face wore its fiercest scowl. Cap'n Bill gathered a lot of leaves and, assisted by Trot, prepared two nice beds in opposite corners of the shed. Pessim slept in a hammock which he swung between two trees.

They required no dishes, as all their food consisted of fruits and nuts picked from the trees; they made no fire, for the weather was warm and there was nothing to cook; the shed had no furniture other than the rude stool which the little man was accustomed to sit upon. He called it his "throne" and they let him keep it.

So they lived upon the island for three days, and rested and ate to their hearts' content. Still, they were not at all happy in this life because of Pessim. He continually found fault with them, and all that they did, and all their surroundings. He could see nothing good or admirable in all the world and Trot soon came to understand why the little man's former neighbors had brought him to this island and left him there, all alone, so he could not annoy anyone. It was their misfortune that they had been led to this place by their adventures, for often they would have preferred the company of a wild beast to that of Pessim.

On the fourth day a happy thought came to the Ork. They had all been racking their brains for a possible way to leave the island, and discussing this or that method, without finding a plan that was practical. Cap'n Bill had said he could make a raft of the trees, big enough to float them all, but he had no tools except those two pocket-knives and it was not possible to chop down tree with such small blades.

"And s'pose we got afloat on the ocean," said Trot, "where would we drift to, and how long would it take us to get there?"

Cap'n Bill was forced to admit he didn't know. The Ork could fly away from the island any time it wished to, but the queer creature was loyal to his new friends and refused to leave them in such a lonely, forsaken place.

It was when Trot urged him to go, on this fourth morning, that the Ork had his happy thought.

"I will go," said he, "if you two will agree to ride upon my back."

"We are too heavy; you might drop us," objected Cap'n Bill.

"Yes, you are rather heavy for a long journey," acknowledged the Ork, "but you might eat of those lavender berries and become so small that I could carry you with ease."

This quaint suggestion startled Trot and she looked gravely at the speaker while she considered it, but Cap'n Bill gave a scornful snort and asked:

"What would become of us afterward? We wouldn't be much good if we were some two or three inches high. No, Mr. Ork, I'd rather stay here, as I am, than be a hop-o'-my-thumb somewhere else."

"Why couldn't you take some of the dark purple berries along with you, to eat after we had reached our destination?" inquired the Ork. "Then you could grow big again whenever you pleased."

Trot clapped her hands with delight.

"That's it!" she exclaimed. "Let's do it, Cap'n Bill."

The old sailor did not like the idea at first, but he thought it over carefully and the more he thought the better it seemed.

"How could you manage to carry us, if we were so small?" he asked.

"I could put you in a paper bag, and tie the bag around my neck."

"But we haven't a paper bag," objected Trot.

The Ork looked at her.

"There's your sunbonnet," it said presently, "which is hollow in the middle and has two strings that you could tie around my neck."

Trot took off her sunbonnet and regarded it critically. Yes, it might easily hold both her and Cap'n Bill, after they had eaten the lavender berries and been reduced in size. She tied the strings around the Ork's neck and the sunbonnet made a bag in which two tiny people might ride without danger of falling out. So she said:

"I b'lieve we'll do it that way, Cap'n."

Cap'n Bill groaned but could make no logical objection except that the plan seemed to him quite dangerous—and dangerous in more ways than one.

"I think so, myself," said Trot soberly. "But nobody can stay alive without getting into danger sometimes, and danger doesn't mean getting hurt, Cap'n; it only means we *might* get hurt. So I guess we'll have to take the risk."

"Let's go and find the berries," said the Ork.

They said nothing to Pessim, who was sitting on his stool and scowling dismally as he stared at the ocean, but started at once to seek the trees that bore the magic fruits. The Ork remembered very well where the lavender berries grew and led his companions quickly to the spot.

Cap'n Bill gathered two berries and placed them carefully in his pocket. Then they went around to the east side of the island and found the tree that bore the dark purple berries.

"I guess I'll take four of these," said the sailor-man, "so in case one doesn't make us grow big we can eat another."

"Better take six," advised the Ork. "It's well to be on the safe side, and I'm sure these trees grow nowhere else in all the world."

So Cap'n Bill gathered six of the purple berries and with their precious fruit they returned to the shed to bid good-bye to Pessim. Perhaps they would not have granted the surly little man this courtesy had they not wished to use him to tie the sunbonnet around the Ork's neck.

When Pessim learned they were about to leave him he at first looked greatly pleased, but he suddenly recollected that nothing ought to please him and so began to grumble about being left alone.

"We knew it wouldn't suit you," remarked Cap'n Bill. "It didn't suit you to have us here, and it won't suit you to have us go away."

"That is quite true," admitted Pessim. "I haven't been suited since I can remember; so it doesn't matter to me in the least whether you go or stay."

He was interested in their experiment, however, and willingly agreed to assist, although he prophesied they would fall out of the sunbonnet on their way and be either drowned in the ocean or crushed upon some rocky shore. This uncheerful prospect did not daunt Trot, but it made Cap'n Bill quite nervous.

"I will eat my berry first," said Trot, as she placed her sunbonnet on the ground, in such manner that they could get into it.

Then she ate the lavender berry and in a few seconds became so small that Cap'n Bill picked her up gently with his thumb and one finger and placed her in the middle of the sunbonnet. Then he placed beside her the six purple berries—each one being about as big as the tiny Trot's head—and all preparations being now made the old sailor ate his lavender berry and became very small—wooden leg and all!

Cap'n Bill stumbled sadly in trying to climb over the edge of the sunbonnet and pitched in beside Trot headfirst, which caused the unhappy Pessim to laugh with glee. Then the King of the Island picked up the sunbonnet—so rudely that he shook its occupants like peas in a pod—and tied it, by means of its strings, securely around the Ork's neck.

"I hope, Trot, you sewed those strings on tight," said Cap'n Bill anxiously.

"Why, we are not very heavy, you know," she replied, "so I think the stitches will hold. But be careful and not crush the berries, Cap'n."

"One is jammed already," he said, looking at them.

"All ready?" asked the Ork.

"Yes!" they cried together, and Pessim came close to the sunbonnet and called out to them: "You'll be smashed or drowned, I'm sure you will! But farewell, and good riddance to you."

The Ork was provoked by this unkind speech, so he turned his tail toward the little man and made it revolve so fast that the rush of air tumbled Pessim over backward and he rolled several times upon the ground before he could stop himself and sit up. By that time the Ork was high in the air and speeding swiftly over the ocean.

CHAPTER VI

THE FLIGHT OF THE MIDGETS

CAP'N BILL AND TROT RODE VERY COMFORTABLY IN THE SUNBONNET. THE MOTION was quite steady, for they weighed so little that the Ork flew without effort. Yet they were both somewhat nervous about their future fate and could not help wishing they were safe on land and their natural size again.

"You're terr'ble small, Trot," remarked Cap'n Bill, looking at his companion.

"Same to you, Cap'n," she said with a laugh; "but as long as we have the purple berries we needn't worry about our size."

"In a circus," mused the old man, "we'd be curiosities. But in a sunbonnet—high up in the air—sailin' over a big, unknown ocean—they ain't no word in any book-tionary to describe us."

"Why, we're midgets, that's all," said the little girl.

The Ork flew silently for a long time. The slight swaying of the sunbonnet made Cap'n Bill drowsy, and he began to doze. Trot, however, was wide awake, and after enduring the monotonous journey as long as she was able she called out:

"Don't you see land anywhere, Mr. Ork?"

"Not yet," he answered. "This is a big ocean and I've no idea in which direction the nearest land to that island lies; but if I keep flying in a straight line I'm sure to reach some place some time."

That seemed reasonable, so the little people in the sunbonnet remained as patient as possible; that is, Cap'n Bill dozed and Trot tried to remember her geography lessons so she could figure out what land they were likely to arrive at.

For hours and hours the Ork flew steadily, keeping to the straight line and searching with his eyes the horizon of the ocean for land. Cap'n Bill was fast asleep and snoring and Trot had laid her head on his shoulder to rest it when suddenly the Ork exclaimed:

"There! I've caught a glimpse of land, at last."

At this announcement they roused themselves. Cap'n Bill stood up and tried to peek over the edge of the sunbonnet.

"What does it look like?" he inquired.

"Looks like another island," said the Ork; "but I can judge it better in a minute or two."

"I don't care much for islands, since we visited that other one," declared Trot.

Soon the Ork made another announcement.

"It is surely an island, and a little one, too," said he. "But I won't stop, because I see a much bigger land straight ahead of it."

"That's right," approved Cap'n Bill. "The bigger the land, the better it will suit us."

"It's almost a continent," continued the Ork after a brief silence, during which he did not decrease the speed of his flight. "I wonder if it can be Orkland, the place I have been seeking so long?"

"I hope not," whispered Trot to Cap'n Bill—so softly that the Ork could not hear her—"for I shouldn't like to be in a country where only Orks live. This one Ork isn't a bad companion, but a lot of him wouldn't be much fun."

After a few more minutes of flying the Ork called out in a sad voice:

"No! this is not my country. It's a place I have never seen before, although I have wandered far and wide. It seems to be all mountains and deserts and green valleys and queer cities and lakes and rivers—mixed up in a very puzzling way."

"Most countries are like that," commented Cap'n Bill. "Are you going to land?"

"Pretty soon," was the reply. "There is a mountain peak just ahead of me. What do you say to our landing on that?"

"All right," agreed the sailor-man, for both he and Trot were getting tired of riding in the sunbonnet and longed to set foot on solid ground again.

So in a few minutes the Ork slowed down his speed and then came to a stop so easily that they were scarcely jarred at all. Then the creature squatted down until the sunbonnet rested on the ground, and began trying to unfasten with its claws the knotted strings.

This proved a very clumsy task, because the strings were tied at the back of the Ork's neck, just where his claws would not easily reach. After much fumbling he said:

"I'm afraid I can't let you out, and there is no one near to help me."

This was at first discouraging, but after a little thought Cap'n Bill said:

"If you don't mind, Trot, I can cut a slit in your sunbonnet with my knife."

"Do," she replied. "The slit won't matter, 'cause I can sew it up again afterward, when I am big."

So Cap'n Bill got out his knife, which was just as small, in proportion, as he was, and after considerable trouble managed to cut a long slit in the sunbonnet. First he squeezed through the opening himself and then helped Trot to get out.

When they stood on firm ground again their first act was to begin eating the dark purple berries which they had brought with them. Two of these Trot had guarded carefully during the long journey, by holding them in her lap, for their safety meant much to the tiny people.

"I'm not very hungry," said the little girl as she handed a berry to Cap'n Bill, "but hunger doesn't count, in this case. It's like taking medicine to make you well, so we must manage to eat 'em, somehow or other."

But the berries proved quite pleasant to taste and as Cap'n Bill and Trot nibbled at their edges their forms began to grow in size—slowly but steadily. The bigger they grew the easier it was for them to eat the berries, which of course became smaller to them, and by the time the fruit was eaten our friends had regained their natural size.

The little girl was greatly relieved when she found herself as large as she had ever been, and Cap'n Bill shared her satisfaction; for, although they had seen the effect of the berries on the Ork, they had not been sure the magic fruit would have the same effect on human beings, or that the magic would work in any other country than that in which the berries grew.

"What shall we do with the other four berries?" asked Trot, as she picked up her sunbonnet, marveling that she had ever been small enough to ride in it. "They're no good to us now, are they, Cap'n?"

"I'm not sure as to that," he replied. "If they were eaten by one who had never eaten the lavender berries, they might have no effect at all; but then, contrarywise, they might. One of 'em has got badly jammed, so I'll throw it away, but the other three I b'lieve I'll carry with me. They're magic things, you know, and may come handy to us some time."

He now searched in his big pockets and drew out a small wooden box with a sliding cover. The sailor had kept an assortment of nails, of various sizes, in this box, but those he now dumped loosely into his pocket and in the box placed the three sound purple berries.

When this important matter was attended to they found time to look about them and see what sort of place the Ork had landed them in.

CHAPTER VII

THE BUMPY MAN

THE MOUNTAIN ON WHICH THEY HAD ALIGHTED WAS NOT A BARREN WASTE, BUT HAD on its sides patches of green grass, some bushes, a few slender trees and here and there masses of tumbled rocks. The sides of the slope seemed rather steep, but with care one could climb up or down them with ease and safety. The view from where they now stood showed pleasant valleys and fertile hills lying below the heights. Trot thought she saw some houses of queer shapes scattered about the lower landscape, and there were moving dots that might be people or animals, yet were too far away for her to see them clearly.

Not far from the place where they stood was the top of the mountain, which seemed to be flat, so the Ork proposed to his companions that he would fly up and see what was there.

"That's a good idea," said Trot, " 'cause it's getting toward evening and we'll have to find a place to sleep."

The Ork had not been gone more than a few minutes when they saw him appear on the edge of the top which was nearest them.

"Come on up!" he called.

So Trot and Cap'n Bill began to ascend the steep slope and it did not take them long to reach the place where the Ork awaited them.

Their first view of the mountain top pleased them very much. It was a level space of wider extent than they had guessed and upon it grew grass of a brilliant green color. In the very center stood a house built of stone and very neatly constructed. No one was in sight, but smoke was coming from the chimney, so with one accord all three began walking toward the house.

"I wonder," said Trot, "in what country we are, and if it's very far from my home in California."

"Can't say as to that, partner," answered Cap'n Bill, "but I'm mighty certain we've come a long way since we struck that whirlpool."

"Yes," she agreed, with a sigh, "it must be miles and miles!"

"Distance means nothing," said the Ork. "I have flown pretty much all over the world, trying to find my home, and it is astonishing how many little countries there are, hidden away in the cracks and corners of this big globe of Earth. If one travels, he may find some new country at every turn, and a good many of them have never yet been put upon the maps."

"P'raps this is one of them," suggested Trot.

They reached the house after a brisk walk and Cap'n Bill knocked upon the door. It was at once opened by a rugged looking man who had "bumps all over him," as Trot afterward declared. There were bumps on his head, bumps on his body and bumps on his arms and legs and hands. Even his fingers had bumps on the ends of them. For dress he wore an old gray suit of fantastic design, which fitted him very badly because of the bumps it covered but could not conceal.

But the Bumpy Man's eyes were kind and twinkling in expression and as soon as he saw his visitors he bowed low and said in a rather bumpy voice:

"Happy day! Come in and shut the door, for it grows cool when the sun goes down. Winter is now upon us."

"Why, it isn't cold a bit, outside," said Trot, "so it can't be winter yet."

"You will change your mind about that in a little while," declared the Bumpy Man. "My bumps always tell me the state of the weather, and they feel just now as if a snowstorm was coming this way. But make yourselves at home, strangers. Supper is nearly ready and there is food enough for all."

Inside the house there was but one large room, simply but comfortably furnished. It had benches, a table and a fireplace, all made of stone. On the hearth a pot was bubbling and steaming, and Trot thought it had a rather nice smell. The visitors seated

themselves upon the benches—except the Ork, which squatted by the fireplace—and
the Bumpy Man began stirring the kettle briskly.

"May I ask what country this is, sir?" inquired Cap'n Bill.

"Goodness me—fruit-cake and apple-sauce!—don't you know where you
are?" asked the Bumpy Man, as he stopped stirring and looked at the speaker in
surprise.

"No," admitted Cap'n Bill. "We've just arrived."

"Lost your way?" questioned the Bumpy Man.

"Not exactly," said Cap'n Bill. "We didn't have any way to lose."

"Ah!" said the Bumpy Man, nodding his bumpy head. "This," he announced, in
a solemn, impressive voice, "is the famous Land of Mo."

"Oh!" exclaimed the sailor and the girl, both in one breath. But, never having heard of the Land of Mo, they were no wiser than before.

"I thought that would startle you," remarked the Bumpy Man, well pleased, as he resumed his stirring. The Ork watched him a while in silence and then asked:

"Who may *you* be?"

"Me?" answered the Bumpy Man. "Haven't you heard of me? Gingerbread and lemon-juice! I'm known, far and wide, as the Mountain Ear."

They all received this information in silence at first, for they were trying to think what he could mean. Finally Trot mustered up courage to ask:

"What is a Mountain Ear, please?"

For answer the man turned around and faced them, waving the spoon with which he had been stirring the kettle, as he recited the following verses in a singsong tone of voice:

"Here's a mountain, hard of hearing,
  That's sad-hearted and needs cheering,
  So my duty is to listen to all sounds that Nature makes,
  So the hill won't get uneasy—
  Get to coughing, or get sneezy—
  For this monster bump, when frightened, is quite liable to quakes.

"*You* can hear a bell that's ringing;
  I can feel some people's singing;
  But a mountain isn't sensible of what goes on, and so
  When I hear a blizzard blowing
  Or it's raining hard, or snowing,
  I tell it to the mountain and the mountain seems to know.

"Thus I benefit all people
  While I'm living on this steeple,
  For I keep the mountain steady so my neighbors all may thrive.
  With my list'ning and my shouting
  I prevent this mount from spouting,
  And that makes me so important that I'm glad that I'm alive."

When he had finished these lines of verse the Bumpy Man turned again to resume his stirring. The Ork laughed softly and Cap'n Bill whistled to himself and Trot made up her mind that the Mountain Ear must be a little crazy. But the Bumpy Man seemed satisfied that he had explained his position fully and presently he placed four stone plates upon the table and then lifted the kettle from the fire and poured some of its contents on each of the plates. Cap'n Bill and Trot at once approached the table, for they were hungry, but when she examined her plate the little girl exclaimed:

"Why, it's molasses candy!"

"To be sure," returned the Bumpy Man, with a pleasant smile. "Eat it quick, while it's hot, for it cools very quickly this winter weather."

With this he seized a stone spoon and began putting the hot molasses candy into his mouth, while the others watched him in astonishment.

"Doesn't it burn you?" asked the girl.

"No indeed," said he. "Why don't you eat? Aren't you hungry?"

"Yes," she replied, "I am hungry. But we usually eat our candy when it is cold and hard. We always pull molasses candy before we eat it."

"Ha, ha, ha!" laughed the Mountain Ear. "What a funny idea! Where in the world did you come from?"

"California," she said.

"California! Pooh! there isn't any such place. I've heard of every place in the Land of Mo, but I never before heard of California."

"It isn't in the Land of Mo," she explained.

"Then it isn't worth talking about," declared the Bumpy Man, helping himself again from the steaming kettle, for he had been eating all the time he talked.

"For my part," sighed Cap'n Bill, "I'd like a decent square meal, once more, just by way of variety. In the last place there was nothing but fruit to eat, and here it's worse, for there's nothing but candy."

"Molasses candy isn't so bad," said Trot. "Mine's nearly cool enough to pull, already. Wait a bit, Cap'n, and you can eat it."

A little later she was able to gather the candy from the stone plate and begin to work it back and forth with her hands. The Mountain Ear was greatly amazed at this and watched her closely. It was really good candy and pulled beautifully, so that Trot was soon ready to cut it into chunks for eating.

Cap'n Bill condescended to eat one or two pieces and the Ork ate several, but the Bumpy Man refused to try it. Trot finished the plate of candy herself and then asked for a drink of water.

"Water?" said the Mountain Ear wonderingly. "What is that?"

"Something to drink. Don't you have water in Mo?"

"None that ever I heard of," said he. "But I can give you some fresh lemonade. I caught it in a jar the last time it rained, which was only day before yesterday."

"Oh, does it rain lemonade here?" she inquired.

"Always; and it is very refreshing and healthful."

With this he brought from a cupboard a stone jar and a dipper, and the girl found it very nice lemonade, indeed. Cap'n Bill liked it, too; but the Ork would not touch it.

"If there is no water in this country, I cannot stay here for long," the creature declared. "Water means life to man and beast and bird."

"There must be water in lemonade," said Trot.

"Yes," answered the Ork, "I suppose so; but there are other things in it, too, and they spoil the good water."

The day's adventures had made our wanderers tired, so the Bumpy Man brought them some blankets in which they rolled themselves and then lay down before the fire, which their host kept alive with fuel all through the night. Trot wakened several times and found the Mountain Ear always alert and listening intently for the slightest sound. But the little girl could hear no sound at all except the snores of Cap'n Bill.

CHAPTER VIII

BUTTON-BRIGHT IS LOST AND FOUND AGAIN

"WAKE UP—WAKE UP!" CALLED THE VOICE OF THE BUMPY MAN. "DIDN'T I TELL you winter was coming? I could hear it coming with my left ear, and the proof is that it is now snowing hard outside."

"Is it?" said Trot, rubbing her eyes and creeping out of her blanket. "Where I live, in California, I have never seen snow, except far away on the tops of high mountains."

"Well, this is the top of a high mountain," returned the bumpy one, "and for that reason we get our heaviest snowfalls right here."

The little girl went to the window and looked out. The air was filled with falling white flakes, so large in size and so queer in form that she was puzzled.

"Are you certain this is snow?" she asked.

"To be sure. I must get my snow-shovel and turn out to shovel a path. Would you like to come with me?"

"Yes," she said, and followed the Bumpy Man out when he opened the door. Then she exclaimed: "Why, it isn't cold a bit!"

"Of course not," replied the man. "It was cold last night, before the snowstorm; but snow, when it falls, is always crisp and warm."

Trot gathered a handful of it.

"Why, it's popcorn!" she cried.

"Certainly; all snow is popcorn. What did you expect it to be?"

"Popcorn is not snow in my country."

"Well, it is the only snow we have in the Land of Mo, so you may as well make the best of it," said he, a little impatiently. "I'm not responsible for the absurd things that happen in your country, and when you're in Mo you must do as the Momen do. Eat some of our snow, and you will find it is good. The only fault I find with our snow is that we get too much of it at times."

With this the Bumpy Man set to work shoveling a path and he was so quick and industrious that he piled up the popcorn in great banks on either side of the trail that led to the mountain-top from the plains below. While he worked, Trot ate popcorn and found it crisp and slightly warm, as well as nicely salted and buttered. Presently Cap'n Bill came out of the house and joined her.

"What's this?" he asked.

"Mo snow," said she. "But it isn't real snow, although it falls from the sky. It's popcorn."

Cap'n Bill tasted it; then he sat down in the path and began to eat. The Ork came out and pecked away with its bill as fast as it could. They all liked popcorn and they all were hungry this morning.

Meantime the flakes of "Mo snow" came down so fast that the number of them almost darkened the air. The Bumpy Man was now shoveling quite a distance down the mountain-side, while the path behind him rapidly filled up with fresh-fallen popcorn. Suddenly Trot heard him call out:

"Goodness gracious—mince pie and pancakes!—here is some one buried in the snow."

She ran toward him at once and the others followed, wading through the corn and crunching it underneath their feet. The Mo snow was pretty deep where the Bumpy Man was shoveling and from beneath a great bank of it he had uncovered a pair of feet.

"Dear me! Someone has been lost in the storm," said Cap'n Bill. "I hope he is still alive. Let's pull him out and see."

He took hold of one foot and the Bumpy Man took hold of the other. Then they both pulled and out from the heap of popcorn came a little boy. He was dressed in a brown velvet jacket and knickerbockers, with brown stockings, buckled shoes and a blue shirt-waist that had frills down its front. When drawn from the heap the boy was chewing a mouthful of popcorn and both his hands were full of it. So at first he

couldn't speak to his rescuers but lay quite still and eyed them calmly until he had swallowed his mouthful. Then he said:

"Get my cap," and stuffed more popcorn into his mouth.

While the Bumpy Man began shoveling into the corn-bank to find the boy's cap, Trot was laughing joyfully and Cap'n Bill had a broad grin on his face. The Ork looked from one to another and asked:

"Who is this stranger?"

"Why, it's Button-Bright, of course," answered Trot. "If anyone ever finds a lost boy, he can make up his mind it's Button-Bright. But how he ever came to be lost in this far-away country is more'n I can make out."

"Where does he belong?" inquired the Ork.

"His home used to be in Philadelphia, I think; but I'm quite sure Button-Bright doesn't belong anywhere."

"That's right," said the boy, nodding his head as he swallowed the second mouthful.

"Everyone belongs somewhere," remarked the Ork.

"Not me," insisted Button-Bright. "I'm half way 'round the world from Philadelphia, and I've lost my Magic Umbrella, that used to carry me anywhere. Stands to reason that if I can't get back I haven't any home. But I don't care much. This is a pretty good country, Trot. I've had lots of fun here."

By this time the Mountain Ear had secured the boy's cap and was listening to the conversation with much interest.

"It seems you know this poor, snow-covered cast-away," he said.

"Yes, indeed," answered Trot. "We made a journey together to Sky Island, once, and were good friends."

"Well, then I'm glad I saved his life," said the Bumpy Man.

"Much obliged, Mr. Knobs," said Button-Bright, sitting up and staring at him, "but I don't believe you've saved anything except some popcorn that I might have eaten had you not disturbed me. It was nice and warm in that bank of popcorn, and there was plenty to eat. What made you dig me out? And what makes you so bumpy everywhere?"

"As for the bumps," replied the man, looking at himself with much pride, "I was born with them and I suspect they were a gift from the fairies. They make me look rugged and big, like the mountain I serve."

"All right," said Button-Bright and began eating popcorn again.

It had stopped snowing, now, and great flocks of birds were gathering around the mountain-side, eating the popcorn with much eagerness and scarcely noticing the people at all. There were birds of every size and color, most of them having gorgeous feathers and plumes.

"Just look at them!" exclaimed the Ork scornfully. "Aren't they dreadful creatures, all covered with feathers?"

"I think they're beautiful," said Trot, and this made the Ork so indignant that he went back into the house and sulked.

Button-Bright reached out his hand and caught a big bird by the leg. At once it rose into the air and it was so strong that it nearly carried the little boy with it. He let go the leg in a hurry and the bird flew down again and began to eat of the popcorn, not being frightened in the least.

This gave Cap'n Bill an idea. He felt in his pocket and drew out several pieces of stout string. Moving very quietly, so as to not alarm the birds, he crept up to several of the biggest ones and tied cords around their legs, thus making them prisoners. The birds were so intent on their eating that they did not notice what had happened to them, and when about twenty had been captured in this manner Cap'n Bill tied the ends of all the strings together and fastened them to a huge stone, so they could not escape.

The Bumpy Man watched the old sailor's actions with much curiosity.

"The birds will be quiet until they've eaten up all the snow," he said, "but then they will want to fly away to their homes. Tell me, sir, what will the poor things do when they find they can't fly?"

"It may worry 'em a little," replied Cap'n Bill, "but they're not going to be hurt if they take it easy and behave themselves."

Our friends had all made a good breakfast of the delicious popcorn and now they walked toward the house again. Button-Bright walked beside Trot and held her hand in his, because they were old friends and he liked the little girl very much. The boy was not so old as Trot, and small as she was he was half a head shorter in height. The most remarkable thing about Button-Bright was that he was always quiet and composed, whatever happened, and nothing was ever able to astonish him. Trot liked him because he was not rude and never tried to plague her. Cap'n Bill liked him because he had found the boy cheerful and brave at all times, and willing to do anything he was asked to do.

When they came to the house Trot sniffed the air and asked: "Don't I smell perfume?"

"I think you do," said the Bumpy Man. "You smell violets, and that proves there is a breeze springing up from the south. All our winds and breezes are perfumed and for that reason we are glad to have them blow in our direction. The south breeze always has a violet odor; the north breeze has the fragrance of wild roses; the east breeze is perfumed with lilies-of-the-valley and the west wind with lilac blossoms. So we need no weathervane to tell us which way the wind is blowing. We have only to smell the perfume and it informs us at once."

Inside the house they found the Ork, and Button-Bright regarded the strange, bird-like creature with curious interest. After examining it closely for a time he asked:

"Which way does your tail whirl?"

"Either way," said the Ork.

Button-Bright put out his hand and tried to spin it.

"Don't do that!" exclaimed the Ork.

"Why not?" inquired the boy.

"Because it happens to be my tail, and I reserve the right to whirl it myself," explained the Ork.

"Let's go out and fly somewhere," proposed Button-Bright. "I want to see how the tail works."

"Not now," said the Ork. "I appreciate your interest in me, which I fully deserve; but I only fly when I am going somewhere, and if I got started I might not stop."

"That reminds me," remarked Cap'n Bill, "to ask you, friend Ork, how we are going to get away from here?"

"Get away!" exclaimed the Bumpy Man. "Why don't you stay here? You won't find any nicer place than Mo."

"Have you been anywhere else, sir?"

"No; I can't say that I have," admitted the Mountain Ear.

"Then permit me to say you're no judge," declared Cap'n Bill. "But you haven't answered my question, friend Ork. How are we to get away from this mountain?"

The Ork reflected a while before he answered.

"I might carry one of you—the boy or the girl—upon my back," said he, "but three big people are more than I can manage, although I have carried two of you for a short distance. You ought not to have eaten those purple berries so soon."

"P'r'aps we did make a mistake," Cap'n Bill acknowledged.

"Or we might have brought some of those lavender berries with us, instead of so many purple ones," suggested Trot regretfully.

Cap'n Bill made no reply to this statement, which showed he did not fully agree with the little girl; but he fell into deep thought, with wrinkled brows, and finally he said:

"If those purple berries would make anything grow bigger, whether it'd eaten the lavender ones or not, I could find a way out of our troubles."

They did not understand this speech and looked at the old sailor as if expecting him to explain what he meant. But just then a chorus of shrill cries rose from outside.

"Here! Let me go—let me go!" the voices seemed to say. "Why are we insulted in this way? Mountain Ear, come and help us!"

Trot ran to the window and looked out.

"It's the birds you caught, Cap'n," she said. "I didn't know they could talk."

"Oh, yes; all the birds in Mo are educated to talk," said the Bumpy Man. Then he looked at Cap'n Bill uneasily and added: "Won't you let the poor things go?"

"I'll see," replied the sailor, and walked out to where the birds were fluttering and complaining because the strings would not allow them to fly away.

"Listen to me!" he cried, and at once they became still. "We three people who are strangers in your land want to go to some other country, and we want three of you

birds to carry us there. We know we are asking a great favor, but it's the only way we can think of—excep' walkin', an' I'm not much good at that because I've a wooden leg. Besides, Trot an' Button-Bright are too small to undertake a long and tiresome journey. Now, tell me: Which three of you birds will consent to carry us?"

The birds looked at one another as if greatly astonished. Then one of them replied:

"You must be crazy, old man. Not one of us is big enough to fly with even the smallest of your party."

"I'll fix the matter of size," promised Cap'n Bill. "If three of you will agree to carry us, I'll make you big an' strong enough to do it, so it won't worry you a bit."

The birds considered this gravely. Living in a magic country, they had no doubt but that the strange one-legged man could do what he said. After a little, one of them asked:

"If you make us big, would we stay big always?"

"I think so," replied Cap'n Bill.

They chattered a while among themselves and then the bird that had first spoken said: "I'll go, for one."

"So will I," said another; and after a pause a third said: "I'll go, too."

Perhaps more would have volunteered, for it seemed that for some reason they all longed to be bigger than they were; but three were enough for Cap'n Bill's purpose and so he promptly released all the others, who immediately flew away.

The three that remained were cousins, and all were of the same brilliant plumage and in size about as large as eagles. When Trot questioned them she found they were quite young, having only abandoned their nests a few weeks before. They were strong young birds, with clear, brave eyes, and the little girl decided they were the most beautiful of all the feathered creatures she had ever seen.

Cap'n Bill now took from his pocket the wooden box with the sliding cover and removed the three purple berries, which were still in good condition.

"Eat these," he said, and gave one to each of the birds. They obeyed, finding the fruit very pleasant to taste. In a few seconds they began to grow in size and grew so fast that Trot feared they would never stop. But they finally did stop growing, and then they were much larger than the Ork, and nearly the size of full-grown ostriches.

Cap'n Bill was much pleased by this result.

"You can carry us now, all right," said he.

The birds strutted around with pride, highly pleased with their immense size.

"I don't see, though," said Trot doubtfully, "how we're going to ride on their backs without falling off."

"We're not going to ride on their backs," answered Cap'n Bill. "I'm going to make swings for us to ride in."

He then asked the Bumpy Man for some rope, but the man had no rope. He had, however, an old suit of gray clothes which he gladly presented to Cap'n Bill, who cut the cloth into strips and twisted it so that it was almost as strong as rope. With this material he attached to each bird a swing that dangled below its feet, and Button-Bright made a trial flight in one of them to prove that it was safe and comfortable. When all this had been arranged one of the birds asked:

"Where do you wish us to take you?"

"Why, just follow the Ork," said Cap'n Bill. "He will be our leader, and wherever the Ork flies you are to fly, and wherever the Ork lands you are to land. Is that satisfactory?"

The birds declared it was quite satisfactory, so Cap'n Bill took counsel with the Ork.

"On our way here," said that peculiar creature, "I noticed a broad, sandy desert at the left of me, on which was no living thing."

"Then we'd better keep away from it," replied the sailor.

"Not so," insisted the Ork. "I have found, on my travels, that the most pleasant countries often lie in the midst of deserts; so I think it would be wise for us to fly over this desert and discover what lies beyond it. For in the direction we came from lies the ocean, as we well know, and beyond here is this strange Land of Mo, which we do not care to explore. On one side, as we can see from this mountain, is a broad expanse of plain, and on the other the desert. For my part, I vote for the desert."

"What do you say, Trot?" inquired Cap'n Bill.

"It's all the same to me," she replied.

No one thought of asking Button-Bright's opinion, so it was decided to fly over the desert. They bade good-bye to the Bumpy Man and thanked him for his kindness and hospitality. Then they seated themselves in the swings—one for each bird—and told the Ork to start away and they would follow.

The whirl of the Ork's tail astonished the birds at first, but after he had gone a short distance they rose in the air, carrying their passengers easily, and flew with strong, regular strokes of their great wings in the wake of their leader.

CHAPTER IX

THE KINGDOM OF JINXLAND

Trot rode with more comfort than she had expected, although the swing swayed so much that she had to hold on tight with both hands. Cap'n Bill's bird followed the Ork, and Trot came next, with Button-Bright trailing behind her. It was quite an imposing procession, but unfortunately there was no one to see it, for the Ork had headed straight for the great sandy desert and in a few minutes after starting they were flying high over the broad waste, where no living thing could exist.

The little girl thought this would be a bad place for the birds to lose strength, or for the cloth ropes to give way; but although she could not help feeling a trifle nervous and fidgety she had confidence in the huge and brilliantly plumaged bird that bore her, as well as in Cap'n Bill's knowledge of how to twist and fasten a rope so it would hold.

That was a remarkably big desert. There was nothing to relieve the monotony of view and every minute seemed an hour and every hour a day. Disagreeable fumes and gases rose from the sands, which would have been deadly to the travelers had they not been so high in the air. As it was, Trot was beginning to feel sick, when a breath of fresher air filled her nostrils and on looking ahead she saw a great cloud of pink-tinted mist. Even while she wondered what it could be, the Ork plunged boldly into the mist and the other birds followed. She could see nothing for a time, nor could the bird which carried her see where the Ork had gone, but it kept flying as sturdily as ever and in a few moments the mist was passed and the girl saw a most beautiful landscape spread out below her, extending as far as her eye could reach.

She saw bits of forest, verdure clothed hills, fields of waving grain, fountains, rivers and lakes; and throughout the scene were scattered groups of pretty houses and a few grand castles and palaces.

Over all this delightful landscape—which from Trot's high perch seemed like a magnificent painted picture—was a rosy glow such as we sometimes see in the west at sunset. In this case, however, it was not in the west only, but everywhere.

No wonder the Ork paused to circle slowly over this lovely country. The other birds followed his action, all eyeing the place with equal delight. Then, as with one accord, the four formed a group and slowly sailed downward. This brought them to that part of the newly-discovered land which bordered on the desert's edge; but it was just as pretty here as anywhere, so the Ork and the birds alighted and the three passengers at once got out of their swings.

"Oh, Cap'n Bill, isn't this fine an' dandy?" exclaimed Trot rapturously. "How lucky we were to discover this beautiful country!"

"The country seems rather high class, I'll admit, Trot," replied the old sailorman, looking around him, "but we don't know, as yet, what its people are like."

"No one could live in such a country without being happy and good—I'm sure of that," she said earnestly. "Don't you think so, Button-Bright?"

"I'm not thinking, just now," answered the little boy. "It tires me to think, and I never seem to gain anything by it. When we see the people who live here we will know what they are like, and no 'mount of thinking will make them any different."

"That's true enough," said the Ork. "But now I want to make a proposal. While you are getting acquainted with this new country, which looks as if it contains everything to make one happy, I would like to fly along—all by myself—and see if I can find my home on the other side of the great desert. If I do, I will stay there, of course. But if I fail to find Orkland I will return to you in a week, to see if I can do anything more to assist you."

They were sorry to lose their queer companion, but could offer no objection to the plan; so the Ork bade them good-bye and rising swiftly in the air, he flew over the country and was soon lost to view in the distance.

The three birds which had carried our friends now begged permission to return by the way they had come, to their own homes, saying they were anxious to show their families how big they had become. So Cap'n Bill and Trot and Button-Bright all thanked them gratefully for their assistance and soon the birds began their long flight toward the Land of Mo.

Being now left to themselves in this strange land, the three comrades selected a pretty pathway and began walking along it. They believed this path would lead them to a splendid castle which they espied in the distance, the turrets of which towered far above the tops of the trees which surrounded it. It did not seem very far away, so they sauntered on slowly, admiring the beautiful ferns and flowers that lined the pathway and listening to the singing of the birds and the soft chirping of the grasshoppers.

Presently the path wound over a little hill. In a valley that lay beyond the hill was a tiny cottage surrounded by flower beds and fruit trees. On the shady porch of the cottage they saw, as they approached, a pleasant faced woman sitting amidst a group of children, to whom she was telling stories. The children quickly discovered the strangers and ran toward them with exclamations of astonishment, so that Trot and her friends became the center of a curious group, all chattering excitedly. Cap'n Bill's wooden leg seemed to arouse the wonder of the children, as they could not understand why he had not two meat legs. This attention seemed to please the old sailor, who patted the heads of the children kindly and then, raising his hat to the woman, he inquired:

"Can you tell us, madam, just what country this is?"

She stared hard at all three of the strangers as she replied briefly: "Jinxland."

"Oh!" exclaimed Cap'n Bill, with a puzzled look. "And where is Jinxland, please?"

"In the Quadling Country," said she.

"What!" cried Trot, in sudden excitement. "Do you mean to say this is the Quadling Country of the Land of Oz?"

"To be sure I do," the woman answered. "Every bit of land that is surrounded by the great desert is the Land of Oz, as you ought to know as well as I do; but I'm sorry to say that Jinxland is separated from the rest of the Quadling Country by that row of high mountains you see yonder, which have such steep sides that no one can cross them. So we live here all by ourselves, and are ruled by our own King, instead of by Ozma of Oz."

"I've been to the Land of Oz before," said Button-Bright, "but I've never been here."

"Did you ever hear of Jinxland before?" asked Trot.

"No," said Button-Bright.

"It is on the Map of Oz, though," asserted the woman, "and it's a fine country, I assure you. If only," she added, and then paused to look around her with a frightened expression. "If only—" here she stopped again, as if not daring to go on with her speech.

"If only what, ma'am?" asked Cap'n Bill.

The woman sent the children into the house. Then she came closer to the strangers and whispered: "If only we had a different King, we would be very happy and contented."

"What's the matter with your King?" asked Trot, curiously. But the woman seemed frightened to have said so much. She retreated to her porch, merely saying:

"The King punishes severely any treason on the part of his subjects."

"What's treason?" asked Button-Bright.

"In this case," replied Cap'n Bill, "treason seems to consist of knockin' the King; but I guess we know his disposition now as well as if the lady had said more."

"I wonder," said Trot, going up to the woman, "if you could spare us something to eat. We haven't had anything but popcorn and lemonade for a long time."

"Bless your heart! Of course I can spare you some food," the woman answered, and entering her cottage she soon returned with a tray loaded with sandwiches, cakes and cheese. One of the children drew a bucket of clear, cold water from a spring and the three wanderers ate heartily and enjoyed the good things immensely.

When Button-Bright could eat no more he filled the pockets of his jacket with cakes and cheese, and not even the children objected to this. Indeed, they all seemed pleased to see the strangers eat, so Cap'n Bill decided that no matter what the King of Jinxland was like, the people would prove friendly and hospitable.

"Whose castle is that, yonder, ma'am?" he asked, waving his hand toward the towers that rose above the trees.

"It belongs to his Majesty, King Krewl." she said.

"Oh, indeed; and does he live there?"

"When he is not out hunting with his fierce courtiers and war captains," she replied.

"Is he hunting now?" Trot inquired.

"I do not know, my dear. The less we know about the King's actions the safer we are."

It was evident the woman did not like to talk about King Krewl and so, having finished their meal, they said good-bye and continued along the pathway.

"Don't you think we'd better keep away from that King's castle, Cap'n?" asked Trot.

"Well," said he, "King Krewl would find out, sooner or later, that we are in his country, so we may as well face the music now. Perhaps he isn't quite so bad as that woman thinks he is. Kings aren't always popular with their people, you know, even if they do the best they know how."

"Ozma is pop'lar," said Button-Bright.

"Ozma is diff'rent from any other Ruler, from all I've heard," remarked Trot musingly, as she walked beside the boy. "And, after all, we are really in the Land of Oz, where Ozma rules ev'ry King and ev'rybody else. I never heard of anybody getting hurt in her dominions, did you, Button-Bright?"

"Not when she knows about it," he replied. "But those birds landed us in just the wrong place, seems to me. They might have carried us right on, over that row of mountains, to the Em'rald City."

"True enough," said Cap'n Bill; "but they didn't, an' so we must make the best of Jinxland. Let's try not to be afraid."

"Oh, I'm not very scared," said Button-Bright, pausing to look at a pink rabbit that popped its head out of a hole in the field near by.

"Nor am I," added Trot. "Really, Cap'n, I'm so glad to be anywhere at all in the wonderful Fairyland of Oz that I think I'm the luckiest girl in all the world. Dorothy lives in the Em'rald City, you know, and so does the Scarecrow and the Tin Woodman and Tik-Tok and the Shaggy Man—and all the rest of 'em that we've heard so much about—not to mention Ozma, who must be the sweetest and loveliest girl in all the world!"

"Take your time, Trot," advised Button-Bright. "You don't have to say it all in one breath, you know. And you haven't mentioned half of the curious people in the Em'rald City."

"That 'ere Em'rald City," said Cap'n Bill impressively, "happens to be on the other side o' those mountains, that we're told no one is able to cross. I don't want to discourage of you, Trot, but we're a'most as much separated from your Ozma an' Dorothy as we were when we lived in Californy."

There was so much truth in this statement that they all walked on in silence for some time. Finally they reached the grove of stately trees that bordered the grounds of the King's castle. They had gone halfway through it when the sound of sobbing, as of someone in bitter distress, reached their ears and caused them to halt abruptly.

CHAPTER X

PON, THE GARDENER'S BOY

It was Button-Bright who first discovered, lying on his face beneath a broad spreading tree near the pathway, a young man whose body shook with the force of his sobs. He was dressed in a long brown smock and had sandals on his feet, betokening one in humble life. His head was bare and showed a shock of brown, curly hair. Button-Bright looked down on the young man and said:

"Who cares, anyhow?"

"I do!" cried the young man, interrupting his sobs to roll over, face upward, that he might see who had spoken. "I care, for my heart is broken!"

"Can't you get another one?" asked the little boy.

"I don't want another!" wailed the young man.

By this time Trot and Cap'n Bill arrived at the spot and the girl leaned over and said in a sympathetic voice:

"Tell us your troubles and perhaps we may help you."

The youth sat up, then, and bowed politely. Afterward he got upon his feet, but still kept wringing his hands as he tried to choke down his sobs. Trot thought he was very brave to control such awful agony so well.

"My name is Pon," he began. "I'm the gardener's boy."

"Then the gardener of the King is your father, I suppose," said Trot.

"Not my father, but my master," was the reply

"I do the work and the gardener gives the orders. And it was not my fault, in the least, that the Princess Gloria fell in love with me."

"Did she, really?" asked the little girl.

"I don't see why," remarked Button-Bright, staring at the youth.

"And who may the Princess Gloria be?" inquired Cap'n Bill.

"She is the niece of King Krewl, who is her guardian. The Princess lives in the castle and is the loveliest and sweetest maiden in all Jinxland. She is fond of flowers and used to walk in the gardens with her attendants. At such times, if I was working at my tasks, I used to cast down my eyes as Gloria passed me; but one day I glanced up and found her gazing at me with a very tender look in her eyes. The next day she dismissed her attendants and, coming to my side, began to talk with me. She said I had touched her heart as no other young man had ever done. I kissed her hand. Just then the King came around a bend in the walk. He struck me with his fist and kicked me with his foot. Then he seized the arm of the Princess and rudely dragged her into the castle."

"Wasn't he awful!" gasped Trot indignantly.

"He is a very abrupt King," said Pon, "so it was the least I could expect. Up to that time I had not thought of loving Princess Gloria, but realizing it would be impolite not to return her love, I did so. We met at evening, now and then, and she told me the King wanted her to marry a rich courtier named Googly-Goo, who is old enough to be Gloria's father. She has refused Googly-Goo thirty-nine times, but he still persists and has brought many rich presents to bribe the King. On that account King Krewl has commanded his niece to marry the old man, but the Princess has assured me, time and again, that she will wed only me. This morning we happened to meet in the grape arbor and as I was respectfully saluting the cheek of the Princess, two of the King's guards seized me and beat me terribly before the very eyes of Gloria, whom the King himself held back so she could not interfere."

"Why, this King must be a monster!" cried Trot.

"He is far worse than that," said Pon, mournfully.

"But, see here," interrupted Cap'n Bill, who had listened carefully to Pon. "This King may not be so much to blame, after all. Kings are proud folks, because they're so high an' mighty, an' it isn't reasonable for a royal Princess to marry a common gardener's boy."

"It isn't right," declared Button-Bright. "A Princess should marry a Prince."

"I'm not a common gardener's boy," protested Pon. "If I had my rights I would be the King instead of Krewl. As it is, I'm a Prince, and as royal as any man in Jinxland."

"How does that come?" asked Cap'n Bill.

"My father used to be the King and Krewl was his Prime Minister. But one day while out hunting, King Phearse—that was my father's name—had a quarrel with Krewl and tapped him gently on the nose with the knuckles of his closed hand. This so provoked the wicked Krewl that he tripped my father backward, so that he fell into a deep pond. At once Krewl threw in a mass of heavy stones, which so weighted down

my poor father that his body could not rise again to the surface. It is impossible to kill anyone in this land, as perhaps you know, but when my father was pressed down into the mud at the bottom of the deep pool and the stones held him so he could never escape, he was of no more use to himself or the world than if he had died. Knowing this, Krewl proclaimed himself King, taking possession of the royal castle and driving all my father's people out. I was a small boy, then, but when I grew up I became a gardener. I have served King Krewl without his knowing that I am the son of the same King Phearse whom he so cruelly made away with."

"My, but that's a terr'bly exciting story!" said Trot, drawing a long breath. "But tell us, Pon, who was Gloria's father?"

"Oh, he was the King before my father," replied Pon. "Father was Prime Minister for King Kynd, who was Gloria's father. She was only a baby when King Kynd fell into the Great Gulf that lies just this side of the mountains—the same mountains that separate Jinxland from the rest of the Land of Oz. It is said the Great Gulf has no bottom; but, however that may be, King Kynd has never been seen again and my father became King in his place."

"Seems to me," said Trot, "that if Gloria had her rights she would be Queen of Jinxland."

"Well, her father was a King," admitted Pon, "and so was my father; so we are of equal rank, although she's a great lady and I'm a humble gardener's boy. I can't see why we should not marry if we want to—except that King Krewl won't let us."

"It's a sort of mixed-up mess, taken altogether," remarked Cap'n Bill. "But we are on our way to visit King Krewl, and if we get a chance, young man, we'll put in a good word for you."

"Do, please!" begged Pon.

"Was it the flogging you got that broke your heart?" inquired Button-Bright.

"Why, it helped to break it, of course," said Pon.

"I'd get it fixed up, if I were you," advised the boy, tossing a pebble at a chipmunk in a tree. "You ought to give Gloria just as good a heart as she gives you."

"That's common sense," agreed Cap'n Bill. So they left the gardener's boy standing beside the path, and resumed their journey toward the castle.

CHAPTER XI

THE WICKED KING AND GOOGLY-GOO

WHEN OUR FRIENDS APPROACHED THE GREAT DOORWAY OF THE CASTLE THEY FOUND it guarded by several soldiers dressed in splendid uniforms. They were armed with swords and lances. Cap'n Bill walked straight up to them and asked:

"Does the King happen to be at home?"

"His Magnificent and Glorious Majesty, King Krewl, is at present inhabiting his Royal Castle," was the stiff reply.

"Then I guess we'll go in an' say how-d'ye-do," continued Cap'n Bill, attempting to enter the doorway. But a soldier barred his way with a lance.

"Who are you, what are your names, and where do you come from?" demanded the soldier.

"You wouldn't know if we told you," returned the sailor, "seein' as we're strangers in a strange land."

"Oh, if you are strangers you will be permitted to enter," said the soldier, lowering his lance. "His Majesty is very fond of strangers."

"Do many strangers come here?" asked Trot.

"You are the first that ever came to our country," said the man. "But his Majesty has often said that if strangers ever arrived in Jinxland he would see that they had a very exciting time."

Cap'n Bill scratched his chin thoughtfully. He wasn't very favorably impressed by this last remark. But he decided that as there was no way of escape from Jinxland it would be wise to confront the King boldly and try to win his favor. So they entered the castle, escorted by one of the soldiers.

It was certainly a fine castle, with many large rooms, all beautifully furnished. The passages were winding and handsomely decorated, and after following several of these the soldier led them into an open court that occupied the very center of the huge building. It was surrounded on every side by high turreted walls, and contained beds of flowers, fountains and walks of many colored marbles which were matched together in quaint designs. In an open space near the middle of the court they saw a group of courtiers and their ladies, who surrounded a lean man who wore upon his head a jeweled crown. His face was hard and sullen and through the slits of his half-closed eyelids the eyes glowed like coals of fire. He was dressed in brilliant satins and velvets and was seated in a golden throne-chair.

This personage was King Krewl, and as soon as Cap'n Bill saw him the old sailor knew at once that he was not going to like the King of Jinxland.

"Hello! who's here?" said his Majesty, with a deep scowl.

"Strangers, Sire," answered the soldier, bowing so low that his forehead touched the marble tiles.

"Strangers, eh? Well, well; what an unexpected visit! Advance, strangers, and give an account of yourselves."

The King's voice was as harsh as his features. Trot shuddered a little but Cap'n Bill calmly replied:

"There ain't much for us to say, 'cept as we've arrived to look over your country an' see how we like it. Judgin' from the way you speak, you don't know who we are, or you'd be jumpin' up to shake hands an' offer us seats. Kings usually treat us pretty well, in the great big Outside World where we come from, but in this little kingdom—which don't amount to much, anyhow—folks don't seem to 'a' got much culchure."

The King listened with amazement to this bold speech, first with a frown and then gazing at the two children and the old sailor with evident curiosity. The courtiers were dumb with fear, for no one had ever dared speak in such a manner to their self-willed, cruel King before. His Majesty, however, was somewhat frightened, for cruel people are always cowards, and he feared these mysterious strangers might possess magic powers that would destroy him unless he treated them well.

So he commanded his people to give the new arrivals seats, and they obeyed with trembling haste.

After being seated, Cap'n Bill lighted his pipe and began puffing smoke from it, a sight so strange to them that it filled them all with wonder. Presently the King asked:

"How did you penetrate to this hidden country? Did you cross the desert or the mountains?"

"Desert," answered Cap'n Bill, as if the task were too easy to be worth talking about.

"Indeed! No one has ever been able to do that before," said the King.

"Well, it's easy enough, if you know how," asserted Cap'n Bill, so carelessly that it greatly impressed his hearers. The King shifted in his throne uneasily. He was more afraid of these strangers than before.

"Do you intend to stay long in Jinxland?" was his next anxious question.

"Depends on how we like it," said Cap'n Bill. "Just now I might suggest to your Majesty to order some rooms got ready for us in your dinky little castle here. And a royal banquet, with some fried onions an' pickled tripe, would set easy on our stomicks an' make us a bit happier than we are now."

"Your wishes shall be attended to," said King Krewl, but his eyes flashed from between their slits in a wicked way that made Trot hope the food wouldn't be poisoned. At the King's command several of his attendants hastened away to give the proper orders to the castle servants and no sooner were they gone than a skinny old man entered the courtyard and bowed before the King.

This disagreeable person was dressed in rich velvets, with many furbelows and laces. He was covered with golden chains, finely wrought rings and jeweled ornaments.

He walked with mincing steps and glared at all the courtiers as if he considered himself far superior to any or all of them.

"Well, well, your Majesty; what news—what news?" he demanded, in a shrill, cracked voice.

The King gave him a surly look.

"No news, Lord Googly-Goo, except that strangers have arrived," he said.

Googly-Goo cast a contemptuous glance at Cap'n Bill and a disdainful one at Trot and Button-Bright. Then he said:

"Strangers do not interest me, your Majesty. But the Princess Gloria is very interesting—very interesting, indeed! What does she say, Sire? Will she marry me?"

"Ask her," retorted the King.

"I have, many times; and every time she has refused."

"Well?" said the King harshly.

"Well," said Googly-Goo in a jaunty tone, "a bird that *can* sing, and *won't* sing, must be *made* to sing."

"Huh!" sneered the King. "That's easy, with a bird; but a girl is harder to manage."

"Still," persisted Googly-Goo, "we must overcome difficulties. The chief trouble is that Gloria fancies she loves that miserable gardener's boy, Pon. Suppose we throw Pon into the Great Gulf, your Majesty?"

"It would do you no good," returned the King. "She would still love him."

"Too bad, too bad!" sighed Googly-Goo. "I have laid aside more than a bushel of precious gems—each worth a King's ransom—to present to your Majesty on the day I wed Gloria."

The King's eyes sparkled, for he loved wealth above everything; but the next moment he frowned deeply again.

"It won't help us to kill Pon," he muttered. "What we must do is kill Gloria's love for Pon."

"That is better, if you can find a way to do it," agreed Googly-Goo. "Everything would come right if you could kill Gloria's love for that gardener's boy. Really, Sire, now that I come to think of it, there must be fully a bushel and a half of those jewels!"

Just then a messenger entered the court to say that the banquet was prepared for the strangers. So Cap'n Bill, Trot and Button-Bright entered the castle and were taken to a room where a fine feast was spread upon the table.

"I don't like that Lord Googly-Goo," remarked Trot as she was busily eating.

"Nor I," said Cap'n Bill. "But from the talk we heard I guess the gardener's boy won't get the Princess."

"Perhaps not," returned the girl; "but I hope old Googly doesn't get her, either."

"The King means to sell her for all those jewels," observed Button-Bright, his mouth half full of cake and jam.

"Poor Princess!" sighed Trot. "I'm sorry for her, although I've never seen her. But if she says no to Googly-Goo, and means it, what can they do?"

"Don't let us worry about a strange Princess," advised Cap'n Bill. "I've a notion we're not too safe, ourselves, with this cruel King."

The two children felt the same way and all three were rather solemn during the remainder of the meal.

When they had eaten, the servants escorted them to their rooms. Cap'n Bill's room was way to one end of the castle, very high up, and Trot's room was at the opposite end, rather low down. As for Button-Bright, they placed him in the middle, so that all were as far apart as they could possibly be. They didn't like this arrangement very well, but all the rooms were handsomely furnished and being guests of the King they dared not complain.

After the strangers had left the courtyard the King and Googly-Goo had a long talk together, and the King said:

"I cannot force Gloria to marry you just now, because those strangers may interfere. I suspect that the wooden-legged man possesses great magical powers, or he would never have been able to carry himself and those children across the deadly desert."

"I don't like him; he looks dangerous," answered Googly-Goo. "But perhaps you are mistaken about his being a wizard. Why don't you test his powers?"

"How?" asked the King.

"Send for the Wicked Witch. She will tell you in a moment whether that wooden-legged person is a common man or a magician."

"Ha! that's a good idea," cried the King. "Why didn't I think of the Wicked Witch before? But the woman demands rich rewards for her services."

"Never mind; I will pay her," promised the wealthy Googly-Goo.

So a servant was dispatched to summon the Wicked Witch, who lived but a few leagues from King Krewl's castle. While they awaited her, the withered old courtier proposed that they pay a visit to Princess Gloria and see if she was not now in a more complaisant mood. So the two started away together and searched the castle over without finding Gloria.

At last Googly-Goo suggested she might be in the rear garden, which was a large park filled with bushes and trees and surrounded by a high wall. And what was their anger, when they turned a corner of the path, to find in a quiet nook the beautiful Princess, and kneeling before her, Pon, the gardener's boy!

With a roar of rage the King dashed forward; but Pon had scaled the wall by means of a ladder, which still stood in its place, and when he saw the King coming he ran up the ladder and made good his escape. But this left Gloria confronted by her angry guardian, the King, and by old Googly-Goo, who was trembling with a fury he could not express in words.

Seizing the Princess by her arm the King dragged her back to the castle. Pushing her into a room on the lower floor he locked the door upon the unhappy girl. And at that moment the arrival of the Wicked Witch was announced.

Hearing this, the King smiled, as a tiger smiles, showing his teeth. And Googly-Goo smiled, as a serpent smiles, for he had no teeth except a couple of fangs. And having frightened each other with these smiles the two dreadful men went away to the Royal Council Chamber to meet the Wicked Witch.

CHAPTER XII

THE WOODEN-LEGGED GRASSHOPPER

Now it so happened that Trot, from the window of her room, had witnessed the meeting of the lovers in the garden and had seen the King come and drag Gloria away. The little girl's heart went out in sympathy for the poor Princess, who seemed to her to be one of the sweetest and loveliest young ladies she had ever seen, so she crept along the passages and from a hidden niche saw Gloria locked in her room.

The key was still in the lock, so when the King had gone away, followed by Googly-Goo, Trot stole up to the door, turned the key and entered. The Princess lay prone upon a couch, sobbing bitterly. Trot went up to her and smoothed her hair and tried to comfort her.

"Don't cry," she said. "I've unlocked the door, so you can go away any time you want to."

"It isn't that," sobbed the Princess. "I am unhappy because they will not let me love Pon, the gardener's boy!"

"Well, never mind; Pon isn't any great shakes, anyhow, seems to me," said Trot soothingly. "There are lots of other people you can love."

Gloria rolled over on the couch and looked at the little girl reproachfully.

"Pon has won my heart, and I can't help loving him," she explained. Then with sudden indignation she added: "But I'll never love Googly-Goo—never, as long as I live!"

"I should say not!" replied Trot. "Pon may not be much good, but old Googly is very, very bad. Hunt around, and I'm sure you'll find someone worth your love. You're very pretty, you know, and almost anyone ought to love you."

"You don't understand, my dear," said Gloria, as she wiped the tears from her eyes with a dainty lace handkerchief bordered with pearls. "When you are older you will realize that a young lady cannot decide whom she will love, or choose the most worthy. Her heart alone decides for her, and whomsoever her heart selects, she must love, whether he amounts to much or not."

Trot was a little puzzled by this speech, which seemed to her unreasonable; but she made no reply and presently Gloria's grief softened and she began to question the little girl about herself and her adventures. Trot told her how they had happened to come to Jinxland, and all about Cap'n Bill and the Ork and Pessim and the Bumpy Man.

While they were thus conversing together, getting more and more friendly as they became better acquainted, in the Council Chamber the King and Googly-Goo were talking with the Wicked Witch.

This evil creature was old and ugly. She had lost one eye and wore a black patch over it, so the people of Jinxland had named her "Blinkie." Of course witches are forbidden to exist in the Land of Oz, but Jinxland was so far removed from the center of Ozma's dominions, and so absolutely cut off from it by the steep mountains and the bottomless gulf, that the Laws of Oz were not obeyed very well in that country. So there were several witches in Jinxland who were the terror of the people, but King Krewl favored them and permitted them to exercise their evil sorcery.

Blinkie was the leader of all the other witches and therefore the most hated and feared. The King used her witchcraft at times to assist him in carrying out his cruelties and revenge, but he was always obliged to pay Blinkie large sums of money or heaps of precious jewels before she would undertake an enchantment. This made him hate the old woman almost as much as his subjects did, but to-day Lord Googly-Goo had agreed to pay the witch's price, so the King greeted her with gracious favor.

"Can you destroy the love of Princess Gloria for the gardener's boy?" inquired his Majesty.

The Wicked Witch thought about it before she replied:

"That's a hard question to answer. I can do lots of clever magic, but love is a stubborn thing to conquer. When you think you've killed it, it's liable to bob up again as strong as ever. I believe love and cats have nine lives. In other words, killing love is a hard job, even for a skillful witch, but I believe I can do something that will answer your purpose just as well."

"What is that?" asked the King.

"I can freeze the girl's heart. I've got a special incantation for that, and when Gloria's heart is thoroughly frozen she can no longer love Pon."

"Just the thing!" exclaimed Googly-Goo, and the King was likewise much pleased.

They bargained a long time as to the price, but finally the old courtier agreed to pay the Wicked Witch's demands. It was arranged that they should take Gloria to Blinkie's house the next day, to have her heart frozen.

Then King Krewl mentioned to the old hag the strangers who had that day arrived in Jinxland, and said to her:

"I think the two children—the boy and the girl—are unable to harm me, but I have a suspicion that the wooden-legged man is a powerful wizard."

The witch's face wore a troubled look when she heard this.

"If you are right," she said, "this wizard might spoil my incantation and interfere with me in other ways. So it will be best for me to meet this stranger at once and match my magic against his, to decide which is the stronger."

"All right," said the King. "Come with me and I will lead you to the man's room."

Googly-Goo did not accompany them, as he was obliged to go home to get the money and jewels he had promised to pay old Blinkie, so the other two climbed several flights of stairs and went through many passages until they came to the room occupied by Cap'n Bill.

The sailor-man, finding his bed soft and inviting, and being tired with the adventures he had experienced, had decided to take a nap. When the Wicked Witch and the King softly opened his door and entered, Cap'n Bill was snoring with such vigor that he did not hear them at all.

Blinkie approached the bed and with her one eye anxiously stared at the sleeping stranger.

"Ah," she said in a soft whisper, "I believe you are right, King Krewl. The man looks to me like a very powerful wizard. But by good luck I have caught him asleep, so I shall transform him before he wakes up, giving him such a form that he will be unable to oppose me."

"Careful!" cautioned the King, also speaking low. "If he discovers what you are doing he may destroy you, and that would annoy me because I need you to attend to Gloria."

But the Wicked Witch realized as well as he did that she must be careful. She carried over her arm a black bag, from which she now drew several packets carefully wrapped in paper. Three of these she selected, replacing the others in the bag. Two of the packets she mixed together and then she cautiously opened the third.

"Better stand back, your Majesty," she advised, "for if this powder falls on you you might be transformed yourself."

The King hastily retreated to the end of the room. As Blinkie mixed the third powder with the others she waved her hands over it, mumbled a few words, and then backed away as quickly as she could.

Cap'n Bill was slumbering peacefully, all unconscious of what was going on. Puff! A great cloud of smoke rolled over the bed and completely hid him from view. When the smoke rolled away, both Blinkie and the King saw that the body of the stranger had quite disappeared, while in his place, crouching in the middle of the bed, was a little gray grasshopper.

One curious thing about this grasshopper was that the last joint of its left leg was made of wood. Another curious thing—considering it was a grasshopper—was that it began talking, crying out in a tiny but sharp voice:

"Here—you people! What do you mean by treating me so? Put me back where I belong, at once, or you'll be sorry!"

The cruel King turned pale at hearing the grasshopper's threats, but the Wicked Witch merely laughed in derision. Then she raised her stick and aimed a vicious blow at the grasshopper, but before the stick struck the bed the tiny hopper made a marvelous jump—marvelous, indeed, when we consider that it had a wooden leg. It rose in the air and sailed across the room and passed right through the open window, where it disappeared from their view.

"Good!" shouted the King. "We are well rid of this desperate wizard." And then they both laughed heartily at the success of the incantation, and went away to complete their horrid plans.

After Trot had visited a time with Princess Gloria, the little girl went to Button-Bright's room but did not find him there. Then she went to Cap'n Bill's room, but he was not there because the witch and the King had been there before her. So she made her way downstairs and questioned the servants. They said they had seen the little boy

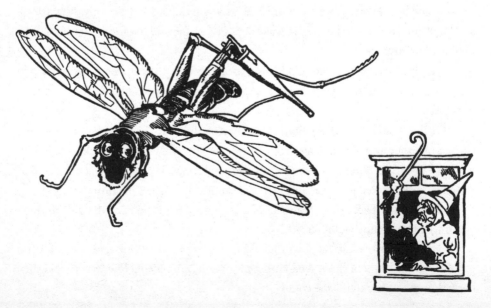

go out into the garden, some time ago, but the old man with the wooden leg they had not seen at all.

Therefore Trot, not knowing what else to do, rambled through the great gardens, seeking for Button-Bright or Cap'n Bill and not finding either of them. This part of the garden, which lay before the castle, was not walled in, but extended to the roadway, and the paths were open to the edge of the forest; so, after two hours of vain search for her friends, the little girl returned to the castle.

But at the doorway a soldier stopped her.

"I live here," said Trot, "so it's all right to let me in. The King has given me a room."

"Well, he has taken it back again," was the soldier's reply. "His Majesty's orders are to turn you away if you attempt to enter. I am also ordered to forbid the boy, your companion, to again enter the King's castle."

"How 'bout Cap'n Bill?" she inquired.

"Why, it seems he has mysteriously disappeared," replied the soldier, shaking his head ominously. "Where he has gone to, I can't make out, but I can assure you he is no longer in this castle. I'm sorry, little girl, to disappoint you. Don't blame me; I must obey my master's orders."

Now, all her life Trot had been accustomed to depend on Cap'n Bill, so when this good friend was suddenly taken from her she felt very miserable and forlorn indeed. She was brave enough not to cry before the soldier, or even to let him see her grief and anxiety, but after she was turned away from the castle she sought a quiet bench in the garden and for a time sobbed as if her heart would break.

It was Button-Bright who found her, at last, just as the sun had set and the shades of evening were falling. He also had been turned away from the King's castle, when he tried to enter it, and in the park he came across Trot.

"Never mind," said the boy. "We can find a place to sleep."

"I want Cap'n Bill," wailed the girl.

"Well, so do I," was the reply. "But we haven't got him. Where do you s'pose he is, Trot?

"I don't s'pose anything. He's gone, an' that's all I know 'bout it."

Button-Bright sat on the bench beside her and thrust his hands in the pockets of his knickerbockers. Then he reflected somewhat gravely for him.

"Cap'n Bill isn't around here," he said, letting his eyes wander over the dim garden, "so we must go somewhere else if we want to find him. Besides, it's fast getting dark, and if we want to find a place to sleep we must get busy while we can see where to go."

He rose from the bench as he said this and Trot also jumped up, drying her eyes on her apron. Then she walked beside him out of the grounds of the King's castle.

They did not go by the main path, but passed through an opening in a hedge and found themselves in a small but well-worn roadway. Following this for some distance, along a winding way, they came upon no house or building that would afford them refuge for the night. It became so dark that they could scarcely see their way, and finally Trot stopped and suggested that they camp under a tree.

"All right," said Button-Bright, "I've often found that leaves make a good warm blanket. But—look there, Trot!—isn't that a light flashing over yonder?"

"It certainly is, Button-Bright. Let's go over and see if it's a house. Whoever lives there couldn't treat us worse than the King did."

To reach the light they had to leave the road, so they stumbled over hillocks and brushwood, hand in hand, keeping the tiny speck of light always in sight.

They were rather forlorn little waifs, outcasts in a strange country and forsaken by their only friend and guardian, Cap'n Bill. So they were very glad when finally they reached a small cottage and, looking in through its one window, saw Pon, the gardener's boy, sitting by a fire of twigs.

As Trot opened the door and walked boldly in, Pon sprang up to greet them. They told him of Cap'n Bill's disappearance and how they had been turned out of the King's castle. As they finished the story Pon shook his head sadly.

"King Krewl is plotting mischief, I fear," said he, "for to-day he sent for old Blinkie, the Wicked Witch, and with my own eyes I saw her come from the castle and hobble away toward her hut. She had been with the King and Googly-Goo, and I was afraid they were going to work some enchantment on Gloria so she would no longer love me. But perhaps the witch was only called to the castle to enchant your friend, Cap'n Bill."

"Could she do that?" asked Trot, horrified by the suggestion.

"I suppose so, for old Blinkie can do a lot of wicked magical things."

"What sort of an enchantment could she put on Cap'n Bill?"

"I don't know. But he has disappeared, so I'm pretty certain she has done something dreadful to him. But don't worry. If it has happened, it can't be helped, and if it hasn't happened we may be able to find him in the morning."

With this Pon went to the cupboard and brought food for them. Trot was far too worried to eat, but Button-Bright made a good supper from the simple food and then lay down before the fire and went to sleep. The little girl and the gardener's boy, however, sat for a long time staring into the fire, busy with their thoughts. But at last Trot, too, became sleepy and Pon gently covered her with the one blanket he possessed. Then he threw more wood on the fire and laid himself down before it, next to Button-Bright. Soon all three were fast asleep. They were in a good deal of trouble; but they were young, and sleep was good to them because for a time it made them forget.

CHAPTER XIII

GLINDA THE GOOD AND THE SCARECROW OF OZ

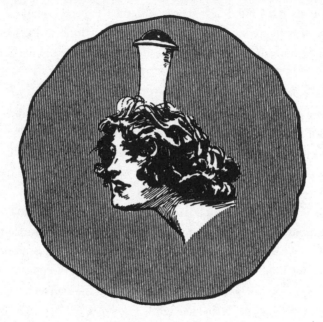

THAT COUNTRY SOUTH OF THE EMERALD CITY, IN THE LAND OF OZ, IS KNOWN AS the Quadling Country, and in the very southernmost part of it stands a splendid palace in which lives Glinda the Good.

Glinda is the Royal Sorceress of Oz. She has wonderful magical powers and uses them only to benefit the subjects of Ozma's kingdom. Even the famous Wizard of Oz pays tribute to her, for Glinda taught him all the real magic he knows, and she is his superior in all sorts of sorcery.

Everyone loves Glinda, from the dainty and exquisite Ruler, Ozma, down to the humblest inhabitant of Oz, for she is always kindly and helpful and willing to listen to their troubles, however busy she may be. No one knows her age, but all can see how beautiful and stately she is. Her hair is like red gold and finer than the finest silken strands. Her eyes are blue as the sky and always frank and smiling. Her cheeks are the envy of peach-blows and her mouth is enticing as a rosebud. Glinda is tall and wears splendid gowns that trail behind her as she walks. She wears no jewels, for her beauty would shame them.

For attendants Glinda has half a hundred of the loveliest girls in Oz. They are gathered from all over Oz, from among the Winkies, the Munchkins, the Gillikins and the Quadlings, as well as from Ozma's magnificent Emerald City, and it is considered a great favor to be allowed to serve the Royal Sorceress.

Among the many wonderful things in Glinda's palace is the Great Book of Records. In this book is inscribed everything that takes place in all the world, just the instant it happens; so that by referring to its pages Glinda knows what is taking place far and near, in every country that exists. In this way she learns when and where she can help any in distress or danger, and although her duties are confined to assisting those who inhabit the Land of Oz, she is always interested in what takes place in the unprotected outside world.

So it was that on a certain evening Glinda sat in her library, surrounded by a bevy of her maids, who were engaged in spinning, weaving and embroidery, when an attendant announced the arrival at the palace of the Scarecrow.

This personage was one of the most famous and popular in all the Land of Oz. His body was merely a suit of Munchkin clothes stuffed with straw, but his head was a round sack filled with bran, with which the Wizard of Oz had mixed some magic brains of a very superior sort. The eyes, nose and mouth of the Scarecrow were painted upon the front of the sack, as were his ears, and since this quaint being had been endowed with life, the expression of his face was very interesting, if somewhat comical.

The Scarecrow was good all through, even to his brains, and while he was naturally awkward in his movements and lacked the neat symmetry of other people, his disposition was so kind and considerate and he was so obliging and honest, that all who knew him loved him, and there were few people in Oz who had not met our Scarecrow and made his acquaintance. He lived part of the time in Ozma's palace at the Emerald City, part of the time in his own corncob castle in the Winkie Country, and part of the time he traveled over all Oz, visiting with the people and playing with the children, whom he dearly loved.

It was on one of his wandering journeys that the Scarecrow had arrived at Glinda's palace, and the Sorceress at once made him welcome. As he sat beside her, talking of his adventures, he asked:

"What's new in the way of news?"

Glinda opened her Great Book of Records and read some of the last pages.

"Here is an item quite curious and interesting," she announced, an accent of surprise in her voice. "Three people from the big Outside World have arrived in Jinxland."

"Where is Jinxland?" inquired the Scarecrow.

"Very near here, a little to the east of us," she said. "In fact, Jinxland is a little slice taken off the Quadling Country, but separated from it by a range of high mountains, at the foot of which lies a wide, deep gulf that is supposed to be impassable."

"Then Jinxland is really a part of the Land of Oz," said he.

"Yes," returned Glinda, "but Oz people know nothing of it, except what is recorded here in my book."

"What does the Book say about it?" asked the Scarecrow.

"It is ruled by a wicked man called King Krewl, although he has no right to the title. Most of the people are good, but they are very timid and live in constant fear of their fierce ruler. There are also several Wicked Witches who keep the inhabitants of Jinxland in a state of terror."

"Do those witches have any magical powers?" inquired the Scarecrow.

"Yes, they seem to understand witchcraft in its most evil form, for one of them has just transformed a respectable and honest old sailor—one of the strangers who arrived there—into a grasshopper. This same witch, Blinkie by name, is also planning to freeze the heart of a beautiful Jinxland girl named Princess Gloria."

"Why, that's a dreadful thing to do!" exclaimed the Scarecrow.

Glinda's face was very grave. She read in her book how Trot and Button-Bright were turned out of the King's castle, and how they found refuge in the hut of Pon, the gardener's boy.

"I'm afraid those helpless earth people will endure much suffering in Jinxland, even if the wicked King and the witches permit them to live," said the good Sorceress, thoughtfully. "I wish I might help them."

"Can I do anything?" asked the Scarecrow, anxiously. "If so, tell me what to do, and I'll do it."

For a few moments Glinda did not reply, but sat musing over the records. Then she said: "I am going to send you to Jinxland, to protect Trot and Button-Bright and Cap'n Bill."

"All right," answered the Scarecrow in a cheerful voice. "I know Button-Bright already, for he has been in the Land of Oz before. You remember he went away from the Land of Oz in one of our Wizard's big bubbles."

"Yes," said Glinda, "I remember that." Then she carefully instructed the Scarecrow what to do and gave him certain magical things which he placed in the pockets of his ragged Munchkin coat.

"As you have no need to sleep," said she, "you may as well start at once."

"The night is the same as day to me," he replied, "except that I cannot see my way so well in the dark."

"I will furnish a light to guide you," promised the Sorceress.

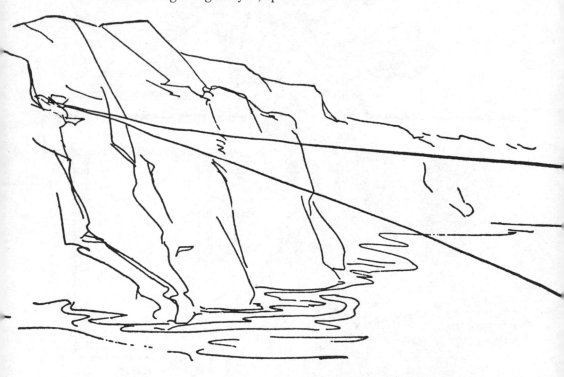

So the Scarecrow bade her good-bye and at once started on his journey. By morning he had reached the mountains that separated the Quadling Country from Jinxland. The sides of these mountains were too steep to climb, but the Scarecrow took a small rope from his pocket and tossed one end upward, into the air. The rope unwound itself for hundreds of feet, until it caught upon a peak of rock at the very top of a mountain, for it was a magic rope furnished him by Glinda. The Scarecrow climbed the rope and, after pulling it up, let it down on the other side of the mountain range. When he descended the rope on this side he found himself in Jinxland, but at his feet yawned the Great Gulf, which must be crossed before he could proceed any farther.

The Scarecrow knelt down and examined the ground carefully, and in a moment he discovered a fuzzy brown spider that had rolled itself into a ball. So he took two tiny pills from his pocket and laid them beside the spider, which unrolled itself and quickly ate up the pills. Then the Scarecrow said in a voice of command:

"Spin!" and the spider obeyed instantly.

In a few moments the little creature had spun two slender but strong strands that reached way across the gulf, one being five or six feet above the other. When these were completed the Scarecrow started across the tiny bridge, walking upon one strand as a person walks upon a rope, and holding to the upper strand with his hands to prevent him from losing his balance and toppling over into the gulf. The tiny threads held him safely, thanks to the strength given them by the magic pills.

Presently he was safe across and standing on the plains of Jinxland. Far away he could see the towers of the King's castle and toward this he at once began to walk.

CHAPTER XIV

THE FROZEN HEART

IN THE HUT OF PON, THE GARDENER'S BOY, BUTTON-BRIGHT WAS THE FIRST TO waken in the morning. Leaving his companions still asleep, he went out into the fresh morning air and saw some blackberries growing on bushes in a field not far away. Going to the bushes he found the berries ripe and sweet, so he began eating them. More bushes were scattered over the fields, so the boy wandered on, from bush to bush, without paying any heed to where he was wandering. Then a butterfly fluttered by. He gave chase to it and followed it a long way. When finally he paused to look around him, Button-Bright could see no sign of Pon's house, nor had he the slightest idea in which direction it lay.

"Well, I'm lost again," he remarked to himself. "But never mind; I've been lost lots of times. Someone is sure to find me."

Trot was a little worried about Button-Bright when she awoke and found him gone. Knowing how careless he was, she believed that he had strayed away, but felt that he would come back in time, because he had a habit of not staying lost. Pon got the little girl some food for her breakfast and then together they went out of the hut and stood in the sunshine.

Pon's house was some distance off the road, but they could see it from where they stood and both gave a start of surprise when they discovered two soldiers walking along the roadway and escorting Princess Gloria between them. The poor girl had her hands bound together, to prevent her from struggling, and the soldiers rudely dragged her forward when her steps seemed to lag.

Behind this group came King Krewl, wearing his jeweled crown and swinging in his hand a slender golden staff with a ball of clustered gems at one end.

"Where are they going?" asked Trot. "To the house of the Wicked Witch, I fear," Pon replied. "Come, let us follow them, for I am sure they intend to harm my dear Gloria."

"Won't they see us?" she asked timidly.

"We won't let them. I know a short cut through the trees to Blinkie's house," said he.

So they hurried away through the trees and reached the house of the witch ahead of the King and his soldiers. Hiding themselves in the shrubbery, they watched the approach of poor Gloria and her escort, all of whom passed so near to them that Pon could have put out a hand and touched his sweetheart, had he dared to.

Blinkie's house had eight sides, with a door and a window in each side. Smoke was coming out of the chimney and as the guards brought Gloria to one of the doors it was opened by the old witch in person. She chuckled with evil glee and rubbed her skinny hands together to show the delight with which she greeted her victim, for Blinkie was pleased to be able to perform her wicked rites on one so fair and sweet as the Princess.

Gloria struggled to resist when they bade her enter the house, so the soldiers forced her through the doorway and even the King gave her a shove as he followed close behind. Pon was so incensed at the cruelty shown Gloria that he forgot all caution and rushed forward to enter the house also; but one of the soldiers prevented him, pushing the gardener's boy away with violence and slamming the door in his face.

"Never mind," said Trot soothingly, as Pon rose from where he had fallen. "You couldn't do much to help the poor Princess if you were inside. How unfortunate it is that you are in love with her!"

"True," he answered sadly, "it is indeed my misfortune. If I did not love her, it would be none of my business what the King did to his niece Gloria; but the unlucky circumstance of my loving her makes it my duty to defend her."

"I don't see how you can, duty or no duty," observed Trot.

"No; I am powerless, for they are stronger than I. But we might peek in through the window and see what they are doing."

Trot was somewhat curious, too, so they
crept up to one of the windows and looked in,
and it so happened that those inside the
witch's house were so busy they did
not notice that Pon and Trot were
watching them.

Gloria had been tied to a stout
post in the center of the
room and the King was
giving the Wicked Witch
a quantity of money and
jewels, which Googly-Goo had provided
in payment. When this had been done the
King said to her:

"Are you perfectly sure you can freeze
this maiden's heart, so that she will no longer love that low gardener's boy?"

"Sure as witchcraft, your Majesty," the
creature replied.

"Then get to work," said the King. "There
may be some unpleasant features about the ceremony that would annoy me, so I'll bid you good
day and leave you to carry out your contract. One
word, however: If you fail, I shall burn you at the
stake!" Then he beckoned to his soldiers to follow
him, and throwing wide the door of the house
walked out.

This action was so sudden that King
Krewl almost caught Trot and Pon eavesdropping, but they managed to run around
the house before he saw them. Away he marched, up the road, followed by his men,
heartlessly leaving Gloria to the mercies of old Blinkie.

When they again crept up to the window, Trot and Pon saw Blinkie gloating
over her victim. Although nearly fainting from fear, the proud Princess gazed with
haughty defiance into the face of the wicked creature; but she was bound so tightly to
the post that she could do no more to express her loathing.

Pretty soon Blinkie went to a kettle that was swinging by a chain over the fire and
tossed into it several magical compounds. The kettle gave three flashes, and at every
flash another witch appeared in the room.

These hags were very ugly but when one-eyed Blinkie whispered her orders to them they grinned with joy as they began dancing around Gloria. First one and then another cast something into the kettle, when to the astonishment of the watchers at the window all three of the old women were instantly transformed into maidens of exquisite beauty, dressed in the daintiest costumes imaginable. Only their eyes could not be disguised, and an evil glare still shone in their depths. But if the eyes were cast down or hidden, one could not help but admire these beautiful creatures, even with the knowledge that they were mere illusions of witchcraft.

Trot certainly admired them, for she had never seen anything so dainty and bewitching, but her attention was quickly drawn to their deeds instead of their persons, and then horror replaced admiration.

Into the kettle old Blinkie poured another mess from a big brass bottle she took from a chest, and this made the kettle begin to bubble and smoke violently. One by one the beautiful witches approached to stir the contents of the kettle and to mutter a magic charm. Their movements were graceful and rhythmic and the Wicked Witch who had called them to her aid watched them with an evil grin upon her wrinkled face.

Finally the incantation was complete. The kettle ceased bubbling and together the witches lifted it from the fire. Then Blinkie brought a wooden ladle and filled it from the contents of the kettle. Going with the spoon to Princess Gloria she cried:

"Love no more! Magic art
Now will freeze your mortal heart!"

With this she dashed the contents of the ladle full upon Gloria's breast.

Trot saw the body of the Princess become transparent, so that her beating heart showed plainly. But now the heart turned from a vivid red to gray, and then to white. A layer of frost formed about it and tiny icicles clung to its surface. Then slowly the body of the girl became visible again and the heart was hidden from view. Gloria seemed to have fainted, but now she recovered and, opening her beautiful eyes, stared coldly and without emotion at the group of witches confronting her.

Blinkie and the others knew by that one cold look that their charm had been successful. They burst into a chorus of wild laughter and the three beautiful ones began dancing again, while Blinkie unbound the Princess and set her free.

Trot rubbed her eyes to prove that she was wide awake and seeing clearly, for her astonishment was great when the three lovely maidens turned into ugly, crooked hags again, leaning on broomsticks and canes. They jeered at Gloria, but the Princess regarded them with cold disdain. Being now free, she walked to a door, opened it and passed out. And the witches let her go.

Trot and Pon had been so intent upon this scene that in their eagerness they had pressed quite hard against the window. Just as Gloria went out of the house the window-sash broke loose from its fastenings and fell with a crash into the room. The witches uttered a chorus of screams and then, seeing that their magical incantation had been observed, they rushed for the open window with uplifted broomsticks and canes. But Pon was off like the wind, and Trot followed at his heels. Fear lent them strength to run, to leap across ditches, to speed up the hills and to vault the low fences as a deer would.

The band of witches had dashed through the window in pursuit; but Blinkie was so old, and the others so crooked and awkward, that they soon realized they would be unable to overtake the fugitives. So the three who had been summoned by the Wicked Witch put their canes or broomsticks between their legs and flew away through the air, quickly disappearing against the blue sky. Blinkie, however, was so enraged at Pon and Trot that she hobbled on in the direction they had taken, fully determined to catch them, in time, and to punish them terribly for spying upon her witchcraft.

When Pon and Trot had run so far that they were confident they had made good their escape, they sat down near the edge of a forest to get their breath again, for both were panting hard from their exertions. Trot was the first to recover speech, and she said to her companion:

"My! wasn't it terr'ble?"

"The most terrible thing I ever saw," Pon agreed.

"And they froze Gloria's heart; so now she can't love you any more."

"Well, they froze her heart, to be sure," admitted Pon, "but I'm in hopes I can melt it with my love."

"Where do you s'pose Gloria is?" asked the girl, after a pause.

"She left the witch's house just before we did. Perhaps she has gone back to the King's castle," he said.

"I'm pretty sure she started off in a diff'rent direction," declared Trot. "I looked over my shoulder, as I ran, to see how close the witches were, and I'm sure I saw Gloria walking slowly away toward the north."

"Then let us circle around that way," proposed Pon, "and perhaps we shall meet her."

Trot agreed to this and they left the grove and began to circle around toward the north, thus drawing nearer and nearer to old Blinkie's house again. The Wicked Witch did not suspect this change of direction, so when she came to the grove she passed through it and continued on.

Pon and Trot had reached a place less than half a mile from the witch's house when they saw Gloria walking toward them. The Princess moved with great dignity and with no show of haste whatever, holding her head high and looking neither to right nor left.

Pon rushed forward, holding out his arms as if to embrace her and calling her sweet names. But Gloria gazed upon him coldly and repelled him with a haughty gesture. At this the poor gardener's boy sank upon his knees and hid his face in his arms, weeping bitter tears; but the Princess was not at all moved by his distress. Passing him by, she drew her skirts aside, as if unwilling they should touch him, and then she walked up the path a way and hesitated, as if uncertain where to go next.

Trot was grieved by Pon's sobs and indignant because Gloria treated him so badly. But she remembered why.

"I guess your heart is frozen, all right," she said to the Princess. Gloria nodded gravely, in reply, and then turned her back upon the little girl. "Can't you like even me?" asked Trot, half pleadingly.

"No," said Gloria.

"Your voice sounds like a refrig'rator," sighed the little girl. "I'm awful sorry for you, 'cause you were sweet an' nice to me before this happened. You can't help it, of course; but it's a dreadful thing, jus' the same."

"My heart is frozen to all mortal loves," announced Gloria, calmly. "I do not love even myself."

"That's too bad," said Trot, "for, if you can't love anybody, you can't expect anybody to love you."

"I do!" cried Pon. "I shall always love her."

"Well, you're just a gardener's boy," replied Trot, "and I didn't think you 'mounted to much, from the first. I can love the old Princess Gloria, with a warm heart an' nice manners, but this one gives me the shivers."

"It's her icy heart, that's all," said Pon.

"That's enough," insisted Trot. "Seeing her heart isn't big enough to skate on, I can't see that she's of any use to anyone. For my part, I'm goin' to try to find Button-Bright an' Cap'n Bill."

"I will go with you," decided Pon. "It is evident that Gloria no longer loves me and that her heart is frozen too stiff for me to melt it with my own love; therefore I may as well help you to find your friends."

As Trot started off, Pon cast one more imploring look at the Princess, who returned it with a chilly stare. So he followed after the little girl.

As for the Princess, she hesitated a moment and then turned in the same direction the others had taken, but going far more slowly. Soon she heard footsteps pattering behind her, and up came Googly-Goo, a little out of breath with running.

"Stop, Gloria!" he cried. "I have come to take you back to my mansion, where we are to be married."

She looked at him wonderingly a moment, then tossed her head disdainfully and walked on. But Googly-Goo kept beside her.

"What does this mean?" he demanded. "Haven't you discovered that you no longer love that gardener's boy, who stood in my way?"

"Yes; I have discovered it," she replied. "My heart is frozen to all mortal loves. I cannot love you, or Pon, or the cruel King my uncle, or even myself. Go your way, Googly-Goo, for I will wed no one at all."

He stopped in dismay when he heard this, but in another minute he exclaimed angrily:

"You *must* wed me, Princess Gloria, whether you want to or not! I paid to have your heart frozen; I also paid the King to permit our marriage. If you now refuse me it will mean that I have been robbed—robbed—robbed of my precious money and jewels!"

He almost wept with despair, but she laughed a cold, bitter laugh and passed on. Googly-Goo caught at her arm, as if to restrain her, but she whirled and dealt him a blow that sent him reeling into a ditch beside the path. Here he lay for a long time, half covered by muddy water, dazed with surprise.

Finally the old courtier arose, dripping, and climbed from the ditch. The Princess had gone; so, muttering threats of vengeance upon her, upon the King and upon Blinkie, old Googly-Goo hobbled back to his mansion to have the mud removed from his costly velvet clothes.

CHAPTER XV

TROT MEETS THE SCARECROW

TROT AND PON COVERED MANY LEAGUES OF GROUND, SEARCHING THROUGH forests, in fields and in many of the little villages of Jinxland, but could find no trace of either Cap'n Bill or Button-Bright. Finally they paused beside a cornfield and sat upon a stile to rest. Pon took some apples from his pocket and gave one to Trot. Then he began eating another himself, for this was their time for luncheon. When his apple was finished Pon tossed the core into the field.

"Tchuk-tchuk!" said a strange voice. "What do you mean by hitting me in the eye with an apple-core?"

Then rose up the form of the Scarecrow, who had hidden himself in the cornfield while he examined Pon and Trot and decided whether they were worthy to be helped.

"Excuse me," said Pon. "I didn't know you were there."

"How did you happen to be there, anyhow?" asked Trot.

The Scarecrow came forward with awkward steps and stood beside them.

"Ah, you are the gardener's boy," he said to Pon. Then he turned to Trot. "And you are the little girl who came to Jinxland riding on a big bird, and who has had the misfortune to lose her friend, Cap'n Bill, and her chum, Button-Bright."

"Why, how did you know all that?" she inquired.

"I know a lot of things," replied the Scarecrow, winking at her comically. "My brains are the Carefully-Assorted, Double-Distilled, High-Efficiency sort that the Wizard of Oz makes. He admits, himself, that my brains are the best he ever manufactured."

"I think I've heard of you," said Trot slowly, as she looked the Scarecrow over with much interest; "but you used to live in the Land of Oz."

"Oh, I do now," he replied cheerfully. "I've just come over the mountains from the Quadling Country to see if I can be of any help to you."

"Who, me?" asked Pon.

"No, the strangers from the big world. It seems they need looking after."

"I'm doing that myself," said Pon, a little ungraciously. "If you will pardon me for saying so, I don't see how a Scarecrow with painted eyes can look after anyone."

"If you don't see that, you are more blind than the Scarecrow," asserted Trot. "He's a fairy man, Pon, and comes from the Fairyland of Oz, so he can do 'most anything. I hope," she added, turning to the Scarecrow, "you can find Cap'n Bill for me."

"I will try, anyhow," he promised. "But who is that old woman who is running toward us and shaking her stick at us?"

Trot and Pon turned around and both uttered an exclamation of fear. The next instant they took to their heels and ran fast up the path. For it was old Blinkie, the Wicked Witch, who had at last traced them to this place. Her anger was so great that she was determined not to abandon the chase of Pon and Trot until she had caught and punished them.

The Scarecrow understood at once that the old woman meant harm to his new friends, so as she drew near he stepped before her. His appearance was so sudden and unexpected that Blinkie ran into him and toppled him over, but she tripped on his straw body and went rolling in the path beside him.

The Scarecrow sat up and said: "I beg your pardon!" but she whacked him with her stick and knocked him flat again. Then, furious with rage, the old witch sprang upon her victim and began pulling the straw out of his body. The poor Scarecrow was helpless to resist and in a few moments all that was left of him was an empty suit of clothes and a heap of straw beside it. Fortunately, Blinkie did not harm his head, for it rolled into a little hollow and escaped her notice. Fearing that Pon and Trot would escape her, she quickly resumed the chase and disappeared over the brow of a hill, following the direction in which she had seen them go.

Only a short time elapsed before a gray grasshopper with a wooden leg came hopping along and lit directly on the upturned face of the Scarecrow's head.

"Pardon me, but you are resting yourself upon my nose," remarked the Scarecrow.

"Oh! are you alive?" asked the grasshopper.

"That is a question I have never been able to decide," said the Scarecrow's head. "When my body is properly stuffed I have animation and can move around as well as any live person. The brains in the head you are now occupying as a throne, are of very superior quality and do a lot of very clever thinking. But whether that is being alive, or not, I cannot prove to you; for one who lives is liable to death, while I am only liable to destruction."

"Seems to me," said the grasshopper, rubbing his nose with his front legs, "that in your case it doesn't matter—unless you're destroyed already."

"I am not; all I need is re-stuffing," declared the Scarecrow; "and if Pon and Trot escape the witch, and come back here, I am sure they will do me that favor."

"Tell me! Are Trot and Pon around here?" inquired the grasshopper, its small voice trembling with excitement.

The Scarecrow did not answer at once, for both his eyes were staring straight upward at a beautiful face that was slightly bent over his head. It was, indeed, Princess Gloria, who had wandered to this spot, very much surprised when she heard the Scarecrow's head talk and the tiny gray grasshopper answer it.

"This," said the Scarecrow, still staring at her, "must be the Princess who loves Pon, the gardener's boy."

"Oh, indeed!" exclaimed the grasshopper—who of course was Cap'n Bill—as he examined the young lady curiously.

"No," said Gloria frigidly, "I do not love Pon, or anyone else, for the Wicked Witch has frozen my heart."

"What a shame!" cried the Scarecrow. "One so lovely should be able to love. But would you mind, my dear, stuffing that straw into my body again?"

The dainty Princess glanced at the straw and at the well-worn blue Munchkin clothes and shrank back in disdain. But she was spared from refusing the Scarecrow's request by the appearance of Trot and Pon, who had hidden in some bushes just over the brow of the hill and waited until old Blinkie had passed them by. Their hiding place was on the same side as the witch's blind eye, and she rushed on in the chase of the girl and the youth without being aware that they had tricked her.

Trot was shocked at the Scarecrow's sad condition and at once began putting the straw back into his body. Pon, at sight of Gloria, again appealed to her to take pity on him, but the frozen-hearted Princess turned coldly away and with a sigh the gardener's boy began to assist Trot.

Neither of them at first noticed the small grasshopper, which at their appearance had skipped off the Scarecrow's nose and was now clinging to a wisp of grass beside the path, where he was not likely to be stepped upon. Not until the Scarecrow had been neatly restuffed and set upon his feet again—when he bowed to his restorers

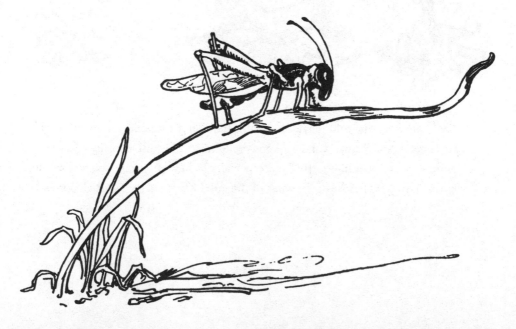

and expressed his thanks—did the grasshopper move from his perch. Then he leaped lightly into the path and called out:

"Trot—Trot! Look at me. I'm Cap'n Bill! See what the Wicked Witch has done to me."

The voice was small, to be sure, but it reached Trot's ears and startled her greatly. She looked intently at the grasshopper, her eyes wide with fear at first; then she knelt down and, noticing the wooden leg, she began to weep sorrowfully.

"Oh, Cap'n Bill—dear Cap'n Bill! What a cruel thing to do!" she sobbed.

"Don't cry, Trot," begged the grasshopper. "It didn't hurt any, and it doesn't hurt now. But it's mighty inconvenient an' humiliatin', to say the least."

"I wish," said the girl indignantly, while trying hard to restrain her tears, "that I was big 'nough an' strong 'nough to give that horrid witch a good beating. She ought to be turned into a toad for doing this to you, Cap'n Bill!"

"Never mind," urged the Scarecrow, in a comforting voice, "such a transformation doesn't last always, and as a general thing there's some way to break the enchantment. I'm sure Glinda could do it, in a jiffy."

"Who is Glinda?" inquired Cap'n Bill.

Then the Scarecrow told them all about Glinda, not forgetting to mention her beauty and goodness and her wonderful powers of magic. He also explained how the Royal Sorceress had sent him to Jinxland especially to help the strangers, whom she knew to be in danger because of the wiles of the cruel King and the Wicked Witch.

CHAPTER XVI

PON SUMMONS THE KING TO SURRENDER

GLORIA HAD DRAWN NEAR TO THE GROUP TO LISTEN TO THEIR TALK, AND IT SEEMED to interest her in spite of her frigid manner. They knew, of course, that the poor Princess could not help being cold and reserved, so they tried not to blame her.

"I ought to have come here a little sooner," said the Scarecrow, regretfully; "but Glinda sent me as soon as she discovered you were here and were likely to get into trouble. And now that we are all together—except Button-Bright, over whom it is useless to worry—I propose we hold a council of war, to decide what is best to be done."

That seemed a wise thing to do, so they all sat down upon the grass, including Gloria, and the grasshopper perched upon Trot's shoulder and allowed her to stroke him gently with her hand.

"In the first place," began the Scarecrow, "this King Krewl is a usurper and has no right to rule this Kingdom of Jinxland."

"That is true," said Pon, eagerly. "My father was King before him, and I—"

"You are a gardener's boy," interrupted the Scarecrow. "Your father had no right to rule, either, for the rightful King of this land was the father of Princess Gloria, and only she is entitled to sit upon the throne of Jinxland."

"Good!" exclaimed Trot. "But what'll we do with King Krewl? I s'pose he won't give up the throne unless he has to."

"No, of course not," said the Scarecrow. "Therefore it will be our duty to *make* him give up the throne."

"How?" asked Trot.

"Give me time to think," was the reply. "That's what my brains are for. I don't know whether you people ever think, or not, but my brains are the best that the Wizard of Oz ever turned out, and if I give them plenty of time to work, the result usually surprises me."

"Take your time, then," suggested Trot. "There's no hurry."

"Thank you," said the straw man, and sat perfectly still for half an hour. During this interval the grasshopper whispered in Trot's ear, to which he was very close, and Trot whispered back to the grasshopper sitting upon her shoulder. Pon cast loving glances at Gloria, who paid not the slightest heed to them.

Finally the Scarecrow laughed aloud.

"Brains working?" inquired Trot.

"Yes. They seem in fine order to-day. We will conquer King Krewl and put Gloria upon his throne as Queen of Jinxland."

"Fine!" cried the little girl, clapping her hands together gleefully. "But how?"

"Leave the *how* to me," said the Scarecrow proudly. "As a conqueror I'm a wonder. We will, first of all, write a message to send to King Krewl, asking him to surrender. If he refuses, then we will make him surrender."

"Why ask him, when we *know* he'll refuse?" inquired Pon.

"Why, we must be polite, whatever we do," explained the Scarecrow. "It would be very rude to conquer a King without proper notice."

They found it difficult to write a message without paper, pen and ink, none of which was at hand; so it was decided to send Pon as a messenger, with instructions to ask the King, politely but firmly, to surrender.

Pon was not anxious to be the messenger. Indeed, he hinted that it might prove a dangerous mission. But the Scarecrow was now the acknowledged head of the Army of Conquest, and he would listen to no refusal. So off Pon started for the King's castle, and the others accompanied him as far as his hut, where they had decided to await the gardener's boy's return.

I think it was because Pon had known the Scarecrow such a short time that he lacked confidence in the straw man's wisdom. It was easy to say: "We will conquer King Krewl," but when Pon drew near to the great castle he began to doubt the ability of a straw-stuffed man, a girl, a grasshopper and a frozen-hearted Princess to do it. As for himself, he had never thought of defying the King before.

That was why the gardener's boy was not very bold when he entered the castle and passed through to the enclosed court where the King was just then seated, with his favorite courtiers around him. None prevented Pon's entrance, because he was known to be the gardener's boy, but when the King saw him he began to frown fiercely. He considered Pon to be to blame for all his trouble with Princess Gloria, who since her heart had been frozen had escaped to some unknown place, instead of returning to the castle to wed Googly-Goo, as she had been expected to do. So the King bared his teeth angrily as he demanded:

"What have you done with Princess Gloria?"

"Nothing, your Majesty! I have done nothing at all," answered Pon in a faltering voice. "She does not love me any more and even refuses to speak to me."

"Then why are you here, you rascal?" roared the King.

Pon looked first one way and then another, but saw no means of escape; so he plucked up courage.

"I am here to summon your Majesty to surrender."

"What!" shouted the King. "Surrender? Surrender to whom?"

Pon's heart sank to his boots.

"To the Scarecrow," he replied.

Some of the courtiers began to titter, but King Krewl was greatly annoyed. He sprang up and began to beat poor Pon with the golden staff he carried. Pon howled lustily and would have run away had not two of the soldiers held him until his Majesty was exhausted with punishing the boy. Then they let him go and he left the castle and returned along the road, sobbing at every step because his body was so sore and aching.

"Well," said the Scarecrow, "did the King surrender?"

"No; but he gave me a good drubbing!" sobbed poor Pon.

Trot was very sorry for Pon, but Gloria did not seem affected in any way by her lover's anguish.

The grasshopper leaped to the Scarecrow's shoulder and asked him what he was going to do next.

"Conquer," was the reply. "But I will go alone, this time, for beatings cannot hurt me at all; nor can lance thrusts—or sword cuts—or arrow pricks."

"Why is that?" inquired Trot.

"Because I have no nerves, such as you meat people possess. Even grasshoppers have nerves, but straw doesn't; so whatever they do—except just one thing—they cannot injure me. Therefore I expect to conquer King Krewl with ease."

"What is that one thing you excepted?" asked Trot.

"They will never think of it, so never mind. And now, if you will kindly excuse me for a time, I'll go over to the castle and do my conquering."

"You have no weapons," Pon reminded him.

"True," said the Scarecrow. "But if I carried weapons I might injure some-one—perhaps seriously—and that would make me unhappy. I will just borrow that riding-whip, which I see in the corner of your hut, if you don't mind. It isn't exactly proper to walk with a riding-whip, but I trust you will excuse the inconsistency."

Pon handed him the whip and the Scarecrow bowed to all the party and left the hut, proceeding leisurely along the way to the King's castle.

CHAPTER XVII

THE ORK RESCUES BUTTON-BRIGHT

I MUST NOW TELL YOU WHAT HAD BECOME OF BUTTON-BRIGHT SINCE HE WANDERED away in the morning and got lost. This small boy, as perhaps you have discovered, was almost as destitute of nerves as the Scarecrow. Nothing ever astonished him much; nothing ever worried him or made him unhappy. Good fortune or bad fortune he accepted with a quiet smile, never complaining, whatever happened. This was one reason why Button-Bright was a favorite with all who knew him—and perhaps it was the reason why he so often got into difficulties, or found himself lost.

To-day, as he wandered here and there, over hill and down dale, he missed Trot and Cap'n Bill, of whom he was fond, but nevertheless he was not unhappy. The birds sang merrily and the wildflowers were beautiful and the breeze had a fragrance of new-mown hay.

"The only bad thing about this country is its King," he reflected; "but the country isn't to blame for that."

A prairie-dog stuck its round head out of a mound of earth and looked at the boy with bright eyes.

"Walk around my house, please," it said, "and then you won't harm it or disturb the babies."

"All right," answered Button-Bright, and took care not to step on the mound. He went on, whistling merrily, until a petulant voice cried:

"Oh, stop it! Please stop that noise. It gets on my nerves."

Button-Bright saw an old gray owl sitting in the crotch of a tree, and he replied with a laugh: "All right, old Fussy," and stopped whistling until he had passed out of the owl's hearing. At noon he came to a farm-house where an aged couple lived. They gave him a good dinner and treated him kindly, but the man was deaf and the woman was dumb, so they could answer no questions to guide him on the way to Pon's house. When he left them he was just as much lost as he had been before.

Every grove of trees he saw from a distance he visited, for he remembered that the King's castle was near a grove of trees and Pon's hut was near the King's castle; but always he met with disappointment. Finally, passing through one of these groves, he came out into the open and found himself face to face with the Ork.

"Hello!" said Button-Bright. "Where did *you* come from?"

"From Orkland," was the reply. "I've found my own country, at last, and it is not far from here, either. I would have come back to you sooner, to see how you are getting along, had not my family and friends welcomed my return so royally that a great

celebration was held in my honor. So I couldn't very well leave Orkland again until the excitement was over."

"Can you find your way back home again?" asked the boy.

"Yes, easily; for now I know exactly where it is. But where are Trot and Cap'n Bill?"

Button-Bright related to the Ork their adventures since it had left them in Jinxland, telling of Trot's fear that the King had done something wicked to Cap'n Bill, and of Pon's love for Gloria, and how Trot and Button-Bright had been turned out of the King's castle. That was all the news that the boy had, but it made the Ork anxious for the safety of his friends.

"We must go to them at once, for they may need us," he said.

"I don't know where to go," confessed Button-Bright. "I'm lost."

"Well, I can take you back to the hut of the gardener's boy," promised the Ork, "for when I fly high in the air I can look down and easily spy the King's castle. That was how I happened to spy you, just entering the grove; so I flew down and waited until you came out."

"How can you carry me?" asked the boy.

"You'll have to sit straddle my shoulders and put your arms around my neck. Do you think you can keep from falling off?"

"I'll try," said Button-Bright. So the Ork squatted down and the boy took his seat and held on tight. Then the skinny creature's tail began whirling and up they went, far above all the tree-tops.

After the Ork had circled around once or twice, its sharp eyes located the towers of the castle and away it flew, straight toward the place. As it hovered in the air, near by the castle, Button-Bright pointed out Pon's hut, so they landed just before it and Trot came running out to greet them.

Gloria was introduced to the Ork, who was surprised to find Cap'n Bill transformed into a grasshopper.

"How do you like it?" asked the creature.

"Why, it worries me good deal," answered Cap'n Bill, perched upon Trot's shoulder. "I'm always afraid o' bein' stepped on, and I don't like the flavor of grass an' can't seem to get used to it. It's my nature to eat grass, you know, but I begin to suspect it's an acquired taste."

"Can you give molasses?" asked the Ork.

"I guess I'm not that kind of a grasshopper," replied Cap'n Bill. "But I can't say what I might do if I was squeezed—which I hope I won't be."

"Well," said the Ork, "it's a great pity, and I'd like to meet that cruel King and his Wicked Witch and punish them both severely. You're awfully small, Cap'n Bill, but I think I would recognize you anywhere by your wooden leg."

Then the Ork and Button-Bright were told all about Gloria's frozen heart and how the Scarecrow had come from the Land of Oz to help them. The Ork seemed rather disturbed when it learned that the Scarecrow had gone alone to conquer King Krewl.

"I'm afraid he'll make a fizzle of it," said the skinny creature, "and there's no telling what that terrible King might do to the poor Scarecrow, who seems like a very interesting person. So I believe I'll take a hand in this conquest myself."

"How?" asked Trot.

"Wait and see," was the reply. "But, first of all, I must fly home again—back to my own country—so if you'll forgive my leaving you so soon, I'll be off at once. Stand away from my tail, please, so that the wind from it, when it revolves, won't knock you over."

They gave the creature plenty of room and away it went like a flash and soon disappeared in the sky.

"I wonder," said Button-Bright, looking solemnly after the Ork, "whether he'll ever come back again."

"Of course he will!" returned Trot. "The Ork's a pretty good fellow, and we can depend on him. An' mark my words, Button-Bright, whenever our Ork does come back, there's one cruel King in Jinxland that'll wish he hadn't."

CHAPTER XVIII

THE SCARECROW MEETS AN ENEMY

THE SCARECROW WAS NOT A BIT AFRAID OF KING KREWL. INDEED, HE RATHER enjoyed the prospect of conquering the evil King and putting Gloria on the throne of Jinxland in his place. So he advanced boldly to the royal castle and demanded admittance.

Seeing that he was a stranger, the soldiers allowed him to enter. He made his way straight to the throne room, where at that time his Majesty was settling the disputes among his subjects.

"Who are you?" demanded the King.

"I'm the Scarecrow of Oz, and I command you to surrender yourself my prisoner."

"Why should I do that?" inquired the King, much astonished at the straw man's audacity.

"Because I've decided you are too cruel a King to rule so beautiful a country. You must remember that Jinxland is a part of Oz, and therefore you owe allegiance to Ozma of Oz, whose friend and servant I am."

Now, when he heard this, King Krewl was much disturbed in mind, for he knew the Scarecrow spoke the truth. But no one had ever before come to Jinxland from the Land of Oz and the King did not intend to be put out of his throne if he could help it. Therefore he gave a harsh, wicked laugh of derision and said:

"I'm busy, now. Stand out of my way, Scarecrow, and I'll talk with you by and by."

But the Scarecrow turned to the assembled courtiers and people and called in a loud voice:

"I hereby declare, in the name of Ozma of Oz, that this man is no longer ruler of Jinxland. From this moment Princess Gloria is your rightful Queen, and I ask all of you to be loyal to her and to obey her commands."

The people looked fearfully at the King, whom they all hated in their hearts, but likewise feared. Krewl was now in a terrible rage and he raised his golden sceptre and struck the Scarecrow so heavy a blow that he fell to the floor.

But he was up again, in an instant, and with Pon's riding-whip he switched the King so hard that the wicked monarch roared with pain as much as with rage, calling on his soldiers to capture the Scarecrow.

They tried to do that, and thrust their lances and swords into the straw body, but without doing any damage except to make holes in the Scarecrow's clothes. However, they were many against one and finally old Googly-Goo brought a rope which he wound around the Scarecrow, binding his legs together and his arms to his sides, and after that the fight was over.

The King stormed and danced around in a dreadful fury, for he had never been so switched since he was a boy—and perhaps not then. He ordered the Scarecrow thrust into the castle prison, which was no task at all because one man could carry him easily, bound as he was.

Even after the prisoner was removed the King could not control his anger. He tried to figure out some way to be revenged upon the straw man, but could think of nothing that could hurt him.

At last, when the terrified people and the frightened courtiers had all slunk away, old Googly-Goo approached the King with a malicious grin upon his face.

"I'll tell you what to do," said he. "Build a big bonfire and burn the Scarecrow up, and that will be the end of him."

The King was so delighted with this suggestion that he hugged old Googly-Goo in his joy.

"Of course!" he cried. "The very thing. Why did I not think of it myself?"

So he summoned his soldiers and retainers and bade them prepare a great bonfire in an open space in the castle park. Also he sent word to all his people to assemble and witness the destruction of the Scarecrow who had dared to defy his power. Before

long a vast throng gathered in the park and the servants had heaped up enough fuel
to make a fire that might be seen for miles away—even in the daytime.

When all was prepared, the King had his throne brought out for him to sit upon
and enjoy the spectacle, and then he sent his soldiers to fetch the Scarecrow.

Now the one thing in all the world that the straw man really feared was fire. He
knew he would burn very easily and that his ashes wouldn't amount to much afterward. It wouldn't hurt him to be destroyed in such a manner, but he realized that many
people in the Land of Oz, and especially Dorothy and the Royal Ozma, would feel sad
if they learned that their old friend the Scarecrow was no longer in existence.

In spite of this, the straw man was brave and faced his fiery fate like a hero. When
they marched him out before the concourse of people he turned to the King with great
calmness and said:

"This wicked deed will cost you your throne, as well as much suffering, for my
friends will avenge my destruction."

"Your friends are not here, nor will they know what I have done to you, when you
are gone and cannot tell them," answered the King in a scornful voice.

Then he ordered the Scarecrow bound to a stout stake that he had had driven into
the ground, and the materials for the fire were heaped all around him. When this had
been done, the King's brass band struck up a lively tune and old Googly-Goo came
forward with a lighted match and set fire to the pile.

At once the flames shot up and crept closer and closer toward the Scarecrow. The
King and all his people were so intent upon this terrible spectacle that none of them
noticed how the sky grew suddenly dark. Perhaps they thought that the loud buzzing sound—like the noise of a dozen moving railway trains—came from the blazing
fagots; that the rush of wind was merely a breeze. But suddenly down swept a flock
of Orks, half a hundred of them at the least, and the powerful currents of air caused
by their revolving tails sent the bonfire scattering in every direction, so that not one
burning brand ever touched the Scarecrow.

But that was not the only effect of this sudden tornado. King Krewl was blown
out of his throne and went tumbling heels over head until he landed with a bump
against the stone wall of his own castle, and before he could rise a big Ork sat upon
him and held him pressed flat to the ground. Old Googly-Goo shot up into the air like
a rocket and landed on a tree, where he hung by the middle on a high limb, kicking
the air with his feet and clawing the air with his hands, and howling for mercy like the
coward he was.

The people pressed back until they were jammed close together, while all the
soldiers were knocked over and sent sprawling to the earth. The excitement was
great for a few minutes, and every frightened inhabitant of Jinxland looked with awe

and amazement at the great
Orks whose descent had
served to rescue the
Scarecrow and con-
quer King Krewl
at one and the
same time.

The Ork, who was
the leader of the band,
soon had the Scarecrow
free of his bonds. Then he
said: "Well, we were just in
time to save you, which is better
than being a minute too late.
You are now the master
here, and we are deter-
mined to see your orders obeyed."

With this the Ork picked up Krewl's
golden crown, which had fallen off his
head, and placed it upon the head of the
Scarecrow, who in his awkward way then
shuffled over to the throne and sat down in it.

Seeing this, a rousing cheer broke from the crowd of people, who tossed their hats
and waved their handkerchiefs and hailed the Scarecrow as their King. The soldiers
joined the people in the cheering, for now they fully realized that their hated master
was conquered and it would be wise to show their good will to the conqueror. Some
of them bound Krewl with ropes and dragged him forward, dumping his body on the
ground before the Scarecrow's throne. Googly-Goo struggled until he finally slid off
the limb of the tree and came tumbling to the ground. He then tried to sneak away and
escape, but the soldiers seized and bound him beside Krewl.

"The tables are turned," said the Scarecrow, swelling out his chest until the straw
within it crackled pleasantly, for he was highly pleased; "but it was you and your people
who did it, friend Ork, and from this time you may count me your humble servant."

CHAPTER XIX

THE CONQUEST OF THE WITCH

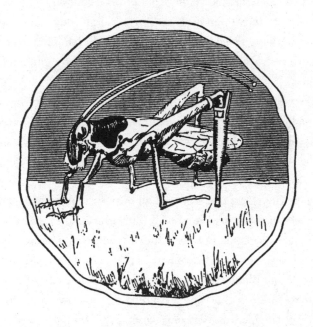

Now as soon as the conquest of King Krewl had taken place, one of the Orks had been dispatched to Pon's house with the joyful news. At once Gloria and Pon and Trot and Button-Bright hastened toward the castle. They were somewhat surprised by the sight that met their eyes, for there was the Scarecrow, crowned King, and all the people kneeling humbly before him. So they likewise bowed low to the new ruler and then stood beside the throne. Cap'n Bill, as the gray grasshopper, was still perched upon Trot's shoulder, but now he hopped to the shoulder of the Scarecrow and whispered into the painted ear:

"I thought Gloria was to be Queen of Jinxland."

The Scarecrow shook his head.

"Not yet," he answered. "No Queen with a frozen heart is fit to rule any country." Then he turned to his new friend, the Ork, who was strutting about, very proud of what he had done, and said: "Do you suppose you, or your followers, could find old Blinkie the Witch?"

"Where is she?" asked the Ork.

"Somewhere in Jinxland, I'm sure."

"Then," said the Ork, "we shall certainly be able to find her."

"It will give me great pleasure," declared the Scarecrow. "When you have found her, bring her here to me, and I will then decide what to do with her."

The Ork called his followers together and spoke a few words to them in a low tone. A moment after they rose into the air—so suddenly that the Scarecrow, who was very light in weight, was blown quite out of his throne and into the arms of Pon, who replaced him carefully upon his seat. There was an eddy of dust and ashes, too, and the grasshopper only saved himself from being whirled into the crowd of people by jumping into a tree, from where a series of hops soon brought him back to Trot's shoulder again.

The Orks were quite out of sight by this time, so the Scarecrow made a speech to the people and presented Gloria to them, whom they knew well already and were fond of. But not all of them knew of her frozen heart, and when the Scarecrow related the story of the Wicked Witch's misdeeds, which had been encouraged and paid for by Krewl and Googly-Goo, the people were very indignant.

Meantime the fifty Orks had scattered all over Jinxland, which is not a very big country, and their sharp eyes were peering into every valley and grove and gully. Finally one of them spied a pair of heels sticking out from underneath some bushes, and with a shrill whistle to warn his comrades that the witch was found the Ork flew down and dragged old Blinkie from her hiding-place. Then two or three of the Orks seized the clothing of the wicked woman in their strong claws and, lifting her high in the air, where she struggled and screamed to no avail, they flew with her straight to the royal castle and set her down before the throne of the Scarecrow.

"Good!" exclaimed the straw man, nodding his stuffed head with satisfaction. "Now we can proceed to business. Mistress Witch, I am obliged to request, gently but firmly, that you undo all the wrongs you have done by means of your witchcraft."

"Pah!" cried old Blinkie in a scornful voice. "I defy you all! By my magic powers I can turn you all into pigs, rooting in the mud, and I'll do it if you are not careful."

"I think you are mistaken about that," said the Scarecrow, and rising from his throne he walked with wobbling steps to the side of the Wicked Witch. "Before I left the Land of Oz, Glinda the Royal Sorceress gave me a box, which I was not to open except in an emergency. But I feel pretty sure that this occasion is an emergency; don't you, Trot?" he asked, turning toward the little girl.

"Why, we've got to do *something*," replied Trot seriously. "Things seem in an awful muddle here, jus' now, and they'll be worse if we don't stop this witch from doing more harm to people."

"That is my idea, exactly," said the Scarecrow, and taking a small box from his pocket he opened the cover and tossed the contents toward Blinkie.

The old woman shrank back, pale and trembling, as a fine white dust settled all about her. Under its influence she seemed to the eyes of all observers to shrivel and grow smaller.

"Oh, dear—oh, dear!" she wailed, wringing her hands in fear. "Haven't you the antidote, Scarecrow? Didn't the great Sorceress give you another box?"

"She did," answered the Scarecrow.

"Then give it me—quick!" pleaded the witch. "Give it me—and I'll do anything you ask me to!"

"You will do what I ask first," declared the Scarecrow, firmly.

The witch was shriveling and growing smaller every moment.

"Be quick, then!" she cried. "Tell me what I must do and let me do it, or it will be too late."

"You made Trot's friend, Cap'n Bill, a grasshopper. I command you to give him back his proper form again," said the Scarecrow.

"Where is he? Where's the grasshopper? Quick—quick!" she screamed.

Cap'n Bill, who had been deeply interested in this conversation, gave a great leap from Trot's shoulder and landed on that of the Scarecrow. Blinkie saw him alight and at once began to make magic passes and to mumble magic incantations. She was in a desperate hurry, knowing that she had no time to waste, and the grasshopper was so suddenly transformed into the old sailor-man, Cap'n Bill, that he had no opportunity to jump off the Scarecrow's shoulder; so his great weight bore the stuffed Scarecrow to the ground. No harm was done, however, and the straw man got up and brushed the dust from his clothes while Trot delightedly embraced Cap'n Bill.

"The other box! Quick! Give me the other box," begged Blinkie, who had now shrunk to half her former size.

"Not yet," said the Scarecrow. "You must first melt Princess Gloria's frozen heart."

"I can't; it's an awful job to do that! I can't," asserted the witch, in an agony of fear—for still she was growing smaller.

"You must!" declared the Scarecrow, firmly.

The witch cast a shrewd look at him and saw that he meant it; so she began dancing around Gloria in a frantic manner. The Princess looked coldly on, as if not at all interested in the proceedings, while Blinkie tore a handful of hair from her own head and ripped a strip of cloth from the bottom of her gown. Then the witch sank upon her knees, took a purple powder from her black bag and sprinkled it over the hair and cloth.

"I hate to do it—I hate to do it!" she wailed, "for there is no more of this magic compound in all the world. But I must sacrifice it to save my own life. A match! Give me a match, quick!" and panting from lack of breath she gazed imploringly from one to another.

Cap'n Bill was the only one who had a match, but he lost no time in handing it to Blinkie, who quickly set fire to the hair and the cloth and the purple powder. At once a purple cloud enveloped Gloria, and this gradually turned to a rosy pink color—brilliant and quite transparent. Through the rosy cloud they could all see the beautiful Princess, standing proud and erect. Then her heart became visible, at first frosted with ice but slowly growing brighter and warmer until all the frost had disappeared and it was beating as softly and regularly as any other heart. And now the cloud dispersed and disclosed Gloria, her face suffused with joy, smiling tenderly upon the friends who were grouped about her.

Poor Pon stepped forward—timidly, fearing a repulse, but with pleading eyes and arms fondly outstretched toward his former sweetheart—and the Princess saw him and her sweet face lighted with a radiant smile. Without an instant's hesitation she threw herself into Pon's arms and this reunion of two loving hearts was so affecting that the people turned away and lowered their eyes so as not to mar the sacred joy of the faithful lovers.

But Blinkie's small voice was shouting to the Scarecrow for help.

"The antidote!" she screamed. "Give me the other box—quick!"

The Scarecrow looked at the witch with his quaint, painted eyes and saw that she was now no taller than his knee. So he took from his pocket the second box and scattered its contents on Blinkie. She ceased to grow any smaller, but she could never regain her former size, and this the wicked old woman well knew.

She did not know, however, that the second powder had destroyed all her power to work magic, and seeking to be revenged upon the Scarecrow and his friends she at once began to mumble a charm so terrible in its effect that it would have destroyed half the population of Jinxland—had it worked. But it did not work at all, to the amazement of old Blinkie. And by this time the Scarecrow noticed what the little witch was trying to do, and said to her:

"Go home, Blinkie, and behave yourself. You are no longer a witch, but an ordinary old woman, and since you are powerless to do more evil I advise you to try to do some good in the world. Believe me, it is more fun to accomplish a good act than an evil one, as you will discover when once you have tried it."

But Blinkie was at that moment filled with grief and chagrin at losing her magic powers. She started away toward her home, sobbing and bewailing her fate, and not one who saw her go was at all sorry for her.

CHAPTER XX

QUEEN GLORIA

NEXT MORNING THE SCARECROW CALLED UPON ALL THE COURTIERS AND THE people to assemble in the throne room of the castle, where there was room enough for all that were able to attend. They found the straw man seated upon the velvet cushions of the throne, with the King's glittering crown still upon his stuffed head. On one side of the throne, in a lower chair, sat Gloria, looking radiantly beautiful and fresh as a new-blown rose. On the other side sat Pon, the gardener's boy, still dressed in his old smock frock and looking sad and solemn; for Pon could not make himself believe that so splendid a Princess would condescend to love him when she had come to her own and was seated upon a throne. Trot and Cap'n Bill sat at the feet of the Scarecrow and were much interested in the proceedings. Button-Bright had lost himself before breakfast, but came into the throne room before the ceremonies were over. Back of the throne stood a row of the great Orks, with their leader in the center, and the entrance to the palace was guarded by more Orks, who were regarded with wonder and awe.

When all were assembled, the Scarecrow stood up and made a speech. He told how Gloria's father, the good King Kynd, who had once ruled them and been loved by everyone, had been destroyed by King Phearce, the father of Pon, and how King

Phearce had been destroyed by King Krewl. This last King had been a bad ruler, as they knew very well, and the Scarecrow declared that the only one in all Jinxland who had the right to sit upon the throne was Princess Gloria, the daughter of King Kynd.

"But," he added, "it is not for me, a stranger, to say who shall rule you. You must decide for yourselves, or you will not be content. So choose now who shall be your future ruler."

And they all shouted: "The Scarecrow! The Scarecrow shall rule us!"

Which proved that the stuffed man had made himself very popular by his conquest of King Krewl, and the people thought they would like him for their King. But the Scarecrow shook his head so vigorously that it became loose, and Trot had to pin it firmly to his body again.

"No," said he, "I belong in the Land of Oz, where I am the humble servant of the lovely girl who rules us all—the royal Ozma. You must choose one of your own inhabitants to rule over Jinxland. Who shall it be?"

They hesitated for a moment, and some few cried: "Pon!" but many more shouted: "Gloria!"

So the Scarecrow took Gloria's hand and led her to the throne, where he first seated her and then took the glittering crown off his own head and placed it upon that of the young lady, where it nestled prettily amongst her soft curls. The people cheered and shouted then, kneeling before their new Queen; but Gloria leaned down and took Pon's hand in both her own and raised him to the seat beside her.

"You shall have both a King and a Queen to care for you and to protect you, my dear subjects," she said in a sweet voice, while her face glowed with happiness; "for Pon was a King's son before he became a gardener's boy, and because I love him he is to be my Royal Consort."

That pleased them all, especially Pon, who realized that this was the most important moment of his life. Trot and Button-Bright and Cap'n Bill all congratulated him on winning the beautiful Gloria; but the Ork sneezed twice and said that in his opinion the young lady might have done better.

Then the Scarecrow ordered the guards to bring in the wicked Krewl, King no longer, and when he appeared, loaded with chains and dressed in fustian, the people hissed him and drew back as he passed so their garments would not touch him.

Krewl was not haughty or overbearing any more; on the contrary he seemed very meek and in great fear of the fate his conquerors had in store for him. But Gloria and Pon were too happy to be revengeful and so they offered to appoint Krewl to the position of gardener's boy at the castle, Pon having resigned to become King. But they said he must promise to reform his wicked ways and to do his duty faithfully, and he must change his name from Krewl to Grewl. All this the man eagerly promised to do,

and so when Pon retired to a room in the castle to put on princely raiment, the old brown smock he had formerly worn was given to Grewl, who then went out into the garden to water the roses.

The remainder of that famous day, which was long remembered in Jinxland, was given over to feasting and merrymaking. In the evening there was a grand dance in the courtyard, where the brass band played a new piece of music called the "Ork Trot" which was dedicated to "Our Glorious Gloria, the Queen."

While the Queen and Pon were leading this dance, and all the Jinxland people were having a good time, the strangers were gathered in a group in the park outside the castle. Cap'n Bill, Trot, Button-Bright and the Scarecrow were there, and so was their old friend the Ork; but of all the great flock of Orks which had assisted in the conquest but three remained in Jinxland, besides their leader, the others having returned to their own country as soon as Gloria was crowned Queen. To the young Ork who had accompanied them in their adventures Cap'n Bill said:

"You've surely been a friend in need, and we're mighty grateful to you for helping us. I might have been a grasshopper yet if it hadn't been for you, an' I might remark that bein' a grasshopper isn't much fun."

"If it hadn't been for you, friend Ork," said the Scarecrow, "I fear I could not have conquered King Krewl."

"No," agreed Trot, "you'd have been just a heap of ashes by this time."

"And I might have been lost yet," added Button-Bright. "Much obliged, Mr. Ork."

"Oh, that's all right," replied the Ork. "Friends must stand together, you know, or they wouldn't be friends. But now I must leave you and be off to my own country, where there's going to be a surprise party on my uncle, and I've promised to attend it."

"Dear me," said the Scarecrow, regretfully. "That is very unfortunate."

"Why so?" asked the Ork.

"I hoped you would consent to carry us over those mountains, into the Land of Oz. My mission here is now finished and I want to get back to the Emerald City."

"How did you cross the mountains before?" inquired the Ork.

"I scaled the cliffs by means of a rope, and crossed the Great Gulf on a strand of spider web. Of course I can return in the same manner, but it would be a hard journey—and perhaps an impossible one—for Trot and Button-Bright and Cap'n Bill. So I thought that if you had the time you and your people would carry us over the mountains and land us all safely on the other side, in the Land of Oz."

The Ork thoughtfully considered the matter for a while. Then he said:

"I mustn't break my promise to be present at the surprise party; but, tell me, could you go to Oz to-night?"

"What, now?" exclaimed Trot.

"It is a fine moonlight night," said the Ork, "and I've found in my experience that there's no time so good as right away. The fact is," he explained, "it's a long journey

to Orkland and I and my cousins here are all rather tired by our day's work. But if you will start now, and be content to allow us to carry you over the mountains and dump you on the other side, just say the word and—off we go!"

Cap'n Bill and Trot looked at one another questioningly. The little girl was eager to visit the famous Fairyland of Oz and the old sailor had endured such hardships in Jinxland that he would be glad to be out of it.

"It's rather impolite of us not to say good-bye to the new King and Queen," remarked the Scarecrow, "but I'm sure they're too happy to miss us, and I assure you it will be much easier to fly on the backs of the Orks over those steep mountains than to climb them as I did."

"All right; let's go!" Trot decided. "But where's Button-Bright?"

Just at this important moment Button-Bright was lost again, and they all scattered in search of him. He had been standing beside them just a few minutes before, but his friends had an exciting hunt for him before they finally discovered the boy seated among the members of the band, beating the end of the bass drum with the bone of a turkey-leg that he had taken from the table in the banquet room.

"Hello, Trot," he said, looking up at the little girl when she found him. "This is the first chance I ever had to pound a drum with a reg'lar drum stick. And I ate all the meat off the bone myself."

"Come quick. We're going to the Land of Oz."

"Oh, what's the hurry?" said Button-Bright; but she seized his arm and dragged him away to the park, where the others were waiting.

Trot climbed upon the back of her old friend, the Ork leader, and the others took their seats on the backs of his three cousins. As soon as all were placed and clinging to the skinny necks of the creatures, the revolving tails began to whirl and up rose the four monster Orks and sailed away toward the mountains. They were so high in the air that when they passed the crest of the highest peak it seemed far below them. No sooner were they well across the barrier than the Orks swooped downward and landed their passengers upon the ground.

"Here we are, safe in the Land of Oz!" cried the Scarecrow joyfully.

"Oh, are we?" asked Trot, looking around her curiously.

She could see the shadows of stately trees and the outlines of rolling hills; beneath her feet was soft turf, but otherwise the subdued light of the moon disclosed nothing clearly.

"Seems jus' like any other country," was Cap'n Bill's comment.

"But it isn't," the Scarecrow assured him. "You are now within the borders of the most glorious fairyland in all the world. This part of it is just a corner of the Quadling Country, and the least interesting portion of it. It's not very thickly settled, around here, I'll admit, but—"

He was interrupted by a sudden whir and a rush of air as the four Orks mounted into the sky.

"Good night!" called the shrill voices of the strange creatures, and although Trot shouted "Good night!" as loudly as she could, the little girl was almost ready to cry because the Orks had not waited to be properly thanked for all their kindness to her and to Cap'n Bill.

But the Orks were gone, and thanks for good deeds do not amount to much except to prove one's politeness.

"Well, friends," said the Scarecrow, "we mustn't stay here in the meadows all night, so let us find a pleasant place to sleep. Not that it matters to me, in the least, for I never sleep; but I know that meat people like to shut their eyes and lie still during the dark hours."

"I'm pretty tired," admitted Trot, yawning as she followed the straw man along a tiny path, "so, if you don't find a house handy, Cap'n Bill and I will sleep under the trees, or even on this soft grass."

But a house was not very far off, although when the Scarecrow stumbled upon it there was no light in it whatever. Cap'n Bill knocked on the door several times, and there being no response the Scarecrow boldly lifted the latch and walked in, followed by the others. And no sooner had they entered than a soft light filled the room. Trot couldn't tell where it came from, for no lamp of any sort was visible, but she did not waste much time on this problem, because directly in the center of the room stood a table set for three, with lots of good food on it and several of the dishes smoking hot.

The little girl and Button-Bright both uttered exclamations of pleasure, but they looked in vain for any cook stove or fireplace, or for any person who might have prepared for them this delicious feast.

"It's fairyland," muttered the boy, tossing his cap in a corner and seating himself at the table. "This supper smells 'most as good as that turkey-leg I had in Jinxland. Please pass the muffins, Cap'n Bill."

Trot thought it was strange that no people but themselves were in the house, but on the wall opposite the door was a gold frame bearing in big letters the word:

"WELCOME."

So she had no further hesitation in eating of the food so mysteriously prepared for them.

"But there are only places for three!" she exclaimed.

"Three are quite enough," said the Scarecrow. "I never eat, because I am stuffed full already, and I like my nice clean straw better than I do food."

Trot and the sailor-man were hungry and made a hearty meal, for not since they had left home had they tasted such good food. It was surprising that Button-Bright could eat so soon after his feast in Jinxland, but the boy always ate whenever there was an opportunity. "If I don't eat now," he said, "the next time I'm hungry I'll wish I had."

"Really, Cap'n," remarked Trot, when she found a dish of ice-cream appear beside her plate, "I b'lieve this is fairyland, sure enough."

"There's no doubt of it, Trot," he answered gravely

"I've been here before," said Button-Bright, "so I know."

After supper they discovered three tiny bedrooms adjoining the big living room of the house, and in each room was a comfortable white bed with downy pillows. You may be sure that the tired mortals were not long in bidding the Scarecrow good night and creeping into their beds, where they slept soundly until morning.

For the first time since they set eyes on the terrible whirlpool, Trot and Cap'n Bill were free from anxiety and care. Button-Bright never worried about anything. The Scarecrow, not being able to sleep, looked out of the window and tried to count the stars.

CHAPTER XXI

DOROTHY, BETSY AND OZMA

I SUPPOSE MANY OF MY READERS HAVE READ DESCRIPTIONS OF THE BEAUTIFUL AND magnificent Emerald City of Oz, so I need not describe it here, except to state that never has any city in any fairyland ever equaled this one in stately splendor. It lies almost exactly in the center of the Land of Oz, and in the center of the Emerald City rises the wall of glistening emeralds that surrounds the palace of Ozma. The palace is almost a city in itself and is inhabited by many of the Ruler's especial friends and those who have won her confidence and favor.

As for Ozma herself, there are no words in any dictionary I can find that are fitted to describe this young girl's beauty of mind and person. Merely to see her is to love her for her charming face and manners; to know her is to love her for her tender sympathy, her generous nature, her truth and honor. Born of a long line of Fairy Queens, Ozma is as nearly perfect as any fairy may be, and she is noted for her wisdom as well as for her other qualities. Her happy subjects adore their girl Ruler and each one considers her a comrade and protector.

At the time of which I write, Ozma's best friend and most constant companion was a little Kansas girl named Dorothy, a mortal who had come to the Land of Oz in a very curious manner and had been offered a home in Ozma's palace. Furthermore, Dorothy had been made a Princess of Oz, and was as much at home in the royal palace as was the gentle Ruler. She knew almost every part of the great country and almost all of its numerous inhabitants. Next to Ozma she was loved better than anyone in all Oz, for Dorothy was simple and sweet, seldom became angry and had such a friendly, chummy way that she made friends wherever she wandered. It was she who first brought the Scarecrow and the Tin Woodman and the Cowardly Lion to the Emerald City. Dorothy had also introduced to Ozma the Shaggy Man and the Hungry Tiger, as well as Billina the Yellow Hen, Eureka the Pink Kitten, and many other delightful characters and creatures. Coming as she did from our world, Dorothy was much like many other girls we know; so there were times when she was not so wise as she might have been, and other times when she was obstinate and got herself into trouble. But life in a fairyland had taught the little girl to accept all sorts of surprising things as matters-of-course, for while Dorothy was no fairy—but just as mortal as we are—she had seen more wonders than most mortals ever do.

Another little girl from our outside world also lived in Ozma's palace. This was Betsy Bobbin, whose strange adventures had brought her to the Emerald City, where Ozma had cordially welcomed her. Betsy was a shy little thing and could never get used to the marvels that surrounded her, but she and Dorothy were firm friends and thought themselves very fortunate in being together in this delightful country.

One day Dorothy and Betsy were visiting Ozma in the girl Ruler's private apartment, and among the things that especially interested them was Ozma's Magic Picture, set in a handsome frame and hung upon the wall of the room. This picture was a magic one because it constantly changed its scenes and showed events and adventures happening in all parts of the world.

Thus it was really a "moving picture" of life, and if the one who stood before it wished to know what any absent person was doing, the picture instantly showed that person, with his or her surroundings.

The two girls were not wishing to see anyone in particular, on this occasion, but merely enjoyed watching the shifting scenes, some of which were exceedingly

curious and remarkable. Suddenly Dorothy exclaimed: "Why, there's Button-Bright!" and this drew Ozma also to look at the picture, for she and Dorothy knew the boy well.

"Who is Button-Bright?" asked Betsy, who had never met him.

"Why, he's the little boy who is just getting off the back of that strange flying creature," exclaimed Dorothy. Then she turned to Ozma and asked: "What is that thing, Ozma? A bird? I've never seen anything like it before."

"It is an Ork," answered Ozma, for they were watching the scene where the Ork and the three big birds were first landing their passengers in Jinxland, after the long flight across the desert. "I wonder," added the girl Ruler, musingly, "why those strangers dare venture into that unfortunate country, which is ruled by a wicked King."

"That girl, and the one-legged man, seem to be mortals from the outside world," said Dorothy.

"The man isn't one-legged," corrected Betsy; "he has one wooden leg."

"It's almost as bad," declared Dorothy, watching Cap'n Bill stump around.

"They are three mortal adventurers," said Ozma, "and they seem worthy and honest. But I fear they will be treated badly in Jinxland, and if they meet with any misfortune there it will reflect upon me, for Jinxland is a part of my dominions."

"Can't we help them in any way?" inquired Dorothy. "That seems like a nice little girl. I'd be sorry if anything happened to her."

"Let us watch the picture for a while," suggested Ozma, and so they all drew chairs before the Magic Picture and followed the adventures of Trot and Cap'n Bill and Button-Bright. Presently the scene shifted and showed their friend the Scarecrow crossing the mountains into Jinxland, and that somewhat relieved Ozma's anxiety, for she knew at once that Glinda the Good had sent the Scarecrow to protect the strangers.

The adventures in Jinxland proved very interesting to the three girls in Ozma's palace, who during the succeeding days spent much of their time in watching the picture. It was like a story to them.

"That girl's a reg'lar trump!" exclaimed Dorothy, referring to Trot, and Ozma answered:

"She's a dear little thing, and I'm sure nothing very bad will happen to her. The old sailor is a fine character, too, for he has never once grumbled over being a grasshopper, as so many would have done."

When the Scarecrow was so nearly burned up the girls all shivered a little, and they clapped their hands in joy when the flock of Orks came and saved him.

So it was that when all the exciting adventures in Jinxland were over and the four Orks had begun their flight across the mountains to carry the mortals into the Land of Oz, Ozma called the Wizard to her and asked him to prepare a place for the strangers to sleep.

The famous Wizard of Oz was a quaint little man who inhabited the royal palace and attended to all the magical things that Ozma wanted done. He was not as powerful as Glinda, to be sure, but he could do a great many wonderful things. He proved this by placing a house in the uninhabited part of the Quadling Country where the Orks landed Cap'n Bill and Trot and Button-Bright, and fitting it with all the comforts I have described in the last chapter.

Next morning Dorothy said to Ozma:

"Oughtn't we to go meet the strangers, so we can show them the way to the Emerald City? I'm sure that little girl will feel shy in this beautiful land, and I know if 'twas me I'd like somebody to give me a welcome."

Ozma smiled at her little friend and answered:

"You and Betsy may go to meet them, if you wish, but I cannot leave my palace just now, as I am to have a conference with Jack Pumpkinhead and Professor Woggle-Bug on important matters. You may take the Saw-Horse and the Red Wagon, and if you start soon you will be able to meet the Scarecrow and the strangers at Glinda's palace."

"Oh, thank you!" cried Dorothy, and went away to tell Betsy and to make preparations for the journey.

CHAPTER XXII

THE WATERFALL

GLINDA'S CASTLE WAS A LONG WAY FROM THE MOUNTAINS, BUT THE SCARECROW began the journey cheerfully, since time was of no great importance in the Land of Oz and he had recently made the trip and knew the way. It never mattered much to Button-Bright where he was or what he was doing; the boy was content in being alive and having good companions to share his wanderings. As for Trot and Cap'n Bill, they now found themselves so comfortable and free from danger, in this fine fairy-land, and they were so awed and amazed by the adventures they were encountering, that the journey to Glinda's castle was more like a pleasure trip than a hardship, so many wonderful things were there to see.

Button-Bright had been in Oz before, but never in this part of it, so the Scarecrow was the only one who knew the paths and could lead them. They had eaten a hearty breakfast, which they found already prepared for them and awaiting them on the table when they arose from their refreshing sleep, so they left the magic house in a contented mood and with hearts lighter and more happy than they had known for many a day. As they marched along through the fields, the sun shone brightly and the breeze was laden with delicious fragrance, for it carried with it the breath of millions of wildflowers.

At noon, when they stopped to rest by the banks of a pretty river, Trot said with a long-drawn breath that was much like a sigh:

"I wish we'd brought with us some of the food that was left from our breakfast, for I'm getting hungry again."

Scarcely had she spoken when a table rose up before them, as if from the ground itself, and it was loaded with fruits and nuts and cakes and many other good things to eat. The little girl's eyes opened wide at this display of magic, and Cap'n Bill was not sure that the things were actually there and fit to eat until he had taken them in his hand and tasted them. But the Scarecrow said with a laugh:

"Someone is looking after your welfare, that is certain, and from the looks of this table I suspect my friend the Wizard has taken us in his charge. I've known him to do things like this before, and if we are in the Wizard's care you need not worry about your future."

"Who's worrying?" inquired Button-Bright, already at the table and busily eating.

The Scarecrow looked around the place while the others were feasting, and finding many things unfamiliar to him he shook his head and remarked:

"I must have taken the wrong path, back in that last valley, for on my way to Jinxland I remember that I passed around the foot of this river, where there was a great waterfall."

"Did the river make a bend, after the waterfall?" asked Cap'n Bill.

"No, the river disappeared. Only a pool of whirling water showed what had become of the river; but I suppose it is underground, somewhere, and will come to the surface again in another part of the country."

"Well," suggested Trot, as she finished her luncheon, "as there is no way to cross this river, I s'pose we'll have to find that waterfall, and go around it."

"Exactly," replied the Scarecrow; so they soon renewed their journey, following the river for a long time until the roar of the waterfall sounded in their ears. By and by they came to the waterfall itself, a sheet of silver dropping far, far down into a tiny lake which seemed to have no outlet. From the top of the fall, where they stood, the banks gradually sloped away, so that the descent by land was quite easy, while the river could do nothing but glide over an edge of rock and tumble straight down to the depths below.

"You see," said the Scarecrow, leaning over the brink, "this is called by our Oz people the Great Waterfall, because it is certainly the highest one in all the land; but I think—Help!"

He had lost his balance and pitched headforemost into the river. They saw a flash of straw and blue clothes, and the painted face looking upward in surprise. The next moment the Scarecrow was swept over the waterfall and plunged into the basin below.

The accident had happened so suddenly that for a moment they were all too horrified to speak or move.

"Quick! We must go to help him or he will be drowned," Trot exclaimed.

Even while speaking she began to descend the bank to the pool below, and Cap'n Bill followed as swiftly as his wooden leg would let him. Button-Bright came more slowly, calling to the girl:

"He can't drown, Trot; he's a Scarecrow."

But she wasn't sure a Scarecrow couldn't drown and never relaxed her speed until she stood on the edge of the pool, with the spray dashing in her face. Cap'n Bill, puffing and panting, had just voice enough to ask, as he reached her side:

"See him, Trot?"

"Not a speck of him. Oh, Cap'n, what do you s'pose has become of him?"

"I s'pose," replied the sailor, "that he's in that water, more or less far down, and I'm 'fraid it'll make his straw pretty soggy. But as fer his bein' drowned, I agree with Button-Bright that it can't be done."

There was small comfort in this assurance and Trot stood for some time searching with her eyes the bubbling water, in the hope that the Scarecrow would finally come to the surface. Presently she heard Button-Bright calling: "Come here, Trot!" and looking around she saw that the boy had crept over the wet rocks to the edge of the waterfall and seemed to be peering behind it. Making her way toward him, she asked:

"What do you see?"

"A cave," he answered. "Let's go in. P'r'aps we'll find the Scarecrow there."

She was a little doubtful of that, but the cave interested her, and so did it Cap'n Bill. There was just space enough at the edge of the sheet of water for them to crowd in behind it, but after that dangerous entrance they found room enough to walk upright and after a time they came to an opening in the wall of rock. Approaching this opening, they gazed within it and found a series of steps, cut so that they might easily descend into the cavern.

Trot turned to look inquiringly at her companions. The falling water made such din and roaring that her voice could not be heard. Cap'n Bill nodded his head, but before he could enter the cave, Button-Bright was before him, clambering down the steps without a particle of fear. So the others followed the boy.

The first steps were wet with spray, and slippery, but the remainder were quite dry. A rosy light seemed to come from the interior of the cave, and this lighted their way. After the steps there was a short tunnel, high enough for them to walk erect in, and then they reached the cave itself and paused in wonder and admiration.

They stood on the edge of a vast cavern, the walls and domed roof of which were lined with countless rubies, exquisitely cut and flashing sparkling rays from one to another. This caused a radiant light that permitted the entire cavern to be distinctly seen, and the effect was so marvelous that Trot drew in her breath with a sort of a gasp, and stood quite still in wonder.

But the walls and roof of the cavern were merely a setting for a more wonderful scene. In the center was a bubbling caldron of water, for here the river rose again, splashing and dashing till its spray rose high in the air, where it took the ruby color of the jewels and seemed like a seething mass of flame. And while they gazed into the tumbling, tossing water, the body of the Scarecrow suddenly rose in the center, struggling and kicking, and the next instant wholly disappeared from view.

"My, but he's wet!" exclaimed Button-Bright; but none of the others heard him.

Trot and Cap'n Bill discovered that a broad ledge—covered, like the walls, with glittering rubies—ran all around the cavern; so they followed this gorgeous path to the rear and found where the water made its final dive underground, before it disappeared entirely. Where it plunged into this dim abyss the river was black and dreary looking, and they stood gazing in awe until just beside them the body of the Scarecrow again popped up from the water.

CHAPTER XXIII

THE LAND OF OZ

THE STRAW MAN'S APPEARANCE ON THE WATER WAS SO SUDDEN THAT IT STARTLED Trot, but Cap'n Bill had the presence of mind to stick his wooden leg out over the water and the Scarecrow made a desperate clutch and grabbed the leg with both hands. He managed to hold on until Trot and Button-Bright knelt down and seized his clothing, but the children would have been powerless to drag the soaked Scarecrow ashore had not Cap'n Bill now assisted them. When they laid him on the ledge of rubies he was the most useless looking Scarecrow you can imagine—his straw sodden and dripping with water, his clothing wet and crumpled, while even the sack upon which his face was painted had become so wrinkled that the old jolly expression of their stuffed friend's features was entirely gone. But he could still speak, and when Trot bent down her ear she heard him say:

"Get me out of here as soon as you can."

That seemed a wise thing to do, so Cap'n Bill lifted his head and shoulders, and Trot and Button-Bright each took a leg; among them they partly carried and partly dragged the damp Scarecrow out of the Ruby Cavern, along the tunnel, and up the flight of rock steps. It was somewhat difficult to get him past the edge of the waterfall,

but they succeeded, after much effort, and a few minutes later laid their poor comrade on a grassy bank where the sun shone upon him freely and he was beyond the reach of the spray.

Cap'n Bill now knelt down and examined the straw that the Scarecrow was stuffed with.

"I don't believe it'll be of much use to him, any more," said he, "for it's full of polliwogs an' fish eggs, an' the water has took all the crinkle out o' the straw an' ruined it. I guess, Trot, that the best thing for us to do is to empty out all his body an' carry his head an' clothes along the road till we come to a field or a house where we can get some fresh straw."

"Yes, Cap'n," she agreed, "there's nothing else to be done. But how shall we ever find the road to Glinda's palace, without the Scarecrow to guide us?"

"That's easy," said the Scarecrow, speaking in a rather feeble but distinct voice. "If Cap'n Bill will carry my head on his shoulders, eyes front, I can tell him which way to go."

So they followed that plan and emptied all the old, wet straw out of the Scarecrow's body. Then the sailor-man wrung out the clothes and laid them in the sun till they were quite dry. Trot took charge of the head and pressed the wrinkles out of the face as it dried, so that after a while the Scarecrow's expression became natural again, and as jolly as before.

This work consumed some time, but when it was completed they again started upon their journey, Button-Bright carrying the boots and hat, Trot the bundle of clothes, and Cap'n Bill the head. The Scarecrow, having regained his composure and being now in a good humor, despite his recent mishaps, beguiled their way with stories of the Land of Oz.

It was not until the next morning, however, that they found straw with which to restuff the Scarecrow. That evening they came to the same little house they had slept in before, only now it was magically transferred to a new place. The same bountiful supper as before was found smoking hot upon the table and the same cosy beds were ready for them to sleep in.

They rose early and after breakfast went out of doors, and there, lying just beside the house, was a heap of clean, crisp straw. Ozma had noticed the Scarecrow's accident in her Magic Picture and had notified the Wizard to provide the straw, for she knew the adventurers were not likely to find straw in the country through which they were now traveling.

They lost no time in stuffing the Scarecrow anew, and he was greatly delighted at being able to walk around again and to assume the leadership of the little party.

"Really," said Trot, "I think you're better than you were before, for you are fresh and sweet all through and rustle beautifully when you move."

"Thank you, my dear," he replied gratefully. "I always feel like a new man when I'm freshly stuffed. No one likes to get musty, you know, and even good straw may be spoiled by age."

"It was water that spoiled you, the last time," remarked Button-Bright, "which proves that too much bathing is as bad as too little. But, after all, Scarecrow, water is not as dangerous for you as fire."

"All things are good in moderation," declared the Scarecrow. "But now, let us hurry on, or we shall not reach Glinda's palace by nightfall."

CHAPTER XXIV

THE ROYAL RECEPTION

AT ABOUT FOUR O'CLOCK OF THAT SAME DAY THE RED WAGON DREW UP AT THE
entrance to Glinda's palace and Dorothy and Betsy jumped out. Ozma's Red Wagon
was almost a chariot, being inlaid with rubies and pearls, and it was drawn by Ozma's
favorite steed, the wooden Saw-Horse.

"Shall I unharness you," asked Dorothy, "so you can come in and visit?"

"No," replied the Saw-Horse. "I'll just stand here and think. Take your time.
Thinking doesn't seem to bore me at all."

"What will you think of?" inquired Betsy.

"Of the acorn that grew the tree from which I was made."

So they left the wooden animal and went in to see Glinda, who welcomed the little
girls in her most cordial manner.

"I knew you were on your way," said the good Sorceress when they were seated
in her library, "for I learned from my Record Book that you intended to meet Trot
and Button-Bright on their arrival here."

"Is the strange little girl named Trot?" asked Dorothy.

"Yes; and her companion, the old sailor, is named Cap'n Bill. I think we shall like them very much, for they are just the kind of people to enjoy and appreciate our fairy-land and I do not see any way, at present, for them to return again to the outside world."

"Well, there's room enough here for them, I'm sure," said Dorothy. "Betsy and I are already eager to welcome Trot. It will keep us busy for a year, at least, showing her all the wonderful things in Oz."

Glinda smiled.

"I have lived here many years," said she, "and I have not seen all the wonders of Oz yet."

Meantime the travelers were drawing near to the palace, and when they first caught sight of its towers Trot realized that it was far more grand and imposing than was the King's castle in Jinxland. The nearer they came, the more beautiful the palace appeared, and when finally the Scarecrow led them up the great marble steps, even Button-Bright was filled with awe.

"I don't see any soldiers to guard the place," said the little girl.

"There is no need to guard Glinda's palace," replied the Scarecrow. "We have no wicked people in Oz, that we know of, and even if there were any, Glinda's magic would be powerful enough to protect her."

Button-Bright was now standing on the top steps of the entrance, and he suddenly exclaimed:

"Why, there's the Saw-Horse and the Red Wagon! Hip, hooray!" and next moment he was rushing down to throw his arms around the neck of the wooden horse, which good-naturedly permitted this familiarity when it recognized in the boy an old friend.

Button-Bright's shout had been heard inside the palace, so now Dorothy and Betsy came running out to embrace their beloved friend, the Scarecrow, and to welcome Trot and Cap'n Bill to the Land of Oz.

"We've been watching you for a long time, in Ozma's Magic Picture," said Dorothy, "and Ozma has sent us to invite you to her own palace in the Em'rald City. I don't know if you realize how lucky you are to get that invitation, but you'll understand it better after you've seen the royal palace and the Em'rald City."

Glinda now appeared in person to lead all the party into her Azure Reception Room. Trot was a little afraid of the stately Sorceress, but gained courage by holding fast to the hands of Betsy and Dorothy. Cap'n Bill had no one to help him feel at ease, so the old sailor sat stiffly on the edge of his chair and said: "Yes, ma'am," or "No, ma'am," when he was spoken to, and was greatly embarrassed by so much splendor.

The Scarecrow had lived so much in palaces that he felt quite at home, and he chatted to Glinda and the Oz girls in a merry, light-hearted way. He told all about his adventures in Jinxland, and at the Great Waterfall, and on the journey hither—most of which his hearers knew already—and then he asked Dorothy and Betsy what had happened in the Emerald City since he had left there.

They all passed the evening and the night at Glinda's palace, and the Sorceress was so gracious to Cap'n Bill that the old man by degrees regained his self-possession and began to enjoy himself. Trot had already come to the conclusion that in Dorothy and Betsy she had found two delightful comrades, and Button-Bright was just as much at home here as he had been in the fields of Jinxland or when he was buried in the popcorn snow of the Land of Mo.

The next morning they arose bright and early and after breakfast bade good-bye to the kind Sorceress, whom Trot and Cap'n Bill thanked earnestly for sending the Scarecrow to Jinxland to rescue them. Then they all climbed into the Red Wagon.

There was room for all on the broad seats, and when all had taken their places—Dorothy, Trot and Betsy on the rear seat and Cap'n Bill, Button-Bright and the Scarecrow in front—they called "Gid-dap!" to the Saw-Horse and the wooden steed moved briskly away, pulling the Red Wagon with ease.

It was now that the strangers began to perceive the real beauties of the Land of Oz, for they were passing through a more thickly settled part of the country and the population grew more dense as they drew nearer to the Emerald City. Everyone they met had a cheery word or a smile for the Scarecrow, Dorothy and Betsy Bobbin, and some of them remembered Button-Bright and welcomed him back to their country.

It was a happy party, indeed, that journeyed in the Red Wagon to the Emerald City, and Trot already began to hope that Ozma would permit her and Cap'n Bill to live always in the Land of Oz.

When they reached the great city they were more amazed than ever, both by the concourse of people in their quaint and picturesque costumes, and by the splendor of the city itself. But the magnificence of the Royal Palace quite took their breath away, until Ozma received them in her own pretty apartment and by her charming manners and assuring smiles made them feel they were no longer strangers.

Trot was given a lovely little room next to that of Dorothy, while Cap'n Bill had the cosiest sort of a room next to Trot's and overlooking the gardens. And that evening Ozma gave a grand banquet and reception in honor of the new arrivals. While Trot had read of many of the people she then met, Cap'n Bill was less familiar with them and many of the unusual characters introduced to him that evening caused the old sailor to open his eyes wide in astonishment.

He had thought the live Scarecrow about as curious as anyone could be, but now he met the Tin Woodman, who was all made of tin, even to his heart, and carried a gleaming axe over his shoulder wherever he went. Then there was Jack

Pumpkinhead, whose head was a real pumpkin with the face carved upon it; and Professor Woggle-Bug, who had the shape of an enormous bug but was dressed in neat fitting garments. The Professor was an interesting talker and had very polite manners, but his face was so comical that it made Cap'n Bill smile to look at it. A great friend of Dorothy and Ozma seemed to be a machine man called Tik-Tok, who ran down several times during the evening and had to be wound up again by someone before he could move or speak.

At the reception appeared the Shaggy Man and his brother, both very popular in Oz, as well as Dorothy's Uncle Henry and Aunt Em, two happy old people who lived in a pretty cottage near the palace.

But what perhaps seemed most surprising to both Trot and Cap'n Bill was the number of peculiar animals admitted into Ozma's parlors, where they not only conducted themselves quite properly but were able to talk as well as anyone.

There was the Cowardly Lion, an immense beast with a beautiful mane; and the Hungry Tiger, who smiled continually; and Eureka the Pink Kitten, who lay curled upon a cushion and had rather supercilious manners; and the wooden Saw-Horse; and nine tiny piglets that belonged to the Wizard; and a mule named Hank, who belonged to Betsy Bobbin. A fuzzy little terrier dog, named Toto, lay at Dorothy's feet but seldom took part in the conversation, although he listened to every word that was said. But the most wonderful of all to Trot was a square beast with a winning smile, that squatted in a corner of the room and wagged his square head at everyone in quite a jolly way. Betsy told Trot that this unique beast was called the Woozy, and there was no other like him in all the world.

Cap'n Bill and Trot had both looked around expectantly for the Wizard of Oz, but the evening was far advanced before the famous little man entered the room. But he went up to the strangers at once and said:

"I know you, but you don't know me; so let's get acquainted."

And they did get acquainted, in a very short time, and before the evening was over Trot felt that she knew every person and animal present at the reception, and that they were all her good friends.

Suddenly they looked around for Button-Bright, but he was nowhere to be found.

"Dear me!" cried Trot. "He's lost again."

"Never mind, my dear," said Ozma, with her charming smile, "no one can go far astray in the Land of Oz, and if Button-Bright isn't lost occasionally, he isn't happy."

CONTENTS

CHAPTER I

THE PRINCE OF PINGAREE

IF YOU HAVE A MAP OF THE LAND OF OZ HANDY, YOU WILL FIND THAT THE GREAT Nonestic Ocean washes the shores of the Kingdom of Rinkitink, between which and the Land of Oz lies a strip of the country of the Nome King and a Sandy Desert. The Kingdom of Rinkitink isn't very big and lies close to the ocean, all the houses and the King's palace being built near the shore. The people live much upon the water, boating and fishing, and the wealth of Rinkitink is gained from trading along the coast and with the islands nearest it.

Four days' journey by boat to the north of Rinkitink is the Island of Pingaree, and as our story begins here I must tell you something about this island. At the north end of Pingaree, where it is widest, the land is a mile from shore to shore, but at the south end it is scarcely half a mile broad; thus, although Pingaree is four miles long, from north to south, it cannot be called a very big island. It is exceedingly pretty, however, and to the gulls who approach it from the sea it must resemble a huge green wedge lying upon the waters, for its grass and trees give it the color of an emerald.

The grass came to the edge of the sloping shores; the beautiful trees occupied all the central portion of Pingaree, forming a continuous grove where the branches met high overhead and there was just space beneath them for the cosy houses of the inhabitants. These houses were scattered everywhere throughout the island, so that there was no town or city, unless the whole island might be called a city. The canopy of leaves, high overhead, formed a shelter from sun and rain, and the dwellers in the grove could all look past the straight tree-trunks and across the grassy slopes to the purple waters of the Nonestic Ocean.

At the big end of the island, at the north, stood the royal palace of King Kitticut, the lord and ruler of Pingaree. It was a beautiful palace, built entirely of snow-white marble and capped by domes of burnished gold, for the King was exceedingly wealthy. All along the coast of Pingaree were found the largest and finest pearls in the whole world.

These pearls grew within the shells of big oysters, and the people raked the oysters from their watery beds, sought out the milky pearls and carried them dutifully to their King. Therefore, once every year His Majesty was able to send six of his boats, with sixty rowers and many sacks of the valuable pearls, to the Kingdom of Rinkitink, where there was a city called Gilgad, in which King Rinkitink's palace stood on a rocky headland and served, with its high towers, as a lighthouse to guide sailors to the harbor. In Gilgad the pearls from Pingaree were purchased by the King's treasurer, and the boats went back to the island laden with stores of rich merchandise and such supplies of food as the people and the royal family of Pingaree needed.

The Pingaree people never visited any other land but that of Rinkitink, and so there were few other lands that knew there was such an island. To the southwest was an island called the Isle of Phreex, where the inhabitants had no use for pearls. And far north of Pingaree—six days' journey by boat, it was said—were twin islands named Regos and Coregos, inhabited by a fierce and warlike people.

Many years before this story really begins, ten big boatloads of those fierce warriors of Regos and Coregos visited Pingaree, landing suddenly upon the north end of the island. There they began to plunder and conquer, as was their custom, but the people of Pingaree, although neither so big nor so strong as their foes, were able to defeat them and drive them all back to the sea, where a great storm overtook the raiders from Regos and Coregos and destroyed them and their boats, not a single warrior returning to his own country.

This defeat of the enemy seemed the more wonderful because the pearl-fishers of Pingaree were mild and peaceful in disposition and seldom quarreled even among themselves. Their only weapons were their oyster rakes; yet the fact remains that they drove their fierce enemies from Regos and Coregos from their shores.

King Kitticut was only a boy when this remarkable battle was fought, and now his hair was gray; but he remembered the day well and, during the years that followed, his one constant fear was of another invasion of his enemies. He feared they might send a more numerous army to his island, both for conquest and revenge, in which case there could be little hope of successfully opposing them.

This anxiety on the part of King Kitticut led him to keep a sharp lookout for strange boats, one of his men patrolling the beach constantly, but he was too wise to allow any fear to make him or his subjects unhappy. He was a good King and lived very contentedly in his fine palace, with his fair Queen Garee and their one child, Prince Inga.

The wealth of Pingaree increased year by year; and the happiness of the people increased, too. Perhaps there was no place, outside the Land of Oz, where contentment and peace were more manifest than on this pretty island, hidden in the bosom of the Nonestic Ocean. Had these conditions remained undisturbed, there would have been no need to speak of Pingaree in this story.

Prince Inga, the heir to all the riches and the kingship of Pingaree, grew up surrounded by every luxury; but he was a manly little fellow, although somewhat too grave and thoughtful, and he could never bear to be idle a single minute. He knew where the finest oysters lay hidden along the coast and was as successful in finding pearls as any of the men of the island, although he was so slight and small. He had a little boat of his own and a rake for dragging up the oysters and he was very proud indeed when he could carry a big white pearl to his father.

There was no school upon the island, as the people of Pingaree were far removed from the state of civilization that gives our modern children such advantages as schools and learned professors, but the King owned several manuscript books, the pages being made of sheepskin. Being a man of intelligence, he was able to teach his son something of reading, writing and arithmetic.

When studying his lessons Prince Inga used to go into the grove near his father's palace and climb into the branches of a tall tree, where he had built a platform with a comfortable seat to rest upon, all hidden by the canopy of leaves. There, with no one to disturb him, he would pore over the sheepskin on which were written the queer characters of the Pingarese language.

King Kitticut was very proud of his little son, as well he might be, and he soon felt a high respect for Inga's judgment and thought that he was worthy to be taken into the confidence of his father in many matters of state. He taught the boy the needs of the people and how to rule them justly, for some day he knew that Inga would be King in his place. One day he called his son to his side and said to him:

"Our island now seems peaceful enough, Inga, and we are happy and prosperous, but I cannot forget those terrible people of Regos and Coregos. My constant fear is that they will send a fleet of boats to search for those of their race whom we defeated many years ago, and whom the sea afterwards destroyed. If the warriors come in great numbers we may be unable to oppose them, for my people are little trained to fighting at best; they surely would cause us much injury and suffering."

"Are we, then, less powerful than in my grandfather's day?" asked Prince Inga.

The King shook his head thoughtfully.

"It is not that," said he. "That you may fully understand that marvelous battle, I must confide to you a great secret. I have in my possession three Magic Talismans, which I have ever guarded with utmost care, keeping the knowledge of their existence from anyone else. But, lest I should die and the secret be lost, I have decided to tell you what these talismans are and where they are hidden. Come with me, my son."

He led the way through the rooms of the palace until they came to the great banquet hall. There, stopping in the center of the room, he stooped down and touched a hidden spring in the tiled floor. At once one of the tiles sank downward and the King reached within the cavity and drew out a silken bag.

This bag he proceeded to open, showing Inga that it contained three great pearls, each one as big around as a marble. One had a blue tint and one was of a delicate rose color, but the third was pure white.

"These three pearls," said the King, speaking in a solemn, impressive voice, "are the most wonderful the world has ever known. They were gifts to one of my ancestors from the Mermaid Queen, a powerful fairy whom he once had the good fortune to rescue from her enemies. In gratitude for this favor she presented him with these pearls. Each of the three possesses an astonishing power, and whoever is their owner may count himself a fortunate man. This one having the blue tint will give to the person who carries it a strength so great that no power can resist him. The one with the pink glow will protect its owner from all dangers that may threaten him, no matter from what source they may come. The third pearl—this one of pure white—can speak, and its words are always wise and helpful."

"What is this, my father!" exclaimed the Prince, amazed; "do you tell me that a pearl can speak? It sounds impossible."

"Your doubt is due to your ignorance of fairy powers," returned the King, gravely. "Listen, my son, and you will know that I speak the truth."

He held the white pearl to Inga's ear and the Prince heard a small voice say distinctly: "Your father is right. Never question the truth of what you fail to understand, for the world is filled with wonders."

"I crave your pardon, dear father," said the Prince, "for clearly I heard the pearl speak, and its words were full of wisdom."

"The powers of the other pearls are even greater," resumed the King. "Were I poor in all else, these gems would make me richer than any other monarch the world holds."

"I believe that," replied Inga, looking at the beautiful pearls with much awe. "But tell me, my father, why do you fear the warriors of Regos and Coregos when these marvelous powers are yours?"

"The powers are mine only while I have the pearls upon my person," answered King Kitticut, "and I dare not carry them constantly for fear they might be lost. Therefore, I keep them safely hidden in this recess. My only danger lies in the chance that my watchmen might fail to discover the approach of our enemies and allow the warrior invaders to seize me before I could secure the pearls. I should, in that case, be quite powerless to resist. My father owned the magic pearls at the time of the Great Fight, of which you have so often heard, and the pink pearl protected him from harm, while the blue pearl enabled him and his people to drive away the enemy. Often have I suspected that the destroying storm was caused by the fairy mermaids, but that is a matter of which I have no proof."

"I have often wondered how we managed to win that battle," remarked Inga thoughtfully. "But the pearls will assist us in case the warriors come again, will they not?"

"They are as powerful as ever," declared the King. "Really, my son, I have little to fear from any foe. But lest I die and the secret be lost to the next King, I have now given it into your keeping. Remember that these pearls are the rightful heritage of all Kings of Pingaree. If at any time I should be taken from you, Inga, guard this treasure well and do not forget where it is hidden."

"I shall not forget," said Inga.

Then the King returned the pearls to their hiding place and the boy went to his own room to ponder upon the wonderful secret his father had that day confided to his care.

CHAPTER II

THE COMING OF KING RINKITINK

A FEW DAYS AFTER THIS, ON A BRIGHT AND SUNNY MORNING WHEN THE BREEZE blew soft and sweet from the ocean and the trees waved their leaf-laden branches, the Royal Watchman, whose duty it was to patrol the shore, came running to the King with news that a strange boat was approaching the island.

At first the King was sore afraid and made a step toward the hidden pearls, but the next moment he reflected that one boat, even if filled with enemies, would be power-less to injure him, so he curbed his fear and went down to the beach to discover who the strangers might be. Many of the men of Pingaree assembled there also, and Prince Inga followed his father. Arriving at the water's edge, they all stood gazing eagerly at the oncoming boat.

It was quite a big boat, they observed, and covered with a canopy of purple silk, embroidered with gold. It was rowed by twenty men, ten on each side. As it came nearer, Inga could see that in the stern, seated upon a high, cushioned chair of state, was a little man who was so very fat that he was nearly as broad as he was high This man was dressed in a loose silken robe of purple that fell in folds to his feet, while upon his head was a cap of white velvet curiously worked with golden threads and having a circle of diamonds sewn around the band. At the opposite end of the boat stood an oddly shaped cage, and several large boxes of sandalwood were piled near the center of the craft.

As the boat approached the shore the fat little man got upon his feet and bowed several times in the direction of those who had assembled to greet him, and as he bowed he flourished his white cap in an energetic manner. His face was round as an apple and nearly as rosy. When he stopped bowing he smiled in such a sweet and happy way that Inga thought he must be a very jolly fellow.

The prow of the boat grounded on the beach, stopping its speed so suddenly that the little man was caught unawares and nearly toppled headlong into the sea. But he managed to catch hold of the chair with one hand and the hair of one of his rowers with the other, and so steadied himself. Then, again waving his jeweled cap around his head, he cried in a merry voice:

"Well, here I am at last!"

"So I perceive," responded King Kitticut, bowing with much dignity.

The fat man glanced at all the sober faces before him and burst into a rollicking laugh. Perhaps I should say it was half laughter and half a chuckle of merriment, for the sounds he emitted were quaint and droll and tempted every hearer to laugh with him.

"Heh, heh—ho, ho, ho!" he roared. "Didn't expect me, I see. Keek-eek-eek-eek! This is funny—it's really funny. Didn't know I was coming, did you? Hoo, hoo, hoo, hoo! This is certainly amusing. But I'm here, just the same."

"Hush up!" said a deep, growling voice. "You're making yourself ridiculous."

Everyone looked to see where this voice came from; but none could guess who had uttered the words of rebuke. The rowers of the boat were all solemn and silent and certainly no one on the shore had spoken. But the little man did not seem astonished in the least, or even annoyed.

King Kitticut now addressed the stranger, saying courteously:

"You are welcome to the Kingdom of Pingaree. Perhaps you will deign to come ashore and at your convenience inform us whom we have the honor of receiving as a guest."

"Thanks; I will," returned the little fat man, waddling from his place in the boat and stepping, with some difficulty, upon the sandy beach. "I am King Rinkitink, of the City of Gilgad in the Kingdom of Rinkitink, and I have come to Pingaree to see for myself the monarch who sends to my city so many beautiful pearls. I have long wished to visit this island; and so, as I said before, here I am!"

"I am pleased to welcome you," said King Kitticut. "But why has Your Majesty so few attendants? Is it not dangerous for the King of a great country to make distant journeys in one frail boat, and with but twenty men?"

"Oh, I suppose so," answered King Rinkitink, with a laugh. "But what else could I do? My subjects would not allow me to go anywhere at all, if they knew it. So I just ran away."

"Ran away!" exclaimed King Kitticut in surprise.

"Funny, isn't it? Heh, heh, heh—woo, hoo!" laughed Rinkitink, and this is as near as I can spell with letters the jolly sounds of his laughter. "Fancy a King running away from his own people—hoo, hoo—keek, eek, eek, eek! But I had to, don't you see!"

"Why?" asked the other King.

"They're afraid I'll get into mischief. They don't trust me. Keek-eek-eek—Oh, dear me! Don't trust their own King. Funny, isn't it?"

"No harm can come to you on this island," said Kitticut, pretending not to notice the odd ways of his guest. "And, whenever it pleases you to return to your own country, I will send with you a fitting escort of my own people. In the meantime, pray accompany me to my palace, where everything shall be done to make you comfortable and happy."

"Much obliged," answered Rinkitink, tipping his white cap over his left ear and heartily shaking the hand of his brother monarch. "I'm sure you can make me comfortable if you've plenty to eat. And as for being happy—ha, ha, ha, ha!—why, that's my trouble. I'm *too* happy. But stop! I've brought you some presents in those boxes. Please order your men to carry them up to the palace."

"Certainly," answered King Kitticut, well pleased, and at once he gave his men the proper orders.

"And, by the way," continued the fat little King, "let them also take my goat from his cage."

"A goat!" exclaimed the King of Pingaree.

"Exactly; my goat Bilbil. I always ride him wherever I go, for I'm not at all fond of walking, being a trifle stout—eh, Kitticut?—a trifle stout! Hoo, hoo, hoo—keek, eek!"

The Pingaree people started to lift the big cage out of the boat, but just then a gruff voice cried: "Be careful, you villains!" and as the words seemed to come from the goat's mouth the men were so astonished that they dropped the cage upon the sand with a sudden jar.

"There! I told you so!" cried the voice angrily. "You've rubbed the skin off my left knee. Why on earth didn't you handle me gently?"

"There, there, Bilbil," said King Rinkitink soothingly; "don't scold, my boy. Remember that these are strangers, and we their guests." Then he turned to Kitticut and remarked: "You have no talking goats on your island, I suppose."

"We have no goats at all," replied the King; "nor have we any animals, of any sort, who are able to talk."

"I wish my animal couldn't talk, either," said Rinkitink, winking comically at Inga and then looking toward the cage. "He is very cross at times, and indulges in language that is not respectful. I thought, at first, it would be fine to have a talking goat, with whom I could converse as I rode about my city on his back; but—keek-eek-eek-eek!—the rascal treats me as if I were a chimney sweep instead of a King. Heh, heh, heh, keek, eek! A chimney sweep—hoo, hoo, hoo!—and me a King! Funny, isn't it?" This last was addressed to Prince Inga, whom he chucked familiarly under the chin, to the boy's great embarrassment.

"Why do you not ride a horse?" asked King Kitticut.

"I can't climb upon his back, being rather stout; that's why. Kee, kee, keek, eek!—rather stout—hoo, hoo, hoo!" He paused to wipe the tears of merriment from his eyes and then added: "But I can get on and off Bilbil's back with ease."

He now opened the cage and the goat deliberately walked out and looked about him in a sulky manner. One of the rowers brought from the boat a saddle made of red velvet and beautifully embroidered with silver thistles, which he fastened upon the goat's back. The fat King put his leg over the saddle and seated himself comfortably, saying:

"Lead on, my noble host, and we will follow."

"What! Up that steep hill?" cried the goat. "Get off my back at once, Rinkitink, or I won't budge a step."

"But—consider, Bilbil," remonstrated the King. "How am I to get up that hill unless I ride?"

"Walk!" growled Bilbil.

"But I'm too fat. Really, Bilbil, I'm surprised at you. Haven't I brought you all this distance so you may see something of the world and enjoy life? And now you are so ungrateful as to refuse to carry me! Turn about is fair play, my boy. The boat carried you to this shore, because you can't swim, and now you must carry me up the hill, because I can't climb. Eh, Bilbil, isn't that reasonable?"

"Well, well, well," said the goat, surlily, "keep quiet and I'll carry you. But you make me very tired, Rinkitink, with your ceaseless chatter."

After making this protest Bilbil began walking up the hill, carrying the fat King upon his back with no difficulty whatever.

Prince Inga and his father and all the men of Pingaree were much astonished to overhear this dispute between King Rinkitink and his goat; but they were too polite to make critical remarks in the presence of their guests. King Kitticut walked beside the goat and the Prince followed after, the men coming last with the boxes of sandalwood.

When they neared the palace, the Queen and her maidens came out to meet them and the royal guest was escorted in state to the splendid throne room of the palace. Here the boxes were opened and King Rinkitink displayed all the beautiful silks and laces and jewelry with which they were filled. Every one of the courtiers and ladies received a handsome present, and the King and Queen had many rich gifts and Inga not a few. Thus the time passed pleasantly until the Chamberlain announced that dinner was served.

Bilbil the goat declared that he preferred eating of the sweet, rich grass that grew abundantly in the palace grounds, and Rinkitink said that the beast could never bear being shut up in a stable; so they removed the saddle from his back and allowed him to wander wherever he pleased.

During the dinner Inga divided his attention between admiring the pretty gifts he had received and listening to the jolly sayings of the fat King, who laughed when he was not eating and ate when he was not laughing and seemed to enjoy himself immensely.

"For four days I have lived in that narrow boat," said he, "with no other amusement than to watch the rowers and quarrel with Bilbil; so I am very glad to be on land again with such friendly and agreeable people."

"You do us great honor," said King Kitticut, with a polite bow.

"Not at all—not at all, my brother. This Pingaree must be a wonderful island, for its pearls are the admiration of all the world; nor will I deny the fact that my kingdom would be a poor one without the riches and glory it derives from the trade in your pearls. So I have wished for many years to come here to see you, but my people said: 'No! Stay at home and behave yourself, or we'll know the reason why.' "

"Will they not miss Your Majesty from your palace at Gilgad?" inquired Kitticut.

"I think not," answered Rinkitink. "You see, one of my clever subjects has written a parchment entitled 'How to be Good,' and I believed it would benefit me to study it, as I consider the accomplishment of being good one of the fine arts. I had just scolded severely my Lord High Chancellor for coming to breakfast without combing his eyebrows, and was so sad and regretful at having hurt the poor man's feelings that I decided to shut myself up in my own room and study the scroll until I knew how to be good—hee, heek, keek, eek, eek!—to be good! Clever idea, that, wasn't it? Mighty

clever! And I issued a decree that no one should enter my room, under pain of my royal displeasure, until I was ready to come out. They're awfully afraid of my royal displeasure, although not a bit afraid of me. Then I put the parchment in my pocket and escaped through the back door to my boat—and here I am. Oo, hoo-hoo, keek-eek! Imagine the fuss there would be in Gilgad if my subjects knew where I am this very minute!"

"I would like to see that parchment," said the solemn-eyed Prince Inga, "for if it indeed teaches one to be good it must be worth its weight in pearls."

"Oh, it's a fine essay," said Rinkitink, "and beautifully written with a goosequill. Listen to this: You'll enjoy it—tee, hee, hee!—enjoy it."

He took from his pocket a scroll of parchment tied with a black ribbon, and having carefully unrolled it, he proceeded to read as follows:

" 'A Good Man is One who is Never Bad.' How's that, eh? Fine thought, what? 'Therefore, in order to be Good, you must avoid those Things which are Evil.' Oh, hoo-hoo-hoo!—how clever! When I get back I shall make the man who wrote that a royal hippolorum, for, beyond question, he is the wisest man in my kingdom—as he has often told me himself." With this, Rinkitink lay back in his chair and chuckled his queer chuckle until he coughed, and coughed until he choked and choked until he sneezed. And he wrinkled his face in such a jolly, droll way that few could keep from laughing with him, and even the good Queen was forced to titter behind her fan.

When Rinkitink had recovered from his fit of laughter and had wiped his eyes upon a fine lace handkerchief, Prince Inga said to him:

"The parchment speaks truly."

"Yes, it is true beyond doubt," answered Rinkitink, "and if I could persuade Bilbil to read it he would be a much better goat than he is now. Here is another selection: 'To avoid saying Unpleasant Things, always Speak Agreeably.' That would hit Bilbil, to a dot. And here is one that applies to you, my Prince: 'Good Children are seldom punished, for the reason that they deserve no punishment.' Now, I think that is neatly put, and shows the author to be a deep thinker. But the advice that has impressed me the most is in the following paragraph: 'You may not find it as Pleasant to be Good as it is to be Bad, but Other People will find it more Pleasant.' Haw-hoo-ho! keek-eek! 'Other people will find it more pleasant!'—hee, hee, heek, keek!—'more pleasant.' Dear me—dear me! Therein lies a noble incentive to be good, and whenever I get time I'm surely going to try it."

Then he wiped his eyes again with the lace handkerchief and, suddenly remembering his dinner, seized his knife and fork and began eating.

CHAPTER III

THE WARRIORS FROM THE NORTH

KING RINKITINK WAS SO MUCH PLEASED WITH THE ISLAND OF PINGAREE THAT HE continued his stay day after day and week after week, eating good dinners, talking with King Kitticut and sleeping. Once in a while he would read from his scroll. "For," said he, "whenever I return home, my subjects will be anxious to know if I have learned 'How to be Good,' and I must not disappoint them."

The twenty rowers lived on the small end of the island, with the pearl fishers, and seemed not to care whether they ever returned to the Kingdom of Rinkitink or not. Bilbil the goat wandered over the grassy slopes, or among the trees, and passed his days exactly as he pleased. His master seldom cared to ride him. Bilbil was a rare curiosity to the islanders, but since there was little pleasure in talking with the goat they kept away from him. This pleased the creature, who seemed well satisfied to be left to his own devices.

Once Prince Inga, wishing to be courteous, walked up to the goat and said: "Good morning, Bilbil."

"It isn't a good morning," answered Bilbil grumpily. "It is cloudy and damp, and looks like rain."

"I hope you are contented in our kingdom," continued the boy, politely ignoring the other's harsh words.

"I'm not," said Bilbil. "I'm never contented; so it doesn't matter to me whether I'm in your kingdom or in some other kingdom. Go away—will you?"

"Certainly," answered the Prince, and after this rebuff he did not again try to make friends with Bilbil.

Now that the King, his father, was so much occupied with his royal guest, Inga was often left to amuse himself, for a boy could not be allowed to take part in the conversation of two great monarchs. He devoted himself to his studies, therefore, and day after day he climbed into the branches of his favorite tree and sat for hours in his "tree-top rest," reading his father's precious manuscripts and thinking upon what he read.

You must not think that Inga was a molly-coddle or a prig, because he was so solemn and studious. Being a King's son and heir to a throne, he could not play with the other boys of Pingaree, and he lived so much in the society of the King and Queen, and was so surrounded by the pomp and dignity of a court, that he missed all the jolly times that boys usually have. I have no doubt that had he been able to live as other boys do, he would have been much like other boys; as it was, he was subdued by his surroundings, and more grave and thoughtful than one of his years should be.

Inga was in his tree one morning when, without warning, a great fog enveloped the Island of Pingaree. The boy could scarcely see the tree next to that in which he sat, but the leaves above him prevented the dampness from wetting him, so he curled himself up in his seat and fell fast asleep.

All that forenoon the fog continued. King Kitticut, who sat in his palace talking with his merry visitor, ordered the candles lighted, that they might be able to see one another. The good Queen, Inga's mother, found it was too dark to work at her embroidery, so she called her maidens together and told them wonderful stories of bygone days, in order to pass away the dreary hours.

But soon after noon the weather changed. The dense fog rolled away like a heavy cloud and suddenly the sun shot his bright rays over the island.

"Very good!" exclaimed King Kitticut. "We shall have a pleasant afternoon, I am sure," and he blew out the candles.

Then he stood a moment motionless, as if turned to stone, for a terrible cry from without the palace reached his ears—a cry so full of fear and horror that the King's heart almost stopped beating. Immediately there was a scurrying of feet as every one in the palace, filled with dismay, rushed outside to see what had happened. Even fat little Rinkitink sprang from his chair and followed his host and the others through the arched vestibule.

After many years the worst fears of King Kitticut were realized.

Landing upon the beach, which was but a few steps from the palace itself, were hundreds of boats, every one filled with a throng of fierce warriors. They sprang upon the land with wild shouts of defiance and rushed to the King's palace, waving aloft their swords and spears and battle-axes.

King Kitticut, so completely surprised that he was bewildered, gazed at the approaching host with terror and grief.

"They are the men of Regos and Coregos!" he groaned. "We are, indeed, lost!"

Then he bethought himself, for the first time, of his wonderful pearls. Turning quickly, he ran back into the palace and hastened to the hall where the treasures were hidden. But the leader of the warriors had seen the King enter the palace and bounded after him, thinking he meant to escape. Just as the King had stooped to press the secret spring in the tiles, the warrior seized him from the rear and threw him backward upon the floor, at the same time shouting to his men to fetch ropes and bind the prisoner. This they did very quickly and King Kitticut soon found himself helplessly bound and in the power of his enemies. In this sad condition he was lifted by the warriors and carried outside, when the good King looked upon a sorry sight.

The Queen and her maidens, the officers and servants of the royal household and all who had inhabited this end of the Island of Pingaree had been seized by the invaders and bound with ropes. At once they began carrying their victims to the boats, tossing them in as unceremoniously as if they had been bales of merchandise.

The King looked around for his son Inga, but failed to find the boy among the prisoners. Nor was the fat King, Rinkitink, to be seen anywhere about.

The warriors were swarming over the palace like bees in a hive, seeking anyone who might be in hiding, and after the search had been prolonged for some time the leader asked impatiently: "Do you find anyone else?"

"No," his men told him. "We have captured them all."

"Then," commanded the leader, "remove everything of value from the palace and tear down its walls and towers, so that not one stone remains upon another!"

While the warriors were busy with this task we will return to the boy Prince, who, when the fog lifted and the sun came out, wakened from his sleep and began to climb down from his perch in the tree. But the terrifying cries of the people, mingled with the shouts of the rude warriors, caused him to pause and listen eagerly.

Then he climbed rapidly up the tree, far above his platform, to the topmost swaying branches. This tree, which Inga called his own, was somewhat taller than the other trees that surrounded it, and when he had reached the top he pressed aside the leaves and saw a great fleet of boats upon the shore—strange boats, with banners that he had never seen before. Turning to look upon his father's palace, he found it surrounded by a horde of enemies. Then Inga knew the truth: that the island had been invaded by

the barbaric warriors from the north. He grew so faint from the terror of it all that he might have fallen had he not wound his arms around a limb and clung fast until the dizzy feeling passed away. Then with his sash he bound himself to the limb and again ventured to look out through the leaves.

The warriors were now engaged in carrying King Kitticut and Queen Garee and all their other captives down to the boats, where they were thrown in and chained one to another. It was a dreadful sight for the Prince to witness, but he sat very still, concealed from the sight of anyone below by the bower of leafy branches around him. Inga knew very well that he could do nothing to help his beloved parents, and that if he came down he would only be forced to share their cruel fate.

Now a procession of the Northmen passed between the boats and the palace, bearing the rich furniture, splendid draperies and rare ornaments of which the royal palace had been robbed, together with such food and other plunder as they could lay their hands upon. After this, the men of Regos and Coregos threw ropes around the marble domes and towers and hundreds of warriors tugged at these ropes until the domes and towers toppled and fell in ruins upon the ground. Then the walls themselves were torn down, till little remained of the beautiful palace but a vast heap of white marble blocks tumbled and scattered upon the ground.

Prince Inga wept bitter tears of grief as he watched the ruin of his home; yet he was powerless to avert the destruction. When the palace had been demolished, some of the warriors entered their boats and rowed along the coast of the island, while the others marched in a great body down the length of the island itself. They were so numerous that they formed a line stretching from shore to shore and they destroyed every house they came to and took every inhabitant prisoner.

The pearl fishers who lived at the lower end of the island tried to escape in their boats, but they were soon overtaken and made prisoners, like the others. Nor was there any attempt to resist the foe, for the sharp spears and pikes and swords of the invaders terrified the hearts of the defenseless people of Pingaree, whose sole weapons were their oyster rakes.

When night fell the whole of the Island of Pingaree had been conquered by the men of the North, and all its people were slaves of the conquerors. Next morning the men of Regos and Coregos, being capable of no further mischief, departed from the scene of their triumph, carrying their prisoners with them and taking also every boat to be found upon the island. Many of the boats they had filled with rich plunder, with pearls and silks and velvets, with silver and gold ornaments and all the treasure that had made Pingaree famed as one of the richest kingdoms in the world. And the hundreds of slaves they had captured would be set to work in the mines of Regos and the grain fields of Coregos.

So complete was the victory of the Northmen that it is no wonder the warriors sang songs of triumph as they hastened back to their homes. Great rewards were awaiting them when they showed the haughty King of Regos and the terrible Queen of Coregos the results of their ocean raid and conquest.

CHAPTER IV

THE DESERTED ISLAND

ALL THROUGH THAT TERRIBLE NIGHT PRINCE INGA REMAINED HIDDEN IN HIS TREE. In the morning he watched the great fleet of boats depart for their own country, carrying his parents and his countrymen with them, as well as everything of value the Island of Pingaree had contained.

Sad, indeed, were the boy's thoughts when the last of the boats had become a mere speck in the distance, but Inga did not dare leave his perch of safety until all of the craft of the invaders had disappeared beyond the horizon. Then he came down, very slowly and carefully, for he was weak from hunger and the long and weary watch, as he had been in the tree for twenty-four hours without food.

The sun shone upon the beautiful green isle as brilliantly as if no ruthless invader had passed and laid it in ruins. The birds still chirped among the trees and the butterflies darted from flower to flower as happily as when the land was filled with a prosperous and contented people.

Inga feared that only he was left of all his nation. Perhaps he might be obliged to pass his life there alone. He would not starve, for the sea would give him oysters and fish, and the trees fruit; yet the life that confronted him was far from enticing.

The boy's first act was to walk over to where the palace had stood and search the ruins until he found some scraps of food that had been overlooked by the enemy. He sat upon a block of marble and ate of this, and tears filled his eyes as he gazed upon the desolation around him. But Inga tried to bear up bravely, and having satisfied his hunger he walked over to the well, intending to draw a bucket of drinking water.

Fortunately, this well had been overlooked by the invaders and the bucket was still fastened to the chain that wound around a stout wooden windlass. Inga took hold of the crank and began letting the bucket down into the well, when suddenly he was startled by a muffled voice crying out:

"Be careful, up there!"

The sound and the words seemed to indicate that the voice came from the bottom of the well, so Inga looked down. Nothing could be seen, on account of the darkness.

"Who are you?" he shouted.

"It's I—Rinkitink," came the answer, and the depths of the well echoed: "Tink-i-tink-i-tink!" in a ghostly manner.

"Are you in the well?" asked the boy, greatly surprised.

"Yes, and nearly drowned. I fell in while running from those terrible warriors, and I've been standing in this damp hole ever since, with my head just above the water. It's lucky the well was no deeper, for had my head been under water, instead of above it—hoo, hoo, hoo, keek, eek!—under instead of over, you know—why, then I wouldn't be talking to you now! Ha, hoo, hee!" And the well dismally echoed: "Ha, hoo, hee!" which you must imagine was a laugh half merry and half sad.

"I'm awfully sorry," cried the boy, in answer. "I wonder you have the heart to laugh at all. But how am I to get you out?"

"I've been considering that all night," said Rinkitink, "and I believe the best plan will be for you to let down the bucket to me, and I'll hold fast to it while you wind up the chain and so draw me to the top."

"I will try to do that," replied Inga, and he let the bucket down very carefully until he heard the King call out:

"I've got it! Now pull me up—slowly, my boy, slowly—so I won't rub against the rough sides."

Inga began winding up the chain, but King Rinkitink was so fat that he was very heavy and by the time the boy had managed to pull him halfway up the well his strength was gone. He clung to the crank as long as possible, but suddenly it slipped from his grasp and the next minute he heard Rinkitink fall "plump!" into the water again.

"That's too bad!" called Inga, in real distress; "but you were so heavy I couldn't help it."

"Dear me!" gasped the King, from the darkness below, as he spluttered and coughed to get the water out of his mouth. "Why didn't you tell me you were going to let go?"

"I hadn't time," said Inga, sorrowfully.

"Well, I'm not suffering from thirst," declared the King, "for there's enough water inside me to float all the boats of Regos and Coregos—or at least it feels that way. But never mind! So long as I'm not actually drowned, what does it matter?"

"What shall we do next?" asked the boy anxiously.

"Call someone to help you," was the reply.

"There is no one on the island but myself," said the boy; "—excepting you," he added, as an afterthought.

"I'm not on it—more's the pity!—but *in* it," responded Rinkitink. "Are the warriors all gone?"

"Yes," said Inga, "and they have taken my father and mother, and all our people, to be their slaves," he added, trying in vain to repress a sob.

"So—so!" said Rinkitink softly; and then he paused a moment, as if in thought. Finally he said: "There are worse things than slavery, but I never imagined a well could be one of them. Tell me, Inga, could you let down some food to me? I'm nearly starved, and if you could manage to send me down some food I'd be *well* fed—hoo, hoo, heek, keek, eek!—well fed. Do you see the joke, Inga?"

"Do not ask me to enjoy a joke just now, Your Majesty," begged Inga in a sad voice; "but if you will be patient I will try to find something for you to eat."

He ran back to the ruins of the palace and began searching for bits of food with which to satisfy the hunger of the King, when to his surprise he observed the goat, Bilbil, wandering among the marble blocks.

"What!" cried Inga. "Didn't the warriors get you, either?"

"If they had," calmly replied Bilbil, "I shouldn't be here."

"But how did you escape?" asked the boy.

"Easily enough. I kept my mouth shut and stayed away from the rascals," said the goat. "I knew that the soldiers would not care for a skinny old beast like me, for to the eye of a stranger I seem good for nothing. Had they known I could talk, and that my head contained more wisdom than a hundred of their own noddles, I might not have escaped so easily."

"Perhaps you are right," said the boy.

"I suppose they got the old man?" carelessly remarked Bilbil.

"What old man?"

"Rinkitink."

"Oh, no! His Majesty is at the bottom of the well," said Inga, "and I don't know how to get him out again."

"Then let him stay there," suggested the goat.

"That would be cruel. I am sure, Bilbil, that you are fond of the good King, your master, and do not mean what you say. Together, let us find some way to save poor King Rinkitink. He is a very jolly companion, and has a heart exceedingly kind and gentle."

"Oh, well; the old boy isn't so bad, taken altogether," admitted Bilbil, speaking in a more friendly tone. "But his bad jokes and fat laughter tire me dreadfully, at times."

Prince Inga now ran back to the well, the goat following more leisurely.

"Here's Bilbil!" shouted the boy to the King. "The enemy didn't get him, it seems."

"That's lucky for the enemy," said Rinkitink. "But it's lucky for me, too, for perhaps the beast can assist me out of this hole. If you can let a rope down the well, I am sure that you and Bilbil, pulling together, will be able to drag me to the earth's surface."

"Be patient and we will make the attempt," replied Inga encouragingly, and he ran to search the ruins for a rope. Presently he found one that had been used by the warriors in toppling over the towers, which in their haste they had neglected to remove, and with some difficulty he untied the knots and carried the rope to the mouth of the well.

Bilbil had lain down to sleep and the refrain of a merry song came in muffled tones from the well, proving that Rinkitink was making a patient endeavor to amuse himself.

"I've found a rope!" Inga called down to him; and then the boy proceeded to make a loop in one end of the rope, for the King to put his arms through, and the other end he placed over the drum of the windlass. He now aroused Bilbil and fastened the rope firmly around the goat's shoulders.

"Are you ready?" asked the boy, leaning over the well.

"I am," replied the King.

"And I am not," growled the goat, "for I have not yet had my nap out. Old Rinki will be safe enough in the well until I've slept an hour or two longer."

"But it is damp in the well," protested the boy, "and King Rinkitink may catch the rheumatism, so that he will have to ride upon your back wherever he goes."

Hearing this, Bilbil jumped up at once.

"Let's get him out," he said earnestly.

"Hold fast!" shouted Inga to the King. Then he seized the rope and helped Bilbil to pull. They soon found the task more difficult than they had supposed. Once or twice the King's weight threatened to drag both the boy and the goat into the well, to keep Rinkitink company. But they pulled sturdily, being aware of this danger, and at last the King popped out of the hole and fell sprawling full length upon the ground.

For a time he lay panting and breathing hard to get his breath back, while Inga and Bilbil were likewise worn out from their long strain at the rope; so the three rested quietly upon the grass and looked at one another in silence.

Finally Bilbil said to the King:

"I'm surprised at you. Why were you so foolish as to fall down that well? Don't you know it's a dangerous thing to do? You might have broken your neck in the fall, or been drowned in the water."

"Bilbil," replied the King solemnly, "you're a goat. Do you imagine I fell down the well on purpose?"

"I imagine nothing," retorted Bilbil. "I only know you were there."

"There? Heh-heh-heek-keek-eek! To be sure I was there," laughed Rinkitink. "There in a dark hole, where there was no light; there in a watery well, where the wetness soaked me through and through—keek-eek-eek-eek!—through and through!"

"How did it happen?" inquired Inga.

"I was running away from the enemy," explained the King, "and I was carelessly looking over my shoulder at the same time, to see if they were chasing me. So I did not see the well, but stepped into it and found myself tumbling down to the bottom. I struck the water very neatly and began struggling to keep myself from drowning, but presently I found that when I stood upon my feet on the bottom of the well, that my chin was just above the water. So I stood still and yelled for help; but no one heard me."

"If the warriors had heard you," said Bilbil, "they would have pulled you out and carried you away to be a slave. Then you would have been obliged to work for a living, and that would be a new experience."

"Work!" exclaimed Rinkitink. "Me work? Hoo, hoo, heek-keek-eek! How absurd! I'm so stout—not to say chubby—not to say fat—that I can hardly walk, and I couldn't earn my salt at hard work. So I'm glad the enemy did not find me, Bilbil. How many others escaped?"

"That I do not know," replied the boy, "for I have not yet had time to visit the other parts of the island. When you have rested and satisfied your royal hunger, it might be well for us to look around and see what the thieving warriors of Regos and Coregos have left us."

"An excellent idea," declared Rinkitink. "I am somewhat feeble from my long confinement in the well, but I can ride upon Bilbil's back and we may as well start at once."

Hearing this, Bilbil cast a surly glance at his master but said nothing, since it was really the goat's business to carry King Rinkitink wherever he desired to go.

They first searched the ruins of the palace, and where the kitchen had once been they found a small quantity of food that had been half hidden by a block of marble. This they carefully placed in a sack to preserve it for future use, the little fat King having first eaten as much as he cared for. This consumed some time, for Rinkitink had been exceedingly hungry and liked to eat in a leisurely manner. When he had finished the meal he straddled Bilbil's back and set out to explore the island, Prince Inga walking by his side.

They found on every hand ruin and desolation. The houses of the people had been pilfered of all valuables and then torn down or burned. Not a boat had been left upon the shore, nor was there a single person, man or woman or child, remaining upon the island, save themselves. The only inhabitants of Pingaree now consisted of a fat little King, a boy and a goat.

Even Rinkitink, merry hearted as he was, found it hard to laugh in the face of this mighty disaster. Even the goat, contrary to its usual habit, refrained from saying anything disagreeable. As for the poor boy whose home was now a wilderness, the tears came often to his eyes as he marked the ruin of his dearly loved island.

When, at nightfall, they reached the lower end of Pingaree and found it swept as bare as the rest, Inga's grief was almost more than he could bear. Everything had been swept from him—parents, home and country—in so brief a time that his bewilderment was equal to his sorrow.

Since no house remained standing, in which they might sleep, the three wanderers crept beneath the overhanging branches of a cassa tree and curled themselves up as comfortably as possible. So tired and exhausted were they by the day's anxieties and griefs that their troubles soon faded into the mists of dreamland. Beast and King and boy slumbered peacefully together until wakened by the singing of the birds which greeted the dawn of a new day.

CHAPTER V

THE THREE PEARLS

When King Rinkitink and Prince Inga had bathed themselves in the sea and eaten a simple breakfast, they began wondering what they could do to improve their condition.

"The poor people of Gilgad," said Rinkitink cheerfully, "are little likely ever again to behold their King in the flesh, for my boat and my rowers are gone with everything else. Let us face the fact that we are imprisoned for life upon this island, and that our lives will be short unless we can secure more to eat than is in this small sack."

"I'll not starve, for I can eat grass," remarked the goat in a pleasant tone—or a tone as pleasant as Bilbil could assume.

"True, quite true," said the King. Then he seemed thoughtful for a moment and turning to Inga he asked: "Do you think, Prince, that if the worst comes, we could eat Bilbil?"

The goat gave a groan and cast a reproachful look at his master as he said:

"Monster! Would you, indeed, eat your old friend and servant?"

"Not if I can help it, Bilbil," answered the King pleasantly. "You would make a remarkably tough morsel, and my teeth are not as good as they once were."

While this talk was in progress Inga suddenly remembered the three pearls which his father had hidden under the tiled floor of the banquet hall. Without doubt King Kitticut had been so suddenly surprised by the invaders that he had found no opportunity to get the pearls, for otherwise the fierce warriors would have been defeated and driven out of Pingaree. So they must still be in their hiding place, and Inga believed they would prove of great assistance to him and his comrades in this hour of need. But the palace was a mass of ruins; perhaps he would be unable now to find the place where the pearls were hidden.

He said nothing of this to Rinkitink, remembering that his father had charged him to preserve the secret of the pearls and of their magic powers. Nevertheless, the thought of securing the wonderful treasures of his ancestors gave the boy new hope.

He stood up and said to the King:

"Let us return to the other end of Pingaree. It is more pleasant than here in spite of the desolation of my father's palace. And there, if anywhere, we shall discover a way out of our difficulties."

This suggestion met with Rinkitink's approval and the little party at once started upon the return journey. As there was no occasion to delay upon the way, they reached the big end of the island about the middle of the day and at once began searching the ruins of the palace.

They found, to their satisfaction, that one room at the bottom of a tower was still habitable, although the roof was broken in and the place was somewhat littered with stones. The King was, as he said, too fat to do any hard work, so he sat down on a block of marble and watched Inga clear the room of its rubbish. This done, the boy hunted through the ruins until he discovered a stool and an armchair that had not been broken beyond use. Some bedding and a mattress were also found, so that by nightfall the little room had been made quite comfortable.

The following morning, while Rinkitink was still sound asleep and Bilbil was busily cropping the dewy grass that edged the shore, Prince Inga began to search the tumbled heaps of marble for the place where the royal banquet hall had been. After climbing over the ruins for a time he reached a flat place which he recognized, by means of the tiled flooring and the broken furniture scattered about, to be the great hall he was seeking. But in the center of the floor, directly over the spot where the pearls were hidden, lay several large and heavy blocks of marble, which had been torn from the dismantled walls.

This unfortunate discovery for a time discouraged the boy, who realized how helpless he was to remove such vast obstacles; but it was so important to secure the pearls that he dared not give way to despair until every human effort had been made, so he sat him down to think over the matter with great care.

Meantime Rinkitink had risen from his bed and walked out upon the lawn, where he found Bilbil reclining at ease upon the greensward.

"Where is Inga?" asked Rinkitink, rubbing his eyes with his knuckles because their vision was blurred with too much sleep.

"Don't ask me," said the goat, chewing with much satisfaction a cud of sweet grasses.

"Bilbil," said the King, squatting down beside the goat and resting his fat chin upon his hands and his elbows on his knees, "allow me to confide to you the fact that I am bored, and need amusement. My good friend Kitticut has been kidnapped by the barbarians and taken from me, so there is no one to converse with me intelligently. I am the King and you are the goat. Suppose you tell me a story."

"Suppose I don't," said Bilbil, with a scowl, for a goat's face is very expressive.

"If you refuse, I shall be more unhappy than ever, and I know your disposition is too sweet to permit that. Tell me a story, Bilbil."

The goat looked at him with an expression of scorn. Said he:

"One would think you are but four years old, Rinkitink! But there—I will do as you command. Listen carefully, and the story may do you some good—although I doubt if you understand the moral."

"I am sure the story will do me good," declared the King, whose eyes were twinkling.

"Once on a time," began the goat.

"When was that, Bilbil?" asked the King gently.

"Don't interrupt; it is impolite. Once on a time there was a King with a hollow inside his head, where most people have their brains, and—"

"Is this a true story, Bilbil?"

"And the King with a hollow head could chatter words, which had no sense, and laugh in a brainless manner at senseless things. That part of the story is true enough, Rinkitink."

"Then proceed with the tale, sweet Bilbil. Yet it is hard to believe that any King could be brainless—unless, indeed, he proved it by owning a talking goat."

Bilbil glared at him a full minute in silence. Then he resumed his story:

"This empty-headed man was a King by accident, having been born to that high station. Also the King was empty-headed by the same chance, being born without brains."

"Poor fellow!" quoth the King. "Did he own a talking goat?"

"He did," answered Bilbil.

"Then he was wrong to have been born at all. Cheek-eek-eek-eek, oo, hoo!" chuckled Rinkitink, his fat body shaking with merriment. "But it's hard to prevent oneself from being born; there's no chance for protest, eh, Bilbil?"

"Who is telling this story, I'd like to know," demanded the goat, with anger.

"Ask someone with brains, my boy; I'm sure I can't tell," replied the King, bursting into one of his merry fits of laughter.

Bilbil rose to his hoofs and walked away in a dignified manner, leaving Rinkitink chuckling anew at the sour expression of the animal's face.

"Oh, Bilbil, you'll be the death of me, some day—I'm sure you will!" gasped the King, taking out his lace handkerchief to wipe his eyes; for, as he often did, he had laughed till the tears came.

Bilbil was deeply vexed and would not even turn his head to look at his master. To escape from Rinkitink he wandered among the ruins of the palace, where he came upon Prince Inga.

"Good morning, Bilbil," said the boy. "I was just going to find you, that I might consult you upon an important matter. If you will kindly turn back with me I am sure your good judgment will be of great assistance."

The angry goat was quite mollified by the respectful tone in which he was addressed, but he immediately asked:

"Are you also going to consult that empty-headed King over yonder?"

"I am sorry to hear you speak of your kind master in such a way," said the boy gravely. "All men are deserving of respect, being the highest of living creatures, and Kings deserve respect more than others, for they are set to rule over many people."

"Nevertheless," said Bilbil with conviction, "Rinkitink's head is certainly empty of brains."

"That I am unwilling to believe," insisted Inga. "But anyway his heart is kind and gentle and that is better than being wise. He is merry in spite of misfortunes that would cause others to weep and he never speaks harsh words that wound the feelings of his friends."

"Still," growled Bilbil, "he is—"

"Let us forget everything but his good nature, which puts new heart into us when we are sad," advised the boy.

"But he is—"

"Come with me, please," interrupted Inga, "for the matter of which I wish to speak is very important."

Bilbil followed him, although the boy still heard the goat muttering that the King had no brains. Rinkitink, seeing them turn into the ruins, also followed, and upon joining them asked for his breakfast.

Inga opened the sack of food and while he and the King ate of it the boy said:

"If I could find a way to remove some of the blocks of marble which have fallen in the banquet hall, I think I could find means for us to escape from this barren island."

"Then," mumbled Rinkitink, with his mouth full, "let us move the blocks of marble."

"But how?" inquired Prince Inga. "They are very heavy."

"Ah, how, indeed?" returned the King, smacking his lips contentedly. "That is a serious question. But—I have it! Let us see what my famous parchment says about it." He wiped his fingers upon a napkin and then, taking the scroll from a pocket inside his embroidered blouse, he unrolled it and read the following words: " 'Never step on another man's toes.' "

The goat gave a snort of contempt; Inga was silent; the King looked from one to the other inquiringly.

"That's the idea, exactly!" declared Rinkitink.

"To be sure," said Bilbil scornfully, "it tells us exactly how to move the blocks of marble."

"Oh, does it?" responded the King, and then for a moment he rubbed the top of his bald head in a perplexed manner. The next moment he burst into a peal of joyous laughter. The goat looked at Inga and sighed.

"What did I tell you?" asked the creature. "Was I right, or was I wrong?"

"This scroll," said Rinkitink, "is indeed a masterpiece. Its advice is of tremendous value. 'Never step on another man's toes.' Let us think this over. The inference is that

we should step upon our own toes, which were given us for that purpose. Therefore, if I stepped upon another man's toes, I would be the other man. Hoo, hoo, hoo!—the other man—hee, hee, heek-keek-eek! Funny, isn't it?"

"Didn't I say—" began Bilbil.

"No matter what you said, my boy," roared the King. "No fool could have figured that out as nicely as I did."

"We have still to decide how to remove the blocks of marble," suggested Inga anxiously.

"Fasten a rope to them, and pull," said Bilbil. "Don't pay any more attention to Rinkitink, for he is no wiser than the man who wrote that brainless scroll. Just get the rope, and we'll fasten Rinkitink to one end of it for a weight and I'll help you pull."

"Thank you, Bilbil," replied the boy. "I'll get the rope at once."

Bilbil found it difficult to climb over the ruins to the floor of the banquet hall, but there are few places a goat cannot get to when it makes the attempt, so Bilbil succeeded at last, and even fat little Rinkitink finally joined them, though much out of breath.

Inga fastened one end of the rope around a block of marble and then made a loop at the other end to go over Bilbil's head. When all was ready the boy seized the rope and helped the goat to pull; yet, strain as they might, the huge block would not stir from its place. Seeing this, King Rinkitink came forward and lent his assistance,

the weight of his body forcing the heavy marble to slide several feet from where it had lain.

But it was hard work and all were obliged to take a long rest before undertaking the removal of the next block.

"Admit, Bilbil," said the King, "that I am of some use in the world."

"Your weight was of considerable help," acknowledged the goat, "but if your head were as well filled as your stomach the task would be still easier."

When Inga went to fasten the rope a second time he was rejoiced to discover that by moving one more block of marble he could uncover the tile with the secret spring. So the three pulled with renewed energy and to their joy the block moved and rolled upon its side, leaving Inga free to remove the treasure when he pleased.

But the boy had no intention of allowing Bilbil and the King to share the secret of the royal treasures of Pingaree; so, although both the goat and its master demanded to know why the marble blocks had been moved, and how it would benefit them, Inga begged them to wait until the next morning, when he hoped to be able to satisfy them that their hard work had not been in vain.

Having little confidence in this promise of a mere boy, the goat grumbled and the King laughed; but Inga paid no heed to their ridicule and set himself to work rigging up a fishing rod, with line and hook. During the afternoon he waded out to some rocks near the shore and fished patiently until he had captured enough yellow perch for their supper and breakfast.

"Ah," said Rinkitink, looking at the fine catch when Inga returned to the shore; "these will taste delicious when they are cooked; but do you know how to cook them?"

"No," was the reply. "I have often caught fish, but never cooked them. Perhaps Your Majesty understands cooking."

"Cooking and majesty are two different things," laughed the little King. "I could not cook a fish to save me from starvation."

"For my part," said Bilbil, "I never eat fish, but I can tell you how to cook them, for I have often watched the palace cooks at their work." And so, with the goat's assistance, the boy and the King managed to prepare the fish and cook them, after which they were eaten with good appetite.

That night, after Rinkitink and Bilbil were both fast asleep, Inga stole quietly through the moonlight to the desolate banquet hall. There, kneeling down, he touched the secret spring as his father had instructed him to do and to his joy the tile sank downward and disclosed the opening. You may imagine how the boy's heart throbbed with excitement as he slowly thrust his hand into the cavity and felt around to see if the precious pearls were still there. In a moment his fingers touched the silken bag and, without pausing to close the recess, he pressed the treasure against his

breast and ran out into the moonlight to examine it. When he reached a bright place he started to open the bag, but he observed Bilbil lying asleep upon the grass near by. So, trembling with the fear of discovery, he ran to another place, and when he paused he heard Rinkitink snoring lustily. Again he fled and made his way to the seashore, where he squatted under a bank and began to untie the cords that fastened the mouth of the bag. But now another fear assailed him.

"If the pearls should slip from my hand," he thought, "and roll into the water, they might be lost to me forever. I must find some safer place."

Here and there he wandered, still clasping the silken bag in both hands, and finally he went to the grove and climbed into the tall tree where he had made his platform and seat. But here it was pitch dark, so he found he must wait patiently until morning before he dared touch the pearls. During those hours of waiting he had time for reflection and reproached himself for being so frightened by the possession of his father's treasures.

"These pearls have belonged to our family for generations," he mused, "yet no one has ever lost them. If I use ordinary care I am sure I need have no fears for their safety."

When the dawn came and he could see plainly, Inga opened the bag and took out the Blue Pearl. There was no possibility of his being observed by others, so he took time to examine it wonderingly, saying to himself: "This will give me strength."

Taking off his right shoe he placed the Blue Pearl within it, far up in the pointed toe. Then he tore a piece from his handkerchief and stuffed it into the shoe to hold the pearl in place. Inga's shoes were long and pointed, as were all the shoes worn in Pingaree, and the points curled upward, so that there was quite a vacant space beyond the place where the boy's toes reached when the shoe was upon his foot.

After he had put on the shoe and laced it up he opened the bag and took out the Pink Pearl. "This will protect me from danger," said Inga, and removing the shoe from his left foot he carefully placed the pearl in the hollow toe. This, also, he secured in place by means of a strip torn from his handkerchief.

Having put on the second shoe and laced it up, the boy drew from the silken bag the third pearl—that which was pure white—and holding it to his ear he asked.

"Will you advise me what to do, in this my hour of misfortune?"

Clearly the small voice of the pearl made answer:

"I advise you to go to the Islands of Regos and Coregos, where you may liberate your parents from slavery."

"How could I do that?" exclaimed Prince Inga, amazed at receiving such advice.

"To-night," spoke the voice of the pearl, "there will be a storm, and in the morning a boat will strand upon the shore. Take this boat and row to Regos and Coregos."

"How can I, a weak boy, pull the boat so far?" he inquired, doubting the possibility.

"The Blue Pearl will give you strength," was the reply.

"But I may be shipwrecked and drowned, before ever I reach Regos and Coregos," protested the boy.

"The Pink Pearl will protect you from harm," murmured the voice, soft and low but very distinct.

"Then I shall act as you advise me," declared Inga, speaking firmly because this promise gave him courage, and as he removed the pearl from his ear it whispered:

"The wise and fearless are sure to win success."

Restoring the White Pearl to the depths of the silken bag, Inga fastened it securely around his neck and buttoned his waist above it to hide the treasure from all prying eyes. Then he slowly climbed down from the tree and returned to the room where King Rinkitink still slept.

The goat was browsing upon the grass but looked cross and surly. When the boy said good morning as he passed, Bilbil made no response whatever. As Inga entered the room the King awoke and asked:

"What is that mysterious secret of yours? I've been dreaming about it, and I haven't got my breath yet from tugging at those heavy blocks. Tell me the secret."

"A secret told is no longer a secret," replied Inga, with a laugh. "Besides, this is a family secret, which it is proper I should keep to myself. But I may tell you one thing, at least: We are going to leave this island to-morrow morning."

The King seemed puzzled by this statement.

"I'm not much of a swimmer," said he, "and, though I'm fat enough to float upon the surface of the water, I'd only bob around and get nowhere at all."

"We shall not swim, but ride comfortably in a boat," promised Inga.

"There isn't a boat on this island!" declared Rinkitink, looking upon the boy with wonder.

"True," said Inga. "But one will come to us in the morning." He spoke positively, for he had perfect faith in the promise of the White Pearl; but Rinkitink, knowing nothing of the three marvelous jewels, began to fear that the little Prince had lost his mind through grief and misfortune.

For this reason the King did not question the boy further but tried to cheer him by telling him witty stories. He laughed at all the stories himself, in his merry, rollicking way, and Inga joined freely in the laughter because his heart had been lightened by the prospect of rescuing his dear parents. Not since the fierce warriors had descended upon Pingaree had the boy been so hopeful and happy.

With Rinkitink riding upon Bilbil's back, the three made a tour of the island and found in the central part some bushes and trees bearing ripe fruit. They gathered this freely, for—aside from the fish which Inga caught—it was the only food they now had, and the less they had, the bigger Rinkitink's appetite seemed to grow.

"I am never more happy," said he with a sigh, "than when I am eating."

Toward evening the sky became overcast and soon a great storm began to rage. Prince Inga and King Rinkitink took refuge within the shelter of the room they had fitted up and there Bilbil joined them. The goat and the King were somewhat disturbed by the violence of the storm, but Inga did not mind it, being pleased at this evidence that the White Pearl might be relied upon.

All night the wind shrieked around the island; thunder rolled, lightning flashed and rain came down in torrents. But with morning the storm abated and when the sun arose no sign of the tempest remained save a few fallen trees.

CHAPTER VI

THE MAGIC BOAT

PRINCE INGA WAS UP WITH THE SUN AND, ACCOMPANIED BY BILBIL, BEGAN WALKING along the shore in search of the boat which the White Pearl had promised him. Never for an instant did he doubt that he would find it and before he had walked any great distance a dark object at the water's edge caught his eye.

"It is the boat, Bilbil!" he cried joyfully, and running down to it he found it was, indeed, a large and roomy boat. Although stranded upon the beach, it was in perfect order and had suffered in no way from the storm.

Inga stood for some moments gazing upon the handsome craft and wondering where it could have come from. Certainly it was unlike any boat he had ever seen. On the outside it was painted a lustrous black, without any other color to relieve it; but all the inside of the boat was lined with pure silver, polished so highly that the surface resembled a mirror and glinted brilliantly in the rays of the sun. The seats had white velvet cushions upon them and the cushions were splendidly embroidered with threads of gold. At one end, beneath the broad seat, was a small barrel with silver hoops, which the boy found was filled with fresh, sweet water. A great chest of sandalwood, bound and ornamented with silver, stood in the other end of the boat. Inga raised the lid and discovered the chest filled with sea-biscuits, cakes, tinned meats and ripe, juicy melons; enough good and wholesome food to last the party a long time.

Lying upon the bottom of the boat were two shining oars, and overhead, but rolled back now, was a canopy of silver cloth to ward off the heat of the sun.

It is no wonder the boy was delighted with the appearance of this beautiful boat; but on reflection he feared it was too large for him to row any great distance. Unless, indeed, the Blue Pearl gave him unusual strength.

While he was considering this matter, King Rinkitink came waddling up to him and said:

"Well, well, well, my Prince, your words have come true! Here is the boat, for a certainty, yet how it came here—and how you knew it would come to us—are puzzles that mystify me. I do not question our good fortune, however, and my heart is bubbling with joy, for in this boat I will return at once to my City of Gilgad, from which I have remained absent altogether too long a time."

"I do not wish to go to Gilgad," said Inga.

"That is too bad, my friend, for you would be very welcome. But you may remain upon this island, if you wish," continued Rinkitink, "and when I get home I will send some of my people to rescue you."

"It is my boat, Your Majesty," said Inga quietly.

"May be, may be," was the careless answer, "but I am King of a great country, while you are a boy Prince without any kingdom to speak of. Therefore, being of greater importance than you, it is just and right that I take your boat and return to my own country in it."

"I am sorry to differ from Your Majesty's views," said Inga, "but instead of going to Gilgad I consider it of greater importance that we go to the Islands of Regos and Coregos."

"Hey? What!" cried the astounded King. "To Regos and Coregos! To become slaves of the barbarians, like the King, your father? No, no, my boy! Your Uncle Rinki may have an empty noddle, as Bilbil claims, but he is far too wise to put his head in the lion's mouth. It's no fun to be a slave."

"The people of Regos and Coregos will not enslave us," declared Inga. "On the contrary, it is my intention to set free my dear parents, as well as all my people, and to bring them back again to Pingaree."

"Cheek-eek-eek-eek-eek! How funny!" chuckled Rinkitink, winking at the goat, which scowled in return. "Your audacity takes my breath away, Inga, but the adventure has its charm, I must confess. Were I not so fat, I'd agree to your plan at once, and could probably conquer that horde of fierce warriors without any assistance at all—any at all—eh, Bilbil? But I grieve to say that I am fat, and not in good fighting trim. As for your determination to do what I admit I can't do, Inga, I fear you forget that you are only a boy, and rather small at that."

"No, I do not forget that," was Inga's reply.

"Then please consider that you and I and Bilbil are not strong enough, as an army, to conquer a powerful nation of skilled warriors. We could attempt it, of course, but you are too young to die, while I am too old. Come with me to my City of Gilgad, where you will be greatly honored. I'll have my professors teach you how to be good. Eh? What do you say?"

Inga was a little embarrassed how to reply to these arguments, which he knew King Rinkitink considered were wise; so, after a period of thought, he said:

"I will make a bargain with Your Majesty, for I do not wish to fail in respect to so worthy a man and so great a King as yourself. This boat is mine, as I have said, and in my father's absence you have become my guest; therefore I claim that I am entitled to some consideration, as well as you."

"No doubt of it," agreed Rinkitink. "What is the bargain you propose, Inga?"

"Let us both get into the boat, and you shall first try to row us to Gilgad. If you succeed, I will accompany you right willingly; but should you fail, I will then row the boat to Regos, and you must come with me without further protest."

"A fair and just bargain!" cried the King, highly pleased. "Yet, although I am a man of mighty deeds, I do not relish the prospect of rowing so big a boat all the way to Gilgad. But I will do my best and abide by the result."

The matter being thus peaceably settled, they prepared to embark. A further supply of fruits was placed in the boat and Inga also raked up a quantity of the delicious oysters that abounded on the coast of Pingaree but which he had before been unable to reach for lack of a boat. This was done at the suggestion of the ever-hungry Rinkitink, and when the oysters had been stowed in their shells behind the water barrel and a plentiful supply of grass brought aboard for Bilbil, they decided they were ready to start on their voyage.

It proved no easy task to get Bilbil into the boat, for he was a remarkably clumsy goat and once, when Rinkitink gave him a push, he tumbled into the water and nearly drowned before they could get him out again. But there was no thought of leaving the quaint animal behind. His power of speech made him seem almost human in the eyes of the boy, and the fat King was so accustomed to his surly companion that nothing could have induced him to part with him. Finally Bilbil fell sprawling into the bottom of the boat, and Inga helped him to get to the front end, where there was enough space for him to lie down.

Rinkitink now took his seat in the silver-lined craft and the boy came last, pushing off the boat as he sprang aboard, so that it floated freely upon the water.

"Well, here we go for Gilgad!" exclaimed the King, picking up the oars and placing them in the row-locks. Then he began to row as hard as he could, singing at the same time an odd sort of a song that ran like this:

> "The way to Gilgad isn't bad
> For a stout old King and a brave young lad,
> For a cross old goat with a dripping coat,
> And a silver boat in which to float.
> So our hearts are merry, light and glad
> As we speed away to fair Gilgad!"

"Don't, Rinkitink; please don't! It makes me seasick," growled Bilbil.

Rinkitink stopped rowing, for by this time he was all out of breath and his round face was covered with big drops of perspiration. And when he looked over his shoulder he found to his dismay that the boat had scarcely moved a foot from its former position.

Inga said nothing and appeared not to notice the King's failure. So now Rinkitink, with a serious look on his fat, red face, took off his purple robe and rolled up the sleeves of his tunic and tried again.

However, he succeeded no better than before and when he heard Bilbil give a gruff laugh and saw a smile upon the boy Prince's face, Rinkitink suddenly dropped the oars and began shouting with laughter at his own defeat. As he wiped his brow with a yellow silk handkerchief he sang in a merry voice:

> "A sailor bold am I, I hold,
> But boldness will not row a boat.
> So I confess I'm in distress
> And just as useless as the goat."

"Please leave me out of your verses," said Bilbil with a snort of anger.

"When I make a fool of myself, Bilbil, I'm a goat," replied Rinkitink.

"Not so," insisted Bilbil. "Nothing could make you a member of my superior race."

"Superior? Why, Bilbil, a goat is but a beast, while I am a King!"

"I claim that superiority lies in intelligence," said the goat.

Rinkitink paid no attention to this remark, but turning to Inga he said:

"We may as well get back to the shore, for the boat is too heavy to row to Gilgad or anywhere else. Indeed, it will be hard for us to reach land again."

"Let me take the oars," suggested Inga. "You must not forget our bargain."

"No, indeed," answered Rinkitink. "If you can row us to Regos, or to any other place, I will go with you without protest."

So the King took Inga's place in the stern of the boat and the boy grasped the oars and commenced to row. And now, to the great wonder of Rinkitink—and even to Inga's surprise—the oars became light as feathers as soon as the Prince took hold of them. In an instant the boat began to glide rapidly through the water and, seeing this, the boy turned its prow toward the north. He did not know exactly where Regos and Coregos were located, but he did know that the islands lay to the north of Pingaree, so he decided to trust to luck and the guidance of the pearls to carry him to them.

Gradually the Island of Pingaree became smaller to their view as the boat sped onward, until at the end of an hour they had lost sight of it altogether and were wholly surrounded by the purple waters of the Nonestic Ocean.

Prince Inga did not tire from the labor of rowing; indeed, it seemed to him no labor at all. Once he stopped long enough to place the poles of the canopy in the holes that had been made for them, in the edges of the boat, and to spread the canopy of silver over the poles, for Rinkitink had complained of the sun's heat. But the canopy shut out the hot rays and rendered the interior of the boat cool and pleasant.

"This is a glorious ride!" cried Rinkitink, as he lay back in the shade. "I find it a decided relief to be away from that dismal Island of Pingaree.

"It may be a relief for a short time," said Bilbil, "but you are going to the land of your enemies, who will probably stick your fat body full of spears and arrows."

"Oh, I hope not!" exclaimed Inga, distressed at the thought.

"Never mind," said the King calmly, "a man can die but once, you know, and when the enemy kills me I shall beg him to kill Bilbil, also, that we may remain together in death as in life."

"They may be cannibals, in which case they will roast and eat us," suggested Bilbil, who wished to terrify his master.

"Who knows?" answered Rinkitink, with a shudder. "But cheer up, Bilbil; they may not kill us after all, or even capture us; so let us not borrow trouble. Do not look so cross, my sprightly quadruped, and I will sing to amuse you."

"Your song would make me more cross than ever," grumbled the goat.

"Quite impossible, dear Bilbil. You couldn't be more surly if you tried. So here is a famous song for you."

While the boy rowed steadily on and the boat rushed fast over the water, the jolly King, who never could be sad or serious for many minutes at a time, lay back on his embroidered cushions and sang as follows:

> "A merry maiden went to sea—
>   Sing too-ral-oo-ral-i-do!
> She sat upon the Captain's knee
> And looked around the sea to see
> What she could see, but she couldn't see me—
>   Sing too-ral-oo-ral-i-do!"

"How do you like that, Bilbil?"

"I don't like it," complained the goat. "It reminds me of the alligator that tried to whistle."

"Did he succeed, Bilbil?" asked the King.

"He whistled as well as you sing."

"Ha, ha, ha, ha, heek, keek, eek!" chuckled the King. "He must have whistled most exquisitely, eh, my friend?"

"I am not your friend," returned the goat, wagging his ears in a surly manner.

"I am yours, however," was the King's cheery reply; "and to prove it I'll sing you another verse."

"Don't, I beg of you!"

But the King sang as follows:

> "The wind blew off the maiden's shoe—
>   Sing too-ral-oo-ral-i-do!
> And the shoe flew high to the sky so blue
> And the maiden knew 'twas a new shoe, too;
> But she couldn't pursue the shoe, 'tis true—
>   Sing too-ral-oo-ral-i-do!"

"Isn't that sweet, my pretty goat?"

"Sweet, do you ask?" retorted Bilbil. "I consider it as sweet as candy made from mustard and vinegar."

"But not as sweet as your disposition, I admit. Ah, Bilbil, your temper would put honey itself to shame."

"Do not quarrel, I beg of you," pleaded Inga. "Are we not sad enough already?"

"But this is a jolly quarrel," said the King, "and it is the way Bilbil and I often amuse ourselves. Listen, now, to the last verse of all:

"The maid who shied her shoe now cried—
    Sing too-ral-oo-ral-i-do!
Her tears were fried for the Captain's bride
Who ate with pride her sobs, beside,
And gently sighed 'I'm satisfied'—
    Sing to-ral-oo-ral-i-do!"

"Worse and worse!" grumbled Bilbil, with much scorn. "I am glad that is the last verse, for another of the same kind might cause me to faint."

"I fear you have no ear for music," said the King.

"I have heard no music, as yet," declared the goat. "You must have a strong imagination, King Rinkitink, if you consider your songs music. Do you remember the story of the bear that hired out for a nursemaid?"

"I do not recall it just now," said Rinkitink, with a wink at Inga.

"Well, the bear tried to sing a lullaby to put the baby to sleep."

"And then?" said the King.

"The bear was highly pleased with its own voice, but the baby was nearly frightened to death."

"Heh, heh, heh, heh, whoo, hoo, hoo! You are a merry rogue, Bilbil," laughed the King; "a merry rogue in spite of your gloomy features. However, if I have not amused you, I have at least pleased myself, for I am exceedingly fond of a good song. So let us say no more about it."

All this time the boy Prince was rowing the boat. He was not in the least tired, for the oars he held seemed to move of their own accord. He paid little heed to the conversation of Rinkitink and the goat, but busied his thoughts with plans of what he should do when he reached the Islands of Regos and Coregos and confronted his enemies. When the others finally became silent, Inga inquired:

"Can you fight, King Rinkitink?"

"I have never tried," was the answer. "In time of danger I have found it much easier to run away than to face the foe."

"But *could* you fight?" asked the boy.

"I might try, if there was no chance to escape by running. Have you a proper weapon for me to fight with?"

"I have no weapon at all," confessed Inga.

"Then let us use argument and persuasion instead of fighting. For instance, if we could persuade the warriors of Regos to lie down, and let me step on them, they would be crushed with ease."

Prince Inga had expected little support from the King, so he was not discouraged by this answer. After all, he reflected, a conquest by battle would be out of the question, yet the White Pearl would not have advised him to go to Regos and Coregos had the mission been a hopeless one. It seemed to him, on further reflection, that he must rely upon circumstances to determine his actions when he reached the islands of the barbarians.

By this time Inga felt perfect confidence in the Magic Pearls. It was the White Pearl that had given him the boat, and the Blue Pearl that had given him strength to row it. He believed that the Pink Pearl would protect him from any danger that might arise; so his anxiety was not for himself, but for his companions. King Rinkitink and the goat had no magic to protect them, so Inga resolved to do all in his power to keep them from harm.

For three days and three nights the boat with the silver lining sped swiftly over the ocean. On the morning of the fourth day, so quickly had they traveled, Inga saw before him the shores of the two great Islands of Regos and Coregos.

"The pearls have guided me aright!" he whispered to himself. "Now, if I am wise, and cautious, and brave, I believe I shall be able to rescue my father and mother and my people."

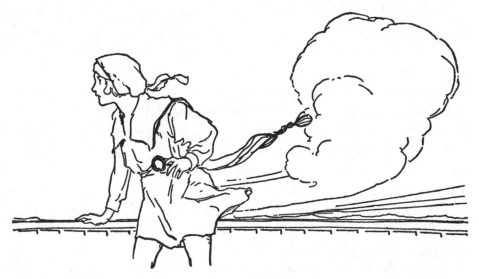

CHAPTER VII

THE TWIN ISLANDS

THE ISLAND OF REGOS WAS TEN MILES WIDE AND FORTY MILES LONG AND IT WAS ruled by a big and powerful King named Gos. Near to the shores were green and fertile fields, but farther back from the sea were rugged hills and mountains, so rocky that nothing would grow there. But in these mountains were mines of gold and silver, which the slaves of the King were forced to work, being confined in dark underground passages for that purpose. In the course of time huge caverns had been hollowed out by the slaves, in which they lived and slept, never seeing the light of day. Cruel overseers with whips stood over these poor people, who had been captured in many countries by the raiding parties of King Gos, and the overseers were quite willing to lash the slaves with their whips if they faltered a moment in their work.

Between the green shores and the mountains were forests of thick, tangled trees, between which narrow paths had been cut to lead up to the caves of the mines. It was on the level green meadows, not far from the ocean, that the great City of Regos had been built, wherein was located the palace of the King. This city was inhabited by thousands of the fierce warriors of Gos, who frequently took to their boats and spread over the sea to the neighboring islands to conquer and pillage, as they had done at Pingaree. When they were not absent on one of these expeditions, the City of Regos swarmed with them and so became a dangerous place for any peaceful person to live in, for the warriors were as lawless as their King.

The Island of Coregos lay close beside the Island of Regos; so close, indeed, that one might have thrown a stone from one shore to another. But Coregos was only half the size of Regos and instead of being mountainous it was a rich and pleasant country, covered with fields of grain. The fields of Coregos furnished food for the warriors and citizens of both countries, while the mines of Regos made them all rich.

Coregos was ruled by Queen Cor, who was wedded to King Gos; but so stern and cruel was the nature of this Queen that the people could not decide which of their sovereigns they dreaded most.

Queen Cor lived in her own City of Coregos, which lay on that side of her island facing Regos, and her slaves, who were mostly women, were made to plow the land and to plant and harvest the grain.

From Regos to Coregos stretched a bridge of boats, set close together, with planks laid across their edges for people to walk upon. In this way it was easy to pass from one island to the other and in times of danger the bridge could be quickly removed.

The native inhabitants of Regos and Coregos consisted of the warriors, who did nothing but fight and ravage, and the trembling servants who waited on them. King Gos and Queen Cor were at war with all the rest of the world. Other islanders hated and feared them, for their slaves were badly treated and absolutely no mercy was shown to the weak or ill.

When the boats that had gone to Pingaree returned loaded with rich plunder and a host of captives, there was much rejoicing in Regos and Coregos and the King and Queen gave a fine feast to the warriors who had accomplished so great a conquest. This feast was set for the warriors in the grounds of King Gos's palace, while with them in the great throne room all the captains and leaders of the fighting men were assembled with King Gos and Queen Cor, who had come from her island to attend the ceremony. Then all the goods that had been stolen from the King of Pingaree were divided according to rank, the King and Queen taking half, the captains a quarter, and the rest being divided amongst the warriors.

The day following the feast King Gos sent King Kitticut and all the men of Pingaree to work in his mines under the mountains, having first chained them together so they could not escape. The gentle Queen of Pingaree and all her women, together with the captured children, were given to Queen Cor, who set them to work in her grain fields.

Then the rulers and warriors of these dreadful islands thought they had done forever with Pingaree. Despoiled of all its wealth, its houses torn down, its boats captured and all its people enslaved, what likelihood was there that they might ever again hear of the desolated island? So the people of Regos and Coregos were surprised and puzzled when one morning they observed approaching their shores from the direction of the south a black boat containing a boy, a fat man and a goat. The warriors asked one another who these could be, and where they had come from? No one ever came to those islands of their own accord, that was certain.

Prince Inga guided his boat to the south end of the Island of Regos, which was the landing place nearest to the city, and when the warriors saw this action they went down to the shore to meet him, being led by a big captain named Buzzub.

"Those people surely mean us no good," said Rinkitink uneasily to the boy. "Without doubt they intend to capture us and make us their slaves."

"Do not fear, sir," answered Inga, in a calm voice. "Stay quietly in the boat with Bilbil until I have spoken with these men."

He stopped the boat a dozen feet from the shore, and standing up in his place made a grave bow to the multitude confronting him. Said the big Captain Buzzub in a gruff voice:

"Well, little one, who may you be? And how dare you come, uninvited and all alone, to the Island of Regos?"

"I am Inga, Prince of Pingaree," returned the boy, "and I have come here to free my parents and my people, whom you have wrongfully enslaved."

When they heard this bold speech a mighty laugh arose from the band of warriors, and when it had subsided the captain said:

"You love to jest, my baby Prince, and the joke is fairly good. But why did you willingly thrust your head into the lion's mouth? When you were free, why did you not stay free? We did not know we had left a single person in Pingaree! But since you managed to escape us then, it is really kind of you to come here of your own free will, to be our slave. Who is the funny fat person with you?"

"It is His Majesty, King Rinkitink, of the great City of Gilgad. He has accompanied me to see that you render full restitution for all you have stolen from Pingaree."

"Better yet!" laughed Buzzub. "He will make a fine slave for Queen Cor, who loves to tickle fat men, and see them jump."

King Rinkitink was filled with horror when he heard this, but the Prince answered as boldly as before, saying:

"We are not to be frightened by bluster, believe me; nor are we so weak as you imagine. We have magic powers so great and terrible that no host of warriors can possibly withstand us, and therefore I call upon you to surrender your city and your island to us, before we crush you with our mighty powers."

The boy spoke very gravely and earnestly, but his words only aroused another shout of laughter. So while the men of Regos were laughing Inga drove the boat well up onto the sandy beach and leaped out. He also helped Rinkitink out, and when the goat had unaided sprung to the sands, the King got upon Bilbil's back, trembling a little internally, but striving to look as brave as possible.

There was a bunch of coarse hair between the goat's ears, and this Inga clutched firmly in his left hand. The boy knew the Pink Pearl would protect not only himself, but all whom he touched, from any harm, and as Rinkitink was astride the goat and Inga had his hand upon the animal, the three could not be injured by anything the warriors could do. But Captain Buzzub did not know this, and the little group of three seemed so weak and ridiculous that he believed their capture would be easy. So he turned to his men and with a wave of his hand said:

"Seize the intruders!"

Instantly two or three of the warriors stepped forward to obey, but to their amazement they could not reach any of the three; their hands were arrested as if by an invisible wall of iron. Without paying any attention to these attempts at capture, Inga advanced slowly and the goat kept pace with him. And when Rinkitink saw that he was safe from harm he gave one of his big, merry laughs, and it startled the warriors and made them nervous. Captain Buzzub's eyes grew big with surprise as the three steadily advanced and forced his men backward; nor was he free from terror himself at the magic that protected these strange visitors. As for the warriors, they presently became terror-stricken and fled in a panic up the slope toward the city, and Buzzub was obliged to chase after them and shout threats of punishment before he could halt them and form them into a line of battle.

All the men of Regos bore spears and bows-and-arrows, and some of the officers had swords and battle-axes; so Buzzub ordered them to stand their ground and shoot and slay the strangers as they approached. This they tried to do. Inga being in advance, the warriors sent a flight of sharp arrows straight at the boy's breast, while others cast their long spears at him.

It seemed to Rinkitink that the little Prince must surely perish as he stood facing this hail of murderous missiles; but the power of the Pink Pearl did not desert him, and when the arrows and spears had reached to within an inch of his body they bounded back again and fell harmlessly at his feet. Nor were Rinkitink or Bilbil injured in the least, although they stood close beside Inga.

Buzzub stood for a moment looking upon the boy in silent wonder. Then, recovering himself, he shouted in a loud voice:

"Once again! All together, my men. No one shall ever defy our might and live!"

Again a flight of arrows and spears sped toward the three, and since many more of the warriors of Regos had by this time joined their fellows, the air was for a moment darkened by the deadly shafts. But again all fell harmless before the power of the Pink

Pearl, and Bilbil, who had been growing very angry at the attempts to injure him and his party, suddenly made a bolt forward, casting off Inga's hold, and butted into the line of warriors, who were standing amazed at their failure to conquer.

Taken by surprise at the goat's attack, a dozen big warriors tumbled in a heap, yelling with fear, and their comrades, not knowing what had happened but imagining that their foes were attacking them, turned about and ran to the city as hard as they could go. Bilbil, still angry, had just time to catch the big captain as he turned to follow his men, and Buzzub first sprawled headlong upon the ground, then rolled over two or three times, and finally jumped up and ran yelling after his defeated warriors. This butting on the part of the goat was very hard upon King Rinkitink, who nearly fell off Bilbil's back at the shock of encounter; but the little fat King wound his arms around the goat's neck and shut his eyes and clung on with all his might. It was not until he heard Inga say triumphantly, "We have won the fight without striking a blow!" that Rinkitink dared open his eyes again. Then he saw the warriors rushing into the City of Regos and barring the heavy gates, and he was very much relieved at the sight.

"Without striking a blow!" said Bilbil indignantly. "That is not quite true, Prince Inga. You did not fight, I admit, but I struck a couple of times to good purpose, and I claim to have conquered the cowardly warriors unaided."

"You and I together, Bilbil," said Rinkitink mildly. "But the next time you make a charge, please warn me in time, so that I may dismount and give you all the credit for the attack."

There being no one now to oppose their advance, the three walked to the gates of the city, which had been closed against them. The gates were of iron and heavily barred, and upon the top of the high walls of the city a host of the warriors now appeared armed with arrows and spears and other weapons. For Buzzub had gone straight to the palace of King Gos and reported his defeat, relating the powerful magic of the boy, the fat King and the goat, and had asked what to do next.

The big captain still trembled with fear, but King Gos did not believe in magic, and called Buzzub a coward and a weakling. At once the King took command of his men personally, and he ordered the walls manned with warriors and instructed them to shoot to kill if any of the three strangers approached the gates.

Of course, neither Rinkitink nor Bilbil knew how they had been protected from harm and so at first they were inclined to resent the boy's command that the three must always keep together and touch one another at all times. But when Inga explained that his magic would not otherwise save them from injury, they agreed to obey, for they had now seen enough to convince them that the Prince was really protected by some invisible power.

As they came before the gates another shower of arrows and spears descended upon them, and as before not a single missile touched their bodies. King Gos, who was upon the wall, was greatly amazed and somewhat worried, but he depended upon the strength of his gates and commanded his men to continue shooting until all their weapons were gone.

Inga let them shoot as much as they wished, while he stood before the great gates and examined them carefully.

"Perhaps Bilbil can batter down the gates," suggested Rinkitink.

"No," replied the goat; "my head is hard, but not harder than iron."

"Then," returned the King, "let us stay outside; especially as we can't get in."

But Inga was not at all sure they could not get in. The gates opened inward, and three heavy bars were held in place by means of stout staples riveted to the sheets of steel. The boy had been told that the power of the Blue Pearl would enable him to accomplish any feat of strength, and he believed that this was true.

The warriors, under the direction of King Gos, continued to hurl arrows and darts and spears and axes and huge stones upon the invaders, all without avail. The ground below was thickly covered with weapons, yet not one of the three before the gates had been injured in the slightest manner. When everything had been cast that was available and not a single weapon of any sort remained at hand, the amazed warriors saw the boy put his shoulder against the gates and burst asunder the huge staples that held the bars in place. A thousand of their men could not have accomplished this feat, yet the small, slight boy did it with seeming ease. The gates burst open, and Inga advanced into the city street and called upon King Gos to surrender.

But Gos was now as badly frightened as were his warriors. He and his men were accustomed to war and pillage and they had carried terror into many countries, but here was a small boy, a fat man and a goat who could not be injured by all his skill in warfare, his numerous army and thousands of death-dealing weapons. Moreover, they not only defied King Gos's entire army but they had broken in the huge gates of the city—as easily as if they had been made of paper—and such an exhibition of enormous strength made the wicked King fear for his life. Like all bullies and marauders, Gos was a coward at heart, and now a panic seized him and he turned and fled before the calm advance of Prince Inga of Pingaree. The warriors were like their master, and having thrown all their weapons over the wall and being helpless to oppose the strangers, they all swarmed after Gos, who abandoned his city and crossed the bridge of boats to the Island of Coregos. There was a desperate struggle among these cowardly warriors to get over the bridge, and many were pushed into the water and obliged to swim; but finally every fighting man of Regos had gained the shore of Coregos and then they tore away the bridge of boats and drew them up on their own side, hoping the stretch of open water would prevent the magic invaders from following them.

The humble citizens and serving people of Regos, who had been terrified and abused by the rough warriors all their lives, were not only greatly astonished by this sudden conquest of their masters but greatly delighted. As the King and his army fled to Coregos, the people embraced one another and danced for very joy, and then they turned to see what the conquerors of Regos were like.

CHAPTER VIII

RINKITINK MAKES A GREAT MISTAKE

THE FAT KING RODE HIS GOAT THROUGH THE STREETS OF THE CONQUERED CITY AND the boy Prince walked proudly beside him, while all the people bent their heads humbly to their new masters, whom they were prepared to serve in the same manner they had King Gos.

Not a warrior remained in all Regos to oppose the triumphant three; the bridge of boats had been destroyed; Inga and his companions were free from danger—for a time, at least.

The jolly little King appreciated this fact and rejoiced that he had escaped all injury during the battle. How it had all happened he could not tell, nor even guess, but he was content in being safe and free to take possession of the enemy's city. So, as they passed through the lines of respectful civilians on their way to the palace, the King tipped his crown back on his bald head and folded his arms and sang in his best voice the following lines:

"Oh, here comes the army of King Rinkitink!
It isn't a big one, perhaps you may think,
But it scattered the warriors quicker than wink—
    Rink-i-tink, tink-i-tink, tink!
Our Bilbil's a hero and so is his King;
Our foemen have vanished like birds on the wing;
I guess that as fighters we're quite the real thing—
Rink-i-tink, tink-i-tink, tink!"

"Why don't you give a little credit to Inga?" inquired the goat. "If I remember aright, he did a little of the conquering himself."

"So he did," responded the King, "and that's the reason I'm sounding our own praise, Bilbil. Those who do the least, often shout the loudest and so get the most glory. Inga did so much that there is danger of his becoming more important than we are, and so we'd best say nothing about him."

When they reached the palace, which was an immense building, furnished throughout in regal splendor, Inga took formal possession and ordered the majordomo to show them the finest rooms the building contained. There were many pleasant apartments, but Rinkitink proposed to Inga that they share one of the largest bedrooms together.

"For," said he, "we are not sure that old Gos will not return and try to recapture his city, and you must remember that I have no magic to protect me. In any danger, were I alone, I might be easily killed or captured, while if you are by my side you can save me from injury."

The boy realized the wisdom of this plan, and selected a fine big bedroom on the second floor of the palace, in which he ordered two golden beds placed and prepared for King Rinkitink and himself. Bilbil was given a suite of rooms on the other side of the palace, where servants brought the goat fresh-cut grass to eat and made him a soft bed to lie upon.

That evening the boy Prince and the fat King dined in great state in the lofty-domed dining-hall of the palace, where forty servants waited upon them. The royal chef, anxious to win the favor of the conquerors of Regos, prepared his finest and most savory dishes for them, which Rinkitink ate with much appetite and found so delicious that he ordered the royal chef brought into the banquet hall and presented him with a gilt button which the King cut from his own jacket.

"You are welcome to it," said he to the chef, "because I have eaten so much that I cannot use that lower button at all."

Rinkitink was mightily pleased to live in a comfortable palace again and to dine at a well spread table. His joy grew every moment, so that he came in time to be as

merry and cheery as before Pingaree was despoiled. And, although he had been much frightened during Inga's defiance of the army of King Gos, he now began to turn the matter into a joke.

"Why, my boy," said he, "you whipped the big black-bearded King exactly as if he were a schoolboy, even though you used no warlike weapon at all upon him. He was cowed through fear of your magic, and that reminds me to demand from you an explanation. How did you do it, Inga? And where did the wonderful magic come from?"

Perhaps it would have been wise for the Prince to have explained about the Magic Pearls, but at that moment he was not inclined to do so. Instead, he replied:

"Be patient, Your Majesty. The secret is not my own, so please do not ask me to divulge it. Is it not enough, for the present, that the magic saved you from death to-day?"

"Do not think me ungrateful," answered the King earnestly. "A million spears fell on me from the wall, and several stones as big as mountains, yet none of them hurt me!"

"The stones were not as big as mountains, sire," said the Prince with a smile. "They were, indeed, no larger than your head."

"Are you sure about that?" asked Rinkitink.

"Quite sure, Your Majesty."

"How deceptive those things are!" sighed the King. "This argument reminds me of the story of Tom Tick, which my father used to tell."

"I have never heard that story," Inga answered.

"Well, as he told it, it ran like this:

"When Tom walked out, the sky to spy,
A naughty gnat flew in his eye;
But Tom knew not it was a gnat—
He thought, at first, it was a cat.

"And then, it felt so very big,
He thought it surely was a pig
Till, standing still to hear it grunt,
He cried: 'Why, it's an *elephunt*!'

"But—when the gnat flew out again
And Tom was free from all his pain,
He said: 'There flew into my eye
A leetle, teenty-tiny fly.'"

"Indeed," said Inga, laughing, "the gnat was much like your stones that seemed as big as mountains."

After their dinner they inspected the palace, which was filled with valuable goods stolen by King Gos from many nations. But the day's events had tired them and they retired early to their big sleeping apartment.

"In the morning," said the boy to Rinkitink, as he was undressing for bed, "I shall begin the search for my father and mother and the people of Pingaree. And, when they are found and rescued, we will all go home again, and be as happy as we were before."

They carefully bolted the door of their room, that no one might enter, and then got into their beds, where Rinkitink fell asleep in an instant. The boy lay awake for a while thinking over the day's adventures, but presently he fell sound asleep also, and so weary was he that nothing disturbed his slumber until he awakened next morning with a ray of sunshine in his eyes, which had crept into the room through the open window by King Rinkitink's bed.

Resolving to begin the search for his parents without any unnecessary delay, Inga at once got out of bed and began to dress himself, while Rinkitink, in the other bed, was still sleeping peacefully. But when the boy had put on both his stockings and began looking for his shoes, he could find but one of them. The left shoe, that containing the Pink Pearl, was missing.

Filled with anxiety at this discovery, Inga searched through the entire room, looking underneath the beds and divans and chairs and behind the draperies and in the corners and every other possible place a shoe might be. He tried the door, and found it still bolted; so, with growing uneasiness, the boy was forced to admit that the precious shoe was not in the room.

With a throbbing heart he aroused his companion.

"King Rinkitink," said he, "do you know what has become of my left shoe?"

"Your shoe!" exclaimed the King, giving a wide yawn and rubbing his eyes to get the sleep out of them. "Have you lost a shoe?"

"Yes," said Inga. "I have searched everywhere in the room, and cannot find it."

"But why bother me about such a small thing?" inquired Rinkitink. "A shoe is only a shoe, and you can easily get another one. But, stay! Perhaps it was your shoe which I threw at the cat last night."

"The cat!" cried Inga. "What do you mean?"

"Why, in the night," explained Rinkitink, sitting up and beginning to dress himself, "I was wakened by the mewing of a cat that sat upon a wall of the palace, just outside my window. As the noise disturbed me, I reached out in the dark and caught up something and threw it at the cat, to frighten the creature away. I did not know what it was that I threw, and I was too sleepy to care; but probably it was your shoe, since it is now missing."

"Then," said the boy, in a despairing tone of voice, "your carelessness has ruined me, as well as yourself, King Rinkitink, for in that shoe was concealed the magic power which protected us from danger."

The King's face became very serious when he heard this and he uttered a low whistle of surprise and regret.

"Why on earth did you not warn me of this?" he demanded. "And why did you keep such a precious power in an old shoe? And why didn't you put the shoe under a pillow? You were very wrong, my lad, in not confiding to me, your faithful friend, the secret, for in that case the shoe would not now be lost."

To all this Inga had no answer. He sat on the side of his bed, with hanging head, utterly disconsolate, and seeing this, Rinkitink had pity for his sorrow.

"Come!" cried the King; "let us go out at once and look for the shoe which I threw at the cat. It must even now be lying in the yard of the palace."

This suggestion roused the boy to action. He at once threw open the door and in his stocking feet rushed down the staircase, closely followed by Rinkitink. But although they looked on both sides of the palace wall and in every possible crack and corner where a shoe might lodge, they failed to find it.

After a half hour's careful search the boy said sorrowfully:

"Someone must have passed by, as we slept, and taken the precious shoe, not knowing its value. To us, King Rinkitink, this will be a dreadful misfortune, for we are surrounded by dangers from which we have now no protection. Luckily I have the other shoe left, within which is the magic power that gives me strength; so all is not lost."

Then he told Rinkitink, in a few words, the secret of the wonderful pearls, and how he had recovered them from the ruins and hidden them in his shoes, and how they had enabled him to drive King Gos and his men from Regos and to capture the city. The King was much astonished, and when the story was concluded he said to Inga:

"What did you do with the other shoe?"

"Why, I left it in our bedroom," replied the boy.

"Then I advise you to get it at once," continued Rinkitink, "for we can ill afford to lose the second shoe, as well as the one I threw at the cat."

"You are right!" cried Inga, and they hastened back to their bedchamber.

On entering the room they found an old woman sweeping and raising a great deal of dust.

"Where is my shoe?" asked the Prince, anxiously.

The old woman stopped sweeping and looked at him in a stupid way, for she was not very intelligent.

"Do you mean the one odd shoe that was lying on the floor when I came in?" she finally asked.

"Yes—yes!" answered the boy. "Where is it? Tell me where it is!"

"Why, I threw it on the dust-heap, outside the back gate," said she, "for, it being but a single shoe, with no mate, it can be of no use to anyone."

"Show us the way to the dust-heap—at once!" commanded the boy, sternly, for he was greatly frightened by this new misfortune which threatened him.

The old woman hobbled away and they followed her, constantly urging her to hasten; but when they reached the dust-heap no shoe was to be seen.

"This is terrible!" wailed the young Prince, ready to weep at his loss. "We are now absolutely ruined, and at the mercy of our enemies. Nor shall I be able to liberate my dear father and mother."

"Well," replied Rinkitink, leaning against an old barrel and looking quite solemn, "the thing is certainly unlucky, any way we look at it. I suppose someone has passed along here and, seeing the shoe upon the dust-heap, has carried it away. But no one could know the magic power the shoe contains and so will not use it against us. I believe, Inga, we must now depend upon our wits to get us out of the scrape we are in."

With saddened hearts they returned to the palace, and entering a small room where no one could observe them or overhear them, the boy took the White Pearl from its silken bag and held it to his ear, asking:

"What shall I do now?"

"Tell no one of your loss," answered the Voice of the Pearl. "If your enemies do not know that you are powerless, they will fear you as much as ever. Keep your secret, be patient, and fear not!"

Inga heeded this advice and also warned Rinkitink to say nothing to anyone of the loss of the shoes and the powers they contained. He sent for the shoemaker of King Gos, who soon brought him a new pair of red leather shoes that fitted him quite well. When these had been put upon his feet, the Prince, accompanied by the King, started to walk through the city.

Wherever they went the people bowed low to the conqueror, although a few, remembering Inga's terrible strength, ran away in fear and trembling. They had been used to severe masters and did not yet know how they would be treated by King Gos's successor. There being no occasion for the boy to exercise the powers he had displayed the previous day, his present helplessness was not suspected by any of the citizens of Regos, who still considered him a wonderful magician.

Inga did not dare to fight his way to the mines, at present, nor could he try to conquer the Island of Coregos, where his mother was enslaved; so he set about the regulation of the City of Regos, and having established himself with great state in the royal palace he began to govern the people by kindness, having consideration for the most humble.

The King of Regos and his followers sent spies across to the island they had abandoned in their flight, and these spies returned with the news that the terrible boy conqueror was still occupying the city. Therefore none of them ventured to go back to Regos but continued to live upon the neighboring island of Coregos, where they passed the days in fear and trembling and sought to plot and plan ways how they might overcome the Prince of Pingaree and the fat King of Gilgad.

CHAPTER IX

A PRESENT FOR ZELLA

NOW IT SO HAPPENED THAT ON THE MORNING OF THAT SAME DAY WHEN THE PRINCE of Pingaree suffered the loss of his priceless shoes, there chanced to pass along the road that wound beside the royal palace a poor charcoal-burner named Nikobob, who was about to return to his home in the forest.

Nikobob carried an axe and a bundle of torches over his shoulder and he walked with his eyes to the ground, being deep in thought as to the strange manner in which the powerful King Gos and his city had been conquered by a boy Prince who had come from Pingaree.

Suddenly the charcoal-burner espied a shoe lying upon the ground, just beyond the high wall of the palace and directly in his path. He picked it up and, seeing it was a pretty shoe, although much too small for his own foot, he put it in his pocket.

Soon after, on turning a corner of the wall, Nikobob came to a dust-heap where, lying amidst a mass of rubbish, was another shoe—the mate to the one he had before found. This also he placed in his pocket, saying to himself:

"I have now a fine pair of shoes for my daughter Zella, who will be much pleased to find I have brought her a present from the city."

And while the charcoal-burner turned into the forest and trudged along the path toward his home, Inga and Rinkitink were still searching for the missing shoes. Of course, they could not know that Nikobob had found them, nor did the honest man think he had taken anything more than a pair of cast-off shoes which nobody wanted.

Nikobob had several miles to travel through the forest before he could reach the little log cabin where his wife, as well as his little daughter Zella, awaited his return, but he was used to long walks and tramped along the path whistling cheerfully to beguile the time.

Few people, as I said before, ever passed through the dark and tangled forests of Regos, except to go to the mines in the mountain beyond, for many dangerous creatures lurked in the wild jungles, and King Gos never knew, when he sent a messenger to the mines, whether he would reach there safely or not.

The charcoal-burner, however, knew the wild forest well, and especially this part of it lying between the city and his home. It was the favorite haunt of the ferocious beast Choggenmugger, dreaded by every dweller in the Island of Regos. Choggenmugger was so old that everyone thought it must have been there since the world was made, and each year of its life the huge scales that covered its body grew thicker and harder and its jaws grew wider and its teeth grew sharper and its appetite grew more keen than ever.

In former ages there had been many dragons in Regos, but Choggenmugger was so fond of dragons that he had eaten all of them long ago. There had also been great serpents and crocodiles in the forest marshes, but all had gone to feed the hunger of Choggenmugger. The people of Regos knew well there was no use opposing the Great Beast, so when one unfortunately met with it he gave himself up for lost.

All this Nikobob knew well, but fortune had always favored him in his journeys through the forest, and although he had at times met many savage beasts and fought them with his sharp axe, he had never to this day encountered the terrible Choggenmugger. Indeed, he was not thinking of the Great Beast at all as he walked along, but suddenly he heard a crashing of broken trees and felt a trembling of the earth and saw the immense jaws of Choggenmugger opening before him. Then Nikobob gave himself up for lost and his heart almost ceased to beat.

He believed there was no way of escape. No one ever dared oppose Choggenmugger. But Nikobob hated to die without showing the monster, in some way, that he was eaten only under protest. So he raised his axe and brought it down upon the red, protruding tongue of the monster—and cut it clean off!

For a moment the charcoal-burner scarcely believed what his eyes saw, for he knew nothing of the pearls he carried in his pocket or the magic power they lent his

arm. His success, however, encouraged him to strike again, and this time the huge scaly jaw of Choggenmugger was severed in twain and the beast howled in terrified rage.

Nikobob took off his coat, to give himself more freedom of action, and then he earnestly renewed the attack. But now the axe seemed blunted by the hard scales and made no impression upon them whatever. The creature advanced with glaring, wicked eyes, and Nikobob seized his coat under his arm and turned to flee.

That was foolish, for Choggenmugger could run like the wind. In a moment it overtook the charcoal-burner and snapped its four rows of sharp teeth together. But they did not touch Nikobob, because he still held the coat in his grasp, close to his body, and in the coat pocket were Inga's shoes, and in the points of the shoes were the magic pearls. Finding himself uninjured, Nikobob put on his coat, again seized his axe, and in a short time had chopped Choggenmugger into many small pieces—a task that proved not only easy but very agreeable.

"I must be the strongest man in all the world!" thought the charcoal-burner, as he proudly resumed his way, "for Choggenmugger has been the terror of Regos since the world began, and I alone have been able to destroy the beast. Yet it is singular that never before did I discover how powerful a man I am."

He met no further adventure and at midday reached a little clearing in the forest where stood his humble cabin.

"Great news! I have great news for you," he shouted, as his wife and little daughter came to greet him. "King Gos has been conquered by a boy Prince from the far island of Pingaree, and I have this day—unaided—destroyed Choggenmugger by the might of my strong arm."

This was, indeed, great news. They brought Nikobob into the house and set him in an easy chair and made him tell everything he knew about the Prince of Pingaree and the fat King of Gilgad, as well as the details of his wonderful fight with mighty Choggenmugger.

"And now, my daughter," said the charcoal-burner, when all his news had been related for at least the third time, "here is a pretty present I have brought you from the city."

With this he drew the shoes from the pocket of his coat and handed them to Zella, who gave him a dozen kisses in payment and was much pleased with her gift. The little girl had never worn shoes before, for her parents were too poor to buy her such luxuries, so now the possession of these, which were not much worn, filled the child's heart with joy. She admired the red leather and the graceful curl of the pointed toes. When she tried them on her feet, they fitted as well as if made for her.

All the afternoon, as she helped her mother with the housework, Zella thought of her pretty shoes. They seemed more important to her than the coming to Regos of the conquering Prince of Pingaree, or even the death of Choggenmugger.

When Zella and her mother were not working in the cabin, cooking or sewing, they often searched the neighboring forest for honey which the wild bees cleverly hid in hollow trees. The day after Nikobob's return, as they were starting out after honey, Zella decided to put on her new shoes, as they would keep the twigs that covered the ground from hurting her feet. She was used to the twigs, of course, but what is the use of having nice, comfortable shoes, if you do not wear them?

So she danced along, very happily, followed by her mother, and presently they came to a tree in which was a deep hollow. Zella thrust her hand and arm into the space and found that the tree was full of honey, so she began to dig it out with a wooden paddle. Her mother, who held the pail, suddenly cried in warning:

"Look out, Zella; the bees are coming!" and then the good woman ran fast toward the house to escape.

Zella, however, had no more than time to turn her head when a thick swarm of bees surrounded her, angry because they had caught her stealing their honey and intent on stinging the girl as a punishment. She knew her danger and expected to be badly injured by the multitude of stinging bees, but to her surprise the little creatures were unable to fly close enough to her to stick their dart-like stingers into her flesh. They swarmed about her in a dark cloud, and their angry buzzing was terrible to hear, yet the little girl remained unharmed.

When she realized this, Zella was no longer afraid but continued to ladle out the honey until she had secured all that was in the tree. Then she returned to the cabin, where her mother was weeping and bemoaning the fate of her darling child, and the good woman was greatly astonished to find Zella had escaped injury.

Again they went to the woods to search for honey, and although the mother always ran away whenever the bees came near them, Zella paid no attention to the creatures but kept at her work, so that before supper time came the pails were again filled to overflowing with delicious honey.

"With such good fortune as we have had this day," said her mother, "we shall soon gather enough honey for you to carry to Queen Cor." For it seems the wicked Queen was very fond of honey and it had been Zella's custom to go, once every year, to the City of Coregos, to carry the Queen a supply of sweet honey for her table. Usually she had but one pail.

"But now," said Zella, "I shall be able to carry two pailsful to the Queen, who will, I am sure, give me a good price for it."

"True," answered her mother, "and, as the boy Prince may take it into his head to conquer Coregos, as well as Regos, I think it best for you to start on your journey to Queen Cor to-morrow morning. Do you not agree with me, Nikobob?" she added, turning to her husband, the charcoal-burner, who was eating his supper.

"I agree with you," he replied. "If Zella must go to the City of Coregos, she may as well start to-morrow morning."

CHAPTER X

THE CUNNING OF QUEEN COR

You may be sure the Queen of Coregos was not well pleased to have King Gos and all his warriors living in her city after they had fled from their own. They were savage natured and quarrelsome men at all times, and their tempers had not improved since their conquest by the Prince of Pingaree. Moreover, they were eating up Queen Cor's provisions and crowding the houses of her own people, who grumbled and complained until their Queen was heartily tired.

"Shame on you!" she said to her husband, King Gos, "to be driven out of your city by a boy, a roly-poly King and a billy goat! Why do you not go back and fight them?"

"No human can fight against the powers of magic," returned the King in a surly voice. "That boy is either a fairy or under the protection of fairies. We escaped with our lives only because we were quick to run away; but, should we return to Regos, the same terrible power that burst open the city gates would crush us all to atoms."

"Bah! you are a coward," cried the Queen, tauntingly.

"I am not a coward," said the big King. "I have killed in battle scores of my enemies; by the might of my sword and my good right arm I have conquered many nations; all my life people have feared me. But no one would dare face the tremendous power of the Prince of Pingaree, boy though he is. It would not be courage, it would be folly, to attempt it."

"Then meet his power with cunning," suggested the Queen. "Take my advice, and steal over to Regos at night, when it is dark, and capture or destroy the boy while he sleeps."

"No weapon can touch his body," was the answer. "He bears a charmed life and cannot be injured."

"Does the fat King possess magic powers, or the goat?" inquired Cor.

"I think not," said Gos. "We could not injure them, indeed, any more than we could the boy, but they did not seem to have any unusual strength, although the goat's head is harder than a battering-ram."

"Well," mused the Queen, "there is surely some way to conquer that slight boy. If you are afraid to undertake the job, I shall go myself. By some stratagem I shall manage to make him my prisoner. He will not dare to defy a Queen and no magic can stand against a woman's cunning."

"Go ahead, if you like," replied the King, with an evil grin, "and if you are hung up by the thumbs or cast into a dungeon, it will serve you right for thinking you can succeed where a skilled warrior dares not make the attempt."

"I'm not afraid," answered the Queen. "It is only soldiers and bullies who are cowards."

In spite of this assertion, Queen Cor was not so brave as she was cunning. For several days she thought over this plan and that, and tried to decide which was most likely to succeed. She had never seen the boy Prince but had heard so many tales of him from the defeated warriors, and especially from Captain Buzzub, that she had learned to respect his power.

Spurred on by the knowledge that she would never get rid of her unwelcome guests until Prince Inga was overcome and Regos regained for King Gos, the Queen of Coregos finally decided to trust to luck and her native wit to defeat a simple-minded boy, however powerful he might be. Inga could not suspect what she was going to do, because she did not know herself. She intended to act boldly and trust to chance to win.

It is evident that had the cunning Queen known that Inga had lost all his magic, she would not have devoted so much time to the simple matter of capturing him, but like all others she was impressed by the marvelous exhibition of power he had shown in capturing Regos, and had no reason to believe the boy was less powerful now.

One morning Queen Cor boldly entered a boat, and, taking four men with her as an escort and bodyguard, was rowed across the narrow channel to Regos. Prince Inga was sitting in the palace playing checkers with King Rinkitink when a servant came to him, saying that Queen Cor had arrived and desired an audience with him.

With many misgivings lest the wicked Queen discover that he had now lost his magic powers, the boy ordered her to be admitted, and she soon entered the room and bowed low before him, in mock respect.

Cor was a big woman, almost as tall as King Gos. She had flashing black eyes and the dark complexion you see on gypsies. Her temper, when irritated, was something dreadful, and her face wore an evil expression which she tried to cover by smiling sweetly—often when she meant the most mischief.

"I have come," said she in a low voice, "to render homage to the noble Prince of Pingaree. I am told that Your Highness is the strongest person in the world, and invincible in battle, and therefore I wish you to become my friend, rather than my enemy."

Now Inga did not know how to reply to this speech. He disliked the appearance of the woman and was afraid of her and he was unused to deception and did not know how to mask his real feelings. So he took time to think over his answer, which he finally made in these words:

"I have no quarrel with Your Majesty, and my only reason for coming here is to liberate my father and mother, and my people, whom you and your husband have made your slaves, and to recover the goods King Gos has plundered from the Island of Pingaree. This I hope soon to accomplish, and if you really wish to be my friend, you can assist me greatly."

While he was speaking Queen Cor had been studying the boy's face stealthily, from the corners of her eyes, and she said to herself: "He is so small and innocent that I believe I can capture him alone, and with ease. He does not seem very terrible and I suspect that King Gos and his warriors were frightened at nothing." Then, aloud, she said to Inga:

"I wish to invite you, mighty Prince, and your friend, the great King of Gilgad, to visit my poor palace at Coregos, where all my people shall do you honor. Will you come?"

"At present," replied Inga, uneasily, "I must refuse your kind invitation."

"There will be feasting, and dancing girls, and games and fireworks," said the Queen, speaking as if eager to entice him and at each word coming a step nearer to where he stood.

"I could not enjoy them while my poor parents are slaves," said the boy, sadly.

"Are you sure of that?" asked Queen Cor, and by that time she was close beside Inga. Suddenly she leaned forward and threw both of her long arms around Inga's body, holding him in a grasp that was like a vise.

Now Rinkitink sprang forward to rescue his friend, but Cor kicked out viciously with her foot and struck the King squarely on his stomach—a very tender place to be kicked, especially if one is fat. Then, still hugging Inga tightly, the Queen called aloud:

"I've got him! Bring in the ropes."

Instantly the four men she had brought with her sprang into the room and bound the boy hand and foot. Next they seized Rinkitink, who was still rubbing his stomach, and bound him likewise.

With a laugh of wicked triumph, Queen Cor now led her captives down to the boat and returned with them to Coregos.

Great was the astonishment of King Gos and his warriors when they saw that the mighty Prince of Pingaree, who had put them all to flight, had been captured by a woman. Cowards as they were, they now crowded around the boy and jeered at him, and some of them would have struck him had not the Queen cried out:

"Hands off! He is my prisoner, remember—not yours."

"Well, Cor, what are you going to do with him?" inquired King Gos.

"I shall make him my slave, that he may amuse my idle hours. For he is a pretty boy, and gentle, although he did frighten all of you big warriors so terribly."

The King scowled at this speech, not liking to be ridiculed, but he said nothing more. He and his men returned that same day to Regos, after restoring the bridge of boats. And they held a wild carnival of rejoicing, both in the King's palace and in the city, although the poor people of Regos who were not warriors were all sorry that the kind young Prince had been captured by his enemies and could rule them no longer.

When her unwelcome guests had all gone back to Regos and the Queen was alone in her palace, she ordered Inga and Rinkitink brought before her and their bonds removed. They came sadly enough, knowing they were in serious straits and at the mercy of a cruel mistress. Inga had taken counsel of the White Pearl, which had advised him to bear up bravely under his misfortune, promising a change for the better very soon. With this promise to comfort him, Inga faced the Queen with a dignified bearing that indicated both pride and courage.

"Well, youngster," said she, in a cheerful tone because she was pleased with her success, "you played a clever trick on my poor husband and frightened him badly, but for that prank I am inclined to forgive you. Hereafter I intend you to be my page, which means that you must fetch and carry for me at my will. And let me advise you to obey my every whim without question or delay, for when I am angry I become ugly, and when I am ugly someone is sure to feel the lash. Do you understand me?"

Inga bowed, but made no answer. Then she turned to Rinkitink and said:

"As for you, I cannot decide how to make you useful to me, as you are altogether too fat and awkward to work in the fields. It may be, however, that I can use you as a pincushion."

"What!" cried Rinkitink in horror, "would you stick pins into the King of Gilgad?"

"Why not?" returned Queen Cor. "You are as fat as a pincushion, as you must yourself admit, and whenever I needed a pin I could call you to me." Then she laughed at his frightened look and asked: "By the way, are you ticklish?"

This was the question Rinkitink had been dreading. He gave a moan of despair and shook his head.

"I should love to tickle the bottom of your feet with a feather," continued the cruel woman. "Please take off your shoes."

"Oh, your Majesty!" pleaded poor Rinkitink, "I beg you to allow me to amuse you in some other way. I can dance, or I can sing you a song."

"Well," she answered, shaking with laughter, "you may sing a song—if it be a merry one. But you do not seem in a merry mood."

"I *feel* merry—indeed, Your Majesty, I do!" protested Rinkitink, anxious to escape the tickling. But even as he professed to "feel merry" his round, red face wore an expression of horror and anxiety that was realty comical.

"Sing, then!" commanded Queen Cor, who was greatly amused.

Rinkitink gave a sigh of relief and after clearing his throat and trying to repress his sobs he began to sing this song—gently, at first, but finally roaring it out at the top of his voice:

> "Oh!
>   There was a Baby Tiger lived in a men-ag-er-ie—
>   Fizzy-fezzy-fuzzy—they wouldn't set him free;
>   And ev'rybody thought that he was gentle as could be—
>   Fizzy-fezzy-fuzzy—Ba-by Ti-ger!
>
> "Oh!
>   They patted him upon his head and shook him by the paw—
>   Fizzy-fezzy-fuzzy—he had a bone to gnaw;
>   But soon he grew the biggest Tiger that you ever saw—
>   Fizzy-fezzy-fuzzy—what a Ti-ger!
>
> "Oh!
>   One day they came to pet the brute and he began to fight—
>   Fizzy-fezzy-fuzzy—how he did scratch and bite!
>   He broke the cage and in a rage he darted out of sight—
>   Fizzy-fezzy-fuzzy was a Ti-ger!"

"And is there a moral to the song?" asked Queen Cor, when King Rinkitink had finished his song with great spirit.

"If there is," replied Rinkitink, "it is a warning not to fool with tigers."

The little Prince could not help smiling at this shrewd answer, but Queen Cor frowned and gave the King a sharp look.

"Oh," said she; "I think I know the difference between a tiger and a lapdog. But I'll bear the warning in mind, just the same."

For, after all her success in capturing them, she was a little afraid of these people who had once displayed such extraordinary powers.

CHAPTER XI

ZELLA GOES TO COREGOS

THE FOREST IN WHICH NIKOBOB LIVED WITH HIS WIFE AND DAUGHTER STOOD between the mountains and the City of Regos, and a well-beaten path wound among the trees, leading from the city to the mines. This path was used by the King's messengers, and captured prisoners were also sent by this way from Regos to work in the underground caverns.

Nikobob had built his cabin more than a mile away from this path, that he might not be molested by the wild and lawless soldiers of King Gos, but the family of the charcoal-burner was surrounded by many creatures scarcely less dangerous to encounter, and often in the night they could hear savage animals growling and prowling about the cabin. Because Nikobob minded his own business and never hunted the wild creatures to injure them, the beasts had come to regard him as one of the natural dwellers in the forest and did not molest him or his family. Still Zella and her mother seldom wandered far from home, except on such errands as carrying honey to Coregos, and at these times Nikobob cautioned them to be very careful.

So when Zella set out on her journey to Queen Cor, with the two pails of honey in her hands, she was undertaking a dangerous adventure and there was no certainty that she would return safely to her loving parents. But they were poor, and Queen

Cor's money, which they expected to receive for the honey, would enable them to purchase many things that were needed; so it was deemed best that Zella should go. She was a brave little girl and poor people are often obliged to take chances that rich ones are spared.

A passing woodchopper had brought news to Nikobob's cabin that Queen Cor had made a prisoner of the conquering Prince of Pingaree and that Gos and his warriors were again back in their city of Regos; but these struggles and conquests were

matters which, however interesting, did not concern the poor charcoal-burner or his family. They were more anxious over the report that the warriors had become more reckless than ever before, and delighted in annoying all the common people; so Zella was told to keep away from the beaten path as much as possible, that she might not encounter any of the King's soldiers.

"When it is necessary to choose between the warriors and the wild beasts," said Nikobob, "the beasts will be found the more merciful."

The little girl had put on her best attire for the journey and her mother threw a blue silk shawl over her head and shoulders. Upon her feet were the pretty red shoes her father had brought her from Regos. Thus prepared, she kissed her parents good-bye and started out with a light heart, carrying the pails of honey in either hand.

It was necessary for Zella to cross the path that led from the mines to the city, but once on the other side she was not likely to meet with anyone, for she had resolved to cut through the forest and so reach the bridge of boats without entering the City of Regos, where she might be interrupted. For an hour or two she found the walking easy enough, but then the forest, which in this part was unknown to her, became badly tangled. The trees were thicker and creeping vines intertwined between them. She had to turn this way and that to get through at all, and finally she came to a place where a network of vines and branches effectually barred her farther progress.

Zella was dismayed, at first, when she encountered this obstacle, but setting down her pails she made an endeavor to push the branches aside. At her touch they parted as if by magic, breaking asunder like dried twigs, and she found she could pass freely. At another place a great log had fallen across her way, but the little girl lifted it easily and cast it aside, although six ordinary men could scarcely have moved it.

The child was somewhat worried at this evidence of a strength she had heretofore been ignorant that she possessed. In order to satisfy herself that it was no delusion, she tested her new-found power in many ways, finding that nothing was too big nor too heavy for her to lift. And, naturally enough, the girl gained courage from these experiments and became confident that she could protect herself in any emergency. When, presently, a wild boar ran toward her, grunting horribly and threatening her with its great tusks, she did not climb a tree to escape, as she had always done before on meeting such creatures, but stood still and faced the boar. When it had come quite close and Zella saw that it could not injure her—a fact that astonished both the beast and the girl—she suddenly reached down and seizing it by one ear threw the great beast far off amongst the trees, where it fell headlong to the earth, grunting louder than ever with surprise and fear.

The girl laughed merrily at this incident and, picking up her pails, resumed her journey through the forest. It is not recorded whether the wild boar told his adventure

to the other beasts or they had happened to witness his defeat, but certain it is that
Zella was not again molested. A brown bear watched her pass without making any
movement in her direction and a great puma—a beast much dreaded by all men—
crept out of her path as she approached, and disappeared among the trees.

Thus everything favored the girl's journey and she made such good speed that by
noon she emerged from the forest's edge and found she was quite near to the bridge of
boats that led to Coregos. This she crossed safely and without meeting any of the rude
warriors she so greatly feared, and five minutes later the daughter of the charcoal-
burner was seeking admittance at the back door of Queen Cor's palace.

CHAPTER XII

THE EXCITEMENT OF BILBIL THE GOAT

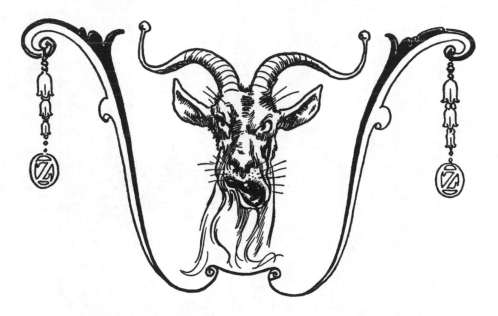

OUR STORY MUST NOW RETURN TO ONE OF OUR CHARACTERS WHOM WE HAVE BEEN forced to neglect. The temper of Bilbil the goat was not sweet under any circumstances, and whenever he had a grievance he was inclined to be quite grumpy. So, when his master settled down in the palace of King Gos for a quiet life with the boy Prince, and passed his time in playing checkers and eating and otherwise enjoying himself, he had no use whatever for Bilbil, and shut the goat in an upstairs room to prevent his wandering through the city and quarreling with the citizens. But this Bilbil did not like at all. He became very cross and disagreeable at being left alone and he did not speak nicely to the servants who came to bring him food; therefore those people decided not to wait upon him any more, resenting his conversation and not liking to be scolded by a lean, scraggly goat, even though it belonged to a conqueror. The servants kept away from the room and Bilbil grew more hungry and more angry every hour. He tried to eat the rugs and ornaments, but found them not at all nourishing. There was no grass to be had unless he escaped from the palace.

When Queen Cor came to capture Inga and Rinkitink, both the prisoners were so filled with despair at their own misfortune that they gave no thought whatever to the goat, who was left in his room. Nor did Bilbil know anything of the changed fortunes of his comrades until he heard shouts and boisterous laughter in the courtyard below. Looking out of a window, with the intention of rebuking those who dared thus to disturb him, Bilbil saw the courtyard quite filled with warriors and knew from this that the palace had in some way again fallen into the hands of the enemy.

Now, although Bilbil was often exceedingly disagreeable to King Rinkitink, as well as to the Prince, and sometimes used harsh words in addressing them, he was intelligent enough to know them to be his friends, and to know that King Gos and his people were his foes. In sudden anger, provoked by the sight of the warriors and the knowledge that he was in the power of the dangerous men of Regos, Bilbil butted his head against the door of his room and burst it open. Then he ran to the head of the staircase and saw King Gos coming up the stairs followed by a long line of his chief captains and warriors.

The goat lowered his head, trembling with rage and excitement, and just as the King reached the top stair the animal dashed forward and butted His Majesty so fiercely that the big and powerful King, who did not expect an attack, doubled up and tumbled backward. His great weight knocked over the man just behind him and he in turn struck the next warrior and upset him, so that in an instant the whole line of Bilbil's foes was tumbling heels over head to the bottom of the stairs, where they piled up in a heap, struggling and shouting and in the mix-up hitting one another with their fists, until every man of them was bruised and sore.

Finally King Gos scrambled out of the heap and rushed up the stairs again, very angry indeed. Bilbil was ready for him and a second time butted the King down the stairs; but now the goat also lost his balance and followed the King, landing full upon the confused heap of soldiers. Then he kicked out so viciously with his heels that he soon freed himself and dashed out of the doorway of the palace.

"Stop him!" cried King Gos, running after.

But the goat was now so wild and excited that it was not safe for anyone to stand in his way. None of the men were armed and when one or two tried to head off the goat, Bilbil sent them sprawling upon the ground. Most of the warriors, however, were wise enough not to attempt to interfere with his flight.

Coursing down the street, Bilbil found himself approaching the bridge of boats and without pausing to think where it might lead him he crossed over and proceeded on his way. A few moments later a great stone building blocked his path. It was the palace of Queen Cor, and seeing the gates of the courtyard standing wide open, Bilbil rushed through them without slackening his speed.

CHAPTER XIII

ZELLA SAVES THE PRINCE

THE WICKED QUEEN OF COREGOS WAS IN A VERY BAD HUMOR THIS MORNING, FOR one of her slave drivers had come from the fields to say that a number of slaves had rebelled and would not work.

"Bring them here to me!" she cried savagely. "A good whipping may make them change their minds."

So the slave driver went to fetch the rebellious ones and Queen Cor sat down to eat her breakfast, an ugly look on her face.

Prince Inga had been ordered to stand behind his new mistress with a big fan of peacock's feathers, but he was so unused to such service that he awkwardly brushed her ear with the fan. At once she flew into a terrible rage and slapped the Prince twice with her hand—blows that tingled, too, for her hand was big and hard and she was not inclined to be gentle. Inga took the blows without shrinking or uttering a cry, although they stung his pride far more than his body. But King Rinkitink, who was acting as the Queen's butler and had just brought in her coffee, was so startled at seeing the young Prince punished that he tipped over the urn and the hot coffee streamed across the lap of the Queen's best morning gown.

Cor sprang from her seat with a scream of anger and poor Rinkitink would doubtless have been given a terrible beating had not the slave driver returned at this moment and attracted the woman's attention. The overseer had brought with him all of the women slaves from Pingaree, who had been loaded down with chains and were so weak and ill they could scarcely walk, much less work in the fields.

Prince Inga's eyes were dimmed with sorrowful tears when he discovered how his poor people had been abused, but his own plight was so helpless that he was unable to aid them. Fortunately the boy's mother, Queen Garee, was not among these slaves, for Queen Cor had placed her in the royal dairy to make butter.

"Why do you refuse to work?" demanded Cor in a harsh voice, as the slaves from Pingaree stood before her, trembling and with downcast eyes.

"Because we lack strength to perform the tasks your overseers demand," answered one of the women.

"Then you shall be whipped until your strength returns!" exclaimed the Queen, and turning to Inga, she commanded: "Get me the whip with the seven lashes."

As the boy left the room, wondering how he might manage to save the unhappy women from their undeserved punishment, he met a girl entering by the back way, who asked:

"Can you tell me where to find Her Majesty, Queen Cor?"

"She is in the chamber with the red dome, where green dragons are painted upon the walls," replied Inga; "but she is in an angry and ungracious mood to-day. Why do you wish to see her?"

"I have honey to sell," answered the girl, who was Zella, just come from the forest. "The Queen is very fond of my honey."

"You may go to her, if you so desire," said the boy, "but take care not to anger the cruel Queen, or she may do you a mischief."

"Why should she harm me, who brings her the honey she so dearly loves?" inquired the child innocently. "But I thank you for your warning; and I will try not to anger the Queen."

As Zella started to go, Inga's eyes suddenly fell upon her shoes and instantly he recognized them as his own. For only in Pingaree were shoes shaped in this manner: high at the heel and pointed at the toes.

"Stop!" he cried in an excited voice, and the girl obeyed, wonderingly. "Tell me," he continued, more gently, "where did you get those shoes?"

"My father brought them to me from Regos," she answered.

"From Regos!"

"Yes. Are they not pretty?" asked Zella, looking down at her feet to admire them. "One of them my father found by the palace wall, and the other on an ash-heap. So he brought them to me and they fit me perfectly."

By this time Inga was trembling with eager joy, which of course the girl could not understand.

"What is your name, little maid?" he asked.

"I am called Zella, and my father is Nikobob, the charcoal-burner."

"Zella is a pretty name. I am Inga, Prince of Pingaree," said he, "and the shoes you are now wearing, Zella, belong to me. They were not cast away, as your father supposed, but were lost. Will you let me have them again?"

Zella's eyes filled with tears.

"Must I give up my pretty shoes, then?" she asked. "They are the only ones I have ever owned."

Inga was sorry for the poor child, but he knew how important it was that he regain possession of the Magic Pearls. So he said, pleadingly:

"Please let me have them, Zella. See! I will exchange for them the shoes I now have on, which are newer and prettier than the others."

The girl hesitated. She wanted to please the boy Prince, yet she hated to exchange the shoes which her father had brought her as a present.

"If you will give me the shoes," continued the boy, anxiously, "I will promise to make you and your father and mother rich and prosperous. Indeed, I will promise to grant any favors you may ask of me," and he sat down upon the floor and drew off the shoes he was wearing and held them toward the girl.

"I'll see if they will fit me," said Zella, taking off her left shoe—the one that contained the Pink Pearl—and beginning to put on one of Inga's.

Just then Queen Cor, angry at being made to wait for her whip with the seven lashes, rushed into the room to find Inga. Seeing the boy sitting upon the floor beside Zella, the woman sprang toward him to beat him with her clenched fists; but Inga had now slipped on the shoe and the Queen's blows could not reach his body.

Then Cor espied the whip lying beside Inga and snatching it up she tried to lash him with it—all to no avail.

While Zella sat horrified by this scene, the Prince, who realized he had no time to waste, reached out and pulled the right shoe from the girl's foot, quickly placing it upon his own. Then he stood up and, facing the furious but astonished Queen, said to her in a quiet voice:

"Madam, please give me that whip."

"I won't!" answered Cor. "I'm going to lash those Pingaree women with it."

The boy seized hold of the whip and with irresistible strength drew it from the Queen's hand. But she drew from her bosom a sharp dagger and with the swiftness of lightning aimed a blow at Inga's heart. He merely stood still and smiled, for the blade rebounded and fell clattering to the floor.

Then, at last, Queen Cor understood the magic power that had terrified her husband but which she had ridiculed in her ignorance, not believing in it. She did not know that Inga's power had been lost, and found again, but she realized the boy was no common foe and that unless she could still manage to outwit him her reign in the Island of Coregos was ended. To gain time, she went back to the red-domed chamber and seated herself in her throne, before which were grouped the weeping slaves from Pingaree.

Inga had taken Zella's hand and assisted her to put on the shoes he had given her in exchange for his own. She found them quite comfortable and did not know she had lost anything by the transfer.

"Come with me," then said the boy Prince, and led her into the presence of Queen Cor, who was giving Rinkitink a scolding. To the overseer Inga said:

"Give me the keys which unlock these chains, that I may set these poor women at liberty."

"Don't you do it!" screamed Queen Cor.

"If you interfere, madam," said the boy, "I will put you into a dungeon."

By this Rinkitink knew that Inga had recovered his Magic Pearls and the little fat King was so overjoyed that he danced and capered all around the room. But the Queen was alarmed at the threat and the slave driver, fearing the conqueror of Regos, tremblingly gave up the keys.

Inga quickly removed all the shackles from the women of his country and comforted them, telling them they should work no more but would soon be restored to their homes in Pingaree. Then he commanded the slave driver to go and get all the children who had been made slaves, and to bring them to their mothers. The man obeyed and left at once to perform his errand, while Queen Cor, growing more and more uneasy, suddenly sprang from her throne and before Inga could stop her had rushed through the room and out into the courtyard of the palace, meaning to make her escape. Rinkitink followed her, running as fast as he could go.

It was at this moment that Bilbil, in his mad dash from Regos, turned in at the gates of the courtyard, and as he was coming one way and Queen Cor was going the other they bumped into each other with great force. The woman sailed through the air, over Bilbil's head, and landed on the ground outside the gates, where her crown rolled into a ditch and she picked herself up, half dazed, and continued her flight. Bilbil was also somewhat dazed by the unexpected encounter, but he continued his rush rather blindly and so struck poor Rinkitink, who was chasing after Queen Cor. They rolled over one another a few times and then Rinkitink sat up and Bilbil sat up and they looked at each other in amazement.

"Bilbil," said the King, "I'm astonished at you!"

"Your Majesty," said Bilbil, "I expected kinder treatment at your hands."

"You interrupted me," said Rinkitink.

"There was plenty of room without your taking my path," declared the goat.

And then Inga came running out and said: "Where is the Queen?"

"Gone," replied Rinkitink, "but she cannot go far, as this is an island. However, I have found Bilbil, and our party is again reunited. You have recovered your magic powers, and again we are masters of the situation. So let us be thankful."

Saying this, the good little King got upon his feet and limped back into the throne room to help comfort the women.

Presently the children of Pingaree, who had been gathered together by the overseer, were brought in and restored to their mothers, and there was great rejoicing among them, you may be sure.

"But where is Queen Garee, my dear mother?" questioned Inga; but the women did not know and it was some time before the overseer remembered that one of the slaves from Pingaree had been placed in the royal dairy. Perhaps this was the woman the boy was seeking.

Inga at once commanded him to lead the way to the butter house, but when they arrived there Queen Garee was nowhere in the place, although the boy found a silk scarf which he recognized as one that his mother used to wear. Then they began a search throughout the island of Coregos, but could not find Inga's mother anywhere.

When they returned to the palace of Queen Cor, Rinkitink discovered that the bridge of boats had again been removed, separating them from Regos, and from this they suspected that Queen Cor had fled to her husband's island and had taken Queen Garee with her. Inga was much perplexed what to do and returned with his friends to the palace to talk the matter over.

Zella was now crying because she had not sold her honey and was unable to return to her parents on the island of Regos, but the boy Prince comforted her and promised she should be protected until she could be restored to her home. Rinkitink found Queen Cor's purse, which she had had no time to take with her, and gave Zella several gold pieces for the honey. Then Inga ordered the palace servants to prepare a feast for all the women and children of Pingaree and to prepare for them beds in the great palace, which was large enough to accommodate them all.

Then the boy and the goat and Rinkitink and Zella went into a private room to consider what should be done next.

CHAPTER XIV

THE ESCAPE

"Our fault," said Rinkitink, "is that we conquer only one of these twin islands at a time. When we conquered Regos, our foes all came to Coregos, and now that we have conquered Coregos, the Queen has fled to Regos. And each time they removed the bridge of boats, so that we could not follow them."

"What has become of our own boat, in which we came from Pingaree?" asked Bilbil.

"We left it on the shore of Regos," replied the Prince, "but I wonder if we could not get it again."

"Why don't you ask the White Pearl?" suggested Rinkitink.

"That is a good idea," returned the boy, and at once he drew the White Pearl from its silken bag and held it to his ear. Then he asked: "How may I regain our boat?"

The Voice of the Pearl replied: "Go to the south end of the Island of Coregos, and clap your hands three times and the boat will come to you.

"Very good!" cried Inga, and then he turned to his companions and said: "We shall be able to get our boat whenever we please; but what then shall we do?"

"Take me home in it!" pleaded Zella.

"Come with me to my City of Gilgad," said the King, "where you will be very welcome to remain forever."

"No," answered Inga, "I must rescue my father and mother, as well as my people. Already I have the women and children of Pingaree, but the men are with my father in the mines of Regos, and my dear mother has been taken away by Queen Cor. Not until all are rescued will I consent to leave these islands."

"Quite right!" exclaimed Bilbil.

"On second thought," said Rinkitink, "I agree with you. If you are careful to sleep in your shoes, and never take them off again, I believe you will be able to perform the task you have undertaken."

They counseled together for a long time as to their mode of action and it was finally considered best to make the attempt to liberate King Kitticut first of all, and with him the men from Pingaree. This would give them an army to assist them and afterward they could march to Regos and compel Queen Cor to give up the Queen of Pingaree. Zella told them that they could go in their boat along the shore of Regos to a point opposite the mines, thus avoiding any conflict with the warriors of King Gos.

This being considered the best course to pursue, they resolved to start on the following morning, as night was even now approaching. The servants being all busy in caring for the women and children, Zella undertook to get a dinner for Inga and Rinkitink and herself and soon prepared a fine meal in the palace kitchen, for she was a good little cook and had often helped her mother. The dinner was served in a small room overlooking the gardens and Rinkitink thought the best part of it was the sweet honey, which he spread upon the biscuits that Zella had made. As for Bilbil, he wandered through the palace grounds and found some grass that made him a good dinner.

During the evening Inga talked with the women and cheered them, promising soon to reunite them with their husbands who were working in the mines and to send them back to their own island of Pingaree.

Next morning the boy rose bright and early and found that Zella had already prepared a nice breakfast. And after the meal they went to the most southern point of the island, which was not very far away, Rinkitink riding upon Bilbil's back and Inga and Zella following behind them, hand in hand.

When they reached the water's edge the boy advanced and clapped his hands together three times, as the White Pearl had told him to do. And in a few moments they saw in the distance the black boat with the silver lining, coming swiftly toward them from the sea. Presently it grounded on the beach and they all got into it.

Zella was delighted with the boat, which was the most beautiful she had ever seen, and the marvel of its coming to them through the water without anyone to row it, made her a little afraid of the fairy craft. But Inga picked up the oars and began to row and at once the boat shot swiftly in the direction of Regos. They rounded the point of that island where the city was built and noticed that the shore was lined with warriors who had discovered their boat but seemed undecided whether to pursue it or not. This was probably because they had received no commands what to do, or perhaps they had learned to fear the magic powers of these adventurers from Pingaree and were unwilling to attack them unless their King ordered them to.

The coast on the western side of the Island of Regos was very uneven and Zella, who knew fairly well the location of the mines from the inland forest path, was puzzled to decide which mountain they now viewed from the sea was the one where the entrance to the underground caverns was located. First she thought it was this peak, and then she guessed it was that; so considerable time was lost through her uncertainty.

They finally decided to land and explore the country, to see where they were, so Inga ran the boat into a little rocky cove where they all disembarked. For an hour they searched for the path without finding any trace of it and now Zella believed they had gone too far to the north and must return to another mountain that was nearer to the city.

Once again they entered the boat and followed the winding coast south until they thought they had reached the right place. By this time, however, it was growing dark, for the entire day had been spent in the search for the entrance to the mines, and Zella warned them that it would be safer to spend the night in the boat than on the land, where wild beasts were sure to disturb them. None of them realized at this time how fatal this day of search had been to their plans and perhaps if Inga had realized what was going on he would have landed and fought all the wild beasts in the forest rather than quietly remain in the boat until morning.

However, knowing nothing of the cunning plans of Queen Cor and King Gos, they anchored their boat in a little bay and cheerfully ate their dinner, finding plenty of food and drink in the boat's lockers. In the evening the stars came out in the sky and tipped the waves around their boat with silver. All around them was delightfully still save for the occasional snarl of a beast on the neighboring shore.

They talked together quietly of their adventures and their future plans and Zella told them her simple history and how hard her poor father was obliged to work, burning charcoal to sell for enough money to support his wife and child. Nikobob might be the humblest man in all Regos, but Zella declared he was a good man, and honest, and it was not his fault that his country was ruled by so wicked a King.

Then Rinkitink, to amuse them, offered to sing a song, and although Bilbil protested in his gruff way, claiming that his master's voice was cracked and disagreeable, the little King was encouraged by the others to sing his song, which he did.

> "A red-headed man named Ned was dead;
>   Sing fiddle-cum-faddle-cum-fi-do!
> In battle he had lost his head;
>   Sing fiddle-cum-faddle-cum-fi-do!
> 'Alas, poor Ned,' to him I said,
> 'How did you lose your head so red?'
>   Sing fiddle-cum-faddle-cum-fi-do!
>
> "Said Ned: 'I for my country bled,'
>   Sing fiddle-cum-faddle-cum-fi-do!
> 'Instead of dying safe in bed,'
>   Sing fiddle-cum-faddle-cum-fi-do!
> 'If I had only fled, instead,
>   I then had been a head ahead.'
>   Sing fiddle-cum-faddle-cum-fi-do!
>
> "I said to Ned—"

"Do stop, Your Majesty!" pleaded Bilbil. "You're making my head ache."

"But the song isn't finished," replied Rinkitink, "and as for your head aching, think of poor Ned, who hadn't any head at all!"

"I can think of nothing but your dismal singing," retorted Bilbil. "Why didn't you choose a cheerful subject, instead of telling how a man who was dead lost his red head? Really, Rinkitink, I'm surprised at you."

"I know a splendid song about a live man," said the King."

"Then don't sing it," begged Bilbil.

Zella was both astonished and grieved by the disrespectful words of the goat, for she had quite enjoyed Rinkitink's singing and had been taught a proper respect for Kings and those high in authority. But as it was now getting late they decided to go to sleep, that they might rise early the following morning, so they all reclined upon the bottom of the big boat and covered themselves with blankets which they found stored underneath the seats for just such occasions. They were not long in falling asleep and did not waken until daybreak.

After a hurried breakfast, for Inga was eager to liberate his father, the boy rowed the boat ashore and they all landed and began searching for the path. Zella found it within the next half hour and declared they must be very close to the entrance to the mines; so they followed the path toward the north, Inga going first, and then Zella following him, while Rinkitink brought up the rear riding upon Bilbil's back.

Before long they saw a great wall of rock towering before them, in which was a low arched entrance, and on either side of this entrance stood a guard, armed with a sword and a spear. The guards of the mines were not so fierce as the warriors of King Gos, their duty being to make the slaves work at their tasks and guard them from escaping; but they were as cruel as their cruel master wished them to be, and as cowardly as they were cruel.

Inga walked up to the two men at the entrance and said:

"Does this opening lead to the mines of King Gos?"

"It does," replied one of the guards, "but no one is allowed to pass out who once goes in."

"Nevertheless," said the boy, "we intend to go in and we shall come out whenever it pleases us to do so. I am the Prince of Pingaree, and I have come to liberate my people, whom King Gos has enslaved."

Now when the two guards heard this speech they looked at one another and laughed, and one of them said: "The King was right, for he said the boy was likely to come here and that he would try to set his people free. Also the King commanded that we must keep the little Prince in the mines, and set him to work, together with his companions."

"Then let us obey the King," replied the other man.

Inga was surprised at hearing this, and asked:

"When did King Gos give you this order?"

"His Majesty was here in person last night," replied the man, "and went away again but an hour ago. He suspected you were coming here and told us to capture you if we could."

This report made the boy very anxious, not for himself but for his father, for he feared the King was up to some mischief. So he hastened to enter the mines and the guards did nothing to oppose him or his companions, their orders being to allow him to go in but not to come out.

The little group of adventurers passed through a long rocky corridor and reached a low, wide cavern where they found a dozen guards and a hundred slaves, the latter being hard at work with picks and shovels digging for gold, while the guards stood over them with long whips.

Inga found many of the men from Pingaree among these slaves, but King Kitticut was not in this cavern; so they passed through it and entered another corridor that led to a second cavern. Here also hundreds of men were working, but the boy did not find his father amongst them, and so went on to a third cavern.

The corridors all slanted downward, so that the farther they went the lower into the earth they descended, and now they found the air hot and close and difficult to

breathe. Flaming torches were stuck into the walls to give light to the workers, and these added to the oppressive heat.

The third and lowest cavern was the last in the mines, and here were many scores of slaves and many guards to keep them at work. So far, none of the guards had paid any attention to Inga's party, but allowed them to proceed as they would, and while the slaves cast curious glances at the boy and girl and man and goat, they dared say nothing. But now the boy walked up to some of the men of Pingaree and asked news of his father, telling them not to fear the guards as he would protect them from the whips.

Then he learned that King Kitticut had indeed been working in this very cavern until the evening before, when King Gos had come and taken him away—still loaded with chains.

"Seems to me," said King Rinkitink, when he heard this report, "that Gos has carried your father away to Regos, to prevent us from rescuing him. He may hide poor Kitticut in a dungeon, where we cannot find him."

"Perhaps you are right," answered the boy, "but I am determined to find him, wherever he may be."

Inga spoke firmly and with courage, but he was greatly disappointed to find that King Gos had been before him at the mines and had taken his father away. However, he tried not to feel disheartened, believing he would succeed in the end, in spite of all opposition. Turning to the guards, he said:

"Remove the chains from these slaves and set them free."

The guards laughed at this order, and one of them brought forward a handful of chains, saying: "His Majesty has commanded us to make you, also, a slave, for you are never to leave these caverns again."

Then he attempted to place the chains on Inga, but the boy indignantly seized them and broke them apart as easily as if they had been cotton cords. When a dozen or more of the guards made a dash to capture him, the Prince swung the end of the chain like a whip and drove them into a corner, where they cowered and begged for mercy.

Stories of the marvelous strength of the boy Prince had already spread to the mines of Regos, and although King Gos had told them that Inga had been deprived of all his magic power, the guards now saw this was not true, so they deemed it wise not to attempt to oppose him.

The chains of the slaves had all been riveted fast to their ankles and wrists, but Inga broke the bonds of steel with his hands and set the poor men free—not only those from Pingaree but all who had been captured in the many wars and raids of King Gos. They were very grateful, as you may suppose, and agreed to support Prince Inga in whatever action he commanded.

He led them to the middle cavern, where all the guards and overseers fled in terror at his approach, and soon he had broken apart the chains of the slaves who had been working in that part of the mines. Then they approached the first cavern and liberated all there.

The slaves had been treated so cruelly by the servants of King Gos that they were eager to pursue and slay them, in revenge; but Inga held them back and formed them into companies, each company having its own leader. Then he called the leaders together and instructed them to march in good order along the path to the City of Regos, where he would meet them and tell them what to do next.

They readily agreed to obey him, and, arming themselves with iron bars and pick-axes which they brought from the mines, the slaves began their march to the city.

Zella at first wished to be left behind, that she might make her way to her own home, but neither Rinkitink nor Inga thought it was safe for her to wander alone through the forest, so they induced her to return with them to the city.

The boy beached his boat this time at the same place as when he first landed at Regos, and while many of the warriors stood on the shore and before the walls of the city, not one of them attempted to interfere with the boy in any way. Indeed, they seemed uneasy and anxious, and when Inga met Captain Buzzub the boy asked if anything had happened in his absence.

"A great deal has happened," replied Buzzub. "Our King and Queen have run away and left us, and we don't know what to do."

"Run away!" exclaimed Inga. "Where did they go to?"

"Who knows?" said the man, shaking his head despondently. "They departed together a few hours ago, in a boat with forty rowers, and they took with them the King and Queen of Pingaree!"

CHAPTER XV

THE FLIGHT OF THE RULERS

Now it seems that when Queen Cor fled from her island to Regos, she had wit enough, although greatly frightened, to make a stop at the royal dairy, which was near to the bridge, and to drag poor Queen Garee from the butter-house and across to Regos with her. The warriors of King Gos had never before seen the terrible Queen Cor frightened, and therefore when she came running across the bridge of boats, dragging the Queen of Pingaree after her by one arm, the woman's great fright had the effect of terrifying the waiting warriors.

"Quick!" cried Cor. "Destroy the bridge, or we are lost."

While the men were tearing away the bridge of boats the Queen ran up to the palace of Gos, where she met her husband.

"That boy is a wizard!" she gasped. "There is no standing against him."

"Oh, have you discovered his magic at last?" replied Gos, laughing in her face. "Who, now, is the coward?"

"Don't laugh!" cried Queen Cor. "It is no laughing matter. Both our islands are as good as conquered, this very minute. What shall we do, Gos?"

"Come in," he said, growing serious, "and let us talk it over."

So they went into a room of the palace and talked long and earnestly.

"The boy intends to liberate his father and mother, and all the people of Pingaree, and to take them back to their island," said Cor. "He may also destroy our palaces and make us his slaves. I can see but one way, Gos, to prevent him from doing all this, and whatever else he pleases to do."

"What way is that?" asked King Gos.

"We must take the boy's parents away from here as quickly as possible. I have with me the Queen of Pingaree, and you can run up to the mines and get the King. Then we will carry them away in a boat and hide them where the boy cannot find

them, with all his magic. We will use the King and Queen of Pingaree as hostages, and send word to the boy wizard that if he does not go away from our islands and allow us to rule them undisturbed, in our own way, we will put his father and mother to death. Also we will say that as long as we are let alone his parents will be safe, although still safely hidden. I believe, Gos, that in this way we can compel Prince Inga to obey us, for he seems very fond of his parents."

"It isn't a bad idea," said Gos, reflectively; "but where can we hide the King and Queen, so that the boy cannot find them?"

"In the country of the Nome King, on the mainland away at the south," she replied. "The Nomes are our friends, and they possess magic powers that will enable them to protect the prisoners from discovery. If we can manage to get the King and Queen of Pingaree to the Nome Kingdom before the boy knows what we are doing, I am sure our plot will succeed."

Gos gave the plan considerable thought in the next five minutes, and the more he thought about it the more clever and reasonable it seemed. So he agreed to do as Queen Cor suggested and at once hurried away to the mines, where he arrived before Prince Inga did. The next morning he carried King Kitticut back to Regos.

While Gos was gone, Queen Cor busied herself in preparing a large and swift boat for the journey. She placed in it several bags of gold and jewels with which to bribe the Nomes, and selected forty of the strongest oarsmen in Regos to row the boat. The instant King Gos returned with his royal prisoner all was ready for departure. They quickly entered the boat with their two important captives and without a word of explanation to any of their people they commanded the oarsmen to start, and were soon out of sight upon the broad expanse of the Nonestic Ocean.

Inga arrived at the city some hours later and was much distressed when he learned that his father and mother had been spirited away from the islands.

"I shall follow them, of course," said the boy to Rinkitink, "and if I cannot overtake them on the ocean I will search the world over until I find them. But before I leave here I must arrange to send our people back to Pingaree."

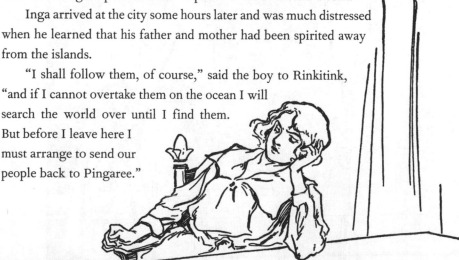

CHAPTER XVI

NIKOBOB REFUSES A CROWN

ALMOST THE FIRST PERSONS THAT ZELLA SAW WHEN SHE LANDED FROM THE SILVER-lined boat at Regos were her father and mother. Nikobob and his wife had been greatly worried when their little daughter failed to return from Coregos, so they had set out to discover what had become of her. When they reached the City of Regos, that very morning, they were astonished to hear news of all the strange events that had taken place; still, they found comfort when told that Zella had been seen in the boat of Prince Inga, which had gone to the north. Then, while they wondered what this could mean, the silver-lined boat appeared again, with their daughter in it, and they ran down to the shore to give her a welcome and many joyful kisses.

Inga invited the good people to the palace of King Gos, where he conferred with them, as well as with Rinkitink and Bilbil.

"Now that the King and Queen of Regos and Coregos have run away," he said, "there is no one to rule these islands. So it is my duty to appoint a new ruler, and as Nikobob, Zella's father, is an honest and worthy man, I shall make him the King of the Twin Islands."

"Me?" cried Nikobob, astounded by this speech. "I beg Your Highness, on my bended knees, not to do so cruel a thing as to make me King!"

"Why not?" inquired Rinkitink. "I'm a King, and I know how it feels. I assure you, good Nikobob, that I quite enjoy my high rank, although a jeweled crown is rather heavy to wear in hot weather."

"With you, noble sir, it is different," said Nikobob, "for you are far from your kingdom and its trials and worries and may do as you please. But to remain in Regos, as King over these fierce and unruly warriors, would be to live in constant anxiety and peril, and the chances are that they would murder me within a month. As I have done no harm to anyone and have tried to be a good and upright man, I do not think that I should be condemned to such a dreadful fate."

"Very well," replied Inga, "we will say no more about your being King. I merely wanted to make you rich and prosperous, as I had promised Zella."

"Please forget that promise," pleaded the charcoal-burner, earnestly; "I have been safe from molestation for many years, because I was poor and possessed nothing that anyone else could envy. But if you make me rich and prosperous I shall at once become the prey of thieves and marauders and probably will lose my life in the attempt to protect my fortune."

Inga looked at the man in surprise.

"What, then, can I do to please you?" he inquired.

"Nothing more than to allow me to go home to my poor cabin," said Nikobob.

"Perhaps," remarked King Rinkitink, "the charcoal-burner has more wisdom concealed in that hard head of his than we gave him credit for. But let us use that wisdom, for the present, to counsel us what to do in this emergency."

"What you call my wisdom," said Nikobob, "is merely common sense. I have noticed that some men become rich, and are scorned by some and robbed by others. Other men become famous, and are mocked at and derided by their fellows. But the poor and humble man who lives unnoticed and unknown escapes all these troubles and is the only one who can appreciate the joy of living."

"If I had a hand, instead of a cloven hoof, I'd like to shake hands with you, Nikobob," said Bilbil the goat. "But the poor man must not have a cruel master, or he is undone."

During the council they found, indeed, that the advice of the charcoal-burner was both shrewd and sensible, and they profited much by his words.

Inga gave Captain Buzzub the command of the warriors and made him promise to keep his men quiet and orderly—if he could. Then the boy allowed all of King Gos's former slaves, except those who came from Pingaree, to choose what boats they required and to stock them with provisions and row away to their own countries.

When these had departed, with grateful thanks and many blessings showered upon the boy Prince who had set them free, Inga made preparations to send his own people home, where they were told to rebuild their houses and then erect a new royal palace. They were then to await patiently the coming of King Kitticut or Prince Inga.

"My greatest worry," said the boy to his friends, "is to know whom to appoint to take charge of this work of restoring Pingaree to its former condition. My men are all pearl fishers, and although willing and honest, have no talent for directing others how to work."

While the preparations for departure were being made, Nikobob offered to direct the men of Pingaree, and did so in a very capable manner. As the island had been despoiled of all its valuable furniture and draperies and rich cloths and paintings and statuary and the like, as well as gold and silver and ornaments, Inga thought it no more than just that they be replaced by the spoilers. So he directed his people to search through the storehouses of King Gos and to regain all their goods and chattels that could be found. Also he instructed them to take as much else as they required to make their new homes comfortable, so that many boats were loaded full of goods that would enable the people to restore Pingaree to its former state of comfort.

For his father's new palace the boy plundered the palaces of both Queen Cor and King Gos, sending enough wares away with his people to make King Kitticut's new residence as handsomely fitted and furnished as had been the one which the ruthless invaders from Regos had destroyed.

It was a great fleet of boats that set out one bright, sunny morning on the voyage to Pingaree, carrying all the men, women and children and all the goods for refitting their homes. As he saw the fleet depart, Prince Inga felt that he had already successfully accomplished a part of his mission, but he vowed he would never return to Pingaree in person until he could take his father and mother there with him; unless, indeed, King Gos wickedly destroyed his beloved parents, in which case Inga would become the King of Pingaree and it would be his duty to go to his people and rule over them.

It was while the last of the boats were preparing to sail for Pingaree that Nikobob, who had been of great service in getting them ready, came to Inga in a thoughtful mood and said:

"Your Highness, my wife and my daughter Zella have been urging me to leave Regos and settle down in your island, in a new home. From what your people have told me, Pingaree is a better place to live than Regos, and there are no cruel warriors or savage beasts there to keep one in constant fear for the safety of those he loves. Therefore, I have come to ask to go with my family in one of the boats."

Inga was much pleased with this proposal and not only granted Nikobob permission to go to Pingaree to live, but instructed him to take with him sufficient goods

to furnish his new home in a comfortable manner. In addition to this, he appointed Nikobob general manager of the buildings and of the pearl fisheries, until his father or he himself arrived, and the people approved this order because they liked Nikobob and knew him to be just and honest.

As soon as the last boat of the great flotilla had disappeared from the view of those left at Regos, Inga and Rinkitink prepared to leave the island themselves. The boy was anxious to overtake the boat of King Gos, if possible, and Rinkitink had no desire to remain in Regos.

Buzzub and the warriors stood silently on the shore and watched the black boat with its silver lining depart, and I am sure they were as glad to be rid of their unwelcome visitors as Inga and Rinkitink and Bilbil were to leave.

The boy asked the White Pearl what direction the boat of King Gos had taken and then he followed after it, rowing hard and steadily for eight days without becoming at all weary. But, although the black boat moved very swiftly, it failed to overtake the barge which was rowed by Queen Cor's forty picked oarsmen.

CHAPTER XVII

THE NOME KING

THE KINGDOM OF THE NOMES DOES NOT BORDER ON THE NONESTIC OCEAN, FROM which it is separated by the Kingdom of Rinkitink and the Country of the Wheelers, which is a part of the Land of Ev. Rinkitink's country is separated from the country of the Nomes by a row of high and steep mountains, from which it extends to the sea. The Country of the Wheelers is a sandy waste that is open on one side to the Nonestic Ocean and on the other side has no barrier to separate it from the Nome Country, therefore it was on the coast of the Wheelers that King Gos landed—in a spot quite deserted by any of the curious inhabitants of that country.

The Nome Country is very large in extent, and is only separated from the Land of Oz, on its eastern borders, by a Deadly Desert that cannot be crossed by mortals, unless they are aided by the fairies or by magic.

The Nomes are a numerous and mischievous people, living in underground caverns of wide extent, connected one with another by arches and passages. The word "Nome" means "one who knows," and these people are so called because they know where all the gold and silver and precious stones are hidden in the earth—a knowledge that no other living creatures share with them. The Nomes are busy people, constantly digging up gold in one place and taking it to another place, where they secretly bury it, and perhaps this is the reason they alone know where to find it. The Nomes were ruled, at the time of which I write, by a King named Kaliko.

King Gos had expected to be pursued by Inga in his magic boat, so he made all the haste possible, urging his forty rowers to their best efforts night and day. To his joy he was not overtaken but landed on the sandy beach of the Wheelers on the morning of the eighth day.

The forty rowers were left with the boat, while Queen Cor and King Gos, with their royal prisoners, who were still chained, began the journey to the Nome King.

It was not long before they passed the sands and reached the rocky country belonging to the Nomes, but they were still a long way from the entrance to the underground caverns in which lived the Nome King. There was a dim path, winding between stones and boulders, over which the walking was quite difficult, especially as the path led up hills that were small mountains, and then down steep and abrupt slopes where any misstep might mean a broken leg. Therefore it was the second day of their journey before they climbed halfway up a rugged mountain and found themselves at the entrance of the Nome King's caverns.

On their arrival, the entrance seemed free and unguarded, but Gos and Cor had been there before, and they were too wise to attempt to enter without announcing themselves, for the passage to the caves was full of traps and pitfalls. So King Gos stood still and shouted, and in an instant they were surrounded by a group of crooked Nomes, who seemed to have sprung from the ground.

One of these had very long ears and was called The Long-Eared Hearer. He said: "I heard you coming early this morning."

Another had eyes that looked in different directions at the same time and were curiously bright and penetrating. He could look over a hill or around a corner and was called The Lookout. Said he: "I saw you coming yesterday."

"Then," said King Gos, "perhaps King Kaliko is expecting us."

"It is true," replied another Nome, who wore a gold collar around his neck and carried a bunch of golden keys. "The mighty Nome King expects you, and bids you follow me to his presence."

With this he led the way into the caverns and Gos and Cor followed, dragging their weary prisoners with them, for poor King Kitticut and his gentle Queen had been obliged to carry, all through the tedious journey, the bags of gold and jewels which were to bribe the Nome King to accept them as slaves.

Through several long passages the guide led them and at last they entered a small cavern which was beautifully decorated and set with rare jewels that flashed from every part of the wall, floor and ceiling. This was a waiting-room for visitors, and there their guide left them while he went to inform King Kaliko of their arrival.

Before long they were ushered into a great domed chamber, cut from the solid rock and so magnificent that all of them—the King and Queen of Pingaree and the King and Queen of Regos and Coregos—drew long breaths of astonishment and opened their eyes as wide as they could.

In an ivory throne sat a little round man who had a pointed beard and hair that rose to a tall curl on top of his head. He was dressed in silken robes, richly embroidered, which had large buttons of cut rubies. On his head was a diamond crown and in his hand he held a golden sceptre with a big jeweled ball at one end of it. This was Kaliko, the King and ruler of all the Nomes. He nodded pleasantly enough to his visitors and said in a cheery voice:

"Well, Your Majesties, what can I do for you?"

"It is my desire," answered King Gos, respectfully, "to place in your care two prisoners, whom you now see before you. They must be carefully guarded, to prevent them from escaping, for they have the cunning of foxes and are not to be trusted. In return for the favor I am asking you to grant, I have brought Your Majesty valuable presents of gold and precious gems."

He then commanded Kitticut and Garee to lay before the Nome King the bags of gold and jewels, and they obeyed, being helpless.

"Very good," said King Kaliko, nodding approval, for like all the Nomes he loved treasures of gold and jewels. "But who are the prisoners you have brought here, and why do you place them in my charge instead of guarding them yourself? They seem gentle enough, I'm sure."

"The prisoners," returned King Gos, "are the King and Queen of Pingaree, a small island north of here. They are very evil people and came to our Islands of Regos and Coregos to conquer them and slay our poor people. Also they intended to plunder us of all our riches, but by good fortune we were able to defeat and capture them. However, they have a son who is a terrible wizard and who by magic art is trying to find this awful King and Queen of Pingaree, and to set them free, that they may continue their wicked deeds. Therefore, as we have no magic to defend ourselves with, we have brought the prisoners to you for safe keeping."

"Your Majesty," spoke up King Kitticut, addressing the Nome King with great indignation, "do not believe this tale, I implore you. It is all a lie!"

"I know it," said Kaliko. "I consider it a clever lie, though, because it is woven without a thread of truth. However, that is none of my business. The fact remains that my good friend King Gos wishes to put you in my underground caverns, so that you will be unable to escape. And why should I not please him in this little matter? Gos is a mighty King and a great warrior, while your island of Pingaree is desolated and your people scattered. In my heart, King Kitticut, I sympathize with you, but as a matter of

business policy we powerful Kings must stand together and trample the weaker ones under our feet."

King Kitticut was surprised to find the King of the Nomes so candid and so well informed, and he tried to argue that he and his gentle wife did not deserve their cruel fate and that it would be wiser for Kaliko to side with them than with the evil King of Regos. But Kaliko only shook his head and smiled, saying:

"The fact that you are a prisoner, my poor Kitticut, is evidence that you are weaker than King Gos, and I prefer to deal with the strong. By the way," he added, turning to the King of Regos, "have these prisoners any connection with the Land of Oz?"

"Why do you ask?" said Gos.

"Because I dare not offend the Oz people," was the reply. "I am very powerful, as you know, but Ozma of Oz is far more powerful than I; therefore, if this King and Queen of Pingaree happened to be under Ozma's protection, I would have nothing to do with them."

"I assure Your Majesty that the prisoners have nothing to do with the Oz people," Gos hastened to say. And Kitticut, being questioned, admitted that this was true.

"But how about that wizard you mentioned?" asked the Nome King.

"Oh, he is merely a boy; but he is very ferocious and obstinate and he is assisted by a little fat sorcerer called Rinkitink and a talking goat."

"Oho! A talking goat, do you say? That certainly sounds like magic; and it also sounds like the Land of Oz, where all the animals talk," said Kaliko, with a doubtful expression.

But King Gos assured him the talking goat had never been to Oz.

"As for Rinkitink, whom you call a sorcerer," continued the Nome King, "he is a neighbor of mine, you must know, but as we are cut off from each other by high mountains beneath which a powerful river runs, I have never yet met King Rinkitink. But I have heard of him, and from all reports he is a jolly rogue, and perfectly harmless. However, in spite of your false statements and misrepresentations, I will earn the treasure you have brought me, by keeping your prisoners safe in my caverns.

"Make them work," advised Queen Cor. "They are rather delicate, and to make them work will make them suffer delightfully."

"I'll do as I please about that," said the Nome King sternly. "Be content that I agree to keep them safe."

The bargain being thus made and concluded, Kaliko first examined the gold and jewels and then sent it away to his royal storehouse, which was well filled with like treasure. Next the captives were sent away in charge of the Nome with the golden collar and keys, whose name was Klik, and he escorted them to a small cavern and gave them a good supper.

"I shall lock your door," said Klik, "so there is no need of your wearing those heavy chains any longer." He therefore removed the chains and left King Kitticut and his Queen alone. This was the first time since the Northmen had carried them away from Pingaree that the good King and Queen had been alone together and free of all bonds, and as they embraced lovingly and mingled their tears over their sad fate they were also grateful that they had passed from the control of the heartless King Gos into the more considerate care of King Kaliko. They were still captives but they believed they would be happier in the underground caverns of the Nomes than in Regos and Coregos.

Meantime, in the King's royal cavern a great feast had been spread. King Gos and Queen Cor, having triumphed in their plot, were so well pleased that they held high revelry with the jolly Nome King until a late hour that night. And the next morning, having cautioned Kaliko not to release the prisoners under any consideration without their orders, the King and Queen of Regos and Coregos left the caverns of the Nomes to return to the shore of the ocean where they had left their boat.

CHAPTER XVIII

INGA PARTS WITH HIS PINK PEARL

THE WHITE PEARL GUIDED INGA TRULY IN HIS PURSUIT OF THE BOAT OF KING GOS, but the boy had been so delayed in sending his people home to Pingaree that it was a full day after Gos and Cor landed on the shore of the Wheeler Country that Inga's boat arrived at the same place.

There he found the forty rowers guarding the barge of Queen Cor, and although they would not or could not tell the boy where the King and Queen had taken his father and mother, the White Pearl advised him to follow the path to the country and the caverns of the Nomes.

Rinkitink didn't like to undertake the rocky and mountainous journey, even with Bilbil to carry him, but he would not desert Inga, even though his own kingdom lay just beyond a range of mountains which could be seen towering southwest of them. So the King bravely mounted the goat, who always grumbled but always obeyed his master, and the three set off at once for the caverns of the Nomes.

They traveled just as slowly as Queen Cor and King Gos had done, so when they were about halfway they discovered the King and Queen coming back to their boat.

The fact that Gos and Cor were now alone proved that they had left Inga's father and mother behind them; so, at the suggestion of Rinkitink, the three hid behind a high rock until the King of Regos and the Queen of Coregos, who had not observed them, had passed them by. Then they continued their journey, glad that they had not again been forced to fight or quarrel with their wicked enemies.

"We might have asked them, however, what they had done with your poor parents," said Rinkitink.

"Never mind," answered Inga. "I am sure the White Pearl will guide us aright."

For a time they proceeded in silence and then Rinkitink began to chuckle with laughter in the pleasant way he was wont to do before his misfortunes came upon him.

"What amuses Your Majesty?" inquired the boy.

"The thought of how surprised my dear subjects would be if they realized how near to them I am, and yet how far away. I have always wanted to visit the Nome Country, which is full of mystery and magic and all sorts of adventures, but my devoted subjects forbade me to think of such a thing, fearing I would get hurt or enchanted."

"Are you afraid, now that you are here?" asked Inga.

"A little, but not much, for they say the new Nome King is not as wicked as the old King used to be. Still, we are undertaking a dangerous journey and I think you ought to protect me by lending me one of your pearls."

Inga thought this over and it seemed a reasonable request.

"Which pearl would you like to have?" asked the boy.

"Well, let us see," returned Rinkitink; "you may need strength to liberate your captive parents, so you must keep the Blue Pearl. And you will need the advice of the White Pearl, so you had best keep that also. But in case we should be separated I would have nothing to protect me from harm, so you ought to lend me the Pink Pearl."

"Very well," agreed Inga, and sitting down upon a rock he removed his right shoe and after withdrawing the cloth from the pointed toe took out the Pink Pearl—the one which protected from any harm the person who carried it.

"Where can you put it, to keep it safely?" he asked.

"In my vest pocket," replied the King. "The pocket has a flap to it and I can pin it down in such a way that the pearl cannot get out and become lost. As for robbery, no one with evil intent can touch my person while I have the pearl."

So Inga gave Rinkitink the Pink Pearl and the little King placed it in the pocket of his red-and-green brocaded velvet vest, pinning the flap of the pocket down tightly.

They now resumed their journey and finally reached the entrance to the Nome King's caverns. Placing the White Pearl to his ear, Inga asked: "What shall I do now?" and the Voice of the Pearl replied: "Clap your hands together four times and call aloud

the word 'Klik.' Then allow yourselves to be conducted to the Nome King, who is now holding your father and mother captive."

Inga followed these instructions and when Klik appeared in answer to his summons the boy requested an audience of the Nome King. So Klik led them into the presence of King Kaliko, who was suffering from a severe headache, due to his revelry the night before, and therefore was unusually cross and grumpy.

"I know what you've come for," said he, before Inga could speak. "You want to get the captives from Regos away from me; but you can't do it, so you'd best go away again."

"The captives are my father and mother, and I intend to liberate them," said the boy firmly.

The King stared hard at Inga, wondering at his audacity. Then he turned to look at King Rinkitink and said:

"I suppose you are the King of Gilgad, which is in the Kingdom of Rinkitink."

"You've guessed it the first time," replied Rinkitink.

"How round and fat you are!" exclaimed Kaliko.

"I was just thinking how fat and round *you* are," said Rinkitink. "Really, King Kaliko, we ought to be friends, we're so much alike in everything but disposition and intelligence."

Then he began to chuckle, while Kaliko stared hard at him, not knowing whether to accept his speech as a compliment or not. And now the Nome's eyes wandered to Bilbil, and he asked:

"Is that your talking goat?"

Bilbil met the Nome King's glowering look with a gaze equally surly and defiant, while Rinkitink answered: "It is, Your Majesty."

"Can he really talk?" asked Kaliko, curiously.

"He can. But the best thing he does is to scold. Talk to His Majesty, Bilbil."

But Bilbil remained silent and would not speak.

"Do you always ride upon his back?" continued Kaliko, questioning Rinkitink.

"Yes," was the answer, "because it is difficult for a fat man to walk far, as perhaps you know from experience.

"That is true," said Kaliko. "Get off the goat's back and let me ride him a while, to see how I like it. Perhaps I'll take him away from you, to ride through my caverns."

Rinkitink chuckled softly as he heard this, but at once got off Bilbil's back and let Kaliko get on. The Nome King was a little awkward, but when he was firmly astride the saddle he called in a loud voice: "Giddap!"

When Bilbil paid no attention to the command and refused to stir, Kaliko kicked his heels viciously against the goat's body, and then Bilbil made a sudden start. He ran swiftly across the great cavern, until he had almost reached the opposite wall, when he stopped so abruptly that King Kaliko sailed over his head and bumped against the jeweled wall. He bumped so hard that the points of his crown were all mashed out of shape and his head was driven far into the diamond-studded band of the crown, so that it covered one eye and a part of his nose. Perhaps this saved Kaliko's head from being cracked against the rock wall, but it was hard on the crown.

Bilbil was highly pleased at the success of his feat and Rinkitink laughed merrily at the Nome King's comical appearance; but Kaliko was muttering and growling as he picked himself up and struggled to pull the battered crown from his head, and it was evident that he was not in the least amused. Indeed, Inga could see that the King was very angry, and the boy knew that the incident was likely to turn Kaliko against the entire party.

The Nome King sent Klik for another crown and ordered his workmen to repair the one that was damaged. While he waited for the new crown he sat regarding his visitors with a scowling face, and this made Inga more uneasy than ever. Finally, when the new crown was placed upon his head, King Kaliko said: "Follow me, strangers!" and led the way to a small door at one end of the cavern.

Inga and Rinkitink followed him through the doorway and found themselves standing on a balcony that overlooked an enormous domed cave—so extensive that it seemed miles to the other side of it. All around this circular cave, which was brilliantly lighted from an unknown source, were arches connected with other caverns.

Kaliko took a gold whistle from his pocket and blew a shrill note that echoed through every part of the cave. Instantly Nomes began to pour in through the side arches in great numbers, until the immense space was packed with them as far as the eye could reach. All were armed with glittering weapons of polished silver and gold, and Inga was amazed that any King could command so great an army.

They began marching and countermarching in very orderly array until another blast of the gold whistle sent them scurrying away as quickly as they had appeared. And as soon as the great cave was again empty Kaliko returned with his visitors to his own royal chamber, where he once more seated himself upon his ivory throne.

"I have shown you," said he to Inga, "a part of my bodyguard. The royal armies, of which this is only a part, are as numerous as the sands of the ocean, and live in many thousands of my underground caverns. You have come here thinking to force me to give up the captives of King Gos and Queen Cor, and I wanted to convince you that my power is too mighty for anyone to oppose. I am told that you are a wizard, and depend upon magic to aid you; but you must know that the Nomes are not mortals, and understand magic pretty well themselves, so if we are obliged to fight magic with magic the chances are that we are a hundred times more powerful than you can be. Think this over carefully, my boy, and try to realize that you are in my power. I do not believe you can force me to liberate King Kitticut and Queen Garee, and I know that you cannot coax me to do so, for I have given my promise to King Gos. Therefore, as I do not wish to hurt you, I ask you to go away peaceably and let me alone."

"Forgive me if I do not agree with you, King Kaliko," answered the boy. "However difficult and dangerous my task may be, I cannot leave your dominions until every effort to release my parents has failed and left me completely discouraged."

"Very well," said the King, evidently displeased. "I have warned you, and now if evil overtakes you it is your own fault. I've a headache to-day, so I cannot entertain you properly, according to your rank; but Klik will attend you to my guest chambers and to-morrow I will talk with you again."

This seemed a fair and courteous way to treat one's declared enemies, so they politely expressed the wish that Kaliko's headache would be better, and followed their guide, Klik, down a well-lighted passage and through several archways until they finally reached three nicely furnished bedchambers which were cut from solid gray rock and well lighted and aired by some mysterious method known to the Nomes.

The first of these rooms was given King Rinkitink, the second was Inga's and the third was assigned to Bilbil the goat. There was a swinging rock door between the third and second rooms and another between the second and first, which also had a door that opened upon the passage. Rinkitink's room was the largest, so it was here that an excellent dinner was spread by some of the Nome servants, who, in spite of their crooked shapes, proved to be well trained and competent.

"You are not prisoners, you know," said Klik; "neither are you welcome guests, having declared your purpose to oppose our mighty King and all his hosts. But we bear you no ill will, and you are to be well fed and cared for as long as you remain in our caverns. Eat hearty, sleep tight, and pleasant dreams to you."

Saying this, he left them alone and at once Rinkitink and Inga began to counsel together as to the best means to liberate King Kitticut and Queen Garee. The White Pearl's advice was rather unsatisfactory to the boy, just now, for all that the Voice said in answer to his questions was: "Be patient, brave and determined."

Rinkitink suggested that they try to discover in what part of the series of underground caverns Inga's parents had been confined, as that knowledge was necessary before they could take any action; so together they started out, leaving Bilbil asleep in his room, and made their way unopposed through many corridors and caverns.

In some places were great furnaces, where gold dust was being melted into bricks. In other rooms workmen were fashioning the gold into various articles and ornaments. In one cavern immense wheels revolved which polished precious gems, and they found many caverns used as storerooms, where treasure of every sort was piled high. Also they came to the barracks of the army and the great kitchens.

There were Nomes everywhere—countless thousands of them—but none paid the slightest heed to the visitors from the earth's surface. Yet, although Inga and Rinkitink walked until they were weary, they were unable to locate the place where the boy's father and mother had been confined, and when they tried to return to their own rooms they found that they had hopelessly lost themselves amid the labyrinth of passages. However, Klik presently came to them, laughing at their discomfiture, and led them back to their bedchambers.

Before they went to sleep they carefully barred the door from Rinkitink's room to the corridor, but the doors that connected the three rooms one with another were left wide open.

In the night Inga was awakened by a soft grating sound that filled him with anxiety because he could not account for it. It was dark in his room, the light having disappeared as soon as he got into bed, but he managed to feel his way to the door that led to Rinkitink's room and found it tightly closed and immovable. Then he made his way to the opposite door, leading to Bilbil's room, to discover that also had been closed and fastened.

The boy had a curious sensation that all of his room—the walls, floor and ceiling—was slowly whirling as if on a pivot, and it was such an uncomfortable feeling that he got into bed again, not knowing what else to do. And as the grating noise had ceased and the room now seemed stationary, he soon fell asleep again.

When the boy wakened, after many hours, he found the room again light. So he dressed himself and discovered that a small table, containing a breakfast that was smoking hot, had suddenly appeared in the center of his room. He tried the two doors, but finding that he could not open them he ate some breakfast, thoughtfully wondering who had locked him in and why he had been made a prisoner. Then he again went to the door which he thought led to Rinkitink's chamber and to his surprise the latch lifted easily and the door swung open.

Before him was a rude corridor hewn in the rock and dimly lighted. It did not look inviting, so Inga closed the door, puzzled to know what had become of Rinkitink's room and the King, and went to the opposite door. Opening this, he found a solid wall of rock confronting him, which effectually prevented his escape in that direction.

The boy now realized that King Kaliko had tricked him, and while professing to receive him as a guest had plotted to separate him from his comrades. One way had been left, however, by which he might escape and he decided to see where it led to.

So, going to the first door, he opened it and ventured slowly into the dimly lighted corridor. When he had advanced a few steps he heard the door of his room slam shut behind him. He ran back at once, but the door of rock fitted so closely into the wall that he found it impossible to open it again. That did not matter so much, however, for the room was a prison and the only way of escape seemed ahead of him.

Along the corridor he crept until, turning a corner, he found himself in a large domed cavern that was empty and deserted. Here also was a dim light that permitted him to see another corridor at the opposite side; so he crossed the rocky floor of the cavern and entered a second corridor. This one twisted and turned in every direction but was not very long, so soon the boy reached a second cavern, not so large as the first. This he found vacant also, but it had another corridor leading out of it, so Inga entered that. It was straight and short and beyond was a third cavern, which differed little from the others except that it had a strong iron grating at one side of it.

All three of these caverns had been roughly hewn from the rock and it seemed they had never been put to use, as had all the other caverns of the Nomes he had visited. Standing in the third cavern, Inga saw what he thought was still another corridor

at its farther side, so he walked toward it. This opening was dark, and that fact, and the solemn silence all around him, made him hesitate for a while to enter it. Upon reflection, however, he realized that unless he explored the place to the very end he could not hope to escape from it, so he boldly entered the dark corridor and felt his way cautiously as he moved forward.

Scarcely had he taken two paces when a crash resounded back of him and a heavy sheet of steel closed the opening into the cavern from which he had just come. He paused a moment, but it still seemed best to proceed, and as Inga advanced in the dark, holding his hands outstretched before him to feel his way, handcuffs fell upon his wrists and locked themselves with a sharp click, and an instant later he found he was chained to a stout iron post set firmly in the rock floor.

The chains were long enough to permit him to move a yard or so in any direction and by feeling the walls he found he was in a small circular room that had no outlet except the passage by which he had entered, and that was now closed by the door of steel. This was the end of the series of caverns and corridors.

It was now that the horror of his situation occurred to the boy with full force. But he resolved not to submit to his fate without a struggle, and realizing that he possessed the Blue Pearl, which gave him marvelous strength, he quickly broke the chains and set himself free of the handcuffs. Next he twisted the steel door from its hinges, and creeping along the short passage, found himself in the third cave.

But now the dim light, which had before guided him, had vanished; yet on peering into the gloom of the cave he saw what appeared to be two round disks of flame, which cast a subdued glow over the floor and walls. By this dull glow he made out the form of an enormous man, seated in the center of the cave, and he saw that the iron grating had been removed, permitting the man to enter.

The giant was unclothed and its limbs were thickly covered with coarse red hair. The round disks of flame were its two eyes and when it opened its mouth to yawn Inga saw that its jaws were wide enough to crush a dozen men between the great rows of teeth.

Presently the giant looked up and perceived the boy crouching at the other side of the cavern, so he called out in a hoarse, rude voice:

"Come hither, my pretty one. We will wrestle together, you and I, and if you succeed in throwing me I will let you pass through my cave."

The boy made no reply to the challenge. He realized he was in dire peril and regretted that he had lent the Pink Pearl to King Rinkitink. But it was now too late for vain regrets, although he feared that even his great strength would avail him little against this hairy monster. For his arms were not long enough to span a fourth of the giant's huge body, while the monster's powerful limbs would be likely to crush out Inga's life before he could gain the mastery.

Therefore the Prince resolved to employ other means to combat this foe, who had doubtless been placed there to bar his return. Retreating through the passage he reached the room where he had been chained and wrenched the iron post from its socket. It was a foot thick and four feet long, and being of solid iron was so heavy that three ordinary men would have found it hard to lift.

Returning to the cavern, the boy swung the great bar above his head and dashed it with mighty force full at the giant. The end of the bar struck the monster upon its forehead, and with a single groan it fell full length upon the floor and lay still.

When the giant fell, the glow from its eyes faded away, and all was dark. Cautiously, for Inga was not sure the giant was dead, the boy felt his way toward the opening that led to the middle cavern. The entrance was narrow and the darkness was intense, but, feeling braver now, the boy stepped boldly forward. Instantly the floor began to sink beneath him and in great alarm he turned and made a leap that enabled him to grasp the rocky sides of the wall and regain a footing in the passage through which he had just come.

Scarcely had he obtained this place of refuge when a mighty crash resounded throughout the cavern and the sound of a rushing torrent came from far below. Inga felt in his pocket and found several matches, one of which he lighted and held before him. While it flickered he saw that the entire floor of the cavern had fallen away, and knew that had he not instantly regained his footing in the passage he would have plunged into the abyss that lay beneath him.

By the light of another match he saw the opening at the other side of the cave and the thought came to him that possibly he might leap across the gulf. Of course, this could never be accomplished without the marvelous strength lent him by the Blue Pearl, but Inga had the feeling that one powerful spring might carry him over the chasm into safety. He could not stay where he was, that was certain, so he resolved to make the attempt.

He took a long run through the first cave and the short corridor; then, exerting all his strength, he launched himself over the black gulf of the second cave. Swiftly he flew and, although his heart stood still with fear, only a few seconds elapsed before his feet touched the ledge of the opposite passageway and he knew he had safely accomplished the wonderful feat.

Only pausing to draw one long breath of relief, Inga quickly traversed the crooked corridor that led to the last cavern of the three. But when he came in sight of it he paused abruptly, his eyes nearly blinded by a glare of strong light which burst upon them. Covering his face with his hands, Inga retreated behind a projecting corner of rock and by gradually getting his eyes used to the light he was finally able to gaze without blinking upon the strange glare that had so quickly changed the condition of the cavern. When he had passed through this vault it had been entirely empty. Now the flat floor of rock was covered everywhere with a bed of glowing coals, which shot up little tongues of red and white flames. Indeed, the entire cave was one monster furnace and the heat that came from it was fearful.

Inga's heart sank within him as he realized the terrible obstacle placed by the cunning Nome King between him and the safety of the other caverns. There was no turning back, for it would be impossible for him again to leap over the gulf of the second cave, the corridor at this side being so crooked that he could get no run before he jumped. Neither could he leap over the glowing coals of the cavern that faced him, for it was much larger than the middle cavern. In this dilemma he feared his great strength would avail him nothing and he bitterly reproached himself for parting with the Pink Pearl, which would have preserved him from injury.

However, it was not in the nature of Prince Inga to despair for long, his past adventures having taught him confidence and courage, sharpened his wits and given him the genius of invention. He sat down and thought earnestly on the means of escape from his danger and at last a clever idea came to his mind. This is the way to

get ideas: never to let adverse circumstances discourage you, but to believe there is a way out of every difficulty, which may be found by earnest thought.

There were many points and projections of rock in the walls of the crooked corridor in which Inga stood and some of these rocks had become cracked and loosened, although still clinging to their places. The boy picked out one large piece, and, exerting all his strength, tore it away from the wall. He then carried it to the cavern and tossed it upon the burning coals, about ten feet away from the end of the passage. Then he returned for another fragment of rock, and wrenching it free from its place, he threw it ten feet beyond the first one, toward the opposite side of the cave. The boy continued this work until he had made a series of stepping-stones reaching straight across the cavern to the dark passageway beyond, which he hoped would lead him back to safety if not to liberty.

When his work had been completed, Inga did not long hesitate to take advantage of his stepping-stones, for he knew his best chance of escape lay in his crossing the bed of coals before the rocks became so heated that they would burn his feet. So he leaped to the first rock and from there began jumping from one to the other in quick succession. A withering wave of heat at once enveloped him, and for a time he feared he would suffocate before he could cross the cavern; but he held his breath, to keep the hot air from his lungs, and maintained his leaps with desperate resolve.

Then, before he realized it, his feet were pressing the cooler rocks of the passage beyond and he rolled helpless upon the floor, gasping for breath. His skin was so red that it resembled the shell of a boiled lobster, but his swift motion had prevented his being burned, and his shoes had thick soles, which saved his feet.

After resting a few minutes, the boy felt strong enough to go on. He went to the end of the passage and found that the rock door by which he had left his room was still closed, so he returned to about the middle of the corridor and was thinking what he should do next, when suddenly the solid rock before him began to move and an opening appeared through which shone a brilliant light. Shielding his eyes, which were somewhat dazzled, Inga sprang through the opening and found himself in one of the Nome King's inhabited caverns, where before him stood King Kaliko, with a broad grin upon his features, and Klik, the King's chamberlain, who looked surprised, and King Rinkitink seated astride Bilbil the goat, both of whom seemed pleased that Inga had rejoined them.

CHAPTER XIX

RINKITINK CHUCKLES

W<small>E WILL NOW RELATE WHAT HAPPENED TO</small> R<small>INKITINK AND</small> B<small>ILBIL THAT MORNING,</small> while Inga was undergoing his trying experience in escaping the fearful dangers of the three caverns.

The King of Gilgad wakened to find the door of Inga's room fast shut and locked, but he had no trouble in opening his own door into the corridor, for it seems that the boy's room, which was the middle one, whirled around on a pivot, while the adjoining rooms occupied by Bilbil and Rinkitink remained stationary. The little King also found a breakfast magically served in his room, and while he was eating it, Klik came to him and stated that His Majesty, King Kaliko, desired his presence in the royal cavern.

So Rinkitink, having first made sure that the Pink Pearl was still in his vest pocket, willingly followed Klik, who ran on some distance ahead. But no sooner had Rinkitink set foot in the passage than a great rock, weighing at least a ton, became dislodged and dropped from the roof directly over his head. Of course, it could not harm him, protected as he was by the Pink Pearl, and it bounded aside and crashed upon the floor, where it was shattered by its own weight.

"How careless!" exclaimed the little King, and waddled after Klik, who seemed amazed at his escape.

Presently another rock above Rinkitink plunged downward, and then another, but none touched his body. Klik seemed much perplexed at these continued escapes and certainly Kaliko was surprised when Rinkitink, safe and sound, entered the royal cavern.

"Good morning," said the King of Gilgad. "Your rocks are getting loose, Kaliko, and you'd better have them glued in place before they hurt someone." Then he began to chuckle: "Hoo, hoo, hoo-hee, hee-heek, keek, eek!" and Kaliko sat and frowned because he realized that the little fat King was poking fun at him.

"I asked Your Majesty to come here," said the Nome King, "to show you a curious skein of golden thread which my workmen have made. If it pleases you, I will make you a present of it."

With this he held out a small skein of glittering gold twine, which was really pretty and curious. Rinkitink took it in his hand and at once the golden thread began to unwind—so swiftly that the eye could not follow its motion. And, as it unwound, it coiled itself around Rinkitink's body, at the same time weaving itself into a net, until it had enveloped the little King from head to foot and placed him in a prison of gold.

"Aha!" cried Kaliko; "*this* magic worked all right, it seems.

"Oh, did it?" replied Rinkitink, and stepping forward he walked right through the golden net, which fell to the floor in a tangled mass.

Kaliko rubbed his chin thoughtfully and stared hard at Rinkitink.

"I understand a good bit of magic," said he, "but Your Majesty has a sort of magic that greatly puzzles me, because it is unlike anything of the sort that I ever met with before."

"Now, see here, Kaliko," said Rinkitink; "if you are trying to harm me or my companions, give it up, for you will never succeed. We're harm-proof, so to speak, and you are merely wasting your time trying to injure us.

"You may be right, and I hope I am not so impolite as to argue with a guest," returned the Nome King. "But you will pardon me if I am not yet satisfied that you are stronger than my famous magic. However, I beg you to believe that I bear you no ill will, King Rinkitink; but it is my duty to destroy you, if possible, because you and that insignificant boy Prince have openly threatened to take away my captives and have positively refused to go back to the earth's surface and let me alone. I'm very tender-hearted, as a matter of fact, and I like you immensely and would enjoy having you as a friend, but—" Here he pressed a button on the arm of his throne chair and the section of the floor where Rinkitink stood suddenly opened and disclosed a black pit beneath, which was a part of the terrible Bottomless Gulf.

But Rinkitink did not fall into the pit; his body remained suspended in the air until he put out his foot and stepped to the solid floor, when the opening suddenly closed again.

"I appreciate Your Majesty's friendship," remarked Rinkitink, as calmly as if nothing had happened, "but I am getting tired with standing. Will you kindly send for my goat, Bilbil, that I may sit upon his back to rest?"

"Indeed I will!" promised Kaliko. "I have not yet completed my test of your magic, and as I owe that goat a slight grudge for bumping my head and smashing my second-best crown, I will be glad to discover if the beast can also escape my delightful little sorceries."

So Klik was sent to fetch Bilbil and presently returned with the goat, which was very cross this morning because it had not slept well in the underground caverns.

Rinkitink lost no time in getting upon the red velvet saddle which the goat constantly wore, for he feared the Nome King would try to destroy Bilbil and knew that as long as his body touched that of the goat the Pink Pearl would protect them both; whereas, if Bilbil stood alone, there was no magic to save him.

Bilbil glared wickedly at King Kaliko, who moved uneasily in his ivory throne. Then the Nome King whispered a moment in the ear of Klik, who nodded and left the room.

"Please make yourselves at home here for a few minutes, while I attend to an errand," said the Nome King, getting up from the throne. "I shall return pretty soon, when I hope to find you pieceful—ha, ha, ha!—that's a joke you can't appreciate now but will later. Be pieceful—that's the idea. Ho, ho, ho! How funny." Then he waddled from the cavern, closing the door behind him.

"Well, why didn't you laugh when Kaliko laughed?" demanded the goat, when they were left alone in the cavern.

"Because he means mischief of some sort," replied Rinkitink, "and we'll laugh after the danger is over, Bilbil. There's an old adage that says: 'He laughs best who laughs last,' and the only way to laugh last is to give the other fellow a chance. Where did that knife come from, I wonder."

For a long, sharp knife suddenly appeared in the air near them, twisting and turning from side to side and darting here and there in a dangerous manner, without any support whatever. Then another knife became visible—and another and another—until all the space in the royal cavern seemed filled with them. Their sharp points and edges darted toward Rinkitink and Bilbil perpetually and nothing could have saved them from being cut to pieces except the protecting power of the Pink Pearl. As it was, not a knife touched them and even Bilbil gave a gruff laugh at the failure of Kaliko's clever magic.

The goat wandered here and there in the cavern, carrying Rinkitink upon his back, and neither of them paid the slightest heed to the whirring knives, although the glitter of the hundreds of polished blades was rather trying to their eyes. Perhaps for ten minutes the knives darted about them in bewildering fury; then they disappeared as suddenly as they had appeared.

Kaliko cautiously stuck his head through the doorway and found the goat chewing the embroidery of his royal cloak, which he had left lying over the throne, while Rinkitink was reading his manuscript on "How to be Good" and chuckling over its advice. The Nome King seemed greatly disappointed as he came in and resumed his seat on the throne. Said Rinkitink with a chuckle:

"We've really had a peaceful time, Kaliko, although not the pieceful time you expected. Forgive me if I indulge in a laugh—hoo, hoo, hoo-hee, heek-keek-eek! And now, tell me; aren't you getting tired of trying to injure us?"

"Eh-heh," said the Nome King. "I see now that your magic can protect you from all my arts. But is the boy Inga as well protected as Your Majesty and the goat?'

"Why do you ask?" inquired Rinkitink, uneasy at the question because he remembered he had not seen the little Prince of Pingaree that morning.

"Because," said Kaliko, "the boy has been undergoing trials far greater and more dangerous than any you have encountered, and it has been hundreds of years since anyone has been able to escape alive from the perils of my Three Trick Caverns."

King Rinkitink was much alarmed at hearing this, for although he knew that Inga possessed the Blue Pearl, that would only give to him marvelous strength, and perhaps strength alone would not enable him to escape from danger. But he would not let Kaliko see the fear he felt for Inga's safety, so he said in a careless way:

"You're a mighty poor magician, Kaliko, and I'll give you my crown if Inga hasn't escaped any danger you have threatened him with."

"Your whole crown is not worth one of the valuable diamonds in my crown," answered the Nome King, "but I'll take it. Let us go at once, therefore, and see what has become of the boy Prince, for if he is not destroyed by this time I will admit he cannot be injured by any of the magic arts which I have at my command."

He left the room, accompanied by Klik, who had now rejoined his master, and by Rinkitink riding upon Bilbil. After traversing several of the huge caverns they entered one that was somewhat more bright and cheerful than the others, where the Nome King paused before a wall of rock. Then Klik pressed a secret spring and a section of the wall opened and disclosed the corridor where Prince Inga stood facing them.

"Tarts and tadpoles!" cried Kaliko in surprise. "The boy is still alive!"

CHAPTER XX

DOROTHY TO THE RESCUE

ONE DAY WHEN PRINCESS DOROTHY OF OZ WAS VISITING GLINDA THE GOOD, WHO is Ozma's Royal Sorceress, she was looking through Glinda's Great Book of Records—wherein is inscribed all important events that happen in every part of the world—when she came upon the record of the destruction of Pingaree, the capture of King Kitticut and Queen Garee and all their people, and the curious escape of Inga, the boy Prince, and of King Rinkitink and the talking goat. Turning over some of the following pages, Dorothy read how Inga had found the Magic Pearls and was rowing the silver-lined boat to Regos to try to rescue his parents.

The little girl was much interested to know how well Inga succeeded, but she returned to the palace of Ozma at the Emerald City of Oz the next day and other events made her forget the boy Prince of Pingaree for a time. However, she was one day idly looking at Ozma's Magic Picture, which shows any scene you may wish to see, when the girl thought of Inga and commanded the Magic Picture to show what the boy was doing at that moment.

It was the time when Inga and Rinkitink had followed the King of Regos and Queen of Coregos to the Nome King's country and she saw them hiding behind the rock as Cor and Gos passed them by after having placed the King and Queen of Pingaree in the keeping of the Nome King. From that time Dorothy followed, by means of the Magic Picture, the adventures of Inga and his friends in the Nome King's caverns, and the danger and helplessness of the poor boy aroused the little girl's pity and indignation.

So she went to Ozma and told the lovely girl Ruler of Oz all about Inga and Rinkitink.

"I think Kaliko is treating them dreadfully mean," declared Dorothy, "and I wish you'd let me go to the Nome Country and help them out of their troubles."

"Go, my dear, if you wish to," replied Ozma, "but I think it would be best for you to take the Wizard with you."

"Oh, I'm not afraid of the Nomes," said Dorothy, "but I'll be glad to take the Wizard, for company. And may we use your Magic Carpet, Ozma?"

"Of course. Put the Magic Carpet in the Red Wagon and have the Saw-Horse take you and the Wizard to the edge of the desert. While you are gone, Dorothy, I'll watch you in the Magic Picture, and if any danger threatens you I'll see you are not harmed."

Dorothy thanked the Ruler of Oz and kissed her good-bye, for she was determined to start at once. She found the Wizard of Oz, who was planting shoe-trees in the garden, and when she told him Inga's story he willingly agreed to accompany the little girl to the Nome King's caverns. They had both been there before and had conquered the Nomes with ease, so they were not at all afraid.

The Wizard, who was a cheery little man with a bald head and a winning smile, harnessed the wooden Saw-Horse to the Red Wagon and loaded on Ozma's Magic Carpet. Then he and Dorothy climbed to the seat and the Saw-Horse started off and carried them swiftly through the beautiful Land of Oz to the edge of the Deadly Desert that separated their fairyland from the Nome Country.

Even Dorothy and the clever Wizard would not have dared to cross this desert without the aid of the Magic Carpet, for it would have quickly destroyed them; but when the roll of carpet had been placed upon the edge of the sands, leaving just enough lying flat for them to stand upon, the carpet straightway began to unroll before them and as they walked on it continued to unroll, until they had safely passed over the stretch of Deadly Desert and were on the border of the Nome King's dominions.

This journey had been accomplished in a few minutes, although such a distance would have required several days' travel had they not been walking on the Magic Carpet. On arriving they at once walked toward the entrance to the caverns of the Nomes.

The Wizard carried a little black bag containing his tools of wizardry, while Dorothy carried over her arm a covered basket in which she had placed a dozen eggs, with which to conquer the Nomes if she had any trouble with them.

Eggs may seem to you to be a queer weapon with which to fight, but the little girl well knew their value. The Nomes are immortal; that is, they do not perish, as mortals do, *unless they happen to come in contact with an egg*. If an egg touches them—either the outer shell or the inside of the egg—the Nomes lose their charm of perpetual life and thereafter are liable to die through accident or old age, just as all humans are.

For this reason the sight of an egg fills a Nome with terror and he will do anything to prevent an egg from touching him, even for an instant. So, when Dorothy took her basket of eggs with her, she knew that she was more powerfully armed than if she had a regiment of soldiers at her back.

CHAPTER XXI

THE WIZARD FINDS AN ENCHANTMENT

AFTER KALIKO HAD FAILED IN HIS ATTEMPTS TO DESTROY HIS GUESTS, AS HAS BEEN related, the Nome King did nothing more to injure them but treated them in a friendly manner. He refused, however, to permit Inga to see or to speak with his father and mother, or even to know in what part of the underground caverns they were confined.

"You are able to protect your lives and persons, I freely admit," said Kaliko; "but I firmly believe you have no power, either of magic or otherwise, to take from me the captives I have agreed to keep for King Gos."

Inga would not agree to this. He determined not to leave the caverns until he had liberated his father and mother, although he did not then know how that could be accomplished. As for Rinkitink, the jolly King was well fed and had a good bed to sleep upon, so he was not worrying about anything and seemed in no hurry to go away.

Kaliko and Rinkitink were engaged in pitching a game with solid gold quoits, on the floor of the royal chamber, and Inga and Bilbil were watching them, when Klik came running in, his hair standing on end with excitement, and cried out that the Wizard of Oz and Dorothy were approaching.

Kaliko turned pale on hearing this unwelcome news and, abandoning his game, went to sit in his ivory throne and try to think what had brought these fearful visitors to his domain.

"Who is Dorothy?" asked Inga.

"She is a little girl who once lived in Kansas," replied Klik, with a shudder, "but she now lives in Ozma's palace at the Emerald City and is a Princess of Oz—which means that she is a terrible foe to deal with."

"Doesn't she like the Nomes?" inquired the boy.

"It isn't that," said King Kaliko, with a groan, "but she insists on the Nomes being goody-goody, which is contrary to their natures. Dorothy gets angry if I do the least thing that is wicked, and tries to make me stop it, and that naturally makes me downhearted. I can't imagine why she has come here just now, for I've been behaving very well lately. As for that Wizard of Oz, he's chock-full of magic that I can't overcome, for he learned it from Glinda, who is the most powerful sorceress in the world. Woe is me! Why didn't Dorothy and the Wizard stay in Oz, where they belong?"

Inga and Rinkitink listened to this with much joy, for at once the idea came to them both to plead with Dorothy to help them. Even Bilbil pricked up his ears when he heard the Wizard of Oz mentioned, and the goat seemed much less surly, and more thoughtful than usual.

A few minutes later a Nome came to say that Dorothy and the Wizard had arrived and demanded admittance, so Klik was sent to usher them into the royal presence of the Nome King.

As soon as she came in the little girl ran up to the boy Prince and seized both his hands.

"Oh, Inga!" she exclaimed, "I'm so glad to find you alive and well."

Inga was astonished at so warm a greeting. Making a low bow he said:

"I don't think we have met before, Princess."

"No, indeed," replied Dorothy, "but I know all about you and I've come to help you and King Rinkitink out of your troubles." Then she turned to the Nome King and continued: "You ought to be ashamed of yourself, King Kaliko, to treat an honest Prince and an honest King so badly."

"I haven't done anything to them," whined Kaliko, trembling as her eyes flashed upon him.

"No; but you tried to, an' that's just as bad, if not worse," said Dorothy, who was very indignant. "And now I want you to send for the King and Queen of Pingaree and have them brought here *immejitly*!"

"I won't," said Kaliko.

"Yes, you will!" cried Dorothy, stamping her foot at him. "I won't have those poor people made unhappy any longer, or separated from their little boy. Why, it's *dreadful*, Kaliko, an' I'm su'prised at you. You must be more wicked than I thought you were."

"I can't do it, Dorothy," said the Nome King, almost weeping with despair. "I promised King Gos I'd keep them captives. You wouldn't ask me to break my promise, would you?"

"King Gos was a robber and an outlaw," she said, "and p'r'aps you don't know that a storm at sea wrecked his boat, while he was going back to Regos, and that he and Queen Cor were both drowned."

"Dear me!" exclaimed Kaliko. "Is that so?"

"I saw it in Glinda's Record Book," said Dorothy. "So now you trot out the King and Queen of Pingaree as quick as you can."

"No," persisted the contrary Nome King, shaking his head. "I won't do it. Ask me anything else and I'll try to please you, but I can't allow these friendly enemies to triumph over me.

"In that case," said Dorothy, beginning to remove the cover from her basket, "I'll show you some eggs."

"Eggs!" screamed the Nome King in horror. "Have you eggs in that basket?"

"A dozen of 'em," replied Dorothy.

"Then keep them there—I beg—I implore you!—and I'll do anything you say," pleaded Kaliko, his teeth chattering so that he could hardly speak.

"Send for the King and Queen of Pingaree," said Dorothy.

"Go, Klik," commanded the Nome King, and Klik ran away in great haste, for he was almost as much frightened as his master.

It was an affecting scene when the unfortunate King and Queen of Pingaree entered the chamber and with sobs and tears of joy embraced their brave and adventurous son. All the others stood silent until greetings and kisses had been exchanged and Inga had told his parents in a few words of his vain struggles to rescue them and how Princess Dorothy had finally come to his assistance.

Then King Kitticut shook the hands of his friend King Rinkitink and thanked him for so loyally supporting his son Inga, and Queen Garee kissed little Dorothy's forehead and blessed her for restoring her husband and herself to freedom.

The Wizard had been standing near Bilbil the goat and now he was surprised to hear the animal say:

"Joyful reunion, isn't it? But it makes me tired to see grown people cry like children."

"Oho!" exclaimed the Wizard. "How does it happen, Mr. Goat, that you, who have never been to the Land of Oz, are able to talk?"

"That's my business," returned Bilbil in a surly tone.

The Wizard stooped down and gazed fixedly into the animal's eyes. Then he said, with a pitying sigh: "I see; you are under an enchantment. Indeed, I believe you to be Prince Bobo of Boboland."

Bilbil made no reply but dropped his head as if ashamed.

"This is a great discovery," said the Wizard, addressing Dorothy and the others of the party. "A good many years ago a cruel magician transformed the gallant Prince of Boboland into a talking goat, and this goat, being ashamed of his condition, ran away and was never after seen in Boboland, which is a country far to the south of here but bordering on the Deadly Desert, opposite the Land of Oz. I heard of this story long ago and know that a diligent search has been made for the enchanted Prince, without result. But I am well assured that, in the animal you call Bilbil, I have discovered the unhappy Prince of Boboland."

"Dear me, Bilbil," said Rinkitink, "why have you never told me this?"

"What would be the use?" asked Bilbil in a low voice and still refusing to look up.

"The use?" repeated Rinkitink, puzzled.

"Yes, that's the trouble," said the Wizard. "It is one of the most powerful enchantments ever accomplished, and the magician is now dead and the secret of the anti-charm lost. Even I, with all my skill, cannot restore Prince Bobo to his proper form. But I think Glinda might be able to do so and if you will all return with Dorothy and me to the Land of Oz, where Ozma will make you welcome, I will ask Glinda to try to break this enchantment."

This was willingly agreed to, for they all welcomed the chance to visit the famous Land of Oz. So they bade good-bye to King Kaliko, whom Dorothy warned not to be wicked any more if he could help it, and the entire party returned over the Magic Carpet to the Land of Oz. They filled the Red Wagon, which was still waiting for them, pretty full; but the Saw-Horse didn't mind that and with wonderful speed carried them safely to the Emerald City.

CHAPTER XXII

OZMA'S BANQUET

Ozma had seen in her Magic Picture the liberation of Inga's parents and the departure of the entire party for the Emerald City, so with her usual hospitality she ordered a splendid banquet prepared and invited all her quaint friends who were then in the Emerald City to be present that evening to meet the strangers who were to become her guests.

Glinda, also, in her wonderful Record Book had learned of the events that had taken place in the caverns of the Nome King and she became especially interested in the enchantment of the Prince of Boboland. So she hastily prepared several of her most powerful charms and then summoned her flock of sixteen white storks, which swiftly bore her to Ozma's palace. She arrived there before the Red Wagon did and was warmly greeted by the girl Ruler.

Realizing that the costume of Queen Garee of Pingaree must have become sadly worn and frayed, owing to her hardships and adventures, Ozma ordered a royal outfit prepared for the good Queen and had it laid in her chamber ready for her to put on as soon as she arrived, so she would not be shamed at the banquet. New costumes were also provided for King Kitticut and King Rinkitink and Prince Inga, all cut and made and embellished in the elaborate and becoming style then prevalent in the Land of

Oz, and as soon as the party arrived at the palace Ozma's guests were escorted by her servants to their rooms, that they might bathe and dress themselves.

Glinda the Sorceress and the Wizard of Oz took charge of Bilbil the goat and went to a private room where they were not likely to be interrupted. Glinda first questioned Bilbil long and earnestly about the manner of his enchantment and the ceremony that had been used by the magician who enchanted him. At first Bilbil protested that he did not want to be restored to his natural shape, saying that he had been forever disgraced in the eyes of his people and of the entire world by being obliged to exist as a scrawny, scraggly goat. But Glinda pointed out that any person who incurred the enmity of a wicked magician was liable to suffer a similar fate, and assured him that his misfortune would make him better beloved by his subjects when he returned to them freed from his dire enchantment.

Bilbil was finally convinced of the truth of this assertion and agreed to submit to the experiments of Glinda and the Wizard, who knew they had a hard task before them and were not at all sure they could succeed. We know that Glinda is the most complete mistress of magic who has ever existed, and she was wise enough to guess that the clever but evil magician who had enchanted Prince Bobo had used a spell that would puzzle any ordinary wizard or sorcerer to break; therefore she had given the matter much shrewd thought and hoped she had conceived a plan that would succeed. But because she was not positive of success she would have no one present at the incantation except her assistant, the Wizard of Oz.

GOAT   LAMB   OSTRICH

First she transformed Bilbil the goat into a lamb, and this was done quite easily. Next she transformed the lamb into an ostrich, giving it two legs and feet instead of four. Then she tried to transform the ostrich into the original Prince Bobo, but this incantation was an utter failure. Glinda was not discouraged, however, but by a powerful spell transformed the ostrich into a tottenhot—which is a lower form of a man. Then the tottenhot was transformed into a mifket, which was a great step in advance and, finally, Glinda transformed the mifket into a handsome young man, tall and shapely, who fell on his knees before the great Sorceress and gratefully kissed her hand, admitting that he had now recovered his proper shape and was indeed Prince Bobo of Boboland.

This process of magic, successful though it was in the end, had required so much time that the banquet was now awaiting their presence. Bobo was already dressed in princely raiment and although he seemed very much humbled by his recent lowly condition, they finally persuaded him to join the festivities.

When Rinkitink saw that his goat had now become a Prince, he did not know whether to be sorry or glad, for he felt that he would miss the companionship of the quarrelsome animal he had so long been accustomed to ride upon, while at the same time he rejoiced that poor Bilbil had come to his own again.

Prince Bobo humbly begged Rinkitink's forgiveness for having been so disagreeable to him, at times, saying that the nature of a goat had influenced him and the surly disposition he had shown was a part of his enchantment. But the jolly King assured the

TOTTENHOT

MIFKET

PRINCE

OZMA

DOROTHY

Prince that he had really enjoyed Bilbil's grumpy speeches and forgave him readily. Indeed, they all discovered the young Prince Bobo to be an exceedingly courteous and pleasant person, although he was somewhat reserved and dignified.

Ah, but it was a great feast that Ozma served in her gorgeous banquet hall that night and everyone was as happy as could be. The Shaggy Man was there, and so was Jack Pumpkinhead and the Tin Woodman and Cap'n Bill. Beside Princess Dorothy sat Tiny Trot and Betsy Bobbin, and the three little girls were almost as sweet to look upon as was Ozma, who sat at the head of her table and outshone all her guests in loveliness.

King Rinkitink was delighted with the quaint people of Oz and laughed and joked with the tin man and the pumpkin-headed man and found Cap'n Bill a very agreeable companion. But what amused the jolly King most were the animal guests, which Ozma always invited to her banquets and seated at a table by themselves, where they talked and chatted together as people do but were served the sort of food their natures required. The Hungry Tiger and Cowardly Lion and the Glass Cat were much admired by Rinkitink, but when he met a mule named Hank, which Betsy Bobbin had brought to Oz, the King found the creature so comical that he laughed and chuckled until his friends thought he would choke. Then while the banquet was still in progress, Rinkitink composed and sang a song to the mule and they all joined in the chorus, which was something like this:

BETSY

TROT

> "It's very queer how big an ear
> Is worn by Mr. Donkey;
> And yet I fear he could not hear
> If it were on a monkey.
> 'Tis thick and strong and broad and long
> And also very hairy;
> It's quite becoming to our Hank
> But might disgrace a fairy!"

This song was received with so much enthusiasm that Rinkitink was prevailed upon to sing another. They gave him a little time to compose the rhyme, which he declared would be better if he could devote a month or two to its composition, but the sentiment he expressed was so admirable that no one criticized the song or the manner in which the jolly little King sang it.

Dorothy wrote down the words on a piece of paper, and here they are:

> "We're merry comrades all, to-night,
> Because we've won a gallant fight
> And conquered all our foes.
> We're not afraid of anything,
> So let us gayly laugh and sing
> Until we seek repose.

"We've all our grateful hearts can wish;
  King Gos has gone to feed the fish,
    Queen Cor has gone, as well;
  King Kitticut has found his own,
  Prince Bobo soon will have a throne
    Relieved of magic spell.

"So let's forget the horrid strife
  That fell upon our peaceful life
    And caused distress and pain;
  For very soon across the sea
  We'll all be sailing merrily
    To Pingaree again."

CHAPTER XXIII

THE PEARL KINGDOM

IT WAS UNFORTUNATE THAT THE FAMOUS SCARECROW—THE MOST POPULAR PERSON in all Oz, next to Ozma—was absent at the time of the banquet, for he happened just then to be making one of his trips through the country; but the Scarecrow had a chance later to meet Rinkitink and Inga and the King and Queen of Pingaree and Prince Bobo, for the party remained several weeks at the Emerald City, where they were royally entertained, and where both the gentle Queen Garee and the noble King Kitticut recovered much of their good spirits and composure and tried to forget their dreadful experiences.

At last, however, the King and Queen desired to return to their own Pingaree, as they longed to be with their people again and see how well they had rebuilt their homes. Inga also was anxious to return, although he had been very happy in Oz, and King Rinkitink, who was happy anywhere except at Gilgad, decided to go with his former friends to Pingaree. As for Prince Bobo, he had become so greatly attached to King Rinkitink that he was loth to leave him.

On a certain day they all bade good-bye to Ozma and Dorothy and Glinda and the Wizard and all their good friends in Oz, and were driven in the Red Wagon to the edge of the Deadly Desert, which they crossed safely on the Magic Carpet. They then made their way across the Nome Kingdom and the Wheeler Country, where no one molested them, to the shores of the Nonestic Ocean. There they found the boat with the silver lining still lying undisturbed on the beach.

There were no important adventures during the trip and on their arrival at the pearl kingdom they were amazed at the beautiful appearance of the island they had left in ruins. All the houses of the people had been rebuilt and were prettier than before, with green lawns before them and flower gardens in the back yards. The marble towers of King Kitticut's new palace were very striking and impressive, while the palace itself proved far more magnificent than it had been before the warriors from Regos destroyed it.

Nikobob had been very active and skillful in directing all this work, and he had also built a pretty cottage for himself, not far from the King's palace, and there Inga found Zella, who was living very happy and contented in her new home. Not only had Nikobob accomplished all this in a comparatively brief space of time, but he had started the pearl fisheries again and when King Kitticut returned to Pingaree he found a quantity of fine pearls already in the royal treasury.

So pleased was Kitticut with the good judgment, industry and honesty of the former charcoal-burner of Regos, that he made Nikobob his Lord High Chamberlain and put him in charge of the pearl fisheries and all the business matters of the island kingdom.

They all settled down very comfortably in the new palace and the Queen gathered her maids about her once more and set them to work embroidering new draperies for the royal throne. Inga placed the three Magic Pearls in their silken bag and again deposited them in the secret cavity under the tiled flooring of the banquet hall, where they could be quickly secured if danger ever threatened the now prosperous island.

King Rinkitink occupied a royal guest chamber built especially for his use and seemed in no hurry to leave his friends in Pingaree. The fat little King had to walk wherever he went and so missed Bilbil more and more; but he seldom walked far and he was so fond of Prince Bobo that he never regretted Bilbil's disenchantment.

Indeed, the jolly monarch was welcome to remain forever in Pingaree, if he wished to, for his merry disposition set smiles on the faces of all his friends and made everyone near him as jolly as he was himself. When King Kitticut was not too busy with affairs of state he loved to join his guest and listen to his brother monarch's songs and stories. For he found Rinkitink to be, with all his careless disposition, a shrewd philosopher, and in talking over their adventures one day the King of Gilgad said:

"The beauty of life is its sudden changes. No one knows what is going to happen next, and so we are constantly being surprised and entertained. The many ups and downs should not discourage us, for if we are down, we know that a change is coming

and we will go up again; while those who are up are almost certain to go down. My grandfather had a song which well expresses this and if you will listen I will sing it."

"Of course I will listen to your song," returned Kitticut, "for it would be impolite not to."

So Rinkitink sang his grandfather's song:

> "A mighty King once ruled the land—
>   But now he's baking pies.
> A pauper, on the other hand,
>   Is ruling, strong and wise.
>
> "A tiger once in jungles raged—
>   But now he's in a zoo;
> A lion, captive-born and caged,
>   Now roams the forest through.
>
> "A man once slapped a poor boy's pate
>   And made him weep and wail.
> The boy became a magistrate
>   And put the man in jail.
>
> "A sunny day succeeds the night;
>   It's summer—then it snows!
> Right oft goes wrong and wrong comes right,
>   As ev'ry wise man knows."

CHAPTER XXIV

THE CAPTIVE KING

ONE MORNING, JUST AS THE ROYAL PARTY WAS FINISHING BREAKFAST, A SERVANT came running to say that a great fleet of boats was approaching the island from the south. King Kitticut sprang up at once, in great alarm, for he had much cause to fear strange boats. The others quickly followed him to the shore to see what invasion might be coming upon them.

Inga was there with the first, and Nikobob and Zella soon joined the watchers. And presently, while all were gazing eagerly at the approaching fleet, King Rinkitink suddenly cried out:

"Get your pearls, Prince Inga—get them quick!"

"Are these our enemies, then?" asked the boy, looking with surprise upon the fat little King, who had begun to tremble violently.

"They are my people of Gilgad!" answered Rinkitink, wiping a tear from his eye. "I recognize my royal standards flying from the boats. So, please, dear Inga, get out your pearls to protect me!"

"What can you fear at the hands of your own subjects?" asked Kitticut, astonished.

But before his frightened guest could answer the question Prince Bobo, who was standing beside his friend, gave an amused laugh and said:

"You are caught at last, dear Rinkitink. Your people will take you home again and oblige you to reign as King."

Rinkitink groaned aloud and clasped his hands together with a gesture of despair, an attitude so comical that the others could scarcely forbear laughing.

But now the boats were landing upon the beach. They were fifty in number, beautifully decorated and upholstered and rowed by men clad in the gay uniforms of the King of Gilgad. One splendid boat had a throne of gold in the center, over which was draped the King's royal robe of purple velvet, embroidered with gold buttercups.

Rinkitink shuddered when he saw this throne; but now a tall man, handsomely dressed, approached and knelt upon the grass before his King, while all the other occupants of the boats shouted joyfully and waved their plumed hats in the air.

"Thanks to our good fortune," said the man who kneeled, "we have found Your Majesty at last!"

"Pinkerbloo," answered Rinkitink sternly, "I must have you hanged, for thus finding me against my will."

"You think so now, Your Majesty, but you will never do it," returned Pinkerbloo, rising and kissing the King's hand.

"Why won't I?" asked Rinkitink.

"Because you are much too tender-hearted, Your Majesty."

"It may be—it may be," agreed Rinkitink, sadly. "It is one of my greatest failings. But what chance brought you here, my Lord Pinkerbloo?"

"We have searched for you everywhere, sire, and all the people of Gilgad have been in despair since you so mysteriously disappeared. We could not appoint a new King, because we did not know but that you still lived; so we set out to find you, dead or alive. After visiting many islands of the Nonestic Ocean we at last thought of Pingaree, from where come the precious pearls; and now our faithful quest has been rewarded."

"And what now?" asked Rinkitink.

"Now, Your Majesty, you must come home with us, like a good and dutiful King, and rule over your people," declared the man in a firm voice.

"I will not."

"But you must—begging Your Majesty's pardon for the contradiction."

"Kitticut," cried poor Rinkitink, "you must save me from being captured by these, my subjects. What! must I return to Gilgad and be forced to reign in splendid state when I much prefer to eat and sleep and sing in my own quiet way? They will make me sit in a throne three hours a day and listen to dry and tedious affairs of state; and I must stand up for hours at the court receptions, till I get corns on my heels; and forever must I listen to tiresome speeches and endless petitions and complaints!"

"But someone must do this, Your Majesty," said Pinkerbloo respectfully, "and since you were born to be our King you cannot escape your duty."

" 'Tis a horrid fate!" moaned Rinkitink. "I would die willingly, rather than be a King—if it did not hurt so terribly to die."

"You will find it much more comfortable to reign than to die, although I fully appreciate Your Majesty's difficult position and am truly sorry for you," said Pinkerbloo.

King Kitticut had listened to this conversation thoughtfully, so now he said to his friend:

"The man is right, dear Rinkitink. It is your duty to reign, since fate has made you a King, and I see no honorable escape for you. I shall grieve to lose your companionship, but I feel the separation cannot be avoided."

Rinkitink sighed.

"Then," said he, turning to Lord Pinkerbloo, "in three days I will depart with you for Gilgad; but during those three days I propose to feast and make merry with my good friend King Kitticut."

Then all the people of Gilgad shouted with delight and eagerly scrambled ashore to take their part in the festival.

Those three days were long remembered in Pingaree, for never—before nor since—has such feasting and jollity been known upon that island. Rinkitink made the most of his time and everyone laughed and sang with him by day and by night.   ·

Then, at last, the hour of parting arrived and the King of Gilgad and Ruler of the Dominion of Rinkitink was escorted by a grand procession to his boat and seated upon his golden throne. The rowers of the fifty boats paused, with their glittering oars pointed into the air like gigantic uplifted sabres, while the people of Pingaree—men, women and children—stood upon the shore shouting a royal farewell to the jolly King.

Then came a sudden hush, while Rinkitink stood up and, with a bow to those assembled to witness his departure, sang the following song, which he had just composed for the occasion.

> "Farewell, dear Isle of Pingaree—
> The fairest land in all the sea!
> No living mortals, kings or churls,
> Would scorn to wear thy precious pearls.

> "King Kitticut, 'tis with regret
> I'm forced to say farewell; and yet
> Abroad no longer can I roam
> When fifty boats would drag me home.

> "Good-bye, my Prince of Pingaree;
> A noble King some time you'll be
> And long and wisely may you reign
> And never face a foe again!"

They cheered him from the shore; they cheered him from the boats; and then all the oars of the fifty boats swept downward with a single motion and dipped their blades into the purple-hued waters of the Nonestic Ocean.

As the boats shot swiftly over the ripples of the sea Rinkitink turned to Prince Bobo, who had decided not to desert his former master and his present friend, and asked anxiously:

"How did you like that song, Bilbil—I mean Bobo? Is it a masterpiece, do you think?"

And Bobo replied with a smile:

"Like all your songs, dear Rinkitink, the sentiment far excels the poetry."

THE END